Praise for *Quietus*

"Vivian Schilling's *Quietus* is a great gothic raven perched somewhere between, say, Anne Rice and Iris Murdoch. It's a spooky, sweeping book of death, dreams and psychosexual intrigue. Schilling herself—in her deft melding of mythic animus and modern anxiety—seems like the bastard daughter of Carl Jung and Mary Wollstonecraft Shelley. *Quietus* should come with a guarantee: Will keep you up at night (either turning pages or jumping at shadows . . . probably both) or your money back. I loved it."
—James Ireland Baker, *Time Out New York*

"Schilling has crafted a complex and creepy thriller. An Anne Rice novel without the goth trappings." —*Publishers Weekly*

"A profoundly insightful and engaging thriller."
—*The Cleveland Plain Dealer*

"Award-winning author Vivian Schilling's novel *Quietus* is a bold and terrifying tale of suspense as survivors of a deadly crash awaken in a hospital with untrustworthy memories and uncertain futures. A tense, involving, complex, deftly written and highly recommended saga about unraveling the defenses of the human mind one by one. *Quietus* is aptly titled after the moment of release of life, and haunting to the very end."
—*Midwest Book Review*

"Using extensive research obtained from ancient religious apocrypha of the world's major religions, Schilling has crafted stunning and plausible insights that question what we have come to know as 'death.' The result is an epic and chilling new thriller that will please readers on both a visceral and intellectual level." —*West Coast Literary Review*

"Haunting and passionate . . . A chilling and foreboding tale about fate, death and the afterlife. Gripping and thought-provoking . . . Highly recommended."
—*Dark Realms*

"Beautifully written, this is a tale of suspense and introspection."
—Amy Rosenfeld, Joseph Beth Bookseller

"Rich and intelligent." —*The Women's Connection*

PENGUIN BOOKS

QUIETUS

Vivian Schilling is a screenwriter as well as a novelist, her previous works garnering the Saturn Award and the Golden Scroll Award for Outstanding Achievement in Literature. She divides her time between Los Angeles and Fayetteville, Arkansas.

QUIETUS

A NOVEL BY

Vivian Schilling

PENGUIN BOOKS

To Eric
My beloved
&
To Shari
My forever friend

PENGUIN BOOKS
Published by the Penguin Group
Penguin Group (USA) Inc., 375 Hudson Street, New York, New York 10014, U.S.A.
Penguin Books Ltd, 80 Strand, London WC2R 0RL, England
Penguin Books Australia Ltd, 250 Camberwell Road, Camberwell, Victoria 3124, Australia
Penguin Books Canada Ltd, 10 Alcorn Avenue, Toronto, Ontario, Canada M4V 3B2
Penguin Books India (P) Ltd, 11 Community Centre,
Panchsheel Park, New Delhi – 110 017, India
Penguin Books (N.Z.) Ltd, Cnr Rosedale and Airborne Roads,
Albany, Auckland, New Zealand
Penguin Books (South Africa) (Pty) Ltd, 24 Sturdee Avenue,
Rosebank, Johannesburg 2196, South Africa

Penguin Books Ltd, Registered Offices: 80 Strand, London WC2R 0RL, England

First published in the United States of America by Hannover House 2002
Published in Penguin Books 2003

1   3   5   7   9   10   8   6   4   2

PUBLISHER'S NOTE
This is a work of fiction. Names, characters, places, and incidents either are the product
of the author's imagination or are used fictitiously, and any resemblance to actual persons,
living or dead, business establishments, events, or locales is entirely coincidental.

THE LIBRARY OF CONGRESS HAS CATALOGED THE HARDCOVER EDITION AS FOLLOWS:
Schilling, Vivian.
Quietus : a novel / by Vivian Schilling.
p.   cm.
Includes bibliographical references.
ISBN 0-9637846-1-7 (hc.)
ISBN 0 14 20.0306 9 (pbk.)
1. Near-death experiences—Fiction.   2. Suspense fiction.   I. Title.
PS3569.C492Q54   2001   813'.54   2001094402
QBI01-700963

Printed in the United States of America

BOOK ONE

PART ONE

One

THE TEMPERATURE IN THE WHITE MOUNTAINS HAD DROPPED TO negative five degrees with a wind-chill factor of minus forty. The ten-passenger twin-engine aircraft floated across the vast gray sky, slowly gaining altitude. In spite of strong warnings from Air Traffic Control, the Merlin IV had taken off and had been in the air for nearly fifteen minutes.

Although all VFR-rated pilots at the Errol airport had been grounded, the pilot of the plane, Bud Graves, was Instrument-rated, therefore free to fly through the storm if he elected. The flight was filled to capacity with six of his colleagues, both male and female attorneys at Benson, Graves & Sneed, and two couples that had unofficially chartered their seats. They had already boarded and were ready to go when he had received the Center Weather Advisory. A storm was moving into the White Mountain region at an alarming rate, yet Graves had an important case in court the next day and couldn't take a chance the system would snow him in. The advisory had warned of adverse conditions with turbulence, low level wind shear and clear ice in the clouds, but Graves was not to be daunted. He had picked his way through many a storm without incident and wasn't about to let even the northern wilds of New Hampshire keep him down. By his calculations, he would be landing in Boston a mere two-hundred and ten miles away, just in time for supper.

"My radar's working fine," he had responded to the report. "I'll find a hole in the pattern just like I always do." Yet in touting his competence to Air Traffic Control, there was one factor he failed to mention: he hadn't waited the mandatory eight-hour turnaround required by the FAA between the time a pilot consumes alcohol and the time his feet leave the ground.

. . .

KYLIE O'ROURKE had just drifted asleep when the turbulence first hit. The plane dropped suddenly, then immediately rose again. Her husband, Jack, instinctively grabbed her hand.

"What was that?" he asked, looking about. The group of attorneys at the front of the plane were passing around a bottle of Scotch, unfazed by the jolt.

"It's alright Jack," Kylie said and kissed his cheek. "It's just a little bad weather." Just then the floor seemed to fall from beneath them then forcefully rush back up. It repeated the motion several more times drawing screeches from the passengers. Their drinks were spilled and their bags tossed about, until finally, the plane leveled out again. Sunlight broke through the windows and a cheer came from the group of drunken attorneys.

Kylie peered out the window at the storm cloud that had released them. She looked over at Jack whose lips had gone white. Tiny beads of sweat had formed at his temples. "Are you okay?" she asked.

He gave her a half-smile and adjusted his body in the seat. She could see that he was terrified and felt guilty for dragging him onto the flight. His father had died in a plane crash when Jack was fifteen. That had been twenty years ago but the fear of flying had stayed with him, making him apprehensive from the moment the trip had been proposed.

"Fly? Why do we have to fly? New Hampshire's the next state over. It's silly to take a plane," he had argued. His point had been reasonable enough: the Dixville Notch area was a mere four hours from Boston in good weather. Yet the chartered seats on the aircraft had been part of a gift from an appreciative client—a ski-package to the famed Balsam's Resort. Located within the northern region of New Hampshire near the Canadian border, the four-star destination was not exactly Kylie and Jack's style, but they knew it would be a much needed break. After ten years of hard work building their own interior design firm, it was time to enjoy the perks. "But we can't just take part of the gift," Kylie had argued, fearful of offending their client. "Besides, the weather up there is so unpredictable. It could take forever if the roads are bad."

With thought of having to trudge through the back country on a snow-packed highway, Jack had finally conceded and until that moment, the trip had been a success.

Kylie's best friend, Amelia Blackwell and her husband Dix, had flown up from Savannah to join them, both couples taking the last leg of the journey together. After six days of non-stop skiing and warm pampered nights inside the luxurious hotel, the two couples had caught the flight bound to Boston where Kylie and Jack would remain, while Amelia and Dix continued back to Savannah. Kylie would report back to her client, Alex Newhunger, that the trip had been a pleasure and tell him that the next time he needed one of his mansions refurbished, she and Jack would be there for him again.

With another jolt of the plane, Kylie squeezed her husband's hand. "We'll be on the ground soon," she promised.

He threw her a glance. "That's what I'm afraid of," he grumbled.

"Now, now," she whispered, kissing him tenderly on the cheek. As much as she hated to see him uneasy, she couldn't help but admire the way it made him look. He was a handsome if not beautiful man with long lean angles to his delicate face and lanky body—attributes he had acquired from his mother, much to his father's dismay. His father, who had been a stocky, beer-drinking, cigar-smoking man, believed it necessary to instill in his winsome young son a strong sense of manhood to counterbalance his almost feminine comeliness. Jack's high cheek bones, small up-turned nose and soft skin had long since been roughed and scarred by years of football, basketball and every other type of activity that proved he was more than a pretty boy. His body was strong and muscular, and his hands worn from sixteen years of work as a carpenter . . . certainly a respectable occupation for the son of a brawny factory worker from South Boston. After years of tough discipline his father had succeeded in his quest and had turned out an insecure son that would never be accepting of his beauty or of anything else that he encountered; but Jack was masculine if nothing else.

From the moment Kylie had met him, she had been intrigued by the vibrant intensity with which he approached life, as though by sheer concentration he could change anything around him or within himself; even obliterate all traces of vulnerability or grace. It was the glimpses into the man that should have been that kept Kylie riveted. As he sat beside her clutching her hand, his face lost its virile stranglehold and took on the frightened innocence of a child. His curly blonde hair, blue eyes and pouting lips gave him the guileless look of a cherub; but a cherub Jack was not. It was an interesting juxtaposition that brought a smile to Kylie's face.

"What are you smiling at?" he asked, the tiny line between his eyes returning.

"Nothing, Jack," Kylie said, unable to remove the grin from her face. "I was just thinking about how cute you are," she said.

"Give me a break," Jack grumbled, slouching back in his seat.

Dix Hamilton peered around from the seat ahead of them, his short black hair standing on end. "Looking a little pale there, Jack," he said with a mischievous smile.

"You're one to talk, you bloodless albino," Jack retorted to Dix's delight. "Just turn your cheerful, earring-ed butt around, 'cause I don't want to look at it."

Dix laughed and disappeared again.

"You're lucky he's got a sense of humor," Kylie said.

"He just likes to torment me," Jack said.

"That's because it's so easy," she said, unable to suppress another smile.

"There you go again," said Jack with genuine irritation. "You're enjoying this aren't you? . . . Getting me on this damn plane. These guys are idiots, I'm telling you," he scowled, glowering at the loud attorneys.

"Jack, just relax," said Kylie, suddenly growing irritated herself.

Amelia's head slowly appeared over the seat. She glanced at Jack who sat pouting, then turned to Kylie with a heavy smile.

"Don't worry," said Kylie, motioning toward Jack. "If he doesn't behave we'll stick him out on the wing."

"Kylie," reprimanded Amelia. "Leave him alone."

The two smiled at one another. They had wanted to sit together but Jack was insistent on having Kylie next to him. It was painful for the two women, who lived 703 miles apart, to be so close yet unable to talk. From the time they were seven years old, when they had met on the playground of St. Mary's School for Girls in the Historic District of Savannah, the friends had been inseparable. Even after Kylie had moved from Savannah back to her hometown of Boston at the age of twenty-two, the distance hadn't kept them apart. In the following twelve years they had talked daily and visited often. While most friendships would have dwindled, theirs had only deepened.

"Hey, you're bleeding," Amelia said.

Kylie suddenly became aware of the sweet taste of blood in her mouth. She touched her lip and felt a small cut.

"It must have happened during the turbulence," she said reaching for her bag.

"Here," Amelia said, offering a tissue.

"Thanks."

Amelia smiled and disappeared once again onto the other side of the seat. Kylie pulled out a compact and dabbed the blood from her lip. Adjusting her long auburn hair, she frowned to see that her eyes were still swollen from the night before. She and Jack had argued until nearly daylight. The long night's tears and lack of sleep had created a puffed look, that, in spite of her concern, went unnoticed by anyone other than Amelia. Most strangers would be too taken with Kylie's clover-green eyes and long dark lashes to notice any temporary flaw. In fact, most found it hard to look into her strong gaze for long without looking away. Her lion-like mane of hair, full lips, tawny freckled skin and self-possessed confidence made them cower under her attention. Her casual attitude toward her appearance only seemed to add to her disheveled beauty. With the exception of ruby lipstick, she rarely wore make-up. It was simply too time-consuming. She was indifferent to her looks, except of course, when they revealed more than she cared to tell. Her eyes had betrayed her that morning. When she had descended the long stairs of the hotel, Amelia knew instantly it had been one of many rough nights and Kylie felt embarrassed. They usually experienced each other's problems from afar, with seven hundred miles of phone line to ease the reality of marriage or lack thereof. It always made for an awkward adjustment every time they saw each other and realized that the voice had a body and face that time was slowly changing.

Kylie sighed as she closed the compact and returned the bag to the floor. Within eight hours, her closest friend and strongest source of stability, would be hundreds of miles away from her in Savannah. She had implored Amelia to stay in Boston for awhile, but her beloved friend had to get back for work. Saying good-bye was always the hardest part, and it left her feeling sad. Though the friends came from totally different backgrounds, they had formed a life-long bond that gave them both a profound feeling of security. Upon their first meeting, they had connected instantly, finding in each other what their own self was lacking.

Kylie had been born into a poor, volatile household, where every day brought about a new adventure of one countenance or another. She was Boston-Irish: curvy, strong-willed and with a temper to match. In spite of her buoyancy and a firm sense of survival, grim happenings always seemed to seep into her roller coaster life. There was no middle ground of experiences in Kylie's life, only extreme highs and extreme lows. While some would consider her to be the luckiest person on earth, others would consider her ill-fated.

Amelia, on the other hand, had been raised by wealthy, cultured parents steeped in the strong traditions of a Southern wealth. It was a quiet household governed by the stifling forces of unbroken formalities. She was blonde, thin and delicately sublime, her tenor equally clandestine and tender. She had been sheltered and protected, and within the overly maternal walls a timorous spirit had formed.

The most stable influence Kylie would ever know was Amelia. She learned from Amelia the importance of boundaries and that her erratic energy could be focused so that the demons within would not destroy her. Whenever she ventured too far, Amelia was always there to pull her back. When she lacked the refinement of one born into the socially elite, Amelia smoothed her rough edges and taught her poise.

Kylie, in turn, showed Amelia how to risk in order to live. When Amelia lacked the confidence of a rebel, Kylie led the way. As an adult, Kylie helped to bring the single most important love into Amelia's life: Dix Hamilton. She had given Amelia the strength to marry the penniless, young musician against her mother's wishes.

It was a perfect friendship in every way; so perfect that Kylie felt the same understanding and accord lacking within her own troubled marriage; but she loved Jack and was committed to making it work. She had been drawn to him for the very reasons they now suffered. Theirs had been a rocky relationship that followed in the same pattern as everything else in her life: no middle ground. The good times were incredible and the bad times, devastating. They struggled to learn where the middle ground was, but neither knew how to find it.

Kylie suddenly felt like holding him, just taking him into her arms and keeping him there; instead, she merely took his hand. He was unusually quiet watching the attorneys party instead of joining in. She knew by his pursed lips and stunned gaze that he was afraid, but was lost as to how to comfort him.

She lay her head back onto the seat and looked out at the billowing clouds looming ahead. They created a surrealistic wall that seemed impenetrable. She looked out at the wing of the plane as it glided through the turbulence. She had often wondered how the appendages could withstand the constant pressure, the rivets holding all of the many pieces together. The bright light danced on the silvery surface as the arm quivered. She looked down at the mountains below, their uneven edges appearing so distant. Just looking at the vast frozen area made her shiver. She took Jack's hand and nestled into the seat, her gaze falling once again to the wing of the plane. The roar of the engines had replaced the voices around her. She lay back and let the steady blare lull her into a drowsy calm, when she saw something out of the corner of her eye move onto the wing. Her stomach dropped as she turned. It was a bird—a large black raven facing sideways, and it seemed to be staring in at her.

"Jack, look!" she exclaimed, clutching her husband's arm, but when they turned back to the window the bird was gone.

"What?" Jack asked with alarm.

"I just saw a bird. It landed on the wing and—"

"Jesus Kylie, you scared the hell out of me," he groaned, wiping his brow. "How could a bird land on the wing? We must be going two hundred miles an hour," he argued.

"It did," she said defensively. "It was just standing there."

"There's no way."

"It was," she grumbled, but when she turned back to the window, to the smooth surface of the wing, her conviction waned. She had been drowsing, so it was possible that her eyes had deceived her. "Maybe it just lit there for a second," she said quietly, but Jack was already onto his own thoughts. His quick dismissal of the subject left her feeling saddened and chilled. She sighed heavily and closed her eyes, but the image of the bird refused to leave her. It stood solidly on the wing, its tiny eyes peering into her soul. The wind rushed past but it was unmoved. She abruptly became aware of the speed of the plane, herself trapped in the belly of the roaring beast. With a start, she quickly opened her eyes. She was prone to claustrophobia and recognized the beginnings of an attack. To her dismay, she found herself in the worst seat imaginable. Not only were they in the back of the plane, but luggage—strapped by a cargo net—formed a wall behind them. Sitting in anything other than an aisle seat was always a mistake, but she had relinquished it to Jack so that he would feel more comfortable. She looked over at her husband who sat twisting a napkin in his hands. She shook her head and smiled to herself. "What a pair . . . the brave Irish O'Rourkes," she said softly. The comment drew a smile from Jack. Kylie's heart warmed, for he was simply beautiful when he smiled. As she looked into the childlike eyes, a shadow passed over the cabin. Both O'Rourkes turned to the window. They had finally reached the wall of clouds, the billowing thunder heads rising around them like skyscrapers, the plane carefully making its way through a valley between them.

"God, I've never seen anything like this," murmured Kylie, Jack silent beside her.

As the plane penetrated one of the storm cells, the cabin was swallowed by the darkness.

Two

Jacy Greers sat at the radar scope inside the Air Route Traffic Control Center with headsets on and a space heater at her feet. She had a twin-engine requesting assistance through an impossible storm over the White Mountains—a range notorious for bad weather. The pilot was foolishly attempting to penetrate a solid line of thunderstorms and needed guidance through. She had been handling the flight for the past twenty miles and had been anticipating the call with mounting anxiety.

"Irresponsible dumb-ass," she grumbled as she scanned the monitor for a hole in the hazardous line of weather. If the macho-types would just stay out of the skies on days like this, it would make her job a lot easier. She shook her head and just as she was about to depress the push-to-talk-switch an impatient voice came back through the radio. It was the voice of Bud Graves.

"Center, Merlin Niner-Six Alpha. I'm getting knocked all over the place up here. I need to stay out of these cells. Every time I go in, I pick up more ice."

"No shit," she grumbled to herself. She herself had warned the pilot of the storm as soon as he had come onto her frequency, but it had not deterred him. Now he wanted options and she had none to give. She knew from the Center Weather Advisory that the storm cells were towering to 45,000 feet. The Merlin IV was incapable of climbing over the storm and if the pilot tried to get under it, he would run the risk of boxing the plane inside a canyon without power enough to clear the mountaintops.

Before she could respond, Bud Graves came back over the airwave. "Center, Merlin Niner-Six Alpha, I'm getting severe icing here at seven-thousand feet. I need to get lower now," he said emphatically.

"Negative, Merlin Niner-Six Alpha," she responded. "Minimum Vectoring Altitude in your area is 6500 feet. I can't take you any lower."

"Center, Merlin Niner-Six Alpha. Cancel my IFR flight plan."

Jacy shook her head. The pilot was cutting his cord to Air Traffic Control so that he could engage in scud running—a term given to the dangerous endeavor of an aircraft picking its way through unfamiliar terrain beneath low-lying clouds. But there was nothing she could do to stop him. Now that he was dumping his flight plan, he could go wherever he wanted as long as he stayed out of the IFR governed clouds.

"IFR cancellation received," she reluctantly responded. "Remain on that squawk code for flight following."

With shoulders tensed, she watched the plane's descent until it sank below her radar coverage. "Merlin Niner-Six Alpha, I've lost radar contact," she said.

"Roger."

"You're on your own," she said softly as she stared at the place on the scope where the signal had vanished.

"WHO NEEDS you anyway?" Graves muttered, the sour taste of indigestion rising into his mouth. He stared nervously through his ice-covered windshield at the canyon before him. After changing his heading, he found the skies beneath the heavy clouds more suitable, but he was concerned about the new, unfamiliar course. He had flown in and out of the Dixville Notch area several times before and had always been able to follow the same flight path. Since he had deviated from that plan, he was forced to take the terrain as it came at him, but at the moment his reflexes were slower than he would have liked and his head felt like someone had rammed a poker into his skull. For the first time in his life, he was regretting those last few Scotch and sodas.

THEIR NEW altitude seemed dangerously low to Kylie. She stared intently out the window watching the sides of the mountains pass so closely it felt as though they were going to scrape one of them. The cabin of the aircraft was completely quiet, the party had stopped and no one seemed to be laughing anymore. It was clear when they had abruptly dropped into a ravine that Bud Graves was not exactly in control of the situation. The misty clouds were squeezing down on them, while the dark wooded terrain seemed to be closing in from both sides.

The sliding door to the cockpit was suddenly yanked open. Graves looked back into the cabin, his face taut. "Murphy, get up here and help me with the charts," he directed at what appeared to be the drunkest of the attorneys.

Jack straightened in his seat. "You've got to be kidding. That guy's going to help him?"

"That's right buddy," Graves said, overhearing the comment. "Unless you happen to be a pilot."

"He's been knocking back booze the whole flight," Jack retorted.

"Don't worry about it," chirped Murphy pivoting back to him. "I'm not going to fly the plane—I'm just going to check the charts for him. Isn't that right, Bud?"

"Just get your butt up here," said Graves.

Murphy obediently made his way to the co-pilot's seat where he began rummaging through a flight bag on the floor. "Jesus Bud, you've got the whole country in here. Which chart is it?"

"The Montreal Sectional."

The passengers watched in silence, their confidence in the situation waning as the attorney fumbled to unfold the awkward paper. When he finally wrestled it open, the stiff chart nearly filled the cockpit. Graves had to bat it aside to see through his windshield.

"We're about twenty miles southwest of Berlin," Graves said. "What's the highest altitude in our area?"

"Let me see," muttered Murphy. "6288."

"Check it again," Graves said under his breath.

"6288 feet," Murphy repeated.

Graves looked at the chart himself and was clearly disturbed by what he saw. He abruptly reached back and yanked the cockpit door shut closing the passengers off from further view.

THE MERLIN IV advanced up the rising canyon at 170 knots with maximum power. The nose of the plane pointed upward as the small aircraft struggled to out-climb the steep grade. The passengers inside were thrust back in their seats, the severity of the situation apparent to all, everyone aware of the straining engines.

Kylie looked out the window but the steep angle of the plane made her instantly nauseated. Never before had she experienced such a sheer climb. She could see the precipitous wall of rock moving beneath them but the top of the mountain was nowhere in sight.

A man in the rear of the cabin began praying softly, "'Hail Mary, full of grace . . .'"

"Oh Jack, I'm sorry," Kylie whispered, looking into his frightened face. "I'm sorry."

"Hey, there's nothing to be sorry about," he said with feigned good spirits.

As the plane struggled higher and higher, Kylie felt as though a huge rock was bearing down on her chest. The ceiling of the plane seemed suddenly lower than before, and the seat ahead of her appeared to be pressing toward her legs. It felt as if the oxygen had been sucked from the cabin, leaving behind a stale void. She began to hyper-ventilate. The luggage behind her moaned as the curve of the wall threatened to crush her if she didn't get out of its way. She tried to lift her head from the seat but the force of the climb pushed it down. She gripped the arm rest to pull herself up but there was nowhere to go. She could see Amelia peering back at her through the crack in the seats, her friend's worried face fueling her panic even more.

"I can't breathe," she whispered.

Jack grabbed her hand with a firm grip, "It's okay," he said.

The prayer in front of them continued in the ritualistic drone. "'Blessed art thou among women and blessed is the fruit of thy womb—'"

"We'll be alright," Jack said, but she could tell he was not convinced. She squeezed his hand tighter and began to weep.

"I can't believe this," she said. She felt foolish for panicking, even though she was still in the midst of the terror. She smiled a genuine smile, the tears streaming down her face. "You're the one who's afraid to fly, remember?"

The man continued to pray, his voice becoming louder and louder. "'Holy Mary, Mother of God, pray for us sinners, now and at the hour of our death—'"

"—Amen! Now shut the hell up!" an anonymous voice yelped.

Suddenly, the plane leveled and they could see the jagged top of the mountain. Sunlight burst through the clouds and the ground was falling away.

"We're going to make it!" an attorney announced.

Just as the passengers cheered with relief, there was a massive jolt. Clipping a dead tree, the plane swung violently to the side. The passengers were yanked sideways as the plane lurched and then thrust into weightlessness as it knife-edged downward, the nose angling toward the floor of the valley. Within a second they were in a full nosedive, the passengers' torsos held tight by their seat belts, their arms and legs dangling like rag dolls. Objects hurtled through the air, pummeling against the suspended bodies.

Jack's hoarse scream seemed an illusion that danced around Kylie's head. She felt her body going limp as her jumbled vision began to fade.

Out of the chaos, the plane rolled back upright and they were once again flying level. Like a hideous ride at an amusement park, the insanity had ended as abruptly as it had started. On the brink of hysteria, the passengers were lulled back into a hesitant ease.

The cabin was eerily quiet as the moans began. Kylie and Jack were still in their seats, Kylie's sweater spattered with blood.

"Where are you hurt?" Jack asked as he inspected her for the source of the crimson stains.

"I'm fine," Kylie replied, as they both realized that the blood had come from an attorney at their feet. He was lying face up, his broken nose bleeding profusely. His eyes were dazed as he lifted himself from the floor and silently stumbled to a seat at the front of the plane.

Jack kissed Kylie's cheeks and her lips then pulled her into his embrace. She quickly undid her seat buckle and stood to look over the seats at Amelia and Dix. They were both shaking and pale.

"Quite a spin, huh?" said Dix, the smile on his lips betraying the terror in his eyes. He had a cut on his ear that was dripping blood onto his black leather jacket.

"You're bleeding," Kylie said softly.

"We're alright," said Amelia, her arm securely around Dix. "You'd better sit back down."

"Buckle back in, Kylie," Jack said, pulling her into the seat. She looked out the window and saw that they were once again over a valley. She let Jack strap her in, then rested her head against his thumping chest and began to cry. He held her tight, his strong lean arms wrapped about her, as he whispered soothingly into her ear. Suddenly, his body went rigid and he was instantly silent. Kylie pulled back and saw the horror in his eyes: he was looking out the window. She followed his line of sight but at first didn't see anything. The wing was vibrating just as before, the air was clear and the storm seemed to be behind them. Then, her eyes were caught by the moving wing. Something was different. It jumped out at her like a grotesque amputation of a man's hand, only there was no blood or hanging arteries, only hanging wires. There was a void where the tip of the wing had been severed.

IT WAS ONLY a matter of minutes before the plane would reach the next ridge. It had already started the precipitous climb, but the damaged wing was creating additional drag and vibration. With the sounding alarms, the incessant praying had begun again, accompanied by panic-stricken outbursts.

In the midst of the chaos, Kylie and Jack hovered together; both were silent.

The cockpit door slid open, Murphy struggling from the co-pilot's seat covered in vomit.

"Mayday, mayday, mayday," came the desperate voice of Graves.

"Merlin Niner-Six Alpha. I've got damage to my flight controls. I need a heading to the nearest airport."

A female voice came back over the radio. "Merlin Niner-Six Alpha. You're not in radar contact. State your position."

"Somewhere around . . . I don't know," said Graves, panic overtaking him. "I . . . don't . . ."

"Merlin Niner-Six Alpha, say fuel on board . . . souls on board," came the female voice.

Graves turned back to the passengers, his eyes red and terror-stricken. "I uh . . . eleven souls on board and my fuel is about . . . eight-hundred pounds," he stammered as he looked back to his gauges.

The praying grew frenzied, as the noise and vibrations intensified. Kylie and Jack clutched tighter together, both starting to weep. They looked into each other's eyes, each with a gentleness; never before had the bond been so strong. Ten years of pain and regret passed through them, all the missed moments when they should have said they were sorry. It had been a long road but they had made it through. Kylie brushed her cheek against her husband's, then tenderly kissed him on the lips.

The shudder of the plane grew frenzied as Graves struggled for control of the crippled aircraft.

"Oh Jesus God!" came the scream from an attorney.

It tore at Kylie's heart to hear Amelia crying in the row ahead of her. "It's okay Melia," she said, but her voice faltered. She knew that it was a lie; they were going to crash. She looked out at the mountain which moved toward them like a vast dream. Shards of sunlight broke from the clouds reflecting off the brilliant snow-covered surface, stabbing into the black woods.

"Put your head down," Jack said, but Kylie couldn't move, couldn't release her gaze from the window. With her surging adrenaline, her focus felt sharper, the deep colors intensifying. The dark trees rustled softly, the shadows playing between them. As the screams around her faded, drowned by her own heightened pulse, she felt something beneath the twisting shades . . . an unseen force that seemed to be drawing them inward. At first it looked like branches casting shapes over the ivory mountain, but as the plane drew nearer, the dark streaks looked almost human, a grouping of shadows that spread distinctly over the white sheet of snow. She could see the trace of clothing, the posturing of unseen heads, and eyes as gray as night peering upward. It looked as if someone or something waited beneath. At once, the cold terror filled her, and her mouth opened in a silent, agonized scream. The plane hurtled downward, yet she couldn't take her eyes off the shrouded presence beneath. "God help us," her mind whispered, as the darkness swallowed her.

Three

NIGHT HAD ALREADY FALLEN OVER THE EAST COAST WHEN DILLON O'Rourke got the call from the police station. He had just gotten home from a long shift at Massachusetts General where he had been up for nearly twenty-six hours monitoring a nine-year-old cardiac patient who had undergone surgery. With the shrill ring, he grabbed for the phone, certain it meant the child had taken a turn for the worse.

"Dr. Dillon O'Rourke?" came the hesitant voice.

"Speaking."

"This is Officer Frank Cummins with the Boston City Police. Are you any relation to Jack O'Rourke of 412 North Battery Street?"

The moment Dillon heard the somber tone of the question his heart fell. "I'm his younger brother," he answered, reluctant to hear what would follow.

The officer continued, speaking slowly and deliberately. His brother Jack had been aboard a small aircraft which had gone down two hours earlier somewhere in the White Mountains; the exact location of the wreckage was still uncertain. The ARTCC had lost radar contact some time before and little was known about the circumstances of the crash. A second storm had moved into the area reaching blizzard proportions. Although they had no information on the condition of the pilot and ten passengers, one thing was certain: casualties were expected.

Dillon's legs became suddenly unstable. He turned on an extra light in the den in hope of steadying his balance.

"We're still trying to locate relatives of his wife, Kylie. We haven't had any luck through our regular channels and we were hoping you could shed some light on it for us."

Dillon knew little about Kylie's family other than she had suffered the loss of her mother and two brothers. Her older brother, Aidan, whom she rarely spoke of, had died when she was a young girl. Then, when she was twenty-two years old, her mother and younger brother had been killed in a tragic car accident. Her father was the only immediate family she had left and Dillon's only encounter with the towering man was a brief meeting at his brother's wedding. "Her father's a fisherman up in Swampscott," he answered weakly, removing his reading glasses.

"Do you have a number for him, sir?"

"No, but I could probably get it."

Dillon remembered the tired, sad face of the fisherman and he felt sick at the idea of a complete stranger calling him to relay the ghastly news. "If it's okay, I'll notify him," he offered.

Dillon scarcely remembered replacing the receiver, or throwing on his rain boots. He knew he should call the rest of his family, particularly his grandmother who had watched after the two brothers from the time they were fourteen and fifteen, but he wanted to approach the situation with extreme caution. He didn't want his family worrying before he had all of the facts. After getting his affairs in order, he would set out for New Hampshire where he could assess the situation himself. There were no flights going in or out of the area and his BMW would never make the treacherous journey through the blizzard. He would have to stop by Kylie and Jack's to exchange his car for their Jeep and pick up a set of chains along the way.

First and foremost, though, he needed to notify Kylie's father of the accident. Rather than the callousness of a phone call, he decided to drive up the coast to tell him in person. If he took the highway, the small fishing village was only about thirty minutes northeast. He had called information for the exact address, only to find it unlisted. Fortunately, he had seen pictures of the old boat that her father owned. Perhaps he would get lucky and spot it against the dock; if not, surely he would find someone to steer him in the right direction. Grabbing his cell phone and the keys to his BMW, he headed for the door.

Although the silence inside the car was more than he could bear,

Dillon couldn't bring himself to turn on the radio. The flapping wipers smeared the sleet and the windows were fogged. He pulled back the sleeve of his jacket and wiped the inside of the window with his sweater. The defroster had been broken all winter but he hadn't had time to take the car to the shop. As a cardiologist, he found the cold weather months to be an exceptionally busy time of the year. While in the summer people were more prone to overexertion, winter took the gravest toll with inertia and depression. "People need sunshine," his grandmother had always told him. He was beginning to believe she was right.

He felt a hollow feeling in his stomach and his head was pounding. The vagueness of the officer's news swirled through his mind with visions of Jack and Kylie lying bloodied in the middle of the freezing mountains with no help in sight. As much as he tried not to, he assumed the worst. He struggled to concentrate on the dark road ahead of him, but he kept veering into the next lane. Twice the screeching horn of a passing car had reeled past narrowly missing the side of his tiny car.

"Take it easy," he said aloud, the sound of his voice breaking the silence. Jack was probably okay. He was a survivor, right? And Kylie. He smiled a painful smile. Hell, Kylie had the resilience of a cat. He thought of the time she fell from the second story of an apartment building she and Jack had been hired to redecorate. She had been measuring the walls and forgot that the railing around the stairwell was only two feet high. She had fallen to the ground floor and landed on her feet. She looked slightly surprised, then climbed back up the stairs without missing a beat. Kylie was tough.

"Living with Jack she has to be," he said aloud. He instantly felt guilty for the comment even though there was no one except his conscience to hear it. While the two brothers were only eleven months apart in age and were the best of friends, their relationship had its weaknesses. When Dillon had been accepted into Harvard, trouble erupted between them for the first time ever. They had grown up in the lower class section of South Boston . . . not the most prestigious neighborhood in a city where social class wars are ever present. Jack, who had gone on to become a carpenter, felt daunted when his younger brother went to the famed university on the other side of the Charles River. While Dillon was proud of his brother's achievements,

Jack didn't reciprocate. Dillon was Harvard which meant traitor. He had visions of Dillon hanging out with high-brow intellectuals in tweed jackets discussing the relative theories of this or that. Jack's perceptions, while far from the truth, had caused many an argument over the years.

Jack's tumultuous marriage had also been a source of tension between the brothers. While Jack liked that Kylie and Dillon were close, he hated it when his brother came to his wife's rescue. Years ago, Dillon had made the mistake of offering Kylie a ride home after Jack had left her stranded at a party following an argument between the couple. While it had been an innocent act that had taken place nearly ten years earlier, Jack never forgave him. To Jack it was proof that his brother didn't approve of the way he ran his marriage or his life. In reality, Dillon never interfered nor gave comment. While he certainly wished that Jack treated Kylie with a little more appreciation, he knew that Kylie loved his brother and saw something in him worth wanting. After all, Jack was handsome, bright, and truly in love with his wife. The couple loved each other; they just simply couldn't get along. As long as Dillon remained neutral on the couple's disagreements, Jack left the subject alone.

In spite of all the unsteady ground between them, the three managed to remain the closest of friends. They saw each other every weekend, and had dinners together on a regular basis. The thought of losing either one of them was too much for Dillon to take.

Tears suddenly flooded his eyes, smearing his vision of the dark road ahead. "Don't jump to conclusions," he said aloud. "They're fine."

TINY LIGHTS dotted the darkened coastline of Nahant Bay. The sleet had been replaced by a brisk northern wind. The icy chill whipped against Dillon's face as he stood out on the pier overlooking the water. Several boats swayed between the floating chunks of ice, but they were all too far away to read the names on the hulls or to differentiate between the colors. He was irritated with himself for not bringing the binoculars. He looked out over the expansive shoreline. The houses were randomly placed with no set distance or format between them. To the north the houses were large and stately. Closer to the docks,

they became smaller, resembling cottages rather than family homes—
the more likely place for a widowed fisherman to live.

He made his way back down the rickety, long dock, holding tight to
the wobbly railing. The walkway was so narrow that there would
scarcely be room enough to pass another person. He shuddered at the
thought of losing his footing, and plunging into the frigid water—a
fatal fall that would surely result in hypothermia. He looked down
through the wooden planks, and as he got closer to the shore the ice
that floated beneath him became more and more dense until it formed
one solid sheet. Suddenly he envisioned Jack's face beneath the glass-
like surface frozen in a hideous scream. He jolted from his own abhorrent imagination and tried to erase the sight from his eyes. "He'll be
fine," he said again as if by saying it would make it so.

At the base of the pier he spotted a small boat docked a couple of
hundred yards up. He couldn't read the letters painted on the side, but
he could see that the boat was red. He quickly made his way along the
snow-covered frozen sand, the wind scraping against the exposed
flesh of his face. Finally the name of the boat was clear: MISS LILA was
painted across the side of the hull just as he remembered from the
photo. Lila had been the name of Kylie's mother. The deck was empty
and there was no light emanating from the small cabin. He followed
the wooden planking to the house that butted against the dock. Not
much bigger than a tiny shack, the red and white house seemed almost
like a cartoon drawing. A warm light shone from the front window
and a line of gray smoke danced from the chimney.

As he approached the house his stomach began to churn. What
would he possibly say to the man? Kylie was all the family the fisherman had left. Through the murky windowpanes he could see Sean
McCallum seated at a small kitchen table with a bowl of food and a
bottle of rye-whiskey in front of him. A black and white television cast
a bluish glow upon the rugged face.

Dillon opened the screen-door and pulled back the rustic knocker.
He instantly regretted not combing his hair. He quickly ran his fingers
through it and straightened his collar.

After a moment the door opened and the friendly face appeared on
the other side. Dillon was struck by how much the man had aged since
the wedding ten years earlier. He had the rugged skin of a fisherman,
the sun and wind having carved deep wrinkles around his eyes and

along his ruddy cheeks. He was a man of considerable height, none of which had been lost with age. Beneath the harsh exterior, he very much resembled his beautiful daughter. His eyes were warm and gentle, his smile wide and friendly. "What can I do for you lad?" he asked, with only a trace of an Irish accent.

Dillon could tell that McCallum didn't recognize him. "Uh, Mr. McCallum, my name is Dillon O'Rourke . . ."

The fisherman's smile wavered as he tried to place the strangely familiar face standing outside his door. It was a handsome, healthy face with bright blue eyes and clear, pale skin. It was the face of his son-in-law Jack with more refinement and intellect, and the hair that blew about it was dark-brown instead of a sun-bleached blonde.

Once again, Dillon straightened his disheveled hair. "Jack's brother, sir."

"Oh, of course," McCallum bellowed, instantly shoving a large brawny hand at Dillon. "I'm sorry I didn't recognize you, son. Come on in."

Dillon paused a moment at the door, wondering whether or not he had made the right decision. Hesitant, he followed McCallum inside and shut the door behind himself. The front room was small and square with a kitchen on one side and a swayed couch and a rocker on the other. The cozy room smelled of fish, tobacco and booze. A stew simmered on the stove mixing with the other odors for a strangely appetizing aroma. The sight of the big man in the tiny house seemed very odd to Dillon. He appeared a giant beside the flimsy kitchen table. "Have a seat," the giant offered, obviously baffled by the unexpected visit.

Dillon fidgeted under the fisherman's observation. In the masculine surroundings, he suddenly felt effeminate in his cotton khakis and button-down shirt. To his chagrin, he was playing the role that Jack had so often accused him of—that of an intellectual.

"Thank you, sir," he said nervously.

"We're family. Why don't you call me Sean?" McCallum asked, taking a seat at the opposite side of the table. "Whiskey?" he offered.

Dillon hesitated a moment. "Sure," he said.

McCallum poured a glass of liquor and scooted it across the waxy surface of the table. "What brings you here, son?"

Dillon could see the worry in the big man's eyes, who clearly knew the visit wasn't a social call.

"Well, I don't know how to say this," Dillon started weakly, wishing he had opted for the telephone to relay the bad news.

"Just spit it out," urged McCallum.

"It's your daughter, sir. She's been in a plane accident. The authorities aren't sure whether or not she's alive. There's a big storm there and they know the plane went down but haven't found it yet, so she could still be alive." He had blurted the information out so quickly that he wasn't sure exactly what he had said and what he had left out. "Jack was with her," he added softly.

In an instant the large, tough fisherman seemed to diminish into the size of a shriveled old man. He pressed his lips together and stared right through Dillon. "Where?"

"The White Mountains," said Dillon. "I'm driving up tonight."

McCallum pushed back his chair and silently stood. There was such pain behind the hazel eyes that Dillon had to look away.

"I'd like to come with you," McCallum said quietly.

Dillon looked into the downcast face. "I'd be glad to have your company, sir. It'll be tough going through the storm, but I figure if we take it slow, we'll make it just after midnight."

McCallum reached for his glass of whiskey and downed it. As he set the glass back on the table Dillon noticed that the big hands were trembling.

Four

THE CHAINED WHEELS OF THE HALF-TON CHEVY BLAZER GROUND against the twelve-foot base of snow, bringing the huge black truck to a standstill. The powerful engine sat idling, the headlights slicing into the dark woods, thousands of snowflakes scurrying in front of the beams.

Haskell Shaw sat motionless behind the wheel, staring out the windshield at the strange object that had embedded itself in a pine tree and was overhanging into his path. It appeared to be the tail-end of an airplane—but surely his eyes were deceiving him.

"What the hell do you suppose that is, Sal?" he asked the panting German shepherd perched on the passenger's side of the cabin.

Sal began to whine and squirm anxiously.

Haskell reached into the glove box and removed a packet of Redman, all the while his eyes riveted to the roadway. He pulled out a clump of the cherry-flavored tobacco and stuck it in the side of his mouth.

"Let's go take a look," he said, grasping a kerosene lantern from the Chevy floor. After he had it lit, he shoved the door to the Blazer open, the wind gusting against him. Sal jumped down onto the snow beside him, barking frantically. Haskell looked toward the ebony woods, then reached behind the seat for his rifle.

He passed the front of the truck and approached the metal object cautiously. While it posed no obvious threat to the sizable man, Haskell had learned at an early age to always expect the unexpected in the backwoods of New Hampshire. Like his ancestors of years ago, he had been tortured and beaten by those of a different skin color. He was three-quarters Pennacook Indian, a fact not lost on most New Englanders. His cheekbones were high, his hair long and black, and his face smooth with the lack of facial hair. When he was sixteen he had accidentally stumbled upon two bigoted convicts who had escaped from a prison in Concord and were hiding out in the nearby woods. Three hours and a nasty scar later, Haskell managed to overcome them and flee. Since then, he carried a gun with him at all times.

Upon closer inspection of the foreign object, Haskell let the barrel of the rifle fall to his side. "Well, I'll be damned," he muttered. He ran his finger alongside the wing buried deep within the bark of the pine. Honey-colored sap oozed down the side of the tree from the large gash.

Sal had disappeared into the woods and was barking incessantly.

"Sal!" Haskell called, swinging the lantern in the direction of the dog. He glanced back to his idling Chevy then turned again to the dark trees.

"Damn," he muttered, then headed toward the barking.

As the long rays from the headlights followed him into the forest, the bright beams slivered into fragments. The wind continued to howl through the trees stirring debris with it. Pine needles pricked painfully into Haskell's exposed cheeks and forehead. He shielded his eyes from the flying rubble with a wool scarf he had wrapped around his neck.

As he got deeper into the woods, the truck lights slowly disappeared, and were replaced with an eerie darkness. The light from the lantern engulfed his steps in a harsh ring, making the night ahead even blacker. When the snow became suddenly speckled with metallic debris, he stopped in his tracks and held the lantern high. The light spread outward illuminating the monstrous sight: the twisted body of a Merlin IV aircraft formed a wall before him. The nose and tail were practically joined together, the center of the plane split down the middle and bent onto itself. It appeared to have skidded sideways through the trees before two large oaks broke its back.

"Lord have mercy," he said aloud.

Sal was on the other side of the mound of gnarled metal, her bark now replaced with a steady howl. Haskell hurried around to the other side, astonished at the phenomenal sight of the white plane glowing in the night.

When Sal saw her master, she jumped excitedly in the air.

"I'm coming, I'm coming," said Haskell.

The side of the plane was split open, the guts of it spilling out onto the snow. Broken luggage, clothes, and ski equipment were strewn about the ground. He stepped over the personal belongings with care, more respectful of them than if the owners were standing in front of him. Though reluctant to witness the inevitable carnage, he moved forward. He peered into the metal cave formed by the buckled plane and saw his first victim. His stomach turned at the sight of a man's dead body strapped within his seat. His chair had been jarred from the aircraft and was sitting upright on the ground facing eerily outward. The wind lashed at the body which appeared to be freezing solid. The middle-aged man had been wearing only a light shirt and pants.

Sal had disappeared inside of the plane and was barking again. Haskell held the light above his head, exposing the aft portion of the cabin. He could see glimpses of Sal bouncing about.

"Hold on there, girl," said Haskell, bending to avoid a sheet of metal. As he stepped into the cabin he stumbled to the side. He had not been expecting the slant of the floor and accidentally banged the lantern against a crushed wall. The light flickered a moment, then glowed bright again.

Haskell took a moment to steady himself, the sight even more grue-some than he had anticipated. The dead were belted in their seats, covered in dark blood. The temperature inside was considerably warmer and the air was nearly silent as the wind and snow beat against the outside of the aircraft. Fearing all the passengers were dead, he was relieved to hear muttering coming from the very back of the plane where Sal was prancing about. He quickly rushed forward to locate the owner of the voice. It was a young man in a black leather jacket slumped on the floor beneath a pile of luggage that had broken free from a cargo net. His eyes were swollen shut, and his ashen face was streaked with blood.

"Is somebody there?" he asked softly, his voice faint and quivering.

"My name's Haskell Shaw," the big Indian said evenly, touching the young man's foot.

The information registered briefly with the barely cognizant man, before he began muttering incoherently once again.

Debating whether or not to move him, Haskell quickly placed the lantern on the floor and began pulling away the ski equipment and luggage piled upon him, shoving it back into the cargo area. Suddenly, the young man clasped Haskell's coat sleeve. There was a piece of metal embedded between his blue fingers.

"Is my wife okay?" he asked feverishly. "Her name is Amelia. She has a red sweater."

As Haskell stared down at the bleeding hand, his stomach fluttered.

"Please mister," the young man said weakly. "I can't see."

The Indian looked behind him at a blonde woman who sat alone, belted into her seat. At first she appeared to be dead, but with the help of the lantern he could see a light mist coming from her mouth. Vomit was covering her multi-colored sweater which was predominately red. "She's fine, son," he said, hoping to hell he had the right woman. Just then a gurgling sound came from the woman's throat.

"What's happening?" panicked the young man. "Is she okay?"

"She's fine," said Haskell, leaning the woman forward so that she would not choke on her own vomit.

"Behind her . . ." the young man said, feeling outward with his hands. "Just right here, there's a couple. They're our friends. Kylie and Jack."

Haskell turned the lantern toward his left. Luggage had piled so high, that he had not even realized there was another row of seats. He quickly pulled the bags away, revealing a young blonde man with a gash in his leg. His face was ashen with the loss of blood, his clothing soaked through with it, but the fine flow of breath emitted from his mouth. The side of the plane was crushing in on the woman next to him, cramping her body into a small space. Ever so slightly he could hear her sporadic breath, but the weight pressing upon her seemed to be crushing the air from her lungs. He quickly leaned across the man beside her and undid her seatbelt, her breath instantly becoming freer. He brushed her long auburn hair back from her bloodied face and in spite of the blood and swollen tissue he was touched by her beauty.

"Mister, are they alive?" the young man begged.

"Yes," replied Haskell, startled by the quaver in his own voice. Looking once again to the man's bleeding leg, he quickly removed the scarf from his own neck, along with his belt and created a compress to form a pressure point to slow the bleeding. Painfully aware of the freezing temperatures and of their exposed skin, he then removed his jacket and spread it across the couple as well as he could.

Then he did a quick survey of the rest of the victims. Halfway down the aisle he found an elderly man whose head was bloodied and his eyes clasped shut, yet his torso was trembling as if in the beginnings of a seizure. Haskell reached down to a dead woman, pulling a blanket from her grasp and tucked it tight around the unconscious man. As he started to turn away, the sharp chin and beaklike nose pulled his attention back. It was a profile he recognized from the news, a famous attorney named Benson. He didn't know what case he knew him from, or even what kind of law the attorney practiced, all he knew was the old man was one step away from death.

As Haskell paused within the center of the cabin, surrounded by the mutilated bodies and the dying, he became suddenly overwhelmed: it would be solely up to him to save the wounded. Due to the freezing temperatures, an expedient rescue was of the essence. It would take too long for help from the nearby town of Bethlehem to ascend the mountain. Even though the storm was slowly subsiding, the victims would surely freeze to death or die of shock if he didn't evacuate them soon.

"I'm going to pull my truck down," he said, turning to the young

man with the swollen eyes, but he had already slipped back into delirium. "Come on Sal," he said, with a pat against his pant leg. As the
dog loped toward him, he took one last glance around. With the lantern in tow, he forged out into the night, leaving the cabin of the plane
once again in darkness.

INHALING the bitter air in gulps, Haskell approached the ragged opening to the aircraft for the fifth time, his heart pounding wildly. His
hands were bleeding and numb with the cold, his back was aching, and
his arms felt like putty, yet in spite of his sixty-one-year-old body, he
had managed to pull four of the five survivors from the wreckage and
place them into the covered truck-bed. Ascending into the plane one
final time, his stomach churned with the difficult task of the last victim. As he made his way down the aisle toward the young woman
named Kylie, he could hear that her breath had become louder. She
was so painfully cramped within the small space that he saw no choice
but to forcefully pull her from the entangled mess of plastic.

After summoning his strength he reached for her, just as the
woman's icy fingers grazed his hand. He was startled to see that she
was conscious. Her pale face had turned toward him, her terrified
eyes beseeching his own.

"Hurry..." she whispered hoarsely. Her labored breathing turned
to gasps as she teetered on the brink of quiet hysteria. As he looked
downward, he was sickened to see for the first time, a piece of metal
protruding from between her ribs.

"You'll be out of here soon," he promised, but his determination
failed to soothe her.

"Don't let them . . ." she whispered, tears choking into her throat.
"Don't let . . ."

"Just be calm," he said reaching again, but she made a sudden move
back.

"Please," she gasped, her terror-stricken eyes focusing behind him.
"They might come . . . *back* . . ."

With a sudden chill, he followed the woman's line of sight past him.
The cabin remained dark, silent with the dead. "Who?" he asked, his
voice catching in his throat.

The woman's eyes were pleading, but only a small sound made it from her throat. "Not . . . human," she murmured. As the energy drained from her frenetic touch, her focus softened. "Beasts . . ." she muttered deliriously. For a few more seconds she struggled to form words, but her lips moved in silence. Then her eyes rolled white as she lost consciousness.

Unsettled, Haskell took one more look around the cabin, then turned back to the woman, trying to collect his thoughts. Assessing the object in her side, he decided to leave it in place, moving her as carefully as possible. With less effort than he thought, he was able to lift her into his embrace, her head falling gently back.

After resting the young woman alongside the others, Haskell jumped into the cab, put the Blazer in gear and pulled away from the wreckage. Looking at his clock, he saw that it had taken him fifteen minutes to load the victims. It would take another half hour to get back down the mountain. Hopefully the critically ill would survive the bumpy journey.

"We'll get there old girl," he said to Sal who whimpered from the passenger's side, nagging him to hurry.

He took the path through the trees slowly and steadily, trying not to lose his head. He wanted to gun the engine and race down the mountain, but knew if he did he risked getting stuck in the drifting snow.

As Sal slumped down on the seat in resignation, Haskell turned up the heater as high as it would go, pointing the vents toward the back of the Blazer where the victims lay.

In the eerie silence of his passengers, Haskell's thoughts returned to the young woman, Kylie. He could still feel her icy fingers against his wrist and see the distant look of death in her eyes. He had served in the front lines of Vietnam where he had witnessed that same detached terror on the faces of his fellow soldiers—the chilling images staying with him over the years. The intimate last pleas had filled his nightmares, the lost faces like those of drowning victims sucked downward from some unseen force. If the woman did not make the journey, once again the dying voice would haunt him, trying desperately to make him understand, to see what she had seen. Steering the truck through a stand of birch where the road slanted downward, Haskell hoped for her safe deliverance, for he could not bear to tell her loved ones that her last words had been in fear.

Five

IN A SMALL DINER AT THE SOUTHERN EDGE OF THE WHITE MOUNTAINS, Dillon O'Rourke and Sean McCallum heard the news. They had stopped to pick up coffee in Plymouth, when they saw the report on the television overhanging the register.

"A small aircraft that went down in the White Mountains yesterday evening has been located," announced the female anchor grimly. "Six people are confirmed dead and the number could be rising." Out of the five survivors, four were in critical condition. They had been taken to the northern town of Bethlehem where they were being treated at the local hospital. The roster of the dead was being withheld, pending notification of the families.

As the newscast moved on to the weather, Dillon and Sean remained frozen, both staring at—but not hearing—the smiling anchor.

"Where's your pay phone?" asked Dillon numbly, for his cell phone had gone hopelessly dead.

The kid behind the counter jerked his head toward the outside.

"Won't do you any good," said a disgruntled trucker in passing. "I just tried it and the lines are all down."

For a moment longer, the two men remained frozen.

"Shall we?" said Sean, the words more a directive than a suggestion. With coffee in hand, he turned for the door.

On the way across the icy parking lot, Dillon nearly broke into a run. His heart thudded with the uncertainty and the dwindling clock. If Kylie and Jack were alive, they needed him by their side, not stuck out on some highway in the middle of nowhere. The trip through the storm was taking longer and had been more treacherous than he had anticipated. What normally would have taken a couple of hours, had already taken six. They had slid off into a ditch just outside of Canterbury, and several times they had to pull over and wait for the winds to die down. As it was, they still had to cross the mountain range to reach the little town fifty miles north.

With no words between them, the two men got into the truck and headed back out onto the highway. With an exact destination and a clearer picture now set, they drove the remainder of the journey in silence.

Six

By FOUR A.M. THE MEDIA HAD ALREADY ARRIVED IN THE QUIET TOWN OF Bethlehem. Due to its high-profile cases, Benson, Graves & Sneed was one of the most famous law firms in the country; therefore news of the tragedy traveled quickly.

When Dillon and Sean stepped from the Jeep, they were nearly knocked to the ground by over-zealous reporters. Concluding from their Boston plates that they were family members of the victims, the reporters closed in on them eager for a morsel of grief to tantalize their early morning viewers. McCallum, who carried a deep, long-rooted resentment toward the media, pushed his way through the flashing lights and extended microphones as if he had entered a war zone.

"I've got no use for you bastards," McCallum growled openly, daring the scrambling reporters to challenge him.

Dillon followed closely in the wake of the big man, wondering how an Irishman who spent his days in the isolated waters of the northern Atlantic could come to detest the media. But there was no time for questions as McCallum cleared the way toward the double doors of the St. Thomas Aquinas Hospital. Once inside, they found the lobby empty with the exception of a camera crew and a reporter that had cornered a large Native American that was shyly turning away from the questions and the bright camera lights.

"This way," said Dillon, following the long hall toward the emergency room. He knew if Kylie and Jack were among the survivors, that's where they would be.

Still unsure of what sort of grief awaited them, the two men hurried through the corridor, their legs unsteady, their guts filled with fear. Unwilling to take the time to ask, they bounded through the shiny doors to see for themselves.

It appeared that the entire staff of the hospital had descended upon the emergency room. The eerily hushed tone of doctors and nurses milling about was disturbed only by the rantings of what at first sounded like a lunatic. "I don't give a damn! I want to see my wife!"

The two men instantly recognized the voice. It was Jack.

They quickly ran toward the disturbance which was coming from a bed on the left side of the unit. Several nurses and a doctor were surrounding Jack, holding him down.

"I've already given him a milligram of versad and 50 of demoral!" cried the nurse to her superior. "Should I give him more?"

"That won't be necessary," Dillon said, approaching. "Take it easy, Jack."

When Jack saw his brother he instantly laid back and calmed. "Dillon, they won't let me see her," he cried, his features beaten and swollen almost to the point of nonrecognition. Before Dillon could respond, his brother's eyes started to droop and within seconds he was out cold.

The winded doctor looked up at the two men. "What's your relationship to this patient?" he asked.

"I'm his brother," said Dillon.

"We had to sedate him, sir," the doctor said. "He's dislocated his shoulder with a possible fracture. If he had continued to move he could have caused serious damage."

McCallum looked frantically about the beds. "My daughter," he said. "Where's my daughter?"

"Well, sir, we're having a hard time identifying all of the victims. Not only was there a plane crash but there was an auto accident . . ." McCallum and Dillon didn't wait for the rest. They were rushing through the aisles, scanning the faces of the injured.

They made their way down the last row of beds, passing patient after patient, until finally there was only one left. Emotion choked into McCallum's throat as his heavy legs took him closer and closer to a bed imprisoned by machines. Shrouded beneath the twisting hoses was the pale and battered face of his unconscious daughter.

"Kylie Rose," he said softly, tears escaping down his cheeks.

With all of his might, he held his gaze on the ravaged face. His daughter's hair was wet and matted to the pillow, and her gown was soaked with sweat. Black stitches were sewn across the lower part of her chin, holding her delicate skin together. There were tiny cuts and scrapes covering her cheeks and forehead and her left eye was blackened and swollen shut. An oxygen tube was taped along her lips and with each sound of the machine her chest rose and fell. A long clear hose stuck out of her side, sucking blood-tainted liquid into a clear box on the floor.

"What is that?" McCallum demanded, his eyes fixed upon the grotesque box, his face filled with horror. "What in God's name are they doing to her?"

"They're draining blood that's trapped in her pleural cavity," said Dillon. "She must have a torn lung," he said, gently examining her chest and sides with his hands. After a moment, he requested the chart from the nurse assigned to the station.

"But sir," she argued, "we can't just—"

"I'm a doctor," he interrupted.

The nurse reluctantly complied and Dillon began reading the report.

McCallum reached down with trembling hands and merely touched the hot-fevered fingers of his daughter, fearing if he took the battered hand into his own, it would cause her pain.

"This patient's had a crit drop of 12 points," Dillon said, looking at the nurse. "Has anybody looked at her spleen?"

She began to answer but then decided against it. "I'll get Doctor Horton," she said.

Dillon turned toward McCallum. "They're clearly short on personnel," he said wearily. "She needs a CAT scan to determine if her spleen has ruptured. If it has, she'll need another surgery."

"Another surgery?"

Dillon swallowed dryly and looked at the father. "She had a tear in her aorta," he said slowly. "A Doctor Rosen repaired it late last night, but it was a major surgery requiring a graft."

"Her heart?" asked McCallum, somehow unable to grasp the information. "They did surgery on her heart?"

"It'll be okay, sir," said Dillon. "Gortex patches are commonly used with a very high probability of no future complications."

McCallum took a moment to digest it all. "And this other surgery?" he finally said. "The one she needs now?"

"It would be a splenectomy—the removal of her spleen."

Sean looked back to Kylie, overwrought. "Who would do it?" he asked, his voice hauntingly low. "Would you be the one?"

"I'm only licensed to practice in Massachusetts and aside from that, medical ethics prohibit me from operating on my own family."

Sean looked with suspicion at the staff before him.

"They're clearly competent," said Dillon. "They're just over-whelmed."

"I'd feel better with you," insisted the father.

"I can't, sir, I'm sorry. I can't be her official doctor but I can still advise them and oversee her treatment."

Sean looked at the young doctor desperately, fear clearly silencing him.

Dillon rested his hand on the man's shoulder. "I'll stay by her every step of the way."

Seven

"LORD JESUS, MARY AND JOSEPH . . . PLEASE DON'T TAKE MY BABY," McCallum begged.

The father's soft-spoken plea floated over the sounds of the machinery that breathed and sighed like a vast creature, prodding and coaxing the life beneath it.

Within twenty-four hours, his daughter's condition had deteriorated. The splenectomy had gone without incident, but her x-rays showed evidence of pneumonia settling in. Her breathing had become coarse and wheezy, her lips and fingers turning blue with her failing lungs—the mechanical ventilator still not getting the much needed oxygen to her blood.

It's not enough, Sean, came the doctor's voice again and again. *Not enough.*

McCallum stared at the tube leading into his daughter's mouth, as if by sheer will he could force the oxygen into her blood.

"Breathe, baby, breathe," he pleaded softly.

OUT OF THE depths the fire erupted in her skull like acid-tipped needles. She was suddenly aware of each breath that she took as the oxygen scorched down her windpipe and into her lungs. Her first impulse was to cry out, to beg for mercy, but something was clamped down upon her face, refusing her the release of the primal scream.

She heard the garbled sound of words that were slow to assimilate in her confused and terrified mind. Then she realized the voice was calling out to her, pulling her away from the black sarcophagus. "Kylie?", it repeated again and again. "Can you hear me, baby?"

The erratic sound of a heart monitor jolted her into the light and the blurry vision of her father came into view. He was standing beside the bed, peering through what looked like a plastic sheeting, his image diffused through the translucent surface like an impressionistic water-color that eerily moved with the subject's intent. His teary eyes lightened and his lips parted.

"You're going to be fine, baby girl," the encouragement sounded after the movement of his mouth.

Daddy, help me, she wanted to beg but couldn't manage a sound. There was an object in her mouth forcing excruciating surges of air into her blazing lungs. She could hear her heart beating and with each swell of blood it felt as if her skull would split. The pain was insufferable. Her feet, her chest, her back, her stomach all ached but nothing compared to the sharp, unrelenting pressure in her head.

"Nurse!" her father's voice suddenly boomed. "She's awake and she needs something for the pain!"

Another face suddenly appeared on the other side of the blurred space. It was Dillon, wearing what appeared to be a doctor's surgical gown. Though the image of his face smeared with a smile, she could see the distress in his movements.

"Welcome back," he said sweetly.

Kylie suddenly remembered that she wasn't alone in her nightmare. Jack had been with her and so had Amelia and Dix. She nearly bolted from the bed but Dillon quickly reassured her.

"Jack's fine," he said as if reading her mind. "He's doing really well. Your friends are fine, also. Banged up, but okay." His eyes flinched and although he tried not to lose his smile, it faded slowly from his face. "You got the worst of it." He leaned in closer and his features became clearer. "Kylie, we're gonna need to transport you."

Transport me? she wanted to ask, unable to remember where she was.

"You hung in there really well on the surgeries, but you have to keep fighting," he said, like a coach coaxing a losing team through a difficult game. "We need to move you back to Boston in the morning. I've arranged for a Medivac to transfer you. I know you're probably not too fond of flying right now but it's important. There's a treatment there that can help you. Jack's already agreed to go. And your father and I will be with you in the . . ."

His words faded into the alcove of her mind as her thoughts drifted. She needed to tell him about the darkness that had entered her world and threatened her very being, but at the moment she couldn't differentiate the tangible from the intangible. There was a sense of urgency, but for what her mind wouldn't say.

"Hey," whispered Dillon. "You'll be fine."

"You've got to give her something for the pain," her father insisted quietly.

"I'll tell the nurse," Dillon said then turned back to her. "Get some rest," he said softly. "We'll be leaving . . ." but she didn't hear the rest. She drifted once again toward the void where the pain receded into black.

Eight

DILLON POURED HIMSELF A CUP OF LUKEWARM COFFEE AND HEADED across the green cafeteria toward the cashier. He had been up for twenty hours straight and needed the black liquid to keep him going through the night. Though he knew his brother was fine and no longer needed his attention, he didn't feel comfortable leaving Kylie alone with the late-night staff. In his own experience as a doctor, no matter how competent a medical staff was, the night always seemed to bring about a certain apathy and Kylie's critical condition couldn't withstand inattentiveness. He had instructed the head nurse of the intensive care unit to page him if her condition changed.

"That'll be fifty cents," said the woman behind the register, her face shadowed behind the *Bethlehem Daily News*. The headline read: SAVED BY GRAFTON COUNTY RESIDENT, FAMOUS ATTORNEY MIRACULOUSLY SURVIVES PLANE CRASH. The rest of the page boasted colorful photos of the gruesome accident, complete with blood and guts and the testimony of the shy local hero, Haskell Shaw.

Dillon held the two quarters out to her, but she was completely absorbed by the paper. He lay the change on the counter and looked about for a comfortable seat where he could do some work. Just on the other side of a partition he noticed Kylie's father sitting at a table by himself smoking a cigarette. The fisherman looked terribly lonely inside the otherwise empty cafeteria. His slumped position and contemplative gaze sent a pang of sadness through Dillon.

"Sean?" he said, walking toward him, but McCallum was entrenched in his own thoughts. A cup of coffee rested on the table with a bottle of whiskey beside it.

Dillon was within a couple of feet before McCallum noticed him. "What are you doing here?" the tall man asked.

"I was about to ask you the same," Dillon said. "I thought you were headed back to the hotel."

McCallum took a swig of the diluted coffee. "Have a seat," he ordered without looking up.

Dillon looked down at the empty chair and suddenly felt nervous. He had driven the tedious trek from Boston with the imposing man, had spent the last few days informing him of Kylie's progress, but not once had they sat down together over coffee.

"Unless you'd rather be by yourself," offered McCallum.

"No, not at all," said Dillon as he quickly took a seat.

The cafeteria was silent with the exception of the cashier shuffling the pages of the paper. Dillon's mind was reeling in search of something to say. Even though he was thirty-four years old, he had the butterflies of a jittery teenager speaking to a friend's parent.

McCallum turned his knowing eyes toward Dillon as if by looking at him he could sum up the youthful man's entire essence. "You care about my daughter, don't you son?"

"Yes sir, very much."

The fisherman stared into Dillon's face searching for something more. After a moment, he took another drink of the coffee and returned to his heavy contemplation.

When he spoke again, his tone had softened. "Her mother was a beautiful lady—a Georgia woman with coal black hair. Lila was her name," McCallum said with apparent admiration and respect. "She and our seven-year-old son were killed in a car accident. Lila died in three and a half days, but our boy lay in a coma for months. The doctors told me he would live. Promised it," he said, returning to his thoughts.

Dillon saw the malevolence pass through the tired, weary eyes and it made him shudder.

"Would you like some?" McCallum suddenly asked, nodding to the bottle of whiskey.

"No thank you, sir," Dillon answered. "I need to stay sharp."

The big man seemed to like the answer. He took the last drag off the self-rolled cigarette and snuffed it out in the ashtray. "I don't know much about medicine," he said, "but something tells me you're the best." The father turned his shrewd gaze back up at him. "I can see it. I hear it in the nurse's voices, I see it in their eyes. You're the one keeping my daughter alive."

"Well sir, Dr. Rosen—"

"Is an idiot," interrupted McCallum. "There's no point in modesty. You're the one." He paused a moment, taking a pensive drink of the coffee. He set the cup down and twisted it round under his brawny hands. "You also strike me as an honest man. Am I right?"

"I try to be," said Dillon.

"I can take you for your word?"

"Yes, sir."

"Then I need an honest answer out of you. I don't like this Doctor Rosen. He's the kind of lily-livered bloke who pats you on the back and tells you it's all going to be alright just to save you a little grief. I'm relying on you for more than that, son."

Dillon bit his lip, anticipating and already knowing what the question would be.

"Will my daughter live?"

Dillon took a deep breath and tried to keep the emotion from his voice. He tried not to think of it as Kylie . . . and not to think of the man before him as her father, a parent that in spite of his desire for the truth, would be devastated by it. "Once we get her to Boston, her condition should improve," he began slowly. "This ECMO, or Extra Corporeal Membrane Oxygenation, is kind of like a by-pass machine. They'll extract her blood, oxygenate it, then put it back in. The procedure has been used with great success, but it's still in experimental stages and they're not sure . . . it's not quite . . ." He felt the eyes of the desperate father upon him and he knew that in spite of himself he was hedging. "It'll give her a fighting chance," he finally concluded.

"What kind of a chance?"

"I've lined up the best—"

"What kind of a chance?" repeated the fisherman.

"Ten percent with a median survival of about two weeks."

The big man's eyes flinched but he held his stare.

"I'm sorry, sir," said Dillon gravely. "Your daughter's tough, but there's still a long road ahead. With ECMO, some patients fight the ventilator, they try to breathe out of sync with the machine. They're given a drug to paralyze them. Then given another drug to calm them and to make them unaware that they're paralyzed. She'll have intermittent lucidity . . . weaning can sometimes be difficult."

"These drugs," said McCallum. "Will they stop the pain?"

"For the most part, yes."

"Promise me that," said the father, tears abruptly washing his eyes. With jaw clenched, he looked down at the cup, staring at it in silence. When he finally continued, his voice was low and grave. "No matter what happens, no matter what the outcome, I want her heavily sedated until it's over. I watched my wife suffer for eighty-four hours and thirty-six minutes because some doctor refused the necessary dosage to relieve her misery. And by God that's not going to happen to Kylie. If my daughter's gonna die, she's gonna do it without pain."

"You have my word," Dillon promised.

Nine

THE SWEET AROMA OF HONEYSUCKLES AND LILACS FILLED HER HEAD, drawing her toward the light. Kylie forced her eyes open against the blinding sun reflecting off a mirror across the room. It was the same scratched mirror that sat atop her mahogany armoire in the bedroom of her childhood. She was home, once again in the lovely, old wood-frame house she cherished so dearly. She was in Savannah with her mother and her father and her little brother, Tucker. Any moment Tucker would come rushing in and pounce on her, begging her to come to the river for an early morning swim. It would be a hot day, she could tell by the brightness of the sun.

Kylie raised her hand to rub her eyes, but something was stuck to her wrist pulling it back toward the bed. Her blurry vision began to clear as she reached to unravel herself from whatever it was that was holding her down. When she touched the skin above her hand the pain shot up her arm. There was a tube connected beneath the flesh, her hand bruised and swollen around it. Then she realized that the room around her was not the gently inviting bedroom of her youth, but a cold, sterile hospital chamber. She looked at the unfamiliar surroundings, confused as to how she had gotten there. Then visions of Jack holding her tight as the plane plummeted toward the mountain came rushing back at her.

"Oh God," she whispered. Her throat hurt and her voice was faint. She tried to sit up but her muscles ached as if she had been sedentary for months. A small object was attached to her fingertip, its tube leading to some kind of monitor. She easily slipped it off, along with the nasal prongs that brought oxygen to her nose.

She shielded her eyes against the sun which was blasting through the blinds and ricocheting off a framed picture hung on the wall. Next to her bed was a wilting bouquet of roses. Fading floral arrangements of all shapes and sizes covered every available shelf space. A shrinking Mylar balloon that read GET WELL struggled to keep its buoyancy against an overhead vent.

She rubbed her temple, trying to sort out the jumbled visions that followed the accident. She vaguely remembered staring through what looked like plastic, and a myriad of unfamiliar people wearing stethoscopes that poked and prodded at her. Her father had been there and so had Dillon. And the helicopter. She remembered the chopping propeller that blew the cold air about, and the huge New Hampshire sky looming overhead. There were blurred images of Jack watching her with a fretted brow and his lips tight with worry. He had stitches on his lower lip and his arm was in a sling. Or had she dreamt that? She remembered speaking with her mother, hugging her and helping her tend to the garden behind their house. Her mother's long raven curls were pulled back in a peach-colored scarf and she wore an old cotton dress she used especially for gardening. Kylie held the tin bowl while her mother dropped in green onions and turnips she pulled from the warm dirt to be prepared for that evening's supper. Tucker swung so high in the rope swing his toes nearly touched the leaves of the old oak tree. But that had to have been a dream. No amount of confusion could convince her that she was still living in Savannah and that her mother and little brother were alive. Then suddenly she remembered her surgery. She had awakened in the middle of it, sending the doctors and nurses into a panic. "Sedate her! Sedate her!" a pudgy face barked behind a surgical mask. She remembered resisting their hands while they tried to push her back onto the cold table. She had broken free, sat up and looked down past the bloodied sheets. Nothing was there but a nub where her right leg had been. They had amputated her leg!

Kylie gasped as she ripped back the cover but her legs were both there intact. She sighed with relief and wiped her sweating brow with her hand. It was hot in the stuffy room.

"Hey! Look who's awake!" cried the familiar voice.

Dillon was standing in the doorway smiling brightly. He was wearing doctor's fatigues and his blue eyes looked tired.

Kylie smiled. "Dillon," she said through a raspy but delighted voice. "Do you mind telling me where the hell I am and who the wise guy is that brought me here."

Dillon kissed her tenderly on the cheek. "Mass. General. And I'm the wise guy."

"Can you cough for me?" he asked.

She reluctantly complied as he pressed his stethoscope to her chest and back.

"Breathe," he ordered. After a moment he pulled away. "Good."

"What day is this?" she asked, searching the room for a calendar.

"March 12th," he answered.

Kylie couldn't believe it. They had wrecked nearly three weeks earlier, but it seemed like only yesterday. "How did I get here?" she asked.

"I take it that means you don't remember the exciting chopper ride back to Boston," he said. "Jack had to be tranquilized. Something tells me that's his last time flying."

"Where is he by the way? Shouldn't he be glued to my side?"

"He just left an hour ago to do some work. I'll track him down for you. How do you feel?"

"Fine, except that it feels like a truck ran over my head. I can't seem to remember much."

"That's not surprising, considering what you've been through."

"Which is what?" Kylie asked reluctantly.

"Two surgeries . . . an intensive treatment called ECMO . . . lots of heavy sedation."

"Surgery, huh?" she asked. "I remember one but something tells me that was just a dream. What was it for?"

"When you first came in, you had a punctured lung and a torn aorta. The second one was to remove your spleen."

Kylie took a moment to absorb it all. "What the hell does a spleen do?"

"Practically nothing. Without it, you'll be a little more prone to certain types of infections."

"You said a torn aorta. That sounds pretty bad."

The crease in Dillon's brow deepened. "It could have been," he said steadily. "But it was handled quickly. The doctors in New Hampshire patched it up before we arrived. They did a good job—cosmetically even. Instead of cutting along your sternum, they hid the incision along the bottom of your breast, taking it up to your armpit. You might still have some tenderness there."

There was another moment of silence as she sorted her thoughts. "Long term," she said softly. "Just give me the long term of things."

"You'll be as good as new in no time," he said. "You have a gortex patch in your heart that'll outlast us all. You have a scar on your lung. Other than limited exercise tolerance, and short windedness in high altitudes, you can lead a perfectly normal life."

Kylie suddenly remembered the ghostly figure of Amelia peering through the blur, her face ashen and a bruise above her brow. She had been wearing a patient gown and her sapphire eyes had been laced with tears. "How are Amelia and Dix?" she asked.

"They're fine," said Dillon. "They're back in Savannah. She's been calling every day to ask how you're doing."

The horn from a boat sounded from outside the window. "Let me guess," said Kylie. "I'm facing the Charles River."

"Yep," smiled Dillon. "Best room in the house. Saw to it myself."

"Thanks," said Kylie looking toward the sunny window. Suddenly a pigeon fluttered past and Kylie nearly screamed.

"What is it?" Dillon asked with alarm.

"Nothing, I'm fine," she said, but her heart was beating wildly.

"You should take it easy for awhile."

"Yeah," she said, resting back into the bed. A sharp pain jabbed through her skull causing her to flinch. "I just can't seem to remember anything."

"It'll come back," he said assuredly. "You've come a long way but you still have more recovering to do."

Kylie looked up at the warm, sensitive face that smiled down at her. Over the years, Dillon had always been there for her and Jack whenever they made a mess of things. Though she had met the brothers on the same night and had been attracted to both, Jack had been the one to take her breath away. He was the one with the unconquerable energy and the tumultuous eyes that appealed to her own restless nature. Dillon, on the other hand, had become a true friend, with a quiet, intellectual voice and a perceptive vision of life, with a steady hand capable of making the troubles disappear. "So are you the one that put me back together?"

Dillon pulled slightly back as if hesitant to answer. "Your doctor's name is Holbrook, but I've been overseeing your treatment. I hope you don't mind."

Kylie was touched by the embarrassment in her brother-in-law's face. "Dillon," she said, gently touching his hand. "Thank you. I wouldn't have trusted anyone else."

He shyly looked away from her gaze.

"Did I ever tell you you're a sweetheart?" she asked.

Dillon smiled but she could see that he was still worried about her. "The drugs that you've been on," he started slowly, carefully choosing his words, "can be very addictive. Dr. Holbrook's begun the weaning process, so to speak. He'll want you off everything before he releases you. We try not to let patients leave here with a prescription for Percodan tucked in their back pockets."

"I'll be fine," she said.

"I have to warn you that it's not going to be easy," he said. He looked at her for a reaction but received none. "Kylie, there's something else I think you should know. It's about the accident and I think it's important that you hear it as soon as possible."

"Is it Jack?" she asked suddenly alarmed. "I can remember him being okay, standing by my—"

"It's not Jack. Except for his arm in a sling, he's back to normal," Dillon quickly said. "It's the other passengers, Kylie. There were only five survivors. Only one of the attorneys made it."

Kylie heard the words and felt suddenly ill. But somehow, it was information that she already knew and had come to grips with. The survivor's name was Collins. Yes, Gavin Collins. She remembered speaking with him after the accident.

Dillon continued slowly. "In tragic occurrences like these, it's best if the survivors can talk to someone, let them know how they're feeling to—"

"I'm fine, Dillon," Kylie interrupted uneasily. "I'm fine. Do you mind tracking down that no-count brother of yours?"

"Sure," he said. He looked at her a moment longer, then turned toward the door.

"Dillon?" Kylie asked.

He looked back at her.

"I wasn't by any chance walking around after the accident, was I?" she asked.

"I seriously doubt it. The man who found you said you were still strapped in your seat when he got there."

She was looking off into the distance, a narrow canyon laying itself out in her memory. "I remember walking along a valley between the mountains," she said vaguely.

Dillon smiled slightly. "I think you're going to remember a lot of stuff. Morphine has a way of doing that."

"Yeah," she said, though unconvinced.

"I've got a critically ill patient to tend to," he said. "Try to rest."

"I will," she promised as he disappeared around the door.

As she lay back onto the bed, she noticed the greenish bruises on her hands and arms. She squeezed her hands in a fist and then released them again, satisfied that they still worked properly. "Thank you, God," she whispered. Her eyes glanced about the room and landed on a hand-mirror on the table beside the bed. Her heart suddenly thundered as she reached for the shiny little object that would reveal her fate in a matter of seconds. With a deep breath, she pulled the reflective glass up to her face. At first stunned by her pallid image, matted hair and the greenish-yellow splotches of faded bruises, she was relieved that none of it was permanent, none with the exception of a red scar traced across the bottom of her chin. "I can live with that," she said aloud. As her lips moved she felt as if she were observing a stranger, one who had been pillaged of her spirit. As the image stared back at her, tears began to form in the stranger's sunken and frightened eyes. "You survived Kylie Rose," she whispered with a bittersweet smile.

She placed the mirror back on the table and laid her head against the pillow. She was exhausted and ready to sleep again, even though she had only been awake a few minutes. As her eyes rested on the balloon that swayed lightly overhead, glimpses of the roaring plane flashed through her mind like pieces of a forgotten nightmare. She instantly felt the rushing blasts of icy wind and heard the thrashing sound of splitting trees and twisting metal. Then all at once there was silence; the memory ended as abruptly as it had started, leaving behind the black bottomless pit of the unknown. Though her head had begun to pound, she concentrated with all her might to re-create the segment of reality but it eluded her like that of a fleeting dream one tries desperately to hold onto to dissect and decode. Tears fell along her cheeks as she fought to hold back a desolate sadness. Others had died but she and her loved ones had been spared. Three weeks of her consciousness had been reduced to a blink of an eye, but she was all too aware that same three weeks was the minuscule price she paid for what could have been an eternity.

Ten

IN HIS OFFICIAL DARK BLUE BOMBER JACKET, MATCHING SLACKS, AND briefcase in hand, Drew Dodson gave the paradoxical impression of a business-jock. He slipped the promised twenty to the nurse and thanked her for the confidential call that would end his three week stay in the Boston area.

"Room 369," she whispered. "She's only been awake for a few minutes."

"Thank you, miss," Dodson replied. "The United States government thanks you," he stressed and with a nod of his head was off to question his last remaining witness.

KYLIE HAD just drifted to sleep when the knock sounded. She immediately sat up, thrilled to put her arms around Jack and hold him tight. When she saw the sun-tanned face and the artificial smile of the forty-six-year-old man she couldn't help but show her disappointment.

"You must have the wrong room," she said, but then noticed something vaguely familiar about the suave-looking man. Suddenly she remembered him standing over her bed in the ICU with a deep frown on his face.

"Mrs. O'Rourke, my name's Drew Dodson and I'm with the National Transportation Safety Board," he said, advancing toward the bed. "I hope you don't mind if I ask you a few questions about the accident."

"Well, I just woke up not too long ago and I was expecting my husband," she said pulling the sheet up around her chest. "I'd rather we did this some other time when my head is a little clearer. I'm still on medication and—"

"Honestly ma'am, in my line of work it's best to talk to the victims while the accident is still fresh in their minds."

"That's just what I'm trying to tell you, Mr. Dodson. Nothing's clear in my mind at this moment. I need to talk with my husband and try to figure—"

"No, you see, that's exactly what we don't want," he interrupted, pulling a clipboard from the leather attaché. "We like to talk to the victims before their stories become polluted with the media or with other survivors' recollections."

"We?" Kylie asked, resenting the sudden shift to the plural to strengthen his power.

"Why yes," he said glancing down at his jacket. The letters NTSB were embroidered into the material in off-white colors. "The NTSB is a federally subsidized organization that investigates the causes and repercussions of aircraft disasters," he recited as if reading from a manual. "I work for the government, miss."

"It's Mrs.," Kylie corrected.

The man smiled slightly. "Pardon me . . . Mrs.," he said pulling out an expensive-looking pen and clicking it twice. He rested his hand against the pad of paper and looked up at her as if waiting for her to begin.

Kylie sighed with reluctance. She felt inundated at the thought of re-creating the horrific nightmare so soon, but judging by the determination in the investigator's manner she knew the interrogation would not be conducted at her own leisure. "Well if you work for the government then by all means let's hop to it. But first I have to warn you, Mr. Dodson, that you may not like what you get."

The man gave her a dismissing smile and pulled up a chair. "I'm sure I will. Just start at the beginning when you left the airport in Errol."

As Kylie thought back to the day and time that they boarded the small aircraft her heart began to flutter. She was forced to recount the names of the passengers, what they were wearing, where they were seated in the aircraft and most importantly of all, what the pilot was saying or doing if anything. She recounted the events leading to the accident, clearer than she had thought possible.

"Concentrate on the details and the rest will come to you," the investigator had repeated again and again.

As her own words guided her memory closer and closer to the moment of impact her pulse quickened and her breath became heavy as if she were once again within the confining walls of the Merlin IV. The room about her became unbearably hot and the stale air felt as if it would smother her.

"Would you like some water?" the investigator asked in his first real moment of clemency.

"That would be nice," Kylie uttered, her throat aching from speaking more in the past half hour than she had in nearly a month. "Am I going into too much detail?" she asked, hoping the answer would be "yes".

"No," Dodson replied, handing her a cup of water from the sink. "The details are exactly what I want."

The cool water slid down her burning throat while she returned her thoughts to the rushing plane. Jack was seated beside her, with his head back and his face taut with worry. She stared out the tiny window of the Merlin, at the countless rivets holding the metal of the plane intact when suddenly a raven fluttered up to the wing and landed less than a foot from her face.

"Excuse me, did you say a raven?" the investigator interrupted.

"Yes," Kylie answered.

Dodson looked slightly confused. "Continue."

Kylie looked down at the pen working feverishly across the pad of paper. She put the plastic cup once again to her lips. "Just take it slow and relax," Dodson reminded.

Kylie sighed and continued.

A thick layer of clouds rushed beneath the plane, while the sun danced off the quivering wing where the bird was perched. The juxta-position of cloud and light gave the surreal impression that heaven and earth had changed places.

She stared out at the shiny black feathers that caught the light and absorbed it. Though the eyes of the bird were dark and small, a feel-ing rushed through her that there was something peculiar about them. She tried to look away but their strange shape captivated her. As she locked into the creature's gaze, she suddenly saw them, freakishly placed within the raven's feathers. The eyes were human, with tiny white corneas, green retinas, and big dark pupils that were dilated. The hideous organs were staring in at her, examining her through the glass.

Kylie choked on her own memory, sucking the water from the cup into her windpipe. She looked about the hospital room, gasping for air as the liquid worked its way down like scorching fire.

"Miss?! Are you alright?" asked the investigator, jumping to his feet.

After a breathless pause, she coughed a deep guttural sound that drew blood.

"Miss?" repeated the investigator.

"I'm fine," she whispered, finally retrieving the air.

The investigator watched her closely, sweat forming along his hair-line.

"I guess I just forgot how to swallow," she smiled uneasily.

The investigator settled back into his seat. "You were saying that you noticed something unusual about the bird," he said, checking his notes.

"No," she whispered, relieved she hadn't given voice to the bizarre eyes that cropped out of the bird. Her hands were trembling as she set the cup onto the bedside table. "Could we please continue this another—"

"But you're doing so well, ma'am," the investigator said.

Kylie rubbed her dry eyes with her hand, thinking the residual drugs must have fabricated the freakish memory. She remembered looking out the window and seeing the bird and mentioning it to Jack. But the eyes . . . she couldn't have seen such hideous eyes. "I'm just not sure I'm remembering this correctly," she said. "I'm remembering things that—"

"—in more detail?" asked the investigator.

She didn't answer.

"That happens quite often, Mrs. O'Rourke, simply because you're paying closer attention to those details. People are always amazed at their own memories once they concentrate." he said. He watched her a moment as she sat in contemplative silence. "Please, I know this is hard," he said, his voice compassionate. "But I live in Denver and I can't go home until I have a full report from you. I've been waiting for three weeks. You're my last interview. If we could finish today I would be most appreciative," he said.

"Okay," she hesitantly agreed.

When she returned to the moment in her memory, the bird was no longer there.

"What happened next, Mrs. O'Rourke?" Dodson prodded.

"I don't know, I can't seem to remember," she said.

"What about when you first felt the turbulence?"

A flash of Jack's terrified face passed before her eyes but only for a moment before it was gone. "I don't remember right now," she repeated.

"That's okay. We'll come back to it later. Let's go to the point immediately following the actual impact," suggested the investigator.

"I don't really know—"

"Just close your eyes and think about the sounds you must have heard inside the plane," he suggested.

Kylie closed her eyes and listened.

She heard the gusting, howling wind and could feel it lashing about her body. She was stretched out, staring into the darkness, stunned and confused. As she opened her eyes and stood to her feet, she felt the solid ground beneath her.

"I remember a field," she said.

"A field?"

"Yes. I was standing in a snow-covered field," she recalled. "My doctor said that I was found in my seat but there must be some mistake."

"Well it wouldn't be the first time inaccuracies were found in the reports; nor the first time a victim returned to the scene of a crash after being thrown from a plane. I once had a victim go so far as to restrap himself in after a crash. Were you alone?" asked Dodson.

Kylie heard the voice calling over the wail of the wind. "We've got to find the plane!" it screamed. She looked to her right and saw an older man standing to his feet. It was a middle-aged attorney.

"I was with Gavin Collins," Kylie said, envisioning the brilliant white snow and gusting wind which nearly knocked the attorney to the ground. "We've got to find the plane!" he screamed against the shrill blizzard.

"Gavin Collins?" asked the investigator.

"Yes."

"Are you sure it was Gavin Collins?" he asked, shuffling through his briefcase.

"Yes," Kylie answered quietly.

The investigator placed a black and white photo in front of her. "Is that him?" he asked.

Though the photo appeared to be at least ten years old there was no mistaking the warm, gentle eyes of the kind attorney. "Yes, that's him," she answered.

The investigator looked at her strangely. "Uh . . . Mrs. O'Rourke, you must be mistaken."

"No," she said. "I'm certain. And Jack. He was there also but we didn't see him until we got to the bottom of a ravine."

As she stared down at the photo of Collins she suddenly remembered standing in the loft of a dark cottage. Collins was on the lower level, smiling up at her with an old radio in his hands. "He tried to fix the radio," she said softly, dictating from her vacillating memory.

"The wires were rusted . . ." she said, her voice trailing off. But something felt wrong, irrevocably and hideously wrong. Stunned by the sudden rush then disappearance of memory she looked up at the dumbfounded investigator.

"You went to a cottage?" he asked.

"Yes," she said uneasily. "A cabin of sorts."

"Why did you leave it?"

"I don't remember," she said, her voice barely audible.

She felt the eyes of the investigator upon her.

"Mrs. O'Rourke," he said slowly. "Not to dispute what you're saying, but you must have Gavin Collins confused with one of these other men," he insisted, laying several photos in front of her.

Kylie became slightly agitated. "I was there I ought to know."

"Mrs. O'Rourke, please take a moment to look at these other photos. Could it have been Dale Benson?" asked the investigator, shoving the photo of an older, thinner attorney in front of her.

"I remember him, but it's not the same man," she answered handing the photo of Benson back. "It was him," she insisted, pointing at the smiling picture of Gavin Collins. "Without a doubt. Why? What did he say?"

"Nothing," the investigator answered quietly. "He died on impact."

KYLIE STARED at the investigator, unable to utter a sound. Abruptly there was a knock at the door breaking the thick silence. Jack was standing in the doorway with a bright smile and a bouquet of white freesia.

"Jack," she said softly, her voice quivering with tears. "Oh Jack," she whispered as he rushed toward her and took her into his arms. His embrace was strong and comforting, his earthy smell familiar and safe. "I'm so happy to see you," she cried, smothering his face and neck with tender kisses.

"We made it, baby," he whispered in a faltering voice as he held her tight.

"I'll just wait outside," the investigator mumbled to himself, ducking out of the room.

"Let me see you," Kylie said, her face wet with her own tears. Jack pulled back from her, his expression tender and shy.

"I'm still a little banged up," he said, his blue eyes glancing away. The couple had been through hell together, yet the sight of their own wounds seemed strangely intimate and embarrassing. "I'm fine," he said.

"Fine's not the word for it," Kylie said. "You're perfect." Though Jack's skin was also covered in the lime-tinged splotches of faded bruises, his face was exactly as she had remembered it. His eyes were defiant, his cheekbones high and his jaw line determined. His rosy lips formed the same sweet, kissable mouth but they had been slightly hardened with the addition of a tiny scar on his bottom lip.

"Guess I bit myself during it all," he said shyly covering the wound with his hand.

"What happened to the sling?" Kylie asked.

"Oh that damn thing," he said with a dismissive gesture of his hand. "There's no way I'm wearing it for another three weeks."

"Jack, if you're—" she started but then caught herself. She never had been able to convince him of anything that he thought threatened his manhood, and to Jack, a sling would certainly fall under the category of testosterone plungers. She smiled at him, admiring his curly blonde hair and tan skin. "Looks like you've been outside," she observed.

"Yeah, the Greyson house," he said pulling a notebook from under the fragrant flowers. "I brought pictures and a copy of the floor plan in case you felt like doing some work. Or in case you decided to have pity on me and steer me in the right direction."

"I would love to but first I have to finish up with the investigator," she said, her voice dropping.

Noticing the trouble in his wife's eyes, Jack quickly laid the flowers and notebook on the table. "What's the matter?" he asked.

"Jack," she said slowly. "Do you remember Gavin Collins?"

He stared back at her blankly. "He was one of the attorneys wasn't he?"

"Yes. The one who went to the cabin with us after the wreck," she said, watching him carefully for his reaction.

Jack smiled tenderly and touched her cheek. "Dillon said you'd probably be confused when you woke up and that—"

"Do you remember the cabin?" she interrupted.

"Kylie," he said, looking intently into her disquieted eyes. "There wasn't any cabin after we wrecked. We stayed in the plane until a guy named Haskell Shaw rescued us."

"I can't believe you don't remember that," she insisted, the recollection as vivid as the very moment around her. Though the memory was fragmented, the details were sketched with such vibrant clarity that she couldn't possibly have been dreaming. The disjointed components were still fresh in her mind as if they had taken place only yesterday. The light of the storm played against the stone walls of the cottage, as the sound of the rushing storm battered against it. The musty smell of the room mixed with pine, and she could hear the voices. "Amelia was there!" she said, suddenly remembering holding Amelia's hands who was fraught with worry over Dix.

"Kylie, think about what you're saying," Jack interrupted. "Amelia was hurt just like the rest of us. We were all practically dead when they found us," he stressed. "I had a huge gash in my leg, you had a piece of metal sticking out of you. Dillon said that it's a miracle we lived. He said the only thing that saved us was the fact that Haskell Shaw came along when he did. There's no way we left that plane and went traipsing around in the woods."

"We didn't leave the plane, Jack," she said. "We woke up in the middle of nowhere and couldn't find the plane."

"You were dreaming," Jack insisted. "Just like you were dreaming about all kinds of stuff. You were dreaming about your mom and Tucker and your brother, Aidan. Kylie, I haven't heard you mention Aidan in years. I came in one day and you thought I was him. You were just hallucinating. That's all. And talking in your sleep. You were talking about all kinds of stuff. Like your necklace," he said pointing down to the gold chain dangling from her neck.

Kylie looked down and for the first time realized that she was wearing it. Since her mother had passed away, she had worn the cameo locket day and night, and had gotten so used to it that it had become an indiscernible extension of her body.

"When one of the nurses took it off of you for surgery, you went ballistic. You put a welt above the poor woman's eye."

"Oh my God, did I really?" Kylie whispered.

"Yes, really," Jack said with an insuppressible smile. "I hadn't seen you whack someone like that since you decked me at the Harrison party a few years ago," he said with true admiration.

"Jack," Kylie scolded. "You promised not to mention that any-more."

"Well, hell, Kylie, you were like Muhammad Ali in the ring with Frazier," he said, moving around her, throwing playful punches at an invisible partner.

"Stop it," she said, trying to keep herself from smiling. "You de-served it."

"Hey, did I say I didn't?" he asked.

Then the voice of Drew Dodson interrupted them. "Uh . . . Mrs. O'Rourke, do you mind if we continue our conversation?" he asked, leaning his head inside the room.

Kylie sighed heavily and pinched the skin between her eyes. "I really don't see the point since I'm remembering implausible conver-sations with a dead man," she said, shaking her head. "Do you?"

The investigator moved once again into the room. "You're a little confused maybe, but—"

"Look," Jack interrupted harshly. "Isn't it a little early to be badger-ing her with questions? She's still sedated, can't you see that?"

Kylie hated it when Jack used a confrontational tone with strangers, but for once she welcomed his raw instinct to protect. She wanted to pull the covers over her head and hide from the investigator's probing eyes, but instead met his gaze with an exasperated sigh.

"My boss prefers that we interview in person," said Dodson, "but I've already got enough from you to get started and considering the circumstances, how about if we take this up by telephone?"

"That would be best," said Kylie.

As Dodson gathered up his belongings, Kylie wondered when that conversation would take place. It seemed the more she remembered, the more confused she became.

"Mr. O'Rourke?" said the investigator.

"Yeah?" said Jack, waiting for the investigator to finish his thought.

"Did you leave the plane anytime following the accident?"

"Not until I was carried out by Mr. Shaw."

"Well, your wife remembers—"

"We didn't leave the plane," Jack interrupted.

The investigator seemed content with the answer. "Well, you folks have a nice day and Mrs. O'Rourke I'll talk to you soon," he said. Jack followed him to the door, then turned back to his wife.

"Hey," he said, observing her from the doorway. "Forget about it for now."

"You're not leaving too, are you?" she asked.

"I have to get back over to the Greyson place," he answered. "I promised her I would have all the new tiling in the bathroom done today."

"But Jack, you just got here," Kylie said, unable to hide the hurt in her voice. "Why does Dora care when you have the tiles in the bathroom finished? It's not like she's going to be taking a bath there for God's sake," she argued. "She obviously can't live in the place until we're finished with it."

"I just promised her it would be done," he said, walking back toward the bed. "We're already behind by a month, and since she's laid out the money in advance, it's understandable that she's a little worried."

"Well it's not like we've been hanging out with our friends sipping on highballs in Bermuda. We were in a plane accident, Jack," Kylie argued. She could feel the anger welling in her chest and as much as she tried to control it, it continued to mount.

"Kylie, just calm down, okay?"

She tried to slow her beating heart, but instead began to cry. "I'm sorry, Jack," she said softly. "I'm just feeling so off."

"Well, there's no wonder," he said, kissing her lightly on the forehead. "You've been through a lot."

"So have you," she said looking into his tired and sad eyes.

"Well, you haven't had time to sort it all out," he concluded.

"Go ahead and go," she whispered, stroking his soft hair.

"I'll be back later tonight."

"Okay," she said. "Leave the notebook and I'll look it over."

Jack smiled. "I think you'll like what I've done in my boss' absence," he said hopefully.

Kylie kissed him tenderly on the lips. "Thanks for the flowers, Jack Black."

"You're welcome, Wylie Coyote," he said.

He gave her a last kiss and headed toward the door, then turned thoughtfully back. "And don't worry about what happened on the mountain. It'll all come back to you."

Eleven

KYLIE LAY IN THE SHADOWS STARING OUT AT THE EMPTY HALLWAY. THE monotonous sound of the clock ticked through her head like a time bomb. The seconds passed one after the other, the hands moving slowly and deliberately, closer and closer to the hour of the rising sun. It was nearly three A.M. and the moon had already begun to drop in the western sky, peeking its glowing face into her window. All around her time was passing but she had been left behind in the brutal solitude of insomnia.

Hours earlier she had requested a sedative but the nurse had refused. It had been three days since she had regained full consciousness and in those three nights she had slept less than ten hours. She had been in a constant battle with the staff to give her something to help her sleep, but they were unrelenting. Though she understood she was in the midst of withdrawal from the heavy doses of sedatives, she hadn't anticipated such long nights staring up at the dark ceiling with only her thoughts to keep her company. Night had always been her favorite time, but now it had turned on her. At night there were no friends or family to cheer her and keep her mind off the horrible nightmare that loomed in the back of her subconscious, eluding and taunting her.

She had telephoned Amelia every day and she too was going through her own sordid hell. She was suffering from a deep, dark depression.

"Post-traumatic stress," Amelia had repeated again and again. "My doctor said it's totally normal after something really awful happens."

Kylie had noticed the quiver in her friend's voice but when she questioned her further Amelia had shut her out. It was at times like these that the distance between the friends was unbearable. Kylie knew if she could just look into her friend's eyes and hold her tight, the darkness would lighten for both of them. But Amelia was in Savannah and no amount of wishing would bring her closer.

Kylie flipped on the fluorescent light above her head and as it sporadically blinked on, she winced at the hideous tint it cast upon herself and the surrounding blankets. She reached for the notebook on the Greyson house and began thumbing through it. With each passing day, Jack had taken Polaroids of his progress. He was laying tiles in the expansive kitchen and the subtle, yet alluring pattern he had created sent a surge of pride through Kylie. Jack was talented and given the push of unavoidable circumstance he was proving he was more than simply a carpenter. He too could take on the artistic aspects of their business and flourish.

She looked once again at the big round clock hanging on the wall directly in front of her. Jack had promised to call nearly four hours earlier. She lay the notebook aside and reached for the telephone. She slowly lifted the receiver and dialed the Greyson house for the third time that night.

"Answer, Jack" she whispered, but the phone rang nearly two minutes before she hung up. She quickly dialed their home number where her own voice answered in a cheerful tone requesting the caller leave a name and number. She had recorded the message before the accident, in a happier time when life was simpler. Now, it seemed to mock her as it conducted business in a house she hadn't seen in over a month. She hung up the receiver.

"Mrs. O'Rourke?" a voice cackled.

Nurse Clark was standing in the doorway with a look of exasperation on her withered old face. "Honey, you know the rules," she said in a sweet, motherly tone.

"Why should I lie here in the dark when I can't sleep?" Kylie quipped back more sternly than she had intended.

"Why of course you can't sleep, darling," said the nurse with a maternal smile, "you've got a light blaring in your sweet little eyes." And with this declaration she marched over to Kylie's bed and flipped off the fluorescent light, then briskly fluffed the pillow behind her head.

Kylie felt her lips pressing together as she tried to contain her frustration. For the past three nights the nurse had insisted on Kylie's curtains being shut and her light off, regardless of whether or not she was sleeping. By the time she got her exasperation under control, the efficient nurse had already hobbled back out of the room.

"Damn it all to hell," she hissed, throwing the blanket aside. She reached for her robe, put her bare feet onto the cold smooth floor, and headed for the door.

"Mrs. O'Rourke!" called the old nurse from her station. "What in heaven's name do you think you're doing?"

"I'm going for a walk," Kylie said with determination as she headed down the hall.

"But Mrs. O'Rourke—" the nurse called rushing after her.

"I'm going for a walk," Kylie repeated, turning back to the nurse. "And I don't need your permission," she said, her face flushed with blood and her heart thumping against her sore ribs. "If you don't like it, call the hospital police, drag me back to my bed, but unless you plan to stand guard over me all night, then you might as well forget it, because I'm not lying there anymore staring up at the goddamned ceiling while my goddamned husband is out screwing some goddamned slut from Beacon Hill!"

Kylie felt her legs shaking, saw the stunned look on the nurse's face and still couldn't believe what had just come out of her mouth. She covered her eyes with her trembling hands. "I'm sorry. I can't believe I said that," she whispered. She didn't even know she had been thinking it. The elderly nurse was silent, staring at her with astonishment on her shriveled, pouting lips. Kylie wanted to say something, anything to erase the horrible outburst, but knew any attempt would be futile. Instead, she simply turned and continued down the hallway.

Jack had been out late every night for the past three nights and given his past record there was only one conclusion that Kylie's mind would draw: he was having an affair.

"I can't believe you said that," she whispered aloud as her hand rested upon the cool metal of the hallway railing. After all, hadn't they both made the commitment to make it work? "You're being ridiculous. He's probably out with Dillon," she said. "Or working. You're just over-reacting as usual," she scolded in a whispered hiss.

She turned to the right and then to the left and not a single person was in sight. The lights in each room were off and the patients were sleeping soundly. Then she came upon the doors of the maternity ward and her heart lifted. She entered the brightly lit corridor strung with pink and blue streamers.

She placed her hands against the glass wall that divided the newborns from the rest of the germ-filled world and stared in at all the beautiful little babies with their tiny feet and hands. A nurse wearing a mask noticed Kylie standing on the other side of the glass in her robe and mistook her for a mother. She pointed to one of the newborns, and gestured as if he were Kylie's. Kylie shook her head "no" and after a confused moment, the nurse went back to her job. Kylie looked down at the delicate, dark-haired baby and tears suddenly filled her eyes. "Tuckie," she whispered and turned away from the glass.

Tucker McCallum had entered her life when she was fifteen years old on a glorious Easter Sunday. The unexpected appearance of the bright-eyed little baby her mother bore was a sigh of relief in her parents' sad and disillusioned marriage. Tucker had been a gift to all and to Kylie he was hers. For seven years she adored him, took care of him, loved him, then one rainy night he was yanked from her life by a semi-truck. On that night, she not only lost a second brother, but a child she had nurtured and loved as her own and in the agonizing grief she vowed to never feel such pain again. In the years to follow, her refusal to have children was the first rift in her troublesome marriage to Jack.

As Kylie made her way down the long hallway, her legs became progressively weaker and her breathing labored. The next corridor would lead past the nurse's station and on to her room. She would apologize to Nurse Clark and return to her bed like a good, obedient patient. But then when she passed through a set of double doors, she realized that she had mistaken the last corridor for another. She was back where she had started, standing before the glass of the maternity ward looking in at the newborns. One of the babies was crying in pitiful whelps as the nurse bent back its tiny hand in a desperate attempt to find a blood vein. The small hand was twisted in such an unnatural position that it made Kylie's stomach flutter and her head swim. She quickly looked away and started in the opposite direction from which she came. She felt a trickling sensation on her skin and when she swiped it away, she found sweat running along the sides of her cheeks. As she continued down the shadowy hallway the walls began closing in on her and the old familiar feeling of claustrophobia began to take hold. She tried to slow her pace in order to calm herself, but instead, began moving faster in an attempt to emerge from the hallway as soon as possible. When she glanced behind her, she realized that the passageway had indeed become more narrow and dark. The maternity ward had spilled out into the older section of the hospital without noticeable entry. The bright corridor of the new had been replaced by the dim tunnels of the old. The fluorescent lights had been reduced to old fixtures eking out a mere orange glow, while the colorful papered walls had turned to a cemented gray.

With relief, she noticed three people in white standing in a pool of light ahead of her. They were discussing something amongst themselves when Kylie approached unsteadily.

"Could you please help me?" she gasped as she leaned against the wall and braced herself with the railing. "I'm trying to get back to my room and somehow got turned around."

She waited for their response but the three merely looked at her as if she were speaking a language they didn't understand.

The youngest of the two women turned toward the man. "She's looking at us," she said strangely.

"Could you help me please?" Kylie repeated, feeling as if she might faint.

The older man stepped forward, examining her closely as if she were some kind of alien. He was thin and stately, his hair streaked with gray. "She knows we're here," he said back to the two women. The harsh overhead light hollowed out his eye sockets giving his face an ethereal cast. "You're lost, child, is that it?" he asked, his voice kind and warm.

The elder woman immediately touched the man's arm. "We mustn't interfere," she said, her tone cool.

Kylie stared with confusion at the inquisitive faces, at the crude shadows that darkened their eyes, when her vision began to deceive her. While the corridor that stretched into the distance maintained its sharp edges and precise angles, the three people in front of her began to blur. She put her hand to her temple trying to clear her sight. "I'm not seeing well . . ." she gasped, digging her hot fingers deep into her temple. "Not . . . feeling . . ." but when she looked back, the distortion had worsened. It appeared that their flesh had become malleable, twisting and smearing the three faces and bodies into elongated mutations, the figures swaying like the distorted images in a warped carnival mirror. Kylie clutched for the railing but it had slipped from her hand. With her balance reeling, she tried to back away but her feet had become leaden. In a single step, the floor beneath her suddenly grew brighter. With a trembling hand she shielded her eyes and when she looked back up she saw that the moving forms were glowing a brilliant, transparent white. The light above the three swaying distortions had also become brighter until it appeared the bulb inside the fixture would burst. All at once, the forms turned to white streaks shooting up toward the bulb. Sparks ricocheted off the arched ceiling as the masses of light were absorbed into the electrical currents. With a wavering surge of power, the luminous light dissipated and no sign was left of the three people or their distorted bodies. The hallway was empty again, murky and dark.

Kylie found herself gasping and alone. She looked to the dim bulb, to the dark tunnel. No one. She turned in the opposite direction but her legs would not move, they merely trembled uncontrollably. "I'm not dreaming," she whispered, trying desperately to grasp reason, but her senses were whirling. "I need to get back," she cried, her hand clutching the wall, when all at once it vanished. She was on the mountaintop, the whipping branches and trees taking her breath. She felt herself screaming but the only sound she heard was the screeching wind and blasting snow. "Kylie!" she shrieked, her own voice commanding her back. The hospital hallway was before her again, the shadowy spaces between the lights, deeper and blacker than before. Then they too began rustling and shifting, when out of them came the hideous beasts that had lain in her memory for three days and three nights. At once, her knees were buckling, her body sinking downward. As the floor rolled upward to greet her, the details of the accident came back to her in crystalline clarity. Before the last of the corridor vanished, she remembered every disturbing moment of the mountaintop nightmare that would change her life forever.

Twelve

THE MOON WAS SETTING IN THE WESTERN SKY AS DILLON HEADED over the massive Longfellow Bridge on his way back to Massachusetts General Hospital. It had been shortly after four A.M. when he received the call that Kylie had passed out in the maternity ward and banged her head resulting in four stitches to the back of her skull. As he pulled up to the parking lot across the street from the red brick hospital he took the last sip of black coffee that would sustain him until breakfast.

"Good mornin', Doctor O'Rourke," said the elderly security guard that patrolled the dark lot in the twilight hours. The watchman had worked next door to the hospital at the ominous Charlestown Prison for forty-two years, when one day the old jail suddenly closed. It had been purchased by the hospital to be used as a parking lot for the over-flow of cars generated by the huge medical center. Before its closure, the prison had fallen into disrepair, and was rumored to be rat-infested to the point of public hazard. It had been over two years since the purchase, but still the large gray building stood vacant. The iron gate that opened for the cars was no longer for the sentry of the incar-cerated but for the doctors of the ill. The old guard had often joked that the keepers were still for the imprisoned, they just drove a higher class of car.

As Dillon exited his BMW and headed toward the opening of the gate, his eyes purposefully avoided the towering, dim windows of the prison. Even though he had been parking in the lot for over a year, it still gave him chills to look into the desolate structure with its tangled web of bars that represented human despair.

"Have a good one, Harry," he said to the watchman who closed the rustic gate after him.

"Watch your backside, sir," said the guard, grinning through to-bacco-stained teeth. He had used the greeting for forty-two years and was reluctant to let it go.

When Dillon entered the floor that Kylie was on, Nurse Clark im-mediately rushed up to him. "Dr. O'Rourke," she said, falling in be-side his determined pace. "After I called you I tried to give her the Valium but she wouldn't take it. She's just sitting there in the dark—"

"—You did fine, Betty," Dillon said, dismissing her with a gesture of his hand.

He found Kylie sitting perfectly still in the dark room. The light from the window cut across her chest but left her face hidden in shadow. "Hey," he said, softly tapping on the door.

There was no answer, only silence.

He walked slowly into the room toward the dark figure silhouetted on the bed. "I hear you had some trouble."

"I can't talk right now," said the shaky voice from the shadows.

As Dillon's sight adjusted to the dark, Kylie's soft face came into view. Her eyes were puffy from crying, staring off into the distance refusing to acknowledge him. He had never seen her look so frightened and alone. Her hands were clasped tightly together, her skin turning white from the pressure of her own grip. He suddenly realized his heart was thudding wildly.

"There's a term called 'sundown'," he began softly. "Withdrawals from heavy sedation can be unpredictable, sporadic, even dangerous . . . night time being the worst. Given your situation, it's perfectly normal to have hallucinations—"

"I wasn't hallucinating," she interrupted, her fixed gaze glistening with emotion. "I saw the three people. They were there."

Dillon took a careful breath. "I know you believe that," he said, softly. "After the trauma you've been through, it's normal for your mind to be distorting things, rearranging them. I had a burn patient once who believed that a snake was nesting under his bed—"

"No . . . no," she said, looking fiercely into his eyes. "You don't understand. I remembered the accident. I remembered everything," she confided, tears trickling onto her cheeks. "Everything."

It was an intimate concession that pulled him into the darkness, her eyes begging for understanding and assurance. "I'm scared," she whispered, her chin trembling with the admission.

The words pierced into Dillon's heart. "What are you scared of?" he asked.

The tears rushed upon her but she didn't stop to brush them away. "I can't say," she said. "You won't believe me."

"Try me," he said, wiping her cheeks, the velvety soft liquid seeming to burn into his fingertips.

"I can't," she whispered, wringing her hands together like a child that wants desperately to confide but is forbidden.

He pulled the hair back from her eyes. "Will you talk to someone else then? I have a doctor who's helped some of my other patients deal with post-traumatic stress."

Even though she didn't answer, he saw a glimmer of hope in her face.

"He offices here in the hospital. I think he can help you."

In the silence her shoulders softened. She looked toward him with sad, fearful eyes. "What if he can't?" she asked, her voice trembling.

Dillon wanted desperately to take her into his arms and hold her tight, but instead kept his distance. If she had been any other patient he would have comforted her, but as he looked into the arresting face of his brother's wife he suddenly felt a pang of guilt. He moved away from the bed and tried to distance himself from the patient in order to maintain objectivity. He had always found Kylie attractive, but his platonic admiration had remained within the confinement of a family and friend alliance. Now they shared the intimacy of a doctor-patient relationship and he hadn't quite adjusted to the new domain. For three weeks her life had been his own, and even though he had not held the scalpel, had not written the prescriptions, or updated her charts, he had guided the hands of others, bringing her back to life. For three solid weeks, she had possessed his sleep and his every waking hour.

She took his hand into her own. "You've got to release me from here," she declared, her eyes wild and determined. As he looked at her, her face softened and once again became vulnerable. "Please Dillon, I need to go home," she whispered. She was trusting in him for her very well-being and he knew she would abide by his decision. He also knew it was a power few had ever possessed over the irrepressible Kylie.

"I want you to talk to the doctor first," he said, once again grasping hold of his professional tone. "Then I'll have Dr. Holbrook sign your release."

Her face relaxed with the promise, her head resting back against her pillow. A melancholy smile formed on her delicate lips. "Thank you, Dillon," she whispered. "Thank you for putting me back together." Her shining hair was spread over the pillowcase like a silken halo, the moonlight kissing her tender skin. She truly was the most beautiful creature Dillon had ever seen. He quickly looked away.

"Do you want me to call Jack?" he asked, heading toward the door.

"No," said Kylie sadly. "I just need to sleep for a little while."

"I'll set the appointment for tomorrow," he said and quietly left her to rest.

Thirteen

THOUGH IT WAS MID-AFTERNOON, THE TUNNELED HALLWAY IN WHICH Kylie sat was dark and indifferent to the daylight outside. Dr. Jordan's office was in the Bulfinch Wing located in the old part of the hospital, one floor down from the psych ward and two floors down from the famous Ether Dome where the initial operation using the drug was first performed in 1846. Kylie had learned about the operating theater from a lanky custodian that had come to her rescue when she had gotten off on the wrong floor and ended up outside the strange room with its rising bleachers. The custodian had proudly boasted that the room stood just as it had been left in the early forties. Like the rest of the ward it was untouched by time, leaving Kylie with a strange pit in her stomach. On the way down to Dr. Jordan's office, she and the custodian had passed a sign posted on a set of double doors that read: RESEARCH. When she asked the custodian about what sort of research they performed, the janitor simply shook his head, but said nothing. A chill ran down her spine as she imagined twisted tortures that would warrant such silence.

Waiting outside the doctor's office, she began to feel uneasy about the appointment in the seemingly questionable part of the hospital. It was as if the dark secrets of the medical center were kept in the older Bulfinch Wing where time had come to a screeching halt. Even the chair in which she sat was old, yet eerily shiny and preserved, as was the brown and black checked floor, and the black stenciling on the frosted door-window that read: DR. RUPERT JORDAN, PSYCHIATRIST.

Bracing herself, she debated whether or not to leave. After last night's episode, she didn't want to be alone in the old part of the hospital again. But just as she rose to leave, the door opened revealing a pleasant looking man with silvery hair and chestnut-brown eyes. "You must be Kylie," he said, extending his slender hand to shake.

When she took it, she was embarrassed to find her own palms cold and clammy.

The doctor looked at her kindly. "Not to worry," he said, gesturing for her to enter. "I'm quite harmless, you'll find."

Kylie was surprised to discover that the office resembled more an accountant's than a psychiatrist's. There were no couches, candles or soft lighting; just a simple wooden desk, two chairs, and several filing cabinets. Two windows opened to a red-bricked alleyway where rain was pouring down. "I had no idea it was raining," she said, finding the lull of the spattering drops to be an instant comfort.

"Are you a rain person?" asked Dr. Jordan, taking a seat behind the desk.

She stared at him defensively, wondering if the analysis had already begun.

The doctor smiled. It was a humorous, intelligent smile. "It wasn't a trick question," he said gently.

"I'm sorry," she said. "Yes, I like rain."

The doctor took a deep breath and released it. "Kylie," he said, looking up at her. "I don't want you to feel as though you have to be here. That would waste both of our time. Dr. O'Rourke . . ." he paused a moment. "Dillon, I guess I should call him, said that you were having some problems and asked if I might be an objective listener. That's all."

"When you hear what I have to say, you may never release me," she said, maintaining her position close to the door.

"You'll be released tomorrow regardless of our session. So really, it's a matter of whether or not you wish to discuss what's troubling you. If not, well then you can just tell me where you got that accent. Is it from the Southeast?"

Kylie's hand went to her lips.

"Don't be embarrassed," he said. "It's quite lovely . . . and ever so faint."

"When I'm nervous . . ." she said.

"You'd be amazed at the accents that suddenly come back to my patients in this room."

Kylie looked into the relaxed open face and instantly felt like crying. She had so much weighing on her, so much to tell. "Most of my childhood was spent in Georgia. Thirteen years, actually. My mother was from Savannah."

The doctor had picked up a pen and was jotting down as she spoke. He noticed that her attention had rested upon the paper. "Habit," he said. "Do you mind?"

"Yes," she said.

He looked at her a moment, then placed the pencil back on the desk, then scooted away from it. "How about if I just listen, then?" He reached over and switched on his desk lamp then sat back with his fingers steepled before him. The warm light made the gray room suddenly cozy, drawing her inward.

"Please," he said, gesturing to the chair opposite him. "You've survived quite an ordeal," he said, with a hint of admiration. "It's perfectly normal to be feeling fear, anger, what have you."

With the subject's encroachment, Kylie's glance averted away. "Yes, I suppose," she said softly.

"Your file indicates that you've been suffering from confusion. That there was some discrepancy about what took place right after the accident. That your husband remembers waking in the plane, but you remember something quite different."

Her gaze rested upon the blurred window streaked with rain, the sound of the pelting water drumming with the beat of her heart. The horrific memory lay open and exposed, without the safety net of spaces to be skipped over and filled in at a later date. She waited for her lips to move, to explain, but the lump in her throat kept her silent. "I'm sorry," she gasped, swiping a tear that escaped hotly over her cheek. She turned in her seat, agitated and uncomfortable. Unable to restrain herself any longer, she got up and walked toward the window, her back to the doctor. "It's all so real to me," she said softly. "The moments before we hit as clear as the moments after. But I could be nothing other than mad to think . . . to believe—" she broke off.

"Don't judge it," said the doctor gently. "Just tell it as though telling a story."

Under the doctor's guidance, she plunged inward, forcing her mind to the beginning . . . to the four o'clock hour when they boarded the plane in Errol. Detailing each moment that led up to the deathly crash, she recalled the information as she had for the investigator only this time with greater clarity and a more accurate chronicling of events; the ebony bird still landed on the wing of the plane but it wasn't until much later when she saw in detail the hideous eyes that were hidden within the feathers . . . the eyes that would be watching and waiting.

As the rain pelted against the glass, she was forced once again to enter the speeding plane with the screaming passengers and flying objects. With memory of Jack's nervous grip in her own, the office left her sight, her senses, the harrowing day rising vividly to greet her. As the Merlin IV hurled toward a wall of stone and ice, she could smell the vomit and the blood from the attorney's nose still covering her sweater. A passenger was praying in the background—"Hail Mary, full of grace . . .'"—only this time she knew the passenger's name; it was Gavin Collins. She turned to the front of the plane where an elderly man was scowling and cussing. He was Dale Benson and he would be the only attorney to survive.

"Put your head down," Jack told her, but as he crouched forward she remained sitting upright, captivated by what she saw outside of the window—something that until that moment she had forgotten. In the strange light of a sun falsely prophesying the storm's end, shadows appeared without substance. Over the brilliant white surface of the mountain, stretched the spectral shade of human forms. Just as before, she sensed a gaze, a focus riveted upward, only this time the unseen features had been filled in with pallid flesh, the gray eyes and parted lips colored with the taint of death.

Though she was now safe within the psychiatrist's office, gooseflesh rose over her; for this time she knew what nightmarish creatures lay hidden beneath the shadows. This time she knew what they patiently awaited.

Fourteen

THERE WAS NO SUFFERING WHEN THE PLANE HIT, ONLY A RIPPING force that silenced all. The shredding metal and blasting wind moved in a muted fog obliterating everything until the darkness took hold. Unable to tell if her eyes were open or closed, Kylie stared into the raven abyss. She was aware of her body, yet there was no pain. She felt a trickling sensation scurry across her cheek, but her arms would not move to brush it away. Then suddenly, the darkness was replaced with a blinding white. Her eyes were open and a powerful wind was blowing around her. When her body finally obeyed her command to move, she sat upright, disoriented and unsure what had just happened or where she was. Then she heard groaning coming from behind her. She saw Amelia lying on the ground thirty feet away moving slowly and the middle-aged attorney, Gavin Collins, shuffling about as if waking from a deep sleep. Straining to see through the blowing snow, she looked to the side and then around the other way; Jack was nowhere to be found. She rose to her feet, taking a moment to steady herself. The ground moved precariously beneath her before flattening out. Again she scanned the area, squinting to see through the storm.

"Jack?!" she cried, her voice whipped away by the whistling winds. She ran toward Amelia and helped her to her feet.

"Hey, look!" Collins yelled. The attorney was pointing across a vast canyon to a red-orange glow burning in the dark pines. "That must be the plane!"

At sight of the glinting fire, Amelia began to scream. "Dix!!" she cried, bolting forward toward the edge of the cliff. Kylie quickly grabbed her and held her tight, her own heart aching for Jack.

With Amelia's face buried against her shoulder, Kylie stared down at the ravine, numbed by the vastness of it . . . by the ninety-foot crevice that had separated them from the plane.

THERE WERE no signs of any other passengers along the steep descent; they moved in silence, full of confusion and fear. As they cut across the canyon at the base of the mountain, a figure emerged out of the blasting darkness stumbling aimlessly toward them. Though Kylie saw only his silhouette, she instantly knew it was Jack. She called out to him and he turned, his eyes blank and confused.

"Jack!" she cried, rushing toward him. Wrapping her arms around him, she held him tight. "Don't ever do that to me again," she whispered pressing her lips to his ear.

When he pulled away, he looked bewildered. "I don't know how I got here," he said, turning behind him. "We were in the plane one minute and then . . ." but his voice trailed off. He looked over at Collins and then finally to Amelia. "Where's Dix?" he asked, at sight of her somber face.

Kylie shook her head.

"Do you know where the plane is?" he asked.

"It's atop this mountain," said Collins. "We better keep moving," he advised, looking upward at the fading sky. "It's gonna be dark soon."

. . .

BY THE TIME the group emerged from the canyon, night had already fallen and the storm had picked up significantly. As they ascended into the dark woods in search of the wreckage, the pine trees crackled and bent dangerously overhead. The smoldering fire seen earlier had vanished. Snow whipped in every direction, limiting their vision to a few feet, making it difficult to establish a clear course. Adding to the confusion of the blizzard, was the fact that they had seen the fire from the opposite mountain. Up close the same landmarks became obscure, the space between each distorted.

"Are you sure we're on the right track?" Jack yelled, his voice competing with the torrential winds.

Collins looked bewildered. He had led them to what he thought was the right place but there was nothing. No plane, no wing . . . not a single sign of debris. He lifted a hand to point behind him, but became perplexed as to which direction they had just emerged.

"Let's head this way," said Jack taking the lead. He held Amelia by the arm, for she had been falling behind in a disoriented daze.

Collins obediently followed, and with one foot in front of the next, Kylie took up the rear. With the glow of the woods tunneling before her, the night felt a dream. The blistering cold was on her skin, yet she felt no pain, only a strange awareness of it. Like desperate hands the wind grabbed at her, while the darkness engulfed her. "I think I'm in shock," she said aloud, the words lost in the numbing roar of the blizzard.

THE OLD COTTAGE arose in their path, so oddly placed within the vast wilderness, that it appeared as if out of a storybook. Clearly built in a time long forgotten, it was a two-story stone structure, with an imposing door of darkened wood and iron hinges. A weather vane in the shape of a hatted little man spun round, his outstretched arm pointing eerily in one direction and then the next. Judging by the dark windows, the cabin appeared vacant.

Jack tried the latch and to everyone's surprise, found it unlocked. The group quickly entered and secured the thick door behind them. Stunned by the sudden relief from the wind, they stood motionless. Within the abrupt silence, the faint sound of the howling storm was all that penetrated the stone walls. As the night filtered through the small windows bringing the room before them into sight, Amelia suddenly gasped. Sitting alone in the corner was the silhouette of a man. He shifted forward into the blue light and they all saw it was Dale Benson . . . the senior partner of Benson, Graves & Sneed.

There was anger in his eyes, his shriveled mouth twisting downward. "What the hell is going on here, Collins?" he demanded, ignoring the rest. "Where the devil is the plane?"

Collins shook his head. "Your guess is as good as mine," he said, his voice low.

"I'm not asking for a guess," snapped Benson. "Where are the others?"

Kylie felt nothing but disdain for the elderly man. She had immediately disliked him when she had met him at the airport, thinking him nothing more than an arrogant jerk.

"We haven't seen them," answered Collins, rubbing his hand tiredly through his hair. "None of them," he added softly.

"Does this place have electricity?" asked Jack, feeling along the walls for a light switch.

"If it did, would I be sitting here in the goddamn dark?" Benson quipped.

With a disgusted sigh, Collins broke away from the cantankerous man. "A fire will help," he said, going toward a stone hearth against the back wall.

"We're not staying here are we?" asked Amelia.

Jack turned toward her. "Just for a little while."

"What about the plane?" she asked.

Kylie heard the panic in her friend's voice and stepped toward her. "We'll find it," she said.

"With the first thaw," muttered Benson.

Kylie glared toward the annoying attorney but knew her acerbic expression was lost in the shadowy room.

Jack touched Amelia's shoulder. "We'll find it," he said reaffirming Kylie's promise. "We just need to wait out the storm. Otherwise, we'll just get turned around and lost."

"I say we wait until daylight," insisted Benson.

"No, we can't!" cried Amelia.

"If the storm slows down, we'll go tonight," Jack said firmly, looking in Benson's direction.

"Then you'll go alone," Benson retorted.

"Suit yourself," said Jack.

Benson let out a huff and returned to his darkened corner of the room. In a troubled silence, the group dispersed, each drifting to his own part of the murky cabin.

Kylie saw that Amelia was crying and put her arms around her. "It'll be okay, Melia," she whispered, rocking her gently.

"He's dead, I just know it," she murmured, her body shaking with the painful prediction.

"Shhh," Kylie said. "Once the fire is going, you should rest by it."

Amelia pulled back, her mascara smeared beneath her eyes, the dark smudges making the blue of them even more luminous. Kylie wiped the tears from her friend's cheeks, struck by how dainty and fragile she appeared.

"I'm not cold," said Amelia wiping her brow. Beads of sweat had formed along her hairline.

"Do you have a fever?" Kylie asked.

"No, I'm fine."

"Hey, there's a bed up here," Jack called from above them. He was looking down into the room from an overhead loft.

Kylie gripped Amelia's hand. "Why don't you lie down for awhile?"

Amelia's face tightened with the suggestion, but Kylie held her gaze firm.

"Jack's right," she insisted. "There's nothing we can do until the storm breaks."

Amelia finally conceded and as she began to climb the loft's ladder, Kylie noticed Collins. He had turned away from the dark hearth and had begun ambling toward the back of the stone cabin, apparently having lost interest in the task of a fire. Perplexed, Kylie turned to the fireplace, where the inlaid wood-pit beside it stood empty. Clearly it had been all Collins had needed to simply dismiss the need of a fire. She clenched her fingers together and then pulled them up to look at them; she herself wasn't the least bit cold. She could hear the wind howling outside, she knew the temperature was way below freezing, they had been out in the storm for at least an hour, but even her fingers weren't cold. She looked around at the rest of the group. Their troubled faces were shrouded in fear, but none of them seemed bothered by the frigid temperature. It was almost as if they had just walked in from a seventy degree wind storm. Their hair was tangled and they looked disheveled, but there was no sign of frostbite. There was not even so much as a red nose. Kylie suddenly felt unsteady. Something was terribly off, yet she was the only one who seemed aware of it.

"Hey, look what I found," Collins said, holding up a small transistor radio.

WHILE the storm outside the cabin raged on, Kylie lay listening to the silence around her. She and Amelia shared the bed, while Jack rested on the floor beside them. She could hear the occasional grumbling from downstairs as Collins struggled to re-wire the transistor radio. He was attempting to fix the rusty connections so they could hear the news to see if the plane had been discovered. Benson was sprawled on the sofa, as silent as the rest of them.

Turning toward the paned window beside the bed, Kylie stared out into the darkness. Snow battered against the glass, gathering at the bottom of the window sill. She wondered how long they would be stranded in the wilderness before help arrived. Perhaps the authorities didn't even know where the aircraft had gone down. She imagined Dix trapped in the wreckage slowly freezing to death, his black leather jacket providing little comfort from the cold. She thought of Amelia and her heart saddened, but there was truly nothing they could do— the storm was impossible.

Taking a deep breath, she tried to relax. She looked about the shadowy room and wondered whose life, if any, they were invading. As an interior designer she believed that buildings weren't simply buildings, they were alive with the occupants that inhabited them; yet the room around her felt empty. It was a dusty, barren cottage with little furnishings and no decorations. There were no family photos or memorabilia, no remnants of a life left behind. She thought how strange it was to find the cabin deserted, yet the door unlocked.

As she lay staring up at the ceiling, she heard a sound outside the window. From the darkness of the storm, a raven appeared, and landed on the window box attached to the second-story room. At first startled by the sudden appearance of the large bird, she quickly became mesmerized by its manner. The bird watched her through the glass for a moment, then began tapping its beak against the window as if asking for entry.

"Are you hungry?" she asked, her hand going toward the window to unlatch it. She quietly unlocked the small metal latch and shoved the stubborn window open against the gusts. The wind immediately flooded the room as the bird moved forward and perched on the windowsill. Kylie reached to pull the bird in closer but when her fingers touched the feathers, something caught her attention. The bird's head was cocked and its beak opened slightly, but its face was off balance and unnatural. Then all at once the eyes appeared to her like two deadly creatures camouflaged in the jungles of the wild. They were clear and intense and they were focused on her. They were the intelligent, knowing eyes of a human. Kylie froze in terror with her hands extended, at first unable to move. Then her hand shot quickly up, slamming the window against the abhorrent sight, knocking the bird back onto the planter. She secured the window latch and clamped her hand down over her own mouth to block the hysteria. The bird continued to watch her for a moment longer from outside the window. Finally, it fluttered away, disappearing into the night. Kylie looked over at Jack and started to call out to him, but then hesitated; his back was to her and he appeared as if he might be asleep. When she turned again to the window there was no sign of the bird anywhere. Glancing over the railing she looked to Collins below. She wanted to say something to him, just to hear another human voice, but the words weren't there.

As if feeling her thoughts, Collins looked up at her and gave her a reassuring smile. "I'm making progress," he whispered.

Kylie smiled back uneasily, then turned again to the bed, telling herself that she must have imagined the strange eyes. After all, until that day, she had never really studied a bird up close so she wasn't even sure what their eyes were supposed to look like. She lay back onto the soft pillow and tried to calm herself. She peered once again out the window and suddenly wondered if she had hurt the poor bird by shoving it so roughly. But it was gone and there was nothing she could do about it.

Closing her eyes, she tried to think of something else. As a child, her mother had taught her to think of fond memories or pleasant places to soothe her spirits. Her mind drifted to Savannah where the summers were sultry and warm, and the winters mild. As she thought of the lovely little city, with its shady squares and blossoming magnolias, she eased into a brilliant lifelike dream. She only need wish it and suddenly she was inside a little café on Abercorn Street called "Clary's." Her mother, Lila, was seated across the table with a menu in her hands. Her little brother, Tucker, peered over the edge of the table looking bored, his chin resting on a napkin. Her beautiful mother was close enough to touch. Kylie felt her eyes fill up with tears.

"Oh Mama," she sighed. It had been over ten years since she had seen her. And Tucker. She had missed him so much! She reached over the table and kissed him on the cheek. The act was met with a warning glare.

"Sorry, Tuckie," she quickly said.

Chelsea, a big black waitress, was banging a tray of dishes behind the counter. "Lila, I think that baby gets more and more like you everyday," she said across the small restaurant.

Tucker rolled his big brown eyes in disgust.

Lila studied her son's sour face with serious consideration. "Why I do believe you're right, Chelsea. He's inherited my sunny disposition."

"Well, I was talking about his hair. I've never seen such thick locks," Chelsea said.

Tucker looked to Kylie for reassurance. When she looked into the worried little face she remembered something from long ago. She used to tell him that he wasn't really a little boy: that he was a monkey and she shaved him at night while he was asleep so no one else would know.

"Don't worry about it Tuckie, I'll take care of it tonight," she said, fighting the urge to kiss him again.

He gave a contented grunt and went back to his bored stare.

She looked over at her mother, whose long raven hair curled wildly around her ivory face. Her mother was watching her with understanding eyes.

"I've missed you too Kylie."

Kylie felt the tears well up, then roll down her cheeks. "Oh Mama. Daddy felt so bad when you died. He's still not himself. He just stays out on his boat all the time, drinking."

Her mother's expression turned suddenly sad. "Your father..." she said staring down at her hands. "I hope he doesn't blame me."

"Oh no Mama," Kylie said.

"He asked me not to take the car, but I wouldn't listen. I tried to stop, but the brakes..." Lila paused, looking distant and melancholy, "... they just weren't there. I didn't even see the truck."

"I know Mama," Kylie said, touching her mother's velvety hand.

Lila looked into her daughter's eyes. "I don't know what your Daddy's gonna do without you," she said with a tearful smile.

"Daddy's not without me," Kylie said, her other hand gripping the plastic seat beneath her.

Her mother's face saddened with pity. "But he is, honey," she said. "You're here with me."

Kylie became intensely aware of the room around her, the seat beneath her fingers cool. She could smell the frying ham and eggs and hear the banging dishes. Tucker's little face was within an arm's reach, as he stared at a fly that had landed on the table. Everything around her felt tangible and real, as if she had overstepped a boundary and was somehow trapped in the strange occurrence.

"It's alright, baby," her mother said softly. "It's just a moment. One that you chose."

At once Kylie felt withdrawn and distant, like an observer watching from afar. The waitress approached with a steaming plate but the movements of her body seemed delayed, as if somehow off from the rhythm of the surrounding air. As she placed the plate before Tucker, something about him seemed dimmer. His hands, the waitress' pink apron, the wall behind them all began to soften and fade, while the image of her mother grew with a brilliant intensity, as if she were the only real element.

Lila smiled warmly, her face arresting and wild. "One of my favorites..." she said turning.

At once they were by the dark sea, in her mother's beautiful garden. Lilacs and honeysuckles twirled together, scenting the ocean breeze. Amazed, Kylie looked around her, at the small yard of her earliest childhood in South Boston, the sea gulls wailing sadly overhead.

"Just moments, baby," her mother said, as she began tending the flowers. "Moments that comprise us."

As she watched her mother's hands move over the pale roses, a deep, wrenching sadness rushed upon her. "Mama," she whispered, feeling something had been horribly lost. She suddenly wanted to be in her own home, with her father and Jack. "I want to go back."

"You have no choice," said Lila with a bittersweet smile. "They're coming for you now." At once she was drifting into the distance. "Don't be frightened. It won't hurt a bit." Then suddenly the garden was gone.

KYLIE SAT up in the bed, trembling. "Mama," she whispered cradling herself in her own arms. She brushed the hair back from her face and when she looked up she was startled by the dark silhouette before her. Amelia sat facing her, with two pools of black for eyes and her face drawn taut.

"Dix thinks we're dead," she whispered, her fingers clutching the blanket tight. She looked to the side, as if seeing the moment in her mind. "He was sitting in the dark, with blood on his face and he thinks we're dead. How do I know that?" she asked, turning back to her. "How do I know?" she repeated urgently.

"Amelia," said Kylie gently, taking her hand. "Just lie back and—"

"No," she said, pulling away, her voice growing stronger. Peering around the darkened room she stood from the bed. "Something's wrong. Something doesn't feel right. We need to get to the plane."

Just then, a loud crash sounded from below.

Jack turned from his place on the floor as Kylie and Amelia rushed to the banister. Looking downward they saw Collins standing in the center of the room with his shoulders pinched. The transistor radio had fallen from his hands, as he stared toward the wall.

"Mr. Collins?" said Kylie, her own fear beginning to mount.

The attorney looked up, his face riddled with concentration. "Did you hear that?" he whispered, as Jack came up beside them.

With the question everyone froze and silently listened.

"I don't hear anything," muttered Benson, the uncertainty in his voice betraying his fear. "Just the wind."

"No," said Collins, advancing toward the wall, pressing his fingers against it. "There was a voice."

Kylie shook her head, for she too heard only the wind.

"Can't you hear that?" he implored, looking toward the door.

"Someone's calling my name!" At once his hand was on the latch, swinging the heavy door open.

"Gavin! What the hell are you doing?" screamed Benson.

At once Collins bolted into the night, the icy wind bursting inward, swirling through the cottage. Jack quickly made his way down the ladder and toward the door, with Kylie close behind. Once outside, the wind whipped against them, the pine needles and snow obscuring their vision. "There he is!" cried Jack, pointing into the woods, catching a glimpse of Collins' back as he disappeared over a ridge.

Quickly making their way over the slope that led beneath the cottage, they spotted Collins once again through the black trees where he had suddenly stopped.

"There's someone there!" cried Jack. "There's someone with him!"

Kylie's first thought was that they had been rescued, for she saw the emotion, the sheer euphoria on Collins' face, but as a tree cleared her line of sight, she saw the figure standing beyond him; a woman whose gaze had fixed in a dead stare, her lips expressionless, her eyes cold and detached like those of another species or of another world. At once, Kylie placed her among the vigilant forms on the mountaintop just seconds before the plane crashed; she instantly knew that the shadows had come and that the result would be death. Oblivious to the danger, Collins was moving toward the woman who was reaching out to him, his hand going up to meet her own.

"No!!" Kylie screamed. Abruptly she was angling down the slope with Jack following, past the flailing branches and hurling snow, but when they drew within thirty feet, they brusquely stopped. Falling back in horror, they gaped through the darkened trees at the inexplicable, at Collins who had locked hand in hand with the woman, his body changing, seeming to disintegrate into the thrashing storm. His eyes had fixed in a blank stare and his face showed no pain, yet the grasp the woman held seemed to be decomposing him fragment by fragment. Melding within the wind, the snow and the earth, a luminous current was flowing from his skin upward and outward, escaping through the twisting trees, the light in his eyes fading. Within seconds, the attorney's entire body broke into a massive swirl of particles that blended with the already flowing current. The stream of fragments continued in every direction upward, then, all at once, the funnel dissipated and Gavin Collins was gone. The woman, whose own eyes had closed and her head fallen hideously back, uprighted herself. At once she fixed her gaze through the woods upon Kylie and Jack.

Over her own horrified gasping, Kylie felt her husband pulling her away. Still locked within the dead eyes, she suddenly realized and felt there were others. Turning for the ridge, she was bolting back through the trees beside Jack, struggling upward toward the cottage. As they cleared the ridge, she saw Amelia within the blue light of the loft's window, her hands pressed against the glass, her face in shadow as she watched them approach. Beneath her, the door banged hideously on its hinges, swung violently about by the blasting wind.

Reaching the doorway first and rounding into the cabin, Kylie was taken aback by the wind gusting through the room, blowing objects about. It was chaotic and dark, the strange sound of flapping and cawing birds rushing past her, then a man's low guttural cry rising above the roar. It was Dale Benson. Her gaze searched quickly the corners, the darkened spaces; he was nowhere in sight. Then she spotted him in the loft, cowering against the far wall above her, with his arms drawn tight against himself, staring in horror at something before him.

"Melia!" she gasped. With her fear propelling her forward, she began clawing her way up the ladder. When her sight cleared the floor of the loft, she saw Amelia backed to the far side of the bed, watching in terror a raven that was slipping its way into the window. To the left, the dark figure of a man came out of the rushing shadows and was moving toward Benson. In his quick lithe movement, she saw the dead eyes, the cold face.

"Get away!" the old man croaked, pulling tighter into a ball on the floor.

Just then Jack cried from the darkness beneath. With her own scream deadened in her throat, Kylie turned to see that someone had followed them into the cottage and that there was a struggle, the shadows moving and indecipherable, bodies intertwining with bodies.

"Kylie!" Amelia shrieked.

When Kylie turned back, she saw a figure moving through the darkness, his eyes fixed upon her. With lightning speed he had ascended onto the upper level. "What do you want?" she gasped, edging back. He towered over her, staring at her with the same remote eyes the woman possessed, gray eyes that felt as though they were penetrating into her very soul, exposing it under their detached scrutiny. She was moving back, when her foot slipped. She felt herself falling over the railing of the balcony. She flipped upside down then around, her body landing with a thud on her back. Her eyes were focused on the loft, as the man came straight over the balcony, leaping down toward her, his muscular body streaking through the air, leaving behind a slightly blurred effect, as if his essence were unsynchronized with the encompassing matter. His feet landed evenly upon the floor, his long agile frame perfectly balanced like that of a lion in complete control of an immensely powerful physique. The light flickered from his moist thin lips, as his hand was reaching out, the long fingers extending. She was trying to move back, but as the touch reached her, her body went limp, the room around her fading to encompass only the pale face. "You don't belong here," he was saying, though his lips did not seem to move. "You're lost and we're here to take you." She felt her head falling back, the sights and the sounds smearing to darkness. Then as abruptly as it started, the feeling ceased. The room reappeared and the dark figure was pulling back from her. As he straightened fully erect, a low decree came from his throat. "It's too late," he said, his face pulling back, his hand falling to his side. "They've been found."

Just then, the fighting all around stopped. With the retreat of the shadows, she heard the flapping again, two birds gliding out the door. The storm continued to ravage the cabin, the door banging in its abhorrent rhythm, but the occupants were silent and motionless.

Jack slowly got up from the floor, Amelia and Benson appearing at the top of the balcony. Kylie scrambled to the side and rose quickly to her feet.

Only two of the dark figures remained, the man before her, and the first woman at his side. Shadows danced off the side of the wall making the deadly couple appear ten feet tall.

It was then that Kylie noticed a mark on the underside of the man's arm. There was a tiny rose etched along his vein just at the wrist. The image stunned her. She looked back to the face, and beneath the expressionless exterior, she caught a fleeting glimpse of someone she thought she knew—but from where, she was uncertain. She had seen those same entrancing eyes animated and full of life, and the pink lips and powerful jaw had formed her name. She had seen his ashen hair, which was parted down the middle and hung down to his chin, pulled back and secured with a tiny piece of leather. Somewhere, hidden within the crevices of her memory, she had seen that same muscular hand extended in anger, and she remembered the terror the tiny rose had evoked. Now, he stood before her—a character from a nightmare that had materialized into flesh.

His eyes were moving over the cottage, past Jack, up to Amelia and Benson, then again to Kylie. "There's nothing more we can do," he said simply. "Their bodies are alive."

He looked toward the woman and with a silent declaration, his brows began to change. The dark hairs above his shadowy eyes began to transform into black outgrowths. The shadows beneath his eyes deepened and his ears drew back like that of a Doberman before an attack. His face began to distort and black feathers sprouted from behind his temples.

Mortified by the sight, Kylie stumbled backward. She looked to the woman, whose face and head were also changing. She was mutating into a creature, her dark clothes altering into long black feathers attached at the shoulders. Her fingers had grown abhorrently long, the nails moving backward upon them covering the skin.

The man now resembled a mutant fowl warped into a thin tall mass. The malleable body suddenly became fluid in its appearance as it leapt from the ground. It twisted into a small orb hovering above Kylie's head. Then the wings began to flap, its head extended, and it showed itself to be a bird. It quickly disappeared out the door.

The second creature soared to the upper part of the cabin and it too began flapping its wings. It dropped back down within an arm's reach of Kylie's terrified face, looking into her eyes. Kylie instantly recognized the mortal eyes that observed her. They were the knowing retinas of the raven which had hovered outside her window.

The ebony bird fluttered lithely out the door and was swallowed up by the night.

THE STORMY weather had tamed considerably but still continued to gust and howl from one moment to the next. The four survivors trudged through the woods in search of the aircraft, frightened by every fluttering bird or blowing branch. They were still considerably shaken from the horrendous scene that had played itself out before them. After the mysterious creatures had disappeared, the group had quickly voted to abandon the cottage in search of the plane. As they made their way through the torrential storm they had heatedly explored every conceivable explanation for the supernatural creatures, but had drawn no logical conclusions. The only thing they knew for certain was that the beasts were of another world—a world they had somehow tapped into. They had been walking for what seemed a long time, but none of them were tired or cold—a fact each was acutely aware of, but none willing to discuss. In the absence of answers they had turned to silence.

Kylie felt numb and dazed, the whole incident seeming a twisted fabrication, yet the small feather she clutched tightly between her fingers was a solid reminder that the nightmare was real. Holding it up into the blue light her eyes fixed upon it once again. It was black and less than an inch in length, one she had found on the floor after the last creature had flapped away. "Don't touch it!" Jack had warned when she had reached out for it, but she had been unable to stop herself. It would not explain to the authorities what had happened to Gavin Collins, for the truth was impossible to believe, but it bore testimony to her own sanity. It was real. As real as her own two fingers that clutched it. Had it not been there, she may have already started to doubt her own memory. Rather than the truth, it would have been easier to dismiss everything, to let the dark thoughts disappear into the storm, to attribute it all to some kind of group hysteria. Feeling for the chain around her neck, her fingers slid along it to the cameo that had been her mother's. She opened the clasp and gently rested the feather inside, quick to close it before it could escape. Confident that it was secure, she let the cameo drop once again to her breast.

Amelia walked alongside her but hadn't said a word since leaving the cabin. Dale Benson was lagging behind the group and Jack kept going back to get him. The elderly man needed coddling to get him to cooperate with the rest. As the senior partner in the towering dynasty of Benson, Graves & Sneed, he was used to maintaining control. Now that things weren't going the way he wanted, somebody would pay the price even if it was three strangers that were not to blame for the predicament.

As their steps fell into a common rhythm, Amelia suddenly cried out, "I see it!" She broke into a run through the woods where a glimpse of the aircraft could be seen. Kylie quickly followed, terrified of what her friend might find, but by the time she reached the wreckage, Amelia had already disappeared inside the cabin of the bent plane.

As Kylie entered the cove the huge metal body formed, she was taken aback by the macabre spectacle of a dead man belted within his seat sitting strangely outside the aircraft.

"Oh God," she whispered, quickly looking away. She would have to pass the lifeless victim to reach the metal opening where the side of the plane had split apart. She averted her eyes, concentrating on the ground in front of her. As she slowly approached, she tried desperately not to look at the man sitting silently in front of her, but like a moth to the flame, her eyes began to rise. She was within inches of the body, when her attention was caught by the distinct pattern of his lightweight, cotton shirt. "It can't be," she whispered aloud, daring to peer into the face of the dead man. Frozen in an abominable stare were the unmistakable features of Gavin Collins. His eyes were lifeless, solidified like those of a wax figurine hideously preserved for all to see. Ice was hanging from his eyebrows and eyelashes, his skin a bluish gray.

Kylie heard herself screaming and was backing away when Jack grabbed her from behind. "Kylie!" he cried, gripping her arms to reassure her, but he had yet to see the face of the victim.

Benson came rushing around the corner and immediately discovered what had upset Kylie. He moved slowly toward the body as if expecting it to stand up and walk at any moment. "This is impossible," he said, staring down at his dead colleague. "He was with us!"

"How in the hell?" Jack whispered, his attention riveted on the grotesque sight.

The three looked at one another, each stricken with the queer, inexplicable chain of events.

Kylie suddenly moved toward the cabin of the plane, her mind spinning. If Collins had died in his seat, then how could he have been with them?

"Amelia?!" she cried as she stepped into the slanting aircraft. She frantically looked toward the seats in the back of the plane, but all she could see was a black hole. It was darker inside and her eyes had not adjusted. Then she heard the soft voice of Amelia coming from in front of her.

"He doesn't hear me," said Amelia.

"Is he conscious?" asked Kylie, as she felt blindly along the seats toward the voice.

"We're dead," Amelia said quietly.

"Amelia?" Kylie called, but the voice had silenced.

Slowly, the light began to diffuse through the tiny round windows and the inside of the plane began to glow a deep, purplish blue. As Kylie made her way toward the back, she passed a dead woman strewn across the seats in the middle of the aircraft. Kylie knew the black stains that covered the woman's head and chest were blood. She began to feel trapped inside the crushed plane, the scent of death smothering her. "Amelia?" she repeated softly, the sound of her own shaking voice causing her panic. Then she felt the floor beneath her move and looked back to see Jack and Benson coming in behind her.

As she continued along the seats, her hand landed on the still, bristly face of a man. His wet lips were open, and his relaxed jaw moved with her touch. Kylie gasped aloud, yanking her hand back. When she looked at the passenger, she was horrified to see that it was Dale Benson sitting quietly, still belted in, with a thick blanket tucked all around him. She looked behind her, past her husband to the elderly man approaching her and she felt as if she were losing her mind. It was the same aged attorney she had just reached out and touched with her fingertips. The dark encasement of the plane began to feel like a huge, heavy coffin closing in on her. She pressed her hands against the ceiling and willed her legs forward. She could see the blonde hair of the man in front of her, seated in her husband's chair. He was motionless and silent. "We're dead," she whispered, and though she was more terrified than she ever dreamed possible, she kept moving forward toward the two bodies that were waiting patiently and ever so silently. Within the shadows, she saw the gold flowered ring on the left hand of the man. It was the wedding ring she herself had designed and placed on the finger. She knew the sweater that he wore and the blonde shiny curls. Then she summoned the courage to look into the face of the victim she had already identified. It was her husband. Blood was covering his mouth and sweater, and a makeshift compress had been belted to his leg. He appeared to be dead but then she noticed a fine stream of mist emitting from his lips. She felt the floor beneath her sway as the two men approached her from behind. She turned toward them, toward the vision of Jack who walked down the slender aisle, his face illuminated by the moonlight like a ghostly apparition.

"You're alive," she whispered aloud, looking back to the bodies before her. The wall next to her husband had crushed in and beneath the twisted metal she saw the body of herself trapped under the collapsed cabin. Her hair was soaked with blood and her jeans were ripped open. Blood had saturated the upholstered seats, and into the carpeting at her feet. A man's jacket, one that she had never seen before, was strewn across her and Jack.

"It's okay, I'm here," she heard the soft voice of Amelia say. She was crouched on the floor by the luggage with Dix in her arms. He appeared delirious and was mumbling softly. Blood was oozing from around his black, swollen eyes. Amelia looked up at Kylie as if pleading for her to make the pain in her heart subside. Amelia's lips moved once again but her words faded to silence as she looked to the seat in front of her.

Kylie followed her friend's line of sight to the body of Amelia sitting upright in the seat which she and Dix had initially inhabited. She was unconscious but alive.

Kylie's attention went back to the body trapped under the wall, at the hand that was her own. Her mother's cameo necklace lay gently shining from under the pile of rubble, the small cream-colored jewel covered in blood. Questioning her own eyes, she reached down and touched the fingers of the body to feel if they were an illusion. The moment she felt the sensation of her own cold hand, pain shot through her fingers like fire. It was a twisting, insufferable cramp that crawled up the inside of her arm just under the surface of her skin. It moved through her veins like an acid-tipped spider scampering upward to her shoulder and down to her waist.

She screamed in agony, pulling away with all her might; but her hand had melded with her own, the two images uniting as one. The pain sucked her downward as if drawing her to the injured body that lay motionless. The excruciating torture traveled through her legs and down to her feet. The moonlight began to darken and the images before her scramble.

"Kylie!?" she heard Jack screaming again and again. She was at one minute standing and in the next lying crushed beneath the wall of the plane. She could no longer hear the voice of her husband. She felt the metal weighing down upon her, and it had suddenly become difficult and painful to breathe. Her head felt as if it would burst and she tried to cry out but her voice was faint.

She forced her head back and turned to the side but the only thing she could see was the injured and unconscious body of her husband beside her. She reached her hand out to touch him but the pain was too much; her awareness faded to black.

Fifteen

"I DON'T KNOW WHAT HAPPENED AFTER THAT," KYLIE SAID, RESTING into the wooden seat across the desk from Dr. Jordan.

"You don't remember the man who rescued you?" he asked, pulling his wire-rim glasses from his tired eyes.

"Vaguely," said Kylie.

"But you remember the jacket he put over you?"

"Yes."

The doctor studied her with his keen, all-knowing eyes. Kylie wondered how long he had been watching her so closely. She had been so absorbed in her story that she had scarcely noticed her surroundings the entire afternoon. For the first time in hours, she saw the time. The big round clock above the window read 6:15 P.M. It was still raining but the light outside had grown dim. "I had no idea it was so late," she said, her voice raspy from speaking so long. She pushed the hair back from her face and took a drink of water from the glass placed before her. "So what do you make of it, Doc?" she asked with a slight smile.

"You strike me as a perfectly balanced young woman," he answered matter-of-factly, leaning back into his chair.

"You're kidding, right?"

"No," he said simply. His eyes narrowed as he continued to watch her. "I think the story you've told me is a direct result of the trauma, your injuries, your medication and a lack of sleep."

Kylie had to smile. "Oh, is that all?"

Dr. Jordan chuckled. "That's a lot, I must admit, but the mind is not a simple playground."

"Playground, huh?" Kylie said quietly, looking down at her hands. "That means you think I imagined it all."

The doctor's brow furrowed. "I think you came very close to dying and your mind is trying to sort it out. And while I believe most of your account is a mixture of hallucinations and dreams, part of it shares common elements with a near-death experience."

Kylie could tell that he was waiting for her reaction.

"Are you familiar with the term?" he finally asked.

"Yes."

"NDE's, as we call them, have been documented for centuries in practically every country in the world. They were even the basis for what is thought to be the oldest religion on earth, animism."

"Animism?"

"It's a basic belief in the soul and its life outside of the body. Archeologists think that the animistic system of beliefs originated over 20,000 years ago in tribal societies. These societies, many of which still practice today, believe that the soul can be inadvertently jarred from the body in a violent attack or accident, and that it can wander endlessly unaware of its state. And unless the soul finds its body, the victim remains in a coma, sometimes for years. It's very fascinating," he said. "A bit different from Western beliefs, but still quite interesting. Most NDE's that you hear about are a simple disassociation from the body at the time of death. The statistics from a recent Gallup poll of Americans that believe they've experienced a type of NDE are staggering. So naturally, when a patient like yourself comes to me with visions of dead relatives and recollections of leaving their body while on the verge of death, its difficult to dismiss as mere fantasy. However," he emphasized, leaning forward with his hands gripped together, "there are certain elements that most documented NDE's seem to share. They generally tend to be pleasant experiences rather than nightmarish. And in no cases that I'm aware of, has the experience been shared with another living person, such as with your husband and the others. I think if you experienced an NDE," the doctor said slowly, weighing his words carefully, "then you may be confusing pieces of it with not only nightmares, but memories that happened after you were rescued. Take the jackets and blankets you saw on the bodies inside of the plane. You were obviously conscious for at least part of the rescue. Am I correct?"

"Yes."

"Well, you must have seen them on those around you, obviously placed by the man who rescued you. That portion is simple memory. Some of the other elements were clearly derived from nightmares."

"Which elements?" she asked.

"I think we both know what those are. I don't think there was a cottage in the woods, or mysterious people in dark clothing dispelling spirits." He looked to the locket that hung from her neck. "I take it you've looked inside for the feather?" he asked.

Her fingers grasped the cameo. "Yes," she said, her face flushing with the admission. "I guess it all does sound a little outlandish."

The doctor smiled gently, resting his warm eyes upon her. "Part of the memory, and I stress memory, of the NDE can be derived from one's imagination. What is your religious background, if you don't mind my asking," the doctor said.

"Well, I don't really go to church anymore, but I was raised Catholic."

"Do you believe in angels?" he asked.

Kylie was baffled by the question. She hadn't given much thought to her religious beliefs in quite some time. "I did as a child," she answered.

"The creatures you described sounded very similar to the personification of an angel of death . . . a messenger on assignment to collect a soul, so to speak. The psyche of the human mind struggles to ease the terror of dying by depicting death as something tangible that our eyes can examine and our fingers touch."

Kylie thought about the towering winged figures and she suddenly remembered a famous painting a client of hers had tried to obtain from the Musee d'Orsay in Paris. "Stokes," she said aloud.

"Pardon?" asked the doctor.

"Marianne Stokes. She's the artist of a painting called *Young Girl and Death*. I have a client who wanted to purchase it for her home. I was researching the possibility before the accident. It's an extraordinary painting of a hooded dark angel seated at the foot of a young woman's bed."

"So your research was recent?" asked the doctor.

"Yes."

"Well, that tells us where certain ideas originated, don't you think?"

"Possibly," said Kylie.

"You mentioned that the male assailant looked familiar to you," the doctor said.

Kylie smiled slightly. "Yes. I thought I had seen him before."

"And you probably had. Characters in our dreams are often taken from our day to day encounters. You've probably passed him on the street, or in a grocery store, or maybe he was your waiter at a restaurant."

Kylie thought about it a moment. She knew she had seen the beguiling face, smiling slyly and speaking with her. "I just don't know," she said softly, fixed in contemplation. Then she thought of the abhorrent transformation the familiar face had made. "But what about the ravens?"

"That's really quite simple. Ever since ancient Egyptian mythology black birds such as ravens and crows have been depicted as harbingers of death or carriers of the soul to the afterworld. In fact, in some of the tribal cultures in West Africa it's still customary to tie a bird to the deceased and then kill it so that it will carry the dead person's soul with it to the afterlife."

Kylie was silent. It all seemed so logical yet her mind fought the evident. "But what about the people in . . ." but she stopped herself.

"Yes?"

"I was in the hallway last night and—"

"—something frightened you?"

"Yes. I stopped to ask directions from three people that were dressed in white. They acted very strange . . . like they were scared to speak to me," she said, her voice beginning to shake. "Then they started to change, just like the people in the cottage. Their heads and bodies became stretched, and it looked as though a light was coming from under their skin. I started to run, but I couldn't take my eyes off them. Finally, they disappeared." Kylie looked away in embarrassment. Her eyes had started to water and her hands were shaking.

"Were you frightened they were going to harm you?"

"No, not really."

"Why are you crying?"

"Because last night I wasn't asleep, or in a coma or on drugs. It was real."

"Dillon said that you haven't been sleeping well. Is that true?"

"Yes. I've been going through withdrawal from the medication."

"Well when our bodies don't get sufficient sleep, we can have what are called micro-dreams. They're literally, life-like dreams that burst into the waking hours, much like a hallucination. 'Personal Earthquakes' is what some of the surgeons around here describe them as after they've been up for two or three days straight. I think that what you saw in the hallway was a continuation of what your mind had already fabricated while you were ill. Much like when you dream repeatedly of the same person you've never met or place you've never been to. Only now, your body is out of danger, therefore your mind transformed the angels into something positive. They were in white rather than black and they were harmless."

"You seem to have logical answers, Doctor, but everything I told you seems as clear as the conversation we're having."

"And it will for awhile, but it'll pass," the doctor said.

In spite of his promise, the silence remained heavy with doubt.

The doctor leaned intently forward, his voice compassionate yet firm. "If there's any uncertainty in your mind about your well being, let me reassure you of this . . . No matter what you decide happened to you on that mountain, never once in the thousands of documented NDE's that I've heard of, has an entity of sorts crossed over into the physical world of the recuperated victim."

Kylie sighed heavily, wanting with all her might to trust in his experience and knowledge.

"You survived the accident," the doctor said. "And it had nothing to do with you warding off beasts. Your mind merely fabricated them in an attempt to cope, but once you knew that you had been rescued they left. Just like in a dream—when you turn around and face the monster, you remove his power."

"Yes, I suppose," she agreed softly.

"It's important that you acknowledge the danger is over, so you can get on with your recovery."

"Thank you, Doctor," she said.

He held up a hand as if to warn her. "I'm not saying that your troubles are over by any means. What you, your husband and your friends have been through is devastating. You'll be dealing with the aftermath for quite some time. There are support groups that can help or you can also seek private counsel. Maybe you and your husband could even go together."

Kylie couldn't help but smile. "Obviously you don't know my husband."

"Well, if problems arise I hope he at least considers it," said the doctor gravely. "Repercussions from something so traumatic can be lethal if not dealt with properly."

Sixteen

AMELIA BLACKWELL STOOD BEFORE THE ALTAR IN ST. VINCENT'S Cathedral trying to decide what to do with the orange carpeting that had shredded and worn to a pale puke color. "Those damn seventies," she mumbled, resenting not only the horrid choice of colors the generation had bore, but the distasteful act of installing carpeting over the stone floors.

With the exception of a dim glow that penetrated the stained-glass windows the cathedral was almost dark; bringing her day's work to an end. It was virtually impossible to work at night in the faintly lit church which had been stripped of its electricity in an attempt to re-wire it more efficiently.

The cathedral had been built in the early 1800's and had undergone few improvements in its nearly two hundred years of existence. Several years earlier, after the electrical wiring began to smoke and the walls to leak, the church had been closed and the parish had taken up residence on Bull Street in an abandoned Episcopalian Church. It wasn't until the previous fall, however, that Amelia had been hired to re-do the interior which had fallen into even graver disrepair after its closure. For a salary of little more than minimum wage, she and Dix had moved into the priest's rectory for the duration of the year it would take for her to breathe new life into the church.

Amelia took one last glance around when a voice suddenly echoed behind her.

"Amelia?"

Dix was standing in the archway, gripping the stone wall next to him. Amelia had yet to adjust to the stark white bandages that covered his eyes. Standing in the shadows he looked strangely lost and vulnerable. "Are you there, Bluebird?" he asked.

"Over here," she answered.

"Kylie's on the phone," he said, holding out a cordless receiver.

Amelia quickly went to him and took the phone from his hand. "Thank you, sweetheart," she whispered, kissing him lightly on the cheek.

"How'd it go?" she asked into the receiver.

"Well," the voice came through the line. "He didn't put me in a straight jacket and threaten to commit me. I'm being released tomorrow."

"That's great," said Amelia, following Dix toward the exit. She stepped onto the brick walkway leading to the rectory, pulling the heavy door to the cathedral closed behind them. "Can you tell me about it now—what it is that you remembered?"

"It's pretty far out there," the voice said softly. "Are you alone?"

"Just a minute," said Amelia tenderly. "I'll go into the office." She entered the dark rectory and went into a small study that was off to the left of the entrance. Dix was behind her but he continued on toward the stairwell. "Okay," she said.

"Melia, are you sure you don't remember anything inside the plane? After the crash, I mean?" Kylie asked.

"No," said Amelia, switching on a floor lamp in front of the open window. "Just vague glimpses of the ride to the hospital. Why?"

"Well, I do—impossible things that involve both you and Jack. The doctor had reasonable explanations for it all, but I just . . . I don't know," Kylie said.

Amelia heard the quiver in her friend's voice. "What is it?" she asked. She listened intently as Kylie told of her harrowing recollections and Doctor Jordan's opinion of the situation.

"Well, I have to agree, that's quite a story," said Amelia quietly.

"Do you think I dreamt it?" she asked.

"Yes," said Amelia, her voice gentle. "I'm not saying I don't believe in . . . in near-death experiences. I just think that if something like that happened, Jack and I would remember at least something of it."

"It just seemed so damn real." whispered Kylie.

"Well, it's creepy, I have to admit," said Amelia. "But you've always had an outlandish imagination. Remember those dreams you were having after Tucker's death?"

"But this was different."

"That's what you said then," Amelia countered.

"But it didn't feel like a dream. I'll admit that I probably hallucinated or dreamt most of it. But what if some of it was real? Like the man . . . like the creatures. What if they . . ." the voice stopped.

"They what?" Amelia asked. There was silence on the line. "Kylie," she said steadily. "You said yourself that you'd seen some painting that inspired them."

"You're right," Kylie agreed quietly. "What the hell am I thinking?"

"What did Jack say? Have you mentioned any of this to him?"

"No," said Kylie. "I've rarely seen him since I've been in here. There's no telling what he's up to. I'll be so glad to leave this place. How's Dix?" she asked, clearly wanting to change the subject.

"The bandages come off in three days. Hopefully that will be the last surgery," said Amelia. "I don't know how much more he can take. Every time I look at him I want to cry. You know how Dix is usually bouncing off the walls?"

"Yeah."

"Well, he's gotten so quiet."

"Well, he'll be better once it's all over."

"Yeah," said Amelia, heavily. "I guess it's like your doctor said— we'll be feeling the repercussions for awhile."

Both were silent.

"We're really lucky, you know?" said Amelia. "Everyone says what a miracle it was that we survived. I guess God decided to spare us. You missed all the papers and tabloids. I saved them if you want to look at them. You wouldn't believe some of the cases those attorneys have handled."

"Hmm—God, huh?" said Kylie. "Where did that come from?"

"What do you mean?"

"Well I haven't heard you mention God in awhile. You're not planning on becoming a nun again are you?"

Amelia laughed. "I don't think there's a convent that would take Dix. Besides, that ended in the seventh grade with the Howie Gordon crush." With a heavy sigh, the humor left her voice. "No, I've just felt like I need to get back in touch with . . . with my faith, I guess. Facing death will do that you know. Send you packing to church toting the Bible. You should have seen Mama Mamie's face when I showed up at St. Mary's on Sunday."

"You've got to be kidding," said Kylie. "You went to church? What did she say?"

Amelia's voice became affected with an upper-class drawl. "She just thought it was so nice that I had come back to my senses and was finally letting the Lord wash the devil from my heart." Her voice fell flat. "Afterwards, she got in her usual sarcastic digs."

"What was it this time?"

"Well, in spite of that dozen roses she sent you, she's got a bone to pick with you."

"Me?! Why?"

"Well, Kylie, you know what a bad influence you've always been. She said that every time I go near you it's nothing but trouble."

"Did you tell her that you're the one that volunteered for the trip?" Kylie protested.

"Of course, but all she can think of is all those car accidents you got me in. I can't really blame her. Every time you got behind the wheel we ended up under a truck or something."

"Bad luck. That's all that was," said Kylie. "Your mother hates me."

"Mama loves you," said Amelia.

"Yeah, right."

The two friends laughed. "She does," giggled Amelia. "I think she likes you better than me. She threw a fit that my hair is shorter than Dix's."

"Well I have to agree with her on that one. You always did want to look like a boy. What'd you do to it this time?"

"You should see it," Amelia said, admiring her reflection in the glass of a framed photo. Her sapphire eyes were dark and sunken, her face pale, her blonde hair cropped so short that it stood on end. "I look possessed," she said happily.

"Well then it suits you," teased Kylie. "Hang on," she suddenly said. The phone rustled for a moment, then finally Kylie came back on. "Nurse Ratchett strikes again. I've got to go."

"Okay," said Amelia. "Are you going to be alright?"

"Yeah," said Kylie sadly. "I just need to get my head together."

Amelia found it harder than ever to hang up the phone. She could tell that Kylie was still uneasy but knew there was nothing more she could say. Kylie would only accept a certain amount of advice before she would abruptly put up a wall and keep the problem to herself. When the two lived together in college, Kylie constantly asked Amelia's advice on simple matters such as what to wear, or what to eat, but then almost always went in the opposite direction. At first offended by the pattern, Amelia finally realized that Kylie merely wanted to know there was a safety net of support so she could defiantly choose to hit the ground. Amelia had always been the voice of reason, the voice that for twenty-six years had pulled Kylie back from self-destruction, but she had learned early on that the voice had to be used sparingly and with a light touch.

Feeling strangely off, Amelia looked pensively about the darkened room with its shelves of musty books, its rich wooden walls and the Persian rug at her feet. The decor of the study was dark with one exception—there was a painting of an iridescent angel whispering into the ear of a small child. Amelia thought of the twisted, dark creatures that Kylie had described. "Kylie's Demons," she said aloud, thinking of the vivid nightmares and harrowing imagination that had beset her friend since childhood. "It makes you the better artist," Amelia had said time and again. While they had both attended the New York School of Interior Design, Kylie had been the one to go on to the bigger of success. She was known throughout Boston as the designer that could bring the macabre to life and give it a sophisticated touch of elegance. She had an understanding and respect for the atrocious. "Without pain, there's no measure for pleasure," Kylie had said often.

A breeze drifted in through the open window, the scent of magnolia breaking Amelia's thoughts. While other parts of the country were still buried in snow, Savannah had already begun to blossom. It was her favorite time of the year—when the air was light and perfumed with the blooming array of flowers and bushes.

Moving toward the window to take in the night, she noticed something stir in the dark courtyard tree. She looked closely but the object had stilled. She reached for the floor lamp and pulled it closer to the window. The light illuminated a circle of the courtyard immediately out from the window. Though the image was still dark, she saw the figure of an ebony bird perched on a branch of the swaying tree. The light reflected in its tiny eyes which had fixed in the direction of the window. Amelia's breath stopped and she was motionless as she locked into the gaze of the bird. It was silent except for the sound of the gently swaying leaves. Then suddenly, the bird took flight soaring out of the enclosed patio. The air moved beneath and over as the bird gracefully lifted into the dark sky.

Just then Amelia felt someone standing behind her. She jumped back nearly screaming. "Dix!" she yelped. "I'm going to have to put bells on you."

"Sorry," he smiled mischievously. "What are you doing?"

"Nothing," said Amelia, her heart still thumping. She glanced back out at the moving tree with the empty branch. "Just looking at the night."

PART TWO

Seventeen

THE UNUSUALLY MILD WINTER HAD GIVEN WAY TO THE MOST ERRATIC spring that Boston had seen in over thirty-two years. Though it was the twentieth of April, unprecedented temperatures soared from sweltering highs to freezing lows often within a twenty-four-hour period.

"I can't believe it's snowing!" said Kylie, peering through the windshield at the plump flakes that floated from the night sky. "It was so warm earlier that I didn't even need a sweater."

Jack let out a squeal of laughter as he maneuvered the Cherokee around the slick corner onto Blanchard Road. "Holy Christ," he laughed. "Dillon's gotta be freezing his butt off. I warned him not to cook out this time of year."

As they pulled up to the brightly lit, two-story house, Kylie leaned forward trying to see if she recognized any of the bundled-up guests streaming into the party.

"There's no way he can cook for this many people," said Jack, as the truck coasted slowly by his brother's Cambridge home.

Though they searched for something closer, the nearest parking spot was a block and a half away. The cold ripped through their jackets as they ran toward the house with their faces covered.

When they entered the bustling living room, Kylie was amazed at how many of the guests she didn't know. While there were friends among the gathering that she and Jack shared with Dillon, there were also countless strangers that seemed perfectly at home.

"Look at all these anal-retentive bookworms," mumbled Jack.

"Now, now, Mr. Insecure," she said with a teasing laugh. "You don't recognize a couple of faces and you lose it. Your brother's got a right to his own friends."

"Well, it's about time," said Dillon, approaching them with a big smile and his arms extended.

"You look awfully happy for a man who's got a hundred hungry mouths to feed . . . all of 'em expecting a nice, fat juicy burger," said Jack pulling his jacket off. "I'll take mine well-done."

"I hate to spoil this moment for you, Jack," said Dillon, "but I nixed the barbecue idea two weeks ago in favor of Domiano's delivery." He looked to Kylie with a wink. "If you'd ever return my calls, you would have known that."

"What do you mean?" said Jack defensively.

"I never see or hear from you guys anymore," said Dillon. "What's the deal? I save your lives and that's the thanks I get? You go into hiding?"

"We've been busy with the Greyson house," said Jack.

A dark-headed woman appeared from the guests and grabbed Dillon's arm. "The food's here," she said discreetly from behind him.

"Thanks Theresa," said Dillon.

Kylie recognized the tall, pretty woman from the hospital. Her long straight black hair and violet-colored eyes were hard to forget. The woman noticed that Kylie was looking at her and smiled.

"Oh, I'm sorry," said Dillon. "I guess you guys haven't officially met," he said pulling the woman into the conversation. "Theresa this is my brother, Jack, and his wife, Kylie. This is my friend, Theresa Ollridge."

They exchanged pleasantries. "You work at the hospital, don't you?" asked Kylie.

The graceful woman seemed to find the question amusing. "I'm an anesthesiologist," she said. "I was the one monitoring your sedation . . . making sure you didn't reject the ECMO therapy."

"I'm sorry," said Kylie.

"That's okay," she said kindly. "A lot of my patients don't remember me. You were in pretty bad shape. I'm glad to see that you recovered so nicely."

"Thank you," said Kylie.

The woman turned to Dillon. "We should lay the food out before it gets cold."

"Yeah, I'll talk to you guys in a little bit," said Dillon, following Theresa back toward the kitchen.

"Friend, my butt," quipped Jack with a smile as he watched his brother walk away with the elegant woman.

"Jack Black and the lovely Wylie!"

They turned to find Roger Hinkley smiling back at them. The gangly stockbroker was a good friend of Dillon's who often played basketball with the brothers. "Where the hell have you been?" he asked drawing the couple into the party. "You're like celebrities, you know? Everyone wants to hear all about it."

"About what?" asked Jack, shooting Kylie a glance.

"About what!" boomed Roger, laughing. "About what! How about a drink? Scotch, bourbon?" He turned to Kylie with a mischievous grin, knowing fully well that she had given up alcohol the year before.

"Coke," she answered, noticing a huddle of people she didn't know peering over at them.

"Jack?"

"Wellers."

After retrieving the drinks, Roger turned to the room. "Listen up, everybody. I want to make a toast," he announced, holding his glass high and waiting patiently for all to follow suit.

As silence fell over the room, Kylie's stomach churned for she sensed what was about to follow.

With his face suddenly solemn, Roger turned back to the couple. "To the survivors," he said, swishing the liquid to the rim of his glass.

"Hear, hear," echoed the response and the sound of clinking glass was heard throughout.

As Kylie took a sip of her drink, a young man with horn-rimmed glasses turned toward her. "So what is it that you've survived?" he asked.

"A plane accident," she said, the words catching in her throat. "Two months ago."

"Glad to see you guys out," interrupted a man in a red cardigan sweater. Kylie recognized him from Jack's games but couldn't remember his name. "Forest Jackson," he said, extending his hand to her. "I haven't seen you at the games lately, Jack. I was beginning to worry."

"My shoulder's still a little sore," he said.

"Believe me, I understand," Forest said. "I had a friend in the Mid-Atlantic crash a few years back. I told Dillon that considering what you guys have been through, it wouldn't surprise me if you didn't come around for awhile. But you're looking mighty good."

"He sure as hell is," chimed Roger, patting Jack on the back.

"You must feel pretty damn lucky," said another man, "surviving something like that."

"Considering the alternative," said Jack with an uncomfortable smile.

Kylie noticed that a tiny woman with long manicured nails had sidled up to her and was studying her closely. Though the party was just underway, her heavily made-up eyes betrayed her drunkenness.

"So you're the couple from the accident," she said, with a look of intrigue on her round face.

"Yes," said Kylie, looking helplessly over at Jack, but he remained ensnared by the group. She felt uncomfortable with the woman eyeing her so closely. She could tell that she was staring at the scar on her chin and she felt her face turn crimson. She hadn't expected the scar to be so noticeable and had yet to adjust to the curious stares it evoked.

"I remember reading about it," said the woman. "You're an architect or something aren't you?"

"Designer."

"Yeah," said the woman. "You guys chartered some seats from the attorneys, right?"

"Right."

"I saw a picture in the *Star* of one of the lawyers that was absolutely dreadful! I couldn't believe they printed it," she said with disdain, but beneath the drooping red eyes there was a look of delight. "It was an older guy, maybe forty or fifty. He had completely frozen in his seat. It was awful," she groaned. When she looked up and saw the strained look on Kylie's face she suddenly stopped. "I'm sorry, you didn't know him did you?" she asked.

Kylie thought of Collins' warm gentle smile that had calmed her disquieted heart and she wanted to say "yes," but instead her lips whispered, "no." In spite of Dr. Jordan's dismissal of her memory with Collins, she still felt an illogical attachment to him; remnants of the bond they momentarily shared in their pursuit of survival. Her stomach suddenly felt sick. The woman was babbling again—something about the attorneys—but Kylie couldn't force her attention back.

"Okay guys, chow time!" called Dillon from the dining room.

With relief, Kylie remained still as the crowd melted from around them. Jack shook his head with a perturbed sigh, then took a solid swig of his drink. Kylie reached out for his hand, but he turned away.

IT WAS two o'clock in the morning, before the party finally thinned. In an attempt to escape the last remaining guests, Kylie made her way to the kitchen. She and Jack had been trying to dodge the subject of the crash all night with little success. Nearly everyone had heard of the attorneys and wanted a piece of the story.

In the otherwise empty kitchen, she found Jack at the counter filling his glass once again with bourbon. His shoulders were drooping and his eyes looked cold and sad.

"Jack?" she said softly, for it was the first moment they had been alone all night, yet he didn't turn.

His shoulders remained tensed, his brow pinched with anger. "Still glad we came?" he asked under his breath.

"So this is where he's hiding the grub," exclaimed Roger Hinkley, bursting into the kitchen. To Kylie's dismay, several other guests drifted in with him, perusing the left-overs.

"Got anything sweet, Dill?" Roger asked.

"I've got cheesecake," said Dillon, entering behind the men. "Other than that, you're on your own."

Though Kylie and Jack remained off to the side, one of the men ambled over to them. "How ya' doin' buddy?" he asked Jack, his voice low in comradery.

"Fine and dandy," said Jack, knocking a gulp of the bourbon back.

"I meant to tell you earlier that I'm an attorney," the man said, sliding his card onto the counter between them.

"Well this is a first," grumbled Jack. "Can you believe it, Kylie? An attorney."

Forest turned to the conversation. "Rick represents that friend I was telling you about. The one in the Mid-Atlantic crash. Got him a helluva settlement. What was it again?" he asked.

"Five-hundred-thousand," said the attorney.

"Whatever they offer," said Forest, "Rick can double it."

Kylie saw the anger in Jack's eyes and broke in before he could respond. "They've already covered everything," she said. "We just want to put it behind us now," she added, hoping the men would take the hint.

"Don't rush to sign on the dotted line," said the attorney. "You've got plenty of time to decide what you want."

"I don't need time," Jack quipped, sliding the card back to him.

"Believe me Jack," said Forest. "There's nothing wrong with a suit against them. My friend earned every penny he got for pain and suffering."

"Do I look like I'm suffering?" asked Jack holding his hands out with a smile.

"No, buddy, you surely don't," laughed Roger, clinking his glass against Jack's.

When Jack lowered the drink again, Kylie was startled by the deadened look in his eyes. Immediately turning away to the counter, he began refilling his glass.

"Well, you're adjusting a helluva lot better than my friend did," said Forest, shoving a sliver of pizza in his mouth. "That's all I can say. I mean the poor bastard completely lost it. He had to go into psychotherapy, behavior-therapy and whatever else kind of therapy there is and he still lost his family over the ordeal. His wife divorced him, his kids won't visit. He can't hardly leave his house without freaking out. It's a mess. Can you imagine? Surviving a goddamned plane crash, just to lose your mind later," he asked, shaking his head. "I'd make 'em pay, by God."

"From what I've read, the pilot was pretty negligent," said the attorney.

"Yeah, he was a fool to take the plane up. I heard that storm was one of the worst in twenty years. And that's saying a lot for Mt. Washington . . ."

As the conversation continued off to the side, Jack remained still at the counter. His face had drawn tight and a raw trepidation had begun to seep into his eyes. Kylie looked to Dillon who had also noticed him.

"Jack, you want something to eat?" he asked, trying to draw his attention away, but Jack remained transfixed by the quieted voices of the men.

"I mean, they didn't even know these guys," continued Forest. "Can you imagine accepting chartered passengers and then pulling that kind of drunken kamikaze shit."

"... Someone said that the pilot was cut clean in half."

"No way," said Roger, whistling softly.

"Holy shit," groaned Forest. "Can you imagine what he must have been thinking right before the plane hit? He must have seen it coming."

. "That would call for some quick soul searching," said Roger, letting out a laugh. "God forgive me for cheating on Sally . . . forgive me for that tax return last year!"

"How about forgive me for killing all of these people?" groaned the attorney.

"You know, I've always wondered what it would be like," said Roger. "Those last few seconds. Hey Jack?" he said, the group looking around for him. "What was going through your mind once you knew you were going down?"

As all eyes rested on Jack, there was an abrupt silence. His body had frozen, his face pale, sweat rolling down the sides of his temples.

"Jack?" said Kylie gently, reaching out for his arm but he yanked it away.

"Jesus," he finally said, his voice low and angry. "What the fuck do you think was going through my mind?" he asked, looking up to Roger. "What the fuck do you think?"

"Jack—"

"No, Kylie, they want to hear it, let's tell 'em. Otherwise they're gonna go on and on about this shit."

"Take it easy, buddy—"

"No, fuck you. You want to know what I was thinking when the plane was going down? I wasn't thinking about some goddamned tax return, I'll tell you that. I was thinking about my wife going down with me. I was thinking about my nails digging into my palms and the warm piss filling my pants. That's right, I wet my goddamned pants—"

"Jack stop!" said Kylie sharply.

"Christ," he said, sliding his drink roughly onto the counter. "Don't you guys ever give it a rest?"

Abruptly he left the room, leaving the group in stunned silence.

Kylie looked to Dillon who was glaring toward his friends.

"Jeez, I thought he was okay with it," said Roger defensively.

"Drop it," warned Dillon, as he started after his brother.

"I'll get him," said Kylie, lifting a hand to stop him.

Though the living room was empty and the front door bolted, she felt a cool breeze curling around her ankles. Following the draft down the long corridor toward the rear of the house, she found the back door ajar. With the brisk night stinging her eyes, she spotted Jack's silhouette headed down toward the lake.

As she watched him circle around by the water and disappear into the woods, she could hear Dillon saying good-night to his friends. After a long while, she gently closed the door and rested into a chair at the window.

"What's he doing?" Dillon asked, coming up behind her.

"Just going for a walk," she answered softly, turning away from the dark glass.

"Are you okay?" asked Dillon gently.

Kylie smiled even though she felt like crying. She was tired, the long evening having worn on her as well. "Yeah, I'm fine."

"I'm sorry about this. No wonder you guys haven't been out."

"It's okay," she said, resting her head to the back of the chair.

"I've been worried about you two," Dillon said. "I can't hardly get Jack to return my calls."

Kylie sighed and rubbed her eyes. "He's just having a tough time," she admitted.

"What about you?" he asked.

"I'm fine."

"Hey," he said softly, taking her hand into his own, "this is me you're talking to."

Kylie looked into his warm, concerned gaze. "Honestly, I'm okay. It's funny, I thought I would have a harder time than Jack but he's really the one struggling. Believe it or not, the night's probably been good for us. Talking about it has gotta be better than the silence," she said, looking sadly down at her hands. "We've only discussed the accident once since I got out of the hospital. Whenever I try to bring it up Jack has a fit so I just stopped mentioning it."

"Maybe you two should see a counselor."

"Dillon," she said with a half-smile. "I'd expect that out of Dr. Jordan, but surely you know Jack better than that."

"Well he needs to do something. I don't like to see him like this. The stuff he's been saying really kind of worries me."

"Like what?" she asked.

After a hesitant moment, Dillon finally responded. "A couple of weeks ago, he said he didn't know why he was here. I talked to Dr. Jordan about it, and he thinks Jack's suffering from some sort of survivor guilt."

"What do you mean?" she asked.

"He thinks Jack's feeling guilty that he survived the plane crash when Pop didn't survive his. I said the two accidents had absolutely nothing to do with each other, but then I got to thinking about it and it started to make sense. I know it's gonna sound crazy, but I think Jack feels like he didn't deserve to live."

"But why?" Kylie asked, baffled.

Dillon stared off for a moment. When he spoke, his tone was embittered. "Pop was really hard on Jack—I mean really hard. Jack couldn't walk in the room without him criticizing him. Jack spent his whole life trying to live up to what Pop thought he should be. Just like everything else connected with Pop, Jack feels like he's not worthy. He doesn't understand why he was spared when Pop wasn't."

"But Jack has a life," said Kylie, stung by the theory.

"I know," said Dillon. "I know it sounds crazy but Pop had a way of making Jack feel like he couldn't get anything right . . . now even dying."

Kylie thought of Jack as a small boy suffering his father's abuse and her heart sank even further.

"Jack needs to talk about it," said Dillon. "You both do. This is a really big thing for you guys to be trying to handle on your own."

"I know," said Kylie sadly. "Honestly, I just try not to think about it. I mean, you know how jumbled my memories are on the whole thing anyway."

While she had not told Dillon the story she had confided to Dr. Jordan, he knew of her confusion—confusion that had only deepened with time. Nearly every night she dreamt of the male "creature," and though her mind told her that it was illogical, she continued to feel as if she knew him, really knew him. Not just some acquaintance that she might have passed on the street like the doctor had suggested.

"Not understanding my own memory is the worst part of it," she said.

Dillon was looking at her sympathetically but clearly he couldn't understand the war that had been waging in her dreams. The war between reality and illusion.

"We'll be fine," said Kylie. "Jack and I have made it through—" but she could not say it. They had not made it through "worse." "We just need time," she added softly.

Eighteen

HER TREMBLING FINGERS GRAZED THE SINEWY WINGS, THEN GENTLY traced down along the muscular arms to the long, clawlike hands that bore nails as sharp as daggers. The face was Romanesque, with keen yet lamentable eyes focused woefully forward, the lips parted as if the very breath had been taken suddenly but at any moment would be retrieved. The hair was tousled and wild, with animalistic ears drawn back tight against the wayward locks. The head was held erect, the back arched and the loins slightly bent as if the huge beast had been swiftly calcified in mid-motion into solid rock. He was a horrifically beautiful creature that stood over six feet tall, shadowed within the back room of the art boutique.

Kylie suddenly realized that she had forgotten to breathe. She stepped back from the statue unable to believe her own vision. With the exception of the face, the sculpture very much resembled the celestial phantoms that continued to live and breathe in her nightmares. Even the feet, which were bare and enormous, had transformed into deformed appendages that were part-human, part-bird.

The figure dominated the small room which was cut off from the rest of the boutique by a narrow doorway hung with long curtains. A thin stream of sunlight filtered through a stained-glass window, casting the only light into the musty room.

Though the statue was a frightening piece, portraying a sensual juxtaposition of beauty and beast, it seemed oddly in keeping with its surrounding companions. The Virgin Mary stood silently and gracefully behind it, her tear-stained eyes lowered and her thin hands clasped. Leaning against the back wall was an archaic wooden cross with a life-sized Christ nailed upon it, his face bloodied and forsaken.

Stone chimeras crouched within the shadows, while fantastical gargoyles spouted invisible water from the walls, ceiling, and barred window sill. Man's medieval mind had come to life in the back room of the
Ratchford Art Boutique and the towering white statue of the angel
took center stage. Kylie stared in wonder at the porcelain lips, as if
waiting for the creature to look down at her and begin speaking, perhaps with an entreaty to be set free from the confining walls of the
twenty-first-century structure.

"Isn't he simply marvelous?" cooed a dainty male voice.

Kylie turned to find Arlin Boyce squeezing into the room behind
her. He was a thin man in his mid-forties but carried himself with the
gawky grace of a teenage girl. He looked at the statue as though feasting his eyes upon the embodiment of Adonis.

"I've got the Madonna you ordered," he said, vaguely pointing to
the statue behind the huge beast, "but I see you found something far
more interesting."

Kylie couldn't find a response within herself. She tried to ignore the
terror the statue evoked, but her whole body was shaking. She had
entered the back room expecting to find a statue of the Virgin Mary,
which she had ordered for Dora Greyson's home, not the personification of the horrid creatures she thought would slowly disappear without incident. To stumble upon the haunting statue in such a manner
had caught her off guard, weakening the protective barrier she had
purposefully built around her thoughts.

Arlin waved his finger in warning. "He's going to go fast and if that
old client of yours can't cough up the bucks for a 'beaut' like him,
well then the old bat deserves the Virgin Mary," he declared, walking
around to the side of the statue. He turned back to the silent Kylie,
and for the first time saw her stunned face and noticed the paleness of
her lips. "Honey, are you alright?" he asked touching her shoulder
gently.

"Where did he come from?" Kylie asked barely able to choke off
the words.

"Good God, honey, you look like you're staring at a ghost."

"Arlin," she repeated. "Where did it come from?"

"Eva Ratchford found him at an auction house in Munich," he answered. "His last owner was a rich widow, but he was originally from
the catacombs under St. Stephan's Cathedral in Vienna." Arlin leaned

in closer to her and said in an almost whisper. "You wouldn't believe where they found him standing, honey. I have pictures if you want to see."

Without waiting for a response, Arlin was already digging through a dusty pile of paperwork and photos atop a small desk. "Here they are," he announced, shoving them in front of her.

Kylie looked down at the first picture which sent chills dancing along her arms. The sculpture was perched inside an underground cemetery of winding dirt tunnels. The bright camera-flash brought the creature to life, accentuating the curves and angles of its masculine physique embellishing its already diabolical countenance. Its glowing wings stretched outward and melded into a murky shadow upon the curved ceiling, giving the impression that the creature was about to take flight through the dusky shaft. It appeared to be guarding a barred hole cut into the dirt wall of the cavern. Kylie focused in on the dark cavity and saw that it was an opening to another room where human bones were stacked unceremoniously on top of each other. There were so many dismembered skeletons that it appeared the pieces would at any moment tumble through the rusty bars and fall at the feet of the angel.

"The sculptor and title are unknown, but the piece dates back to the thirteenth century."

Kylie nodded, her stomach feeling nauseous from her reeling thoughts. The hideous birdlike creatures were no longer her own fusion of beast and angel but one that had been depicted centuries earlier in a place she had never seen nor traveled to. How would she possibly have known of such immortals unless her encounter bore some validity?

"These other two," continued Arlin, pulling another photo from the pile, "are what I call his brothers. They're not quite as pretty but they're still worth taking a peak at."

The photo was of two large statues standing at the dismal entrance to the tombs. Both of the figures were part-human with powerful, male bodies, but each bore its own freakish abnormalities. While the body of the one on the right was completely normal, it had the head of a rat. It very much resembled an old Egyptian work of art where the lines between man and animal are clearly drawn. The sculpture on the left was a much more explicit piece that was hard to look at. It was a beautiful man whose body was being warped in every direction. The legs of a spider were sprouting from his stomach and sides, while his shoulders drew upward like a bat. Though his twisted body was appalling, it was even harder to gaze into the exquisite face that seemed to be caught in the midst of the most intimate of moments. His head was thrown back and frozen in an agonizing scream that painfully depicted extreme pleasure.

"Pretty creepy, aren't they?" asked Arlin taking the photo from her fingers. "That's why Eva didn't bring them over. Nobody in the western world wants to think that an angel of death could change into a spider or a rat—too graphic. I guess the bird's a lot easier to deal with."

"Why do you say angels of death?" asked Kylie, his referral one more piece of evidence against her fate.

"Well that's what Eva called him," said Arlin. "Besides, it's standard myth, hon. You ever heard of Charon the Etruscan God of the Dead—the boatman for the River Styx? He's got the head of a bird with all kinds of creepy crawly creatures coming out of his skin. And Lilith, the goddess of death . . . ditto."

He returned to the photo of the angel standing eerily beside the mound of bones. "I guess death was so common in the Middle Ages that the poor bastards had to have some sort of emotional outlet. People were dropping like flies from the Black Plague. That's what all those remains are from," he said, pointing to the thousands of skulls and bones. "I heard they stacked about ten thousand bodies in one hole. Poor fella'," he said sympathetically stroking the image of the statue. "What a place to hang out." He looked over at the lamentable face of the towering statue and touched its leg affectionately. "I just couldn't believe it when Eva brought him in," he sighed. "I've had my sights on this hunk of rock for two years . . . I've been staring at his photo, day in and day out, just hoping some day he would turn up."

"This photo?" asked Kylie, confused.

"No, silly, those came with him," said Arlin with a giggle. "I was talking about that one," he said with a wave of his hand. "He's the same cutie pie that's in that picture up front."

"What picture?"

"Surely you've seen it, hon," said Arlin, pulling back the curtain that divided the two rooms. "The one by the door," he said with a nod of his head toward the entrance of the shop.

Kylie had to see for herself. She quickly went to the front of the boutique to look at the large photo mounted to the wall in an elaborate gold frame. It was an old photograph of the same statue, only this time it stood inside a huge mansion by the entryway to an expansive ballroom. While not recognizing the picture at first, Kylie vaguely remembered passing it many times on her way out the door. Her mind went back to Dr. Jordan's words of expertise; he had been right all along. Her heart lifted and she smiled. As the doctor said, she had taken elements that she knew and placed them like puppets into a nightmare. For the first time in over a month she felt the gnawing weight of doubt begin to lift. The beasts in her memory had finally found their birthplace and it was the front wall of the Ratchford Art Boutique.

"What?" asked Arlin. "What are you smiling at?"

"Well," said Kylie. "Now that I've found him, I've got to have him."

Arlin's face brightened. "You're going to take him?" he asked.

Kylie looked toward the back room where the glowing beast was about to escape. "Tell me your price and we'll see if Dora can afford him."

Nineteen

KYLIE WATCHED THE TINY BLACK SPIDER CRAWL UP THE WALL ABOVE her head, debating whether or not to tell Jack about the statue. Since that afternoon when she had discovered the basis of the imagined beasts, she had begun to feel like there was hope in resolving her memories of the accident once and for all. If the creatures had a logical yet harmless source, then surely the haunting vision of the man she thought she knew and his rose tattoo did as well. To her it was promising news that she wanted to share with Jack, she just wasn't sure how he would take it. She could no longer predict how he would react to information of any kind concerning the accident.

"I'll be out in a sec'," called Jack over the sound of running water. A dim light spilled out from the master bathroom into the darkened loft where Kylie lay silently waiting.

She pulled the soft comforter up around her waist and laid her head back onto the pillow where she could get a better view of the spider's progress. A small shadow went before the tiny creature, making it appear three times its actual size. The needlelike legs that supported the round ebony body, moved slowly and methodically, the shadow resembling a larger spider forging the way. Kylie's attention was drawn away from the spider itself to the dark image that preceded it. She thought of the spiderlike statue that guarded the opening to the tombs and in the meticulous movements of the reflection, looked for the image that could inspire a sculptor to create such a piece. With little concentration, the small body of the spider became the head of the angel, while the front legs formed the pinched shoulders and drawn up arms. The four lower legs of the spider melded into two shadows, forming the muscular trunk of the beast. Within only a moment, the spider's shadow became the distorted body of the statue, crawling painfully up the wall, edging slowly toward the ventilator shaft that whirled overhead.

"Well, that's lovely," she said aloud, surprised that her imagination had so quickly drawn such a hideous picture. At the sound of her voice, the spider quickened its pace and disappeared into a crack at the bottom of the giant fan that rotated round and round in a lulling hum.

As the twirling of the fan streaked shadows across the high, moonlit ceiling, Kylie began to drowse from the soothing sound she had grown accustomed to. When she and Jack had purchased the enormous building on the Waterfront they had debated whether or not to take out the high-placed fan that was the revealing earmark of a warehouse. After much deliberation they had decided to keep it and through the years it had become the most distinguishing part of their unique abode. The constant energy of the moving blades that exposed flashing glimpses of the starlit sky had come to signify the sanctuary of home; a safe place where the rest of the city was forgotten, and the peaceful Boston Harbor stretched out like a glistening moonlit image of tranquility.

The couple had spent over five years renovating the abandoned warehouse, turning it into a livable showpiece where they often entertained prospective clients. "It's positively exquisite," hailed the eminent Dora Greyson who instantly hired the young couple to re-decorate her Beacon Hill home upon seeing it. "Who would ever have thought these old warehouses could be so striking?" she asked in amazement. "It's fresh, yet it has elegance and a respect for the past." Instead of choosing the conventional high-tech approach most de-signers take in the renovation of deserted warehouses, Kylie had opted for the past in an eclectic combination of Gothic, neo-Rococo and Elizabethan.

The light and airiness of the expansively open structure was grounded with long, burgundy velvet drapes that stretched the en-tire length of the two-story windows that faced the Harbor. The abra-sive wooden floorboards had been sanded and polished but kept bare for an imperfect yet interesting and strangely alive feel. The towering fireplace whose hearth stood over six feet tall had been embellished with a richly sculpted white marble firesurround from the second half of the nineteenth century and above the mantel Kylie had hung an eighteenth-century mirror trimmed in gold. A canary chaise lounge, adorned in the silkiest of damask, stretched before the fireplace like an aristocrat from the past whose sole purpose is to dress in the evening's finest and lounge about with dignity. The furnishings were carved out of luxurious cherry, oak and mahogany, antique pieces that Kylie had purchased from all over the world. The sumptuous bed in which she lay had been imported from France, the high head board made of mahogany intricately engraved in the late 1800's. She had draped a long sheer netting on either side that stretched clear to the high ceiling like a long graceful ghost rising up from the place of rest. The bed stood in the center of the loft, facing out toward the towering windows where a huge yellow moon sent shivers of gold upon the water. Kylie had spent many peaceful nights gazing out at the stars, thinking if she wished it hard enough, she could jump from the loft to the hanging chandelier suspended high above the living room, and pivot right out the windows to the sea.

She was nearly asleep when the light in the bathroom went out.

"Hey, Wylie," Jack said softly, sliding under the covers and cud-dling up next to her.

"Jack," she whispered.

"Yeah?" he said, kissing her cheek.

She searched her groggy mind for a way to broach the subject of the crash. She turned toward him, admiring his face in the blue-tinged light. "I've got good news concerning the accident," she said slowly. "When I was at Arlin's today, I saw something that explains part of what I remember."

Jack's relaxed, pleasant face instantly stiffened. "Kylie," he said. "Do we have to talk about this?"

"I think it's important that you know," she said, sitting up.

Jack rolled onto his back with a sigh of exasperation.

Kylie looked down at him, wondering what it was that terrified him so much. "Arlin got a statue in," she continued, "an angel that's part-human and part-bird, just like I dreamt. He'd had a photo of the same statue at the front of the store I must have passed twenty times before the accident."

Jack suddenly sat up and flipped on the bedside light. "Really, I just wish you could let it rest," he said.

"The only reason I even bring it up is that I wanted you to know that I didn't invent the creatures, somebody else did centuries ago." Kylie could see that familiar look of pain enter his eyes. "Jack," she said, tenderly. "It's exciting to me, like the pieces to the puzzle are finally coming together," she said. She leaned into her husband and looked into his eyes. "When I saw the photo it felt like I was a little freer from it all. I was so happy I wanted to buy the statue for myself," she said with the hint of a smile. "You should see it, Jack. It's really beautiful."

"I'd rather not," he said with pouting lips.

She hesitated a moment. "Well, I'm sorry to hear that because it's exactly the kind of thing Dora was wanting."

"Don't tell me you bought it," said Jack.

"Well the reason she hired me was because she wanted a place that was dark, out of the norm."

"You bought it," he groaned.

"Jack, I have to do what's best for the client," she said. "The Madonna was too cliché and even though this was more expensive it's—"

"How much more?" interrupted Jack, a flash of anger burning in his eyes.

"It's within the budget," Kylie said defensively. "What are you getting so upset about?"

"Because you're becoming obsessed," he said.

"I bought a statue Jack, that's all."

"No, that's not all," he said sharply. "You just can't seem to let it go."

"Neither can you, Jack," she said. She studied him a moment, debating whether or not to continue. "You've got a right to survive a plane crash Jack," she said softly. "Even if your dad didn't."

"Jesus Christ," he said bitterly. "I'm trying to get on with my life—"

"But how can you when you've never worked through it? You're so eaten with pain and guilt that in the rare moment that you're actually around, I can't even stand to look at you. What are you so goddamned afraid of?" she begged.

"I'll tell you what I'm afraid of," he said getting up from the bed and going to the closet. "I was looking for the Greyson sketches today and here's what I found." He pulled out Kylie's leather satchel from the closet and lay it on the bed.

The second he began unzipping it, Kylie knew what he was after.

He pulled out a large drawing pad and began flipping through the bulky pages. His hands stopped on a charcoal illustration that was done in broad dark strokes that worked inward toward the precisely defined features of the male creature. His face was detailed and accurate, so skillfully drawn it resembled a photograph rather than a sketch. "This is what I'm afraid of," said Jack turning to the next drawing. It was another charcoal depiction of the same man but from a different angle. The sketch beneath that was of an outstretched hand, and upon the wrist was a rose tattoo. The next drawing was simply of the tattoo as well as the one after that. "Is this what you do instead of work?" he demanded.

"No," she cried, getting up from the bed. "This is what I do instead of sleep. This is what I do instead of talk to you!" she exclaimed. She desperately searched her mind for a way to make him understand something that wasn't even clear to herself. "Just because you ignore something, doesn't mean it'll go away," she whispered intently. "In my mind this man exists. I try not to think about it but I wake up in the middle of the night smothering with no one to talk to. It's like if I don't think about him in the day, he visits me in my dreams and I always end up in the same dark place I've been dreaming about for years—the

tunnel where I can't breathe or move—only this time he's there waiting for me . . . he's waiting for us."

"But he doesn't exist," insisted Jack.

"But he does," she argued. "No matter how illogical I know it
sounds, in my mind he lives. And his expressions and his movements
are as real to me as your own. And until I find him and see that he's just
an ordinary guy with an ordinary life and an ordinary family, and that
he's made of flesh and blood just like you and me, he'll exist as something much stronger than us. He'll be a threat that can come back
again and harm us. It's like Dr. Jordan said," she added softly. "When
you turn around and face the monster, you remove his power."

The couple stared at one another in silence, Jack without expression and Kylie with a yearning for understanding.

"Can't you see that I'm trying to solve it?" she asked, but he remained silent. Finally she turned away, feeling once again alone—
once again she had hit a brick wall of denial where anything that challenged Jack's guarded vision of life simply didn't exist. Her eyes began
to water but she angrily forced the tears back as she replaced the exposed drawings to the satchel and returned it to the closet.

"Hey," Jack said, turning her gently toward him. "You've just got to
trust me. If you give into these things they'll devour you whole."

Kylie felt a gnawing pit in her chest as she looked into the resolute
eyes of her husband—he was so grounded in the physical world of set
rules and restrictive guidelines that he would never understand his
own actions let alone her struggle with the intangible memories.

"You've just got to try harder to forget about it," he said with so
much love and tenderness that Kylie couldn't possibly be angry.
"We're alive," he whispered, his own voice cracking as he looked intently into her sad eyes. "We're alive and no dream, no matter how
terrifying, can take that away from us."

Twenty

Even though his back was turned toward her, she instantly
recognized the tall handsome physique beneath the overcoat and the

ashen blonde hair that hung neatly to his shoulders. His long, muscular hands rested upon the opposite end of the counter inside the tiny
grocery while he bent to inspect the contents beneath the glass case.
As his left hand fell against his side, she caught a glimpse of the rose
tattoo.

"Ms. Kylie," said Ducker Brown from behind the cash register.

Kylie was so stunned by the stranger, that it took her a moment to
respond. "Yes . . . I'm sorry," she said, turning back to the jovial old
black man who was flashing her a yellowed set of dentures.

"If you don't want this change, I'll keep it," he teased with a
chuckle. "Otherwise I wish you'd take it so I can get back to my
show." Behind the elderly store owner a television blared so loudly
that the tiny speakers were distorting the sound of the black and white
sitcom.

"Thank you Ducker," she said under her breath, retrieving the
coins just as the darkly dressed stranger exited the open door into the
sunny streets of the Italian Northend. Kylie quickly placed the bag of
groceries into her walking cart and headed for the door.

Though she made it outside within a minute of the man's exit, he
was nowhere to be seen. She stood on the porch of the store, looking
up and down Salem Street finding no sign of him in the deserted
neighborhood.

The store owner's wife, Elsey Brown, sat in a rocker next to the
door, gently swaying back and forth. "Elsey?" Kylie said but the old
woman's gaze remained distant and sleepy. "Elsey?" she said a little
louder to the half-deaf woman.

The old woman turned her golden-brown eyes toward her and
smiled brightly. "Well, hello there Georgia Peach," she crowed.

Kylie smiled. "Did you see the man who just came out?"

The old woman looked distracted. Kylie could tell she was focused
on the scar on her chin. "It's from a wreck," she quickly offered. "Did
you see the man who just came out?" she repeated anxiously.

"Another wreck?!" exclaimed Elsey. "I thought they wouldn't let
you drive no more."

"Well, I cheated," lied Kylie, reluctant to explain the plane accident.

The comment drew a gleeful laugh from the store owner's wife.

"Georgia Peach, you're gonna get yourself into serious trouble some day," she cackled with a shake of her head.

"Elsey," Kylie repeated. "It's really important. Did you—"

"—I don't know nothin' about any man," the old woman finally answered, her tired eyes clouded. "I must have been napping, 'cause if he came out, I didn't notice."

Kylie felt her heart sink as she looked again up and down the street. "Thanks Elsey," she said kindly, then lowered the cart onto the brick sidewalk and headed up the sloping hill toward the Waterfront.

Though it was a sunny day, there was a brisk chill that churned through the narrow winding streets. The buildings on either side were butted against each other so that they formed a steady unbreakable wall of quaint shops and restaurants. As Kylie passed each establishment, she looked inside hoping to stumble upon the man once again but all she found were the shop owners and an occasional customer.

"He's real," she said aloud, her heart beating wildly from the discovery and the steady climb up the hill. Though she was elated to have found him, she was disappointed to have lost him so suddenly.

The squeak of Elsey's rocker receded further and further behind her until there was no sound—only silence. The neighborhood was unusually quiet for a Sunday afternoon and it left Kylie with a feeling of apprehension. Since the accident she had grown to detest solitude of any kind even in the light of day. As she approached the intersection of Salem and Prince Street, she heard the sound of footsteps behind her. She looked around and saw the man once again. He was back by Ducker's Grocery, headed in her direction.

He appeared to be looking at her, but he was still so far away that she couldn't see the details of his face. While he continued toward her, Kylie sensed that he was uncomfortable with her stare but as much as she tried, she couldn't turn her eyes away. Then he seemed to challenge her gaze and began to walk with more aim, his coat spreading slightly from his muscular legs. She recognized the graceful way in which he carried himself; the refinement only adding to the power which he seemed to possess beneath the dark clothing. For a brief moment, Kylie felt the familiar pang of fear but it immediately dissipated when the sun hit his face and she saw that he was merely a man.

As he drew nearer, his features came slowly into view. He was much more striking than she remembered, perhaps because he no longer carried the terror of her dreams. Just as she had envisioned, his skin was pallid and his lips were thin and pink like those of Northern European descent. He moved with the sureness of one bred into the upper echelon of society, his grey eyes sad and remote yet arrestingly intense. He was within speaking distance when she realized that she hadn't thought of what to say.

"Do I know you?" she asked, but her voice failed her. She quickly cleared her throat. "I'm sorry I don't mean to stare . . ."

The man slowed his pace, then silently stopped about ten feet from her. Kylie felt embarrassed under his observation. He seemed interested yet baffled by her question. "I look familiar to you?" he finally asked, his voice smooth and bespeaking education.

"Yes," she said and she couldn't help but smile. To her own chagrin, she felt her face turning red. He was so strangely appealing with no particularly commanding features, yet the sum total and the air that surrounded him gave him an extraordinary beauty. She suddenly realized that her hair was wind blown and that she must look a mess. "I'm sorry, I know this probably sounds really strange . . ." she said, but then stopped when she noticed him looking at her lips. Her hand went immediately up to hide the scar on her chin, but then she pulled it back down. "I was in an accident," she said. There was an uncomfortable silence as she tried to regroup her thoughts. "I don't want to take up your time, I just thought that I knew you from somewhere and . . ."

He listened without emotion, yet she could tell by his somber eyes that he was intrigued with her words. "What's your name if you don't mind my asking," she finally said.

He watched her a moment, studying her. "Petrie," he said. "Robert Petrie."

Kylie extended her hand. "Mine's Kylie O'Rourke."

He grasped her hand gently and for a moment Kylie wondered if she were dreaming. She glanced down at the distinguishing tattoo and felt her heart falter. He seemed to notice the moment of uncertainty and politely pulled his hand away.

"It's a pleasure," he offered, stepping away from her as if not to frighten her. The sun absorbed into his smooth hair that was parted perfectly down the center.

His voice soothed her shaky feelings. He was flesh and blood just as the doctor had predicted and their paths had finally crossed. Though part of her knew he was a stranger, another felt as if she had known him for years. She knew the intricate details of his face, what it looked like happy and most certainly how it appeared when he was angry. But surely these thoughts were created by her dreams much the same as her imaginary relationship with Collins still carried its own erroneous nuances. "Have you met me before?" she asked, uncertainly.

He studied her a moment. "I'm not sure," he answered.

"I'm a designer . . . interior designer. Could I know you from that?"

"It's doubtful," he answered softly. "I'm a writer."

"Do you mind if I walk with you for a moment?" she asked.

"No," he said simply. Kylie was struck by the sad resignation in his voice. They slowly began walking in the direction of the Waterfront.

Within only a moment, Kylie was pouring out the details of the harrowing accident as if speaking to an old friend. She told him of her jumbled memories and her face flushed as she honestly revealed that he too had been part of the experience. He listened quietly and with reservation, yet his attentiveness set Kylie at ease, allowing her the much needed release. To detail the suffering with the foremost character who tormented her, unbound the burden she had carried for nearly two months. As she spoke of dark forces and demons, he listened to her story without prejudice; if nothing else, he appeared slightly entertained by the account. At one point a tiny smile almost formed on his lips. When she questioned him as to where they had met, he seemed just as interested as she to find an answer.

"Maybe I've seen you in the store," she said. "I've been going in Ducker's for years."

"I don't think that would have been possible," he said. "I've been away for awhile."

"Oh," Kylie said, hesitant to ask.

"I was living down in New York with my wife, Laura," he offered.

"You're married?" asked Kylie.

He thought about it for a moment. "No," he said quietly looking away from her eyes.

Kylie wasn't sure whether he meant he was divorced or that she had died.

"She left me," he said.

"Oh, I'm sorry," said Kylie.

As they left the cozy streets of the historical Northend for the brisk open air of the Harbor, the sun was setting. A brilliant orange glow cracked through the blue sky leaving splinters of fire upon the water. In what seemed like only minutes from the time they had met, they were standing outside of the warehouse Kylie called home. Through the huge arching windows she could see Jack fixing supper in the warmly lit kitchen.

"Do you mind coming up for a moment?" she asked. "I would love for you to meet my husband."

Kylie could see the discomfort in his grey eyes that took on the golden warmth of the dusk.

"How about if I bring him down to you, then?" she asked.

"If you like," he said.

KYLIE LEFT the cart of groceries at the door and rushed up the entry stairs to the main level where the kitchen was located.

"Jack!" she cried.

She found him at the sink washing a bundle of spinach. "Hey Wylie," he said sweetly. "Did you get the olive oil?"

"Jack," she said, pulling his hands from the wet greens. "I've got someone I want you to meet."

"Who is it?" he asked.

"Just come and see," she said impatiently going toward the window while Jack dried his hands. Looking to the street below, she saw no sign of the man beneath the glowing street lamp where she had left him moments earlier. Then she noticed his eloquent figure halfway up the shadowy block, walking slowly away from the warehouse.

"Who is it?" Jack repeated, stepping to the window, just as the man disappeared into the dusky light.

"He's gone," sighed Kylie. "I guess he didn't want to wait."

"Who?" asked Jack impatiently, turning toward his pensive wife.

Kylie looked toward him, unsure whether or not to say. "The man from my nightmares."

Jack's face dropped.

"He has a rose on his wrist just like I dreamt," she continued, unable to hide her excitement. "I ran into him at Ducker's."

Jack was silent for a moment. "What's his name?" he asked.

"Robert Petrie."

"And you let him walk you home?"

"Yes," said Kylie.

"So now he knows where you live?"

Looking into his worried face, Kylie couldn't help but smile. His instinct to protect was touching. "Jack," she said affectionately. "If you saw this man that wouldn't even be a consideration. He's a perfect gentleman."

She turned back toward the window where the shadows of the trees played against the empty street.

Jack suddenly threw his hands up in the air. "Jesus, Kylie, I thought this whole accident thing was over with."

Kylie stared out at the glistening sea as the light faded from the sky and the half-moon rose over the clouds. "It is," she said softly, thinking of the sad, intriguing stranger. His manner had been so interestingly reticent, his eyes so pale, that there was no wonder he had found his way into her dreams. "It's over," she added softly, wishing she could have said good-bye to the man who was not only incapable of the malice but also the joyful abandon her dreams had led her to believe.

Twenty-One

"AMELIA CORRINNE! I THOUGHT I TAUGHT YOU BETTER THAN THAT," scolded Mamie Blackwell, snatching a sweating soda from the antique bed-table.

"Sorry Mama."

"Here, move for a second," the mother snapped, pulling and fussing with the bedclothes beneath her daughter's sprawled body.

"Mama, just give me a few more minutes," Amelia pleaded, cupping her hand over the telephone receiver.

Her mother shot her an exasperated glance and then headed toward the door. "When you hang up with Kylie, come down for breakfast."

"I will Mama."

Amelia watched until the door was completely shut. "God," she groaned, flipping onto her back. "You'd think this was her old room the way she carries on."

Kylie gave a thought-ridden sigh from the other end of the line. "How strange," she finally said.

"What?"

"Oh I don't know. It would just be really strange for me to be in my old bedroom."

"Strange isn't quite the word," said Amelia, her eyes resting on the dolls lining the walls. "It's freaky the way Mama keeps it. You'd think I died at puberty."

"It's nice that you've still got it though," Kylie said. "It must make you feel safe."

Amelia felt an ache, for she understood the wistful sound of Kylie's voice, whose childhood home now lay abandoned in the bayou behind her. She reached out for the pink rosary that dangled from the bedpost. "It is nice," she admitted, lacing the pearly beads between her fingers as she had as a child. "Mama asked if I wanted the guest room, but I sleep best in here."

"How long are you staying?"

"Just till Daddy gets back from his trip. You know how Mama hates being alone. Dix isn't too happy about me being gone, though."

"Jack wouldn't notice," said Kylie. "Not now, anyway."

"No better, huh?"

"Not really, no. His moods are all over the place. I think he's slipping into some kind of mid-life crisis."

"Aren't we too young for that?"

"Apparently not," said Kylie softly. "For the first time in years, he mentioned having a baby."

"And?"

"And nothing," Kylie sighed. "Can you imagine us with a child? Parents are supposed to actually speak to one another."

"And if you did, would you want one?"

Within the silence, Amelia regretted the question—one to which she already knew the answer, one long since put to rest during those dark months following Tucker's death. Kylie had drawn so far into herself, that the brutal depression had nearly destroyed her.

"You think I'm wrong," came her friend's sad voice.

"No," said Amelia with hesitation. *You've got to let him go*, she wanted to say, but knew no advice could mend her friend's crippled heart. "I miss him too," she said softly, remembering the child's warm brown eyes and mischievous smile.

"So when are you coming to visit?" asked Kylie, abruptly changing the subject.

Amelia had to laugh. "You're kidding right? I can't even look at a plane right now."

"Hey, we're done with all of that, remember?" said Kylie playfully. "Now that we know who my monster is, we've decided to move forward, to put all of that post-traumatic mumbo jumbo behind us."

"Good," said Amelia, gripping the rosary tighter. "Can you tell that to Mama? She's driving me nuts. I can't get her to talk about anything else ... about the papers and what they said about the attorneys. About how God could have crushed us, but spared us. I've only been here a couple of days and she's got me convinced I'm gonna burn in hell."

"For what?" asked Kylie with exasperation.

"She thinks the accident was a warning."

"Warning for what?"

"Who knows. You know Mama. Always trying to save my heathen soul. Problem is, her rantings are starting to make sense."

"Don't let that happen," grumbled Kylie.

"Too late. She's got me running scared."

"Scared of what?"

"I don't know. God, I suppose."

"You're scared of your mama's God, Melia. Anybody would be. Trust me, if there is a God, he's not the one your mother would have us believe."

"Let's hope not."

"You'll be leaving there soon, right?"

"Not soon enough," groaned Amelia, her heart lifting with the mere thought of escape. "Never soon enough."

There was a moment of silence between them, wherein Amelia's thoughts returned to the plane, to those terrifying moments before the darkness came. "It's over, isn't it?" she asked quietly.

"Yes," came the soft reply. "We made it."

Twenty-Two

THE TRAIN ROARED OUT OF THE EARTH LIKE A HUGE SNAKE SURFACING momentarily into the light of day, before disappearing once again into the darkened caverns where the underground tracks traced beneath the bustling streets of Boston. It moved below the city, twisting and turning within the belly of the earth, forcing the wind ahead of it in a howling rage. The fluorescent light inside the train cast a deathly appearance upon its listless passengers whose bodies swayed with the enormous reptile's movements. At high noon the businessmen, laymen and tourists were thrust into night where they obediently followed the unspoken law of survival. They were silent and suspicious of all from the time they placed their tokens into the subway gate until they emerged from the stairwell into the street above.

Though the stretch between the Downtown Crossing and the Arlington exit had only two stops, Kylie had already become drowsy. Unlike most, Kylie loved the rocking of the subway, full of energy and force. While others complained of the unpleasant yet necessary means of transportation, Kylie enjoyed it. When her Massachusetts driver's license had been revoked several years earlier for excessive speeding, she had rediscovered the subterranean city of darkness she had known and loved as a child living in Quincy. From the time she was an infant, when her mother used to take her on the subway so that the lulling motion would soothe her colic, she had felt perfectly safe and at home in the trains which moved with such confident speed through the pitch black tunnels. She loved the underground billboards, the writing on the walls, and the sounds of the rushing air that could change from a screeching pitch to a deep guttural moan from one moment to the next. It was the sound of an old powerful friend for whom she had respect; for no matter how comfortable she felt in its care, she never forgot that its grinding steel underbelly could split her in half with the slip of a foot onto the wrong tracks.

"Next stop . . . Arlington," announced an emotionless voice over the muffled speaker. Though the next station was Kylie's exit, she remained seated with her head against the window. Like most of her thoughts lately, her mind was on Jack. Since her discovery two weeks earlier of Robert Petrie, she had let go of the accident and had moved

on to the resolution of her ailing marriage. While she felt that she
had resolved her feelings of the tragedy, Jack seemed to be lost in a
silent depression where he drifted further and further from her. He
was struggling desperately, but with what she could only guess.
Though it was Sunday, a day the couple had reserved as their own,
Jack was spending the afternoon with an old friend, Freddy Hopkins.
While Kylie had nothing against the artist who panhandled in
Harvard Square for a living, it made her nervous that Jack had suddenly started spending time with him again. Freddy was from an era in
the couple's lives when they threw all-night parties of gross overindul-
gence of every kind. It was a reckless lifestyle the couple had abandoned a year earlier in an attempt to reconcile their volatile marriage.
While Kylie had vowed to stop drinking, Jack had promised fidelity
and to quit gambling. Though Jack reassured her that he was absolutely keeping his side of the bargain, she couldn't help but feel apprehensive about the sudden reunion of the friends. While she no longer
worried about him gambling, for she had placed both their personal
and business accounts into only her name, she was uneasy about the
other trouble her husband would find if left to his own devices. "I'll
meet you at seven at the Greyson house," Jack had promised that
morning.

The squealing of the brakes began to slow the rapidly moving train.
"Arlington," announced the tinny voice. As the passengers around her
began standing Kylie glanced through the rear windows to the next
train-car. A man stood at the opposite window staring back at her. After a startled moment, she realized that it was Robert Petrie. His eyes
met hers and he smiled slightly. She herself began to smile but another
passenger cut in front of her as the train came to a halt. The glass
doors opened with a sigh and the passengers began to spew out onto
the cement walkway. As Kylie was carried away from the train by the
rushing mass, she looked to the next car to see if Petrie had de-
boarded. She was happy to see that he was no longer on the train and
therefore in the crowd. Perhaps they could have coffee before she re-
sumed the task of finding a lamp for Greyson's study. She looked
through the sea of pedestrians moving toward the stairwell and
caught a glimpse of the back of his coat.

"Robert!" she called but he didn't turn around. "Robert," she repeated as she touched his shoulder.

The man turned toward her but it was not Robert Petrie. "Yeah lady?" asked the stranger.

"I'm sorry," she said. "I thought you were someone else." She looked quickly about, but to her disappointment, Robert Petrie had once again slipped through her fingers.

The train quickly filled with new passengers, then disappeared into the darkened tunnel. Suddenly alone in the quiet station, Kylie felt a sadness come over her. Since the day that Petrie had left without saying good-bye she had wanted to see him again. "You don't even know him," she said softly to herself, hoping to dismiss the illogical attachment she felt for a man she barely knew. She concentrated on the day's work as her steps echoed toward the light of the stairwell, but as much as she tried, the image of his sad face refused to leave her.

THE RAIN sliced down in sheets as Kylie beat on the door of Dora Greyson's five-story rowhouse. "Jack!" she cried repeatedly, but there was no answer from within. She stepped out of the shelter of the recessed entry and into the muddy garden below the entrance hall window. As the icy rain pelted against her face, she tugged on the shoulder-high latch but it was bolted shut. "Jack," she cried softly, peering into the darkened mansion.

She groaned with defeat and turned away. Never had she seen Pickney Street so flooded or so dark. She looked with hesitation up and down the neighborhood that smeared into one big blur from the torrential rain. "This is what you get for speeding," she muttered to herself as she stepped out into the pouring rain and headed for the nearest pay phone on foot.

She was half-way down the narrow street when the downpour abated to a mild drizzle. "Thank you, God," she whispered, drawing her arms closer into her soaked chest.

The cobblestone sidewalk was shadowed beneath a dense row of trees, the gentle sprinkle adding a creepiness to the long street. Kylie glanced up at the lights wishing the yellowish glow of the gas lanterns was brighter. While providing an Old World charm to the picturesque, nineteenth-century neighborhood, they did little to eliminate the shadowy alcoves between the tightly spaced rowhouses of the wealthy. As Kylie passed each narrow crevice between the dwellings she felt her back stiffen with apprehension. As much as she hated to admit it, she was frightened. Earlier that day she had sensed that she was being followed along the posh Newbury Street, but when she had turned back she had seen no one of suspect in the crowd. Several times on her way to Greyson's, she had heard noises behind her only to find that it was a blowing branch or a scampering cat. The cloudy day had been filled with an uneasiness that had given way to the dark night.

She went toward Charles Street where she had shopped that afternoon for the lamp even though she knew in her heart that all of the boutiques would be closed as well as the exclusive little restaurants. Beacon Hill was a rich, conservative neighborhood whose residents, if not traveling the world, were at home with their families on a Sunday evening, not shopping or eating out. The chances of finding something open were slim, yet there was no other direction in which to go.

The rain finally subsided, leaving behind an eerie stillness broken only by the sound of Kylie's breathing and the click of her shoes along the glistening, uneven sidewalk. As she passed the corner of Cedar Lane, an alleyway too narrow for even a small car to pass through, she debated whether or not to take the shortcut through the tiny passage. It would save her at least a block and the alley was no more dimly lit than the rest of the Hill. If anything, the passage was brighter for there was less space between the close brick buildings to light. She hesitated a moment, then decided in favor of it.

Though her sweater was soaked, she pulled the itchy collar up around her neck. An aching chill set through her body and she began to tremble. "Jack," she whispered angrily, wondering where to call once she managed to reach a telephone.

She was deep into the narrow walkway when suddenly she heard the crunching sound of a shoe against the cobblestones behind her. Her body instantly froze. Surely she had imagined it. After all, her nerves were on edge and she had been listening intently all day for anything out of the ordinary. She slowly turned back but saw no one in the alley behind her. It was silent except for the echo of dripping water from the sodden trees. "See," she whispered calmly to herself, attempting to gain control of her imagination. She took a breath and tried to relax, but as she turned back, she heard the same sound in front of her, this time from the completely opposite end of the alley.

She stood silent and motionless. "Is anyone there?" she asked quietly, her own voice barely louder than her beating heart. Again there was only the sound of dripping water. She slowly forced herself forward toward Mt. Vernon Street.

She went a quarter of a block before she once again heard someone behind her; this time the single step had been replaced with a steady walk. As much as she tried to ignore it, she became aware of her own back as though viewing herself through the eyes of a killer. She quickened her pace, trying hard not to panic, but along with her own, the footsteps also quickened. With a gasp, she began running toward the opening of the alley which was only twenty feet away. As she reached the intersection she turned back just in time to see a shadow duck into a crevice between the buildings. Even though she had distinctly seen the figure of a man, Kylie barely believed her own eyes. It wasn't her imagination, there really was someone following her. Still trying to maintain a sense of control, she turned to the houses around her, searching for a light that signified someone was home. A few houses down, the living room of a rowhouse was aglow. She would pass the home on her way to Charles Street and if she needed, she would knock on the door for help.

She quickly continued toward Charles Street, constantly checking behind her but the stalker had yet to appear from the alleyway. As she approached the business-lined street of Charles, she could see that, just as she had dreaded—all of the windows of the small shops and restaurants were darkened.

"Just keep calm," she said to herself, comforted only by the fact that she was now on a wider street. She could hear the distant hum of the freeway and wished desperately that one of the cars would make its way through the quiet, sleepy neighborhood.

As she rounded the corner onto Beacon Street which bordered the wooded Public Garden, the rain began to pour so suddenly that the roar of it gave her a start. Stealing a glance back through the wall of water, she saw the blurred figure of the man moving toward her. At once she was running along the park toward the lights of Arlington Street, the rumble of the storm exploding around her.

As her body jolted against the hard slick pavement, her lungs burned so painfully it felt as if her chest would explode. She gasped for breath but the thundershower was so thick she feared she would suffocate. She frantically stepped onto Arlington just as a black Volvo came to a screeching halt, its headlights blinding her and the blare of the horn assaulting her.

"What the hell do you think you're doing?" screamed the driver, his wheels spinning as he hit the gas once again.

On the right side of the street ahead of her, a blue and white sign glowed: BUSCH BEER. Within a matter of steps, her bitterly cold hand grasped the rusted handle of the tavern door and forcefully yanked it open.

TEARS filled her eyes as Kylie stood before the clouded mirror of the ladies rest room, her reflection vibrating with the sound of the live band. Her hair lay in damp ringlets, her body soaked beneath the long cotton dress and thick sweater. Glancing into the mirror at the pay phone behind her, she felt her frustration surge. It was an hour and a half past the time Jack was supposed to meet her at Greyson's house and he was nowhere to be found. She had dialed the warehouse and numerous friends but was unable to reach anyone. She had even tried to call a cab but the storm assured at least a forty-five minute wait.

"It'll be okay," she whispered but the hot tears escaped over the rim of her eyes and burned down her cold cheeks. "He's just out with Freddy," she said, pulling the wool sweater over her head and laying it onto the counter. She turned on the warm water and splashed her red face; and though she tried not to think of Jack, her mind imagined him kissing and caressing Alice Newfield.

Though Jack's one-night affair with the clothes designer happened over a year earlier, Kylie couldn't help but wonder if he had been seeing her again. Alice Newfield belonged to the same circle of friends as Freddy Hopkins, whose reappearance into the couple's lives had brought the painful past into the present.

While Kylie hated the insecurity of mistrust and wanted desperately to forgive and forget Jack's indiscretion, she had been losing the battle all along.

At first, her love for Jack and the history they shared had convinced her that she could surmount the infidelity; after all, there was much more to marriage than monogamy and she herself had come close to the same mistake only a few years earlier. But where she had once been an equal partner in the relationship, she suddenly found herself in the role of a victim. While she became less sure of herself in the marriage, Jack became more secure. Though he had committed the adultery, he had been rewarded by proof of Kylie's unconditional love. She, on the other hand, was left to struggle with her self-respect and the limits that he had begun once again to test.

Since the accident, Jack was slowly returning to the old, self-destructive days of missed appointments and walled emotions where Kylie was unable to reach him.

"Damn you Jack, where are you?" she whispered, hating him for slowly destroying the life they had worked so hard to build.

She dried her face with a paper towel, then tugged at the dress that clung like wet paper to her shapely body. It obediently pulled free and hung limply to her boots. She glanced once again at the telephone but then decided against anymore calls; she would have to find her own way home. She grabbed the soggy sweater from the counter and stepped out into the noisy, smoke-filled bar.

Through the neon-lit windows, she saw that the rain had nearly stopped once again. She scanned the room, only to find what few patrons there were, lecherously staring at her from their seats. All eyes were upon her with the exception of a businessman who had entered the tavern after her and had taken a seat at the bar. In his tailored suit-jacket and designer shoes he was oddly out of place in the smoky dive. Kylie felt a surge of trepidation as she examined his profile from across the room. He was just about the build of the man in the alley, but surely he wouldn't be so brazen as to follow her into the bar.

"Can I help you, miss?" asked a husky bartender from behind a wall of whiskey bottles and hanging glasses. "You look a little lost."

"Has that man been sitting there long?" she asked, nodding to the patron.

The bartender glanced over his shoulder at the businessman. "He walked in right after you went into the ladies room," he answered. "I thought he was with you."

"He's not," she said, her face suddenly hot with anger. "Thank you."

She moved toward the bold offender, who continued to stare forward with a cigarette dangling from his fingers. Her anger built with each step, and she was within a few feet when he finally looked up at her. His eyes were vacant and pathetic, like those of a man who was tired and well on his way to intoxication. He was so unaware of her presence that she instantly knew she had been mistaken. While the man may have been the one behind her in the street, he had clearly not been following her, but had been heading to the bar to sit in peace. Feeling suddenly foolish, she continued on past him toward the door. The Arlington train-stop was less than a block from the tavern and the street along the way was well-lit and busy with traffic. If in fact anyone had been following her, she doubted the predator would have the audacity to stalk her in plain sight of others. She had been inside the sanctity of the bar for nearly thirty minutes and saw no reason to wait any longer.

KYLIE glanced both ways outside the door before abandoning the safe haven for the sidewalk. A soft mist floated downward, catching the colored lights of Arlington Street. With the cars whisking past, she headed in the direction of the train-stop, looking several times behind her to make sure no one was following. Within only a few minutes she was dropping her subway token into the gate and stepping into the tunnel where she had exited earlier for the day.

At first thinking the faintly lit station was empty, she noticed a man leaning against a nearby pillar waiting for a train. When he turned toward her, she was surprised to see that it was Robert Petrie. "Hello," he said warmly.

To her annoyance her stomach dropped like a nervous schoolgirl's. "Hello," she replied. After the tense evening it was comforting to see his familiar, calm face. "Going home?" she asked.

"Yes," he said with a nod of his head.

"I saw you earlier," she said, sure that he could see through her feigned nonchalance.

"Yes, I know," he answered softly.

Kylie felt his gray eyes upon her and knew she was blushing. Though he couldn't have been more than a couple of years older than she, his self-possessed confidence made her feel like a child. She looked toward the tracks, anything to escape his absorbing gaze.

"Have you remembered where we might have met?" he asked kindly.

"No," she said, once again meeting his eyes.

The answer brought a surprisingly deep sadness to Petrie's countenance. She could see that he too had the same feeling of familiarity. A lengthy silence followed, but it was a comfortable, safe silence. It had been years since Kylie had felt such a strong attraction to anyone.

"Kylie Rose," he said softly as if the name suddenly appeared in his mind and rolled off his lips.

"Yes, that's my middle name," she said. "Then we must have known each other."

His long body leaned against the column with stately grace. With his eyes upon her she had no choice but to smile. For the first time since she had met him, he too smiled a genuine, exquisite smile. Their eyes locked and for a silent moment, neither looked away.

"I hear the train," she said shyly, eager for the interruption. A low rumble resonated in the distance, and they both turned toward the tracks as a breeze wafted toward them. Chills traveled up Kylie's arms and she began to tremble. He was watching her, his coat rustling in the increasing wind. Then she realized that he was looking at her body whose intricate details were exposed through the clinging dress. She instantly started to cover herself but he gently stopped her hand.

"You're beautiful," he said with such admiration and respect that she felt a warm flush move through her and she relaxed. In spite of herself, she shyly pulled the dress away from her skin.

The train roared up in front of them and came to a screeching halt. The glass doors split open and let out a sigh of invitation.

Like a perfect gentleman, he waited for her to board. The moment she stepped onto the train she noticed with a start the only other passenger. Beneath the fluorescent lights, the pale, stern face of an elderly man watched her from the back of the car. His appearance resembled that of an undertaker, his clothes dark and his face long and thin with a huge scar cut into his cheek. He clutched a cane with large, gnarled fingers and though she smiled uneasily at him, his stony expression didn't change.

She took a seat by the door, where Petrie stood before her with his hand on the overhead railing. He glanced back at the old man who continued to stare at them. "Good evening," said Petrie in the voice of gentry.

At first the deathly man didn't respond, then finally he returned the greeting. "Good evening," he said then turned toward the window as the train slowly began to move.

Kylie watched the disappearing lights of the station, feeling as though she were being carried away into a dream. Her reflection appeared in the blackened windows as the train entered a long tunnel. The rain had turned her hair to long, crimson ringlets that curled wildly around her soft face and neck. Her cheeks and lips were pink, and she was startled to see how alive her own eyes appeared with dark lashes and large black pupils that nearly swallowed the green. The swaying of the car rocked her gently back and forth, as the roaring speed smeared the outside walls into ebony liquid. In the reflection, Petrie met her eyes with such a look of desire that she had to catch her breath and look away.

The vibration of the train sent shivers rolling once again over her body. Though she tried to ignore the thumping in her chest, she was intensely aware of Petrie as he stood over her. His hand reached toward her, at first she thought to offer his jacket, but instead, he delicately touched her neck. She looked up into his darkened eyes, dazed by the advance, but the touch was so warm and with such openness and control that she sat motionless and riveted.

After a silent moment, his jaw clenched with determination and he continued to trace down along her neck, all the while his eyes never leaving hers. His confident touch slowly moved over her wet dress, over the top of her full breasts until he gently caressed her erect nipple through the wet cotton. He brushed it softly as though it were the most precious of jewels, then tenderly squeezed it.

"No please, stop," she said, looking away, her cold hand suddenly grasping his.

He turned her face back to him, his eyes filled with a blatant lust. "It doesn't matter," he whispered as though reading her mind.

She was thinking of Jack, of the pain and the coldness she wanted so desperately to escape and her hand relaxed. She looked into the piercing eyes and as much as she wanted to stop she knew that she wouldn't. She felt her breath growing heavy and her body flushed.

"What is it about you?" he whispered. She could hear the struggle in his deep voice as he too fought the attraction. A look of anger passed through his eyes, then they narrowed as he resigned to the same need burning beneath her skin. His lips moved toward her as if to feast himself upon her. His warm mouth pressed against hers and his soft tongue touched upon her own.

"What am I doing?" she murmured, pulling away with sudden panic. Then his warm lips caressed her neck and her head fell back.

"Kylie Rose," he said again and again. His kiss was so natural so alive and everything she had forgotten yet yearned for and needed. His strong hand spread her legs apart as he laid her back on the seat, and though they were clothed she could feel the heat of his body as he pressed down upon her. The train moaned and writhed beneath them and as it moved through the vast rippling tunnels, she saw the deathly white face of the old man watching from across the car. She felt the top of her dress come open, her breast exposed to the cool air and though she knew it was wrong, the old man's eyes fueled her desire even more.

She felt her breath leave her and suddenly she realized she was moaning. Petrie's velvety soft hair fell upon her cheek as his warm body moved against hers. His skin pressed against her lips and with her breath she recognized his smell. A long dim hallway flashed into her mind and she felt her hand in the comfort of his.

"Oh my God!" she gasped at the glimpse into a clouded memory. Then his hand moved down to her legs and up her dress where the warmth between her legs waited for his touch. As he began stroking her, he caressed her with his whispers. "You're so beautiful . . ."

His adoration pulled her deeper into the passion and she worked her hands up through his clothing to the soft, inviting feel of his stomach.

"So beautiful," he whispered again and again. "So lovely to observe . . . to admire in the night."

Kylie heard the words that slowly started to assimilate in her disoriented mind. Then suddenly a feeling of terror rushed over her . . . *so lovely to observe!* Her heart jolted within its feverish beat as she realized the man atop her had been the one all along. He had been following her since that morning at the station. "No," she gasped trying to pull away from his increasingly forceful hands. "No," she said but his gray eyes suddenly took on the vengeance of a madman. She nearly screamed as the deranged face from her nightmares materialized before her. She frantically pulled away from him, falling onto the floor of the moving train, but his hands grasped her legs and pulled her back.

With a flick of his wrists he turned her over and as much as she fought she was helpless in his powerful grasp.

"No!" she cried as he lowered himself once again upon her, but her entreaty was muffled by the sound of the roaring train. From the floor she could see the old man who continued to watch without expression. Then she felt her dress rip and her panties pull away from her body. "NO!" she cried again and with all her might she shoved her hands against Petrie's face, screaming again and again. She was kicking and beating with everything she had when she suddenly realized that he was no longer upon her and that the train had stopped. Petrie stood to his feet, his face returning to the gentleness of before. He was horrified and stunned.

"I'm so sorry," he gasped, turning his eyes away from her naked legs. "I didn't mean . . . I didn't," but his voice trailed to silence.

Kylie tried to control her rushing tears as she scrambled across the floor. She pulled her ripped dress up around her bare legs and shakily stood to her feet.

She looked to the ghastly man still seated silently in the back of the car. He was looking once again out the window.

She turned to Petrie who had his back toward her. "You've been following me," she said. And while he didn't answer she knew that she was right. "Why?" she asked.

"I have no choice," he said quietly. He turned toward her and his face took on the conviction of a justified warrior. "I need you."

The words sent more terror through her soul than his hands could ever evoke. "Stay away," she warned, her voice heavy and low. She could feel the burning of his kisses upon her lips and as much as she wanted to loathe him, his beautiful gray eyes and graceful body sent a conflicting chill over her. "Stay away," she repeated and turned for the door. She stepped down onto the cement walkway outside the train and didn't look back, for she knew he hadn't moved. The glass doors of the train slammed shut and with a roar it was gone.

Twenty-Three

DILLON TOOK THE SHORTCUT ALONG ESSEX STREET, EVEN THOUGH he felt uneasy about the neighborhood. Chinatown was not safe in the day much less at ten o'clock at night; but his date, Theresa Ollridge, lived off Atlantic Avenue and it was the quickest way to her condo.

"It was much better than the reviews," mused Theresa, still pondering the stage production the two had just seen in the Theater District.

As Dillon steered the BMW past a drunken bum, his headlights illuminated a young woman walking alone in the street. "I don't believe it," he said, peering through the flapping wipers. "That's Kylie."

Theresa slid her manicured hand into his. "What in the world is she doing here?" she asked.

KYLIE knew the neighborhood was questionable, yet she was too tired to be frightened. The bums and the prostitutes passed her by, occasionally throwing comments her way, but her focus remained forward, intent on reaching the warmth of her bed.

She was just half a block from the next train stop when the BMW pulled slowly up to her and coasted alongside her. She continued forward, hoping that if she ignored it, the gawker would simply go away. When she heard the window on the passenger's side roll down, she kept the same pace so as not to show fear.

"Kylie!"

Startled to hear her name, she turned toward the familiar voice. When she saw that it was Dillon staring back at her from behind the wheel, her mouth fell. Theresa's face appeared from the shadows with a look of detached curiosity.

Quickly pulling the rip in her dress together, Kylie brushed back the wet hair from her eyes. "Dillon," she said, her stunned reaction nearly matching his.

He instantly stopped the car and rushed over toward her. "Kylie, what are you doing here?" he asked, noticing the tear in her clothing that she desperately tried to hide. "You're soaking wet," he said, "and you've been crying."

As he searched her face for an answer a flash of protective anger moved across his eyes. "Did someone hurt you?" he asked taking her gently by the shoulders.

"No," she said with a forced smile, but she could not meet his worried gaze. She knew that he didn't believe her. "I was just headed for the train stop. I tried to flag down a cab but none of them would stop."

He was studying her closely, his lips clenched tight, then he tenderly took her into his arms.

"I'm okay, Dillon," she whispered.

"Get in and I'll take you home," he insisted.

He opened the back door for her and as Theresa's eyes looked discreetly away from her, Kylie felt humiliation and shame. She wanted to break away, anything to escape the uncomfortable silence, but instead slid into the back seat where the shadows would hide her from further scrutiny.

"WHAT happened?" asked Jack from the doorway.

Kylie's eyes were vacant with contrition and a deep brewing resentment. "Seems to me I should be asking you the same," she said, brushing past him up the entry stairs.

Jack turned to his brother silhouetted in the newly surfaced moon.

"She was locked out of the Greyson house," explained Dillon.

"How'd her dress get ripped?" asked Jack.

Dillon turned toward the walkway. "She wouldn't say."

Jack could tell by his cool tone that his brother was angry with him. "Hey Dill," he said, "thanks for bringing her home."

Dillon looked back at him with a piercing glance. "I obviously wasn't soon enough," he said before heading back to his car.

LONG after Kylie had finished speaking, Jack stood with his back to her, the firelight creating an orange rim around his tensed shoulders. She had told him about the encounter to hurt him, to jab into his heart the same dagger he had plunged into hers, yet within his silence she felt regret. "Jack," she said softly.

At once he shrugged his shoulders. "I told you," he said simply. "You never should have approached him in the first place."

His arrogance burned across her cold cheeks. "That's it?" she asked from the edge of the chaise lounge. "I tell you that I almost had sex with another man and that's all you can say?"

"What am I supposed to say?" he asked, turning toward her with a vengeance.

They looked at one another in silence—the wall too high for either to climb.

"Where were you, Jack?" she asked bitterly, looking away to the glowing hearth.

"I was out with Freddy."

"Where?"

"Now you want an itinerary?" he snapped.

She looked up at him, her flashing eyes daring him not to answer.

"We were at his place and I lost track of time. I don't think that's any excuse for rolling around in a subway with some—"

"Damn it Jack," she said, putting her head into her hands. "You may think I asked for it . . . but he almost raped me."

Jack looked away from her bruised and cut legs exposed from under the terry robe. "We should call the cops," he said.

"No," said Kylie.

"Then I'm going to give ole Mr. Petrie a call myself," he insisted, heading for the phone.

"No," she repeated.

Jack turned with the response, his face suddenly riddled with suspicion. "Why?" he asked, the anger building behind his vibrant blue eyes as his fists clenched at his sides.

"Jack, don't start with your macho crap."

"No, I want to know why," he insisted. "Some bastard follows my wife all over the city, seduces her in a subway, then nearly rapes her and you don't think I should even give the son-of-a-bitch a telephone call?"

"It's over, Jack," she said quietly, staring into the burning embers. "If he wanted to hurt me, he would have."

"I wouldn't be too sure," said Jack standing before her. He looked down at her smooth skin and lovely full lips. "He's already had a taste—I guarantee he'll be back."

Twenty-Four

THE SHRILL RING OF THE TELEPHONE PIERCED INTO HER SENSES AS she groggily looked for a clock.

"Jack?" Kylie whispered through a hoarse voice, surprised to see that it was already morning. She reached across the bed before she remembered the previous night's events; Jack had spent the night in the guest room downstairs.

As the ringing continued, she threw back the covers and headed for the stairs.

"Jack?" she called down into the empty living room. "Can you get that?", but there was no answer from below.

She descended the stairs and as she passed the spare bedroom, she saw that the unmade bed was empty. She finally grabbed the receiver putting an end to the shrill annoyance.

"Hello," she said.

"Kylie Rose," said the silky, deep voice on the other end.

Her hand faltered and she nearly dropped the phone.

"I'm sorry if I woke you—"

"How did you get this number?" she asked, looking instinctively about as though Petrie were in the room with her.

"That doesn't matter," he said. "I wanted to apologize for my unacceptable conduct last night. I would never intentionally hurt you."

"Look," she said. "I'm married. Last night was a mistake."

"I would never intentionally hurt you," he repeated.

"Then why were you following me?" she asked.

"It wasn't to harm you," he said. "You're too important to me."

"How can I be important to you?" she asked. "You don't even know me."

"But I've been watching you for some time now and I've learned more than you can imagine. I know the tiny details about you that make a person whole. I know that you like oysters, straight up on the half shell," he said. "And that you take your milk warm with honey."

Kylie was stricken with his words. She had eaten oysters at the Haymarket last Sunday, a public place where he could have observed her easily, but the only time she drank milk was in the privacy of her home before bed.

"You're beautiful when you sleep," he said softly.

Kylie looked to the loft, her throat tightening.

"I'm not telling you this to frighten you," he said.

"You're sick."

"We're connected, Kylie Rose," he whispered. "I can feel it."

"Just stay away from me," she said and slammed the receiver back down.

"It's okay," she whispered, pacing back and forth before the window. There's no way he could have watched her while she slept in the sanctity of the second-story loft. She stopped and took a deep breath, trying to keep her fear in check. But then she thought of the rage that surfaced in the train and of the shadowy figure following her through the dark alley. Glancing out to the empty street she thought of Jack's concern that first day when she had let Petrie walk her home. Jack had been right after all—Petrie had indeed revealed himself a threat. Because of her overly-trusting nature, not only did the stranger know where she lived, but also where she worked. He had followed her to the Greyson mansion and now he had managed to find out her unlisted number. While she had been going about her daily life, Petrie had been doing his homework thus putting her at a disadvantage, for she knew nothing about him.

She grabbed the telephone once again and dialed information. "Yes, uh, Boston . . ." she said. "Robert Petrie, please."

"How are you spelling that?" asked the female voice.

"I don't know," said Kylie. "P-e-t-r-i-e."

"There's nothing listed under that name," said the operator.

"Try it without the 'i'," she requested.

"I already did, ma'am."

"Thank you," said Kylie, gently placing the telephone back onto the table. A cool sweat had formed in the palms of her hands. She looked about the bright warehouse, its sunny appearance suddenly taking on a chill. For the first time ever, she felt vulnerable in the open expanse. Through the towering windows, she looked to the sunlit sea but the vast body made her feel even more exposed.

She headed for the kitchen where she would make herself some coffee and put her thoughts in order. As she pulled the freshly ground beans from the cabinet, she suddenly thought of Ducker Brown. Surely the store owner would know Petrie—after all, none of the customers escaped Ducker and Elsey Brown without exposing a complete life history of oneself. She grabbed the cordless telephone and called information once again, this time for the number of the tiny store on Salem Street.

"Ducker's Grocer," said the friendly old voice on the other end.

"Ducker, this is Kylie O'Rourke," she said.

"Georgia Peach!" he exclaimed. "What a pleasant surprise. What can I do for you on this fine morning?"

"Well, there's a man who was in the store a couple of weeks ago," she said. "I was wondering if you might know something about him. He was in there the same time I was. He's tall, about six-foot-two, and he's got blondish hair that's parted down the middle. He was wearing dark clothes and—"

"Why Kylie, I'm an old man," he interrupted. "You can't expect me to remember someone that was in that long ago. Does the fellow have a name?"

"Robert Petrie," she answered.

"Mmm . . . Robert Petrie," mumbled the old man as though it sounded familiar. "And you met him here in the store?"

"Yeah."

"Does he sometimes go by Rob?"

"Maybe. Do you know him?" asked Kylie hopefully.

"He has a wife named Laura?"

"Yes!" said Kylie, her heart lifting. "He used to."

"I know him alright, " Ducker said with a chuckle. "But something tells me he's not who you think he is."

"What do you mean?"

"Well, believe it or not I was just watching Mr. Petrie on TV. Turn your TV—you got a TV don't you?" he asked.

"Yes," she said.

"Turn to channel seven and you'll see him on there right now. He's a writer isn't he?" asked the old man.

"Yes."

"Well," said Ducker. "That's him alright."

Kylie quickly turned the portable television to channel seven but instead of the news as she expected, an old black and white episode of the *Dick van Dyke Show* was playing.

"Ducker," she said into the receiver. "I've got the wrong channel."

"No you don't," he said.

She looked back to the screen where a youthful Mary Tyler Moore and Dick van Dyke bantered across a middle-class living room.

"That's the only Robert and Laura Petrie I know," said Ducker.

"Oh my God," Kylie whispered, her stomach twisting. She had watched the show as a child but hadn't connected the similarities between the sitcom personality and the man whom she had been kissing less than twelve hours earlier.

"Miss Kylie?" asked the old man.

"I'm sorry, Ducker," she said, trying to maintain her composure. "He told me that was his name—"

"Well, he's obviously trying to pull the wool over on you," said Ducker. "I almost always got Dick van Dyke going," he said. "He must have overheard it while he was in. I can't imagine why any fellow wouldn't want to tell a woman as gorgeous as you his real name."

"Thank you Ducker," she said. "I appreciate your help."

"Well, you be careful, Georgia," he said, his tone suddenly serious. "This neighborhood ain't as safe as it used to be. There's no telling what that fellow's up to."

Twenty-Five

As THE DELIVERY MEN WHEELED THE HUGE CRATE UP THE GREYSON entry, the dark clouds that loomed overhead split open with a shattering bolt and it began to pour.

"Son-of-a-bitch!" screamed the burly man behind the dolly. "Move your end around, you dimwit!" he ordered the skinny teenager who was trying to maneuver his side of the container through the narrow entryway.

The inside of the house was faintly lit and cold, the sudden shift in weather catching Kylie and Jack off guard. From inside the door, Jack quickly helped the young kid get his side through the opening, while Kylie cleared paint cans and various debris out of the path of the huge crate.

"Coming through!" warned the man hidden behind the bulky box.

The wooden floor creaked in protest under the weight of the dolly, as the man wheeled it through the foyer.

"The parlor's just upstairs," said Kylie.

With several more heaves and groans the men managed to get the crate up the long winding staircase to the vast room on the left.

"Where does this baby land?" demanded the deep voice.

"Over here," called Kylie from the bay window that arched the entire length of the eight-foot-high wall. The box was finally rested down and the owner of the booming voice appeared from behind it. A soggy cigarette butt hung from his pudgy lips.

"You got a check for me?" he asked, pulling a notebook from his belt.

"Right here," said Kylie, handing him the final payment on the delivery. "Twenty-five thousand," she said.

"Sign here," he ordered, shoving a pen into her face.

Kylie signed and the two men turned for the door.

"We know our way out," said the brawny man, heading for the entrance where the sound of pouring rain thundered beyond. Jack followed and shut the door snugly behind them.

Kylie quickly turned on a floor lamp that stood in the middle of the barren room. She grabbed a hammer and began prying the wooden slats from the crate. "It's really beautiful, Jack," she called, excitedly tugging at the nails with the teeth of the tool.

"I thought you already gave him a check," said Jack, coming back into the room.

"I did but it was only partial payment. That twenty-five was the last of it."

Kylie noticed that Jack's face had gone pale. His lips were pursed and his brow was creased. "What's the matter?" she asked.

"I just wish you hadn't bought it," he said angrily.

"But you haven't even seen it, Jack."

"You did it just to spite me," he said pacing about the creaky floor.

"I bought it because it's the right piece for this room," she said gently.

"I've got to get going," he said, abruptly grabbing his car keys.

"What?" she asked.

"I promised Freddy I would help him move," said Jack.

Kylie looked at him, debating whether or not she was up to an argument. She turned away, deciding against it. "I'll see you later at home, then," she said softly.

Within seconds Jack was out the door.

"Damn," she sighed, her anger fueling her strength as she removed the boards from the crate. She had told Jack about that morning's call and how it had frightened her, yet he was already leaving her alone to find her own way home. He had been sullen all day and though she knew he was still angry about the night before, she hadn't had the energy to make amends. After all, he was the one who had put the distance between them.

The wood came flying off faster than she realized and before she knew it, the towering statue was standing before her, shrouded in a heavy burlap wrap. The porcelain clawlike hands peeked from beneath the encasement sending a shiver up Kylie's arms. For a moment she questioned her own decision to purchase the bestial statue but when she touched the cool stone she remembered the beauty that lay beneath the brown cloth. It was such a striking, expressive piece that she was excited to see how it fit within the room. She grabbed a pair of shears from her tool box and began cutting the protective material, revealing the thick muscular legs, abdomen and chest of the pearly sculpture. She unwrapped the face exposing the restless, forlorn eyes that immediately formed a pit of sadness when one gazed into them. The remaining cloth fell away, unveiling the beautiful wings that stretched upward nearly touching the high ceiling. She stepped across the parlor to the fireplace where she could take in the effect the angel cast upon the room.

"Perfection," she whispered. "Absolute perfection."

WHEN the telephone rang Kylie nearly dropped the chisel in her hand. Since nightfall, she had been working on the tiling, trying to avoid the uncurtained windows and praying the telephone didn't ring. *It can't be him*, she told herself as she picked up the receiver. He would have no way of knowing Dora Greyson's number.

"Kylie Rose," said the voice on the other end.

Instinctively, her eyes darted toward the black windows where her own reflection blocked her view of the outside.

"You have magnificent taste. The sculpture is exquisite."

The angel glowed in the dim light, the bow front windows encasing it in reflection. He had clearly been down there, watching from the street.

"What do you want?" she asked, trying to remain calm. She stared toward the window, wondering if he was still there observing her—looking for the fear.

"Please don't be frightened," he said. "I'm not going to hurt you."

"If that were true, you wouldn't have to tell me that," she challenged, facing the window head on.

There was silence on the line and her thumping heart felt as if it would burst through her throat. Her reflection was motionless, as she gripped the telephone tightly. Though she tried to hold onto the anger which was her only defense, she caught a glimpse of fear in her reflected eyes.

"I've been so lost, for so long," came the voice. "You've reawakened something inside of me . . . something—"

"Stop," she gasped, her voice trembling, for the words had drawn so close they seemed to shiver from within. "What do you want from me?" she asked, her head swimming.

"Your company. Your eyes."

"That's not going to happen," she said steadily.

"It will, my love, soon enough," he promised. "I want you to know, that I have to do it . . . I have no choice."

"Do what?" she asked.

"Your husband makes you unhappy," he said softly. "I can see it in your face when he's around. It's as if he drains the energy from your soul then takes it with him when he leaves." His tone was that of a friend—compassionate and gentle. "And he leaves you so often."

The danger that rumbled beneath his words made Kylie look away from the window. Not only had he been following her, he had been watching Jack.

"Ask your husband where he goes, Kylie," he said. "When he leaves you by yourself, night after night."

"Why don't you tell me your real name?" she asked turning back toward the window.

"You won't realize it at first, but your life will be better without him."

"What do you mean?" she asked, the first sign of panic seeping into her voice.

"It'll be better for both of us when he's gone," and the line abruptly went dead.

WITH shaking hands Kylie dialed the only number she had for Freddy Hopkins. "Pick up the phone, damn it," but the line continued to ring. She quickly hung up and dialed her own number. It rang several times before the machine finally answered.

"Jack," she said into the recorder. "Petrie—" but she stopped herself unsure what to call the nameless stalker. "Petrie—just phoned. I don't trust him, Jack. It sounded as though he might try to do something to you." She held the phone to her lips trying to decide what to do next. "I'm going to take a cab to the warehouse," she said softly. "If you get this message, please come home." She looked about the darkened mansion as she hung up the telephone. She quickly went to the window and peered out into the night. The shadowy trees swayed in the wind, the street wet with the earlier rain, but there was no sign of Petrie. She redialed the telephone and requested a cab.

Twenty-Six

"NO POLICE," JACK DECLARED, CLENCHING HIS MOUTH STUBBORNLY.

"But he could hurt you," Kylie said gravely.

Though his eyes remained pained, a sardonic smile spread across his face. "You should have thought of that before," he said.

Kylie got up from the bed and went over to her husband. "You can't be serious," she said. "You're going to punish me by putting yourself in danger?"

He returned her stare like a defiant little boy with crossed arms and pouting lips.

"This is ridiculous," she argued. "You think if he hurts you it'll make me feel any more sorry for what I've done? Jack, whether you believe it or not, I am sorry," she said. "You were right. I never should have approached him in the first place. And I certainly shouldn't have been rolling around with him in a dirty, filthy train! I was wrong and for that I sincerely apologize."

She stared at him a moment, hoping that her sincerity would penetrate his obstinance, yet he didn't budge. "You're so self-righteous, aren't you Jack?" she said, her anger flaring once again. "Let's not forget that I'm not the only one on trial here," she said coldly. She abruptly turned toward the dresser and grabbed a pair of matches from a wooden box. "I've never heard you mention the Coco Row Club," she said, tossing the shiny matchbook onto the bedspread. "Maybe you could tell me a little about it."

Jack's face reddened as he looked down at the matches. "That's pretty pathetic, Kylie," he said, softly. "Now you're going through my pockets?"

Kylie had to smile. "No, Jack Black, you left them by the phone," she said, shaking her head. "I guess you'll have to start taking your girlfriend elsewhere."

He was motionless, his eyes full of indignation, but when she sighed and turned away, he stopped her. He took her into his arms and pressed his lips against her ear. "There's no girlfriend, Wylie," he whispered intently. "I told you that would never happen again."

Tears filled her eyes. She wanted so badly to believe him. "Then tell me what's going on," she begged holding tightly to his neck. "Petrie said to ask you where you go. Well, that's exactly what I'm doing Jack. Where do you go?" she pleaded.

He pulled away from her and moved to the bed, then back again. He started to say something then stopped, clearly struggling with his own courage. "I was . . . just at Freddy's," he finally answered.

Kylie looked away from him, unable to bear the deceit. "Okay, Jack," she said. "If that's the way you want to play it." She felt tired and beaten. "I can't fight anymore," she said as she flipped off the light and disappeared under the covers.

Jack stood in the darkness a long while, then quietly got in beside her.

"KYLIE ROSE!" echoed the man's voice through the black tunnel that encircled her like a crypt. The threatening sound swirled into her clouded head then disappeared behind her, leaving nothing but the dead calm and the uneven rhythm of her breath. With trembling hands, she felt that her face was wet with tears and sweat was rolling down her chest and back. Her legs were cramped, her knees stinging with the feel of scraped skin. It was dark—so black that her eyes strained for anything that projected light but there was nothing.

"Kylie Rose!" drifted the voice once again from one end of the tunnel to the next. Her predator was drawing closer but there was nowhere else to run. Her hands searched beneath and above her but the restricted space was impenetrable, if anything the tunnel was shrinking around her with each swallow of breath. Trying to silence her thundering heart, she strained to listen, for she no longer heard the voice or the footsteps—it was suspiciously quiet. With the salt of her tears burning across a scratch on her cheek, her ears rang within the long silence.

Then all at once there was a blasting noise, abrupt and piercing. A bright light burst toward her and the figure of a man's head and shoulders appeared in silhouette against the round opening. He was silent, watching her.

"Come here, Kylie Rose," he coaxed, as a streak of light cut across his ashen face. His smooth voice was kind and gentle yet his eyes were determined and cold.

Tightening further into a knot, she crouched within the darkness, refusing to budge. The man's hand reached gently toward her and as the pale flesh came within inches of her bare foot the tiny rose glistened from the wrist.

"I'm not going to hurt you," he promised, but then in a fury the icy fingers clamped down upon her ankle and yanked. He was dragging her toward the light while her hands searched desperately for something to grasp onto.

"No! . . . No! . . . No!" she screamed with all of her might but she was getting closer and closer to the opening.

"Kylie!" she heard the voice calling but this time it was one of panic. "Kylie, wake up!"

She forced her mind to focus, to pull herself from the horrid nightmare.

"Kylie!" said the voice again and she was in Jack's arms crying softly.

"It's okay," he whispered, showering her face with kisses and rocking her tenderly. "I'm sorry, baby... I'm so sorry."

"He's dangerous, Jack," she gasped. "He's dangerous."

"It'll be okay," he said, brushing the hair back from her quivering lips. "Dillon knows someone in the police department. We'll ask him about it tomorrow."

Twenty-Seven

A LUSH ROLLING LAWN STRETCHED FOR HALF AN ACRE TO THE LAKE behind Dillon's Cambridge home. The air was chilly but the sun warmed the patio where Kylie, Dillon and Theresa lounged in lawn furniture after the barbecue.

"Dillon, that was delicious," said Kylie with a smile. She felt content and relaxed, the darkness of the past few days nearly dissipated.

"Perfect," said Theresa, putting her arms around the smiling host. "I'm gonna have to hang onto this one for awhile," she said, winking at Kylie.

A football came flying into the tranquil setting, smacking Dillon squarely in the chest.

"Come on you lazy pig," challenged Jack running out toward the open expanse of green, thick grass. "Let's throw a few rounds!"

Dillon looked to the two smiling beauties. "Duty calls," he said shyly.

"Don't go too far. We have to leave in a minute for the movie," Kylie called. Though there was plenty of time before the film started, she simply didn't want to be left alone with Theresa any longer than necessary. Kylie was still embarrassed about the night in Chinatown, and she had yet to explain her ripped dress and unsightly appearance. Theresa had been watching her all afternoon, as if assessing and studying a specimen. While Theresa's manner was approachable and open, Kylie felt uncomfortable under her gaze. As the brothers romped about the huge yard, the two women sat in silence.

"So you and Dillon met at the hospital?" Kylie finally asked, annoyed that the lack of conversation had only seemed to be awkward for herself.

"Yes," answered Theresa. "We've known each other for quite awhile." Then her large violet eyes turned back to the brothers and another silence fell between them. "They're really lovely, aren't they?" she asked, her gaze focused on the two men as if by watching them she could soak their essence into her golden skin.

It was strange for Kylie to hear such a compliment about the brothers coming from anyone other than herself. To see such an intelligent, attractive woman admiring them, she couldn't help but feel a twinge of jealousy.

"Yes they are," she agreed, looking out over the lawn at the handsome brothers, so alike yet so different. Though their physiques were similar, their demeanor couldn't have been more opposite, or splendid in their own way. Jack played with the reckless abandonment of a child, as if his troubles were a million miles away. Dillon was shy and more reserved, adding a tender grace to his movements.

"The energy between them is the most attractive thing of all," Theresa said, her gaze still focused out over the lawn. "It's rare to see brothers so close."

Kylie laughed. "Oh, believe me," she said, "they have their moments."

The remark drifted off, unheard by the pensive woman seated beside her. Theresa's head was back, lost in her own thoughts. "I envy you," she said simply. "To have them both adore you so much."

"They tolerate me," said Kylie with another laugh.

Theresa looked at her with a curious smile, the probing, intelligent eyes studying her. Then she turned back to the men who continued to toss the ball between them. She picked up the glass beside her and took a long drink of her Margarita. "You and Jack mean everything to him. You should have seen him right after the wreck . . . he was a mess. I had to stop sleeping over because he tossed and turned so much. I couldn't bear to see it."

Kylie was touched by the unexpected sadness in her voice. It was the first time that the confident woman had let her poise slip. Theresa glanced at her but then looked away.

The brothers had stopped playing and were standing together quietly talking.

"Dillon's a good man," said Theresa. "He's very honest with me . . . he always has been. We've been friends for a long time and he's never led me to believe there was anything more." She suddenly laughed and shook her head. "He's still a damn good lover even if his heart's not into it."

As Kylie looked at Dillon with his hair tousled and face flushed she felt embarrassed at the mention of his sexual prowess. She wanted to change the subject but Theresa was absorbed in her own wistful thoughts.

"When he first showed up for his residency at the hospital," she continued, "all the women had bets as to which one of us could nab him, but the months and then years passed and he never really went for any of us. Not even me," she smiled. "And I'm considered a pretty good catch if I don't say so myself. There would be a date here and there but nothing ever serious. The only reason he's with me now is because I pushed for something more," she said confidently. "No," she said, as if speaking to herself. "No matter how good the sex is, we'll never really be more than friends . . . I knew that from the start. I knew his heart was already taken. He just doesn't know it."

Kylie shifted uncomfortably. She assumed Theresa was referring to Hannah, a medical student Dillon had dated a few years back, who had broken their relationship to take her residency in Los Angeles. Yet, as well as she knew Dillon, his romantic life was something that he never discussed with her and she felt uneasy hearing about it from his lover. She looked out to the brothers, the sun catching the light in Dillon's dark hair and she felt a pain in her heart. At times she saw his loneliness and wished for him to find someone of his own.

As the two brothers talked, Dillon suddenly turned toward her and they locked eyes. She knew instantly that Jack had told him about Petrie by the worry in his face. He looked again to Jack and then the two brothers began walking slowly back toward the women.

"Kylie," said Dillon tenderly. "My friend's name is Victor Binaggio. I'll give him a call in the morning. I think he'll be able to help with this guy."

Theresa looked at Dillon strangely. "Binaggio? Isn't he the detective?"

"Yes," he said.

Theresa looked back to Kylie with genuine concern. "Whatever it is, I hope it's nothing serious."

"No, I don't think so," said Kylie, though the feeling of dread had suddenly returned.

Twenty-Eight

THE GRAY MORNING MIST FLOATED HEAVILY THROUGH THE COOL AIR. As Jack pulled the Jeep up to the white building on Sudbury Street that served as the police headquarters for the Waterfront District, Kylie positioned her scarf up around her neck and reached for the door.

"Are you sure you don't want me to come with you?" Jack asked for the second time that morning.

"There's really no need," she said, affectionately kissing him on the lips. "I'll call you when I'm done."

She exited the truck and mounted the stairway toward the double doors.

"What can I do for you, miss?" asked a uniformed officer from behind a desk.

"My name is Kylie O'Rourke and I have an appointment with Victor Binaggio."

The clerk pulled a clipboard from behind him and handed it to her along with a pen. "Just answer what you can and he'll help you with the rest," he instructed.

She took a seat on a long wooden bench that stretched the length of the lobby and began filling out the report. She had been apprehensive all morning wondering whether or not she was doing the right thing. She hadn't heard a word from Petrie since the last call two days earlier. Maybe he had forgotten about the whole business and was going about his own life.

As she debated with herself, footsteps approached, along with a waft of cheap men's cologne. "Mrs. O'Rourke?" said a deep, masculine voice.

She looked up to find a tall, strapping man in his late thirties staring down at her. He was somewhat attractive with dark wavy hair, brown eyes and olive-colored skin. His jacket was worn and crinkled and hung awkwardly over a pair of faded jeans that fit him like a glove. He smiled and extended his brawny hand for her to shake.

"I'm Victor Binaggio," he said through a wad of tobacco that was lodged between his lower lip and gums.

"It's nice to meet you," she said.

"You'll have to pardon me," he said, gesturing to his mouth. "I've been in court all morning . . . Unfortunately, the nicotine shakes from chew can be as bad as cigarette withdrawal." The tobacco gave him a lisp which put an odd twist on his thick Bostonian accent. "Won't you follow me up to my office?" he asked politely, motioning toward the elevator.

They got off on the third floor and passed through a busy area where uniformed and plain-clothed officers milled about, joking with and heckling one another. She followed the detective past a desk where a young, angelic-looking woman was handcuffed to a chair beside an officer who was busy typing out a report. Across the room a rowdy teenager, who was also handcuffed to his chair, was shouting over to her. "Don't tell 'em anything, Becky. They don't know nothing unless you tell 'em."

"In here, Mrs. O'Rourke," said Victor, opening the door to a glassed-in office that held two desks. It was a large, messy room with windows to the outside, overlooking the green dome of Quincy Market.

A small, skinny man with long stringy hair was at one of the desks. He was leaning back in a chair with his legs propped upon the windowsill. He flipped through a newspaper while sipping on a mug of coffee.

Victor turned toward the unshaven man. "Doobie," he said. "Can you give us a little privacy so that—"

"—I don't think so, shithead," said Doobie offhandedly, before Binaggio could even finish the question.

Victor took a cup from atop the messy pile of paperwork and spit into it. "You'll have to excuse my partner, ma'am," he said evenly. "He's been undercover so long that he's forgotten how to act in front of a lady." He glanced back at the insolent man. "I guess the grease and lice have eaten away at his brain. Won't you have a seat?" he asked, gesturing toward a wooden chair that sat across from the empty desk.

He closed the door then took a seat opposite her. As he read over her report, Kylie wondered how Dillon, who was a conservative polished man, had befriended the unlikely affiliate. "How do you know Dillon?" she asked, unable to resist the question.

The detective leaned back in his chair and opened the top of his shirt. A long thin scar ran all the way up his hairy chest. "I got cut in a drug bust and it nearly took out my heart," he said. "Dillon patched me up and kept the ole ticker goin'. My grandpop, my uncles, practically my whole family goes to him now," he said proudly. "My ma loves him."

Kylie smiled.

As the detective rebuttoned his shirt, his expression turned serious. "Tell me a little about what's been going on," he said. "Your brother-in-law didn't know much."

Kylie calmly relayed what had happened, starting with the day in which she approached Petrie in the Northend when he had walked her home. She told the detective about seeing him on the train and how he had followed her through Beacon Hill, but when it came time to mention their frolic on the subway she hesitated.

"Mrs. O'Rourke—"

"Please call me Kylie," she said, uncomfortably.

"Kylie," he corrected, leaning inward. "You got to tell me everything or else you're just wastin' my time. Did you sleep with him?"

"No," she said honestly.

There was an uncomfortable, deafening silence.

"But I almost did," she said softly. The words felt strange coming out of her mouth as if someone else were admitting to the embarrassing truth. She had blocked the moment from her thoughts and in retrospect was amazed that she had come so close to such a sordid display of infidelity. As she went into the details of the humiliating night, Doobie, who was still seated at the next desk, slowly took his attention away from his newspaper and began listening. The fact that he was eavesdropping and that Victor knew Dillon made it twice as difficult to admit the lustful encounter; but in spite of her shame she

managed to keep eye contact with Victor as she summarized the inter-
action. Relieved when that portion of the story was over, she told him
about the subsequent calls.

"Robert Petrie, huh?" asked the detective in deep thought. "Hey
shithead," he called over to his partner. "Run a check on Robert
Petrie."

To Kylie's astonishment, Doobie did as he was told.

"I've got a ninety-two-year-old man out on Martha Road but that's
it," he said, looking into his computer screen.

Victor glanced up at her as if to ask if that was him. She had to
smile. "No," she said with a chuckle.

"Look," said Victor. "I might as well tell you this now. I know this is
gonna sound lame but there's not much we can do unless he actually
tries to harm you. You could file an attempted rape—"

"No," interrupted Kylie. "It wasn't like that."

"Well," said Victor. "I can file this report, but that's about it," he
said shaking his head. "That's not to say that this bastard—excuse my
language—isn't dangerous. If I were you, I'd watch my back and I'd
tell my husband to do the same."

"I understand," said Kylie.

"And if you've got a little time, I'd like for you to look through these
mug-shots for identification purposes," he said, dropping a stack of
three-ring notebooks in front of her. "Just in case we get lucky and
this guy turns up with a record."

KYLIE searched through book after book with mounting despair. The
faces of the accused stared out at her from the photos, belligerent and
disconsolate. The reluctant subjects had been photographed dead-on
as well as from the side, a ruler, painted on the wall behind them,
monitoring their height.

"Do you need more coffee?" asked Doobie, whose attitude had
warmed as the morning ensued.

"No, I still have some, thank you," she said, reaching for another
book from the counter across the room.

While most of the mug-shots from the previous notebooks were in
color, this one contained only black and white photos. She picked up

her half-empty cup of coffee and began scanning the faces once again.

"Still at it, huh?" asked Victor as he reentered the room and took his seat behind the desk.

"Yeah," she said with a sigh, her eyes tired and her neck growing stiff. Then suddenly she saw him, his eyes vacant and sad, his light hair parted down the middle. "There he is!" she exclaimed, unable to believe her own eyes.

Both of the detectives looked up.

"Are you sure?" asked Victor coming around to her side of the desk.

"Positive," she said, her finger pressing down upon the photo as if it might escape.

"Then he's got to be at least fifty-five years old," said Victor. "Where did you get this book?" he asked.

"On the counter," she answered.

"Well, you shouldn't have had this one. It's from 1974."

"No," said Kylie. "That's exactly how he looks now."

Victor took the photo from the slip of plastic and read the information card on the back of it. "Julius Vanderpoel," he read aloud, then he stopped. "You've got the wrong fellow, ma'am," he said.

"No," she argued. "That's definitely him. Even his hair is the same."

The detective shook his head. "This man was convicted of murder over twenty years ago."

"Well maybe he was paroled," she countered.

"I'm afraid not," he said solemnly. "He was executed."

KYLIE felt the blood drain from her face as the cup in her hand fell to the floor.

"Ma'am? Are you alright?" the detectives exclaimed, moving toward her.

"I'm sorry," she gasped, looking down at the coffee-stained rug. The two detectives' pants and boots were wet with the brown liquid.

"Don't worry about it," said Doobie, grabbing a napkin from the desk.

Victor pulled a chair out for her to sit down. "Here, take a seat," he said.

"No, I'm okay," she murmured, turning away from their probing eyes. She was confounded, her mind trying to absorb the information. At once she thought of the plane accident, of her scrambled memory; for once again she found herself speaking in absurdities. She swung back to the detectives. "Maybe they didn't execute him," she said grasping at anything that would explain her encounters with a man that no longer existed. "Maybe the decision was somehow overruled and—"

"—You've got the wrong guy," Victor interrupted gently.

She looked down at the haunting picture of the man, whose face she knew she had kissed and caressed. The eyes were so penetrating and real to her that she couldn't possibly be mistaken. "He's got to be alive," she said.

"It says here he's not," said Victor, picking up the photo once again.

"Well, isn't there some kind of record that would say for sure?" she persisted.

"Other than this, I wouldn't know," he said. "We had a fire in the early eighties that destroyed a lot of our records. The older ones weren't replaced."

"He might have appealed it and we just don't know about it," said Doobie.

"I doubt it," argued Victor. "I've never known the back of a photo to be inaccurate."

Doobie ignored his partner's opinion and continued with his thought. "They used to do the executions at the old Charlestown Prison."

"That place next to the hospital?" Kylie asked.

"Yeah," he said. "It's not open anymore but there's an old security guard there who looks after the lot and—"

"Hey shithead," interrupted Victor gruffly. "Why are you even entertaining the idea that she's got the right guy, for Christ's sake? Their ages don't match—they're not even close." The detective held up the worn photo. "This guy's been dead for twenty years. If it says here he was executed he was executed. The son-of-a-bitch is not running around lusting after women in present day Boston . . . he's burning in hell where he belongs."

Twenty-Nine

Beneath the open hall of Quincy Market the crowd moved in a swarm, some merely browsing the culinary delights, others in search of a late lunch.

Kylie and Jack had settled at an oyster bar, oblivious to the wall of pedestrians perusing past. In spite of Kylie's love for shellfish, she had been unable to take a bite, her mind still on the faded photo of the unforgettable face.

"Maybe I should go to the Charlestown Prison anyway," she said to Jack.

"Why?" he asked.

"I just—" she started but then stopped, shaking her head to dispel her thoughts. "I don't know. To speak to that guard to see if he knows what happened to him."

"Kylie," he said. "It's like the cops said . . . you've got the wrong man."

She looked behind her at the passersby, his conviction failing to remove the pit from her stomach.

"Besides," said Jack. "We've got that Armstrong meeting."

"I'll go later, then," she said.

"I just don't see the point," said Jack reaching for his wallet to pay the check. "The guy's obviously not our friend Petrie—he would be too old."

Kylie looked down at her uneaten plate of food. "Yeah, but I could be off on his age. He looked like he was in his late thirties but—"

"Kylie," interrupted Jack. "You couldn't be off by over twenty years. This Julius Vanderpoel would be in his late fifties or even sixties."

"Yeah, I know," she agreed quietly.

"Then you ought to just let it go," he advised.

She looked at Jack who was so calm and nonchalant when she herself felt like screaming. She bit her lip and looked away. "It's just one weird thing after another," she grumbled.

"What do you mean?" he asked.

"Well this is the second time since the accident that I've identified a dead man," she said. "First there was Collins—"

"Listen to me," interrupted Jack. He swirled on the stool to face his troubled wife. "Don't do this to yourself. This Petrie has no connection to the accident whatsoever other than he was part of a dream. And the guy in the photo today has absolutely nothing to do with it. You can't lump all this into the same thing."

"You have to admit that it's pretty weird, though," she said, her voice rising with frustration.

"Nothing's weird about a mistaken identity... especially when you're basing it on a faded old black and white photo. I mean, am I right? Isn't that what you're going by?"

"Yes," she admitted. "I asked them about the tattoo but their records were so bad that they couldn't even tell me if he had one."

"Well if he did, don't you think that's something they would have listed with his mug-shot?" asked Jack.

"You would think so," she agreed. She sighed, tired of weighing all the illusive facts.

"Don't let your imagination run away with you," he warned. "This has nothing to do with the accident. And this Vanderpoel didn't weasel out of execution either. You've got the wrong guy."

She was silent, desperately wanting to forget the whole situation. Maybe she had misjudged the face in the aged photo. Her husband was right in that it was a poor quality photograph that had diminished over the years.

"Besides," said Jack. "All of this may be for nothing. You haven't heard from him in a couple of days. He's probably moved on to someone else."

"You think so?" she asked hopefully.

"That would be my guess," he said.

As she sat silently debating it, she began to feel ridiculous for pursuing the point. After all, there was a chance she was wasting her energy on something that was no longer even an issue. She and Jack had a new client to meet in Harvard Square and she really couldn't spare the time to play detective to an illogical fallacy.

"Alright, Jack Black... you win," she sighed, grabbing her bag. "Let's get going. The Armstrongs are probably waiting on us."

Thirty

Kylie SIPPED ON THE WARM MILK AS SHE PERUSED THE SKETCHES strewn about her desk. A small light put a glow upon her work as a fire crackled in the hearth in the downstairs living room. She found herself yawning once again and decided it was time to call it a night. It had been a long day and she was eager to put it behind her.

She bundled the sketches together, and as she returned them to her portfolio she noticed the old drawings of the male creature and the rose tattoo. She gently pulled them out and spread them upon the table. She was surprised to see how harsh and broad the outer strokes were, in contrast to the finely drawn features of the face and the elaborate detailing of the tattoo. It was as if the sketches had started in anger and finished with a focused determination. As she gazed down at the drawings, she thought of the many, sleepless nights she had spent working on them and how her mind had been reassured as soon as she met the man she had come to call Petrie. Once again, though, she found herself facing questions that no one could answer. "Julius Vanderpoel," she said aloud, staring into the detached eyes of her own creation. "Julius," she repeated—a chill prickling at the base of her neck. The name took on a heightened sense of power against the mutating creature with its ashen visage and animalistic ears.

"What are you doing?" asked Jack from behind her.

She turned to find her husband leaning against the doorway in a pair of boxers, the warm light trickling through his shiny hair, then melting over his golden skin like butter. His face was pleasant, his long lean body relaxed.

"Julius is an uncommon name, don't you think?" she asked sleepily.

"Yeah," he agreed. "But Vanderpoel says money. I guess if you're loaded you can afford to name your kid something like that."

Kylie looked into the spirited blue eyes of her husband, who stood gripping the door-frame overhead and she felt a rush of attraction for him for the first time in weeks. Over the past two days he had returned to his old loving self, as if the stress and turmoil of the accident had finally passed.

He looked down toward the sketches.

"Why didn't you take those in with you today?" he asked. "They might have saved you and those detectives a lot of time."

Kylie smiled. "I'm sure they would have," she said. "They would have taken one look at them and committed me to Bridgewater."

Jack smiled. "No," he said. "They would have taken one look and fallen madly in love with your talent."

Kylie felt her face blush.

"Wow," said Jack. "I didn't know I could still do that."

She moved toward him, pulling open her robe. "Of course you can," she said, pressing her warm naked body up against his. "I've missed you Jack," she whispered, her round, fair breasts resting against his chest.

He took her into his arms and kissed her softly. "I'm here," he said between sweet, tender kisses. "I'm here."

HER ROBE fell to the floor as they lay back upon the feather bed. The hum of the fan whirled overhead, sending flashes of moonlight across their naked skin. "You're beautiful," Jack said softly, tracing his fingers alongside her pale body. He knew just how to touch her, just where to tantalize and caress.

"Jack," she moaned, pressing her lips to his, and as she began feeding upon them she could taste the tiny scar from the accident. "It's been too long," she murmured, sucking and licking the warm, strong mouth.

His silky tongue traced down her neck and breasts, and then her nipple disappeared inside his warm caressing mouth. The sensation sent shivers dancing along her skin as he gently tugged at her nipple then let it pull away erect and hard. Her fingers moved through his soft hair, as he ran his lips between her breasts as if feasting upon a banquet. As the shadows from the fan whirled across the walls, a startling memory flashed vividly before her. Jack suddenly became Petrie, passionately suckling her breasts, while the train roared under the flashing lights of a tunnel. Her husband moved over her, but she felt the dark looming presence of the stranger who had penetrated her very essence.

Jack suddenly pulled back and looked into her eyes with a raw, blazing fury. "You're mine, Kylie O'Rourke," he whispered intently as if reading her thoughts. He pressed her body to the sheets with his strong torso. "You're mine," he said, moving his hands up her sides, pulling her wrists forcefully above her head. He stated his ownership as blatantly and without apology as if it were the most natural instinct of his being. He held her wrists steadfast with one hand and with the other he roughly spread her legs apart. As her body flushed with anticipation he watched her with a look of sudden detachment, daring her to dispute his claim. "This is me," he warned, then thrust up inside her.

As he entered her, his mind was on the night in the subway—on the man whom he had never met, but who had stolen a piece of his wife's soul. He thrust against the warm yielding flesh as if by sheer, ruthless force he could obliterate any memories that lurked within the shadows of their bedroom.

As he drove into her harder and more brutally her legs began to tremble and give way, falling against the sheets. The heat of his body pushed her further and further into the tormenting bliss, as he held her hands down so tightly her wrists began to burn. "I'm yours, Jack," she moaned like an animal in the wild whose mate was savagely staking his territory. "I'm yours."

Her body writhed beneath his as she pulled him deeper and deeper inside her. "Yes," she moaned. "Yes." She felt the rush of pleasure as the quivering sent her over the edge. She lost herself in the sound of her own cries as her head fell to the side. Her own climax brought Jack with her and as he moved above her, she saw the streaking shadow of a person flash across the wall and then disappear with the rotating blades of the ceiling fan. Her body froze in fear but the pleasure continued to titillate over her loins in waves of elation. Then she saw it again. The shadow flashed for a moment and then disappeared. Someone was standing outside the ventilator shaft.

"Jack!" she gasped.

He heard the terror in her voice and instantly stopped moving. He was still atop her, their sweaty bodies pressed together in silence.

"There's someone on the roof," she whispered, their hearts beating wildly together. She could feel him inside her, pulsing in spite of his stillness. Then he pulled away from her and wrapped her in the safety of the sheet. "Wait here," he whispered then slid from the bed.

He quickly put on his boxers and took a gun from the nightstand. Kylie saw the glistening metal in the moonlight and her throat tightened. "Be careful Jack," she whispered, gathering herself up from the bed.

Within seconds he was down the stairs and opening the front door. He went out toward the street so that he could get a clear view of both the roof of the warehouse and the neighboring building that edged up against theirs. Its roof was lower than the warehouse, and if someone climbed atop it, they could easily see into the loft. Jack saw no one on either roof. The gun relaxed in his hand and he headed back for the open door.

"There's no one up there," he said to Kylie who had put on her robe and was waiting at the door.

"Are you sure, Jack?" she asked. "I could swear I saw the figure of a person."

"Well if there was someone there, they're gone now," he said, bolting the heavy door behind him.

It TOOK her over an hour to succumb to sleep but when she did, the nightmare pulled her in viciously.

She was suddenly in the middle of a long darkened hallway its shiny floor stretching in both directions. She was riveted in the center, confused and disoriented, her heart clenched tight, while tears stung down her face. She was frightened, frozen in indecision. Judging by the brightly painted walls she knew she was in an elementary school and that she needed to run, but in which direction she was unsure. Then she heard the sound of a man's footsteps coming from the intersecting hallways ahead of her. She silently turned in the opposite direction and began running.

As she passed each classroom she quickly looked inside desperately searching for a teacher or student; but there was no one. The desks were all abandoned, the shades drawn and the lights out. With each shadowy, vacant chamber she became more and more frantic. If she didn't find help she knew that she would die. His big hands would clamp down upon her throat and though she would gasp and beg silently for help, her limbs would go limp and the light would fade.

She clutched the wall, turning the corner onto another corridor, this one even darker. His steps were drawing nearer to her own and the tears began to blur her vision so that she could barely see.

"No," she cried softly, "no."

The footsteps were so close that she suddenly stopped; she had no choice but to hide. There was a door that led to a closet, but that would be the first place he would look. Then she noticed the opening to an air vent. Her fingers pried at the gridiron until finally the covering clanked to the floor. She wriggled her body into the opening and scrambled for the darkness. The man's voice echoed off the corridors, receding further and further behind her as she disappeared into the tunnel.

"There's no reason to be afraid," he called. Then the sound of the voice changed, becoming clearer and more crisp as though he were speaking directly into the tubing. "I'm not going to hurt you," he said softly and almost kindly.

She glanced behind her but the opening was no longer in sight. She hadn't bothered to replace the metal screen for she knew that the tall man couldn't squeeze inside the casing where her body barely fit.

She crawled along on her hands and knees, her skin scraping against the metallic bottom. "No," she whispered again and again as the space around her became nearly black. She scrambled as fast as she could through the tunnel that turned sharply to the right and then curved back toward the left. She was deep into the casing before she finally stopped and rested.

She wanted to sit up but there wasn't room enough, so she remained crouched in the darkness, her arms aching and her face smudged with dirt and tears.

"Please Jesus, help me," she whispered, as she wiped at her cheeks with her dirty hands. The soot stung her eyes and she blinked frantically to dislodge the burning. Her vision cleared only to be blurred once again by her tears. "'Our Father, who art in heaven, hallowed be thy name,'" she prayed quietly. "'Thy kingdom come'—no, no," she scolded, interrupting herself. "You've got to be quiet." She concentrated to still her own sniffling so as not to be found. She silently waited, hoping and praying that he had given up.

What seemed like hours passed and still there was no sound. Her legs and shoulders were cramping so badly that all she wanted to do was stand and relieve the pressure. It had been so long since he had

called out to her that she began to wonder if he had given up and decided to let her live. She imagined him getting into his shiny white car
and disappearing over the ridge. She knew that he was from somewhere else—somewhere far away. Maybe he had forgotten about her
and returned to that place. Maybe if she just moved a little she could
somehow stretch out and wait until someone found her the next
morning.

Just as she started to move she heard a noise outside of the wall. She
held her breath, and remained motionless. It was silent once again,
but the adrenaline in her body coursed so abruptly it felt as if her skin
would burst. She stared ahead at the black wall, her eyes straining as if
to see through the metal and plaster board to the hallway on the other
side.

Then suddenly, there was a loud bursting noise that made her
scream. An opening to a nearby vent came crashing off just a few feet
from her and the light came rushing in. The silhouetted man was before her, looking in at her.

"I'm not going to hurt you," he said, his voice shaking as though he
had been crying but the silhouette made it impossible for her to see.
His blonde straight hair was tousled like she had never seen it before.
He had always been so perfect and wonderfully groomed.

"It'll be okay," he vowed, but when she turned to crawl the other
way his deadly hand clamped down upon her foot and began dragging
her toward the light.

"No!!" she screamed. Her hands braised against the uneven bottom
of the tunnel as she searched in vain for something to grab.

"Stop fighting me!" he said, his voice growing angry as he continued to pull her toward him.

She felt her legs and then her waist within his firm grasp when she
pulled the soot from the bottom of the vent and thrust it toward the
voice. He yelped in pain and she began kicking and screaming to release herself from his hands.

"No!" she screamed. "No!!"

KYLIE suddenly sat up out of the dream. The silence surrounded her,
the movement of the sea winking at her through the windows.

"My God," she whispered, her mouth dry and her body still shaky and unsure. Jack was sleeping soundly beside her and the clock read: 3:45 A.M. She brushed the hair back from her face and reached for a glass of water that she kept by the bed. That's when she noticed the shadow once again upon the wall. She instantly turned toward the fan where she saw the gray eyes peering in at her. There was no mistaking the pale features or the distinct blonde hair parted down the middle, silhouetted in the moonlight. She heard herself screaming as she scrambled to get up from the bed.

Jack was instantly awake and saw her looking toward the vent, but the deathly white face had already gone. He grabbed for the gun and raced for the back entrance to the warehouse where a fire-escape would be the quickest way to the roof.

"Jack!" Kylie screamed, remembering the stalker's promise to eliminate her husband. Her shaking hands picked up the telephone and dialed 911.

As the operator came on the line, Kylie tried to speak clearly but a deep tremor took her breath. She was following Jack out, up the rear fire escape.

"Ma'am just stay inside and let your husband—"

"I can't!" she cried reaching the roof. She turned in every direction but saw no one. "He's not here!" she gasped into the receiver. "I don't see him."

"Just remain where you are . . . just remain calm."

When she saw Jack round the far side of the huge boiler, her legs weakened. His silhouette came forward, then he bent from his waist to catch his breath. "Nothing," he said, shaking his head.

"We lost him," she said into the phone.

"Ma'am, I suggest both you and your husband go back inside and wait for our squad car."

"IF THERE was someone there," said the young officer, "they didn't leave anything behind to go off of. No foot prints, cigarette butts or what have you," he said, looking down at the clip board he held in his hands. "I'll file this report but if you've already talked to Detective Binaggio about this I don't think there's anything more we can do for you except advise you to keep your doors and windows locked."

"Thanks," said Jack, leading the officer to the door where his partner silently waited.

"Goodnight," said the officer with a tip of his hat.

"Goodnight," said Kylie, her arms folded tightly across her robe. Jack latched the door and turned toward her with a look of exasperation.

"A lot of good they were," he grumbled. "Let's go to bed."

"There's no way I can sleep after all this," she said, taking a sip from a cup of hot coffee. "I'm going to wait until the sun comes up and then I'm going to head over to the Charlestown Prison to speak to that guard."

Jack looked up at her. "What?" he asked. "You're not still thinking this is that Vanderpoel guy are you?"

"I know the ages don't add up," she said, "but I don't know where else to start. I can't just sit around waiting for this guy to show up again. You and I were having sex Jack! He was watching us have sex!"

Jack took her into his arms. She pulled away, her voice quivering with her lack of sleep and frazzled nerves. "I was thinking that Victor Binaggio said the records were limited... well if they're limited maybe they're even wrong... maybe the dates are inaccurate... I mean the notebooks were all mixed in together... You wouldn't believe the disorganization in that place... And the tattoo... they should have been able to say 'no ma'am this man did not have a tattoo like you described'. I mean for Christ's sake—fire or no fire—they ought to at least know that!"

"Kylie, calm down," said Jack.

"Why should I?" she asked. "I'm pissed. I mean they have to wait for this guy to hurt us, for God's sake, before they even investigate it? This is ridiculous."

Jack sank onto the couch, looking tired and exasperated.

Kylie suddenly turned toward him, her eyes wild with conviction. "I've got a feeling, Jack. I can't explain it but the name Julius Vanderpoel just feels right. When I was looking at those sketches tonight and I said his name, it fit. And the fact that he murdered someone didn't even surprise me. It's as if I expected it. From the very beginning I've felt as if I knew him—like there's a piece of the past that I'm grasping at. Before I woke up tonight, I was dreaming about the dark tunnel again but I finally know what it is. It's an air vent. It's an air vent in an elementary school. For the first time in my life I know what that damn tight spot is! All these years I've never dreamt past the darkness until now. This is it, Jack, and it's somehow connected with this guy. I know it sounds crazy but it's true. I have to go to the prison to find out if that gaurd knows what happened to him. I have to at least give it a try."

"I don't like the idea of you going to a place like that alone," he said.

"Then come with me."

"I can't today," he said. "I've got the plumbers meeting me to tear out Dora's old gas line."

"I'll go alone," she said with so much determination that Jack knew there was no way to convince her otherwise. "I'll be fine," she whispered.

Thirty-One

THE GRAY STONE WALLS OF THE CHARLESTOWN PRISON ROSE FROM the misty earth as if the devil himself had shoved the sooted rocks from the pits of hell. The dark and foreboding edifice of the 1812 penitentiary was flanked on all sides by an encroaching city that had long since forgotten its existence. The freeway roared past, the train whistled across the tracks and the patients of the nearby hospital lay contentedly sleeping, completely oblivious to the dilapidated prison behind the encircling wall and the sordid past that led to its closure.

Kylie remained just inside the iron gate, staring toward the archaic structure of towering barred windows, the grayness of the morning adding to its gloom. She had expected to find the security guard at the opening of the lot but there was no one. With her nerves still on edge from the night before, she glanced hesitantly around the deserted property, before finally finding the courage to approach the building in search of the guard.

To her dismay, there were no doors at the front of the prison, which consisted of four wings that joined in the center with a tower. Underneath the octagon-shaped core there was a tunnel that led to the back side of the grounds. As she entered the underpass she became chilled by the sudden shift in temperature. It was a damp cool morning, and within the stone underbelly of the building the temperature was even lower. A thick wooden door with huge rusted padlocks barred the side entrance. She pressed up to the rotting wood and peered through a five-inch window without glass.

"Hello?" she called. Remnants of the past lay rotting inside the solid shell of stone and steel. A steady stream of water trickled down one of the walls, leaving a long streak of moss in its wake. A sign requesting that visitors leave their firearms at the desk was hanging on its side, the nail protruding crudely from the cracked and paint-chipped wall. "Hello?" she said again. Her voice echoed then disappeared without reply.

Emerging from the tunnel to the rear of the building, she found that a huge cement yard stretched the entire length of the cross-shaped prison. A lookout tower had been placed strategically in the corner of the property, while razor sharp wire swirled along the topside of the perimeter wall. On the backside of the prison, there was an alcove of two more medieval-style portals with tiny unpaned windows. Pigeons that had gathered at the openings scattered with her approach. As she peered inside, she was startled to see the main section of the penitentiary where the prisoners were once housed. "My God," she whispered, taken aback by its massiveness. Endless stacks of cells towered upward, while the murky daylight from the immense windows streaked through the myriad of steel bars. The sound of fluttering wings, ghostly shadows and movement, gave the effect of a giant, surreal bird cage.

At once, fear crept inside of her and she started to turn away, when her eye was caught by the far corner where the edge of a dim fluorescent light glowed from within.

"Hello?" she called uncertainly, her hand gripping the door tightly. After a long moment, she gave it a tug, but it was locked. She pulled at the one next to it and the rusted padlock simply fell away. She hesitated, her heart thundering. She looked behind her to the empty yard and then again to the light. The last place she wanted to venture into was an abandoned prison, but if the light—which was so far inward—signified the guard's presence, he couldn't possibly hear her from where she stood.

Slowly squeezing through the jarred door, she was amazed at the ease of her entry to a place where desperate rapists and murderers had been sequestered. Once inside, she nervously pulled her sweater to her body and continued forward, gaping at the secretive world within. Razors, cigarette butts and a man's shoe lay in the debris, while a series of obscenities had been etched into the cement wall. High pitched whistles heaved in and out of the leaky portholes, swirling between the walls in mournful wails. In spite of the physical departure of its tenants, the forsaken dungeon seemed to live and breathe with the broken spirits that had found no other home. As though trapped within an enormous Pandora's box, the evil was palpable.

Peering into one of the cells which had been eerily left open, Kylie shivered from its barbarity. It was a mere five-foot by seven-foot space allotted for two swaying bunks, a tiny sink and an open drain for bodily functions. She suddenly imagined her stalker standing within the shadowy cell, his sad, gray eyes staring out at her, and the terror she held for him was eclipsed by pity. She envisioned his life in such cruel, humiliating quarters and she suddenly felt guilty as if she were somehow responsible for his demise. But how could she be? Even if Julius Vanderpoel were the right man, how could she possibly be responsible for his ruin? If he had committed murder as the detectives said, wouldn't he be deserving of the punishment? Yet when she pictured the man who had kissed her so tenderly her heart faltered. Never before had she experienced such conflicting feelings for the same person; never before had she swung so rapidly between loathing and affection.

As she turned away from the cell, two rats scurried across the floor at her toes and she stopped. Again she assessed the distance to the light.

"Is anybody there?" she called sharply, her voice cutting into the musty air. A pigeon suddenly took flight and fluttered up to the floor of cells five stories above her. As she followed its ascent, her eyes were caught by a huge raven perched on the upper tiers of the prison. It was silently staring down at her with its head cocked. Staring into the knowing eyes, her entire body shuddered. At once she regretted having come to the grim place of persecution. She wanted nothing more than to turn back toward the door, when she felt the presence of someone behind her, the air moving with a breath other than her own.

Swinging forcefully around, she stared at a tall black man dressed in a security uniform.

"What are you doing in here, miss?" he asked abruptly.

It took Kylie a moment to find her voice. "I . . . just . . . I didn't see anyone at the entrance and—"

"You shouldn't be in here," he interrupted, taking her arm. "This is no place for a young lady."

She moved with him toward the door, apologizing for trespassing. "A detective at the Waterfront police station suggested I come here," she explained.

It wasn't until they were outside that the guard released his mild grip on her and the harsh lines of his expression relaxed.

"How can I help you?" he asked, his tone much gentler.

"I'm doing some research," she said.

"Ahh, a student," he said, as though that explained everything. Accepting his assumption as fact, his face softened even further and he grinned. "I got a grandson up at NYU," he said proudly.

Often mistaken for younger than her thirty-four years, Kylie merely returned the smile.

"Name's Harry Stipple," he said extending his hand.

"Kylie O'Rourke," she offered.

"What can I do for you, Miss O'Rourke?"

"I'm trying to find information on a man named Julius Vanderpoel. He was a prisoner here once," she said.

The man's hand went to his chin as he looked upward into the gray sky. "Julius Vanderpoel," he said rolling the name over his tongue. "I remember him alright," he said. "It's been a long time but I definitely remember him. I think the whole damn city knew him. He made such headlines you know."

"How long ago was it?" she asked.

"Oh, that was way back in the late sixties, or early seventies," he said.

"Do you know what happened to him?" she asked. "Do you know whether or not he's still alive?"

"Alive?" he asked with a sly smile. "No . . . I wouldn't think so," he said chuckling. "I remember the night they electrocuted him . . . the whole damn place dimmed."

"Oh," said Kylie, teetering between disappointment and relief. Now that she knew she had the wrong man, she would have to look elsewhere. Just as a last thought, she asked about the tattoo.

"A tattoo?" asked the old man. "I wouldn't rightly know."

She thanked the guard and as she turned to leave, he continued with his recollection.

"Yeah," he mused. "People couldn't hardly believe rich folk could behave like that. You know he murdered some elementary teacher down in South Boston?"

Kylie suddenly stopped. "Elementary teacher?" she asked, her voice faltering as the darkened hallway of her nightmare flashed before her.

"Yep," he said. "Waited 'til school was out and then choked her to death with his bare hands."

Thirty-Two

KYLIE THREADED THE FILM THROUGH THE OLD MICROTEXT VIEWER inside the Boston Public Library, all the while trying to remain sensible. Since leaving the Charlestown Prison she had repeatedly told herself that it could all be some sort of bizarre, twisted coincidence. Just because she had a nightmare wherein the circumstances were the same as the murder, didn't determine anything. The guard had been unable to confirm the tattoo, leaving the stalker's identification based solely on a black and white photo; and he had verified Vanderpoel's death which would leave no logical explanation for her encounters if he had been dead for over twenty years. Yet in spite of the conflicting information, the surmounting questions were compelling enough that she had to move forward.

After an hour inside the drafty wing of the microtext department, she finally found a span of news-articles covering the South Boston murder beginning in the spring of 1974. She calculated that she herself would have been seven years old at the time, living in Quincy.

The first index listing to name Julius Vanderpoel was on April 6, 1974—three days after the murder. VANDERPOEL REPUTATION BE-SMIRCHED BY SCANDALOUS ARREST was the heading. There were so many listings in the following days that Kylie requested the films on all editions of the *Boston Globe* over a three week span from the clerk.

Her fingers positioned the first roll of film so that the greatly reduced image of a newspaper appeared on the lighted monitor. With her left hand she adjusted the scan on the side of the viewer and a headline zoomed in so largely that the words spilled out onto her lap. She backed it up until the copy was in focus and legible. The headline read: TOWERING WORLD TRADE CENTER OPENS IN NEW YORK.

She checked her index notes; the first article concerning the murder was on the second page, fourth column. She quickly turned the wheel at the side of the viewer to find it. The small article was brief, mentioning only a few particulars of the homicide. The thirty-two-year-old teacher had been found strangled to death in her first grade classroom in Lincoln Elementary. The murder was believed to have taken place on April 3rd, her body discovered by a fellow teacher the following morning. The victim's name was Ellen Young.

"Ellen Young," Kylie whispered aloud. The name sounded familiar but it was common enough that she could be mistaken. She was saddened by the size and placement of the article which gave little importance to the death. It was so short and oddly positioned that it was almost as if it were a last minute filler story.

Once again Kylie checked her notes, then turned the lever on the micro-text viewer. The next article covered Julius Vanderpoel's arrest. It had made front page, headline news because of the prominence of the accused man's family who had come from a long line of fame and wealth. Although the article detailed the apprehension of the married man who had a young son, little else was said about the murder or the incriminating evidence which had led to his incarceration without bail. The main focus of the story centered on his family's pristine reputation and the implications of such a scandalous arrest. His father, Harland Vanderpoel, assured the press that it was a grave mistake made by the authorities and that his son would be vindicated and then seek a counter-suit for wrongful arrest and character defamation. There were no pictures of Julius, only of his father, who had held a press conference in the living room of his Back Bay estate. Photos of the Vanderpoel ancestry lined the wall behind the well-dressed, stately man giving his words the force of a heavily armed battalion.

There were no more related articles in that day's paper so Kylie continued onward. She opened the next box of film and threaded it through the machine, then turned the lever until she reached April 7, 1974. The ebony letters of the heading blurred across the screen then focused before her:

ROSE TATTOO INCRIMINATING LINK IN YOUNG SLAYING

At once Kylie lost her breath. "It can't be," she gasped, but the bold, capsulated headline that glowed from the monitor was undeniably conclusive. Though he had been dead for twenty-seven years, Julius Vanderpoel was alive and well, peering into her windows at night and stalking her through the streets of Boston. His body had been executed with enough voltage to dim an entire prison, yet she had touched the warmth of his skin and felt the power of his deadly grasp marked by the rose tattoo. "It's impossible," she whispered, her mind vying to absorb the inconceivable as she struggled with the boundaries between life and death. "It's impossible."

"Excuse me?" asked a voice from beside her.

She looked to the man at the next monitor but his face was transparent—she saw right through him to the insanity of her own thoughts where Julius Vanderpoel roamed freely. She could feel the warmth of his breath on her cheek, the passionate stroke of his hand, and the weight of his body as his heart resonated with her own.

"Miss, are you alright?" asked the imageless voice once again. Then the features appeared forming the face of an Asian man. He was staring at her through thick glasses as though she had lost her mind.

"I'm sorry," she gasped and turned back to the glowing monitor where the article awaited her. She read the first sentence twice, the second time more slowly and deliberately. Her mind was so stunned that it was difficult to assimilate the words.

ROSE TATTOO INCRIMINATING LINK
TO VANDERPOEL IN YOUNG SLAYING

(South Boston) The tattoo of a rose on the arm of murder
suspect Julius Vanderpoel, along with the testimony of

an eye-witness, provided the final links for police in last week's brutal strangulation of thirty-two-year-old school teacher, Ellen Young.

According to District Attorney, Linden White, Julius Vanderpoel, 35, the son of industrialist tycoon Harland Vanderpoel, was positively identified in a police line-up by a seven-year-old student of Lincoln Elementary School in South Boston.

The young girl, whose identity is being protected, witnessed the murder and was allegedly pursued by Vanderpoel as she fled the scene.

According to a statement released by the District Attorney's office, it is believed that Vanderpoel was linked romantically to the slain teacher. The murder was witnessed by the student who had returned to the classroom to retrieve a lunch box after the school's closure. Following a brief confrontation with Vanderpoel and an ensuing chase, the student managed to hide until the next morning when authorities discovered Young's body.

Due to security concerns and the age of the minor, the identity of the witness will not be disclosed. Sources close to the scene, however, confirm that the rose tattoo on Vanderpoel's left wrist is a direct link to the child's identity.

D.A. White says that the death penalty will be sought for Vanderpoel due to "the especially heinous nature of this crime."

As Kylie finished reading the lighted page, she tried to remain calm but the sickening thought had already moved through her; like the female witness, she was seven years old at the time of the murder.

She backed from the monitor, the facts of the article swirling through her mind. A dark dread moved through her blood bringing with it the apocalyptic words . . . *"rose tattoo direct link to child's identity"*. She thought of the tattoo which had haunted and eluded her—of the tiny petals of the flower that she had frantically sketched night after night. Then she heard the words of Julius Vanderpoel himself . . . *"Kylie Rose,"* he beckoned from the tunnel of her dreams, his outstretched hand bearing the picture of her name.

"Rose," she whispered, a terror ripping through her soul deeper than she had ever known. The pretty flower had suddenly turned deadly, its stem surrounding her and its thorns ensnaring her like barbed wire capturing an unsuspecting prisoner. It connected her to the crime like a bloody umbilical cord to a hideous nightmare. "No," she whispered to the lighted screen, arguing with the words before her. The torturous thought was too much. It was too painful to imagine that somewhere in a dark and illusive past she had witnessed a murder and her testimony had sentenced a man to death.

But in spite of her contention, the article continued to assert its voice of reason . . . 'the student managed to escape and hide until the following morning'.

The air vent. She had hidden in the air vent of her nightmare. The stalker had searched for her relentlessly, he had groped through the tunnel and begged for her to reappear, but she had somehow escaped only to become his undoing.

Kylie's hands twisted nervously together as she pondered the thought that the nightmare had been rooted in reality. She was terrified, not only by the idea of witnessing a murder and then inciting an execution, but by the presumable black space in her childhood memories.

She tried desperately to think back to the spring of 1974. She was attending Allen Elementary and her family was preparing to move to Savannah, Georgia. She lived in Quincy, miles from South Boston where the crime had taken place. As far as she knew, she had never even been to the waterside community that bordered Pleasure Bay, much less attended elementary school there. While Jack and Dillon grew up in the Irish community, they had already moved farther north to live with their grandmother by the time she had met them.

She quickly turned to the front page of the following day and as she suspected it carried more news of the murder: DISTRICT ATTORNEY SEEKS DEATH PENALTY IN VANDERPOEL CASE. Beside the headline there were two black and white photos; the first a portrait of Ellen Young. She was a beautiful yet conservative-looking woman with intelligent, virtuous eyes and a sensitive smile. Her ivory skin was framed by dark shoulder-length hair that curved prettily around her dainty neck.

"Miss Young," Kylie whispered, as a feeling of affection wakened from deep within. A mournful sadness, dull and aching, clenched her throat, yet the incarnate of the spirit continued to elude her. She only vaguely felt the essence of the woman . . . her lilting voice and her lovely smell, but like a creature who had slept through a frozen winter, the element of certainty rolled and grumbled yet it refused to show its face.

Beside the portrait of Young there was a photo that appeared to have been taken at a press conference. There was a heavy-set man standing at a podium and while Kylie didn't recognize the name District Attorney Linden White, there was something familiar about his baggy eyes and drooping jowl. "The man in the suit," she uttered as if the words had escaped from the black pit of her subconscious. "The man in the suit," she whispered again but there was nothing else to accompany the phrase.

While she felt a flutter of recognition for both the teacher and the attorney, there were no solid memories to substantiate either claim. She rested her head in her hands and sat in silence, while heavy skepticism worked its way into her thoughts. Maybe her feelings about the photos weren't from memory at all, but a product of her imagination merely fabricating them to substantiate her suspicions. Maybe her dreams and the link with the tattoo were just coincidental. The whispering voices of those around her frayed against her raw senses. A headache had begun to rumble at the base of her skull and a thick lump had formed beneath her ribs making it difficult to breath and impossible to think. The light from the monitor suddenly became too bright and she reached over and switched it off.

She searched through the air vent and the hallway of her dreams but there was nothing—no memories to be found. She remembered nothing else of the school or the teacher, or for that matter Julius Vanderpoel. Doubt began to overtake the testimony; not only were her conclusions improbable but impossible. Dead men did not rise from the grave to seek revenge on their accusers. But she had felt him, she had touched him, and he had been there after the accident, in the cottage. The accident. The creature's words of demise. *No . . . no, it's too much.* She was trying to connect absurdities like a madman at work on a puzzle of fantasy. To even think of the accident in such a manner would unleash her fears and obliterate any voice of reason.

"This is insanity," she said ruefully, resenting her own nature to even consider such outlandish notions. To even consider that she had contact with a dead man was lunacy. Though most of the world believed in one form of spirituality or another, to actually claim to have contact with an entity was to put one's credibility and sanity on the line. She pushed her wavy hair from her shoulders then grabbed her bag from the table beside the viewer and turned for the door. She would go to Lincoln Elementary in South Boston to look for something tangible. She would see if the school existed as she envisioned in her dreams.

Just as she opened the glass door that led into the hallway, a voice called out to her and she turned back. The teenage clerk behind the counter was frowning at her with disapproval.

"I'm the only person here and I'm not supposed to leave this desk so could you please return the film like you're supposed to?" she asked curtly. "I could get in trouble for checking that many boxes in the first place. I just did it to be nice."

Kylie was so distracted that she had completely forgotten about the micro-text she had left at the viewer. "Yes, of course," she said. "I'll get them."

When she crossed down the aisle to go back for the film, she noticed that the Asian man that was sitting next to her had left—she had been so lost in her own world that she hadn't even noticed his departure. Her watch read 3:35. "Damn," she grumbled, wondering if the school would even be open. She reached down to unthread the film from the monitor and noticed that it was once again on. Strange—she could have sworn she switched it off when she was sitting there. She clicked it off once again and the screen flickered a moment then as it turned to black an image appeared reflected in the glass. The white skin formed the nose, the cheeks and the chin, the hallowed eyes and pink lips the darkness. It was Julius Vanderpoel staring out at her, his reflection coming from behind her. She was frozen, unable to move or to breathe. His gray eyes shifted into the light and in that vanishing moment she felt the turmoil and confusion they beheld. Before she could act, the image slid to the side and disappeared. With a gasp she pivoted around to look behind her but he was gone. There was nothing there except the back of the next aisle of viewers. She quickly looked in each direction; the walkway was empty except for herself. At the end of the aisle, the clerk was eyeing her from behind the counter.

"What is it?" the teenager asked, alarmed by the terror in her silent face.

"Nothing," said Kylie, looking away from the questioning eyes.

You're imagining things, her mind whispered, yet the image had been crystalline clear. She turned back to the viewer, and tried to gather the boxes of film but her hands were shaking so badly that she knocked two of them upon the floor.

"It's okay," said the clerk sympathetically. She came around from the side of the counter and took the film from her hands. "I'll get it."

Thirty-Three

STATION AFTER STATION WHISKED PAST, BUT FOR ONCE THE SOOTHING rhythm of the train could not placate the churning inside of her. While at first she had tried to connect it all, to fill in the paradoxical spaces and to draw a discernible conclusion, she had decided it best to leave it alone. She refused to speculate further until she had more facts. Still, her nerves continued to wreak havoc on her body like the platoon of an army that continues to destroy in spite of the loss of its sergeant. Her stomach was in the grip of pandemonium and the base of her throat tingled with the tumult even though her mind had defected to the dulling division of escape.

As she stared numbly at the worn shoes of the old woman seated in front of her, she felt herself losing ground against the battle of gnawing anticipation; the South Boston exit was drawing near at howling speed.

SHE waited outside the train stop, transfixed by what lay before her; from the moment she had mounted the stairwell into the quiet community, it felt as if she were dreaming. In one engulfing sweep, she knew that she had been to the neighborhood, whether for one day or two years she had no perception, for in her jumbled thoughts time had no bearing. Casey's Place, Walsh & Hayes Hardware, and O'Reilly's Soap-n-Suds had existed somewhere before and now appeared like a mirage before her thirsting memory. She had entered a world full of Irish Pubs and paint-chipped pastel houses that had been stored in the warehouse of her mind like the giant sets to a film that had been resurrected for the next scene to begin.

A breeze brushed her skin lightly and its temperature was neither hot nor cold. It was tepid and only added to the surrealistic reflection before her. Even the sky above had the translucence of a vision. The clouds glided overhead, filtering the sun and sending the ground below into a bright, shadowless gray. She recognized the stillness of the fluttering leaves, the eerie glow that penetrated into every crack and the fragrant scent that wafted through the air; it was the quiet before a storm.

A paper cup twirled in the wind and tumbled toward her as she looked up and down the empty street. She looked behind her at the stairwell leading into the subway but the small crowd that had disembarked with her, had been swallowed up by the silence.

She stood alert, arrested with uncertainty, when she heard the laughter of small children coming from the east. The sound drifted on the wind and disappeared once again. Without even thinking or remembering the cab she had ordered, she began walking in that direction, for somehow she knew that Lincoln Elementary was by the bay.

"God blessed you with a sense of direction, Kylie Rose," her mother cooed as she held her hand and they walked toward the water together.

As she passed the dirt alleys between the dilapidated houses with their crushed wire fences and blooming gardens, the whisperings called out to her like the cries of abandoned babes to their long-lost mother.

"'Ring around the rosy, pocket full of posy, ashes, ashes we all fall down . . .'"

The chant echoed from a yellow house, with fallen shutters and a swaying porch. She wondered if she had ever been inside it or merely one similar, with the same haunting chimney and white picket fence. She glanced to the corner, wanting desperately not to recognize the street names but found them distinctly familiar.

"This way you little scamp," her big brother Aidan called to her, his school books flying as he ran ahead. He pulled her forward, deeper and deeper into the neighborhood that came alive before her very eyes.

"Well, it's about time," huffed a skinny little girl in braids, though her face was smiling. "I've been waiting forever . . . race ya' to the end," she squealed as she turned and ran in the opposite direction.

With a dry clenched throat, Kylie started to follow the vision down the overgrown alley, but then she stopped.

"Oh Jesus, what's happening?" she whispered, looking away abruptly. Until that moment, the dear sweet friend had not even existed, but her heart instantly remembered the pain and the anguish of her unhappy tears and that her mother was crippled and sad. "Sally Sorensen," she said aloud.

Abruptly a yellow cab came screeching up to her, the sound of its straining brakes shattering the memories like glass.

"Are you the lady who called for the cab?" asked a voice from within.

It took her a moment to collect her thoughts. "Well," she said looking toward the train station. "I called for one but it was back—"

"Yeah, I know," interrupted the cabby. "I had to stop and—sorry about the wait. Do you still need me?" he asked.

She hesitated a moment, her impulse telling her to go back to the train where it was safe and the images were silent; but her curiosity was too much. "Yes," she finally answered, pulling the heavy door open and then crawling inside. "Lincoln Elementary, please."

DOUBT tried to descend once again over her thoughts, but the clarity of the memories was too strong to deny.

She nervously pulled a compact from her purse and began adjusting her lipstick. As she peered into the tiny mirror at her tense and uneasy face she felt as if she were staring into the eyes of an impostor—an impersonator who had gone through the motions of a lifetime, all the while shielding her from the past. As she thought of the deception a shot of anger flashed through her eyes. "Repressed memory," she said with a smirk. *God, what a term.* With a nod of her head she returned the compact to her purse. She shuddered at joining the ranks of talk show guests and over-analyzed psychiatric patients suddenly remembering horrific things that their own minds had kept from them. She had always considered such claims nothing more than delusions of a bored housewife in need of more in her life; but the delusions were now pecking at her door and she had no choice but to answer.

"You from around here?" asked the inquisitive eyes in the rear view mirror.

"No," she said decisively, as if the mere negation would reverse the outcome.

"No?" he asked, the floating pair of eyes studying her in the tiny frame. "With the red hair and all I would have thought you were."

Kylie remained silent as she stared out the window, the street corners whisking past. There was no denying the cab driver's observation; with her red hair she fit right into the community. Like many areas in Boston where immigrants banded together and recreated their homeland in the new country, the neighborhood was clearly comprised of Irish. For once, she was not the odd outsider lost among a bevy of blondes and brunettes. Here she was in the majority and it frightened her to her depths.

From the time she was a child, she had been drawn toward the brooding atmosphere of Boston and now she was discovering the reason. The nebulous feeling of darkness had lured her back to the metropolis from the affable South over ten years earlier, and the same darkness she had always associated with the city prevailed even stronger over the Irish community.

"It's the spirits you're feeling," Amelia had insisted time and again, convinced that Boston's dark history of witch-hunts and massacres had left behind a grim presence of unsettled dead.

Though Kylie had laughed, she now knew her friend had been right, only the "unsettled dead" were the denounced characters in the shadows of her own memory.

Thirty-Four

THE LAST OF THE CHILDREN HAD BOARDED THE BUSES, BEEN WHISKED away by family cars, and led back to their homes by protective siblings. Kylie stood on the edge of the abandoned playground, and like a forsaken child that had been dumped on the doorstep of doom, watched the taillights of the taxi disappear.

Rising up behind the colorful equipment of fun-filled recesses, was the dark and looming facade of Lincoln Elementary. She tried not to acknowledge it, with its impending arches and jagged edges—she tried to ignore the dread it awakened in her soul; but there was no denying that she had been inside the mortar and stone building and that its walls had claimed a piece of her past.

With a dry swallow that did nothing to quench her apprehension, she started through the playground toward the entrance. The swings creaked gently but ever so slightly in the breeze. As she passed the colorful giant toys, the laughter and the voices called out to her and beckoned for her to play. A memory more vivid than she had ever experienced grabbed hold of her senses and obliterated all around her.

The clouds suddenly split open to a hot and sunny day. She was laughing, her voice melding with the far away sounds of the other children. A pair of strong hands were linked into her own and she was being twirled round and round through the air. The grass below smeared into an emerald blur as she concentrated on the hands that held her so tightly. Her tiny feet sailed through the air and between each spin she caught a glimpse of a lovely woman standing nearby, smiling.

"Not too fast, Julius," the woman called, and when Kylie heard her voice she knew the woman was her beloved teacher and that her name was Ellen Young.

The hands that twirled her like a feather began to slow and Kylie pushed her head back against the whirling force and looked into the mischievously smiling face of Julius Vanderpoel. "Should I stop, Kylie Rose?" he taunted.

"No!" she cried through uncontrollable giggles, her voice light and angelic. "Faster! Faster!"

The scene was snatched as abruptly as it came and with it took her breath. "God help me," she gasped as she let go of the safety of the merry-go-round and looked toward the building. The darkness awaited and it tugged at her shoulders like strong hands clutching tight, refusing to release her.

The wall of memory had been penetrated and like a flood dam with its first tiny hole, the escaping trickles only hinted at the forceful current that awaited on the other side. The first of the memories were demanding to be heard and not by want, but by sheer coercion, did she move forward. Her step rested upon the cement stairs that led to the double doors of the entrance.

"I'm going to marry you someday, Julius," her memory giggled.

He sat on the stair beside her, his warm hand clasped in her own. "And so I shall wait," he answered in a chivalrous tone.

His hair was shining brilliantly, his gray eyes catching the blue of the

sky. Like a prince from a fairy-tale he visited from faraway and would someday be hers to keep.

Kylie touched her hand to her lips as if to catch the pain and to keep it from escaping. It was that old familiar feeling of affection toward the attractive man, but now she knew from whence it came. "A crush," she said but the word did not suffice.

"Children can love," whispered the impassioned voice of Ellen Young. "Children can love."

THE HALLWAY was just as her dreams had confided, with a white and black checkered floor that led past the open doors made of dark cherry wood. She heard the giggling voice once again drifting from behind, and she turned back but there was no one. The hall was empty and silent, the dim light from outside creating dark shadows upon the walls.

Kylie felt a shiver as she was drawn to the stairs with its swirling wooden banister that led to the next level. Her pale hand slid along the railing like a pale ghost gliding into the past.

With a start she found Sally waiting at the top but the little girl's eyes were not upon her; they were distant as though she had just remembered something and halted in her tracks. Sally turned back to the hallway behind her. "Meet me at my house, forgetful-not," she chided and with a whirl of braids bounced down the stairs past.

Then a voice echoed from above, light and angelic like the one she had heard outside.

"'London Bridge is falling down . . .'"

Kylie stood paralyzed on the landing, halfway between the levels where she saw the floor of one and the ceiling of the next.

"'falling down . . .'"

It was her childhood voice echoing through the empty hall and pirouetting down the steps, but one that was strangely removed as though it belonged to another. She slowly ascended the steps, the hallway stretching out before her.

The delicate child was skipping along the shiny floor, with a small wire cage clutched within her grasp. Even from behind, Kylie recognized the curly auburn hair and the skirt that swished against the dainty legs. It was the dress her Aunt Clara had given her for her sixth birthday.

"It's not real," Kylie whispered, a strange sadness moving over her at the sight of the carefree child.

Abruptly the little girl stopped as if she had heard Kylie behind her. She turned toward her, her big green eyes resolute and determined. Her face was freckled, her long pig-tails tumbling over her tiny shoulders to her back.

"Oh my God," Kylie gasped, unable to contain the emotion at the sight of the little face. It was as if she were gazing into the innocent eyes of a long-lost friend. Turning away, she willed the face from her sight but when she looked back the image was still there. Her pulse was fluttering at a dizzying pace, while a deep vibration moved through her veins. She was losing her mind. Her mind was fabricating something so real that it had to be an hallucination.

"It's you," the vision said simply as if she had been expecting her. "Are you ready?" she asked, the question bravely posed.

A tremor of fear rumbled through Kylie's chest as she noticed the colorful little drawings taped along the wall; they were the same as in her nightmare.

"It's okay, Kylie Rose," the little girl said undaunted. "I'll be here to help you. But first you'll need this," she said, lifting the cage within sight. "Remember Mickey?" she asked.

Kylie looked down into the cage at the little gray mouse running round and round on a rotating wheel. She could hear the squeaking of the wheel and smell the unpleasantly sweet odor of its scampering body.

"He's coming with us," the vision said. Then she reached out her other hand for Kylie to take.

As Kylie touched the tiny fingers, the fears left her and she was instantly calm and content. The song was resonating through her head, the humming coming from within. She suddenly had purpose for she knew what she had come for—she had left her lunch box in the cafeteria. *Hurry . . . hurry, you've got to hurry or there won't be time to play.*

Kylie moved forward in a steady walk, but the tiny feet in her memory began skipping once again, the song rolling off the child's tongue like the smooth sweet taste of honey.

"'London Bridge is falling down, falling down, falling down . . .'"

She peered through the huge barred gates that separated the class rooms from the rest of the floor. She hesitated for not only was that section of the school much darker than the rest, she wondered how she would explain her presence inside the elementary school.

Then the urgency of the memory erupted once again . . . *Hurry, Kylie, hurry or you won't have time to play.*

She stiffened up her chest and continued forward. Her fingers touched upon the cool iron gate and she slowly pushed it open. The gate creaked on its giant hinges but before she slid inside the adjoining hallway she peered into the mouse cage. "You're waiting here, Mickey," she said and set the cage onto the floor.

She passed the gymnasium where the big kids sometimes played; but the lights were out and it was silent. The smell of old books wafted into the hallway and as she passed the darkened library she noticed the dim glow up ahead. A ribbon of light was seeping under the door of the janitor's closet.

As she drew nearer, she heard moaning and soft whispering coming from the small room. She abruptly stopped, her wide eyes peering toward the closet. Then there was silence. She stood frozen a moment, then continued her song in a low constant rhythm, forcing her little feet forward.

"London Bridge is . . ." Once past the closed door, she quickened her pace until she came to the lunch hall. She peeked her head inside, immediately spotting her dented old lunch pail sitting atop one of the tables. From where she stood she could see the comforting face of Sleeping Beauty on the front of it. She summoned her valor and quickly ran to the middle of the benches and grabbed it. Then she headed for the door and turned for the gate. Once again she would have to pass the janitor's closet. As she approached she heard the same moaning and a man's voice speaking softly but she couldn't hear what he was saying.

She tried to call out to announce her presence but her voice was barely audible even to herself. "Hello?" she said. She started to move past but a curiosity stirred deep within herself. She had heard the same sounds coming from the bedroom of her parents.

With a thumping heart she moved toward the slats of the door and peeked inside. Mops and brooms were hanging against a wall and there were cleaners and buckets upon the floor. A bare light bulb was glowing dimly, but the sounds were coming from the other side of the closet. She shuffled to the left and then she saw the movement of clothes and flesh within the shadows. It was Julius leaning into a woman who was against the wall. His hips were moving into her rhythmically, while he spoke quietly.

"Tell me that doesn't feel right," he said in a low commanding groan.

The woman's head moved to the side, and Kylie saw that it was Ellen. Her face was flushed and her eyes were pained yet she cooed in a strange voice like Kylie had never heard. She listened and watched through the slim opening, silent and utterly mesmerized.

"Oh my God," Kylie gasped, confronted by the recollection that was so graphically real. As she had retraced the memory she had opened the door to the janitor's closet finding the same sort of equipment used twenty-seven years earlier. She closed the door and started to turn away but then the voices called out to her once again through the slats.

"Julius, we shouldn't be doing this," said Ellen, her voice breathless and unsteady, as she grabbed him by the shoulders as if to pull away. "This isn't the place."

"But you did it with him," he said as he shoved her crudely back against the dirty wall. She didn't answer, she just stared at him with a contemptuous look.

"Didn't you?" he asked and began kissing her mouth once again.

"Julius," the teacher said more forcefully, pulling her lips away from his own. "Stop it."

"You fucked him here—why not me?" he said, anger rising in his voice.

"That's enough! You're hurting me!" she cried and she roughly pulled away. Her dress was open and hoisted above her bare torso. Moisture glistened from the dark curly hair.

The nudity startled Kylie and she quickly pulled away from the door and when she did the metal lunch box in her hand clanked against the wooden slats. Her heart was suddenly in her throat and she knew she should run and hide, but she was too scared to move.

The movement behind the door instantly stopped and there was nothing but silence. After a moment, Ellen spoke. "Who's there?" she asked nervously.

Kylie knew she shouldn't be outside the door—she knew it was wrong to spy. She watched breathlessly as the doorknob which was in line with her eyes, slowly began to turn. With a shove, it cracked open and Ellen peered out at her.

"Kylie?" she asked hoarsely, as she pushed the tousled hair from her eyes. "What are you doing out there?"

She wanted to answer but her lips wouldn't move. She merely stared up at her teacher with wide eyes.

"Come in here for a moment," said Ellen, opening the door wider. Kylie hesitantly moved past her, noticing that she had already buttoned up her skirt and pulled it back over her knees.

Her teacher turned to Julius who stood with his back to them, leaning into the wall as if thinking. "She was just standing out there," said Ellen.

The tears were welling up in her chest. "I was getting . . . I was getting my—"

Julius suddenly turned toward her, "It's okay, Kylie Rose," he said, bending on one knee to where he was even with her face. He kindly smoothed her hair, all the while Ellen pacing behind him. "What did you see?" he asked.

She tried to answer, to tell him that she wasn't even sure herself what she had witnessed, but the tears were choking her words back.

"Look what you've done," grumbled Ellen as she struck a match to light a cigarette. "She's probably scarred for life."

Julius glanced back at the teacher with an acerbic look. "She's a big girl and understands when two people are making love," he said then turned back to Kylie. "Aren't you honey?"

She merely nodded her head.

"That's a good one, Jules," said Ellen bitterly, the smoke wafting to the top of the closet. Kylie couldn't help but stare at the strange woman who was once her sweet and calm teacher. She paced about the room nervously, shoving her hair from one side to the other and blowing puffs of smoke.

As she watched her teacher, Julius took hold of her chin and gently pulled her attention back toward him. "This will be our little secret, okay?" he asked.

"Okay," she managed to say through a cracking voice.

"Now run on home," he said, opening the door once again. "And remember, don't tell a soul."

"Damn," Kylie whispered as she stared into the empty janitor's closet, humiliated and uncomfortable with the moment even twenty-seven years later. She remembered how embarrassed and confused she had been when she hurriedly left the room. But that couldn't have been all that she saw—she knew the worst was yet to come.

After she had promised Julius, they had sent her on her way. She had obediently left the school but only made it to the outer-skirts of the playground when she remembered she had left Mickey by the gate inside. She had debated whether or not to go back into the school and risk making her teacher angry, but the thought of leaving the mouse abandoned in the darkened hallway all night without food or water was too much. She reentered the school, quickly mounted the stairs and quietly headed for the gate.

Her tiny hand reached down to the cage, all the while her eyes riveted on the closed door of the janitor's closet where she could hear the muffled sound of an argument.

"This isn't the place for this," Ellen hissed. "You're going to get me fired!"

"I want you to break it off," he responded, and he sounded even angrier than she.

"Go back to your wife, Jules," she insisted. "I can't let you do this to me anymore!"

"Ellen please," he murmured in agony, his words bringing about another silence.

Kylie lifted the cage slowly, and began walking toward the stairs. Then the door behind her suddenly burst open and the light splashed onto the opposite wall. She could see the shadow of Ellen and the distorted figure of Julius. He was gripping her arms tightly and she was struggling with him.

"Let go of me!" she exclaimed angrily, wrenching her arms from his grasp.

Kylie's heart fell when she saw her teacher's shadow turn toward the door. She quickly backed into a nearby classroom that was dark and empty and waited for the storm to pass.

Ellen suddenly ran past in the opposite direction toward Kylie's first-grade classroom. Then Julius ran after the teacher, both oblivious to the tiny child just on the other side of the door. She stood motionless as they disappeared into the classroom.

Then the fighting was hushed once again.

She wanted to go to the stairs to run out into the fresh air outside, but she had to pass the classroom. The voices slowly began to rise once again, then there was a banging noise. "No, goddamn it!" screamed Julius. "No!"

It's just a memory, she told herself but the terror in her chest continued to mount.

"Let me go, Julius!" cried Ellen. "You have no claim over me!"

"Let her go," Kylie whispered, though her words were not heard twenty-seven years earlier.

"Did you fuck him today?!" he demanded, his voice growing louder and more angry. "Is the bastard still inside you?!"

"It's not real," Kylie said aloud but the emotions and the sounds were as tangible as her own voice. She stared toward the open door feeling helplessly rooted in her tracks. She needed to move forward, she needed to stop the frantic voices before someone got hurt but she couldn't. "It's not real," she whispered again, as the tears began to stream down her face.

The shouting continued but the words were numbed by her own racing thoughts. Just as she turned to find someone to help, it sounded as though a desk had been overturned. *Do something Kylie*, but her feet would not move. She heard the gasping of Ellen and the sobs that wrenched from her own body. Then there was a sound of silence which terrified her more than the violent outburst. As she slowly moved forward through the door and into the room, she saw the chalkboard with that day's lessons still written in her teacher's hand and she heard the sound of Julius whimpering. Past her teacher's desk, she saw the feet of Ellen laying against the shiny floor. Julius was crouched over her, his big shoulders trembling.

"Get up," he said softly, lifting her head, but her eyes were open and glassed over. Kylie had never before seen death and the sight was more than she could bear.

"No," Kylie whispered, her entire body trembling.

At the sound of her voice Julius quickly looked up and across the desk at her, his face was tear-stained and contorted with pain. Then his eyes changed as if he had just for the first time seen her. "Kylie Rose?" he whispered questioningly.

Abruptly a tiny window banged open with the whistling wind and the questioning eyes and the body of her teacher were instantly gone. Kylie stood in the center of the dark, empty classroom with shaking hands and drenched cheeks. She quickly crossed to the window and fastened it back. The trees below bent with the wind and she was startled to see how quickly the clouds had formed into ominous thunderheads.

It had happened. It had truly happened. She thought of her parents wondering why they had never told her. She thought of her father and wondered what he must have thought of the situation. She thought of the man in the suit—the district attorney who must have questioned her. She thought of his face, of his fleshy sallow skin and then suddenly she remembered being seated at a table in a dark, smoke-filled room with her little hands folded neatly in front of her. The attorney was bent over her smiling, though the rest of his face was taut and strained.

"Who has the rose, Kylie?" he asked sweetly, a dribble of sweat trickling down his forehead.

She could see beneath the smile to the impatience and fury that at any moment would unleash upon her. Her chest began to heave and though she struggled against it, her eyes filled with tears. She concentrated to keep them from spilling, but to her embarrassment, droplets splattered down upon the dirty table.

Her father appeared from the other side of the room. His young face was angry as he looked at the interrogating man. "That's enough, goddamn it!" he bellowed. "She's been through enough!"

The suited man looked up at her father. "The killer knows her, sir. And unless she identifies him and we arrest him to get him off the streets, he'll take care of the loose ends, if you know what I mean."

Though the man spoke in riddles, his words brought a change over her father. The suited man stepped aside as her father bent closer to her. His face was tired and worried, and he gently took her hand.

"Kylie, honey," he said, "I know whoever it is, is a friend of yours, but unless you tell us his name, he might hurt someone else."

"No he won't, Daddy," she said, her voice shaky and soft. "He couldn't have done it on purpose." She was confused and sad. She thought of the friend she had grown to love but whom she now feared.

"Please, love," her father said with more urgency.

"But they'll hurt him," she argued, looking at the distressed face of the man in the suit.

Her father sighed heavily, looking down at the floor. She could tell he had been up all night by the dark circles under his eyes and the way his fiery-red hair lay in every which direction. He looked up at her and smiled, yet his eyes were sadder than she had ever seen them. "We promise not to hurt him, love. Just tell us who he is," he said. "Just whisper in my ear and I'll tell the detective. Nobody will hurt your friend."

"Promise Daddy?" she asked.

"I promise, Kylie Rose," he said.

She leaned into his rough, bristly cheek. The familiar, safe smell of Old Spice filled her senses as she put her lips to his ear. "Julius," she whispered.

The memory faded to the faraway sound of the gusting wind through the glass.

"Oh Daddy," she whispered, thinking of the anguish in his eyes at the deceit. How long he had hidden the secret—how long he must have felt the pain. The wind outside had picked up significantly sending the swings tangling together and the merry-go-round creaking back and forth. Her hands rested against the cool glass and a shiver rippled up her spine from the dropping temperatures. She stood silently thinking, when she suddenly got the feeling that someone was standing behind her in the doorway. She turned back just as a shadow moved through the hallway.

"HELLO?" she said, her voice unsteady. She waited a moment, but there was no response from outside the door.

As the threatening clouds rumbled overhead, the glow through the windows dimmed as though it were night. Unnerved, Kylie took one last glance about the room, cautious to leave it as she had found it, and headed for the door. As she rounded the corner into the hallway, she noticed that the door to the janitor's closet had been opened and the light switched on. She had been so consumed with retracing the memory, she hadn't even noticed doing it. She started for the closet but then a man's voice called out to her from the other end of the adjoining hall.

"Miss?"

She looked around the corner and saw an elderly man standing by the stairs.

"Can I help you?" he asked.

Kylie glanced one more time behind her to the janitor's light, debating whether or not she could quickly turn it off before the old man approached. Deciding to leave it, she turned, just as a soft voice emanated from within the closet. "Ellen?" it whispered, faint and eerie. She pivoted back to the glowing light, her stomach at her feet.

"Miss?" the old man repeated from the stairwell. "Miss, can I help you?"

Breaking her eyes away, she told herself that she had imagined it. After all, it had been a long freakish day. "Yes, I'm sorry," she said, moving reluctantly down the hallway toward him. As he met her in the middle, she instantly recognized the slender frame with the hunched back and the balding head. "Mr. Trumble?" she said, remembering the moody principal whom all the children feared.

"Yes," he said crankily. "Do I know you?"

Suddenly the loud crack of thunder rumbled through the hallway followed by a flicker of the fluorescents.

"No, probably not," she answered, when beneath her own words she heard another sound coming from the direction of the closet, a whimpering, low and mournful. Swinging back, her eyes darted to the end of the hallway but the sound had once again dissipated. For a long moment she stood staring, her heart beating wildly. She had not imagined it. It had been there, beneath her voice.

"Were you here to pick someone up? . . . Miss?" snapped the old man, the irritation in his voice demanding that she face him.

"No," she answered, wrestling her eyes from the end of the hallway. The old man looked puzzled. "Well, then, what can I do for you?"

She struggled to make her mind work. The wind had begun to howl and the sound of a tree beat against a distant window pane. "I used to go to school here and I was just . . . just sort—"

"—of looking around?" asked the principal with impatience.

"Yes," she said.

The old man eyed her suspiciously, as the thunder ripped once again through the hallway. With another flicker of the lights, the sound of torrential rain began pounding against the building.

"We don't allow strangers in our hallways," the principal said, his voice straining to overcome the storm. "It's against school policy to have . . ." as the lips of the old man continued to move Kylie's entire body tingled with the sound behind her, her vision narrowing to encompass only the dim light and the shadows. This time the voice was deep and mournful, a wail lamenting and strong, yet she refused to turn.

"You should follow me downstairs," the principal concluded. He was moving away but she remained still, frozen with the terror of the cry, low and agonizing. Slowly, she turned, her eyes resting on a shadow against the far wall.

The principal was saying something behind her, as another crack of thunder settled into a breathtaking rumble. "Miss!" he demanded, but she couldn't move. Her attention remained riveted on the shadow that grew into the form of a man. It drew closer and closer, then the source finally emerged. The deathly white hand of a man felt blindly along the wall while the voice continued to groan. The dark sleeve moved into sight, and then the ashen hair and the long lean body of Julius Vanderpoel appeared. He was clinging to the walls as if absorbing the stones into his fingertips. His dark figure moved over the cream colored paint like a black spider groping its way to the classroom.

Kylie looked back to the old man, then pulled his line of sight to the wall. "Can you see that?" she gasped, but saw instantly that he couldn't. Pressing her fingers to her eyes, she looked away. She was losing her mind. She was losing her mind right before the old man who stared at her with dumbfound. But the figure was there. "It's there," she gasped, looking back just as the shadow disappeared into the classroom.

Abruptly a loud banging of windows sounded in the room and a gusting wind came howling down the hall. A map tore from the wall and came sliding along the slick floor toward them. Then the sound of thunder split down and the overhead lights faded, plunging them into darkness.

"We should go downstairs!" the principal shouted over the roar of thunder. Feeling blindly in the dark, he tried to pull her toward the stairwell, but she had to see, she had to know if she were truly seeing what she thought.

"Miss!" scolded the old man as she slowly walked toward the open door where the sound of moaning continued to emanate.

As she rounded the corner into the doorway of the classroom, the rush of wind nearly knocked her down. The windows that lined the wall were all open and a storm blasted in so bitter and strong that the loose contents of the room were flying everywhere.

From the doorway the room appeared empty. She moved rigidly toward the windows, but when she reached the teacher's desk, she froze. The image of the man—of Julius Vanderpoel—was crouched upon the floor on the other side of the desk, his body shaking with grief. "Ellen," he said softly again and again oblivious to Kylie or to the wind that seemed to move with his beckoning. She watched him a moment in silence. Then suddenly his head threw back like that of a wounded animal unable to bear the pain. His mouth opened in a silent scream, and though the veins in his neck strained, there was no sound. Then an inhuman cry began screeching from the depths of his throat. It was a high-pitched shriek cutting into her nerves like the sharpest of glass. Clutching her hands to her ears, she fell away from the desk. Only after it stopped, when she pulled her hands away from her ears, did she see that he had noticed her. His head turned toward her, his gray eyes yellowed with sorrow, the whites turned to bloody masses engulfing the retinas. She gasped at the twisted, pain-stricken face that fixed upon her.

His lips parted and the screech escaped for a moment but then he seemed to fight it back as he struggled with the elocution of words. "Why did you come back?" he moaned, the last of his sentence trailing off into the shrill noise once again.

Forcing her hands back to her ears to block the sharpness, her heart beat wildly, tears of hysteria filling her eyes. "He's not there," she heard her own voice cry into itself. "He's not there!"

Then the body before her began to change like the bestial creatures after the accident. His skin blackened as his shoulders pulled upward and inward like a bat's. His head threw back and the screeching sound began to grow once again as if controlling his body. His entire being shook with his gasps as Kylie stood transfixed.

She pressed her hands tighter against her ears as the piercing screech replaced the wind, the sound of crashing objects, and her own sobs and cries for help. The pain slashed through her brain and scalded down her spine, paralyzing her every limb. Her lungs tightened and the air no longer entered between her lips. The black coat of the beast fluttered with the wind and the room grew darker and darker. Then it began to spin, blur and then faded to black.

Thirty-Five

SEAN MCCALLUM OFF-LOADED THE DAY'S CATCH OF LOBSTER INTO THE old Ford pickup, all the while cursing the blowing rain that pelted against his yellow slicker. He had hoped to make it inshore well before the storm hit but it had been a good day with lots of legals inside the traps and it was always hard to quit when his luck was up.

"Go tell Eddie we're coming in with a load," he ordered the young college student whose name he never seemed to remember. He wasn't sure if it was Dave or David, or maybe it was even Dale. In any case, the kid did as he was told and McCallum felt lucky to have him for the spring run which had already begun and would probably last another two weeks. Depending on how the kid performed determined whether or not McCallum would be able to keep him on through the following summer months. As the kid ran across the bridge to deliver the message, McCallum continued to load the wooden traps onto the truck. While some lobstermen chose to off-load their catch in livepool tanks of water, McCallum wrapped the lobster in towels soaked in seawater and returned them to the traps for delivery. "It saves your back," he had explained to the student only moments earlier.

"Saves your back," McCallum mumbled ruefully to himself as he hoisted the traps up onto the truck feeling as though a knife were slicing up his back and ripping out his spine. At fifty-nine his tired body screamed for an easier life but fishing was all he'd ever known. He counted down the crates, all the while reminding himself that a cold beer awaited at O'Brian's Pub.

With the load intact he started up the truck, the engine letting out a protesting groan before it finally turned over and came to life with a puff of smoke. "That's my girl," McCallum purred, his gravelly voice an odd juxtaposition to his tone. He wiped his foggy windshield and then grabbed the bottle of rye from under the seat and took a long well-deserved swig. He put the truck in drive and headed for the shop.

James Hook & Sons stood just across the bridge nestled among a bevy of giant glass towers. The red wooden structure that resembled an old over-grown barn was oddly out of place with the modern vicinity. The Harbor Hotel looked down upon the shop like a tall stately gentleman thumbing his nose, yet when it was time to feed their rich clientele the freshest lobster in New England, the only place they looked was right next door.

Sean parked the truck in the back and whistled for the kid to help unload.

Eddie Hook, one of the unspecified sons of James Hook & Sons, stuck his head out into the pouring rain. "Hey, Sean!" he called. "I got a message for ya'!"

"Get outta here Eddie," McCallum called back. "I've got a date with an icy cold brew."

"It's from Kylie!"

McCallum nearly dropped the crate he was holding. The only other time his daughter had called him at the shop was when his sister had died. He quickly laid the trap on the ground and walked over to the building with his boots sloshing. "What is it?" he asked.

"She wants you to pick her up in Pleasure Bay."

THE MESSAGE had needed no further explanation; Pleasure Bay said it all. With a heavy heart, McCallum steered the boat through Boston Harbor all the while trying to remember the advice the doctor had given him twenty-seven years earlier. "She needs to discover it on her own," the doctor had said. "It may take a week or maybe even a year, but she'll eventually remember everything and when she does it will all seem as though it happened only yesterday."

Though the doctor had reassured him that Kylie would one day remember the murder with astonishing clarity, McCallum had hoped and prayed that day would never come; for as long as the experience didn't exist in his daughter's mind, she would be spared the pain. After watching his daughter suffer through those first tumultuous days when she still remembered the grisly details of the crime, he was relieved when her mind simply chose to forget.

Immediately following the homicide she had suffered from nightmares and from unpredictable, uncontrollable flashbacks. Some of the flashbacks were so vivid and disruptive that she was unable to differentiate them from reality, for when they occurred they completely blotted out the moment at hand. Her seven-year-old capacity for understanding had been unable to grasp the dynamics of the complex, adult situation wherein a loved one had turned so incredibly violent. She became disoriented and at times would even run from people she had known for years, fearing they were going to cause her harm.

At first, his daughter had bravely answered all questions regarding the murder and her friendship with Vanderpoel and Young. She was patient as the police interrogated her for hours, but finally on the third day after the incident she slowly started retreating within herself and began refusing to discuss it with anyone. Then one morning when McCallum awoke, his tiny daughter approached him with a troubled look of confusion he would never forget: she was completely baffled as to why the people with the cameras were hovering around their house and the school playground wanting to speak to her and take her photo. The lapse in memory terrified McCallum and his wife but the doctors reassured them it was only a temporary loss of short-term memory and would pass. It wasn't until a month later, when the family moved to Savannah, that the McCallums realized their daughter was suffering from serious amnesia. Even though they had been gone only a week, she remembered nothing of the three months in which they had moved up from Quincy to stay in South Boston.

The McCallums quickly consulted a physician in Savannah who explained that it was a defense mechanism brought on by post-traumatic stress disorder and it was nothing to worry about. She would eventually regain complete memory, probably within a year. But in spite of the doctor's diagnosis, the years passed and still their daughter never spoke of the missing three months. Time and again, the McCallums debated whether or not to tell her, but the longer it went the easier it became to disregard the entire nightmare.

Over the years McCallum had come to believe that the nightmare would remain in the past, but the moment he got the message at the shop, he knew the monster had once again reared its ugly head. McCallum thought of his daughter facing the shocking memories alone and he felt the oppressive weight of guilt pushing down upon him. There had been so many times when he could have told her, thus sparing her the discovery on her own, but he had taken the easy route of denial. Over the drone of the boat's engine and the rushing of the wet wind, the voice inside him shouted out to him—*You're a chicken-shit McCallum! A lousy chicken-shit!*

He stared into the wind as the boat rounded the curve into Pleasure Bay. It had been years since he himself had been there and just the sight of the shore sent his stomach into knots.

As he pulled into the alcove he found his daughter sitting alone inside a gazebo by the water. Her hair was damp and her face was pale.

"Mother of God forgive me," he muttered to himself.

When his daughter saw him coming she walked slowly out onto the swaying dock that was unprotected from the spattering rain.

He pulled back on the throttle and let the boat coast in. "Hey there darlin'," he called out as casually as he could muster. "Need a ride?"

She smiled weakly and he could see that she had been crying. Her eyes were swollen and red. "On you go," he said, holding out his big, leathery hand for her to steady herself.

"Hi Daddy," she said softly, wrapping her arms around his neck tightly.

"Hi love," he said into the sweet smelling hair. "Let's go for a ride," he said turning away from her and going back to the wheel. He had yet to look into those sad eyes for he knew if he did it would break his heart; doctor's orders or not, he should have told. He pushed the throttle forward and headed out to sea.

THE SUN had gone down by the time they anchored seven nautical miles out to sea. The dark clouds had broken in the west just in time for the crimson orb to burst upon the horizon in one last bloody stand before the night drowned it in darkness.

When they first left the dock the water was choppy, but as the stars appeared the waves had calmed into tiny ripples that slapped gently against the side of the boat. McCallum secured the upper deck, all the while keeping his eyes on his daughter who was down below, with a cup of steaming coffee in her hands. He could see her sitting at the table staring sadly into the glowing lantern. She had changed out of her wet blouse into one of his sweaters. The way she had rolled up the huge sleeves and bundled it around her made her appear even more helpless and frail.

Kylie was aware that her father was watching her through the dirty windows and his concern filled her with further apprehension. She sat quietly with her hands wrapped securely around the warm cup, terrified of the forthcoming conversation for fear of what her lips may say; terrified of how her perceptions would be received.

Two hours earlier, she had awakened in the classroom with several teachers standing around her swabbing her forehead with a wet paper towel and debating amongst themselves if they should call an ambulance. Through her hazy wakening she had heard the principal

explaining to the others that before she fainted she had been screaming about Julius Vanderpoel—the man who had killed the teacher so
long ago. When she finally opened her eyes they instantly became silent and regarded her with caution as though at any moment she
would explode into hysterical rantings. "Excuse me," was all she had
said and without further ado, she stood to her feet and exited the
building into the gusting storm. She found a pay phone and phoned
her father, for she had known nowhere else to turn.

The rocking of the boat had calmed her, yet the memories still
danced around her head like fireflies. The swaying lamp over the table
sent light scampering across the cup before her, while pieces of conversations and faces from the past swirled in and out of her brain, confusing and tormenting her. Her head was throbbing and she simply
wanted to sleep, to forget.

She looked through the window at her father moving busily over
the boat. "Oh Daddy," she whispered, for she could tell that he was
avoiding her. As if sensing her eyes upon him, he turned toward her
and smiled uneasily then moved toward the door.

As he lowered himself into the warm cabin his heart rolled and
trembled for he couldn't bear to see the pain that his little girl tried to
hide. She had been crying again and when she saw he was coming
down, she had used the sleeve of the big sweater to wipe her cheeks.

"Are you warm enough, pumpkin?" he asked, turning toward the
miniature stove.

"I'm fine, Daddy," she said softly.

He turned on the burner beneath the pot of coffee and took a mug
from the sink and swished it beneath the water.

"Daddy," she said, staring down at her fidgeting fingers. "You know
what I'm going to ask, don't you?" she said.

He stood silent a moment with the mug in hand, then grabbed a
bottle of rye from the counter and eased down at the table in front of
her. He uncapped the liquid and filled the cup a quarter full then
looked into the green eyes of his daughter that reminded him so much
of her mother's. "Your mama and I would have told you, love, but the
doctor didn't think it was the right thing to do," he said as steadily as
he could all the while the voice inside shouting—*You're a lousy son-of-
a-bitch McCallum!*

Her eyes filled with tears and her rosy lips tightened. She looked away from him a moment to catch her breath then clenched her jaw and faced him. "Then it's true?" she said.

"Yes," he answered.

She was silent for a moment. "And this man, Julius Vanderpoel . . . he was executed?"

"Yes, love."

"And he's dead?"

"Yes," he answered. "He can't hurt you."

She looked up at him, and then abruptly away. She got up from the table and turned toward the sink where she gripped the shiny wood. "I'm not so sure," she said so softly that he barely heard her. Her shoulders squeezed tightly together and she appeared a child beneath the bulky, oversized sweater. She sighed heavily and ran her fingers through her hair. "I feel like I'm losing . . . like I'm losing my mind," she whispered.

He stood from the chair. "I'm sorry, baby," he said. "The doctor said that something traumatic could make you remember so I should have told you after the plane wreck. I just figured you had made it this far, through Aidan's death and your mama and Tucker's that I didn't think you were ever going to remember. I figured it was gone forever and it was best to leave it in the past."

The boat continued to sway as he helplessly stared at his silent daughter. "I'm sorry, love," he said quietly. "That plane accident is what finally did it."

Kylie abruptly turned toward him and buried her head in his chest like she had when she was a child. He folded his arms around her and held her tight. She was silent but he could tell by the trembling of her shoulders that she was crying.

"I've seen him, Daddy," she said through the quiet tears.

"What do you mean, honey?"

"Julius Vanderpoel. I've seen him. After the accident . . . I know it sounds crazy but I've talked to him and walked with him . . . I've touched him—"

McCallum pulled her back and held her steady with his hands. "It wasn't him, love," he said, remembering how vivid the flashbacks had been for her as a child. "It was only a memory."

"No," she insisted, swiping at the annoying tears. "I went to the school just now and I heard his voice and saw—"

"It was a memory, baby," he interrupted, forcing her to meet his eyes. "The doctor said that when the memories came back they could be as real as if they were happening right then. He said your mind could play tricks on you because it'll be trying to sort the information . . . that you could have nightmares or even in some cases hallucinations—"

"He's come back for me, Daddy," she whispered vehemently. "He brought the storm with him."

"No, baby," he argued. "The storm was forecast all week."

She turned away from him as if his words were painful to her. "You don't understand," she said. "Today wasn't the first time I've seen him. I saw him in the Northend in a grocery store several weeks ago. I walked with him the whole way home . . . then I saw him in the subway and we rode the train together. I've even kissed him, Daddy," she said.

He looked away, embarrassed by the admission. "Then it wasn't him, love. It was someone else," he said certainly.

"It was him," she insisted.

"You've got to trust me on this, love. It's important. If you start telling people that you've seen Julius Vanderpoel in the Northend and on the subway they're going to think—" but he couldn't finish the sentence.

"They're going to think I'm insane," she said softly.

"They wouldn't understand, love," he said tenderly. "The doctors said it would be hard on you when you remembered. They said that something that traumatic happening to someone so young would be really hard to cope with even as an adult. Maybe it would do you good to go and talk to someone that could help you with it all . . . like a doctor."

His daughter looked nervous as she pensively chewed on the sleeve of the sweater. "Maybe so, Daddy," she said distractedly.

He took her pale hand into his own. "I'm sorry to put you through this, love."

"Oh Daddy," she said with a bittersweet smile. "How could it possibly be your fault?"

"I could have told you," he said.

"You were just doing what you thought was best."

He sighed and shook his head. "You look tired," he said.

"No, I'm fine," she answered quickly, rubbing her cheeks.

"Why don't you lay down for awhile?" he suggested.

"No, I need to think," she said, her brow crinkling as she cleared her eyes.

"I'll make us something to eat while you rest," he insisted, pulling a wool blanket up for her to lay back on the tiny bunk. "Then we'll talk some more."

THE tantalizing aroma of steaming lobster and melted butter pulled her from the silent cavern of sleep. She rubbed her eyes, disoriented by the sound of lapping water and the swaying rhythm of the bed. She vaguely remembered the school and the library but it had been a dream—a bad nightmare that had started that morning with Jack. "Jack?" she whispered groggily. She opened her eyes and saw her father staring at her from the stove where a trail of steam was escaping from a huge pot.

"Just in time for dinner, love," he said with a sad smile.

The shadow descended once again over her heavy heart. The day had been real with looming prisons, stormy weather and freakish visions. "How long was I asleep?" she asked sitting up.

"Little over an hour," he said, pulling a loaf of bread from the tiny oven. He nodded toward the table where a stack of newspaper articles lay waiting. "I've been holding onto those for awhile and thought you might want to take a look at them," he said.

Kylie sat down at the table and took the yellowed articles into her hands. She had already seen the first of them at the library but the others continued through the trial and into sentencing.

Her father peeked over her shoulder as he prepared the meal. "His attorneys stalled the execution for almost two years," he said.

Kylie felt nauseous as she stared down at the articles. In one of the photos detailing the execution, she saw the young face of her father in the background.

McCallum noticed his daughter studying the photo. "I was at the execution," he said quietly, setting a bowl of bisque in front of her. She looked up at him but he quickly turned back to the stove to avoid the questioning eyes.

After a moment, he pulled out a chair and sat down beside her.

"The papers and news wouldn't let it alone," he said softly. "They couldn't print your name because you were a kid but everyone knew you were the one because the reporters were already there when they found you. We had to leave. We were just in South Boston temporarily anyway—staying with your Aunt Clara and Uncle Jimmy. Do you remember us living with them?" he asked.

A flash of the blue and white house whisked through her mind. "Yes," she answered uncertainly.

"I had a bad season down in Quincy and they were kind enough to let us stay. We were only there about two months when it all happened. The prosecutor wanted you back for the trial, but by that time, you didn't remember any of it."

McCallum saw his daughter's face tighten once again. She abruptly shoved the photos aside and concentrated on her soup.

"It smells great, Daddy," she said cheerily swallowing back the tears.

McCallum reached out his hand to comfort her. "Love, I know that—"

She looked up at him and for a brief moment, he saw the fear and the anguish before she put up the wall. "Daddy, I'm fine," she said. "It's just a memory."

FROM nearly half a mile away, Kylie could see that the warehouse was dark. The thought of entering it with no one home sent a wave of nausea through her. As the boat gently floated up to the dock, her father looked toward the huge structure.

"Where's Jack?" he asked.

"He's working late," she said, though once again she had no idea where her husband was.

"Do you want me to come up with you?" her father asked.

"No, I'll be fine," she said. "Goodnight, Daddy."

She kissed him on his cold cheek and left the swaying of the boat for the unstable ground that lay ahead. As her father disappeared into the blackness of the sea she opened the door with shaking hands. Not only did she mistrust the warehouse which had once been her haven, she was terrified to be left alone with her own thoughts.

Once inside, she flipped on the lights and stood paralyzed in the doorway. She eyed the telephone and debated whether or not to call Amelia. Her friend was the only one who could bring her comfort, but then again, Kylie would first have to explain something that didn't even make sense to herself. Though she had wanted to embrace her father's theory that everything stemmed from the repressed memories, she could never erase the feel of Julius's touch or the realness of his grey eyes penetrating into her very soul. Either Julius Vanderpoel had risen from the grave and was stalking her, or she was simply losing her mind. "He's real," she whispered but she had no way of proving it. No one had seen him except the old man on the subway who had silently sat by as they kissed, and even he could be dismissed as a phantom of her imagination. After a moment of indecision, she deadbolted the door with her key and numbly tossed her bag onto the stand by the door then mounted the stairwell into her bedroom. She no longer had the energy nor the desire to sort out the hideous events that lay jumbled in her head. She opened the night stand drawer and removed a bottle of Benadryl and took several. A doctor had told her once to take them for sleep when all else failed. After a short while the antihistamines kicked in, and though she remained awake, they relaxed her. She lay motionless in her bed, staring out at the deep sea until Jack came home sometime in the middle of the night. Instead of questioning him as to his whereabouts or telling him about her horrific discoveries, she simply lay her head against his chest and fell fast asleep.

Thirty-Six

"DEAR, WHY DON'T YOU TAKE THE COVER OFF THIS MARVELOUS BEAST?"

Kylie looked up from the hemline of the curtain into Dora Greyson's questioning eyes.

"I'm protecting it while we finish the room," Kylie said softly, quickly looking back to the task of tacking up the draperies so that the luxurious fabric gently kissed the floor.

"Nonsense," Dora chided, pulling the tarp from the statue. "He's survived a lot more than a little dust. Wars, I'd say. He'll give you something to look at while you work." Wrapping the material into a ball, she tossed it aside, then floated through the room and grabbed her purse. "Well I'm off to Sweden for a month, dear. Do you have everything?"

"We're set," said Kylie.

"It's looking exquisite," said Dora, her eyes dancing as she moved toward the door. "Simply exquisite."

Within seconds the socialite was gone from the room leaving behind a waft of perfume that scurried around the looming beast. As the sound of the front door opened and closed, Kylie sighed heavily, staring up at the mutating angel. She regretted the purchase of the macabre sculpture for it was a constant reminder of the unanswered questions that plagued her. It had been several days since the nightmare at the elementary school, the week dwindling past without a sound. Fearful that just looking at the celestial creature would open herself up once again to the shadowy world, she grabbed the tarp and slung it back over the statue.

In the silence of the previous days, she had slowly begun to consider the possibility that her father was right about her encounters; that the man who had been following her wasn't Julius Vanderpoel, but that she had somehow placed the likeness of the dead man upon the face of another. After all, the man had never admitted to being anything other than an admirer. Another—more terrifying—possibility was that the encounters had somehow come out of the emancipated memories. To think that her mind could fabricate such real situations involving all of her senses was terrifying; yet her imagination had clearly proven capable of such deception. The memories in the school were so real that she had even smelled the odor of the mouse in the cage.

Amidst all of the uncertainty she was confident of one thing: the plane accident was greatly affecting the unearthing of the long lost memories. Over the past two nights she had begun dreaming of the crash once again—herself screaming as the plane plummeted toward the mountain. Just as the doctor had forewarned, the repercussions of the tragedy were indeed proving unmanageable. Even Jack had been waking at night, sweating and crying out. She knew they needed to seek counseling, but like Jack, to admit that she was losing grasp of her bearings was too frightening. She found it easiest to just push the problem into a corner and hope that the darkness went away.

She had even kept the secret of her past and the question of Julius's

identity to herself, dodging questions from Jack and immersing herself in her work. She would tell him in time, but first wanted to sort
out her own thoughts on the situation. They had grown so far apart
that it was best to let Jack do his own thing and right now that meant
spending his evenings with Freddy.

She wiped her perspiring brow and mumbled to herself, "Call it a
day, Wylie."

With a sigh, she packed up her bag and headed down Charles Street
toward the subway.

THE HEAT simmered from the pavement as the pedestrians moved in
languid silence. It had been a long, hot Friday with gusting winds, but
the setting sun brought sweltering humidity and a stifling stillness.

As Kylie descended the stairs into the subway she could feel the
cool draft from the depths that brought with it the distinct smell of the
underground world. A chill ran up her bare arms where a thin layer of
sweat had formed. Summer was finally upon the city and the hushed
silence hummed with its energy.

A melody, forlorn and ghostly, grew in intensity as she entered the
dark tunnel. A street musician sat on the floor beside a pillar, his gui-
tar hooked up to a speaker that amplified his music. The bluish monitors overhead displayed the newest in fashion while the bodies stood
silent, waiting for the next train. Kylie let her bag fall to her side and
her thoughts be taken with the sad song and the cool breeze that
drifted from the black tunnel.

As she leaned against a pillar, staring into the anonymous faces she
heard the shuffling sound of feet and a tapping cane move behind her.
Then the voice, cracking and thin, whispered in her direction. "He
should have fucked you."

With a start, Kylie turned around but there was no one behind her.
She looked to the right and then to the left. Then she saw him, thirty
feet away, standing on the opposite side of the tracks smiling at her
through brown rotting teeth and shrivelled lips. His gnarled and
twisted fingers were wrapped around the glistening cane, his long
dark coat fluttering in the drafty cavern.

"Oh Jesus," she gasped, for it was the cold scarred face of the old
man on the train.

His mocking eyes focused on her while the sounds and the faces around her faded to complete silence. She heard only the smacking of his hideous lips as he formed his next words. "Your time is coming, my dear."

She remained frozen, every muscle in her body transfixed, while he moved through the silence as if commanding time itself. With the crisp rustling of his coat he stepped from the safety of the cement overhang. He fell toward the tracks and landed perfectly poised on his feet facing into the black hole.

As abruptly as it had stopped, the sounds flooded back in with the rushing air as the coming train thundered through the tunnel toward the old man.

The low rumble shook through her body and grew steadily along with the wind. Then the old man turned to her with an insidious smile but his lips and teeth had changed. They had drawn forward and his eyes had rounded into the hideous likeness of a deformed rat. In the split second before the train hit, his arms jetted upward and his clawlike hands extended out as if to grasp on to the coming force. Kylie began to scream as the screeching brakes and shattering metal obliterated any sign of the disfigured man.

Her hands went to her face as she tried to shield herself from the horror.

A college student standing nearby saw her looking toward the tracks and screaming. He raced for the emergency button and pushed it frantically to stop the train.

"Was someone hit?" a woman cried.

Kylie looked into the excited eyes of the woman but was unable to respond, for the woman would think she was insane. She turned to run, to get away from the rushing bodies and the frenzied faces, but a large man in uniform stepped in front of her and took her by the shoulders. "What did you see?" he asked and began pulling her toward the safety of a lighted cubicle.

She was crying and her legs were shaking so badly that she could scarcely walk. "Nothing," she whispered but the fingers dug into her arm and pulled her to a chair.

The muscular officer had a telephone in his hand and he was speaking to someone; the train would be stopped and they would search the tracks.

Someone was shoving coffee into her hands. "It's alright, miss. Just tell them what happened."

"Nothing," she said, the tears clouding her eyes and drenching her cheeks. "Nothing happened."

"She was screaming like a lunatic and looking down . . ." the college kid was saying.

With guarded eyes they were watching her and waiting. Only after they had checked the tracks and the conductor had inspected the train at the Downtown Crossing, did they release her. "You're free to go, miss," said the security officer. As she stood to move past them, all eyes were upon her, questioning and suspicious.

WITH hard pounding movements she drove the nails into the wood, as she boarded up the ceiling fan above her bed. Sweat trickled between her breasts and along her back where her cotton dress stuck to her skin like paste. The taste of bourbon had numbed her blistering hands, yet it failed to silence the voice that continued to torment her. *Your time is coming, my dear.*

She pounded harder and harder, each stroke chiseling away at the coffin of darkness that lingered around her. The tiny nail glistened in the moonlight but it was the ratlike face of the old man she saw— twisting and turning before the subway. It was the gray, watching eyes of Julius Vanderpoel and the limp, lifeless body of Ellen Young. It was the tiny mouse that went round and round while the screams of her teacher went unheeded. The smells, the sounds and the colors melded into one—one overpowering force of evil that stalked her; but with each angry slam of the hammer she distanced herself from its danger.

With shoulders aching, she stepped down from the ladder, her balance slightly off from the half-empty bottle of Jack Daniels that stood on the night stand.

She breathlessly looked up at her handiwork to make sure there were no more holes in which the dead eyes could peer. The last crevice had been covered, silencing the fan and blocking out all of the moonlight. As she stared up at the boards which had been so crudely nailed into the surrounding woodwork, a cold chill suddenly prickled over her; in less than ten minutes she had destroyed woodworking that was over a hundred years old. She looked down at her raw hands that had wielded the hammer so frantically and saw they were shaking, trembling with the fear. A loaded shotgun lay at her feet and only minutes earlier she had been hovering over the fire escape like a crazed lunatic, chaining it up and securing it with a padlock.

"Jesus," she said aloud, horrified by the panic that had overtaken her. She scarcely remembered coming home or racing about the warehouse in a frenzy. As she dropped the hammer upon the bed, a different kind of trepidation crawled beneath her skin; she was teetering on the brink of madness.

She looked toward the telephone, her mind urging her to call someone before the fear overtook her again, but she had already tried to call Amelia, then Jack, and had been unable to reach either. She trusted no one else to know that she had lost control of her surroundings. She thought of calling Dillon, then her father's advice drummed through her head once again . . .

You've got to trust me on this, love. It's important. If you start telling people that you've seen Julius Vanderpoel in the Northend and on the subway they're—

"—going to think I'm insane," she said aloud. Even her father knew that her mind had proven untrustworthy, for it had disassembled and hidden the atrocities from her childhood. Just as she had opened up her imagination that afternoon by contemplating the statue, her mind had created the bestial creature in the subway.

"It wasn't real," she said solidly and with conviction though she could still feel the thickness of the air which held the promise of doom.

Her eyes avoided the rest of the darkened warehouse, while she pulled her sandals off and dropped them beside the Winchester. As she climbed behind the sheer netting of the canopy which camouflaged her ghostly face within its folds, she knew her efforts at securing the house had been in vain. Whether the old man had been a harbinger of death or a forewarning of her own madness, no chains, boards, or shotgun would stop the prophecy. He was one with the darkness that was slowly seeping up from the entrails of hell and if she found no escape it would eventually devour her.

PART THREE

Thirty-Seven

Dillon hit the buzzer of the warehouse for the fourth time but still there was no answer. Just as he turned to leave the front door edged open and a sleepy-looking Kylie appeared. Her hair was matted and her dress was wrinkled as if she had slept in it. Dillon's heart dropped for he could smell the stench of last night's bourbon.

She looked confused and disoriented. "Dillon?" she said through a hoarse voice. "What are you doing here?"

"Saturday dinner? Remember?"

"What time is it?" she asked.

"Five-thirty."

"My God," she mumbled, pulling the door open so that he could enter. Dillon silently followed her inside, then latched the door behind himself.

"Grab something to drink," she said numbly, looking into the guest bedroom and then slowly ascending the stairs. "I've got to take a shower."

"Where's Jack?" he asked.

"Your guess is as good as mine," she called from the master bathroom where he could hear the water running.

As he looked toward the loft he noticed that it was darker than usual in the bedroom. Then he saw where the boards had been crudely nailed across the ventilator fan. "What happened to your fan?" he called out but there was no answer, only silence.

Within a few minutes Kylie came back down the steps with wet hair and a freshly scrubbed face. She was wearing a robe and running a brush through her tangled locks.

"I'm sorry, Dillon," she said, with dark, clouded eyes that stared through him. "I'm going to have to run to the store for something to cook. It may just be you and me."

"That's okay," said Dillon sympathetically. He could tell by her life-less voice and distracted gaze that something was terribly wrong, but just as he started to ask, she turned nervously away.

"Hmmm," she said looking toward the blinking light on the phone recorder. "I didn't even hear it ring. Maybe it's from Jack," she said softly, rewinding the message.

A woman's voice, serious in tone, crackled from the tiny machine. "Yeah . . . uh, Ms. O'Rourke, this is Valerie at Boston Savings and Loan. We've got a check here from you to Lindon Flooring for $7050.00 that puts your account into the negative and another for $2600. We don't normally call in these situations, but there's a couple of other substantial checks that have already been returned. Please come in to the branch or call our twenty-four hour customer service line to take care of this . . . Thank you."

Kylie sighed heavily as the message ended. "There must be some mix-up," she said dialing the telephone. "Do you mind if I take care of this real quick?"

"No, not at all," he answered.

He looked away, feeling as though his timing couldn't have been worse. Kylie's voice was tense but polite as she spoke to the person on the other end of the line.

"You're talking about my business account?" she asked as Dillon took a seat on the couch. "But that's impossible. I had forty-two thou-sand in there . . ."

There was a long silence as Kylie paced behind the sofa. "Why didn't someone call sooner?" she asked. "He's not on that account and he can't sign—" Her voice was beginning to escalate but she suddenly stopped and listened intently to the person on the line. "Why didn't they check the signature card?" she finally asked. "How can I press charges against him? He's my husband . . . Okay, I understand." She quietly hung up the phone and sat down on the chaise lounge with her face in her hands.

Dillon was silent, unsure how to respond to the awkward situation. He gently reached out and touched her shoulder.

"I don't believe this," she whispered, her breath short and labored. "He's gambling again . . . I never even thought . . . After last year, I took his name off everything so this wouldn't happen." She turned to him with utter bewilderment upon her tired face. "It's not our money.

It's Dora Greyson's. She advanced it for supplies to go toward her house."

She stared out the big glass window at the twinkling sea. "I don't know how much more I can take," she said, shaking her head. "How could he have done this?"

Then suddenly, as if finally realizing the gravity of the situation, she stood to her feet. "Damn! That lying son-of-a-bitch!" She bolted up the stairs toward her bedroom and began rummaging through the night-stand. "There were some matches," she cried as Dillon ascended the steps after her.

She grasped what she was looking for and pulled it out. "Have you ever heard of the Coco Row?" she asked, holding up a colorful book of matches.

His stomach dropped and he looked to the floor. "Yeah, I met Jack there one night when his Jeep wouldn't start," he said reluctantly, realizing now what hadn't occurred to him then.

"What is it?" she asked.

"It's a billiard room in Chinatown," he said slowly. "They've got a back room."

His words seemed to knock the breath from her. "Why didn't you tell me he was gambling again?"

"He told me he wasn't," he said softly. "He said he was there to watch Freddy play."

The fire flashed in her eyes. "Goddamn it Dillon!" she snapped, standing to her feet. "Goddamn it!" she wailed as she grabbed a pair of jeans from a drawer and began slipping into them beneath the robe.

"I'm sorry, I should have known," he said, turning away as she pulled the robe off.

She threw a tee-shirt over her head and grabbed her sandals and wallet. She started for the stairs but then suddenly turned back. Her eyes were frantic and dark, her face pale. "Forgive me, Dillon," she gasped. "I'm not myself right now. This has nothing to do with you. It's nobody's fault but my own." She rushed down the steps toward the front door.

"Let me drive you," Dillon said, quickly following after her.

"I can take a cab," she called, but Dillon grabbed his keys anyway.

. . .

DARKNESS had fallen upon the city, the colorful lights of Chinatown splattering across the BMW.

Kylie sat silent in the passenger seat, her head throbbing and her nerves jittery from the leftover booze in her bloodstream. She stared out at the bums with their carts and the drunkards in the alleyways pondering the bleakness and the insanity that plagued them. One woman in particular was arguing with the air, waving her hands and expounding her view as though the person before her were contradicting her as she spoke. "She really sees someone," Kylie said aloud, wondering if the woman also saw mutating beasts looming in the night.

She could feel Dillon's questioning gaze upon her. She glanced toward him, but her eyes avoided his, for she knew he could tell she had been drinking again. "We're a helluva pair, me and your brother," she said sadly. "Whenever there's problems we self-destruct. I should have known he'd do something like this . . . I should have known the second I got out of the hospital and he wasn't around."

She looked down at her hands as they fidgeted with the cameo around her neck. "I knew he was hurting, but Jack's like an animal when he's wounded: he won't let anyone touch him and he'll chew off his own leg to get away from the pain." She thought of her husband's sad, childlike face and the emotion rose inside her chest but she swallowed it back. She wondered if the hell he had been cast into resembled hers. "Who would have thought surviving a plane crash could be so devastating?" she asked, gazing out into the neon-lit streets. "Nothing's been sane ever since."

Thirty-Eight

MR. ISHIMOTO STARED AT THE COUPLE WITH HIS LIPS OBSTINATELY pressed together.

"Look, I have no intention of causing you any trouble," Kylie said through a tolerant smile. "But if you keep insisting that there's no back room, we'll have to call our friend at the police station to see if he might be able to find it."

The tense little man took a deep breath and then finally asked, "Who are you looking for?"

"My husband. Jack O'Rourke"

Ishimoto glanced over at Dillon then back at Kylie. "Follow me," he reluctantly grumbled.

"Maybe it would be better if I went back and got him," suggested Dillon looking nervously to the rear of the dank pool hall.

"I'll be fine," said Kylie. "Jack's not going to let anything happen to me."

Dillon hesitated a moment, then said, "I'll be waiting out front in the car."

"Thanks," she said softly. She started to follow Ishimoto, but then slowly turned back. "Maybe he's winning," she said hopefully.

Her frightened eyes saddened him. "Maybe so," he answered.

AS THE smoke rose up from the crowded room, the dealer cut the deck and tossed the cards in five directions. "Ante up, boys," said the gangly man staring at Jack who was holding up the game.

Jack tossed the hundred dollar chip into the stack and looked at his hand. The numbers danced in front of his eyes and he tried to focus, but he had been sitting at the table so long that his senses were beginning to deceive him. With nothing to eat but a stale sandwich in the middle of the night, he had been nurturing a steady buzz from a glass of tequila. His back ached and his head throbbed but he knew if he hung in there his luck would surely change. He tossed away three of the cards and the dealer quickly replenished them.

Come on Jack Black, concentrate, his mind scolded, for he'd been on a losing streak since ten o'clock the previous night.

"I'll bet one-fifty," said the guy on his right, who tossed in the appropriate chips.

Jack looked at his hand, trying to decide whether a pair of tens was worth it. *Take a chance*, his mind whispered numbly. *You never get out of a bad streak until you take a chance.* As he matched the one-fifty and raised fifty, the tiny door to the room opened.

"In or out folks," a cranky voice called over the crowd of richly dressed observers who gathered around the four tables of cards. The door quickly closed scattering the overhang of cigarette smoke into whirling patterns.

The first person Kylie saw when she entered the posh little room was Alice Newfield. Even though Jack's fling with the clothes designer was long in the past, Kylie's already frayed nerves began to quiver as all the old jealousy and rage rushed upon her. While Alice was clearly with the man beside her, just the fact that the socialite was in the same room as Jack sent Kylie's temper soaring.

Though Kylie never understood Jack's attraction toward the strange woman, she nonetheless felt daunted by her presence. As usual, Alice was dressed stylishly with her blonde hair neatly smoothed back and her make-up heavily but perfectly applied. She was from a rich, aristocratic family and her every move meant to convey that to the commoner. It had been a mystery how Jack—who openly professed his aversion to blue bloods—had ended up in bed with such a woman. It was no mystery, though, how Alice had come to be friends with the unsavory crowd that had introduced her to the O'Rourkes; she was a successful artist like the rest, with too much time and money on her hands.

As if feeling the weight of Kylie's stare, Alice glanced toward the door and nearly jumped when their eyes met. The socialite quickly looked away and then turned to Freddy who was standing by the next table. Freddy's head turned so sharply in Kylie's direction that it seemed as if his neck would snap. When she saw the guilty look on his freckled face, her heart sank for she knew it meant Jack was nearby and that he was losing.

As her eyes searched the room for her husband she saw it was filled with the same circle of destructive friends that had nearly caused her and Jack to split a year earlier. When she finally spotted him gambling at one of the tables oblivious to her arrival, her anger escalated so forcefully that she was afraid to move for fear of what she might do. While she had suspected he had fallen back in with the old group of hard-core partiers, to actually see him among them—gambling with everything they had worked so hard for—was more than she could handle. She tried to move forward, for she knew she had to, but a wave of terror gripped her tightly. Jack had defected to the enemy camp taking with him the very bond of trust that held them together.

She had no idea how he would respond for he had joined the ranks against their future together. She was the outsider; for everyone knew she was the one who had insisted that she and Jack break from the crowd in hopes of a more stable life. She felt weakened and humiliated for half of the people in the room knew Jack was betraying her and each and every one of them was gladly a part of it.

As she moved toward her husband, the questioning eyes turned toward her. "Kylie?" a voice said to the side of her as others turned to look. She curtly nodded her head as the familiar faces moved to the side. "Alice," she greeted with another nod. "Freddy."

Jack looked up from the table of chips into the blazing eyes of his wife. "Kylie, what are you doing here?" he asked through dry lips.

She stared down at his tired, desperate face, trying to remain calm. "I just want to know one thing, Jack," she said. "How much do we have left?"

Jack stood from his chair. "Let's go outside," he said taking her arm.

She gently pulled away from his grasp with an acerbic smile. "Your breath is even worse than mine," she said, sickened by the overpowering smell of tequila that seeped from his pores. "How much is left?" she repeated, refusing to move until he answered the question.

"Hey, little lady," said the dealer. "We don't allow—"

Kylie turned to him with a challenging glare. With her green eyes flashing and her long mane of hair she resembled a lion about to devour its prey. "With one phone call you could be serving prison time so you'd better keep your nose where it belongs."

The room grew silent as the people at the other tables stopped playing.

Jack looked about at the inquiring faces, clearly embarrassed to disclose the amount. "I've got fifteen-hundred left," he said under his breath.

Kylie fell slightly back but held her position. "You've gone too far this time," she said simply through vacant and resolute eyes.

Chilled by her calm, Jack stood silently by as his wife disappeared into the gawking crowd.

• • •

SHE FELT nothing until she was in the solitude of the darkened alley behind the pool hall; then the magnitude of the betrayal released upon her like a bursting dam.

"Oh God! . . . Oh God!" she cried, her heart racing as she paced back and forth over the gravel, holding onto her stomach as if her very being had been ripped through her skin. It was gone. Everything she had worked so hard for was gone. In one fell swoop the man whom she trusted and loved had yanked the last shred of stability from beneath her. Not only would the loss threaten her financially, but professionally as well. "No," she whispered again and again, feeling the pressure more than she could take.

The heavy metal door suddenly swung open and Jack came racing out into the night. The second he saw his wife's frantic face in the shadows he immediately stopped.

"This is where you've been?" she cried. "I've been losing my mind and this is where you've been?!

"Kylie, don't worry," he said. "It'll be okay."

His words sent an overpowering rage screaming through her. "You don't even realize what you've done!" she gasped looking into the stupefied face of her husband. "Do you think Dora Greyson is just going to let us walk away with forty-two thousand of her money?! It's called embezzlement, Jack, and they're going to send us to jail for it!"

"It'll be alright!" he insisted.

"This isn't some little fling of yours that'll cost us a couple of grand!" she cried. "We're talking forty-two thousand!"

"We'll make it back!"

"With what?" she exclaimed throwing her arms to her side. "Even if we don't do jail time, this is gonna kill our business. Nobody's gonna hire us and invite us into their million dollar homes if they can't trust us!" As she spoke she grew more and more overwrought. "It's gone Jack. All the work and the sacrifice! And for what?! A few seconds of glory in front of a bunch of people that mean nothing?!"

"I'll get a loan!" he begged.

"And who the hell is going to give it to you?" she exclaimed. "We're up to our ears in the warehouse mortgage! We still owe thirty-three thousand on the business! No bank in the world would lend us money right now!"

"Then I'll have to win it back!"

At first jolted by his declaration, the fury shot through her hands and before she could stop herself she slapped him across the face so hard that his head popped to the side. "Damn you!" she exclaimed. "Won't you ever learn?!"

Caught off guard by the blow, Jack stumbled toward the brick building where he grasped the wall to steady himself.

Kylie stepped backward, stunned by the strength of her own temper. The streetlight flashed across her husband's face where a welt slowly appeared on his cheek. At the sight of the raising skin and the feel of her smarting hand, a touch of regret rumbled in her heart. "Damn you," she whispered again.

She turned to get away from his wrinkled shirt and his sunken, tired eyes, but nothing except the darkened alley lay ahead with the graffitied walls and the tumbling trash. The shadows were lurking and heinous, calling out to her to pass. She took several steps forward but then stopped, for the thought of continuing alone filled her with despair. The trembling overtook her and the tears started to flow. "I can't take this anymore," she said. Her arms wrapped about her stomach and she held herself tight, for she was alone in a world that was losing solidity with each passing moment. Everything had turned to madness; even Jack had fallen off into the deep end of insanity, leaving her behind to fend for herself. She tried to gain control of her panic but the tears rushed faster and faster, her gasping breath quickly turning to sobs.

"You don't even know what's been happening," she cried. "You've been so withdrawn that I was afraid to tell you. Then last night, when I needed you most, you were nowhere! I needed you so badly but I couldn't find you anywhere! I just lay there all night—terrified out of my mind!" She turned to him, her words unleashing with bitterness and fear. "I don't know what's real anymore," she cried, her face twisting with the pain. "I see things that no one else sees and I—" but the cries overtook her. Jack started to move toward her, but she put her hand up to stop him. "No, don't touch me," she said, backing away.

"Kylie," he said helplessly, once again reaching out to her. "I'm sorry I've been—"

"Don't!" she said, bitterly pulling away for he too had become the enemy. "I can't count on you Jack," she said backing into the darkness. "Nothing you say is the truth anymore. If you're not lying about some slut you're screwing, you're destroying everything that we've worked for. I need more stability than this. I can't work my whole life building a foundation to have you gamble it all away on a drunken binge." She looked to him, her swollen eyes nearly closing with the pain. "I have to know that you'll be there for me no matter what and that I'm going to have a roof over my head when I'm fifty or sixty or seventy."

"You will," he said desperately.

"No I won't," she said. "I'll never feel safe knowing you can yank it all away with one night at a pool hall."

The fear in Jack's face grew darker. "Just give me another chance, Kylie. I can change. I did it before."

The sincerity in his eyes made the pain in her gut cut deeper. She wanted to believe him like so many times before, but there was no turning back. The transgression had been too deadly. "There's no trust left between us," she whispered. "It's over," she said. "I want you out of the house tonight."

He reached out his arms and stepped toward her, but she backed away. "Kylie," he said, "you can't mean it."

She tried to avoid his frightened eyes as the lights danced behind her husband's hair like a colorful halo. "I'm sorry, Jack," she said softly. "But I can't let you take me down with you." She quickly turned away and hurried along the side of the building toward the street.

"Kylie!" Jack called from behind her.

She quickened her pace but as she reached the sidewalk at the front of the pool hall Jack caught up to her and grabbed her.

"Kylie, please! I'll never do it again!" he begged.

The plea awakened the rage inside of her for she had heard it so many times before. "You've already done it!" she exclaimed, knocking his hands away as she swung around. She could see by his stunned face that he still had no idea of the damage. "How long did it take you to go through that much money?" she asked. "A week? A month? Two months? How many lies did you have to tell?!"

He stepped away as if to let her calm.

"You could have stopped!" she said, going after him with all of her might. "You chose not to! You chose to destroy us!" she wailed as she lunged toward his chest with her fists. "Ten years of marriage! Ten years of my life GONE!!"

Jack grabbed hold of her lashing arms and pulled her in toward him. "Stop it, Kylie!" he yelled. "Stop it!"

Dillon, who was seated in his BMW, saw the fighting couple and immediately got out of his car.

Kylie's arm twisted behind her back as Jack frantically struggled to keep hold of her. Just as she broke free and started running in the opposite direction, he grabbed her again. "Kylie wait!"

"Jack, let her go!" Dillon said from the street, advancing toward them.

When Jack heard Dillon's voice he released his wife and turned toward his brother. "What the hell are you doing here?" he demanded.

"Just cool down," warned Dillon. "I'm going to take Kylie home and—"

Jack thumped him in the chest with his finger. "I bet you are. Like a vulture just waiting around for the take, aren't you little brother?"

"Jack, leave him alone," Kylie said. "This has nothing to do with him."

"Then what the hell is he doing here?" Jack demanded shoving his finger into his brother's chest once again.

"It's alright, Dillon," said Kylie breathlessly, holding up a shaking hand. "I'll find another way home."

She began walking quickly away from the brothers but Jack forcefully pulled her back. Just as she turned toward him an explosion of fists began flying around her. Jack threw Dillon up against the car, pounding him in the face.

"Jack no!" she screamed and tried to pull him off but he pushed her back.

After several blows from Jack, Dillon pounded his fist into Jack's stomach, sending both of them flying backward. Several people who had come out of the pool hall to witness the scuffle scurried to get out of the way.

"Stop it!" Kylie wailed, throwing herself between the brothers. Out of nowhere, the fist made contact with her eye and the pain shot through her head like lightening. She stumbled to the ground as the blood began running from her nose.

With their faces bloodied and their shirts torn, the brothers abruptly stopped fighting and looked down at her.

"Oh my God," said Dillon.

"Kylie!" Jack exclaimed, moving toward her. He stuck out his hand but she pushed it away.

"I'm fine," she said bitterly through the pain and the tears. Blood was dripping upon her shirt and her eye felt as if it had been shoved up into her head.

As she stood shakily to her feet, she noticed the small crowd that had gathered outside of the entrance to the pool hall. Her gaze met that of Alice Newfield and the socialite's look of smug satisfaction brought a cold seething anger through Kylie's bones. She immediately stiffened her shoulders and pushed her hair back, but the blood that trickled down her face worked against the propriety she tried to summon.

Abruptly, the sound of a siren came rushing around the corner, scattering the crowd of gamblers. Newfield and her date quickly walked toward their white Porsche and with a roar of the engine were gone.

The flashing lights of the police car came to a screeching halt in front of them. As Kylie pulled her tee-shirt up to stop the bleeding from her nose, she felt the desolation rush back upon her.

"How could you do this to us, Jack?" she pleaded, the night air stinging against her throbbing eye. "We were a team . . . we could have had everything."

Jack was silent, the sight of his wounded wife bringing tears streaming down his face.

"I'm sorry, baby," he whispered. "I'm so sorry."

Thirty-Nine

DILLON STARED UP AT THE FLUORESCENT LIGHTS OF THE EMERGENCY room as Elaine Grimmer stitched up the gash on his brow. Even though he cringed under her motherly scowls, Dillon was relieved to find the cranky old doctor the attending physician, for Grimmer remained the most competent and experienced in the ER.

"How's my brother look?" he asked trying to ignore the pain of the needle.

"A lot better than you," Grimmer muttered. "He only had five stitches."

Out of the corner of his eye, Dillon saw the door open and the tall figure of Theresa enter.

"Well, what have we here?" she asked with a smirk. She was wearing her doctor's smock, and even though she wore no make-up and her dark hair was pulled back in a knot, she looked radiant.

"I thought you had to work," he grumbled.

"Well, I got the word from David that you were down here and of course I had to take a gander. After all, it's not every day one of our top doctors is treated for bar room brawling in our emergency room."

"Great. So that's the story, huh?" mumbled Dillon. "It wasn't a bar room brawl. We were in the street."

Theresa let out a laugh. "That's even more interesting. Better be careful," she goaded. "You may just shatter that straight-laced image of yours."

"Can't do that," said Dillon. "Then who would Jack have to resent for his shortcomings?"

"Now, now," scolded Theresa. "I thought the fight was over Kylie."

Dillon could feel his face blush beneath the weight of her stare. "Who told you that?" he asked quietly.

"No one," she said. "But your red cheeks are a pretty good indication that I'm right."

"It wasn't what you think," he said defensively, as Grimmer tied the knot on the last stitch.

"And what do I think?" Theresa asked, her tone suddenly cool.

He pulled away from the doctor's grasp and looked angrily into the violet eyes of the anesthesiologist. "You too?" he snapped.

"Can you two lovebirds discuss this later?" chided Grimmer, pulling Dillon's handsome face back toward her. "I refuse to work in the midst of a lover's quarrel."

"Sorry, Elaine," said Theresa. "I'll leave you two to it." She headed for the door but turned momentarily back. "No woman is worth it, Dill. Not even your brother's wife."

As she disappeared through the swinging door, Dillon called out toward her, "You've got it wrong, Dr. Ollridge." Before the door stopped swinging, a nurse came back through it.

"If you're done, Dr. O'Rourke," she said, looking shyly away from his bandaged brow. "That officer wants to see you before you leave."

Dillon sighed heavily and stepped down from the table.

"Go get 'em, tiger," said Grimmer, with a smirk and a wink.

"I WON'T book you this time," said Officer Gallo. "You look like you've done enough damage to each other to make you think twice. But next time I won't be so understanding." He ripped off the report from his clipboard and handed a carbon copy to Dillon, then one to Jack. He put on his hat and turned to Kylie who was seated alone on a bench, her left eye blackened and swollen.

"Ma'am?" he said. "Are you sure you don't want to press charges?"

"Like I told you, it was an accident," she said.

"Well, I guess I'll have to take your word on that," said the officer looking over at Jack and Dillon with a warning glare. "Next time, boys, watch where the hell you're swinging."

With a tip of his hat, the officer exited through the double doors leaving behind a deafening silence in the room.

Kylie got up from the bench and slowly walked toward the exit. "I'm sorry I got you involved in this, Dillon," she said. She looked over at Jack, her gaze chilly and detached. "I'll be out in the Jeep," she said, then continued through the automatic doors.

Alone in the room, the two brothers looked to one another but both were silent. After a moment, Dillon turned for the hallway that led into the main hospital. "Catch you later," he said with a sigh.

"Hey, Dill?" said Jack quietly.

Dillon looked around, unable to hide the hurt and anger in his voice. "Yeah?"

"I don't know what got into me," said Jack.

Dillon hesitated a moment, then nodded his head. "No problem," he said.

"Better keep ice on that hand," advised Jack. "Otherwise it'll be swollen in the morning."

In spite of himself, Dillon smiled, for even though he was the doctor he had stepped into his brother's domain. "You would know," he said, looking down at his pale hand with its scuffed knuckles. He thought how absurd it was that same fair hand would attempt to heal another come Monday. He thought of Jack's calloused, tan fists and he suddenly realized just how badly his brother could have hurt him if he had chosen to; but he hadn't.

When he looked back up at Jack's dejected face, he saw for the first time the remorse and fear. It saddened him to see the worry and pain behind the restless eyes. He wanted to set his brother's mind at ease, to tell him that he would never betray him by lusting after his wife, but the thumping in his chest kept him silent. He wanted to speak the truth, to plead his own innocence, but instead looked away from the disquieted eyes. He cleared his voice, but the air remained heavy and thick with the unspoken words.

"See you later," Jack finally said with a nod of his head.

"Later," said Dillon, his heart pumping even faster. As he silently watched the automatic doors glide open and his brother disappear into the night, he knew he should stop him and set the matter straight, but his body didn't budge. Then the strange feeling that it would be the last time they would ever speak crept into his thoughts. He swallowed hard, trying to quell the eerie sense of the lost chance. "Call him tomorrow," he said aloud as his own frayed reflection in the doors slid to a standstill in front of him. With a shrug of his shoulders to dislodge the unsettling feeling, he headed for the pharmacy to fill a prescription for Codeine Grimmer had given him. Judging by the pain flaring in his jaw, he was going to need it.

Forty

As THE GRANDFATHER CLOCK STRUCK ONE A.M., THE COUPLE ENTERED the dark warehouse where the heat of the day remained trapped within the stone walls. Slipping off her sandals, Kylie eased with bare step across the creaky floorboards. Without switching on the lights, she moved into the moonlit living room, pulled back the long velvet curtains and shoved the huge windows open. She turned toward the beautiful room with her arms folded pensively in front of her, as the summer breeze floated across her skin.

Jack came up behind her, their blue-tinged reflection glistening from the ornate mirror that hung over the mantel. As Kylie caught a glimpse of their wounded, sorrowful faces she not only felt as if she were staring at the final chapter of their lives together but at the ghosts of their past. Over the years the mirror had reflected the room's change and the couple's growth; like a silent chameleon stationed as a watchman it transformed with the events in their lives, contemplating their smiles and their tears. It had witnessed their first Christmas in the house and the hot summer nights when the sounds of their lovemaking drifted up from the sofa. It had heard their plans for the future, their regrets of their past, and was about to witness their end.

"Arlin can help me arrange an auction," Kylie said, her thin voice distant, receding into the shadows. "He already told me if I ever wanted to sell any of this that he'd help." She looked about like a stunned widow preparing for the worst after the sudden death of her lifelong mate. "And I'll call Rockbury Realtors on Monday. They can get us a good price after all we've invested in this place. At least enough to pay back the mortgage and some of the debt."

Jack turned toward the sea, his shoulders drawn and his head down. "You don't need to do that Kylie," he said quietly. "I can talk to Dora tomorrow to work something out. I got us into this mess and I'll get us out."

"It doesn't matter, I don't want any of it anyway," she said, flatly. "It'll only remind me of the past."

"Keep it, Kylie," he said painfully. "Your soul's in this place. You shouldn't have to give it up because of me."

Kylie looked toward him and even though he had his back to her, she could see that he was wiping away tears. She quickly looked toward the loft, anything to avoid having to witness his pain. "Why don't you sleep upstairs," she said methodically. "I'll take the guest room."

"No, that's okay," he said, refusing to turn around. "I'd rather sleep down here."

"Goodnight, then," she said, heading for the loft stairs. As her hand touched the railing, a tremor moved through her at the thought of ascending into the darkness. What had once been a haven for her and Jack had now become a chamber of terror. The hum of the fan was gone and had been replaced with a deathly silence that pressed upon the canopied bed. She was left to face it alone, for Jack would never again be waiting at the top to comfort her fears and to reassure her. As her legs slowly took her up, step by step, she felt as if she were ascending to the deathbed of her marriage, surrendering to the darkness that had been vying for her soul. The loneliness and fear stabbed into her breast as she gasped for breath. She sunk down upon the stairs, her shoulders trembling with her silent tears.

When Jack saw her he rushed to her and pulled her into his arms. "Shh," he whispered, kissing her lightly on the face.

"Jack, please don't," she cried, starting to pull away but he held her steadfast.

"I'm not going to let you go, Kylie," he said.

"Jack."

"No," he said, pulling her tighter and rocking her gently until he felt her relax in his arms. The wetness of her tears stung into the cut on his cheek, and the sweet smell of her soft hair brushed against his neck. His own chest began to tremble for he knew he would never find another woman like her. "I'm gonna make it right again," he vowed, his own tears escaping. "I'll move out but I'm not gonna give up on you, Wylie. I'm gonna rebuild your trust in me."

She gently pulled away, wiping at her wet face with the back of her hand but the tears kept flowing. "We can't keep going on like this, year after year."

"I know I keep repeating the same mistakes," he said. "So I'll get someone to help me change," he said, taking her face into his big hands. With her red cheeks and lips and her glistening eyes she appeared a delicate flower that had been bruised. "I'll prove myself to you so fast that you'll have me back in no time," he promised with a bittersweet smile.

She disappeared once again into his arms. "Jack, I'm so scared," she cried.

"Shh, it'll be okay," he said. He rubbed his hand along her back, when suddenly his gaze was caught by a strange shadow in the loft. He immediately stiffened as he realized it wasn't a shadow but that the fan had been boarded up. "Kylie," he said. "What happened upstairs?"

"Nothing," she murmured, squeezing her arms around his neck wishing never to let go. "I just can't spend another night up there alone!"

"I'm sorry," he whispered, petting her gently. "After everything that's happened I should never have left you here by yourself."

"I just didn't want anyone to be able to look in," she said. She would tell him in the morning about everything—about her past with Julius Vanderpoel and the man in the subway but at the moment her mind couldn't bear going through all of it again.

"Well I don't think you have to worry about that now," he said with a faint smile of admiration. "It looks like you've taken care of it once and for all."

She looked up at the boards but instead of feeling safer, the feeling of doom pressed upon her.

"Come on . . . I'll go up with you while you get into bed," he said, pulling her to her feet. "I'll bring you some ice for that eye."

Jack hesitated a moment when he saw the shotgun on the floor and the nearly empty bottle of bourbon by the bed. "I'm sorry, Kylie," he said. "I really am."

Embarrassed, she quickly bent to scoot the shotgun under the bed but as the blood rushed to her swollen eye a sharp pain jabbed into her brain. "Damn!" she shrieked, standing back up.

"Lay down and I'll get your ice," said Jack.

"By the way," she moaned. "Which one of you socked me?"

"Probably me," he admitted.

As he went down into the kitchen, she stripped to her underwear, replaced her tee-shirt and climbed into the soft bed. The emptiness of it sent another pang of sadness into her stomach. She thought of Jack within the sheets of another woman's bed, protecting her and making love to her until the wee hours of the morning; but instead of anger she felt an eerie pain. She would no longer be able to claim him as her own. She quickly pushed the image from her mind but she couldn't push the bleak sense of longing from her raw and exposed nerves. The warm summer breeze drifted across her bare legs, while she listened to the sound of him in the kitchen. The loneliness of the big dark warehouse closed in on her and she curled up like a child left in the dark.

After a moment, Jack returned with the ice wrapped in a washcloth and a glass of water. He handed it to her along with two pills. "Here you go," he said.

"Thanks but I don't need pills," she said. "I'm so tired I'll be out in no time."

She sadly watched him as his stitched and bruised hand popped the two pills into his own mouth. He reached for the bottle of bourbon and downed them with a swig. The pit in her stomach grew as she continued to imagine life without him.

"I'll never make it here by myself," she said softly.

Jack's shadowed eyes turned toward her. "Yes you will," he said, his voice practically a whisper. "Once I'm gone you'll do fine."

"No," she said, putting the cool ice to her eye. "I never did like living alone."

Jack sat upon the side of the bed, his muscular arms resting on his legs. He looked tired and sadder than she had ever seen him. Shame and remorse were etched in the tiny lines around his mouth.

"It'll be okay, Jack," she said, rolling toward him.

He shook his head with her words. "I never meant to hurt you," he whispered. "I knew I was screwing up but I just couldn't stop. Ever since the accident everything just keeps getting worse. It just feels like . . . like everything's been off. Like I'm not supposed to . . ." but he stopped, staring down at the bottle in his swollen hand.

"Not supposed to what?"

"Like I don't fit anymore."

"Hey," she said, turning his chin toward her. The cut on his cheek appeared like war paint in the darkness. "You just need to get back on the right track."

"Maybe so," he said.

She brushed her fingers through his hair. "Hey, what happened to that guy who's going to fix it?" she asked gently.

He looked toward her and forced a smile. "Yeah. I will, I promise." He stared back down to the floor, his fingers already picking at the stitches on his hand.

Kylie smiled to herself. "Leave them alone," she said gently.

He looked at his hand as if surprised that he had been trying to pull them out. With the bottle in hand, he stood from the bed. "Well I guess I better let you rest," he said, looking down at her.

There was a moment of silence between them. Though Kylie wanted to trust in the thought that it would all work out, she couldn't help but feel it was the beginning of the end. Jack took another swig of the whiskey and as the bottle tipped back down, his eyes rested upon her with so much longing it sent a wave of warmth through her bare loins. She suddenly imagined someone else on the receiving end of his desire and a rush of jealousy moved through her. He was so handsome with his windblown hair and determined gaze. Then his glassy blue eyes began to water as the craving of the man gave way to the fear of the boy. "I'll be lost without you, Kylie," he said, looking back down at his injured hand. His brow furrowed as he tried to hold back the tears. "I just can't imagine being without you even for a little bit."

She stared up at his golden curly hair and his baby soft lips. "No matter what, Jack Black, I'll always love you," she promised.

He took her hand into his own and kissed it softly. The tears began to trickle down his cheeks as his wet lips moved toward her own.

She pulled away, her heart breaking with the pain. "We can't do this," she said but his warm mouth had already touched hers. The taste of the whiskey drew her inward, his hot breath warming her own. Her resolution melted with the force of his touch, for she had never been able to refuse him. "Jack," she sighed. She kissed him with the passion of the pain and the sorrow as he descended upon her. The desire overtook her every move as she tugged at his jeans. Just as the zipper went down he pulled aside her panties and within seconds he was inside her. The feel of him shot through her and with it her anguish grew, for she couldn't imagine a more perfect fit. The warmth and the force was all that mattered.

"I can't lose you, Kylie," his low voice rumbled with determination.

She kissed his neck, suckling the salty taste of his sweat as if it were the very essence of her lifeblood. He thrust against her then pulled her on top. As she moved over him she could feel his eyes upon her, and knew he was admiring her as she enjoyed the pleasure. He wanted her there, over him, using him for her own. She looked down into the detached but admiring eyes that silently said *I have the power to make you feel.* Her head fell back and she lost herself in the senses.

As they finally fell away from each other, exhausted and spent, the coldness of the impending separation left them empty. Jack sat with his back toward her, while she lay sweaty in the sheets. "Do you want me to sleep downstairs?" he asked.

"No, not tonight," she said. "Please, just stay here with me."

The coolness of his sweat touched against her skin and though she felt safer with him by her side, the boarded up window hovered over her like a dark shadow. "Maybe we should go see that doctor that Dillon had me talk to after the accident," she whispered, as she ran the ice pack over her neck and face. "Maybe he would be able to help."

"Maybe so," Jack said, his voice low but unconvinced.

She swabbed her eye with the ice as she felt Jack's breath deepen and sleep quickly pull him in. For over an hour she lay gazing out at the sea contemplating their uncertain future. She held him tightly wishing the night would pass, clinging to him like a buoy in an ocean of darkness, until finally the moving water lulled her into slumber.

As the naked couple lay beneath the netted canopy of the bed, the silhouette of a tiny black spider edged along the wall then dropped down to the cool floor.

The bell struck three o'clock as the moon passed overhead and dipped toward the western sky.

Forty-One

THE DANCING GLOW ON THE WALL AND THE CRACKLING SOUND FROM below pulled her from her restless dreams. She had kicked the blankets from her body and they lay tangled at the foot of the bed. The ice in the washcloth had melted leaving the sheet damp and uncomfortable beneath her stiff neck. For a groggy moment, Kylie stared up at the ceiling trying to place the time of year, for she didn't remember building a fire in the living room hearth. She slipped from the bed, pulling a robe over her bare shoulders as she walked toward the stairs. Pausing at the banister, she looked down at the fireplace, puzzled by the burning logs. Then a cool ocean breeze wafted in from the open windows and she realized that Jack must have gotten up in the night and started the fire after the temperature dropped. She thought it strange though, that he had left the windows open. "Jack?" she asked softly, looking toward the bed, but his bare back moved only with the gentle breath of slumber.

Her silk robe brushed against her ankles as she quietly descended the stairs and went to the windows. It was a still night, the street below silent except for the whispering of the fluttering leaves. As she pulled the huge window shut, a large white ship glided silently through the harbor. She hooked the brass latch then closed the next window and reached for the thick curtains; the sun would be up soon and the thought of the blasting light after the long, hard night was too much. Just as she started to pull the heavy material over, she noticed a reflection in the window from behind her. Someone was sitting on the chaise lounge facing the fire. She froze for a moment, her heart thrashing with fear, then she slowly released the curtain and turned around.

The figure was unmoving, staring silently into the burning embers, the ashen profile none other than Julius Vanderpoel's.

Just as she started to move, to run from her own abhorrent mind, he turned toward her, his index finger pressing against his lips. "Hush, Kylie Rose," he whispered. "I'm not going to hurt you."

She stood perfectly still fearing the slightest movement could upset the balance of the moment, tipping the scale against her. *It's only in your mind*, her thoughts whispered, though she could feel the warmth of the fire that rounded out the image into an eerily perfect vision. It was as if she had created the sumptuous room for this moment, for never before had anyone appeared so at home in the luxurious setting as the apparition. His anemic complexion was the perfect pallet for the blue of the moonlight and the gold of the fire. His fine hair was pulled neatly back in the sophisticated way she remembered from her childhood. He wore an elegant smoker's jacket that was the brilliant color of scarlet and a beautiful complement to the canary lounge he sat upon. His aura was stately and refined as if he were the missing aristocrat the antique pieces had always longed for.

"Come closer," he beckoned with a gentle voice. But she remained frozen by the window, clutching her robe to her closely.

His confidence seemed to fade with her resistance, his shoulders pulling inward. "I don't blame you for being frightened," he said, his face growing shadowed and suddenly dark. "I must apologize for my unseemly behavior the last time we met. It's all new to me, you see— human emotion. It's hard to remember the proper responses." Then a devious smile escaped across his lips as his eyes flickered playfully. "I fear it's all because of you, my rose," he said. "This reawakening . . . this warring you've started in me."

True to his inference, something about him was different. Unlike the solid presence who had accompanied her through the Northend, or who had caressed her in the subway, there was something horribly unnatural about him. The inflections of his voice and the manner of his expressions were similar to the Julius of her childhood, yet like a duplicate copy that lacked the element of its original form, the pieces were impostors—disjointed and fragmented. He seemed to be fighting his own skin, as if it were difficult to be seated in front of her occupying the satin jacket and precisely fitted trousers. Though the room was still, there was a slight rustling of his clothes as if the air itself also fought against him.

She stood breathless, enthralled with the creature before her. A shiver rippled up her back, with the sound of the latched window creaking open behind her. She turned to see it moving on its own accord, then looked back to the observing eyes. He was watching her, soaking up her essence as if gazing at a long lost friend.

"Little Kylie Rose," he whispered, with a twinge of a smile. "I remember your freckles and that song you used to sing . . . 'London Bridge Is Falling Down.'"

For a fleeting moment, she saw him—Julius Vanderpoel, complete and whole; then as soon as the missing essence had appeared, it scampered away into the vacant eyes. As if noticing the change himself, his voice trailed off and he anxiously turned back toward the flames of the fire. "But time has passed, hasn't it?" he asked quietly.

His hand went to his temple and his brow furrowed as he rose slowly to the mirror that hung over the mantel. Kylie gasped at his fire-lit reflection for it somehow gave him quintessence. His eyes were sunken and dark as he stared into his own pale face.

"This is me," he said distractedly touching his skin. "This is how you remember me, isn't it?" he asked turning toward her. "These clothes?"

"Yes," she answered softly, her hands fidgeting together like they had when she was a child.

As if feeding from her conviction, his presence became more solid, like molten rock taking its form from her cue. He slowly began moving toward her, past the table and the overstuffed chair.

A rush of adrenaline urged her to step away, but she was too mesmerized by the being before her. She felt the wooden slats beneath her feet give way as he came to rest only inches from her.

"When I look into your eyes I know I've existed before," he whispered, the yearning for more vibrating behind his smooth voice. "I was flesh and blood," he said, reaching out to touch her skin, but his hand stopped before it grazed her cheek. "Not just a dream or a shadow moving over the wind. Julius Vanderpoel. That was my name wasn't it?"

She trembled with the feel of his breath upon her skin. He was there before her and as real as the room behind him and the floor at her feet. "Yes," she answered softly.

"I was human once, wasn't I?"

His sad and pitiful face brought tears to her eyes and she had to look away. "Yes," she whispered, a child's love rushing upon her.

"And there were others who knew me? And Ellen," he said. "She was real?"

"Yes," she answered, her own memory of the warmhearted teacher cutting through her.

"I only remember pieces of her," he said, bitterly turning to the side. "Just pieces. I remember a yellow dress that she used to wear . . . the feel of her skin, her sweet smell," he said, his voice trailing off. The glistening of tears formed at the rim of his eyes. "I destroyed her, didn't I?" he asked bitterly.

"Yes," she finally answered.

With his anger his face darkened. Then as quickly as it came, it passed and he looked to her again more gently. "Because of you I remember . . . piece by piece."

He turned again to the firelight as if the flames themselves were penetrating his life force, feeding and sustaining him. He stared into the glowing embers like a heroine addict ensnared by the pleasing effect. "Because of you I see colors," he said. "Flashes of beautiful reds and golden yellows . . . You make me human again."

His words swam about her head, swirling and tormenting her. She had resurrected him from memory—limb by limb and the resuscitation of the past was as painful to the creation as to the creator herself.

As if reading her thoughts, the flash of anger returned and he grasped her hand into his own. The breath left her body as he touched her fingers to the skin of his cheek which was smooth yet textured. "I'm real, Kylie Rose," he said, his flesh clutching down upon hers. "You give me substance in your eyes, but I'm here nonetheless. Not just some piece of your mind . . . not just a memory." A thin layer of moisture appeared above his lips that curled bitterly. "They've changed me, I know," he whispered. "I've become hideous and deformed."

At the sound of the ethereal "they," a chill prickled beneath her skin.

"But there's a part of me that remembers," he said with defiance, turning back toward the flames. ". . . that pulls me from the darkness they've surrounded me with." His attention drew to her once again, and as he assessed and admired her, his face softened. "If it weren't for you . . . if you hadn't defied your own fate, I would never have known."

"Fate?" she echoed.

"Your death, Kylie Rose. On the mountain."

Fear jetted into her throat, but she held it back. He was speaking of the plane crash, of her distorted memory, yet it was all merely part of the same nightmare cruelly repeating itself before moving forward into the next. It was one bad dream relating to another, both weightless and benign. Her lips moved but it took a moment for her voice to follow. "You were part of a dream," she said, the fluttering in her chest moving into her stomach. "That's all."

An amused smile twitched at the corner of his mouth. "A dream, Kylie Rose?" he said. "You disappoint me. From the moment you saw us, you knew what we were. I felt your gaze as the plane sped toward the mountain. I could feel your terror as we waited for you on the peak."

Suddenly the faceless gaze of the mountaintop specters flashed through her mind, the creatures the collective presence he had been speaking of.

"That's right. I've become part of them. Part of the many," he said, his words needling into her brain. "Part of that shadow . . . that glimpse that so few see." He smiled a dark knowing smile that held in itself pity. "But you saw, didn't you Kylie Rose? And you remember. The others don't, but you do. So few escape death," he mused. "So few bring us so completely into this world to reclaim them."

Her face suddenly became hot as she backed away from him. "That was a dream," she repeated, struggling to keep control of her accelerating fear. In an attempt to assimilate and digest, her mind was jumbling the accident with her childhood, with Julius Vanderpoel and the death of Ellen Young. He was simply part of her mind and he knew the words to say, where the files to her memories were stored and he was assimilating them to bring her terror. But the crackling fire beside her was real and the light upon his skin detailed his pores and the tiny hairs around his ear.

"What do you want?" she gasped, wishing for nothing more than to dispel the awful effigy.

"I don't want to hurt you," he said, in the same tender voice she had trusted as a child. "But you've known all along that you couldn't stay."

A chill of terror rushed up her spine at the malevolence that passed through his face. His eyes grew abruptly cold as the flicker of the fire disappeared from them. The brilliant red jacket began to fade to black and his hair slowly came loose from the leather tie and fell downward. "Forgive me," he said, his voice resembling the faraway screech that she heard in the elementary school. "But I'm afraid it's time."

The tolling of the grandfather clock suddenly resonated through the room as the window behind her slammed shut.

"Your husband was right," his voice continued as he turned his back to her and walked toward the fire. "You don't belong here anymore."

Then she saw the bright red can in his hands and smelled the pungent odor of gasoline. "I'm sorry, Kylie Rose," he said painfully, a glimmer of the man she knew breaking through. "But you were never supposed to have made it off that mountain." Then the hideous words escaped from his pale lips. "I've come to set things right."

As the sentence of demise stung through her, she began backing toward the staircase. "No," she whispered, for her worst nightmare was coming to fruition, the main character crossing a boundary into the flesh in order to destroy her and to destroy Jack. Whether risen from mere thought or from solid matter, the darkness had finally shown itself and it beheld the cold cruel features of death.

At once, adrenaline shot through her, yet her every limb remained leaden. There were sudden sounds coming from above her, footsteps on the fire escape and the cries of her husband coming from outside of the house, behind her. With her mind reeling, she looked toward the front door that was bolted shut. Then she heard it again, distinct and panicked.

"Kylie! Get out of the house!"

The smell of gasoline permeated the air as there was a bang at the window.

"Kylie!"

She turned to see Jack in the blue of the moonlight pounding against the windowpane, his face barely clearing the high ledge from the ground below. "He's going to kill you!" he screamed, his neck straining with the howling words. "Get out of the house!"

In a cry of release, she bolted for the door. With fumbling hands she turned the key to the lock and then yanked at the handle.

The cool night air rushed upon her as she fled from the warehouse, her bare feet pressing against the damp earth. She ran toward the front windows where Jack stood silently waiting, his face sorrowful and his eyes filled with tears.

"Jack!" she cried, but as she drew nearer she suddenly slowed for something was terribly off.

"I'm sorry, Kylie Rose," his lips said softly but the words were not his own. As the face continued to move like that of a puppet controlled by another, she looked up through the window above where Julius's lips finished her husband's words. "I'll save you for last, for I need you to feel," he said, his voice penetrating through the glass.

Then the image of Jack faded into thin air. "No!!" she screamed as she turned toward the stone ledge that kept her from reaching the high windows.

The colorless face stared down at her from above, the black coat taking a new form. "Forgive me," he said. Then with a violent swooping of his arms the gasoline splashed about the room, the light from the fireplace glittering in the falling liquid.

"JACK!!" she screamed. Backing away from the window, she strained to see into the loft, but saw no movement from the darkened bedroom. "JACK!!" she shrieked again, for the dark figure was moving up the stairs toward him. "No, you bastard!"

She ran toward the door but just as she reached it, it came flying shut bolting against her from the inside. "NO!!" she screamed pounding and kicking against the steadfast wood. She ran to the back alley, the rocks and rubble cutting into her bare feet. She was clear to the rear of the building before she remembered that she had raised and chained the fire escape from reach. When she saw how high it was from the ground, she nearly collapsed with hysteria for there was no other way into the building. "JACK!" she screamed again and again, hoping that her voice would penetrate the stones and mortar to awaken him.

THE FARAWAY sound of his wife's voice seeped through the black warmth, tugging him from the deep slumber. Jack opened his sleep-filled eyes, but the leftover alcohol and Codeine kept him from focusing. He dragged his legs through the tangled sheets and dropped them alongside the bed. When his feet touched the cool floor they felt strangely wet. The scent worked its way around his aching head then his eyes suddenly shot open and he stared downward; the liquid was gasoline and it lay in tiny puddles around his toes.

"What in the hell?" he gasped jumping to his feet. He heard Kylie's voice again calling to him from somewhere distant.

"Kylie! Where are you?!" he screamed looking about, unable to tell where the voice was coming from. He grabbed his jeans but instantly dropped them—they were saturated with the deadly substance.

He ran toward the stairs but hesitated a moment, for a trail of liquid led down each step into the living room. Just then he saw glimpses of Kylie outside, struggling to peer over the ledge into the high windows, her robe flying in the night, her face stricken with panic.

"He's going to ignite it, Jack!" she screamed looking toward the fireplace.

Jack followed her line of sight but he was confused for he saw no one.

Kylie grew more and more frantic. "Get out Jack! Get out!"

He vaulted down the stairs three and four at a time, but just as he reached the bottom the flames appeared to leap from the hearth on their own. The blast was swift and forceful. The fire instantly engulfed the living room floor in a blazing inferno. He heard Kylie screaming but there was nowhere for him to run.

Like a fuse to a bomb, the flames traveled in a straight line with lightning speed, past his feet and up the stairs to the loft where the pile of his clothes ignited with a tiny blast. He turned back to the windows and just before the floor around him exploded into flames, he saw his wife shriek in horror.

Unable to move forward or backward from the unbearable blaze, the hair on his arms began to sizzle from the heat. He stared down at the tiny singeing hairs unable to believe his own eyes, for there was no escaping; his time to die had come.

"NO!!" Kylie shrieked as she saw the dark figure move through the flames toward Jack, then thrust his hand out toward his chest. The fire engulfed them in a roaring inferno as Jack began flailing in the flames, screaming with pain and agony. "NOOO!!!" she wailed, as the adrenaline moved her forward toward the blazing building. The heat nearly knocked her back but she forged ahead. Her hands gripped the stones beneath the window and she tried to claw herself up, but she repeatedly slid back down to the ground. She could hear the screams of her husband rising above the roar and she caught glimpses of his arms reaching to get away from the pain. "Help him, God!!" she cried looking for anything to break the window with but there was nothing—no rocks, no stones, or even small sticks. "SOMEBODY HELP ME!!!" she screamed with all her might as her eyes searched frantically for a sign of Jack, but there was none. "JACK!!!"

Then like a giant vengeful hand, the heat pressed down upon her and crumpled her to the ground.

Cold fingers gripped her from behind and pulled her away from the blazing building. The frantic face of a middle-aged man was before her, his cheeks red and his brow sweating. "Is someone inside?" he implored.

She tried to say the words but they wouldn't form in her throat. Breaking lose from his steady grasp, she began running back toward the building. Then another set of hands gripped her tightly and pulled her away. It was two paramedics in uniform.

"My husband!" she screamed. "My husband's inside!!"

But they wouldn't release her. They dragged her to the street where a huge fire engine came clamoring up. When she looked back to the glowing inferno, she saw the black figure of Julius emerge through the flames, untouched by the fire around him. He pressed his fingers against the glass of the windowpane, his eyes peering through the commotion, searching her out.

As their eyes joined, the sounds around her crashed to silence and his lips began to move. "He's gone, Kylie Rose. He's gone."

"No," she whispered through her sobs, for she knew he could hear her. "Please, no," she begged.

"I had no choice," were his last words before his body began to change.

The glowing loft behind the dark figure came crashing down, exploding the sounds once again around her. As the black smoke rose up and swirled around his coat, his body began to stretch upward melding in with the smoldering elements.

"Stop him! Somebody stop him!!" Kylie screamed, once again breaking lose from the paramedics. They dragged her to the ground and forcefully began to restrain her.

As the tears choked her, she looked to the side, to the mutating body stretching and twisting upward to the top of the arching window. "Can't you see him?" she begged quietly as the feet rushed around her.

The paramedics looked toward the building, but all they saw was the black smoke swirling round and round.

The hideous creature leapt from the floor and hovered at the top of the room. Then a blast, shattering and thunderous sent the people running. As the windows blew out, the flames reached upward into the dark sky. Without notice, a raven glided silently from the shattered windows and followed the billowing smoke upward into the starlit night.

Forty-Two

THE SUN LIFTED BEHIND THE BLACKENED SHELL LIKE A BALL OF FIRE escaping from the bowels of the soot-filled structure. Though it was only 7:45 A.M. the temperature had already reached ninety-two degrees, the steam from the fire hoses hanging limp within the stagnant air.

Lieutenant Tom Woods stood back on the wet street as the last of the flames were doused and the crackling of the smoldering walls silenced. He took one more sip from the bitter coffee then grabbed an ax from the pumper truck.

"Let's see why this baby went up so fast," he said to the arson team assembled behind him. "Keep Lucky down here until we get that door open," he said to the inspector who held the trained dog on a leash.

As the lieutenant surveyed the faces of the small crew, a·frown creased his thick brow. "Where the hell is the photographer?"

Investigator Smits shook his head. "He's probably still in bed, sir."

"Christ," the Lieutenant grumbled, turning toward the building. "Fulton!" he called to a young stout firefighter who nearly jumped when he heard his name. "Tell Captain Buggs to keep one of those pumpers around for hot spots, and that we need a few men to move debris. And help these two investigators by securing the scene," he said. "We're going inside."

"Yes sir," the young man quickly answered.

"And keep those damn people back!" the lieutenant ordered. "If I end up with another contaminated scene, your ass is on the line."

"Yes, sir," responded the firefighter.

While two of the investigators stayed behind to search the crowd for witnesses, Lieutenant Woods led the arson team up the ladders to the front windows of the stone warehouse. He climbed inside first, the crunching rubble beneath his boots sending tiny particles floating upward.

As he gazed at the blackened mess of charred furniture and heaps of indiscernible remains, that old familiar feeling of despair filled his chest. Though he had been a firefighter for over thirty-five years, he would never adjust to the senseless waste that his lifelong nemesis left in its wake. He knew there was a body to be found but where he did not know. He sighed heavily for it was only a matter of minutes before he would have to face the hardest part of his profession; to find a victim, charred and unrecognizable, frozen in the midst of the most intimate and horrifying moment of their life. To find them exposed so crudely in the privacy of their own home was the worst of all. It not only made him feel like a voyeur trampling upon the sanctity of a private life, but the clues to that existence were more than he cared to know. To see the half burnt tennis shoes, the blackened photographs and the melted dolls was a reminder that no one was immune to the enemy. It could strike at any moment, day or night, and would wait for no one to escape its volatile path.

The lieutenant pushed back the sweat from his graying temple and moved slowly and methodically forward. The churning in his stomach instantly turned to acid when he spotted what he dreaded crouched on the floor at the foot of the stairs.

"Dennis," he said quietly to the fire department chaplain.

The chaplain moved forward with evasive eyes and tight lips and began praying over the dead body. The lieutenant's attention was drawn to the stairs behind the victim. After a lifetime of on-scene in-spections he instantly recognized the irregular burn patterns that were the telltale sign of arson; the wood of the stairs was shiny and black, and the line of charring distinct where flammables had been poured. "Looks like we may have accelerants here, boys," said the lieutenant. "Better get that door open so we can bring Lucky in to sniff it out."

"That's a pour pattern if I've ever seen one," said one of the inves-tigators. "Should we go ahead with the samples so the lab can get started?"

"No, I don't want anything disturbed until that damned photogra-pher shows up," said the lieutenant, shaking his head. "God al-mighty," he hissed, trying to avoid looking down at the body. "I should have known when we arrived and the whole damn place was in-volved."

"Take a look at that, Lieutenant," said the investigator.

Lieutenant Woods followed the pointing finger to the loft where the black soot moved up the walls but stopped short of the boarded up fan. "What in the world?" he grumbled.

"Do you suppose that's got anything to do with the chained up fire escape?"

"Probably so," he said, the acid gaining further ground. "By the looks of it, somebody was trying to keep him in the loft."

Another investigator called from the front entryway. "Lieutenant Woods, you got to see this," said the investigator.

"What is it?"

"Nothing was obstructing the door," he answered.

"You mean it's locked?" called the lieutenant.

"Yep."

"Isn't that the way the wife exited?"

"That's what she's claiming, but she must have jumped out the window. It's bolted from the inside."

THE SWARM of media and spectators had grown substantially by the time the lieutenant descended the ladder. When his heavy boots hit the ground, he spotted what looked like a professional photographer standing inside the yellow tape taking photographs.

"It's about time!" he called angrily, walking toward him. "We can't touch a damn thing until—" But he stopped short when he saw that it was not the staff photographer. It was a balding man in his late forties with light blue eyes and pudgy cheeks. "Who the hell are you?" he asked, but instead of waiting for an answer he turned to Corporal Fulton. "Fulton, what the hell did I tell you about this?!" he yelled.

Fulton instantly turned and his face went red. "Sir, I didn't think you'd mind since that's Clyde Tremblay and all," he said.

"Clyde Tremblay?" asked the lieutenant looking back to the face that wasn't the least bit familiar.

Tremblay nervously stuck out his hand. "It's an honor to see you again, Lieutenant. I worked in the insurance department a few years ago. I filed a claim for you."

The lieutenant took his hand, all the while eyeing the camera around his neck. "Our photographer's decided to take the day off," quipped the lieutenant. "Are you any good with that thing?"

Tremblay's face instantly went brighter. "Yes, sir."

"Mind taking some preliminary photos for us here?" asked the lieutenant. "So we can move on with our work."

Tremblay hesitated a moment then shook his head. "No, I don't think so," he said reluctantly, looking down toward his left arm that dangled stiffly at his side.

For the first time, the lieutenant saw that the camera had been rigged with a long stick to accommodate the dysfunctional appendage.

"I'd hate for them to be out of focus or something," said Tremblay.

The lieutenant nodded his head as he headed toward an approaching squad car. "Just stay out of the way then and don't go inside."

"Yes, sir," said Tremblay, his voice low and dejected.

The lieutenant pulled off his helmet as he leaned his head inside the passenger window of the squad car. "They would have to send you, Binaggio," he said with his first smile of the day.

Victor Binaggio got out of the squad car, his rumpled jacket hanging sloppily over his snug jeans.

"Why don't they teach you dicks how to dress?" asked the lieutenant.

"Blow me," said Binaggio. "What have you got?" he asked squinting toward the torched building.

"Well, even without the lab results it looks like someone doused it, then set a match to it," said the lieutenant, pulling a photo from his pocket. "We found this on the floor. The woman is the survivor and we're assuming the man we found inside is her husband. The body was burnt beyond recognition."

Binaggio looked down at the photo and his stomach took a turn south. "Shit," he sighed heavily.

"What?" asked the lieutenant. "Do you know 'em?"

"She was in the station last Monday, complaining that someone was stalking her and threatening her husband's life."

"Did you find the guy?" asked the lieutenant.

"No," admitted Binaggio with a troubled sigh. "She couldn't identify him from the mugs so there wasn't much we could do. Damn!" he hissed. "If I would have paid more attention the bastard might not have gotten him."

"Well, somebody got to him but I wouldn't be so sure it was a stalker," said the lieutenant. "I think I'd lean more towards the wife."

Binaggio looked up at him.

"She miraculously escaped without a single burn, through a door that was dead bolted from the inside with a key," explained the lieutenant.

He held up a plastic bag with a set of keys in it. "We found these still in the lock."

. . .

AS THE lieutenant and detective headed for the rubble the reporters behind the yellow tape clamored for a statement. The lieutenant turned back to the crowd, then looked to Binaggio with a wry smile.

"Hold on while I placate the savages," he said.

ALICE NEWFIELD clicked on the television atop the marble counter and groggily opened the refrigerator for some oranges. Her mouth was dry, and there was nothing like a stiff screwdriver to combat the venom of a hangover. As she turned for a knife, her eye caught the colorful news story that silently played. She instantly recognized the warehouse behind the reporter, though it was damaged nearly to the point of complete destruction.

"Ray!" she called toward the bedroom, her manicured fingers quickly turning up the volume. "My friend Jack . . . his house is on the news!"

As her lover entered the kitchen, his hair rumpled and a shirt as a make-shift skirt, the reporter's voice vibrated through the tiny speakers of the portable television.

". . . Can you confirm that for us, sir?" asked the neatly dressed reporter, moving the microphone from her own mouth to that of a middle-aged man. The screen beneath his white slicker read: LIEUTENANT TOM WOODS.

The lieutenant spoke confidently and bruskly. "Yes . . . There's one fatality, but pending notification of his family, I can't disclose his name at this time."

Alice gripped the counter and without a sound, her eyes grew shadowed.

"Do you think it's your friend?" asked Ray.

"It's gotta be," she answered certainly. "He and his wife lived there alone."

"Lieutenant Woods, have you determined the cause of the fire?" the reporter asked.

"We've got our arson team inside, right now, doing their job," he hedged. "But it'll be awhile before we can release any kind of statement."

The reporter pushed inward putting the microphone closer to his mouth. "The fire was fully involved within minutes. Could it be arson?" she asked quickly.

"As of now we're classifying it as suspicious in nature," he said. "But until we have samples examined by our chemist and our source and origins man does his job, we won't be able to say for certain," he answered patiently. "Now if you don't mind, I better get back to it," he said and started to turn away but a different reporter and cameraman aggressively stepped in front of him.

"Lieutenant Woods, we've been told that the wife escaped without injury," the reporter said. "Can you confirm this?"

The lieutenant answered curtly, his face in profile. "She's at a local hospital being treated for minor injuries," he said. "That's all I can say." As the surrounding reporters tried to close in on him, the lieutenant escaped back toward the warehouse.

While the live report continued, Alice lowered into a chair with her head in her hands.

"Are you okay?" asked Ray.

She slowly looked up at him, her eyes cold and her voice detached. "She did this," she said.

"What are you talking about?" he asked.

"It's the same couple that was fighting last night," she said. "If it's arson, she did it."

"That's a helluva conclusion, Alice," he chided. "She looked like a nice woman to me."

Alice shot angrily up out of her chair. "They've been having problems for ages, Ray. I thought she was going to kill him when she found out he and I had slept together."

"Well do you blame her?" he scoffed.

"I've seen her temper, Ray," she argued. "Didn't you see the way she stormed out of there last night? Not to mention the way she was brawling in the streets like a cat, for God's sake. I've seen dogs with more class than that," she said heading quickly out of the kitchen.

"What are you doing?" he asked, following her into the bedroom.

"If she did it, she's not going to get away with it," she vowed. Preparing for battle, she grabbed her most conservative suit from the closet and headed for the shower.

Forty-Three

WHEN DILLON GOT THE NEWS OF HIS BROTHER'S DEATH HE WAS CERTAIN there was some mistake. "It can't be," he muttered, looking up from the bed into the stunned face of Theresa.

"I'm sorry, Dillon," she said, her eyes pooling with tears. "That detective friend of yours has been trying to get hold of you but didn't know where to find you. That was David calling from the hospital."

Dillon got up from the bed, feeling nothing but a numbness in his chest and a strange tingling in his lips. "It can't be," he said again, for his mind couldn't even begin to grasp such a freakish thought. He had seen Jack less than twelve hours earlier—he was going to call him that morning as soon as he had breakfast and got back to his own place.

As he moved away from the sheets, Theresa was speaking to him, but her voice was merely a whisper against his goose-fleshed skin. He paused in the center of the room his mind completely numb. People died everyday . . . he was exposed to it all of the time in his profession, their father had died suddenly and his mother had lived with death for a year and a half before she succumbed to it; but this couldn't happen to Jack. Jack was the invincible one—the one who survived anything. Jack was going to be around forever.

"Dillon," Theresa whispered, helplessly moving toward him but he backed away. It was too much. His brother was everything to him; without Jack there was nothing. The touch of her hand would force him to believe, and if he did, it would somehow drive the final stake into his coffin.

Within the silence, a sense of urgency rushed through him. He went toward his pants which lay rumpled on the floor. "I've got to call my grandmother," he said distractedly.

Theresa reached out to him. "Sit down for a minute," she said softly.

"I can't," he said, for he knew there was something important to be done. "I've got to take care of this."

His legs felt heavy and his balance was off but he managed to slip into the jeans. As he reached down to button the fly it felt as if someone else's hands were attached to his arms for his fingers would not

obey his will. He impatiently looked down and when he saw his battered knuckles he immediately stopped for he could still feel the grotesque sensation of Jack's face yielding to his anger. "Jack," he said
softly thinking of his brother's pained and swollen eyes in the emergency room. He was gone. Just like that his best friend and only sib-
ling was gone. Without even a chance to save him, he had been
snatched from his grasp.

Don't just stand there, Dill! his brother's happy sun-kissed face called
from the other side of the court. *If you don't keep moving you'll get anni-
hilated!*

The voice and the person had been real and alive, but he would
never capture the same moment again. There was no turning back, no
negotiations or deals to be made. Jack was gone. He would never see
his brother again, nor touch him anew for he would only exist in his
memory. But the thought of it was too painful to endure. He was being asked to accept something that went against his every instinct.
Humans weren't made to endure such finality; it was too cruel—too
hideous.

He turned to escape from it but was met with the pity and anguish
in Theresa's eyes. He quickly looked away for he couldn't face it. His
chest began to cave as he moved back and forth in front of her trying
to shake the overwhelming sorrow grumbling beneath his skin threatening to devour him.

"I've got to get out of here," he said, his breath stealing away from
him.

"Dillon, stop," Theresa said, moving toward him.

"I've got to get—" he felt her arms grasp upon him as the grief
overtook him.

Forty-four

IN SPITE OF THE HEAT RIPPLING FROM THE ASPHALT OUTSIDE OF THE
hospital, a pack of reporters continued to wait in the sun with cameras
poised, ready for action. When the BMW pulled up to the ambulance
entrance they all turned in the direction of the car, but when they saw
faces they didn't recognize they let their cameras down.

Dillon and Theresa quickly got out of the car, and headed for the emergency room. The doors slung open and along with a parching gust of wind they rushed in, immediately turning toward the room where Kylie was being treated.

As they rounded the corner into the hallway, they saw Victor Binaggio pacing under the fluorescents in front of the treatment room doors.

"She must be in there," said Theresa, handing a brown paper bag of clothes to Dillon. "David said she needed something to wear. I'll wait out here."

When Binaggio saw them coming, his back stiffened and he turned to face them. He could tell that Dillon was angry. With his rumpled shirt, dark mussed hair and bandaged brow, the doctor appeared an equal match for the strapping detective.

Theresa fell slightly back, as Dillon continued angrily forward. "What's this all about, Victor?" he asked crossly, his face flushed and his breath winded. "I heard on the radio that it was arson and that you're thinking of charging Kylie."

"Unless she starts talking, I won't have any choice," Binaggio said gravely.

"You know as well as I do that she's not the one who did this," he said.

The detective stood back as if to calm the situation. "You don't know all the facts."

"I know enough," said Dillon. "I know that I sent her to you because some freak was following her threatening Jack's life . . . and what do you do?" he demanded. "You sit on your ass until he kills my brother then you have the balls to blame it on his wife?!"

"Her story doesn't add up," said Binaggio, looking toward the bare wall to avoid the furious blue eyes of the doctor. "She's the only one who ever saw this phantom stalker. Nobody else can verify that he even exists."

"That's your job!" exclaimed Dillon.

The detective looked patiently down at the floor. "Our officers responded the minute they got a call from her last week saying that someone was lurking around on the roof . . . just listen for a minute. When our officers responded they found nothing. Absolutely no sign of a prowler. Your brother admitted that he hadn't seen him either . . .

only Kylie had. The day before that she came into the office and looked through the mug shots and positively identified a dead man. That was before she knew that he had been executed for murder."

"So what?" asked Dillon. "He obviously looked like the guy."

"No, I think she was just looking for a scapegoat and it backfired. She was positive he was the one," said the detective. "She just didn't have any idea that we kept photos of people that are already dead as reference. It's not uncommon for someone to try to stage something like this . . . claim to others that someone is stalking—"

"I don't even want to hear this," interrupted Dillon. "She didn't do it and you know it."

"Well, somebody did," said the detective. "Pure and simple. It was premeditated, clear down to the fire escape that was chained up."

"The fire escape doesn't have anything to do with this," said Dillon. "She was obviously trying to keep the bastard out. Because you wouldn't protect her, she had to fend for herself," he said, turning for the doorway to the treatment room. "You're the one that let this happen," he said. "You're the one who let the son-of-a-bitch get to my brother."

As he started through the door, Binaggio stuck his hand up to stop him. "Nobody got to your brother but his wife," he said, his face suddenly red. "What was the fight about last night?" he asked.

"Why don't you ask Kylie?" Dillon snapped, his eyes seething.

"I already did, but she wouldn't say," said the detective. "I've got a helluva police report—she's all banged up and you're not looking so pretty yourself."

"And what the hell is that supposed to mean?" asked Dillon.

"Nothing," said the detective, "other than it was a helluva fight."

Dillon could feel the pulse of his heart in his throat as he glared eye to eye with the detective. Theresa stepped toward him and put her hand on his arm. "It's okay, Dill," she said softly.

Her comforting tone made the throbbing pain in his heart erupt once again. He shook his head, trying to dispel the insanity of it all. "Jesus Christ, don't you understand?" he asked through a low faltering voice. "She just lost her husband, her home and everything she owns. Now she has to deal with this?" In spite of the tears welling in his eyes, he looked directly into the detective's gaze. "She loved Jack more than life itself," he said quietly. "The last thing she would have done was to burn him alive in his own home."

The detective looked sadly away. "I'm sorry, Dillon," his deep voice rumbled. "I really am. But I have to do my job. At the time of the fire she was the only one in the building except your brother and unless you can get her to talk, we're left with no choice but to charge her with his murder."

THE MOMENT Dillon opened the door he was taken aback by the strange burnt scent that permeated the room. The sight of Kylie sitting atop the table, broken and sorrowful, made his whole body begin to ache. The bruise around her eye had turned a deep purple, her auburn hair hung in knotted clumps and her robe was ripped and dirty. There were scrapes on her hands and arms, and a nurse was busy bandaging her right foot that had been stitched along her heel.

"Hey Wylie," he said with a bittersweet smile.

When she turned toward him, his heart sank even further; her eyes were so puffy from crying that they completely altered the appearance of her face. She looked as if she had been brutally beaten, shedding every last tear possible; but the moment she saw him, her bloodstained eyes filled once again with grief and began to spill over onto her red cheeks.

"Dillon," she murmured through a cracked hoarse voice, reaching her bandaged arms out toward him.

He had never seen her look so small, or sound so weak and defeated.

As the nurse stepped aside, he gently embraced Kylie and held her tight. "Shh . . ." he said softly.

"He was on fire," she gasped into his ear, her quiet sobs shaking through his body. "I saw him on fire, Dillon."

He tried to ignore the abhorrent vision her confession evoked, but the smoky odor of her hair brought it to life with lucidity. The sickening smell became the burning of his brother's flesh as he screamed and begged for help. His hands fought against the brilliant flames—the skin peeling and melting from his fingers exposing the bloody meat beneath. "Shh," Dillon whispered through clenched teeth, squeezing his eyes tighter together. Tears once again escaped down his cheeks. He wanted to pull away, to flee from the overwhelming pain, but knew if he did she would silence the horrific memory and bear it alone. "It's okay," he said softly, stroking her hair.

After a long moment she calmed and he slowly released her. That's when he noticed the officer standing behind the table watching them. "Can we have some privacy here please?" he asked, angrily wiping his tears with the back of his hand.

"I'm sorry, sir, but I've got my orders to stay near the patient."

Dillon walked swiftly over to the young man in uniform. "Is she under arrest?" he asked quietly yet sternly.

"Uh, no sir," said the officer.

"Then get the hell out of here while I confer with my patient," he ordered.

"We need a sample of her blood," said the officer.

"Then get a warrant."

Kylie didn't even seem to notice that the officer was leaving the room or for that matter had ever been in there. Dillon looked toward the nurse. "Sally, bring me 10 milligrams of Valium."

"Yes, Dr. O'Rourke," said the nurse, quickly disappearing through the door.

Dillon gently took Kylie's bandaged hands into his own. "I'm going to give you something to help you sleep, but first I need to ask you something," he said.

She looked up at him and her brow immediately furrowed as if she anticipated what the question would be. "He asked you to talk to me, didn't he?"

"Yes," he answered.

"I didn't kill him, Dillon," she said, her lower lip quivering as she toyed with the chain around her neck. "I would never—"

"I know that Kylie," he said, softly squeezing her hand. "But unless you tell Binaggio what happened he's going to arrest you."

She pulled away from him and her gaze grew distant. "I can't," she whispered.

"If you don't talk to them they'll think you're trying to hide something."

"I know that Dillon," she said anxiously. "I just need time to think. I can't think right now."

"You don't have to explain anything to him," he said. "He just wants to know what you remember."

She sat silently for a moment, staring down at her necklace. "I'll never be able to convince him of what happened. No matter what, it's going to look like I did it," she said.

"Kylie, nobody's going to think anything wrong," he said. "If you're scared to talk to him, then just tell me what happened."

"I can't."

"Now is not the time for you to be stubborn."

"I can't, damn it!" she suddenly exclaimed. "You would never believe me! And I'll be damned if I'll listen to another person tell me I'm hallucinating or dreaming or imagining things! Jack's dead because I didn't have faith in my own mind!" she said. "If I would have screamed sooner he'd be alive. He'd be alive," she repeated, her chest beginning to heave once again. "It's real and I can't let it happen again," she whispered vehemently, the tears trickling down upon her robe.

The conviction in her voice sent a chill scurrying up Dillon's neck. "What do you mean 'happen again'?" he asked.

"I need to call Amelia," she suddenly declared, stepping down from the table but the pain from her foot caused her to draw upward.

"You should stay sitting."

"No, I've got to keep trying her until I get an answer," she insisted, looking anxiously toward the phone. "If they arrest me I won't be able to call."

"Kylie," he said, taking her by the shoulders so that she was forced to look at him. "They won't arrest you if you just tell the truth. You saw who did this didn't you?"

Even though she squirmed beneath the direct question, the terror that moved through her eyes told him he was right. "It was the man following you, wasn't it?" he asked.

For a moment it seemed as if she would answer, but then she suddenly turned away. "You've got to help me get out of this Dillon. I don't know how to get out of this."

"If you're scared someone's gonna hurt you, the police can protect you," he said. "But you've got to talk to them!"

He held her tight, but like a stubborn child she closed up to him as he had seen her do so many times before. "I can't," she whispered.

Then her full lips pressed together and her eyes became set. Even the tiny freckles on her face seemed to scream out their obstinance.

Abruptly the door opened and Theresa looked inside. "She better—" but then she stopped. "Dillon?" she questioned.

He suddenly realized how tightly he was grasping Kylie's arms and immediately released her. "I'm sorry," he said with a heavy sigh running his hand through his curly hair.

"You'd better get dressed, Kylie," said Theresa solemnly. "I think they're getting ready to arrest you."

CLOSING the door behind them, Dillon and Theresa waited in the hallway for Kylie to dress.

"Did she tell you what happened?" Theresa asked.

"I think it was the guy stalking her but she's scared to say," he sighed, pacing about.

"Well she better start talking," said Theresa nodding toward the emergency room.

Dillon's stomach instantly dropped when he saw Alice Newfield at the other end of the corridor speaking with Binaggio.

"Do you know her?" asked Theresa.

"Yeah," he grumbled, watching the perfectly dressed woman speak with animation. "She's had the hots for Jack for years."

"Well, I think she's trying to stir up trouble," said Theresa. "She went through a lot to track down the detective. I heard her say the station told her where to find him."

"Did you hear anything else?"

"She was saying something about some fight Kylie and Jack had last summer. Something about a bar in Cambridge."

"Damn," said Dillon. "Leave it to Alice Newfield to have the memory of an elephant. Did you hear anything else?"

"No, after that they decided I was listening too closely so they moved down the hall."

"What makes you think that they're getting ready to arrest her?" he asked.

"A minute ago Binaggio called out to that skinny officer to get the squad car and to try to avoid the press."

• • •

EVERY INCH of Kylie's body ached as she painfully stood beside the bed, pulling the khaki pants past her bruised and skinned legs. She reached down to buckle them but her eyes were so swollen that her vision deceived her. The lights of the room splayed into tiny crystals that danced around her fingers and the clasp. The snowflakes began to blur as her tears once again started to fall. "Shh, Wylie," she whispered, imagining Jack's lips saying the words, his voice caressing her. "It'll be okay. It'll be okay."

She pulled the white blouse over her achy shoulders and thought of nothing but her husband beside her, with his steady hands and muscular arms helping her every step of the way. The sandals were slightly larger than her feet, the strap sliding down her heel.

The moment the door swung open and she saw Binaggio's face she knew that he had decided her guilt. Her legs grew weak, but she pushed back her head and stood tall. Dillon came in right after the detective, his face worried and sad yet he gave her a wan smile.

"Mrs. O'Rourke," said Binaggio, rolling her name over his tongue as if it froze his very being. "Dillon tells me that you may have seen who did this."

Dillon faltered a moment under her gaze, then stepped forward. "Tell him what you saw, Kylie. They can protect you."

The moment had come and she knew she needed to come up with an answer but her mind was simply too wrung out to think. They were both waiting for her response but she had none.

"I have a witness who says that you and your husband were fighting over money last night—"

"Wait a minute," interrupted Dillon. "Can't you see that she's just scared to tell you?"

Binaggio gave him an irritated glance, then turned back to Kylie. "Again, Mrs. O'Rourke," he said impatiently. "Did you see someone else in your house last night?"

The two men were watching her . . . waiting. "I think I saw someone," she finally answered.

"Do you think it could have been the man that was stalking you?" asked Dillon.

Binaggio turned angrily to the young doctor. "If you don't let me ask the questions," he snapped, "you're gonna wait out in the hall."

When the detective once again turned toward her, she saw the skepticism in his eyes even before he repeated Dillon's question. "Was it the man who was supposedly stalking you and your husband?"

Kylie's heart was thumping against her chest, telling her to speak the truth, but the insolence in the detective's manner kept her lips from moving. She would not be able to convince him that someone else did it, let alone the dead man she had identified the week before. "I . . . I couldn't say," she answered softly. "It all happened so fast that I was confused."

"How did you get outside, Mrs. O'Rourke?" quipped the detective.

Kylie felt her brow sweating and she nervously wiped it away. "I thought I heard my husband's voice coming from around the house, so I ran out the front door."

"Do you know where he was when the fire started?" asked the detective.

"He was at the foot of the stairs."

The detective suddenly looked up. "Then you saw the fire start?"

"I . . . I'm not sure," she hedged.

"Then what makes you think he was at the foot of the stairs?"

She tried to think, but her mind wouldn't work.

"Okay," sighed the detective. "Let's try another. Where were you when the fire started?"

She knew that if she said she was already outside she would be unable to explain.

"It's a simple question," said the detective.

"I'm sorry, I . . . I don't remember," she finally answered.

The detective gave Dillon a knowing glance, then proceeded with his earlier line of questions. "The fight last night, Mrs. O'Rourke . . . Was it about money?"

"Yes," she answered softly.

"Do you have a life insurance policy out on your husband?" he asked.

"Don't answer the question Kylie," said Dillon.

"Why not?" asked the detective. "Unless of course she has something to hide."

"My husband and I both have life insurance," she said.

"What's the amount on your husband?" asked the detective. "If you know, of course."

Kylie thought of the day she and Jack decided on the policy. They had argued for hours over how much to take out. Jack was insisting on enough to pay off the warehouse and to support the business in case something happened to him. She had reluctantly agreed even though the amount scared her. "Half a million dollars," she said quietly.

The sum hung in the air like a dirty stench. Even Dillon looked stunned.

Binaggio instantly reached for his cuffs from his belt and stepped toward her. "You have the right to remain silent," he said. "Anything you say can and will be used against you in the court of law . . ."

The detective pulled her hands behind her back and latched the ice-cold metal tightly upon her wrists. "If you cannot afford an attorney, one will be appointed to you . . ."

"You're hurting her wrists," Dillon said.

Binaggio spouted something angrily back to him but his voice trailed off as the senses around her dulled and her mind became numb. The bodies and voices moved around her, deciding her fate, while her thoughts drifted to the night before, to Jack's gentle touch under the canopy of their soft bed.

The detective's rough hand clasped down upon her arm as he pulled her toward the hallway. When Theresa saw her come out of the door, her eyes filled with tears and she quickly looked away. There was a uniformed police officer walking briskly in front of them, the clicking of his boots on the shiny floor setting the pace.

"Do you have to take her out that way?" she heard Dillon exclaim from behind them just as she saw the inquiring faces peering through the windows.

"Get back, Dr. O'Rourke, you're obstructing justice," said Binaggio as they burst through the emergency room exit.

The bright sunlight blasted her raw eyes sending pain screeching into her brain. The detective pulled her forward as she heard the shuffling of footsteps upon the pavement and voices mumbling all around her. She struggled to keep her eyes open against the overwhelming heat, but she caught only glimpses of the cameras and the faces.

"Coming through, folks," said Binaggio, his hand holding her tight, guiding her.

As her eyes slowly adjusted she saw the faces staring back at her, cold and without pity. Their contempt took her breath, for they no longer saw her for who she was, but for who they believed her to be: a ruthless murderer. With every click of the camera, she felt something taken from her, something violated and exposed. Her impulse was to look away, but the voice of Jack urged her to keep her head high.

The officer who had been ahead disappeared somewhere into the crowd as several cameramen ran backwards in front of her. Then the squad car suddenly pulled up and Binaggio opened the back door.

Just as she lowered herself onto the dark vinyl seat, a reporter tapped the glass so that she would look at him. "Mrs. O'Rourke, why did you kill your husband?"

The detective's hand slammed the door and shoved the reporter back. "You know better than that," she heard him say through the glass. "There's no talking to the prisoners."

She looked straight ahead to the seat in front of her, the flash of the cameras pinging against the shiny vinyl. At last, they were pulling away, the crowd left behind.

Forty-Five

AFTER BINAGGIO HAD SEEN KYLIE O'ROURKE THROUGH BOOKING, he returned to his office where his partner, Doobie, sat reading the paper.

"Don't you ever work?" he grumbled. "There's a lot of shit to do on this one," he said, grabbing one of the books of mugs and dropping it on his own cluttered desk. He turned to the page of Julius Vanderpoel's photo and removed it from the binder. "Just to be sure, we ought to check the records for anyone who looks like this guy."

"Half a million bucks says she did it," said Doobie.

"Yeah, probably so," said the detective. "But I don't want the fact that we let this go by come back and bite us in the ass later."

He took a seat behind his piled desk, wiping the sweat from his neck. "It's hotter than hell in here," he groused, reaching behind himself to close the blinds tighter against the blinding sun. "It must be a hundred and fifty degrees out there."

"Detective Binaggio?"

The deep Irish-tinged voice had come from the doorway.

Binaggio turned, unsure whether the tense, resonating query held anger or fear. More than once he had too quickly admitted his own identity and ended up in a less than desirable situation. Only a few months earlier an irate lover of a newly arrested drug dealer had walked straight into his office and had nearly shot a hole into his chest. But the man standing before him, while large and obviously powerful, didn't appear to be wielding any weapons.

"What can I do for you?" he asked. As the man moved closer, Binaggio recognized him from somewhere, but exactly where he was uncertain. The stranger's stature reminded him of an old-time film star, one with the poise and power of John Wayne, yet with the sad, disarming eyes of Spencer Tracy.

"I'm Sean McCallum," said the big man.

As Binaggio stood to greet him, it struck him why the man looked familiar. It was his thick lashes, unruly red hair and the way he held his head so full of pride; he could be none other than Kylie O'Rourke's father.

"You must be here about your daughter," he said certainly, taking the calloused hand.

"Yes," came the grave reply.

"Won't you have a seat?"

The offer went ignored, the big man standing silently in front of him, staring at him. A slight flurry of concern began to grumble in Binaggio's belly. Maybe he had misjudged the sorrowful face. Maybe the protective father had come to tear out his heart with his teeth. "We can't allow you to see her today because—"

"I'm not here to see my daughter," said the father, gruffly. "I'm here to take her home."

Binaggio's fingers played with a pencil on his desk. "Well, Mr. McCallum, I'm afraid that's impossible. Your daughter's been charged with first degree murder and is awaiting her arraignment."

McCallum's eyes began to flash with the anger the detective had been expecting. "Dillon O'Rourke told me that someone was stalking her, threatening my son-in-law's life."

"So your daughter claims," said Binaggio.

"He also said that she came to you for help . . . that she identified the wrong man so you just quit looking," he said, thumping his finger down on the desk. "I want to know why my daughter's in jail and why you're sitting on your butts instead of out looking for the lunatic who did this!"

"Why?" asked the detective. "Because we don't believe he exists. We think she was just setting us up so that we would think there was someone after her," he said, motioning to the mug shot as if to dismiss it.

The fisherman's eyes were caught by the photo on the desk and he suddenly froze. "What . . . what is . . ." he stammered.

"This is who she identified," answered the detective, sliding the photo of Vanderpoel toward the father. "And I can guarantee he's not following your daughter . . . he's dead."

The father's face drained of color. "Sweet Jesus," he whispered, wiping his brow.

"You know him?"

The big man looked up at him, his eyes suddenly sorrowful and pained. He started to answer, but then put his head down. "My daughter is very confused right now," he said. "That's why she's not telling you everything."

"Usually when a suspect won't tell us everything it's because they've got something to hide," said Binaggio.

"Or they don't remember," said the father, looking down at the photo.

"Please," Binaggio said motioning to the chair, for the powerful physique was making him nervous.

McCallum reluctantly acquiesced, but the tiny chair seemed barely capable of containing him. "Something happened when she was a child," the father said slowly. "She witnessed the murder of her teacher and she identified the killer to the police. If she saw who did this, she may be blocking it out. That's what she did before. She blocked it out for over twenty years."

"What happened to the killer?" asked Binaggio.

"That's him right there," answered McCallum, nodding to the mug shot.

At first Binaggio was certain he had heard wrong. "This man?" he asked.

"Yes," the father answered gravely. "The memories have just

started coming back to her. She's confused and . . ." but the big man's voice trailed off.

The detective sat utterly confounded. Even Doobie had stopped reading the paper and was staring at the father.

McCallum's head went to his hands and he sighed again as if every breath were a labor to the vast muscles. "I know how this must look," he said. "My daughter's not . . . she's not crazy or anything. She's just confused and upset. That's why she won't talk. If she came to you and said she was seeing Julius Vanderpoel she was telling the truth. It's a symptom of repressed trauma—you can verify that with a doctor. Whether or not she saw the man that did this, I don't know. But I can tell you that if she did, she's either too terrified to say or simply doesn't remember. She didn't do this. I know my daughter and she would never do this."

"They've found no evidence that there was anyone else in the house," said the detective. "The lieutenant of the arson investigation thinks she set it and then went out the window."

McCallum shook his head. "She's just blocking it out." He looked up at the two men. "She just needs someone to help her remember who it was. She doesn't need to be in jail, she needs to speak with a doctor."

The pit in Binaggio's stomach had turned to pity. He had seen so many senseless deaths at the hands of a person who had gone over the edge—and it was the freak, sudden change in a loved one's personality that the families could never conceptualize.

"Get a good lawyer for your daughter," said Binaggio. "Her arraignment is tomorrow at noon. Have her attorney ask the judge to send her for psychiatric evaluation. If she's not fit to stand trial they'll find a facility that can help her."

"My daughter's not a murderer," he said. "She just needs someone to help her remember what happened."

"I understand," said the detective. "I can sympathize with your situation, but I'm not here to help your daughter, that's what lawyers are for. I'm here to protect the rights of the man who's dead."

"All you have to do is look at her and know she's not capable of something like this," argued McCallum.

"Unfortunately, it's not always that easy," said the detective.

"Sometimes it's the ones you would least expect. Believe me, I'd love nothing more than to release your daughter. I consider Dillon a friend of my family's and I know this is killing him. But I have to do my job and right now she's my number one suspect."

Forty-Six

CHECKERED MOONLIGHT DAPPLED THE CEMENT FLOOR, WASHING THE tiny cell in a deep shadowy blue. Kylie lay curled on the narrow cot, her face buried in the musty pillow she clutched between her hands and legs, her body shaking with grief. She was exhausted to near-delirium, yet her mind would not let her rest.

The sight of Jack thrashing in the fire repeated in her thoughts like a torturous scene caught on film to be replayed, time and again, backwards, forwards and in slow motion, herself captive in the theater of her own cruel mind that would not let her escape the effigy. Even the smoky stench of her own body added to the hideous picture of Jack screaming for her help against the licking flames. And no matter how many times it replayed, the outcome was always the same. Time and again she ran from the warehouse, leaving him behind to die. Through the cathedral-like windows she watched the dark figure pour the gasoline, and Jack stand from his bed frightened and confused. Over the sound of her screaming, he leapt down the stairs as the killer dipped his own hands into the flames of the hearth to ignite his handiwork.

"Jack," she whispered, doubling with pain as their home burst into flames all around him.

With regret gnawing at her heart and the wool blanket scratching at her exposed skin, she rubbed her dirty hand against her forehead. She wanted nothing more than to rest, but the thought of yielding to the vast dark realm of sleep was too terrifying. The land of dreams was somehow closer to the heinous dimension of death. The idea that Jack had been caught in the shadowy world full of evil and merciless creatures horrified her. It wasn't the magnificent place she had been promised as a child, filled with billowing clouds of heavenly angels; it was a hellish realm with creatures that mutated into sinister birds and deformed spiders and rats. Never again would the ground feel solid nor the air be simply air. They held a veil that could be ripped back at any moment by the brutal hand of death to snatch at its will. It had taken Jack, dragging him through a doorway of harrowing pain into the evil dominion.

She heard his screams once again ricocheting off the dim walls. "Stop," she groaned, pressing her hands into her eyes that felt like two lumps of dough. She needed to gain control of her grief, but never before had she felt such desolation.

Everything was gone: her husband, her home, her possessions, even her body had come to be ruled by another. She had been processed through the booking like a monstrous criminal dehumanized before the slaughter. They had photographed, registered and examined her, their voices and cold hands still upon her.

The vault around her pressed inward, taking every drop of air and replacing it with despair. "Jack," she whispered, though she knew he could no longer help her. He was gone and in a matter of only hours their life had been shattered, invaded by death then pilfered through by authorities who dissected and analyzed what was left. Their darkest secrets had been exposed to the scrutiny of strangers; even their most intimate of moments had not been left sacred.

What time did you go to bed, Mrs. O'Rourke? goaded Binaggio as he paced behind her chair in the questioning room. *Were you still fighting when you went to bed?*

Kylie squeezed the rough pillow tighter between her legs to ease the hollow aching, but her mind continued to taunt her.

I've requested an examination, said the attorney seated through the visitation glass, his deep-set eyes in shadow.

She squeezed tighter, yet she could still feel the icy utensils poking and prodding, drawing samples from her vagina.

We need them, Mrs. O'Rourke, said the eyeless face. *They won't simply take your word that you had reconciled your differences.*

Even their lovemaking had been put under the scrutiny of a microscope to be viewed in the name of justice.

You've got to talk to them, love, came the voice of her father. *Even if you don't remember, you've got to at least tell them that. They can do whatever they want with you if you don't cooperate.*

But she knew that if she confessed the secrets of her mind, they could do even worse. She imagined herself within the harrowing dungeons of Bridgewater Psychiatric Facility with deadening drugs coursing through her veins. No matter what, the price of her freedom would be demanded for her husband's death. At least in a prison she would still have sovereignty of her own mind.

She sighed deeply and tried not to think of the enclosing cell. If she did, the panic would surely overtake her.

Through hazy eyes she looked up at the black, peaceful sky twinkling beyond the bars. It was hard to believe that it was the same sky that had hurled the Merlin IV toward the mountains, and the same stars that had glittered high above the nightmarish world she and the others had tapped into. A world alluded to by Dr. Jordan of ancient religions where souls could be dislodged and wander aimlessly... where death came in the form of creatures, slipping silently through the nights.

She thought of Amelia, hundreds of miles away in Savannah and her heart sank. Little did her friend know that there had been truth in what she had thought illusion. Whether merely part or all of the dream had been real, they truly had wandered the storm fighting the dark forces of death.

Daddy, you've got to call Amelia ... you've got to warn her for me.

Warn her of what, love?

Just tell her to be careful.

Careful of what, Kylie?

But the question had gone unanswered. How could she have possibly explained that they were supposed to have perished on the mountain and that Julius Vanderpoel had been among the creatures sent to deliver them. Julius Vanderpoel. A murderer from her past, somehow resurrected, somehow twisted and warped into something new, something unspeakable and inhuman. Perhaps she truly was a madwoman. How else to explain that Vanderpoel had now become a spirit of the dead sent to take her and the others to their intended fate? What reality would allow such cruel irony, such absurdity? How would she ever explain such lunacy to her father—a man of the earth and the sea? There had been no chance of it, so she had remained silent.

She imagined her friend working alone in the cathedral, while an unseen creature lurked in the shadows, waiting to snatch her life. Perhaps it had already happened and Amelia lay cold in some dingy morgue. She moaned with the possibility, her cry absorbed by the quiet cell.

Her thoughts turned to the elderly attorney, Dale Benson, who was the only other survivor who had been with them and wondered if a figure prowled in the shadows of his law firm. Or perhaps he had already met with some untimely death; one that was logically explainable to those around him but that she herself would be able to see through.

Tell them, love, came the voice of her father. *Or they'll think you're the one to blame.*

"I am, Daddy," she whispered to the walls. "I am."

She had been given the foresight and if only she had trusted her own mind, Jack would still be alive. With a hushed moan of remorse she shifted on the cot, the shadow of the bars streaking across her face. When morning came she would call the guard and demand a phone call. She would warn Amelia; hopefully it wasn't too late.

"Forgive me, Kylie Rose," whispered the voice from the shadowy corner at her feet.

She immediately recoiled toward the wall behind her, pulling her hands up around her, but there was no one there. The startle gripped tight in her chest for she was certain she had heard the words, yet the shadows remained still and the corner empty. The sound of a coughing inmate echoed down the dim hallway then it returned to silence. Pulling her arms in tight around her, she kept her eyes on the spot as she slumped back against the wall and waited for daylight.

Forty-Seven

THE HUM OF THE GENERATOR KEPT THE LIGHTS BURNING BRIGHTLY AS the arson team worked into the night. Lieutenant Woods was just about to stop and eat the soggy sandwich that awaited him, when he spotted the tip of a red can laying beneath the rubble. He had already removed his plastic gloves, but immediately put them back on.

"Move that light a little closer," he called out as he bent toward the can that had been wedged under a fallen overhang.

The lieutenant pulled the half smashed can from the ashes and held it up carefully. "It's in good enough shape for prints," he surmised as he gently placed it in a five-gallon metal container. The assisting investigator sealed the lid with a piece of tape and wrote a description of the contents across the top of it. The lieutenant turned to the dirty and tired team. "Let's call it a night. I want to take this one to the lab myself."

DETECTIVE Binaggio was packing in for the night, but when Lieutenant Woods walked into his office with a strange look on his face, he knew his night was just beginning.

"What have you got?" grumbled the detective, pressing his fingers into his sockets.

The lieutenant dropped into a heap on the chair and slapped a file on Binaggio's desk. "Your suspect may be telling the truth."

Binaggio looked up at him. "Why?"

"We found a container and there's prints all over it," said the Lieutenant, "but they're not Kylie O'Rourke's."

"Shit," groaned the detective. "Then someone else could have set it?"

"It's possible."

"I thought you said no one else was in the place," snapped Binaggio.

"Well, until now, there's been nothing to prove otherwise," said the lieutenant.

"Except the door being bolted from the inside," argued the detective.

"Well Victor, you know as well as I do that doesn't prove diddly," said the lieutenant. "Whether it was the wife or not—whoever did it had to have escaped through the window. There weren't any other bodies found."

"So you think someone may have locked her out, set the fire, then jumped out the window?"

"It's a good possibility," said the lieutenant. "Some arsonists don't like the thought of victims. Maybe he didn't know the husband was still inside."

"Or maybe he did and wanted the wife for himself," muttered the detective, thinking of the reported stalker. "Damn, it would be my luck that there really was someone after her."

Lieutenant Woods sighed in comradery. "We may have both been off on this one, Victor. Central files is doing a comparative analysis right now to see if they come up with a match."

Forty-Eight

AFTER A LONG WHILE, THE BURNING IN KYLIE'S TIRED EYES BECAME too much and she began closing them for short increments, stealing moments of relief. In spite of her effort to stay alert, her body was relaxing, her mind drifting toward the darkness. As her eyes grew increasingly heavy, the room was re-created inside the back of her lids where the walls softened and became less confining. The light through the bars left an indelible mark and where they met the wall there was only black. Then suddenly she saw the sparkling of the eyes in the darkness, staring out at her. The figure was crouched in the corner, sitting perfectly still. His arms were wrapped upon his legs, the paleness of his fingers catching the blue of the moon. A mouth, warm and inviting pressed against her ear, the voice that of Julius Vanderpoel. "It won't be long, Kylie Rose. They found the can."

With a start, Kylie bolted upright on the cot and for a terrified moment searched the corner with her eyes; there was nothing there but the old grungy toilet and sink. Even though she saw there was no danger, the rush of adrenaline left her feeling vulnerable and exposed; she was trapped within the tiny cubicle with no one to help her if she needed it. Taking a deep breath to relax, she lay her head into her hands. She must have drifted asleep and imagined the voice, yet the words clung to her ear like a chilled damp leaf.

"The can," she whispered aloud. She had completely forgotten about the bright red can but now that she remembered it, she wondered what implications it could possibly have. If Julius Vanderpoel had affected the physical world, then certainly he could leave behind evidence.

Abruptly, a door screeched open at the end of the hallway, pulling her attention toward the corridor that lay beyond the bars. She listened intently for footsteps to follow, but it was silent. Though none of the other prisoners were visible from her cubicle, for all of the cells lined only one side of the corridor, she heard one of them shuffling about in her sleep.

Then the door slammed shut and the sound of someone whistling followed with the clattering of a bucket. She stared toward the murky light of the overhead bulbs that did little to light the passageway. A mop sloshed across the cement floor, the swashing drawing closer. An old black man slowly edged into sight, swinging the handle back and forth. Though she saw only his profile, she recognized the slumping of his bony shoulders and the angle of his crooked back. It was Ducker Brown, the elderly grocer from the Northend.

"Ducker?" she called softly from the cot.

The old man turned toward the cell and squinted his eyes to see in. Kylie stood from the shadows, resting her hands on the cool metal of the bars. When the old man saw her, it took a moment for the shock to register on his face.

"Georgia Peach!" he exclaimed with horror. "What in God's name are you doing here, child? What happened to you?"

Her hands instantly went up to hide her swollen face and black eye. Apparently he hadn't seen the incriminating news. She was so relieved to see the old familiar friend that her puffy eyes began to fill again with emotion.

"Now, now," he said sadly, reaching his wrinkled hand between the bars to touch her own. "It can't be that bad."

"Are you working here now?" she asked, trying to put the focus on him.

His brow crinkled with concern, but still he answered the question. "I've been cleaning up here at nights after the store closes. Elsey's always glad to get rid of me for a few hours."

"She wouldn't part with you for the world," she smiled softly, swiping a wayward tear from her neck.

"I see you've been driving again, Georgia," the old man said with a devilish smile.

A snort of laughter escaped past her lips. "No, Ducker, I gave that up a long time ago," she chuckled hoarsely, even though she knew he had only said it to cheer her up. In spite of the moment of relief, her smile faded. She reluctantly told him of the fire and of Jack's death. When it came time to describe the details she had to stop for it was too painful. "I'm sorry," she whispered, her voice trembling with her effort to squelch the emotion. Ducker touched her face with his rough fingers and wiped away the tears.

Embarrassed by the display of concern by the old man, Kylie exhaled and forced a thin smile. "I saw the arsonist, but I couldn't identify him to the police," she said softly.

While hesitant to tell the police anything that may cause them to hunt for an innocent man—for she knew the true arsonist would never be found—Kylie felt safe in telling Ducker that she had clearly seen the culprit. It even brought a bit of relief. She then explained her own arrest, surprising herself at how painful it was that others believed her capable of such an atrocity.

When she finished and looked back up at Ducker, he seemed very sad but not the least bit surprised.

"Well, Georgia," he said, his chestnut eyes flecked with gold and his black hair with grey. "I know you think it was your fault for not saving him, but you did the best you could."

The statement startled her for she hadn't told him of her own guilt.

Ducker lifted her chin to look deeply into her eyes. "'Who can find a virtuous woman, for her price is far above rubies. The heart of her husband doth safely trust in her.'"

"Ducker, that's lovely."

He smiled handsomely, his black face resembling a dried up raisin. "Ecclesiastics chapter thirty-one, verse twenty-three . . . Elsey would be proud to hear I remembered it." Then his tone changed and his face became drawn. "Ecclesiastics again," he said, holding up a finger as if to quiet her. "'To every thing there is a season, and a time to every purpose under heaven. A time to be born and a time to die.' I'm sure you've heard it . . ."

"Yes."

"Everything happens for a reason, Georgia," he said. "Even death."

She looked down, wanting to change the subject.

"It was Jack's time and there was nothing to be done about it," he said. "Did you ever see that old Jimmy Stewart film called *It's a Wonderful Life?*"

Kylie tried to give a smile but it merely turned into a weary nod.

"If George Bailey had never been born, the people around him would have been greatly affected; his absence would have left a hole. Well, the opposite also holds true. If a man misses his time to die, like you hear of so often—like a man miraculously surviving a deadly fall or a plane crash—"

Kylie's stomach dropped. She was certain that Ducker didn't know of the accident, yet there was something glinting behind his eyes that told her he did.

"You hear of it all the time," he continued, his face in shadows. "Well if the man goes on when he isn't supposed to, he touches lives that he shouldn't. If there was a sequel to the film I think it might be called . . . *It's a Wonderful Death*."

Kylie was stung by the remark. "Ducker," she scolded.

"Well it's true my dear. If George Bailey were scheduled to die ten years later and he cheated death, there would be the same dilemma happening in Bedford Falls as there was if he hadn't been born. Every man's life touches so many others in ways you can't even imagine. It's all interconnected. You, me, all of it. Even when a man walks down the street he's touching lives. He reaches the crosswalk and the woman in the car has to slow so that he can cross, making her slightly late to a friend's house, which in turn makes the gathering last longer, keeping another from getting home in time to keep her child from cutting its hand on a broken plate the baby-sitter dropped because she was getting tired . . . etcetera, etcetera. One big orchestration is what it is, Georgia, and we're mere players upon a stage, as Shakespeare once said."

As she stared into the warm eyes of the old man, it appeared that the flecks of brown were dancing around the pupils, and the murky light overhead was finding its way into corners where it shouldn't. A strange churning began to stir within her. Never had she heard Ducker expounding his theories on life so readily. She felt again as if she were dreaming, as though she had never risen from the cot and Ducker and his strange ideas were merely part of her sleep. Ducker leaned confidentially in, so close that she could feel his breath upon her face. He held her stare within his own, refusing to let her look away.

"Jack had to die," he continued intently, his tone practically a whisper. "Or he would have gone on affecting lives that he shouldn't. It had to happen when it did for it was the only time the pieces fit."

The voice tickled around her head, so light that it seemed as if the words had never been said. "Yes," she said, though she was unsure what she was responding to. Her head was suddenly pounding and her eyes throbbing. She removed her hand from beneath his and backed from the bars. "I'm sorry, Ducker," she whispered, but she wasn't sure that her lips had moved. She looked back at the ancient face that stared so wisely through the steel. There was a sudden darkness that moved beneath the intensity of his gaze.

"Don't feel bad for Clyde Tremblay," he said.

"Clyde Tremblay?"

"You'll meet him soon enough," he said. "He decided his fate long ago. It just happened to fit nicely with Jack's."

Kylie shook her head, feeling as though a piece of the conversation had been omitted. "I'm not sure what you mean," she said faintly.

"'There is not any present moment that is unconnected with some future one,'" he said, but his voice had changed. It had become more youthful, losing its gravelly undertone. "'The transition from cause to effect, from event to event, is often carried on by secret steps, which our foresight cannot divine and our sagacity is unable to trace' . . . Joseph Addison . . . 1723."

His words prickled against her skin like tiny bursts of heat, then there was nothing left but her beating heart and the sound of her breath.

"But of course Ducker wouldn't say something like that would he?" asked the shriveled old man.

Terror shot through her limbs as she stared at the old man, certain she had just heard the voice of Julius Vanderpoel.

Abruptly, the door at the other end of the hall opened. She heard the clattering of a bucket and someone whistling. It was the same tune she had heard the man before her whistling only minutes earlier. She turned toward the door where a foot was scooting a bucket into the corridor. Then the rest of the person emerged and she nearly screamed when she saw that it was Ducker Brown with a mop in his hands.

"My God," she gasped, turning back to the figure before her, but he had vanished along with his mop and bucket.

Her hand went to her mouth as she backed into the shadows. She crouched upon the cot, feeling as if her entire world were slipping away. It had been the second time the creature had taken the form of a loved one, and the second time she had trusted the vision.

As Ducker Brown passed her cell she remained in the shadows without saying a word to him. She edged closer against the wall and closed her eyes until she heard the door on the opposite end of the corridor squeak back and close.

At once she straightened, a name rising back out of the disturbing encounter. "Clyde Tremblay," she whispered aloud. Then a sickening thought began to pry its way into her mind: the stranger would somehow be sucked into the nightmare. Not only had the creature come to justify killing Jack, but to forewarn her of the coming events.

Forty-Nine

THE LONG HAND OF THE CERAMIC CLOWN RIGIDLY COUNTED DOWN the seconds of the clock on the wall above the balding head. Beneath the ruby red glow of the dark room, Clyde Tremblay swished the photo paper in the developer, breathlessly waiting for the image to appear through the rippling solution. With his stiff arm hanging at his side, he stared down at the blank paper, while the sweat formed in the creases of his neck from his mounting anticipation.

In only seconds the waving liquid would bring the impression to life and the scene would be reborn at the grace of his own hand. Every detail would be in place with only a slight variation in the characters. The template on the front of the grayish-white helmet was usually the first to emerge and it was at this point that Tremblay imagined the face that followed to be his own.

He would envision his round cheeks, high balding forehead and beady fair eyes within the liquid, then watch with fascination as they transformed beneath the blood-stained light into that of a handsome firefighter with chiseled features and deep penetrating eyes. Though each time was different, with a sundry of faces and rank of firefighters, the result was always the same: a proud titillating sensation that he had become part of the heroic team that had once again crushed the enemy.

As the shield of the helmet appeared before him, the palpitation it aroused had never been stronger. It was the first time he had ever had the fortuity of occupying the highest most esteemed post of the arson squad.

"Lieutenant Tremblay," he said aloud as the rugged, seasoned face of Tom Woods appeared beneath the helmet.

"Can we ask you a few questions please?" It was the voice of the reporter in the bottom right of the photo shoving the microphone beneath his lips. His subordinates buzzed in the background, as they moved about the black structure removing ladders and wrapping up hoses. The cameras clicked all around, waiting for his official response to the horrendous tragedy that had claimed yet another victim.

Tremblay took a deep breath before he answered, but instead of the chemicals of a dark room, he smelled the deep arresting aroma that he loved so dearly—it was the pungency of a newly doused fire.

"I'll answer all of your questions, but first you must stand back," he replied deeply. "For your own safety."

He could hear their whispers as they admired his suit and his courage. There were so many of them there, to idolize him and to scramble to catch his every word.

With the tongs in hand he grasped the photo from the solution before it became too dark. He dropped it in the next tub and sloshed it around, while nervously thinking of the night that was to follow. He had been looking forward to it for over three months and in spite of the unexpected fire on the Waterfront would still go ahead as planned.

THE RED cans were lined neatly along the south wall of the basement, each of them cleaned and as free from the smell of gasoline as Tremblay could get them. But in spite of his efforts to keep the air clear, including the installation of a special ventilator system, the pungent odor was ever present.

He carried the photo of the lieutenant toward a string that stretched across the north side of the basement. He opened the clip and placed it alongside a photo of the sunrise over the smoldering warehouse. While he couldn't add the photos to the collection taken of his own creations, he could at least admire the handiwork of another. Even though there had been a casualty, it was still quite impressive work. The blaze had warranted over two hundred firefighters on the suppression team, with at least thirty-five exterior streams going at once. It was grand, to say the least.

A twinge of jealousy pecked at his chest, for never had one of his own creations drawn such a swell of fire trucks or media attention. His gaze fell toward the wall behind the string where photos and news-clippings of his past were neatly framed and hung upon the stone.

While all of the articles were smaller than the ones the O'Rourke fire would surely warrant, one of his had made headline news three years earlier: ARSON FIRE CLAIMS LIFE IN DOWNTOWN WAREHOUSE and ARSONIST STRIKES AGAIN had been splashed across the front of the morning papers. Of all his fires it had received the most coverage, presumably because a homeless man had died of smoke inhalation. Even though Tremblay knew that the best reporting went to the fires with victims, he still limited himself to occupant-free dwellings or situations where the victims could be easily rescued. The John Doe had been the only life ever lost under his shift, and though Tremblay had regretted the death, he also knew that in his line of work losses were inevitable. He had done his part by getting to a phone quickly— the newspaper had even printed his name as the man who was first on the scene—Station 44 was the one that hadn't held up their end. He was certain that if their units had responded quicker, the homeless man would still be alive. But in spite of the lost life, he felt a sense of pride when he looked at the yellowed articles. It was his one moment of fame. His work since had barely warranted mention even on the second or third pages of the papers. It was time to do better.

He had been devising a plan for over three months and unlike the O'Rourke fire, his would not have to rely on a death to draw the proper respect. His would rely on something much more valued than human life.

For years he had tried to improve his techniques, to build bigger fires in hopes of achieving better, but it wasn't until he saw a Woody Allen movie one night, that he devised the plan he was about to implement. In the film, one of the characters asked another that if a building were on fire and he had only time enough to save either a human being or the only copy of a Shakespearean play, which would he save? The questioned person was in a quandary of moral indecision until finally the one asking insisted that one must save the play. His reasoning was that humans were expendable, whereas art was not. Tremblay had searched for a museum, but found that impractical due to the tight security of most. Then one day he noticed the towering white steeple of the Old North Church and instantly knew it was right. Boston cherished its history as much as it did its art. He could see the reporters now, distraught and saddened by the loss of the very steeple where the lanterns were hung in 1775 to signal that the British were coming, before the famous Paul Revere ride to Lexington. The destruction of the priceless landmark would certainly draw front page attention, if not national news.

His stomach let out a nervous growl as he noticed the time. It was nearly eleven o'clock. He turned toward the east wall of the basement, where a long work-table stretched ten feet across. At sight of the box waiting atop it, he felt the jittery eruption in his belly grow. Every fire he had ever set had been done with the use of gasoline that he simply poured from a new can—the container then saved as a memento. But this one would have to be done differently. Even though the hundred and ninety-one feet high steeple was devised of wood, the bottom section of the Old North Church was made of brick which would not readily burn. He was concerned that even if he managed to get past the alarm and break inside the church to ignite the wooden interior, the newly added sprinkler system could easily squelch the fire before it worked its way up into the steeple. He had nearly decided to find a different landmark when two weeks ago, the Chamber of Commerce announced that it would commence repairs on the steeple which had suffered storm damage. Like a blessing from God, the scaffolding had been erected and had waited for this night ever since.

Tremblay peered into the contents of the box, double checking to make sure everything was in place. The crate was packed neatly with the following: three Molotov cocktails he had devised out of beer bottles filled with a gas and soap mixture—the openings stuffed with rags; a wide exercise belt that would harness the cocktails to his waist while he climbed the scaffolding; a pair of snug-fitting work gloves with rubber grips; two disposable cigarette lighters; a dark ski mask; and a pack of Rolaids. He reached for the Rolaids and split them open, popping four into his mouth. He placed them back in the box which he pulled from the table with his right arm, his stiff left arm holding it in place.

He took one last glance about the basement, debating whether or not to grab one of the gas cans to take along as backup. His eyes grazed past the corner of the stairwell that rose over the cans, his mind too cluttered to notice the empty space on the floor. "This'll work," he said with a confident nod to the box, then he mounted the wooden stairs completely oblivious that one of the twelve cans was missing.

Fifty

LIEUTENANT WOODS AND DETECTIVE BINAGGIO WERE ON THEIR WAY out the door to grab a fresh cup of coffee, when a lab technician came walking up to them with a big smile on her face.

"Got it," she said, holding up a set of fingerprints. "That can you brought in . . . the prints match a small time arsonist that hasn't struck in awhile."

"Do you have a name?" asked Binaggio.

"No, but the FBI thinks he lives somewhere in Brookline."

Fifty-One

CLYDE TREMBLAY'S SHAKING HAND REACHED FOR THE METAL RUNG OF the last level of the scaffolding, the muscles of his arm so strained they were beginning to cramp. With a groan to boost his energy, he managed to lift his legs and topple onto the wooden platform, careful not to break the three beer bottles strapped to his pudgy waist. Gasping for breath through the hole in the wool mask, he stared out at the sea that lay to the northeast of the church, past the lights of the Northend and the Waterfront. The fishy scent drifted on a hot breeze titillating his dry mouth. What he wouldn't give for just one gulp of the sparkling water, even though it would be laden with salt.

The white steeple rose up above him, the bottom of the wood less than fifteen feet from his reach. It was the perfect distance to light the cocktails, toss them over the railing of the tower, then quickly climb back down before it was overtaken with fire. He would then remove his mask and belt, and put them beneath the tire cover in his old Dodge and run for the pay phone half a block away on Bennet Street.

"Yes," he breathed nervously, imagining the inquiring faces of the reporters. "I just happened to be driving by when I noticed the red glow." He had rehearsed the answer all of the way over from his house in Brookline, but still felt the need to say it a few more times.

Just when he thought his heart couldn't pump any faster, it nearly broke through his shirt when his hand pulled the first of the cocktails from the belt. He wanted to wait just a few more minutes to catch his breath, but knew if he did, he increased the risk of being caught. When he looked up at the overhead railing to gauge how hard he would have to throw the cocktail to break it against the side of the steeple, droplets of sweat dripped down from the mask into his eyes. He started to blink to brush the sweat away and nearly lost his balance. He quickly crouched again and set the cocktail at his feet, horribly aware that the drop to the ground would surely mean his death.

After a moment to steady his footing, he pulled the lighter from his pocket and took a deep breath. He snapped the flame up and held it to the rag of the cocktail resting upon the landing. The rag caught faster than he expected. He quickly dropped the lighter to his feet and picked up the cocktail. With his last bit of energy he hoisted it above his head and sent it flying toward the white steeple. His aim was perfect. It slammed against the side of the steeple then dropped down to the tier below.

"Damn," he sighed, for it hadn't broken and the gas wouldn't ignite without contact with oxygen. He was just about to remove another from his belt, when he heard the sound of the bottle rolling through the railing. He looked up in time to see it flying back toward him like a stick of ignited dynamite. He reached out to grab it, for if it broke, it would immediately erupt into a ball of fire. His fingertips grazed the cool glass but it tumbled past, hit the wooden landing with a thud and then rolled off over the edge toward the dark ground below.

SEVENTEEN-YEAR-OLD Andy Frayne was opening the window to let a little air into the living room when he saw the bush beside the church burst into flames. "Holy shit!" he exclaimed.

His mother, who was napping on the couch in front of the glowing television, turned her groggy head.

"Call 911, Ma!" he exclaimed, running for the door of the apartment. "There's a fire by the church!"

His bare feet scarcely touched the bottom of the stairs and within seconds he was out on the narrow street running toward the flames. He was joined by an older, gray-haired woman at the edge of the sidewalk. They reached the church just as the first wooden landing of the scaffolding caught fire.

"Look!" cried the woman, pointing upward.

At the very top of the scaffolding they could see a slightly overweight man standing completely still as if not to be seen. He was wearing a black ski mask, a white tee-shirt, and a huge belt with two strange objects strapped to his waist.

"Hey buddy!" Andy called out. "What the hell are you doing?"

But the masked man continued to stand perfectly still.

"Hey... We can see you up there," called Andy.

The masked man finally looked toward them, then down at the flames cooking the bottom level of the scaffolding like a bonfire.

"Climb down lower and jump before the fire gets too high!" called the woman. The blaze had nearly reached the second landing, but still the masked man hesitated. He began shuffling nervously back and forth.

"What a dumb ass!" screeched the voice of a fourteen-year-old boy from the small crowd that had already gathered on the street. "He can't come down 'cause he's stuck. If he jumps with that belt on he's history and if he leaves it up there the sparks might ignite it."

Andy and the older woman looked curiously toward the kid who flashed a shiny tinsel smile. "Haven't you ever seen a Molotov cocktail? Those are the things stuck to his hips."

With a collective groan, every face of the crowd turned back to the masked man.

TREMBLAY stared down at the upturned faces of the tiny figures on the ground, his legs shaking and his pants hanging off his sweating hips. Stricken with panic he had watched the bush ignite and the flames travel quickly over to the scaffolding before he had a chance to think what to do. Within seconds, the crowd below had gathered and spotted him.

Smoke curled up around the edge of the platform from the lower tiers of the scaffolding. Every time he leaned over to see how bad the fire was, soot stung his eyes.

The sound of sirens wafted on the ocean breeze and as each new person ran up to the crowd the voices of explanation floated up to him. The bodies below had formed into one collective voice of concern but mostly disgust . . . "Look at that idiot . . . what was he trying to do? Burn down the church? . . . Looks like he missed . . ." then a laugh—a taunting jeer erupted. A home-video camcorder was pointed up at him, recording the humiliating moment. A woman stepped forward, her face riddled with pity. "Look, the poor guy's arm doesn't work . . ."

"Come down mister before you die up there!"

"No! Tell him to stay!"

The tears welled in his eyes and the crowd blurred before him. He could feel the heat rising nearer as the blaring horns of the trucks and ambulance came to rest in the narrow red-brick street. Then he saw the first television van and felt as if his life were ending. "Go away," he said softly through the wool mask.

"Clyde?!" called a familiar voice from below. "Clyde Tremblay is that you?"

It was the young stout firefighter named Fulton who had only that morning stood up for him against the lieutenant. Tremblay backed against the opposite metal pole of the scaffolding.

"Go away!" he called down to the rushing firemen.

Then the landing beneath him began to tremble as they pulled up the hoses and doused the fire. To his humiliation, it was out in less than a minute with the use of only three streams.

He could see they were setting a ladder to come up to him. "Leave me alone!" he called down to the gaping faces.

"Just calm down, Clyde," came the voice of Fulton from the ground. "I'm coming up to you!"

"No!" he cried, but in spite of his disapproval the top of the ladder extended up along the side of the church apart from the scaffolding.

Tremblay paced back and forth as the swarm of vehicles and the crowd below grew. He couldn't be taken down like a scared child in front of them all; it was too much. It was bad enough that he would be known as a bungler and a small-time arsonist, let alone to be branded a coward.

The healthy young face of Fulton appeared beside him, the colorful lights from below flashing across his face. He was perched on the ladder with so much confidence one would believe he were only ten feet off the ground instead of the towering distance.

"Get out of here," sniffed Tremblay, his voice shaking. He was certain the firefighter could tell he was crying in spite of the mask.

Like the woman from below, the firefighter's face was filled with pity. "What are you doing, old boy?" he asked.

Tremblay backed as far away as he could.

"Wooohhh . . . hold on there, Clyde," said Fulton, holding out his perfectly muscular arm as if to steady him from ten feet away.

Tremblay looked down at the lights of the television cameras blaring up at him and he could hear the occasional laugh from the crowd.

"They think I'm a failure," said Tremblay.

"No, don't worry about that old boy."

"No!" said Tremblay, shuffling back and forth again. "They think I don't know what I'm doing . . . that I'm some loser . . ." The sobs overtook him. "They're going to send me to prison."

"Don't think about that now, Clyde. Just hand me those cocktails and come on down."

"Stay away."

"Okay, okay"

"I don't want to go to prison," Tremblay said, the tears choking his voice. "When they find out the fires I've set, they're gonna lock me away forever."

The sirens continued to wail as the cop cars pulled up front.

"I didn't mean for the man to die," said Tremblay. "It wasn't my fault. I did my part. The units didn't get there fast enough."

"What are you talking about Clyde?"

"The man in the warehouse . . . I didn't mean for him to die."

"What man in the . . . no Clyde, no," said Fulton, his head going down. "Don't tell me you were the one that set that fire last night."

Tremblay looked toward him confused, his heart tripping ahead. He had been talking of the homeless man he had accidentally killed a few years back. He started to explain, but then looked back down at the reporters and remembered the respect the O'Rourke fire had drawn. He remembered the concern and the awe-inspiring questions they had asked. "Yes," he said quietly. "Tell them it was me."

"Just give me your hand and . . ."

"NO!!" he screamed backing away. "Tell them I'm the one who set the O'Rourke fire. Tell them that Clyde Tremblay knows how to hit his target!"

Fulton slowly began moving onto the landing as the toes of Tremblay's shoes touched the edge of the scaffolding.

"Just give me your hand," said Fulton, as if speaking with a child.

Tremblay remained still and slowly took off his mask revealing a puffy, red face that was wet with sweat. "Tell them," he said simply, then stepped off the landing, his body silently plummeting toward the earth.

Fifty-Two

WHEN LIEUTENANT WOODS AND DETECTIVE BINAGGIO ENTERED Clyde Tremblay's home in Brookline, they immediately followed the odor of gasoline to the basement. They found the cans along the wall and even without matching the prints, or verifying the confession of Tremblay with any other firefighters, knew that they had the right man.

"Look at all of this stuff," Lieutenant Woods said, amazed by all of the articles and hanging photos. Then he noticed the photo of himself looking straight into the camera and instantly pictured the odd little man on the other side of the lens. "He was there this morning," said Lieutenant Woods. "I talked to him right before you drove up."

But Binaggio wasn't listening. He was staring at a photo of himself leading Kylie O'Rourke from the emergency room to the squad car in cuffs. "God forgive me," he said softly.

Fifty-Three

Her breath was short and sporadic, as Kylie gasped for air within the coffin that lay beneath the pressing earth. The weight of the dirt bore down upon the top of the sarcophagus that shrank around her, crumpling her body inward upon itself. With desperate strokes, her fingers scratched at the top of the encasement but there was no sound from above, only a shrieking silence. Her eyes widened but it was black, completely and utterly black. Blood oozed from her fingernails, ragged from digging against the splintering crypt. She had picked and clawed all around her, peeling the velvety material away until reaching the bare wood of the lid. Her hands pressed against the surface, but still it wouldn't give.

She had been buried alive inside the crudely structured box, the only comfort a soft cushion beneath her. Her fingers pressed downward to the silky material that moved strangely as if over skin. Then her hand met that of another and she recoiled with terror. Someone was beneath her, a still and lifeless body between her and the coffin floor. She edged herself over and turned on her side, slowly raising her hands to the head. She felt the short straight hair and even in the darkness she could tell by the touch it was blonde. Her fingers trembled over the delicate face that felt as if it were frozen in a silent scream. She felt the smooth cheeks of a woman as she worked her hands upward to the eyes. Then, as if a shaft of light had been momentarily granted, the blue eyes were looking at her—the crystal retinas frozen in horror and they were none other than Amelia's.

A vacuum drained her lungs and she tried to scream, to cry out but there was nothing inside, only a hollow void of terror.

Then the face began to move, animated by someone else's hand. The dry lips hideously pressed together and formed the words . . . "Mrs. O'Rourke? . . . Mrs. O'Rourke?"

With a jerk of her head, Kylie's eyes were open, staring into the drooping face of a stranger. "Mrs. O'Rourke?" the woman said. "Come with me."

For a terrifying moment, Kylie felt the presence of the oppressive walls, unable to place where she was. She blinked again, as the woman backed from the bed. When she saw the officer's uniform and smelled the smoky odor of her own body, it all came back to her. She lay crumpled against the wall of the cell, her body aching from her awkward position upon the cot. The cell looked different than before. The shadows had lightened with the pledge of the coming day; the deep purples and icy blues fading to a muted gray. The colorless change made it appear even more bleak than before.

"Come with me," said the voice from the open cell door.

Kylie immediately sat up to follow.

"I NEED to make a phone call," she said as she waited on the other side of the glass.

"That won't be necessary," said the officer, sliding a few articles of clothing beneath the security glass opening. With the exception of the cameo necklace, Kylie at first didn't recognize the clothes, then she remembered Theresa handing them to her inside the door at the hospital. "Am I being released?" she asked.

"Sign here," said the officer, shoving a piece of paper at her.

"What is it?"

"Verification that you received everything you came in with."

Kylie signed the voucher, then was led down a hallway to change.

THE LAST of the huge metal doors buzzed open and with the misfitting sandals once again upon her feet Kylie left the secured area and followed the female officer down a long hallway. The woman opened the door to a fluorescent-lit room with chairs and motioned for Kylie to enter.

She found her father sitting sadly against the wall. His elbows were upon his knees and his head was hung low as if he had been waiting there for hours. When he heard the door, he immediately got up to embrace her, but she was reluctant to touch him for fear her horrible smoky odor would rub off on him.

"Come here, love," he said.

Kylie pressed herself into the safety of the strong chest. The familiar essence of the sea filled her senses and immediately brought her comfort. She was so tired she could have slept standing up as long as he was there to hold her. But the thought of Amelia laying inside the coffin of her dream, caused her to pull back with apprehension.

"Did you call Amelia?" she asked, gripping her hands together fretfully.

Beneath the harsh lighting, her father appeared to have aged from the last time she saw him. Dark creases encircled his blood-shot eyes making him look like an old man.

"I talked to her last night," he replied.

"And she was okay?"

"Yes, love," he said. "Why wouldn't she be?"

Kylie noticed that her father had given a knowing glance to someone behind her. Dillon was on the other side of the room along with the psychiatrist she had spoken to after the accident.

Dillon stepped forward, looking exhausted and disheveled in his wrinkled pants and tee-shirt. "Kylie, you remember Dr. Rupert Jordan?"

The slender, white-haired man stood to shake her hand.

"Yes, of course," she answered, brushing her wavy hair back from her face, but it was so matted that it didn't even feel real. At once she felt as if the insightful eyes of the doctor were studying her.

She looked to her father who hung nervously back. "What's this all about?" she asked. "Have I been released?"

"Yes," said her father. "But first the detective wants to ask you a few more questions. They found the man who set the fire, love."

Kylie's stomach leapt into her throat; surely he couldn't have meant Julius Vanderpoel. "What do you mean they found the man?" she asked.

"He's a small time arsonist the FBI has been tracking for years," sighed Dillon. "His name is Clyde Tremblay."

When she heard the name she felt the blood rush from her face.

Her father moved toward her and took her hand. "I'm sorry that the son-of-a-bitch had to kill Jack before they caught him."

Kylie could barely believe what she was hearing. Just as the counterfeit Ducker had forewarned, Clyde Tremblay had entered her life. She imagined the poor, innocent man sitting within one of the dingy cells fearing for his freedom. "How can they be sure they have the right person without a description?" she asked nervously. "I mean, someone has to at least see him or—"

"He tried it again last night and they caught him red-handed," McCallum said. "They know he's the one . . . they just want to make sure that no one else was with him."

Kylie put her hand to her head and looked away from the probing eyes. She felt raw and drawn out and wanted nothing more than to get away from the confining building, but she couldn't let an innocent man take the blame for something he didn't do. "It wasn't . . ." but then she stopped. It would be easier to point out the loop holes in their theory than to convince them of the truth. "There was a red can," she said. "If they look for it, it'll prove—"

"They already found it," her father interrupted. "And the finger-prints match Tremblay's."

Kylie turned back, unable to hide her astonishment.

"So you saw him then?" asked the doctor.

Kylie looked over at the inquiring, analytical face, resenting his presence in the personal conversation. "Forgive me, Dr. Jordan, but I'm a bit wrung out to mince words. Why are you here?"

"I asked him to come," said Dillon. "I thought he might be able to help."

Her father suddenly stepped toward her. "Kylie, it was my idea," he said apprehensively. "The detective was concerned about releasing you."

"Why?" she asked.

"He wanted to make sure you were okay," he answered. "He . . . uh . . . he told me that you filed a report that Julius Vanderpoel was stalking you," said her father.

Kylie felt her face turn crimson. She suddenly became aware of how ravaged she must appear to the three of them.

"You even told me yourself that you thought you were seeing him, love," reminded her father. ". . . that he had somehow come back to get you . . . and I was . . . I was worried."

"It's not uncommon for someone who's suffered from traumatic memories to be confused," offered the doctor. "Fear that the assail-ant—"

"If I want your advice, Dr. Jordan, I'll ask for it," snapped Kylie.

"Love, he's only trying to help."

"Help what?" she asked sharply. She knew her anger was getting the best of her, but she refused to back down.

There was an uncomfortable silence, no one willing to make the next move. Finally the doctor spoke.

"If you remember the can, then perhaps you remember the face . . . or whether there was more than one person?" he proffered.

All three of the men were watching her, waiting for her response; after all, it was a logical question. She turned away and walked over to a bulletin board. She looked at the tiny pieces of paper, yet she saw none of them. "Without my identification they can't hold him. Anyone could have taken the can and set the fire," she posed.

"They have the right man and there's plenty of other evidence to prove it," said her father.

"Evidence can be misleading," she argued.

"He already confessed, love," said her father.

She froze with the statement.

"He told a firefighter that he did it," said Dillon.

Kylie fell back, stunned. "What if he was lying?" she asked weakly. For the first time the conviction in her voice was waning. "Sometimes people do that to get attention."

"Jack wasn't his first victim," said her father. "He set a fire a few years back that killed a man."

The doctor moved in closer. "You don't need to be frightened of him coming back and harming you—that can't happen."

"He's dead, love," her father said gently. "He confessed, then he committed suicide."

The announcement knocked the wind from any further argument she may have had. She had to look away again for fear that her thoughts would read on her face. It was as if the entire thing had been arranged and no matter what she said to counter it all, the segments fit together as though Vanderpoel had never entered the house that night. Jack had been taken, just as the counterfeit Ducker had said, during the "time that the pieces fit" . . . and Clyde Tremblay was merely a player in the orchestration of events.

"He even showed up afterward to take photos of the warehouse. And he was at the hospital when they arrested you, taking photos."

Kylie grew silent wandering how much of it was Tremblay and how much not.

She looked up at the men, consciously trying to hide the fear brewing beneath her composure. If it were that easy for Jack's life to be snagged without notice, then surely hers and the others could be taken just as easily. It was almost as if there was a parallel plane of reality, where the physical unknowingly accommodated the spiritual with no questions asked.

The door opened and Detective Binaggio entered carrying several cups of coffee on a tray. "You got through your release quicker than I thought," he said, looking toward Kylie. He set down the cardboard tray and went toward her. "My condolences and apologies, Mrs. O'Rourke," he said, extending his hand.

As much as Kylie knew she should, she couldn't take the hand after the previous day's brutal questioning.

The detective pulled his sympathies back and wiped them on his jeans. "I understand," he said with a curt nod. "I know you're tired and want to get the hell . . . heck, out of here so I'll keep it brief. You don't have to worry about this guy—"

"We already told her that he's dead," interrupted Dillon.

"Good, good," he said. "And does she remember whether—" He was directing the question to the doctor.

"I can speak for myself, Detective," she said bluntly.

The detective looked to the doctor and then back to Kylie. "Then maybe you can tell me if this is the man that you saw the night of the fire?" he asked, pulling a photo from a pile of papers.

Kylie took the picture into her hands. Her heart sunk when she saw that it was of a balding, meek-looking man that appeared as though he couldn't hurt a soul. She could feel the eyes of everyone upon her, waiting for her response. "As I told you yesterday," she said. "I only vaguely saw him so I couldn't say for sure."

"Did you see more than one person?" asked the detective.

"No," she answered certainly. "There was only one." Not wanting another innocent man to be accused, even she had become part of the players, nudged about by an unseen hand.

The detective turned to the doctor. "Is she okay to be released?" he asked.

Kylie felt her temper boil. "Detective Binaggio," she said sharply. "I could be as batty as a fruit fly and there's not a damn thing you could do to keep me here."

The detective looked as if she had whipped him across the face with her hand.

Her father stepped forward, clearly anxious to get out of the station. "She's free to go, isn't she?" asked the Irishman.

"Yes of course," said the detective, turning away, but then he quickly turned back. "Just one more thing. Clyde Tremblay doesn't really fit the portrait of a stalker. He wasn't by any chance—?"

"No," she interrupted. "That was just some guy I met in the Northend. He ... uh ... The man following me looked a lot like Julius Vanderpoel. That's why I got confused in your office."

The detective looked to her father and to the doctor for their opinion on the matter, but neither looked interested in interjecting. "So have you heard anything else from this man?"

"No," she said quietly. "Not since the night your officers took a report."

"Hopefully that was enough to scare him off," said the detective. "If you have any more problems with him, please let me know."

Kylie nodded her head.

"Well," said the detective, clearly relieved that his work on the case was finished. "Again, Mrs. O'Rourke ... Dr. O'Rourke, my condolences."

Kylie stood quietly back as the men shook hands and headed for the door. She felt empty at the simplicity of it all. There were no more strings to be tied. Jack had slipped away, his death filed under an innocent man's name, yet the consequences of the fallacy were minimal. Another victim on Clyde Tremblay's record meant little, for the dead arsonist would never have to answer to the charge.

As the men moved about her, oblivious to the truth, a numb feeling crept through her soul. She had become an accomplice to her own husband's murder by refusing to expose the true culprit. She had pledged her loyalty and made a pact of secrecy with the very force that had not only destroyed her mate, but within time, would be back for her and Amelia as well.

"Come home with me, love," her father said from the doorway.

Lost in her own disparaging thoughts, she barely heard the suggestion. She hesitated a moment, then moved forward, for she had nowhere else to go and no one left to go to.

WHEN Kylie and her father reached the double doors of the station,
they were overwhelmed by the amount of media waiting outside in
the gray foggy morning. A blockade of reporters, cameras and lights
had formed down the steps, and the street was lined with television
vans.

"Good God," groaned her father, his thick Irish accent erupting
with his annoyance. "Stay close and we'll be at the truck in no time."

Several of the reporters saw them through the doors and the lights
of the cameras flicked on. The second they stepped from the safety of
the station, the questions were upon them.

"Mrs. O'Rourke? Can we get a statement?"

"How do you feel about being wrongly accused?"

"Please Mrs. O'Rourke!"

The flashes exploded all around her, as she followed closely behind
the broad shoulders of her father who ineffectually tried to shield her
from the lenses. Each burst of light stayed within her eyes making it
more and more difficult to see.

"Mrs. O'Rourke, will you press charges against the state?"

A young man stepped in front of her separating her from her father. "Mrs. O'Rourke," he said stopping in his tracks as though he
were in the midst of an interview with her. "We understand that
you—"

"I have nothing to say," she said stepping around him.

As she searched through the frantic reporters for the familiar plaid
shirt of her father, a piece of the past flashed before her and walked
alongside her toward the street. It was her mother, wearing a flowered red dress, her hair pulled away from her dark eyes. For a brief
moment, the sidewalk beneath her feet became the stone walkway of
her Aunt Clara's house and the truck awaiting her at the curb was her
dad's old '59 Chevy.

Tell us about the man, Kylie McCallum, begged the reporters. *Tell us
about the rose.*

Kylie tried to shake off the memory but when she finally reached a clearing in the bodies, her father waited by the truck just as he had when she was a child.

She slid onto the seat of the '82 Ford and pulled the door shut behind her. As she stared out at the scrambling reporters the eerie sensation inside of her grew. It was as if time had stopped twenty-seven years earlier when Vanderpoel exited her life and had begun once again with his reappearance. And like the minute hand of a delayed clock moving round to the proper hour, it was passing the same points twice. Once again the reporters scrambled for insights into a murder, only this time the death had been Jack's and the secret had been kept. And like the lost hours of a stopped clock, every trace of her life without Vanderpoel had been destroyed and her future rerouted. Once again he had entered her world and his presence demanded her attention. Once again he brought death, only this time when he departed she would not be left behind to forget.

BOOK TWO

PART FOUR

One

AMELIA BLACKWELL HAD BEEN SITTING ON THE UPPER SIDE PORCH OF
the rectory for nearly an hour watching the purplish-orange dawn
break over the treetops of Savannah. She had been so troubled by the
news of Jack's death and Kylie's arrest that she had barely slept a wink
all night. After nearly waking Dix with her tossing, she had finally
gotten up and made herself some sugared iced tea and taken it out on
the bedroom veranda. From there she could see nearly all of Lafayette
Square to the south of the cathedral, with its old winding live oaks,
and the historic Georgian homes that lined the picturesque avenues.
The sky was awakening with the morning, yet the ground beneath
remained in deep shadows. In spite of the lingering shade, the temperature was already stifling.

Amelia took in a deep breath and let it out slowly, then touched the
sweating glass of tea to her pounding temple. A white ceiling fan
churned overhead, but it did little to curb the annoying heat. Her thin
legs were propped up on the wrought iron railing, her cotton robe
hoisted above her knees, but the dew of sweat that covered her body
from May to September was ever present. Agitated, she stood from
the wicker chair and began pacing along the creaking porch trying to
relax, but images of a distraught Kylie pursued her.

Once again her friend had met with disaster, and for the first time
ever, Amelia had been unable to console her. To have her so far away
was simply unbearable. She would go to her as soon as possible, but
there were no available flights until later that evening. With the com-
muter flight to Atlanta and the long one to Boston, the earliest she
would arrive would be well after midnight. She had called the Boston
City Police Station an hour earlier, but they had nearly laughed when
she told them she wanted to speak with one of the prisoners. They had

also refused to give her any kind of information as to the status of Kylie's situation.

As her eyes fixed on the dark ground, shards of light finally broke through the thick foliage of the patio, bringing the colors of the garden to life. She glanced through the screened door at Dix who lay quietly sleeping, and then to the bedside clock. It was still only 6:15 A.M., too early to call Kylie's father for an update. Even though he had promised to call if there were any changes in the situation, she still felt compelled to check in.

She thought of the fisherman's deep voice over the line, cracking with the news, and the sadness in her soul deepened. In all the years she had known Sean McCallum, never had they had such an intimate conversation, nor one that lasted so long. In the hour and a half they spoke, not only did he tell her of the horrible news, he had also told her of the past—of the hidden secret of Julius Vanderpoel and of Kylie's discovery of the truth.

"But why didn't she tell me about it?" Amelia had asked, hurt that her friend had kept it secret from her.

"She was upset and confused," said her father. "It was my fault for not telling her long ago."

It had been a disturbing conversation full of remorse and pain wherein for the first time ever, Amelia felt that the intimidating father saw her as an adult. He had even seemed to take comfort in her voice.

When she thought of the troubles he had been forced to bear, of the pain his family had faced, she was amazed that any of them had survived. To find out that Kylie had witnessed a murder as a child was certainly unsettling, but not the least bit surprising. It actually made some of the pieces fit better, explaining more than even Amelia wanted to admit. Her gaze wandered past the square to the Colonial Park Cemetery on her left. She had remembered Kylie as a child walking along the cemetery on recess break, staring at the old, rotting graves and talking with the tombstones. St. Ann's School for Girls was next to the cemetery and the playground bordered on the burial ground wall. It had been a forbidden zone for all of the children; but as usual, Kylie McCallum had broken the rules.

When Kylie first arrived at the private school, she had been an outsider, remaining off by herself in what appeared to be a shell of contentment. Every morning her beautiful, illusive mother would drop

her off in a rusty sedan and every night the clanking old car would be
waiting to pick her up. Because St. Ann's was a private school usually
reserved for the upper class families of Savannah, the sight of the old
car dropping the child off daily was an oddity. What had been even
stranger was that Kylie's older brother, Aidan, had gone to a public
school while Kylie to a private. The seemingly unfair treatment had
bothered Kylie her entire life, for her brother had clearly not received
the same education as herself. But with the history of the Boston
events finally in light, Amelia understood. It hadn't been that Kylie
was favored over Aidan, it was simply to protect her. The McCallums
had moved their family to Savannah and sent their daughter to the
conservative school in an attempt to shelter her from further tragedy.

But the troubles for the McCallum family hadn't ceased with the
move to Georgia. Lila was originally from the outer bayous of Savannah and had relatives around to ease the transition, but the change had
still proved a formidable one. Sean had a difficult time adjusting his
trade to the Southern waters. He sold his heavier-bottomed boat designed for the harsher sea, for a flatter-bottomed shrimping boat, but
still couldn't make ends meet. Lila had been forced to work as a maid
in the wealthier homes of Savannah, some of which had daughters at
St. Ann's. It was rumored that some of the mothers had even forbidden their daughters from associating with Kylie because of her family's social status. Even Amelia's own mother had warned her about
associating with the family that lived in the dark bayou only a couple
of miles behind the Blackwell mansion on the bank of the Skidaway
River.

"They're from a different class than you," her mother had said in
her gentlest Southern drawl, but the words had fallen on deaf ears.
From the moment the timid Amelia had laid eyes on Kylie, she was
fascinated with the tart little redhead who took no flak from any one,
and with her raven-haired mother who always smiled at her through
the car window. Within a short time, the two little girls had become
unlikely friends and had been so ever since.

Amelia's mother had eventually grown to accept the inseparable
friendship. To make things easier on Kylie and her working mother,
she had even started taking Kylie to school along with her own daughter. Over the years Amelia's parents and the McCallums had met at
the occasional graduation or school function where they exchanged

pleasantries like two alien species interested in one another yet most comfortable with keeping a distance. Once, when Amelia's mother had been in an exceptionally generous mood, she had invited the McCallums over for a dinner party; the request had been politely declined much to everyone's relief. Amelia knew that her mother found the McCallums fascinating if nothing else. She often questioned Amelia when she would return from their tiny house in the bayou, asking what sort of things they discussed at the dinner table and how Lila dressed. Amelia told her as little as possible, for she knew that if her mother learned of the life that the McCallums led, she would probably never again be allowed there. There were no salad forks or butter knives, no linen napkins or guest towels, only the bare necessities and a zest for life lacking in Amelia's home. The conversation at the dinner table was not kind and subdued, but impassioned and at times even angry. The food was plentiful, yet only that which they needed, and the taste was not rich and refined, but robust and fresh. Many of the vegetables had come from Lila's garden and the meat from the surrounding woods. Kylie's uncles lived nearby, their avid hunting providing a steady supply of wild game.

While some of the best times of Amelia's life were spent in the small house, so were some of the worst. She had witnessed many fights between Lila and Sean that bordered on traumatic in comparison to her own quiet household. Most of the time the squabbles had remained subdued, with Sean backing down after a warning glare from Lila. But occasionally the fights had become terrifying with glass sailing through the air and screaming voices. It was at these times that she and Kylie would disappear into the woods where they created a world of their own among the cypress and palmetto. They would disappear for hours until they heard the squeal of a fiddle and the dancing of feet. They would return to find a small party underway—the broken glass vanished and the smiles replaced.

The McCallums had lived their lives to the fullest; they experienced more highs and lows than any family that Amelia had ever seen. In that respect, the news from Kylie's father was normal and expected, but even though the bad had come to be anticipated, the pain it brought never lessened. Amelia ached inside from the torturous happenings and could think of nothing other than getting to Kylie and wrapping her arms around her.

"Hey, what are you doing out here?" asked Dix from behind her. He was standing in the doorway looking as though he had been run over by a truck. His black hair was standing straight up and his skin looked positively ashen. His eyes had healed from their surgery, but whenever faced with bright light he squinted more than he used to.

"Did I wake you up?" she asked running her hand along his bare chest.

"I heard the porch creaking and—"

The phone rattled from the bedside and they both froze. It had to be someone calling about Kylie for nobody phoned that early. Amelia set the glass down and raced into the bedroom. When she heard Kylie on the other line she couldn't help but cry.

"I'm so glad to hear your voice," she sighed through the tears. "Where are you?"

Kylie's response was low and monotone, as if she had been numbed by the trauma. "Don't cry Melia. It'll all be okay. I'm at my dad's house in Swampscott."

"You sound so far away."

"I'm calling from outside, by the dock," she explained. "I wanted to talk to you alone."

"What happened? Why did they let you go?"

Kylie told her about Clyde Tremblay's confession and her release. Amelia was so relieved that her friend had been cleared of the charges that she was finally able to relax back onto the bed. But just as she started to feel that everything was going to be alright, the tone in Kylie's voice grew darker. Her friend was hesitating, clearly frightened to continue.

"What is it?" she asked, sitting up.

After a moment, the quiet voice finally answered. "Clyde Tremblay's not the one who killed Jack."

"What do you mean?"

Again the silence. "You've got to promise . . . you've got to—"

"What is it?" she asked, getting up from the bed.

"Do you remember Dr. Jordan, the psychiatrist who saw me after the accident?"

"Yes," said Amelia.

"Do you remember he said that a spiritual entity couldn't cross over into the physical world to hurt someone?"

A chill rose on Amelia's arms. "Yes, I remember."

"Well he was wrong, Melia. He was wrong."

At first jolted by the assertion, Amelia was finally able to respond. "What are you talking about?"

The explanation that followed was done calmly and efficiently, yet there was a silent terror that lay beneath the words. Her friend started with the day she first saw the dark figure in the Northend and continued through until her release from jail that morning. As she spoke of the fate that awaited them, Amelia quietly listened—her own fear mounting with each passing sentence.

"He was watching us," said Kylie softly. "Not only was he following me, he was following Jack. He was waiting for the perfect time and he found it. Everyone thinks Clyde Tremblay did it. I would have told them, but they never would have believed me . . . the questions had already been answered."

Amelia suddenly noticed that her entire body was quivering and that she was pacing back and forth across the bedroom.

"Are you still there?" asked the voice.

"Yes," she said, her throat tight. "Why didn't you talk to me before this? Why didn't you call me when you first found out about this Vanderpoel?"

"I was scared," she answered. "I thought I was losing my mind."

"Why don't the rest of us remember the stuff from the accident?" asked Amelia, her tone sharper and more frantic than she wanted. "And what about the night of the fire?" she pressed. "If you saw him, why didn't Jack?"

"He said that . . . my mind opens me up to him."

"But why you?"

"I don't know."

For a moment there was only the sound of static between them.

"You don't believe me, do you?" came the distant voice.

Amelia tried to find the words. "It's not that I don't," she said softly. "Just imagine how this sounds. What you're saying is that a killer gets rewarded by getting to kill more." Dix looked up from the edge of the bed. "Murderers are sent to hell, Kylie, not rewarded with—"

"It's not like that," her friend interrupted. "Something's very painful to him about it. I don't know how to describe it. It's like he's caught in it . . . like it controls him."

"But why him?" asked Amelia. "Why the man from your past?"

"He didn't know he was from my past," came the faint response. "His memory has somehow been erased."

"That sounds so satanic." Amelia stopped and shook her head. "I can't . . . I can't believe we're saying these things." In spite of herself, foreboding had wedged in her chest. "This goes against every-thing . . . against the Bible."

There was another silence. "I'm sorry," Kylie said. "I didn't mean to scare you."

"Well you have," snapped Amelia. She turned away from Dix's probing eyes—toward the sunshine and the fluttering birds. "I'm sorry."

"That's okay," said Kylie, drawing distant again. "I understand if you don't believe me. I know it's a lot."

Amelia heard the pain in her friend's voice but she couldn't bring herself to respond.

"Maybe you shouldn't come here," Kylie said softly. "You may think there's no danger—"

"I want to come," she insisted.

"But if you get on the plane and something goes wrong—"

"I won't let you face Jack's funeral alone."

"Then maybe Dix could come with you."

Amelia looked down at her husband's worried face. "His moving business has been doing really well and he can't take the time away right now," she hedged. Amelia didn't have the heart to tell her friend they were broke and that she had borrowed the money for her own ticket from her mother.

"Please be careful," repeated Kylie. "If the weather looks bad don't chance it."

"I won't."

"You should give me your flight information."

"Your dad already has it."

"Be careful," Kylie said. Then her voice finally broke. "No matter what you believe, I swear I thought it was Jack outside that night. I never would have abandoned him if I'd known—"

"I know that, Kylie," she said gently.

"Even if you think that I'm . . . that I'm losing—" but Kylie's own heavy sigh cut herself off. "Please, just be careful."

As Amelia replaced the phone to its cradle she felt dazed. The conversation seemed unreal, as though she had just watched a scene in a film where the words had taken place between two characters. Even Kylie's voice had been drawn and reserved as though she were observing it from afar.

She glanced back down at the phone, half expecting it to ring again and for Kylie to take it all back as some kind of joke, but the calmness of her friend's conviction had been too haunting. Maybe the stress of losing yet another loved one had been the final blow to Kylie's reason; maybe her mind had at last given way to the steady barrage of loss, hardship and pain. But Amelia knew better; Kylie was strong—tough enough to endure nearly anything.

"What was that all about?" asked Dix.

Amelia turned to the questioning eyes. "I don't know," she said looking down at her hands and then at the room around her. For a moment she considered the possibility of her friend's theory: that she really was supposed to have died and that some sort of angels of death were watching them from the shadows, holding vigil until that perfect time to take them. She thought of the spider that had crept along her desk the evening before and the black bird she had spotted in the tree outside, watching her through the window night after night. But no, it was too terrifying to even ponder.

"Amelia?"

The clear sound of her husband's voice pulled her from her thoughts. She turned back to find him staring at her with frightened eyes. She knew in that moment that just the possibility of the unseen shadows would be enough to drive her mad. She wasn't like Kylie who could handle grim happenings and dark thoughts so agilely; she was more fragile and susceptible to her own fear. Dix was protective and overly so, perhaps because he saw her vulnerability.

She suddenly rushed to him and put her arms tight around his neck as if never to release him. "I love you," she whispered. "I love you."

"What is it?" he asked, pulling away to look at her.

"You won't believe what . . ." but then she stopped. She could simply choose not to believe it. It was a crazy time and Kylie was upset.

"What?" he asked.

When she told him of the conversation, the skepticism in his eyes was enough to assuage her fear. He quickly pointed out that not only had the arsonist confessed, but that Kylie was distraught, that she was simply delirious from lack of sleep and from the pain of losing Jack.

"I'm sure she thought she saw something in the smoke," he said. "But she was upset and when a person is in a situation like that there's no telling how they're going to react."

As she silently listened, the tears came upon her, not only out of unease, but for Jack. "But don't you think it's strange that . . . that—"

"That what?"

"That Jack's dead," she finally managed to say. "Don't you think it's weird for him to die so soon after the accident?"

"The two have nothing to do with each other," he said steadily.

"But this isn't like Kylie. She's always been so strong and . . . and what about Mama?" she said, her own argument working her up. "She's been saying that something bad would happen. That if I—"

"If you what?"

"That the accident was a warning—"

"She's just trying to control you," he countered. "Don't you see that?"

"But I've been so scared, Dix!" she said, turning away to catch her breath. "There's been this awful dark feeling that I can't shake! Maybe this is what I've been afraid of," she gasped, the thoughts swarming her. "Maybe Kylie's right. Maybe I shouldn't be flying."

Dix grabbed hold of his wife's hand to calm her. "Hey, hey, little Bluebird," he said pulling her into him. "You're getting ahead of yourself. Believe me, nothing is going to happen to you on that flight," he whispered.

She tried to take in his words but the tightening of her chest grew stronger and her breath less and less accessible. "But what if . . ." she gasped.

"Hey," he said soothingly, stroking the short tufts of her hair.

"I can't . . . breathe," she gasped.

"Just let it go," he said. Obediently, she turned her head into his chest, until her breath finally calmed.

After a long moment, he took her delicate face into his hands. "Don't freak out on this, Amelia," he said gently. "I don't want to see you hurt."

He kissed her gently on the forehead.

"Father Matt is coming this afternoon to look at the storm drains," he said softly. "Maybe you should talk to him about it. Then if you still feel nervous, we can cancel your flight."

"No," she said, shaking her head. Pulling back, she squared her shoulders in resolution. "I need to go. No matter what—I need to be there for Kylie."

Two

SEAN MCCALLUM TUGGED THE CHEST DOWN FROM THE CLOSET SHELF, the box landing on the linoleum floor in a dusty heap. His daughter, who was sitting at the kitchen table, turned back when she heard the noise.

"I thought you could wear some of your mother's old things," he explained.

"That would be nice, Daddy," she responded with a sigh.

They were the first words he had heard her utter in almost an hour. From the moment they had left the police station, his daughter had drawn inward and had barely spoken since. When they first arrived at the cottage, she had immediately gone back out into the foggy morning. "I just need some air," she had explained, but when he glanced out the window he had seen her at a pay phone by the small bait shop. He was certain that she was talking with Amelia. The two had been secretive since childhood and he knew better than to interfere. They were closer than sisters, closer than any two friends he had ever seen and it gave him comfort to know that his daughter had someone in whom she could confide. After Kylie had returned to the house, she had taken a long shower while Sean made breakfast. Through the splashing water, he was certain he had heard her crying. She had emerged from the bathroom nearly twenty minutes later, with her hair wet, wearing the odd-fitting clothes someone had given her at the hospital. She had sat down at the table and remained there since, staring out at the boats disappearing in and out of the gray fog that hung in the bay, the plate of eggs and grits before her untouched.

McCallum pried the lock loose from the rusty metal chest and as he pulled it open his daughter got up from the rickety table. The hinges squealed loudly as the heavy lid banged against the wall. When he saw the dresses of his wife neatly laid upon one another, he felt the intense need for a drink. The clothes were much older and more tattered than he had remembered. He could tell by the look on his daughter's face that she was thinking the same.

"I didn't give your mother much, love," he said. "But maybe they can tide you over until we can get you some more."

Kylie gently lifted the first dress out of the chest as though it were made of thin glass. It was a simple cream sundress that McCallum remembered his wife wearing during the hot summer months in Georgia.

"They're beautiful, Daddy," she said. "I'm glad you saved them."

His daughter disappeared with the dress into the bedroom, just as there was a slight rap on the screen door. Dillon O'Rourke was standing outside on the porch, looking tired and worn.

"Door's open," McCallum called, heading for the kitchen cupboard where he removed a couple of glasses and a bottle of whiskey.

The young man peered through the screen apologetically. "I'm sorry to bother you—"

"You're not bothering anyone," said McCallum gruffly. "When are you gonna remember we're family, son?"

"I know how tired you and Kylie are," the young man said stepping into the paltry room.

"We're all tired," said McCallum, holding out a glass. "Whiskey?"

"No thank you, sir. It would probably put me to sleep," the young man sighed. "Is Kylie around? Or is she sleeping?"

"She's awake," said McCallum pouring himself some of the liquor. "She'll be out in a minute."

Just then, the door to the bedroom swayed open and Kylie appeared in the shadows wearing the cream-colored sundress. McCallum was so stunned at how much his daughter resembled her beautiful mother that the glass in his hand nearly slipped through his fingers.

"Sweet Jesus," he gasped, for the dress was a perfect fit.

Like her mother, Kylie had the curvaceous body of a strong sturdy woman and she filled out every inch of the feminine garment that no longer looked old and tattered. It was just as McCallum had remembered it. The smooth cotton material had regained its essence, and like the rejuvenated fabric, a piece of his wife had also come back to life and was standing before him. Like Lila's, Kylie's hair was wild and long, escaping from the clasp that held it back from her bare shoulders. Her neck was delicate and sublime, like that of an enchantress of another time and another place.

Just as Lila had the first time he saw her, his daughter reminded him of the ship's figurehead he had admired as a child in the waters off of Southern Ireland. It was a beautiful fair maiden who guided the prow of the ship through the stormy seas, always to return it to its homeland, undaunted by the troubled waters. For a moment, he mused that Kylie resembled the memorable figurehead even more than his wife had. Lila's beauty had been more ethereal, while Kylie, whose shoulders, knees and face were sprinkled with tiny freckles, had the earthy quality of a dauntless heroine who could conquer the most brutal of savages.

Kylie shyly looked down, away from the eyes of the two men. "This is a lot cooler than the other stuff," she said softly, wiping the tiny line of perspiration from above her lip.

McCallum had to force himself to look away, for he could tell he was embarrassing his daughter.

At first hesitant, Kylie gained her composure and stepped into the room, slipping her hands into Dillon's.

"Dillon," she said, "I'm sorry if I was rude to Dr. Jordan. It was nice of him to come."

Dillon smiled sadly, he too, seeming to look away from the stunning woman before him. "I'm sure he understands, Kylie."

"What brings you all the way up here?" she asked, for it was a thirty-minute drive from Cambridge to Swampscott.

McCallum instantly knew the answer and it made him want to leap for the door; but in spite of the dastardly impulse, he held his boots firm, the glass of liquor the anchor holding him still.

"I need to talk to you about Jack's funeral," Dillon responded quietly.

McCallum watched the green eyes of his daughter but contrary to what he had expected, they didn't so much as flinch.

"I didn't know when they were going to release you," said Dillon. "I hope you don't mind that I arranged a lot of it yesterday."

Kylie gave him a tender smile. "I'm glad you did."

McCallum was happy that his daughter had found her full strength again, but it left him and the young man standing beside him bumbling about at her mercy. She offered Dillon a seat at the kitchen table, where they began discussing the funeral in detail. McCallum took a seat on the couch and silently listened, but the slumping cushions couldn't sustain him for long. With the talk of burials, coffins and gravestones, he began to feel trapped. He paced about the tiny house, trying to avoid the haunting sight of his daughter sitting at the table.

It was like watching Lila after the death of their son, Aidan, sitting with the preacher in their home in the bayou. She had sat at that very same table planning the funeral for their eldest son after he had over-dosed on heroin at the age of eighteen. When the sheriff had come to the house with the news, Lila had collapsed like a crumpled doll. For two days and nights she ate nothing and spoke not a word. Then finally, on the third day she summoned the preacher and planned the funeral with the calm and grace of a queen. Never again did McCallum see his wife shed a tear over the death, yet the misery it left in her eyes lasted for years. It wasn't until the birth of their son Tucker that the darkness faded. Those years in between the death of one and the birth of another had been the most miserable ones of McCallum's life. Their once lively household became quiet, where he longed for his wife to lash out at him with her beguiling temper, instead of the stolid composure she held herself within. To see his daughter's sad-ness trapped within the same countenance was too much to bear. With a sickened heart, he watched her speak quietly and reserved, wondering how long it would last, and who or what could pull her from it.

Three

MOONLIGHT STREAMED THROUGH THE CLERESTORY WINDOWS OF ST. Vincent's Cathedral, sending soft rays of light into the darkened nave of the structure.

Beneath the scant glow of a workman's lantern draped over a tall ladder, Amelia pulled up the last piece of tarpaulin from under the newly varnished pews and rolled it into a long piece. When she stood back up, her head rushed from the smell of tung oil that clung to the air; in spite of the breeze that wafted in from the open windows, the odor was overpowering. She had been working since early that morning, and even though her temples had been throbbing for hours, her back ached and her legs were stiff, she had continued. Knowing that she would be gone for at least a few days, she had wanted the refinishing of the pews to be complete so the church would have time to air out before her return.

She looked at her watch which read 7:15 P.M. With the job finally complete, she had less than two hours to pack and to make her flight. She quickly dragged the long roll of tarpaulin into the darkened west aisle of the church and scooted it against the wall. Dropping her work gloves on top of it, she went back and pulled the lantern from the ladder and laid it directly on the floor. She dragged the ladder over to the side so that it didn't obstruct Father Matt in case he dropped by to survey her progress during her absence. With a heavy sigh, she looked around the shadowy cathedral and tried to draw a mental calendar of when she would be finished.

The renovation of the church had been a much longer process than she had anticipated, but it was nearly complete. While at first hired to update the cathedral after it had fallen into disrepair, she had convinced Father Matt the best thing to do would be to restore the church to its original grandeur. Her predecessors had ineffectually tried to make the two-hundred-year-old church appear contemporary only to mar the cathedral's integrity. She had resurrected the old statues and fixtures from the basement, stripped the entire church's woodwork of numerous coats of paint and restored it to its natural finish, torn out the hideously inappropriate carpeting and sealed the stone floors. She had sent two statues off for repair and ordered three reproductions from the carving department of St. John The Divine in New York. There had been eleven beautiful tableaux of the fourteen stations of the cross in the basement, where they had been exiled after three had been damaged beyond repair. With the entire family again intact, they stood along the north aisle of the church, clumped together beneath a veil of plastic. Like melancholy actors awaiting their posts in the reenactment of Christ's crucifixion, they stood obediently still and silent. At their feet, lay the iron chandeliers that were to be reattached once the rewiring had been completed.

"Another month," she mused aloud, certain that would be how long it would take her. As she looked up at the empty light sockets, an eerie feeling overtook her—a month was longer than she would have; she would not see the cathedral to its completion. She took a deep breath and tried to shake off the feeling, but the walls themselves seemed to whisper the same. She backed toward the door, suddenly feeling like an outsider in the foreboding atmosphere that she herself had resurrected. In removing the colorful paints and carpets, she had brought the true darkness of the cathedral to life again. The majestic arches, muted statues and shadowy corners bespoke of a secretive world of ages long past, where dark angels and beasts of the night could conceivably roam. To hear Kylie speak of such things in the modern day world had been absurd, but to imagine them within the portentous setting seemed perfectly sane.

Amelia turned toward the darkened chancel that held the towering altar and thought of the words and the rituals the vested priest would enact when the church was reopened. Wearing long robes he would speak of death, resurrection, spirits, angels and miracles, and chant prayers over a chalice of water and wine. The congregation, fresh from their air-conditioned cars with cell phones in pocket would scarcely even notice that they had entered another dominion. With little or forgotten understanding of the archaic rituals they witnessed they would answer with "Amen." They would agree to the notions of rising from the dead and turning water to wine, then return to their televisions and newsstands where they would scoff at anything not scientifically proven. It was safe to believe in another dimension, as long as it was confined to the shackles of what they wanted it to be. But as Amelia felt the cool presence around her, she knew that man could never contain it nor fully understand it. She knew that no matter how long the churches would stand and man would flock to pay homage, he would forever remain the outsider.

With a chill, she wondered if the statues knew what beset the walls in her absence. As she moved toward the side door that led to the rectory, she tried not to notice the stone eyes that watched her. Just as her hand touched the huge handle, she paused a moment and looked back. She was certain she had felt someone behind her, standing in the empty pews. But there was no one there, only the rays of light that shot upward from the floor where she had left the lantern. She quickly walked toward it and clicked it off pitching the church into darkness. She stood frozen as her eyes adjusted. Finally the murky shadows appeared and she started back for the door. As she walked past the last column, her eyes were caught by the shadow of a winged figure cast upon a pillar. Startled, she jumped back, but then relaxed when she saw that the shadow was only a pattern projected from the stained-glass windows that were positioned open.

"Hey," came the voice of Dix from behind her.

She spun around. "Damn it, Dix!"

"I'm sorry," he said. "I just don't want you to miss your flight."

THE BLACK and white suit bags sat neatly in the dusty corner of the at-tic, as far out of sight as possible. After their last use, they had been banished to the inconspicuous spot, where they had remained since.

The couple stood staring down at the luggage as if at any moment it would open up and devour them whole. From where Amelia stood, she could see the tiny scar in the side of the largest bag where the metal of Gavin Collins' chair had ripped into it.

"How much stuff are you going to take?" asked Dix, tugging on the pull-chain that brought the room to light.

"Oh I don't know," she said, casually stepping forward and grab-bing the bag. "Enough for a week I suppose."

Dix touched her arm. "Are you sure you don't want me to call Fa-ther Matt and have him come over?"

"Don't be silly, Dix," she said with a feigned smile. "I'm not going to let a little bag scare me off."

"Here I'll take that one," he said, removing the suitcase from her hand. "How 'bout you grab the duffle?"

The couple descended from the attic down the winding iron stair-case and took the bags into the bedroom. Amelia lay the duffle on the bed and opened the door to the porch; the sound of the night locust and crickets filled the air. After a long miserable day, the temperature had finally dropped with the setting sun.

"I'm gonna be lonely here without you," said Dix, with a truly mel-ancholy sigh.

"Oh you'll be hitting the bars in no time," she laughed.

"Yeah, but I'll still miss you," he said with a devilish grin.

"You rat."

Amelia grabbed some underwear from the dresser and pulled the side pocket of the duffle open. She tried to jam the lingerie down into the compartment, but there was something blocking the way. She reached in and pulled out a colorful booklet. "So that's what happened to this thing," she said.

"What is it?"

"It's the White Mountain guide I bought when Kylie invited us on the trip," she said, thumbing through the thin book. "Don't you remember I was trying to find it when we wanted to go to those hot springs?"

Dix shrugged uncertainly.

Just looking at the familiar pictures sent a wave of nausea through Amelia's stomach. Even the vacation before the crash had been tainted with the accident. She tossed it upon the bed and turned back to the dresser. She grabbed another handful of underwear along with some socks and walked back over to the duffle. Just as she started to stuff them into the bag she noticed the picture staring up at her from the bed and her breath caught. On the back cover of the guide was an old stone cottage just as Kylie had described.

Dix noticed the look on his wife's face. "What's the matter?"

Amelia dropped the lingerie and slowly picked up the book.

"What is it?" asked Dix.

"This is the cabin from Kylie's dream. This is the place," she said. "It's got the paned windows, the door has the black hinges—"

"Come on, Amelia," Dix groaned.

"No," she said, quickly flipping through the book to the corresponding page. Another photo of the cottage was inside, her eyes scanning the text. "It says that the Appalachian Mountain Club has these emergency shelters all over the mountains, old cottages and newer ones they've built. And that they leave the doors unlocked for stranded hikers. This is the place, Dix! It's even got the weather vane on top of it!" she gasped, staring down at the little hatted man with his arm pointing outward.

Dix stammered a moment, before finding his thoughts. "Then you must have shown it to her," he said simply.

"No," she said, the cold hand of fear gripping the back of her neck. "Don't you understand? I put it in this bag, but when we got up there I couldn't find it. Kylie never saw it."

Four

THE THICK FOG THAT HUNG OVER NAHANT BAY LINGERED FROM THE DAY into the night. Sean McCallum sat silently in the living room with the lamp beside him glowing dimly, sipping from the bottle of whiskey and quietly smoking a cigarette.

His daughter had taken refuge to the bedroom a couple of hours earlier where she had remained since. He had peeked in on her thirty minutes earlier and she appeared to be in a deep sleep, the Bible she had been poring over lying open at her side. At first he had thought she was looking for something for Jack's funeral, a comforting quote or a reassuring prophecy, but when he had suggested the only quote that he knew of himself, she looked to him, dazed and seemingly at a loss. Clearly she was looking for something other than funeral rhetoric and judging by her increasingly agitated search throughout the day, she had not found whatever comfort it was that she had been seeking.

McCallum mashed the cigarette nub into the ashtray and then pulled some tobacco and papers from his pocket and began to roll another. He felt confined and nervous and wanted to head down to O'Brian's Pub at the end of the docks, but first wanted to make sure his daughter was resting soundly.

Abruptly the telephone on the kitchen cabinet came to life. Sean sprang from the couch, accidentally spilling tobacco all over himself, to stop the alarming clamor of the old dial ringer before it woke Kylie.

"Yes," he said gruffly into the black receiver.

"Mr. McCallum, it's Amelia," came the thin voice over the line. "I'm sorry to disturb you."

"No disturbance at all," he said. "Are you on your way?"

"I'm still in Savannah," she said.

"Oh. I thought you would have left by now," said the father.

"Well . . . I was . . . just finishing up packing," she said hesitantly. "Is Kylie there?"

"Yeah, but she's sleeping," he whispered. "I hate to wake her. She had a hard day."

There was a troubled pause.

"Is everything okay?" he asked.

"Yeah," she said, but her tone was unconvincing.

"I can wake her up if it's important."

"No . . . that's okay," she answered.

"Do you want me to have her call you?"

Again the silence. "It won't do any good," she finally answered. "I have to leave for the airport now if I'm going to make my flight."

It wasn't until after he hung up the phone that he realized the sound in the young woman's voice had been fear. *It must be the accident,* he thought. She was afraid to fly.

"It'll be okay, love," he said softly as though she could hear him hundreds of miles away.

He knocked the spilled tobacco from his jeans and flannel shirt and walked softly over to the bedroom door. He slowly pushed it ajar, only wide enough to peek inside. His daughter's back was to him and she appeared to be asleep.

"Love?" he whispered faintly, but she remained still. Satisfied that she would sleep for awhile, he grabbed the keys to his truck and boat then locked the front door behind him. At midnight he would pick up Amelia at the airport, but until then, he would wait the evening out at the pub down the walkway. He would then retire for the night upon the *Miss Lila* giving his daughter and her friend the privacy of the house.

Five

WITHIN THE DARKENED BEDROOM, KYLIE LAY SILENTLY LISTENING TO her father pull the front door shut. She waited a moment and then stood from the swayed bed and peered through the cracked door into the front room. The smell of cigarettes and Old Spice cologne lingered in the air, where her father had been only a moment earlier. Though she was relieved that he had finally decided to go out, to see the empty room filled her with apprehension; for the first time since the fire, she was truly alone.

She edged the door open and quickly walked to the front windows. Through the dirty, curtainless panes she looked to the right of the house, past the bait shop to the pub, but the fog was so heavy that the neon sign was a mere colorful smear in the night. Though she could not see him, she was certain that was where her father had gone. After pacing about all day, worrying over her every move, it was good for him to get out and be with his friends. It had been a difficult day with the telephone ringing every five minutes. Only a moment earlier she had heard it ring again and assumed that it was another voice filled with condolences. When she heard her father whispering to the person on the other end, she had pulled herself tighter into a ball, unable to bear yet another bereaved caller phoning to comfort her, only to need consolation themself.

Jack's in a good place, she had taken to saying. Jack's grandmother had told her that very same thing that morning and she had taken the words for own, for she had none other.

"Jack's in a good place," she whispered to her faint reflection in the paned glass, but the sentence was empty and meaningless. As she peered into the murky night, her mind once again returned to the trenches of the unknown where it had searched tirelessly all day for the answers to Amelia's questions. As her friend had said, nowhere in the Bible could she find the creatures. It spoke of heaven and hell, of angels and the devil but not of the force that Julius Vanderpoel belonged. Nowhere could she find that murderers became angels and that angels became hideous creatures scurrying along the darkened alleys and subways of earth.

It's like a dream, came the voice of Dr. Jordan. *When you turn around and face the monster, he loses his power.*

"You were wrong, Doctor," she said bitterly.

Remaining at the window, she felt the vast empty sea swaying beyond the haze. It was the same ocean she had enjoyed from the window of her bedroom loft, but now the solitude of it created a hollow aching. She had to turn away and when she did, she saw the bottle of whiskey sitting alone on the table, the liquor illuminated and golden by the light of the lamp. Swiftly going to it, she pulled out the cork. Her hand was tingling as she took a tin cup from the cabinet and filled it to the top. She brought the rim of the mug slowly to her lips, her nostrils breathing in the numbing intoxication. With a long steady swig, the spirit trickled down her throat, burning away the frozen lump in her chest. Resting down in one of the chairs, she gripped the handle of the cup for stability as her father had earlier that morning.

She took another drink and then another, staring silently toward the gray windows.

"Where are you Jack?" she whispered, willing the answers to her questions to materialize from the careening fog. If she saw spirits of death then why had her mind been opened to them? Why had the hideous nightmare been remembered by her and no one else? She thought of the cottage, of the deformed bird in the windowsill and of the chaotic fight within the blue shadowy light. The only thing that differentiated her from the others was the feather she had taken from the floor of the cabin.

Her fingers grasped the cameo around her neck. She had put the feather inside the locket, yet when she had awakened three weeks later it had been gone. She pulled the necklace from around her neck and let it dangle in front of her, the trinket swinging gently back and forth before her eyes. The tiny peach and cream cameo spun silently round, glittering in the soft glow of the lamp. After a moment it finally stopped, with the face of the cameo insolently turning away from her as if not to reveal its secrets. She removed her hand from the cool mug and snapped the dainty locket open with her fingertips. There was a photo of her mother with the harsh shadows of the Georgia sun beating down upon her pale skin. She was smiling. Kylie pulled the little gold ring away that held the photo in place and laid it upon the linoleum table. Then she slid the photo from the locket and held the bare trinket into the light. At first it appeared normal with nothing out of the ordinary, then like a snake coiled within a garden hose, the warped image struck out at her. As though melted directly into the gold, there was a tiny tracing that curved round forming the faint image of a feather. For a moment she dare not blink for fear the slight tracing would disappear. Her breath caught and her heart silenced, then suddenly it was thumping out of control. Without her knowing, it had been there all along, lying camouflaged against her own beating heart. Abruptly she bolted from the table and went into the bathroom where she opened the medicine chest for a razor.

With the blade in hand, she raced back into the living room and pulled the lamp over onto the kitchen table. She sat back down and put the sharp blade to the locket, but then took a last minute swig from the bottle to steady her shaking hands.

. . .

SHE PUSHED the tip of the blade into the tiny crevice of the locket and started to scrape along the inner-line of the image. Slowly the precious metal began to give beneath the pressure, tiny flecks of gold accumulating at the side of the groove that she formed. After cutting as deeply as she could, she anxiously pulled back the blade and held the locket beneath the light of the lamp; there was nothing under the surface of the warped image.

"There's gotta be," she whispered aloud, for something solid had to have made the distinct pattern within the precious metal. Again she put the barbed blade to the locket and cut deeper. With her head bent in concentration, she had dug as far into the locket as possible, when she heard a faint sound stir within the shadows of the room. She looked up from the glow of the lamp, the blade frozen within her fingertips. Like an icy spider crawling over her scalp, the words crept from behind her.

"I've missed you, Kylie Rose."

The room blurred as she whirled around to find the master of the voice. The figure of Julius Vanderpoel was silhouetted before the window, the distant glow of the pub forming a red halo about his body.

Kylie vaulted from the table, the back of her chair thudding to the floor behind her. She backed toward the kitchen counter, as far away from the creature as possible.

He stood perfectly still, staring at her with a strange calm. His anemic skin blended with the blue shadows of the room, yet his gray eyes picked up the warmth of the lantern.

"I'm sorry I startled you," he said kindly.

Just standing before the beast who had set her husband on fire sent tears of rage screaming down Kylie's cheeks. She loathed the pale skin, the smooth hair and the gentle voice. She wanted to lash out at him but she remained still, her body trembling. "What do you want?" she asked, though her emotion nearly swallowed her voice.

"I just want to be near you a moment," he said gently.

She noticed his clothes and resented the choice. It was a dark aristocratic suit and red scarf that she recognized from her childhood—clearly arranged to put her mind at ease. In spite of the effort, his quintessence seemed in constant battle with the deceiving attire, just as it had when he was dressed in the smoking jacket in her living room. The strange movement was the ever present warning that the figure beneath the clothes was not a man as he appeared, but a creature from another world.

"What did you do with Jack?" she demanded through her tears. "Where did you take him?"

"I merely released him," he said simply. "Then he went on his own."

The creature's attention strayed toward her hand. For the first time, Kylie felt a sharp pain and a strange sensation trickling over her fingers. When she looked down, she saw that there was a steady stream of blood oozing from her fingertips where she had unknowingly clutched the razor within her grasp. She opened her hand to let the blade fall, but it was embedded so deeply in her forefinger that it hideously protruded on its own accord. As she pulled it from her flesh and let it fall to the floor, the figure slowly edged toward her, but she quickly backed along the counter closer to the bedroom.

"I'm not going to hurt you," he said.

It was the same promise he had made the night of the fire, yet he had brought her more pain than she could ever imagine. "You couldn't hurt me worse than you already have," she said bitterly.

The creature's eyes flinched with the accusation. "I didn't want to take him from you," he said. "I had no choice."

At thought of the figure ruthlessly splashing the gas while Jack lay asleep in his bed, the fury inside of her grew. Her impulse was to strike out at him but she remained still. "You could have done it another way," she said bitterly.

"He felt nothing but peace," he said.

"Like hell he did," she spat. "I saw him . . . I saw—"

"It doesn't matter what you saw," said Julius, his head rising with his assertion. "The human eye can be deceptive."

"He was screaming," she wept bitterly, wiping away her tears. "He was crying out—begging . . . and you did nothing but watch!"

Her anger brought a sudden chill to his warm eyes. "He felt no pain," he insisted, his face growing darker.

"Like hell!!" she screamed. Her temper took control and her body shot forward, grabbing the lamp from the table and swinging it toward the hideous phantom. As the room instantly plunged into darkness, the creature moved toward her so quickly and so smoothly that she didn't have time to escape. Without even feeling him take them, her hands were clasped within his. Her finger was throbbing as the blood ran down his wrist, but when he touched the wound the pain ceased.

"I'm the one who felt it," he said sharply.

He ran his own finger into the deepest cut, pulling back the flesh so that the blood flowed faster. Kylie gasped, but still there was no pain.

"I felt it," he whispered vehemently. "I felt the flames. I felt the singeing of the hairs and the melting flesh."

"He was screaming," she wept. "I saw it."

"His body was screaming—his soul felt mercy," he said. "Like an endorphin for the dying . . . for the bleeding, collapsing bodies, I'm the one who feels the torture."

As he stared at her with the bitter proclamation wet on his lips, his face slowly softened again and his eyes seemed to absorb her sorrow. He drew back his breath and removed his touch from her wound.

"If I could take away the pain in your heart, I would," he said softly, folding the bloody lesion together. "But I can't."

The sincerity of his gaze was fixed on her so closely that for a moment it was easy to forget that the being before her was no longer human. The melancholy visage took her in as it melted back to the man she remembered on the playground of her childhood. She felt the breath leave her for it wasn't a creature at all but the man she had admired so as a child—the man who had held her hand as she crossed the street and grasped her into his arms as he swung her about. The long silky lashes curved down upon the entrancing eyes that held the same flustering power over her they had when she was younger; they evoked feelings of attachment while they beheld the memory of terror. Not only was it the friend she had loved but the man who had hunted her through the air vent of the school—who had spawned a lifetime of nightmares and an onerous phobia of tight spaces. The man who would have killed her, had he been given the chance.

At once she knew that he heard her thoughts, for his already despondent face sank deeper into despair. "I didn't want to hurt you," he said, mournfully.

"But you would have," she countered softly.

His silent stare was an admission, one that chilled her, for never before had he confirmed his intent, never before had she truly believed the terrifying pursuit could have ended in her death.

"You were my rose," he murmured with regret.

In spite of herself, the shame in his eyes evoked her pity, the same dark empathy that had filled her when she had stumbled into the classroom years earlier. Never again would she forget the face that turned to her in anguish, with the warm dead body of the teacher lying still on the floor.

"And Ellen," he gasped, as if finding the image in her mind unbearable. Tiny beads of sweat began to roll down the sides of his cheeks and his breath deepened as if the painful emotions were a poison that had entered his bloodstream. His body pulled inward and his very flesh seemed to fight against his will. After a moment, he finally continued but an element of distraction had entered his tone. "She had been with someone," he said. "Someone I knew and trusted. She had seen him that day and I—" but he once again stopped. He seemed perplexed, as though his memory had hit a black void. "It was someone . . . someone . . ." He searched the air for the rest, until bewilderment overtook him and he turned toward the windows.

As he stared out to the shifting fog, the pub illuminated the side of his face, the blue of the moon and the red of the neon sign creating a surrealistic pallor to his sweaty skin. "Ellen," he whispered. His pale hand touched the windowpane and his eyes stared off into the distance. "I see pieces of her and I can feel her," he said painfully. "But they've hidden the rest from me."

He looked back at Kylie as if stealing a glimpse before he would have to turn away again to sustain his composure. Glassy tears had formed beneath the colorless eyes and spilled down upon the smooth skin. "I loved her," he whispered. "I never meant—" but the tortured voice that escaped was tainted with a ghastly screech. The sound was quick and violent, piercing into Kylie's skull like tiny prickles of fire.

As the creature instantly turned away like an animal that had been thwarted to the corner, Kylie was reminded of the danger of the being before her. She remained still, waiting for his next move. After a moment he spoke, his voice clear but embittered.

"They've taken her from me," he said.

To Kylie's unease, she noticed the resentment shifting something inside of him. The suit and bright scarf faded, as his stature became more powerful and resolute. She slowly began edging away, for she recognized the tell-tale signs of the cold creature that was once again emerging—the creature who had approached her in the cottage and who had murdered her husband.

"I can feel your fear," he whispered strangely. His voice was intense, lacking the inflections of Julius Vanderpoel's. "I can hear your heartbeat and feel your breath quickening. You have reason to be frightened, but it's not as it seems. I don't want to be like this. I don't want to be trapped . . . trapped in this . . ." but he stopped.

He was silent, staring out at the lights. "A man is nothing without memory," he said, "nothing but a blank slate."

As he turned toward her, Kylie was taken aback by the seething hatred that shone in his shadowed eyes. "That's what they've made me. A blank slate for others to take refuge in." He looked down at his hand as if really seeing it for the first time. "Hell isn't a pit of fire," he said simply. "It's a body that feels the pain of a thousand deaths but can never be destroyed. They don't want me to know that I was human once," he said, clenching his fist. "Made of flesh and blood that could yield to the pain . . . that I once felt the relief of my own death."

His eyes had turned toward her, but through his bitter words, his gaze stared through her, to the evil entity that had destroyed his essence. Kylie could feel the rage moving through her like a current, her throat tightening as if the anger were emanating from within herself. His face was cold and hard, yet sweat glistened from every pore.

Then, as if called from the depths of a dark forest, the gray eyes pulled back. As they focused on her, she felt a hideous drawing sensation within her stomach. The room about her seemed to dim and her energy drain as if he were taking something from her just by looking at her. There was no sign of Julius Vanderpoel, whose life had receded into the shadows of the vacant eyes. The pupils focused on her like an animal who had spotted its prey and was moving in for the feast.

"Through your eyes," he whispered, "I remembered the relief. When you led me to the prison, I saw it and felt it. I remembered the bars and the stench . . . the guard strapping me in while the priest read me my last rites . . . then the fire . . . the jolting pain." A strange gleam sparkled in the eyes. "It lasted only seconds before the relief came . . . before my blood vessels exploded and gave way to the pressure." He took a deep breath as if sucking the feeling into his very being. Then his gaze fell forward and detached, while his continuing thoughts played out on the wall behind her. "That's when they came to me," he said. "Like vultures, they had been watching and waiting."

When the creature silenced, a loud commotion suddenly came from outside. There were voices coming from the direction of the bar, then footsteps walking briskly down the wooden planking of the deck toward the cottage. Though the creature did not turn back to the window, his face registered the identity of the approaching party. Kylie's stomach turned, for she too recognized the heavy boots hitting the deck; it was her father. She instantly thought of the news-clip detailing Vanderpoel's execution and remembered the photo of her father within the audience. If the creature remembered his death, then maybe he remembered her father's presence and would somehow seek vengeance. Her eyes locked with those of the creature in a silent plea for her father's safety.

A smile of amusement twitched on the pale lips that slowly softened again to those of Julius Vanderpoel. "I didn't come for your father," he said gently.

"Then why did you?" she asked.

There was a moment of silence, the smile fading from the shadowed face. "There'll be no escape for either of us, my little rose. Soon they'll force me to take you," he said, looking downward. "Then the darkness will swallow me again."

The prophetic words reawakened the dread inside of her. She suddenly felt the presence of "they" as if they had been watching all along.

"Don't be frightened," he said gently. "I promise it will be painless."

Abruptly her father's voice cut through the darkness. "Kylie!" he called, as the footsteps quickened.

"And your friend," the voice continued, musing with sadness. "She's such a delicate one."

Kylie's mind shot to Amelia—to the flight that she had assuredly boarded. "What do you mean?" she gasped.

"It's not in my hands," came the quiet response. "It's in those of another."

The figure of her father blurred past the windows, then the doorknob began to turn, but the lock remained bolted.

"Kylie!" her father exclaimed from behind the door, but she could not move to unlock it. Her eyes remained riveted on the creature who remained still. After the jangling of keys, the door suddenly burst open, revealing her father standing breathless and frantic in the doorway. "Love!" he gasped. "Are you alright?! Gordy heard screaming!"

The sight of her father less than two feet from the phantom was more than her senses could bear. She tried to respond, to answer his plea but the freakish situation was too much. As the cool breeze drifted in, she couldn't take her eyes off the being that was silhouetted in the windows.

"Kylie?" her father implored, stepping closer, her silence clearly torturous to him. He glanced toward the corner but then quickly looked back at her.

His inability to see the silent visitor sent a despairing feeling of isolation through her; she was truly alone in the nightmare. Not even her father, who had protected her so vehemently over the years, would be able to save her from the grip of the specter.

"I'm sorry, Daddy," she whispered.

As her father moved to embrace her injured hand, she still could not take her eyes from the pale face that hung in the shadows. With a nod of his head, the creature slipped through the door and faded into the misty night.

Six

MCCALLUM HELD HIS DAUGHTER'S HAND TIGHT, HOPING TO STOP the profuse bleeding with the pressure of his own fingers. "What happened, love?" he implored, looking about the darkened room. The furniture was disheveled and the lamp lay broken on the floor as though a struggle had taken place. "Was someone here?"

The question finally drew his daughter's attention toward him, but the distraction in her eyes remained. "No Daddy," she answered, softly. "No one was here."

Though relieved by her answer, McCallum couldn't keep his legs from shaking. Not only had he sprinted from the bar, but to find his daughter standing in the darkness, with her cream dress smeared with blood and the room in disarray, was too much for his rigid body to handle.

Only minutes earlier, Gordy Smith had come up to him in the tavern and casually mentioned that he had heard screaming from the cottage five or ten minutes prior. After nearly slugging him in the mouth for not telling him sooner, McCallum bolted for the door. He left the bar in a daze, but by the time he reached his house, the full impact of the information had laid its claws into him. He was certain that his daughter's stalker had finally materialized. With each labored step of his rigid body, he imagined the brutal attack that was surely being waged. Upon finding the cottage door locked and the windows intact, he felt relieved that no one had broken in; but the mess inside had sent his imagination reeling once again.

"Are you sure no one else was here?" he asked.

"I'm positive, Daddy," his daughter answered, but her eyes avoided his own. She started to slide her hand from his but he held her tight. "You need stitches, love," he said, removing a hanky from his pocket and wrapping it tightly around her finger.

"No, it's okay," she said, nervously pulling away from him. She turned toward the broken pieces of the lamp which lay scattered across the floor. "I'm sorry for the mess," she said. "I was trying to pull it over and I slipped and . . ." but her voice trailed off as she awkwardly tried to pick up the pieces of the lamp with her shaking hands.

"Don't worry about that, love," he said gently, guiding her back to her feet. "Have a seat while I look for some bandages."

"I'm fine," she insisted. "It'll stop bleeding in a minute." But he led her to the couch in spite of her protest.

He stepped around the broken glass and flipped on the kitchen light. When he saw the open bottle of whiskey and half-empty glass on the table his heart sank. Though an imbiber himself, he knew of the troubled past liquor had caused his daughter and hated to see her take it up again. Not wanting to embarrass her, he meant to look away but his attention was caught by the disassembled locket and the razor on the floor beneath it. He was startled by the sight of the blood on the blade, for he had assumed that his daughter had been cut by the glass of the broken lamp. "What were you doing, love?" he asked quietly, picking up the razor.

His daughter, who had gotten up from the couch and was pacing about the room, stopped when she heard the question. She stared back at him with a look of bewilderment. A chill ran up McCallum's neck when he looked into the dark eyes of his daughter. He could see that she was struggling for an answer but had none to give. "I'll get some bandages," he said gently, dropping the blade into the trash.

As he rummaged beneath the sink for something to dress the wound with, his daughter picked up the phone and began dialing. She nervously looked over at him, as if to explain herself.

"I need to see if Amelia caught her flight," she said with a weak smile, in spite of the tremor in her voice.

"I'm sure she did," he said, standing erect again. "She called earlier to say she was leaving."

His daughter froze with the phone in her hand, the color draining from her flushed face.

"What is it, love?" he asked, but as soon as the question had escaped from his lips he knew the answer: she was worried about her friend flying. "She'll be fine, love," he said certainly.

The doubt in her eyes told him his supposition had been correct. Without responding, she abruptly replaced the phone on its cradle, and then got up from the couch and went into the bedroom.

"Kylie?" he said, following after her. "There's no need to worry."

"No, Daddy. You don't understand," she said, moving about the room in agitation. She pulled at the tousled bed clothes, until her hand landed on the odd-fitting pair of khaki pants she had been wearing earlier that day. "I've got to be there," she said. "I've got to go to the airport—"

"Honey," he said. "Her flight doesn't get in for hours. I was gonna drive out there myself and pick—"

His daughter abruptly turned toward him. "Please, Daddy," she begged. "I want to go now. I want to borrow your truck."

"Listen to me for a minute, love," he insisted. "The chances of what happened to you happening to her again are so—"

"Daddy, please," she said, tears welling in her eyes. "If I stay here I'll worry all night. I want to go out there just in case something—" but her emotion choked back the rest.

"Okay, love," he said, touching her cheek to calm her. "I'll come with you."

"No. I don't want to drag you out—"

"Kylie," he interrupted with an affectionate smile. "I'm coming with you."

Seven

THE 747 HAD BEEN CIRCLING LOGAN AIRPORT FOR TWENTY MINUTES waiting for a break in the heavy fog that obscured the runway. Amelia sat buckled in her seat next to the tiny window, her hands gripping the armrests so tightly that her fingers were numb.

The overhead speakers cracked with the captain's voice. "Folks, we're still waiting for that clearance the tower has been promising. If they keep us up much longer, we'll have to head back to refuel. As of now, though, we're still on track and hopefully will be on the ground shortly."

Amelia leaned over and pulled the window shade up just enough to see that a thick layer of clouds was beneath the plane. She put her head back on the seat and tried to relax but her stomach had been growing increasingly queasy. The smell of coffee and stale baked beef clung beneath her nose.

"Are you alright miss?" asked the old woman from one seat over.

Amelia looked toward the inquiring wrinkled face, just as the woman's malodorous breath wafted her way. "Excuse me," she said, unbuckling her belt, for she was certain she was going to be sick.

She squeezed past the woman, holding tight to the headrest of the seat ahead of her to balance herself. The plane had hit turbulence and had begun to bounce. The narrow, lighted aisle swayed before her as she tried to make her way into one of the rest rooms at the back of the plane. A stewardess came abruptly toward her.

"The captain has the seat belt sign on," she said. "Could you return to your—" but when she saw how pale Amelia's face was she quickly stepped aside so that she could pass. "Is there anything I can do to help you?" she asked.

Amelia couldn't answer. Her hand gripped her mouth as she yanked open the tiny door and slammed it behind her.

. . .

THE LIGHTING inside the cramped bathroom was hideous. Amelia stared into the mirror at her dim reflection as if her fate were etched across her forehead. Her creamy skin appeared green, her blonde hair looked dull and her blue eyes had dark shadows beneath them. She had vomited so forcefully into the swaying toilet that broken capillaries had formed at the corners of her eyes from the overwhelming pressure. "Damn," she grumbled. The floor suddenly dipped away from her feet and she fell slightly back; the image danced before her making her sore stomach cramp once again. She quickly grabbed the sink to steady herself and waited for the turbulence to subside. She looked down at the filthy faucet and contemplated whether the water was fit to drink. Deciding against it, she turned on the tap and merely rinsed her mouth, splashed some on her face, then took a paper towel from the stack and pressed it against her skin. As the plane took another dip, she groaned to herself and unlatched the door.

Eight

PRESSED BENEATH THE LOW LYING CLOUDS, LOGAN AIRPORT WAS silent and waiting. The tower remained alert, while the inside of the main structure seemed a deserted shell of its daytime counterpart. Its sprawling corridors and high-tech terminals were deluged in stark light, giving the structure a feel of unnatural balance. Instead of the shadowy calm one would equate with night, the buzzing of the lights seemed to electrify the empty rows of seats and abandoned stations, punctuating the strange absence of life.

As Kylie's father gently dozed beside her, she stared toward the black windows of the terminal, anxiously awaiting the 747. Her lips moved in a muted prayer, while her thoughts raced from one point to the next—flashes of the creature with his pleading eyes and sorrowful voice burning through her thoughts. His words of electrocution, Ellen Young and of Jack's death besieged her, demanding to be deciphered and analyzed. "He felt no pain," she whispered, pressing her fingers into her eye sockets. *Jack felt no pain.* She repeated it to herself but no matter how desperately she wanted to believe it, her mind would not release the sight of him flailing in the fire. Looking at her bandaged hand, she envisioned the pale fingers that had taken her pain away and though she tried to digest all of which the creature had spoken, it was simply too much to think about; too much to decode and reassemble with Amelia's life hanging in the balance.

Her friend's flight had been scheduled to land at 12:34 A.M., but it was already nearly 1:45. Others waited nearby, grumbling about the delay, but while their discomfort was of impatience—Kylie's was of excruciating fear.

"God please," she begged, wishing for nothing more than the plane to break through the clouds and glide down the runway. "Please," she repeated, though deep inside, she doubted if anyone was listening. God had always remained an illusive figure who had somehow forgotten or abandoned her. At a tender young age when she had believed that God dictated all, she had seen her family ripped apart by death and ravaged by grief. The Catholic teachings of St. Mary's had left an imprint upon her, yet it had failed to convince her that God was for everyone. She had lived her life believing in some kind of spirituality, but it had remained a vague image with no real substance. Even now, when only a few hours earlier she had felt the breath of its existence, she had no real grasp of what the spirit world truly was. She only knew the rules of negotiation with which she had been taught, and like a trained soldier, employed every tactic known to her in fighting her enemies. Again she commenced the Lord's Prayer, then again and again. With every word she remained aware of the tracing that rested against her breast, a reminder that the very being she was appealing to would perhaps be the last to heed her invocation. After all, if the creatures had been sent to split her and her loved ones from life, then who other than God had deemed it so? She suddenly shook her head to dispel her thoughts. The chance that there was nowhere left to turn was too bleak to consider. With a heavy sigh, she concluded the last of the prayer and silenced with "Amen."

She found herself clutching the cameo and gently lay it back against her breast. On their way out the door, her father had picked it up from the table and handed it to her. While she had been reluctant to take it, he had looked at her so strangely that she extended her hand. The cool chain had coiled downward like a lethal serpent gently lowering itself into a resting place in her palm. For a brief moment she had considered taking it off again, but then decided to let it be. She had brought the tracing of the spirit world into her own, and whether or not it was the reason for her insight, there would be no turning back.

She thought of her friend aboard the plane—alone and terrified—and her stomach twisted with pain; Amelia could be nothing other than petrified. She remembered her own fear as the Merlin had plummeted toward the mountain, and couldn't imagine reliving such terror. She looked toward the black glass, wondering if Amelia was also staring out into the night.

Abruptly, she got up and went to the windows. Her hands pressed against the cool glass as she stared out at the runway. "God, please," she whispered. She remained still, thinking the plane would land if only she concentrated hard enough, but a tiny voice inside whispered . . . *God doesn't hear you.* The empty runway mocked her, and the wispy fog danced with delight. Then suddenly a fiery ball fell through the mist and exploded on the cement before her, the sound of her friend's anguish rising above the roar. "Amelia!" she gasped, clenching her eyes together to make the horrible sight disappear. She opened them again to the vacant runway and the still night full of silence and waiting.

Nine

"WE'VE BEEN CLEARED FOR LANDING, FOLKS," THE CAPTAIN REPORTED over the speaker. "Thank you for your patience. It's been a long night."

Amelia put her hands together and tried to stay calm, but as much as she hated take-offs, she hated landings even more—especially after delays. She had little confidence in the control tower's clearance, for the fact that they had been delayed for so long was testimony to the danger that existed. Human error and bad weather had caused the destruction of the Merlin IV, and could easily result in the same once again.

"Miss?" came a voice from the aisle. The heavily made-up face of the stewardess was looking at her as she pointed to the carry-on bag that rested against Amelia's toes. "Could you please stow that under the seat in front of you and raise your window shade?" she requested.

Amelia bent to zip up the bag, then wedged it beneath the seat. She turned toward the window shade and shoved it the rest of the way open, but immediately looked away, for she had no desire to see the black sky, nor the clouds that loomed beneath. Her eyes rested on the floor ahead of her where she was startled to see that the White Mountain guide had fallen from the bag, the stone cottage staring up at her. The hatted little man pointed eerily outward, the hinged door and darkened windows whispering their reproach for an escape of which Amelia remembered nothing.

She quickly picked it up and returned it to the side pocket of the bag, but even through the leather, she felt the chill of its presence.

She tried to shift her thoughts, to get her mind onto something pleasant, but the danger that awaited outside the tiny window vied for her attention. She could feel that the plane had begun a quick descent, dropping dramatically in altitude.

Her eyes slowly gazed outward, past the double-insulated Plexiglas to the clouds beneath. With much consternation, she noticed the fog appeared as thick as before, blanketing everything from sight. Wondering why they had been cleared to land when the bad weather remained, she turned toward a stewardess who whisked past in a flurry toward the back of the plane. As she watched the flight attendants rushing about, picking up last minute articles, she was certain she sensed panic. She straightened in her seat, wondering if the stewardesses felt the same danger as herself, but were keeping it from the passengers. They were certainly moving faster than usual to make it to their seats in time for landing.

Amelia turned again to the window, her heart in her throat. The only explanation for the unexpected descent in spite of the fog had to be that they had finally run out of fuel. It had been at least half an hour since the pilot had mentioned their dwindling supply. Maybe he had waited too late to go back to another airport and was forced to land in spite of the risky weather.

She looked at the other passengers, searching their faces for the same fear that she was feeling, but none of them seemed the least bit concerned. The elderly woman beside her continued to knit a pair of socks, oblivious to the whirlwind around her and the deadly weather that awaited them.

The plane dropped suddenly but ever so slightly upon entering the white mass of clouds. Then the turbulence began once again, snapping the placid passengers to attention. Amelia looked down at her hands, wanting desperately to overcome the fear but it continued to mount inside of her with each jolt of the wings. Every nerve in her body was tingling, her head throbbing with the pressure.

The pilot's voice echoed through the cabin. "Flight attendants prepare for landing."

They were descending through the clouds at an incredible speed, surely too fast to make a safe landing. As the flustered stewardesses buckled themselves in, Amelia lay her head stiffly against the seat and waited for the impact. Within only seconds it came. The rear of the plane dipped as the back wheels scraped against the ground. Amelia nearly screamed as the plane bounced against the surface, its nose still pointing upward. Her head fell to the side and she looked outward toward the rushing landscape. The cement whirled past in a blur as the front of the plane slowly lowered and made contact with the runway. A deafening roar rumbled down the aisles, as the wings tilted back and braced the huge bird against the force of the speed. Her seat shook, the overhead-bins rattled and the floor trembled with the pressure. Then finally, the quivering body began to slow.

"Are you okay?" croaked the old woman beside her.

When Amelia looked into the seasoned eyes, she realized that the danger was over. The plane had landed without its sides ripping off or its nose smashing against a wall of stone.

"I'm fine, thank you," she whispered, resting her head into her hands.

"And a smooth landing, folks," came the voice of the captain. "Thank you for flying with us. We hope you enjoy your stay in the Boston area or wherever your final destination may be."

Ten

"THANK YOU," KYLIE GASPED THROUGH TEARY EYES WHEN SHE SAW THE nose of the plane break through the mist and slowly glide toward the gate. She looked back to her father who had instinctively pulled awake. He was rubbing his eyes as he got up from the seat and headed toward her.

A small crowd materialized out of nowhere and began to bustle around the opening to the gate in anticipation of the departing passengers. Kylie smiled at her father who groggily ambled up to her.

"All that worrying for nothing," he grunted with a sheepish grin. "I'll wait for you back here."

Kylie quickly turned to the sparse crowd and worked her way toward the front of the gate. The first passenger had already emerged and was greeting the man beside her. As she gaped down the narrow tunnel, her heart began to thump and tears of anticipation trickled beneath her eyes. With the exception of groggy glimpses through her sedation, she hadn't seen Amelia since the accident, and the anticipation was overwhelming. Passenger after passenger meandered down the restricted corridor, but she had yet to see Amelia. Just as she began to wonder if she had made the flight, she saw the thin, willowy figure of her friend emerging through the lighted tunnel. Her snowy hair was standing on end and her blue eyes were smiling at her from thirty feet away. Amelia began to rush forward, but her dainty limbs were bogged down with luggage. Kylie fought to restrain herself from entering the restricted area of the tunnel, when finally Amelia reached the opening. Kylie rushed forward and grasped her into her arms, pressing her tear-stained cheeks against her own. She held the trembling shoulders within her strong embrace, thinking her friend felt like a bird—a delicate beautiful bird. "Melia," she whispered, breathing in the sweet smell of her beloved, Southern friend.

"Oh Kylie!" Amelia sighed. "I'm so sorry about Jack."

McCallum stood shyly back, watching the childhood friends embrace. He took a heavy sigh and smiled, for it had been weeks since he had felt such relief.

Eleven

IT WAS NEARLY SUNRISE, YET THE TWO WOMEN HADN'T SLEPT. THEY SAT on the swayed bed, both exhausted from the long night of speculation and uncertainty. They had whispered for hours in the dark of the moonlight, careful not to wake Kylie's father who was sleeping on the old couch in the living room.

"I can't stop looking at it," said Amelia, staring down at the White Mountain guide that lay on the bed between them. Through their long discussion of the terrors that had passed and those that awaited, it served as a needling reminder that the danger was real and tangible. "What about the woman?" she asked. "Do you think she also had a life before?"

Startled by the question, for it was something that Kylie hadn't even considered, she took a moment to think about it. She thought of the deadly bird that had perched on the windowsill, remembering the vacancy in the freakish eyes that had matched those of the female creature. "I don't know," she finally replied. "I suppose she did."

"How horrible," muttered Amelia. "To become a sort of mutation of what you were in life. I just can't imagine a worse hell than to forget everything that you are. To feel nothing but the pain of others. Do you think that's why they were there?" she asked, wringing her hands fretfully together. "Do you think that they're some kind of angels of mercy?"

Kylie once again thought of Julius Vanderpoel's promise about Jack. "If what he said about Jack was true . . . if he really did stop him from feeling . . . from . . ." but she could not finish the rest. "Damn," she sighed, rubbing her eyes. "I don't know what to think anymore."

Silence fell once again over the room as the two women sat in heavy contemplation. Kylie shifted on the bed, her frazzled nerves long since succumbing to a pensive calm. Amelia lay her head against the wall, as Kylie picked at the bandage on her hand.

"I'm sorry," Amelia whispered at length.

Kylie looked up and was startled to see that her friend was crying. "Hey," she said softly, shoving the book from between them.

"I'm sorry I didn't believe you when you called," she gasped. "I just—"

Kylie took her into her arms. "Hey Melia, stop that," she said.

"I just hate that I had to have proof," she whispered with reproach.

"You would have been a lunatic if you hadn't," said Kylie. "Look at me. It was easier to think I was going insane than to accept it all."

"Damn," Amelia sighed, looking tired and worn. "What the hell are we going to do? It's not like we can tell anyone. Dix doesn't even believe it."

Kylie searched for an answer, but merely shook her head. "I don't know," she finally replied. "We're just so overwhelmed right now and . . . just . . . just so overwhelmed," she sighed, rubbing her eyes.

The silence of the night once again overtook them. After a long while, Amelia's pinched shoulders finally relaxed. "I'm so damn tired," she groaned.

Kylie pulled back the curtain and saw that the early morning fishermen were loading their boats. "It'll be light soon," she said, slumping down into the covers. "We better get some sleep."

Just as the two women closed their eyes, the sound of snoring drifted in from the living room.

Kylie cocked her head toward the doorway. "I hope he's okay on that couch," she whispered. "His back is probably killing him."

"Yeah," said Amelia. "I was worried about that. But I'm still glad he's here instead of on his boat."

"Me too," agreed Kylie.

After the awful scene of the broken lamp and bloodied dress, her father had been insistent on remaining in the house, at least for the time being. She felt relieved to have him near, for she was certain that while she was surrounded by people, Julius Vanderpoel would be less likely to reappear. As it was, the remainder of the night passed quietly and without incident.

Twelve

THE SUN ROSE HIGH OVER NAHANT BAY WHERE THE FOG HAD LONG since dissipated. The smell of coffee and sausage gravy filled the cottage wherein McCallum sat at the table reading the morning's paper. He had been up for hours, tiptoeing about the living room and kitchen, careful not to wake the two women sleeping in the bedroom. While he had tried to distract himself with cooking, smoking and the paper, a feeling of dread hung heavily about his shoulders.

. . .

KYLIE'S EYES suddenly opened and stared at the sun-splotched ceiling. Though she remained still, her face felt numb and her chest tingled nervously. It had begun. The day of Jack's funeral.

It was hard to believe that such a morning had arrived, but the dingy walls of her father's house were a startling reminder that her life with Jack was over. Never had she anticipated such an ending. Never had she anticipated having to witness his burial, for she had always imagined that she would die first. "Jack," she whispered, wishing for just one moment to say good-bye. She thought of their last night together, of the angry words that had passed between them, of Jack's swollen hand as he gripped the bottle of bourbon and of his childlike eyes fighting against his sadness. What she wouldn't give for just one moment to hold him again and to make his sorrow disappear. He had been so sad—so sad and so lost. "Jack," she whispered, her tears blurring the uneven paint overhead. She immediately squeezed her eyes tight to stop the emotion from spilling out. She threw her arm over her face and waited for the pain to pass.

Impatiently swiping at her wet cheeks, she rolled over on her side, her eyes resting on the sweet face of Amelia whose shoulders moved gently with slumber. It saddened her to see the tiny wrinkles that had appeared on her friend's forehead in the morning light. The years were passing so quickly. While it seemed like only yesterday, it had been a decade since they had huddled together like children under the same blankets. The last time had been the night before her wedding to Jack, when Amelia had flown to Boston to be her maid of honor. Looking back, they seemed so young and unfettered. Little did they know that the marriage would end in such tragedy and that a cloak of darkness would shroud them in terror.

With a leaden sigh, Kylie slowly rose from the bed, careful its creaky springs did not wake Amelia. She went to the dulled mirror that hung over her father's cluttered dresser and looked at her grave reflection. The sunlight caught her auburn hair and set her image on fire. Her green eyes were glistening and sharp, the darkened bruise around her left eye fading. Her fingers touched her pale lips as she heard the voice of Jack and saw his smiling face gazing at her across their dinner table. *Bring those luscious lips here*, he teased, his eyes full of playful desire.

"How do you want me to look, Jack?" she whispered to her reflection, for it was her first appearance as his widow. When she thought of the answer, a bittersweet smile came to her. He would want her in red, though social convention demanded black. He would want her hair down and her lips painted ruby. "Jack Black," she said softly, once again fighting back the tears. With a deep aching she wished for him by her side, but knew she would have to face the most painfully intimate day of their lives together—alone.

Thirteen

THE BLACK LIMOUSINE GLIDED THROUGH THE GATE OF MOUNT AUBURN Cemetery, and rolled slowly down the flower-laden path, parting a sea of pedestrians dressed in their Sunday best. The sunlight tapped against the ebony exterior of the Lincoln, but like a long, dark shadow, the car stole through the bright day with its passengers carefully hidden from view by heavily-tinted windows.

Kylie stared through the glass at the familiar faces that turned awkwardly away from the limousine, as if they sensed that close family members of Jack were inside, and didn't want to break some unspoken code of propriety. She recognized friends from Jack's high school, from his weekend basketball team, even from his favorite restaurant—acquaintances with whom she knew she would never again be able to speak freely of Jack without their discomfort and sympathy. While she may long to discuss his games, or his favorite foods and films, the topic of her husband from that day forward would remain tainted with pity and the heinous way in which he died. The funeral was merely the beginning of the silence that would keep her from sharing pleasant memories of him with anyone other than those closest to her. She knew, for she had experienced it in the past. Even to this day, it was impossible to speak of her mother and brothers without drawing a sad look or a sigh from those to whom she spoke.

As the car glided past the deflecting eyes, the quarantine of her grief had already begun. The funeral home provided the limousines to ease the onerous day, yet it was the first step in enhancing the forlorn

feeling of isolation. The gentle lull of its long body, the leather uphol-
stery, the dark windows, and the soft music were meant to calm, but
instead hid its passengers from light as if they themselves were the
dead arriving inside of a large, dark casket.

Kylie, once again, readjusted the vent inside the car and pulled at
the black dress that remained close to her skin. Though the cool air
wafted toward her, the smell was musty and stifling. She hated limousines and would have given anything to attend the funeral in her
father's truck, but under the funeral director's insistence, had agreed
to the service. As she had feared, it had been a long, dark ride from
Swampscott to Cambridge, the somber journey wearing on the others
as well. Her father sat next to her, fidgeting with his outdated suit,
while Amelia stared down at her hands. The music that surrounded
them was hideous, the sweet melody abhorrently sad and discomforting. Kylie looked to the driver to ask him to turn it off, but he was as
faceless and reserved as the surrounding pedestrians. During the entire trip, his focus had remained forward as if not to disturb the tranquility the automobile was to impart.

Unable to bear the restraint any longer, Kylie unlocked the door
and just as she was about to demand that the driver stop and let them
walk the rest of the way in the warmth of the sun, the long car turned
up the hill toward Bigelow Chapel. The moment she saw the black
hearse waiting outside the Gothic structure she shrank back, retreating into the darkness she had been fighting so fiercely. Feeling suddenly cornered and frightened, she wanted nothing more than to turn
and run; for it had struck her that Jack was indeed present, yet the
empty shell that made his appearance was as hideously cold and unnatural as the macabre vehicle in which he had arrived.

THROUGH the tinted glass, Kylie spotted Dillon standing by the imposing doors of the chapel entrance. Though he was the perfect image of
togetherness in his polished suit with his dark curly hair gleaming in
the sun, his face was drawn and his eyes vacant. He stood silently
watching the crowd and though he was surrounded by people, he
looked as solitary and pensive as if he were standing alone.

"Are you ready, love?" her father asked, as the driver got out of the
car to open their door for them.

Amelia was looking at her expectantly, her eyes brimming with tears. Kylie reached out and squeezed her friend's hand, then took a deep breath and opened the door herself in spite of the scrambling attendant.

"Let's go," she said with resolution.

When they stepped from the car, the eyes of the crowd turned toward her and while some merely moved to clear a path, most silently greeted her with sad nods and inquisitive stares. Silence prevailed with the exception of one comment from a wealthy-looking woman with overpowering perfume whom Kylie was certain she had never seen before. "How are you, darling?" the woman asked, grasping Kylie's hand into her own cold smooth fingers.

"Fine, thank you," she answered, quickly slipping past and mounting the stairs. When Dillon turned toward her, she saw the light come into his eyes and he seemed to breathe a sigh of relief.

"Father Joseph wants us to sit in the section off to the side at the front," he said, his voice strained and low. "Theresa and the rest of the family are already up there."

Kylie wanted to ask why he wasn't with them, but when his eyes glanced back to the hearse with its open doors and empty cargo space, she instantly knew. She felt her legs weaken as a cool breeze drifted from the darkened chapel where the casket awaited them.

"Come on, Dill," she said softly, grasping his arm into her own. "Let's do this together."

WHEN they stepped into the dark body of the chapel, the damp air sent chills prickling up Kylie's back. With eyes downward, she and Dillon slowly made their way along the aisle leading toward the altar. As they drew near the silver surface of the casket placed at the front of the church, Kylie felt Dillon's arm tense within her own.

"This way," a kind voice bid softly from beside them. It was the funeral director and he was motioning them to the right, to a parlor-like room off the side of the nave, blocked from view of the other church pews by heavy velvet curtains. Inside the small wing, chairs were arranged in rows, the back seats already taken by the rest of the O'Rourke family. Kylie smiled at Jack's aunt and gave his grandmother, Dexter, a kiss on her velvety cheek that smelled of rosewater.

"Keep close to him, dear," said the old woman, motioning toward Dillon. "You're the only one who could bring him inside."

"I'm fine, Grandma," Dillon quickly protested, removing his arm from Kylie's and turning away in embarrassment. Just then, Kylie noticed Theresa staring at her from her seat in the front row. There was a look of anguish in the violet eyes that brought a thump to Kylie's chest. The beautiful woman had clearly heard the grandmother's comment that Dillon had responded to Kylie and to no one else when—unquestionably—Theresa should have been the one to walk him inside. Just as soon as the women's eyes had met, Theresa looked discreetly away. Disquieted by the fleeting moment, Kylie remained still as the others took their seats.

At length, she saw her father looking back at her with his lips anxiously pinched—for everyone else had taken their places. As she reluctantly moved to the chair reserved for her, between her father and Dillon, it felt as if a bird had wedged beneath her ribs and was fluttering frantically to escape. There had been something more in Theresa's eyes that she had yet to identify. Then the fluttering bird suddenly turned to ice and lodged in Kylie's throat; could she be the love Theresa had spoken of that day in Dillon's yard? Her shoulders stiffened and her breath caught, as she remembered the way Dillon had turned toward her in the sunlight when Jack told him about Julius Vanderpoel. *It's impossible*, her thoughts quickly asserted. In spite of Jack's jealousy, there had never been anything but friendship between them. She, Jack and Dillon had been as close as family could be, the brothers best of friends. Of course she and Dillon would care for each other and find solace in each other's presence, for not only had they shared in Jack's love together, they had been friends for over a decade. She instantly felt the need to explain. If there was any doubt in Theresa's mind, she needed to set her at ease. But her pulsating thoughts merely sent her body into a cold sweat. She knew she was over-reacting but couldn't stop the tremor that was moving through her. Just then, Theresa reached across Dillon and tenderly pressed Kylie's hand. When Kylie saw the comforting smile on her calm face, she suddenly felt like crying. She had completely misread the moment. The violet eyes seemed to gaze into her soul, then turned away again, the profile one of grace and dignity. Kylie's eyes fell away from the lovely woman, feeling as if her emotions were raging out of control.

How could she have mistaken such a thing? *Get a hold of yourself,* her mind scolded as she clenched her hands together and looked forward. Feeling as though she were losing her grasp she tried to center her thoughts, but the oppressive walls were escalating her disorientation into muted hysteria.

The coffin was within ten feet of her chair, waiting silently and stoically, with a mound of red roses spilling over its top. She wanted to look away but the presence was too much. She suddenly noticed the sound of Amelia sniffling on the other side of her father, and someone bursting into tears behind her. As her gaze remained fixed on the casket, with the sweet smell of roses drifting toward her, she felt as if she had been plunged into a deep, morose dream. The dark walls of the chapel limited the space of the nightmare, while the edges of the coffin and everything around it seemed softer and less defined than in reality. She pulled her heavy eyelids away, toward the velvet curtains that looked so much like the ones that had adorned the windows in their warehouse she thought for a moment they were the same. They shivered slightly in the draft that whirled across the top of her feet and moved upward with the arching doorway. Her father's hand suddenly reached over and took her own. It was then that she realized her entire body was trembling. Her shoulders were shaking intensely yet she could not stop them.

"It's okay, love," her father whispered as he clasped his arm about her. "Do you want me to find you a jacket?"

"No, I'm fine Daddy," she answered softly. Concentrating with all her might, her muscles finally gave way to her will and she stilled. Like cold groping fingers, the frigid air crawled up from the floor and grasped her ankles. It smoothed over her legs before reaching up her dress as if to defile her.

Pulling her legs in closer together, she turned her attention forward, startled to see that the priest, accompanied by two altar boys, had already entered the church and was sprinkling the coffin with holy water. He wore a long white vestment and spoke in a muted tone as he circled the casket in ritual. "'God, you have called your son, Jack O'Rourke from this life . . . Give him eternal rest O Lord . . .'"

It was startling to hear the priest's words—to find herself witnessing the funeral of the man she loved more than breath itself. It was too hideous to imagine that it was really the body of her mate beneath the heavy lid—his soft lips silenced forever, his calloused hands never to touch her again. Her eyes burned with tears as her soul collapsed inward. The room began to change, the rough arches sinking closer and closer inward, squeezing everything from her consciousness but the scorching sound of the priest's authoritative voice.

"'Father of all mercy, fulfill his faith and hope in you, and lead him safely home to heaven' . . ." An altar boy handed the priest a smoking thurible of incense that dangled on a long chain. As the priest rocked it gently over the coffin—the chain clinking against the metal body of burning coals and perfume—tiny puffs of smoke escaped through the holes and drifted toward the grey top of the chapel. In long wisps the pungent incense encircled Kylie, invading her senses, taking her back to the past, to the funeral of her mother and Tucker. Flowers had jammed the tiny Southern church, adorning candlesticks, doorways and the casket. The vase of her mother's ashes took center stage with the dainty casket of her brother beside it. The small box was open and the still body of her beloved little Tucker was as stiff and artificial as if it were made of wax. She remembered the moment in which she approached the altar and gazed down into his face. The tiny eyes that had laughed and cried the tears of a seven-year-old child, had been crudely sewn shut from the inside. She remembered the feeling of shock and terror—then her screams as she backed from the casket.

Abruptly, her father's voice pulled her from the startling memory. "Are you okay, love?" She was gasping for breath, but couldn't find his face. She could think of nothing but Jack, wondering what horrific things the mortician had done to his body. As she thought of the fire and the way it must have ravaged his beautiful flesh, a warm rush of tears flooded her cheeks.

At once her father took her into his strong embrace and rocked her as he had when she was a child. "Shh baby girl . . . it'll be alright," he whispered into her sobs. "It'll be alright."

Through her sorrow, she heard the sound of Dillon weeping beside her. She saw that his head was down and that he was drawn inward into Theresa's arms. "I'm okay," she whispered hoarsely to her father and pulled herself away. She immediately sat up and looked to Dillon, the sight of his grief slicing into her heart. Without even seeing it coming, she had lost control; she had let her grief escape, causing those around her to also give way. "It's okay, Dillon," she whispered, taking his hot hand into her own.

She wiped the make-up from under her eyes then turned back to the altar, but this time she dared not look at the cold container nor the rituals that surrounded it. Her eyes drifted upward toward the muted sun that broke through the stained-glass window, the priest's words floating along with her thoughts.

"A reading from the Book of Wisdom," he said, as her gaze rested upon the colored glass.

The depiction in the window was of a dark birdlike angel carrying the body of a man toward heaven—its claws grasping him by the chest. Startled by what the image of colors and lights sanctioned, Kylie quickly looked to those around her but none seemed to notice the horrific window above them.

"'The souls of the virtuous are in the hands of God,'" the reading began against the backdrop of reticent light. "'No torment shall ever touch them. In the eyes of the unwise, they did appear to die, their going looked like a disaster, their leaving us, like annihilation; but they are in peace.'"

Kylie drew back her breath and looked to the priest, certain she couldn't have heard his words more clearly. Though he read from the book of the Old Testament, it was the same purport that had been spoken to her the night before—the same message she had weighed so heavily in her mind.

The human eye can be deceptive, said the voice of Julius Vanderpoel. *He felt nothing but peace. His body was screaming but his soul felt mercy.*

Kylie's fingers and lips began to tingle, for the Bible itself was confirming what the creature had told her: Jack had passed without pain. The pieces were there all along, heavily encrypted, but proclaimed none the less.

"'. . . those who are faithful will live with him in love; for grace and mercy await those he has chosen.'"

At once an overwhelming relief consumed her. Her mind had been so clouded with cautious doubt that the complete force of Julius Vanderpoel's words had missed her: Jack had been granted mercy for there was good in his soul. The same love that she had found within him, had been discovered by some other force. Yet as quickly as that wonderful realization had lightened her heart, a darker one eclipsed it. There was another side to the clemency—an underbelly of torture that sent a shadow scampering across her thoughts. The shadow was of Julius Vanderpoel's pained face, illuminated by the distant glow of the pub.

Like an endorphin for the dying, for the bleeding, collapsing bodies, I'm the one that feels the torture.

As surely as Jack had been spared, Julius Vanderpoel had been thrust into hell—a never-ending realm of pain where he paid for the mistake of Ellen Young.

As Kylie's eyes absorbed the colors of the stained-glass angel, her heart filled with pity. She remembered the night of the fire when the creature had been riveted to the brilliant flames as though they were a drug that eased his pain.

Because of you I see colors . . . flashes of beautiful reds and yellows . . .

Along with his memories, he had been denied the colors, the sights, the sensations that would bring him pleasure.

"'Blessed are the merciful,'" said the priest. "'For they shall obtain mercy.'"

Kylie looked to the altar, wondering what kind of world could judge so harshly—to force the being of one to exist in order to shoulder the torture of another. She thought how thin the line between good and evil, and how easily one could fall the wrong way. She had seen the kind side of Julius Vanderpoel, she knew it existed, yet the cold lifeless realm that had swallowed his essence was seemingly indifferent to it.

A chill ran over her as she glanced about the candle-lit church, for the brooding atmosphere seemed a mere glimpse into the darkened world that waited beyond. Like the priest's words that danced along the truth but dared not speak in clearer terms, its murky walls and stained-glass depiction of death provided only clues to the unseen dominion.

The colorful lights of the window beckoned to her like a porthole into a flanking sphere that no one except herself seemed to have discovered. And while those around her remained safely tucked within their lethe, she felt as though she were peering through a door where she dare not tread.

She thought of Jack and wondered what he must have thought at that moment when Julius Vanderpoel assumed his misery—when his soul was released from the earthly bonds of pain. She wondered what sights he beheld as he glimpsed into the bordering existence—at that moment of quietus when his essence passed forth from this life to the next.

Fourteen

THE SMALL CROWD THAT HAD GATHERED AT THE TOP OF THE STAIRS AT 2845 Cypress Path stood in silence. While tufts of clouds floated across the clear blue sky, and fragrant flowers danced beneath the shade of swaying oak, beech, cedar and pine, the casket was lowered into the earth.

The robes of Father Joseph fluttered in the breeze as he read from the Bible.

With each inch that the silver casket descended into its permanent quarters, Kylie felt her link with Jack changing. He had found a new home among the rolling hills and wooded forests. As surely as they had lived in the Waterfront together, he would now reside just four miles west in the silent city of Mt. Auburn.

While those around her bent their heads in prayer, her gaze wandered to the shards of sunlight that broke through the trees and caught the tops of the elaborate tombstones. She watched the squirrels scampering through the thick, perfect grass, as though they hadn't a care in the world. As the casket stilled within the dark earth, the perfection of the overwhelmingly beautiful cemetery brought a strange pit to Kylie's stomach. In spite of the warm air, she felt a coldness settling upon her. Something about the cemetery was too pleasant, too civilized, almost as if it were a living breathing community, where the undead carried on life in the absence of the living. Tailored after Père Lachaise in France, the cemetery was touted as the perfect union between heaven and earth. Visitors could stroll amongst the grassy knolls or sit quietly by its ponds and sparkling streams. And while they would not encounter one single permanent resident walking through the thriving community, they were still called upon to visit their homes as if societal etiquette were to be adhered to as stringently after death as before.

The family residences were marked with the addresses of the after-life, their homes petitioned off by wrought iron gates. Stone stairwells led to their entrances to graciously accept their visitors as though life had not ended but merely shifted to a quieter more civilized realm.

Kylie suddenly felt the impulse to back away from the coffin, for the charred remains that rested in the box were as empty and void of their lifeblood as the beauty of the surrounding hillside. They were as life-less as the cold eyes of the creature that devoured the warmth of Julius Vanderpoel and of the void of memory he fought so desperately against. She became intensely aware that the O'Rourke family lot was partitioned like the rest, with mounting stairs and an elaborate gate, the address stenciled on the curb so that they, too, could accept their visitors. The plot beside the unearthed grave of her husband awaited and beckoned to her, promising that life would continue as before with only a mere alteration in the blueprint.

Over the preacher's voice, she heard a fluttering of wings in the tree overhead. Her eyes followed a black crow that rushed through the branches. It landed on a headstone across the way where it in-tently turned toward the group. Abruptly she noticed two others on the railing next to it and several more in the trees. Their black bodies hung within the heavenly garden, as if some hidden door had been opened and their dark essence allowed in. Their heads cocked with a secret knowledge, and she wondered if any of the eyes knew how long it would be before she would join her husband in the paradoxical society.

As the priest finished the prayer, Kylie drew her breath and caught a straying hair that wisped across her forehead. Amelia's hand sud-denly grasped hers and when Kylie looked to her friend, she saw that her disquieted eyes were fixed toward the hole where the coffin had disappeared. A black spider crawled slowly along the lip of the sunny grave. As the family around them began to disperse, the two women remained frozen, for only they noticed the tiny creature slipping through a crack and disappearing into the earth.

Fifteen

"THIS IS HELL," AMELIA WHISPERED NERVOUSLY, PEERING OUT AT THE lights of the murky bay where a fisherman was pulling in his boat for the night. "Not knowing what's out there . . . wondering if it's watching."

The sound of distant conversation and of people walking along the deck drifted in with the warm breeze of the night.

Kylie looked up from the kitchen table with her heart in her throat, for she too felt the same looming apprehension. Since their arrival back at the cottage, her glance had repeatedly scanned the windows in search of shadowy figures or peering eyes. As with Amelia, the chill of the graveyard had stayed with her throughout the day and into the night and though the women had no chance to speak of it until they were alone, they had both felt the proximity of the dark force that so blatantly touted its presence. It had instilled a sense of urgency in them and as soon as the reception had ended, they boarded the same limousine that had delivered them that morning and headed back to Swampscott where they anxiously awaited the chance to be alone. The moment Kylie's father stepped out for the evening, they began scanning the Bible and old newspaper articles of the murder, grasping for anything to help them understand the situation in order to survive.

For over an hour, Amelia labored over Genesis and Revelations, but an uneasiness drew her toward the black windows where she searched the dark waters and dock for their nemesis. And while Amelia's concentration remained riveted on the shadows, Kylie worked on a series of sketches to detail the pivotal night atop the mountain.

"I'm almost done," she promised, hunching busily over the last drawing. Her blackened fingers smeared the charcoal around the remote eyes of the female creature, then with a darting of the ebony pencil added the harsh lines around her thin lips. As the image slowly emerged from the murky paper, a knot formed in Kylie's chest. Once again she wondered if the woman had a life before and if so, what horrid crime she had committed to suffer such a fate. A chill ran up her spine as she looked into the lifeless face she was creating—at the vacant eyes of death. She felt the cold presence closing in—the empty grave alongside Jack's calling to her from miles away.

"They could be out there right now," Amelia said anxiously, chewing at her short nails. "Not just Vanderpoel, but others."

"You're going to drive yourself crazy," said Kylie. "Why don't you keep reading?"

With one last look out the window, Amelia reluctantly returned to her seat at the table. She turned to the Book of Revelations, as Kylie pulled the light closer in. The two women worked in silence, the ticking of the mantel-clock replacing all sound within the room.

"Listen to this," Amelia said at length, her finger pressing upon a passage. "'During those days men will seek death, but will not find it, they will long to die but death will elude them.' It talks about punishment and torture of the wicked for a thousand years. And how they will be left in a pit of darkness . . . an abyss." Her vibrant blue eyes looked up from the scripture. "Do you think his loss of memory is the darkness?"

"It could be," Kylie answered.

After another long silence, Amelia began shaking her head. "This is like trying to decipher a riddle," she groaned. "It says that murderers will become immortal and that the wicked angels will be set free to take the lives of men, but it doesn't say whether they're one in the same." She rubbed her forehead in frustration. "It's almost like they don't want you to figure it out," she grumbled.

"They don't," interjected Kylie as she stood from the table putting the finishing touches on the last sketch. "It's just supposed to scare the hell out of you."

"Well it's doing a good job," said Amelia, cupping her head in her hands.

"Come look," said Kylie.

Amelia scooted around the table as Kylie laid out the drawings. Like snapshots, the characters were all assembled and frozen in action. In the first—which detailed the inside of the cottage—Amelia, Jack and Kylie peered over the balcony, while the two attorneys stood beneath.

"Collins heard the voice when he was standing down here," said Kylie. "After he went out, he went down into the woods here," she said pointing to the drawing on the right. "By the time we reached him, he was standing with the woman. His face was so consumed with emotion that I could swear he was seeing someone other than her."

"What do you mean?"

"Almost as if he thought he knew her."

"Well you already know they can make you think you're seeing someone you're not," joined Amelia. "Because of Jack."

"And Ducker," said Kylie.

"Maybe the voice was to lure him out to her."

"Well, she succeeded. He went to her willingly and even after I screamed, he reached for her hand."

"Christ," said Amelia, suddenly turning away in thought.

"What is it?"

"I don't know if I ever told you this or not?"

"Told me what?"

"You know my grandma was in a lot of pain with her cancer..."

"Yeah," nodded Kylie.

"Well, right before she died, about ten minutes beforehand, she stopped groaning for the first time in hours. When we looked up, she had the most peaceful look on her face and she was smiling toward the foot of her bed." Amelia's voice began to quiver as she continued. "Just a few minutes before her heart monitor stopped, she turned to Mama and said that my grandpa was there for her—that he had been waiting until the right moment and that it was time to follow him."

Chills prickled over Kylie's skin for Amelia's grandfather had died years before her grandmother.

"She said he was holding his hand out to her," Amelia said softly, her gaze falling to the depiction of Gavin Collins and the dark angel. Her shadowed eyes grew darker and even before she asked the question, Kylie knew what her friend was thinking. "You don't suppose....?"

Kylie stared into the unsettled eyes of her friend wishing she could answer anything but "yes", but she was quickly learning that the distrustful face of death had many facades.

The absence of answer was all the confirmation that Amelia needed. "My God," she gasped, turning away to collect her emotion. She nervously ran her fingers about her hair. "Damn, I wish I still smoked," she murmured. She paced a few steps and then stopped, studying the floor. "The doctor called it a deathbed vision," she said. "He told us that a lot of his patients had them ... that their pain suddenly disappears ... they become peaceful ... they see someone at their bedside and then hours, minutes or even seconds later they die. My God!" she gasped, her dread mounting. "This just keeps getting worse. I mean, whatever happened to death being some wondrous experience full of bright lights and tunnels."

Kylie looked down at her drawing, at the blissful expression of Gavin Collins. "Maybe that's all part of it," she said.

Amelia turned to her with a look of bewilderment.

"They quietly guide your way," Kylie mused, remembering the soft voice of the female creature. "And part of the way is the dark tunnel and bright light that everyone talks about."

Both women fell into silent contemplation, each dealing with their own apprehensions. Amelia returned to the window, while Kylie rested into a chair by the table. Once again the ticking clock exerted its voice of dwindling time. "How long do you think we have?" Amelia asked, her fragile words breaking the silence.

Kylie's breath instantly caught. "I don't know," she replied, avoiding the probing eyes of her frightened friend, for she had not told her all that had happened the night before. When she had recounted the scene with Vanderpoel she had left out the mention of Amelia's death.

As if sensing Kylie's uneasiness, Amelia suddenly left the window ledge and began to pace about the room.

"Do you think Dale Benson is still alive?" she asked.

"I hadn't even thought about it," said Kylie, startled to remember that the attorney's life was also at stake.

"Maybe we should try to call him," said Amelia. "I read in the tabloids that after the accident he retired to some town outside of Salem. Salem's not that far from here, is it?"

"No."

"Well maybe we should go talk to him."

"And tell him what?" Kylie asked. "What could we possibly say?"

The question hung suspended before them, each searching the other for the answer; and while neither of the women spoke, they both remembered the close-minded disposition of the bitter attorney.

Kylie shook her head with dismay. "There's nothing we can do. I can't imagine convincing that old man of anything, much less that he was about to die."

"That's assuming he hasn't already," posed Amelia. Unnerved by her own statement, she looked away. The prospect that the attorney could already be dead lay upon the room like a damp chill. "Maybe we should call to find out," she said softly.

A nervous tremor tickled through Kylie's throat. She wasn't sure that she wanted to know; for as long as the attorney was still alive, it somehow put time on their side.

"We'll just see if he answers," Amelia said, as she went to the telephone and dialed information. Within seconds she pulled the earphone out for Kylie to listen as the recorded voice of the attorney came over the line . . . "This is Dale. I've gone to the lake but will be back in the morning. Leave a message and I'll answer your call as soon as I get in."

Amelia gently replaced the receiver to its cradle. "What do you think?" she asked.

"He's probably fishing," said Kylie certainly, though the flutter had returned to her throat. She envisioned the attorney sitting quietly by a lake, completely unaware of his impending fate. The uneasiness within her heart forced her to look away from her troubled friend. "Well, let's get back to it," she said softly. "The more we know, the better."

The toll of the old clock abruptly resonated, startling both of the women.

"Damn!" gasped Amelia, putting her hand to her head. She glanced toward the clock then back to the Bible that lay open on the table. "We're wasting time," she said, beginning once again to pace. "We can't do this on our own. I'm not a theologian, for God's sake. Maybe we should talk to a priest."

Kylie considered the option, then shook her head. "What's he going to say that we haven't already heard in religion class or at mass?" she asked.

"I don't know," sighed Amelia.

As they contemplated the question, the stained-glass depiction of death that hovered over the chapel rolled through Kylie's thoughts. The congregation sat in oblivion as the dark-winged angel carried the man toward heaven. "'The souls of the virtuous are in the hands of God,'" she whispered, repeating the words of the priest. "'No torment shall ever touch them.'"

"What?" asked Amelia.

Kylie turned distractedly toward her. "The reading today from the

Book of Wisdom," she said. "'In the eyes of the unwise they did appear to die, their going looked like a disaster, their leaving us, like annihilation; but they are in peace.' The priest read the words but he couldn't possibly have known . . . couldn't possibly . . ." Her voice trailed off as she looked once again at her own drawings, to the creature that held her hand out to Collins. "They're there," she said, her voice practically a whisper. "In the Church's art, yet if we went to a priest and told him what we knew he would think we were insane. He would advocate angels of mercy, but not like these."

She swiped the hair from her face and turned to the windows. "It's like the true form of the creatures was known about long ago, but they've somehow been weakened," she said. She turned away again, her mind reeling. Arlin's statues were found in the catacombs beneath St. Stephen's Cathedral in Vienna; therefore the Church must have accepted the depictions or they wouldn't have allowed them to remain. And if the Church sanctioned the pieces in the Middle Ages, in a time when art and religion walked hand in hand—when the Church itself commissioned art as the very means of showing the people what to believe—then why the change? "Why?" she mused aloud. "Why have these angels been—" but she suddenly stopped. "My God," she gasped. "I can't believe I didn't think of this until now."

"Think of what?"

"My God!" she repeated. "Here we are with art degrees and we didn't even think . . . These pieces are from a time when many of the Christian teachings were still based on paganism—on theories of spiritualism that had survived thousands and thousands of years . . . before the Council of Trent advocated censorship—"

"—and set guidelines for the contents of religious imagery," joined Amelia. "The Reformation."

"Yes!" said Kylie. "I can't believe I didn't think of this before. The Reformation," she repeated, for she had studied it well. She had been fascinated by the art of the Middle Ages and how it had changed after the practices of the Catholic Church had fallen under scrutiny. She was amazed how one document, the 95 Theses which had been tacked on the door of the Castle Church by Martin Luther, had sparked such mutiny. Much of the artwork which had been commissioned by the Catholic Church was destroyed—whitewashed or simply smashed and burned by the protesters which later became known as Protestants. In a backlash, the Catholic Church formed the Council of Trent to set guidelines for art in order to escape the scrutiny of the Protestants. The lines between good and evil became much more delineated and most paganistic beliefs were washed from Christianity.

"Streamlined," whispered Kylie. "The angels have survived but they've been softened—made more palatable. To us, the image of an angel of death mutating into a spider or a rat seems so obscene, so sacrilegious when only a few hundred years ago . . . in a society that was so close to death . . ."

"They were accepted," whispered Amelia.

Kylie paced back and forth in a moment of silence. Her hands were shaking and her heart beating wildly. Someone in the past had seen what she had seen, had experienced the terror and awe that she had felt and the ideas had been accepted. "Damn," she hissed. "I wish I still had my art books. I could see what other pieces emerged at that time. There was so much death . . . with the Bubonic Plague and the Hundred Years' War there must have been more." She suddenly turned on her heels and stopped pacing. "We need to find out about those statues. If I can find out more about the inconology behind the pieces, maybe . . . maybe we'll find something that can help us."

"What about Arlin?" asked Amelia quietly. "You think he might know something?"

"He might," said Kylie. "If nothing else, we could look through his books and examine the same period. He's got photos of every piece of art that's ever been displayed in a museum or on the market. If archaeologists can base entire theories of civilizations on art, there's got to be something there that can help us."

"Do you think he would mind?" Amelia asked.

"Not at all," said Kylie. "He and his partner have been in Europe, but they should be back. I'll call him in the morning."

The resolution brought a crisp sense of direction to the air. For the first time all day, Kylie thought of food. "Are you hungry?" she asked, gathering up the pencils from the table. When her question was met with silence, she turned around. She was jolted by the pallor of her friend's face. "Melia?" she said gently.

"I'm sorry," said Amelia, turning away. After only seconds of relief, the anxiety had already returned to her voice, and her shoulders pinched inward. "I wonder what Mama would say about all of this. I feel like I'm gonna burn in hell for even thinking about this stuff."

At a loss—for Kylie knew she could never combat the fear Amelia's mother had instilled in her—she reached out and touched her friend's shoulder. Just then, the sound of her father lumbering up to the cottage broke the silence. "See you later O'Connor," he called out to his friend. The distant response echoed from down the walkway. "Night, Sean. Get some rest."

Kylie looked down at the pile of newspaper articles and drawings strewn about the table. "We better get rid of this stuff," she said.

The women quickly bunched the papers together and just as the door opened Kylie darted into the bedroom where she laid the stack of material. When she returned to the living room, her father was gingerly entering the house as if not to disturb whatever it was the women had been involved with. The poignant smell of beer floated in alongside him.

"Hi, Daddy," Kylie said, smoothing back her hair. The sight of her father's blood-shot eyes made her spirits fall. The sadness in his face reminded her of the long months following her mother's death. For the first time, Kylie realized that Jack's funeral must have brought back the same bad memories for her father as they had for herself. "I was just getting ready to fix some dinner," she said. "Are you hungry?"

"Yes, love," he said shyly, turning away to hang his cap onto a hook by the door.

"Are you sleeping here tonight or on the boat?" she asked.

"The water's gonna be pretty choppy later," he said, rubbing his eyes. "I think I'll take the couch again."

"Okay," Kylie said, looking away to hide her relief. She knew her father was staying to look out for them, for the bay was as smooth as glass. "If you're sure about your back?"

"Oh it's fine, love," he said, settling down at the table. "Don't you worry about a thing."

From behind the fisherman, Amelia smiled weakly, clearly relieved that he would stay.

Kylie wanted to say something to ease her friend's mind, but knew of nothing that would eliminate her apprehension. "Why don't you two relax while I fix supper," she proposed.

"I can make something," said her father.

"Please—Daddy," she said. "It gives me something to do."

Amelia only vaguely seemed to hear the suggestion. With a nod of her head, she strayed once again toward the windows where her attention remained riveted on the night.

Sixteen

MOONLIGHT DANCED UPON THE BLACK WATERS OF THE REMOTE LAKE that lay nestled within the heavy woods. The warm night was calm and still, with only the sound of a quiet drip from a nearby bridge. Amelia's dainty feet pressed upon the soft earth of the shore, the icy water lapping up the bank to touch the tip of her bare toes. She had been walking for miles, uncertain where she was or the path she had taken to get there, but the feel of the sultry breeze set her at ease. With a sigh, she gazed out at the moonlight that glittered upon the water when she noticed a movement beneath the inky surface only ten feet away. Just as she was certain she had imagined it, air suddenly gurgled up as though someone were breathing beneath the veneer of the ebony liquid. At once her heart bolted. She glanced around the thickly wooded area, at the fireflies that fluttered through the air, but there was no one in sight to help investigate. With slow, methodical steps she edged out toward the black depths, the frigid lake clearing her ankles and moving halfway up her calves. She saw the movement again and froze, her eyes fixed on the curious spot within the water. Then quietly, with an almost imperceptible gurgle, the pale face of an elderly man pierced through the black surface, his lifeless features illuminated by the glow of the moon. The hideous face bobbed before her, his neck wrapped tight with fishing wire, his bloated cheeks and open eyes bulging from suffocation. His crinkled lips were blue and his expression distorted; but even after the perversion of a hideous death, the face of the famous attorney was still recognizable.

The morbid visage of Dale Benson stilled within the icy waters like a bloodless apparition peering through the surface from the murky world that lay beneath.

. . .

KYLIE was placing the kettle back onto the stove when she heard the harrowing scream from the bedroom.

She nearly dropped the steaming cup in her hand before resting it on the counter. She raced toward the open doorway to find Amelia sitting up, twisted within the bed sheets. Her hair was damp with sweat and her eyes wild with the nightmare that still clouded her vision.

"He's dead," she gasped through labored breath. "Dale Benson is dead."

Kylie instantly went to the bed and took her friend into her arms. "You were dreaming, Melia," she said gently.

"He was in the water. With fishing wire around his neck."

"It was just a dream," said Kylie, stroking the hot back where the nightgown clung. "Just a nightmare." She went to the window and slid open the thread-bare curtains, allowing the rest of the morning sun to pour in.

Amelia unraveled herself from the sheets that had twisted with her long gown. "I'm going to call and see—"

"I already did," said Kylie softly, her eyes averting away from her friend. "His recorder is still on."

Amelia paused for a moment at the edge of the bed to digest the information. The light slowly washed the dream from her eyes, yet they remained dark and blood-shot. "I feel like shit," she said, running her fingers through her hair but in spite of the effort it continued to stick straight up. "What time is it?" she asked.

"Ten o'clock."

"You're kidding."

"I thought I'd let you sleep," said Kylie, for she knew that Amelia had barely slept a wink all night. Several times she had awakened to her friend standing at the window gazing out into the dark harbor. "I went down to that little boutique on the corner and picked up some stuff," she said, smoothing her hand over her flowered sundress. Though the dress fit nicely, it was cut just at her knees, both shorter and longer than she cared to wear. "It's not exactly the height of fashion but it will do for now."

Amelia looked absently up at her. "It's nice," she said. "I see you got sandals too."

"Yeah and they actually fit," said Kylie. She smiled even though the foreign feel of the stiff leather brought a den of coiling snakes alive in her stomach. There was nothing familiar or comfortable about them. There was nothing familiar or comfortable about the dress she wore or the lemon-scented lotion she had purchased at the drug store. They were all reminders that Jack was gone and that her life in its entirety had been swept away, even the most intimate of basics. The lipstick she had purchased was nearly the same shade as the one she had worn, but it was brighter—somehow strange and hideous to her. Even the clip that held her thick hair back at the base of her neck lacked the familiar warmth and alliance that only time could bring. "I called Arlin's," she said.

The words froze Amelia at the side of the bed. "Was he in?"

"Yeah."

"What did you tell him?" asked Amelia quietly.

"I told him that Dora Greyson wanted to know more about the statue she had bought and he said that he wouldn't be much help but that Eva would talk to us. She's the owner of the boutique," she explained off of Amelia's questioning glance. "She brought the statue over from Europe."

Amelia stood nervously from the bed. "What if she starts asking questions?"

"She won't," said Kylie certainly.

"Well don't you think she'll find it strange that the day after your husband's funeral—"

"She doesn't know about Jack. Neither of them do. They just got back from London last night."

Amelia moved to the window, her arms wrapped tightly about her waist. Kylie felt disheartened when she noticed her thin figure beneath the gown, outlined by the sunlight. She had never seen her looking so gaunt or weary. The circles beneath her eyes were startling, and the lines on her brow seemed to have deepened overnight. She had to glance away, her gaze landing on the clock by the bed. "They're expecting us at twelve-thirty," she said. "You'd better get dressed so we can make the ten-thirty train."

Seventeen

Wɪᴛʜ ᴀ ʏᴀɴᴋ ᴏꜰ ᴛʜᴇ ʟᴇᴠᴇʀ, ᴛʜᴇ ᴘᴀᴄᴋ ᴏꜰ Mᴀʀʟʙᴏʀᴏꜱ ꜱʟɪᴅ ᴛᴏ ᴛʜᴇ bottom of the machine where Amelia's shaking hand pulled them from the slot and tore open the wrapper.

"One little pack isn't gonna hurt," she said to herself, as she flicked the lighter and held it to the tip of the cigarette she had placed between her lips. She let the smoke fill her lungs and within a few seconds she could feel the calming effect of the nicotine. Her glance went to the pay phone against the subway wall, her thoughts on Dale Benson. Even though they had just called his number from the last station and hit his recorder, she was already fighting the urge to try again. She nervously took another puff and then turned toward the tracks where a mother was scolding her child.

Kylie walked slowly along the platform, lost in her own anxious thoughts. To be in the shadowy tunnels once again had set her on edge. Twice she had thought she heard the shriveled old man with the cane, only to discover it was a disabled person ambling by, then a child playing with a stick. She scanned each passing face, all the while avoiding the clock that glowed overhead. Even on the Commuter-Rail from Swampscott to the South Station she had concentrated on anything other than her watch, for the dwindling morning brought credence to Amelia's fear that the attorney was already dead. She had concentrated on her shoes, her hands, her nails, anything to erase the image of Dale Benson's bloodied body floating within muddy waters, or lying still within a patch of trees, but her efforts had been in vain. Repeatedly she saw him plummet to his death from a cliff or crash through his windshield in a collision, and though she told herself that she could do nothing for the crotchety old man, the horrid sense of accountability would not leave her. The fact that she knew of his eminent death, but was doing nothing to prevent it prickled painfully against her conscience. She tried to swallow the lump that had formed in her throat as she turned and began her walk once again toward Amelia. Her gaze passed along the dark wall of the tunnel, when her attention was seized by the unusually ashen appearance of her friend standing by the tracks. She was startled to see that she was smoking.

"What are you doing?" she asked.

"What? This?" said Amelia. "Just one pack." She turned casually away and when she did, her averting glance landed once again on the pay phone by the ticket booth.

Kylie instantly knew that she was thinking of the attorney. "Melia," she said. "We have to give him a chance to get home."

"I know," she said anxiously. "But it's driving me crazy not knowing. He said he would be back in the morning and it's already noon."

Kylie's stomach dropped with the mention of time. She looked up at the big round clock she had been avoiding, just as the little hand clicked, joining the other at twelve.

"Okay," she said with a long breath. "Let's see if he's in."

After depositing enough coins to reach the nearby town of Hamilton, the two women huddled around the receiver while the line connected and began to ring. They stood breathlessly by and with each passing second their apprehension grew stronger. Once again a pang of guilt jabbed through Kylie's chest.

"Maybe we should just leave a message," she said as the phone continued to ring. "There's no sense calling him again and again. I could leave him Arlin's number so that he could call us back."

Amelia looked at her as if she had lost her mind. "And what if he does?" she asked. "What are we going to say?"

"I don't know," sighed Kylie. "Anything."

The recorder picked up the line with a resounding click and for the third time that morning, the voice of the attorney sounded. Kylie gripped the phone tightly as the message beep approached, searching her mind for the words to say. "Mr. Benson . . ." she whispered. "We were just . . . just . . . needed to . . ." With an abrupt beep, the message began to record. "Yes, Mr. Benson," she said. "This is Kylie O'Rourke. I had a question regarding the insurance settlement. Nothing to worry about, I just wanted to make sure that you had the information that you needed. My number is . . ." but then her mind went blank. She had almost given the number to the warehouse. "Yes, um. I'm sorry. You can reach me at . . ." then she proceeded to leave him Arlin's. As soon as she finished the number her finger quickly pressed down on the connection. "Damn," she groaned, as she replaced the receiver to its cradle.

The women stood in silence, until the approaching train rumbled through a nearby tunnel.

After a moment, Amelia spoke softly. "All night long I tried to come up with a way to explain it to him . . . how I could convince my own husband even. Again and again. What I would say to him or to Father Matt or to my mother. There is no explanation," she said, her thin voice breaking with emotion. "We're alone in this. If we try to tell anyone—" but the last of her words were slashed from the air by the squealing of the massive brakes. Her eyes glassed with the emotion of the unspoken words. She turned away as the tears slid down her cheeks and fell upon the dirty pavement. She rubbed her face with the back of her hand and took a long steady drag from the cigarette.

The train stilled in front of them bringing a gust of wind rumpling through their hair. Kylie looked towards its passengers, anything to avoid the sight of the trembling hands that repeatedly held the cigarette to the thin lips. Within the sudden silence, Amelia's voice took on the chill of resolution. "Even if he calls back, we can't help him," she said certainly. "He's on his own."

Eighteen

FLANKED BY HIDEOUS CREATURES ALONG ITS ROOFTOP AND BARS UPON its medieval wooden door and windows, the boutique was oddly nestled along the upscale avenue like a tiny dungeon dropped in the lap of a princess. When the two women pushed open the heavy door to the Ratchford Art Boutique, the cool dark air rushed out at them. Like a huge soothing hand, it enveloped them in its chilly grasp, then pulled them inward into the darkened room. Both women squinted to find their way, helplessly waiting for their eyes to adjust.

"Come in," commanded the throaty voice of a woman who glided through the black toward them.

Kylie blinked, trying to separate the face from the entangled shadows. Though the two had never met, she recognized the voice to be Eva Ratchford's. She had spoken to her many times by telephone but had never had the opportunity to meet the famed scholar in person.

"We were just unpacking some pieces in the back. I'm Eva Ratchford."

The sweet smell of booze drifted along with the woman's perfume and as she stepped into the light to shake their hands, Kylie was struck by how much the older woman reminded her of her own mother. Like Lila's, her hair was dark, her cheekbones high and her build slim, yet there was something other than physical appearance that was chillingly similar. Eva Ratchford had the intimidating gaze of someone on the brink of insanity—someone with one foot firmly planted in reality and the other in another dimension. And while Kylie had been comfortable with her own mother's ethereal qualities, the intuitive gaze of the stranger made her feel instantly self-conscious.

"It's a pleasure to finally meet you," said Kylie, taking the proffered hand. "I'm Kylie O'Rourke."

"Yes," smiled the woman. "I enjoyed your profile in the recent issue of *Architectural Digest*. I must say, your photos don't do you justice."

Kylie felt the intelligent gaze of the woman rest upon the greenish bruise around her eye. She had tried in vain to cover the fading mark, but her effort had left an inept smear of make-up along the tender area. "Thank you," she replied, fighting the urge to turn away. "I recognize you from your photos as well," she offered. "I've got . . . had your book on restoration techniques."

"Ahh," said Eva, her crinkled smile widening. "The Nefetari. All those hellacious, grueling days atop a platform in a cave. I spent so many sleepless nights replacing tiny specks of paint that my eyesight will never be the same," she said. "And this is?" she asked, turning to Amelia.

"Oh I'm sorry. This is my friend, Amelia Blackwell."

"It's a pleasure," said Amelia, stepping forward.

"Oh my God!" came the sudden wail of Arlin Boyce, emerging from the back room. "That accent is to die for!" He wore black pants and a designer silk shirt, with his long, brown hair pulled neatly back. With a playful wink he took Amelia's hand into his own. "I'll have to keep you away from my friend Norton, 'cause he just loves that Southern thing. You must be the doll I've heard so much about."

"Nice to meet you," said Amelia shyly.

Arlin turned to Kylie, his smile softening. "Hi precious," he cooed, pecking her on the cheek. "I see you've met the expert."

"Yes," said Kylie.

"Eva can answer anything about any piece in this place," he touted. "You know she taught a course at Harvard for years on art history."

"I had heard that," said Kylie.

"And she even knows your client, Dora Greyson," he said.

"Years ago she bought a few pieces from me," said Eva. "I must admit I was a little surprised when Arlin mentioned that she was the one who had purchased the angel. Her taste has obviously changed."

"Yes," said Kylie. "After her divorce she wanted nothing from her past."

"So she wants to know more about the piece?" asked Eva.

A rush of heat flooded Kylie's cheeks, for she knew that Dora Greyson couldn't care less about the story behind the twisted angel. "Yes," she replied, her eyes glancing downward. "She's interested in the iconology behind the piece."

"That's understandable," said Eva. "It's not exactly your typical depiction of an angel—it's much more horrifying to say the least. In fact, it's such a confrontational piece that I wasn't sure it would sell. Western culture has done such a brilliant job of reducing angels to castrated shelf-ornaments that I was certain there wouldn't be a buyer out there."

"She's very happy with it," said Kylie.

"Well, if understanding it will make her even more happy, then I'll answer anything you want to know about it or any other work that Arlin has lurking around back there," she said, motioning to the curtained doorway that led to the rear of the store. "But I must warn you . . . even with jet lag, Arlin's hellbent on making a sale this afternoon."

"Speaking of which," said Arlin, clasping his hands together. "I hope you brought your checkbook, sugar. We've got two gorgeous surprises that we brought back from Europe that you're just gonna love! Brothers, to be exact."

Arlin's announcement brought a flutter to Kylie's throat. "Brothers?" she asked, looking toward the darkened curtains of the back room.

THE WHITE, glowing creatures rose nearly to the ceiling, one presiding over the room like an Egyptian god, the other caught savagely in the midst of transformation. There was no mistaking the humanlike bodies that had been twisted with the cruelty of fate; one with a perfectly proportioned male physique juxtaposed against the head of a rat—the other with the agonized face of an Adonis whose belly was ridden with the protruding legs of a spider. They were the siblings of the angel Kylie had purchased—the most lurid of the trio that had been left behind in Europe.

Kylie stood breathless in the doorway, her pulse throbbing so forcefully it felt as if her ribs would snap. Though she had seen photos of the statues, nothing could have prepared her for their sudden appearance. The beasts had scaled the ocean between them, and like a deadly force stealing its way into her life, they had appeared at the least expected moment. Amelia remained frozen beside her, her eyes riveted on the same ghastly sight that dominated the far wall of the dark musty room.

"We thought your client might like the whole family reunited," said Arlin, moving past the two women into the back room. "We nearly ravaged the poor devils trying to unpack them before you got here."

Broken crates lay splintered at the feet of the statues as though their stone muscle had turned to flesh and burst through the boards and filler on their own.

"Aren't they magnificent?" said Eva Ratchford proudly.

Kylie struggled to find her voice. "Yes," she replied softly, trying to mask the silent frenzy raging beneath her skin. Little did the shop owner or art connoisseur know of the fatal misdeeds for which the statues represented—little did they know of the horrendous memories which their presence evoked. Kylie could scarcely look into the haughty face of the rodent's head, for it roused the sight and sound of the hideous old man in the subway with his smacking lips and shrewd smirk that had shifted into that of a rat's. And while she found the contemptuous eyes of the rodent unsettling, Amelia remained stricken by the one with the spiderlike protrusions. Kylie knew that the trepidation that whispered through her heart, rumbled through Amelia's tenfold, for it was the first that she had seen of the creatures.

"When the first one sold so quickly, I decided to hunt down these two," Eva explained. "They had been purchased by a gentleman in Wales."

Amelia moved into the room past them, seemingly drawn to the very matter that brought her terror.

"I tried to call from Europe to tell you the news but your phone was disconnected," said Arlin. "You'll have to make sure that I have the right number."

"Yes, of course," said Kylie, forcing the corners of her mouth into a smile. She thought of the warehouse, of the phone that had disintegrated to mere ashes, of her life that had been erased. She had to look away from the ghastly creatures to gain control over her palpitating heart. The overpowering smell of coffee permeated the room, bringing a flutter to her empty stomach.

The muted sound of Mozart began to drift from a pair of dusty speakers, and wind gently through the darkened room.

"*Mozart's Requiem*," announced Arlin from the stereo across the room. "Considering our subject matter, I think it's apropos."

Kylie winced at the horrible irony of the situation. If only Arlin knew of Jack's death, of the real reason they had come to the shop looking for insight into the beasts. With a pang she noticed the plate of cheese, fruit and pastries that had been placed on the table in hopes of a sale. Guilt plucked at the back of her throat, for Arlin knew Jack. He was fond of him and had no idea he had died in a fire only three days earlier.

"This is a nice addition," she said weakly, grasping for anything to gain her footing again—to pull her friend's focus from the beasts.

While the outer dark rim of the room remained cluttered with paintings, sculptures and tapestries, a small area had been cleared in the center where a Tiffany lamp provided a warm halo around a sitting area. Two sofas covered in a luxurious leather faced one another, the table between them stacked with reference books and a steaming pot of coffee.

"Amelia, isn't this nice?" she asked, trying to break through the wall of fear that kept her friend riveted.

Amelia turned distant eyes toward her.

"That old desk of mine was the worst when it came time for negotiations," said Arlin as he shuffled around bringing more books to the coffee table. "Let me see," he paused, studying the accumulating stack. "There's more in my office."

As he whisked back through the curtains, Eva gestured to the divans. "Why don't you two have a seat while I grab my notebook from up front?"

For an uncertain moment, Amelia's panic seemed ready to overtake her. She leaned toward the door as if to bolt from the stifling room, but at the last minute averted her eyes and took a seat. Lighting a cigarette, she took the smoke deep into her lungs, her gaze drawn once again to the beasts. "My God," she said softly, shaking her head. Her body pulled inward as though shrinking from the cool air. She looked to the floor, the blue of her frightened eyes swallowed by the shadows of the room—the oppressive presence of the beasts clearly more than she could bear.

Eva glided back through the curtains carrying a notebook. "Dora's in luck," she announced. "The gentleman who purchased the pieces knew a lot more about them than their previous owners. As an avid connoisseur of the arts—he really did his homework."

Arlin followed close behind carrying several more reference books to the table.

"Evidently the pieces weren't just some twisted foray into an artist's imagination," said Eva. "They were actually commissioned by the Catholic Church."

Kylie looked up, startled by the comment. "What do you mean?" she asked.

Eva's smile broadened. "It's not the original, but close," she said, pulling a plastic-encased paper from the notebook and laying it before them.

The scrawled hand was in Latin, forcefully penned across the yellowed paper.

"It's an order from the Archbishop authorizing the work," explained Eva. She walked toward the statues, studying them with a shrewd eye. "It's hard to imagine them in a cathedral today," she said. "But they're completely synonymous with the religious imagery in Northern Europe during the Middle Ages, before the Protestant and Catholic Reformations put a strangle-hold on the content of what artists could do. As an artist yourself, I assume you're familiar with the iconoclasm of the Reformation and its effect on religious doctrine?" she asked, turning back toward the women.

"Yes, of course," said Kylie, both relieved and startled to hear her own theory so easily corroborated.

"The date of commission was clearly before the Reformation," said

Eva. "I'm sure the Council of Trent would never have approved such depictions," she added with a touch of rancor.

"No," agreed Kylie quietly.

"They survived the destruction by the Protestant zealots simply because they were in the hidden catacombs beneath the church. I have photos," she said, shuffling through one of the books. "It's important that you see the statues in their original environment in order to understand their origins."

A chilling silence permeated the cool air as they waited for her to find the photos. The contemptuous face of the rodent waited patiently and ever so stoically while the twisted brother threw ominous shadows upon the canvases behind him. Amelia took another drag from her cigarette, her gaze avoiding the looming creatures.

"Here they are," said Eva, laying a notebook open for the women to peruse. The page contained several photos of the three statues standing within the hollowed tunnels of the catacombs.

Amelia shuddered at the sight of the ghastly photos.

"Yes," said Kylie. "I've seen them."

"I think it gives you a sense of the abominable times in which the statues were born," said Eva, taking a seat opposite the two women on the couch. "From the document of commission," she continued slowly, "we now know that the artist's name was Nathaniel Roth, a peasant who rose to brief notoriety in the latter part of the fourteenth century. As with any artist's work, it goes without saying that it's inspired by the times in which it's created—the artist often an interpreter of what wages around him. In 1334 you had the start of the Bubonic Plague, or Black Death as some call it. In over a twenty-year period it wiped out as much as three-quarters of the population in Europe and Asia. Roth's mother, father and younger sister all died of the deadly disease. Shortly after completion of the pieces, he himself fell victim to the disease."

Kylie studied the nervous signature of the artist wondering what atrocities he had witnessed at the time of the commission.

"Death was such a prominent part of life," continued Eva, "that it completely shaped the arts, religion, every single aspect of medieval life. One couldn't step from one's doorstep without being reminded of mortality. Long before the bodies of the dead made it to the catacombs, the corpses were thrown into common pits to decompose. These pits were situated right within the city walls. Up to 10,000 bodies at once were stacked crudely on top of one another and left to the elements. You may have heard of the most notorious one—the Innocents in France?"

Goose flesh prickled over Kylie's arms. "I saw drawings of it in school," she said. "My teacher said that it was so toxic that it could consume flesh within a twenty-four hour period."

"I would have opted for the ole' roast and toast method myself," said Arlin.

Eva smiled, clearly amused by the comment. "First off, cremation was forbidden by the Catholic Church and secondly . . . well, I'm afraid my darling, that you wouldn't have had a choice. Once you died the Church owned your body and would dispose of it as it willed," she said. "No one, not even royalty escaped open burials. Molière, La Fontaine and even Mozart were relegated to them."

"What a hideous thought," said Arlin.

"Emotionally, it must have been heinous," said Eva. "To pass by these pits on a daily basis . . . to smell the stench . . . to see the bodies of loved ones slowly picked to death by rats, insects and vultures. To know that one day you, yourself, would end up in one. No wonder artists such as Nathaniel Roth became obsessed with death. They had to find a way to cope . . . to understand. Accounts of spiders and mice running from the mouths of the dead fueled the old superstition that the soul was actually being carried away by these vermin—that while some were there to feast, others were there to free the soul to the next world. Which brings us to the brothers—to messengers of death taking the guise of rodents," she concluded looking toward the statues.

"Not that the idea of vermin taking the souls of the dead was anything new," she continued. "Many ancient cultures drew the same correlations," she paused for a moment, staring thoughtfully at the statues as she lit a cigarette. "Quite frankly," she said. "I was surprised and a little disappointed that the artist didn't include a fly in the renditions."

"A fly?" asked Kylie, startled by the comment.

"Flies were also noted carriers of the soul," said Eva. "The term 'Beelzebub' directly translates to Lord of the Flies or Lord of Souls.

Beelzebub was originally a Philistine god—a psychopomp who delivered the souls of the dead . . . Arlin, sit down," she suddenly said. "You're making me nervous."

Arlin, who was halfway to the curtained doorway turned back. "I just want to make sure I locked the front door."

"Nonsense," said Eva, looking over at the two women with a devilish grin. "He can't stand it when I start telling him what these pieces are really depicting. It sends him screaming like a little sissy."

"Now don't be a witch," scolded Arlin, moving obediently back to the sofa. "They've only just met you. It's too early to expose your dreadful side."

"Ridiculous," teased the woman. "It's never too early." Then, as if to demonstrate her point, she pulled a jeweled flask from her purse and took a sip. "My deadliest vice," she said under her breath. With a knowing eye and a half-smile, she tilted the bottle toward Kylie. "Sip of cognac?" she asked, as though the two were comrades in their propensities.

Again the probing eyes. Kylie felt her face turn crimson, for the flask had not been offered to anyone else. "No thank you," she said.

Like an elder black sheep that recognizes a younger, Eva smiled. Kylie's chagrin melted, for there was no denying the affinity between them. She understood the eccentric woman's strange clothing, dark make-up and flask of whiskey. She understood the lines and the shadowy eyes of the nonconformist who had suffered more tragedy than most.

"Well I just don't understand why he had to put that gorgeous one in such agony," said Arlin, his brow crinkling with disapproval. "Those legs coming out of his stomach are just too much."

"I beg to differ," said Eva, gazing with admiration toward the statue. "True to the belief of the times, Roth captured him in the midst of transformation to give him life. Shapeshifting—as it's called—was a recurrent theme in Slavonic and Germanic mythology. If you look in the beginning of Stroud's book," she said, pointing to a brown art volume on the table, "you'll see other shapeshifters that are a close relative to these angels. The flesh-eating Scandinavian Valkyries were also known throughout Europe as angels of death."

Inside the book they found the work of the French illustrator Gustave Doré. In the series of Biblical illustrations, angels with jagged wings and vicious faces descended upon battle-worn victims, the thunderous skies splitting open with fury. Like the family photo that opens a dark door to the past, the painting brought the glowing creatures beside them to life, crouching ruthlessly over the dying soldiers.

"Valkyries were known shapeshifters," said Eva. "Though the form they usually took wasn't a rat or spider, but a crow like the brother you purchased," she said. "In fact, I knew that one would sell much easier than these two, simply because much of medieval superstition about crows has remained, making it easier to accept them as an intermediary between the living and the dead. Obviously you've heard of the witch that casts a death spell from the foot of a crow." A smile of amusement suddenly spread across her wrinkled face. "And these," she said pointing to the age lines around her glassy eyes. "Were no doubtedly named crow's feet from the notion that a crow as well as age is an impending sign of death."

"And let's not forget that a flock of crows is considered a murder of crows," added Arlin.

"It's amazing how many remnants from pagan superstitions have survived in spite of the Church's efforts otherwise," Eva mused. "May I?" she asked, taking the thick book from Kylie. After a moment, she landed on the works of Hieronymous Bosch.

"Again you see how other artists of the time worked with similar themes," she said, laying the unsettling work of the artist before them. Half-human, half-insectlike creatures filled the pages in freakish depictions of human demise. "Again the shapeshifters," she said, pointing to a blue angel with sharp facial features, grey insectlike wings and a reptilian body.

"Again redemption," she said, turning back to the statues.

"Redemption?" asked Amelia, the word catching in her throat.

"The Middle Ages are often referred to as the 'Age of Faith', when the salvation of one's soul took precedence above all other goals," explained Eva. "The Church used art as a way of instilling fear, to convince its patrons that their souls needed saving. In fact, the abominable pits were situated next to its cathedrals so that its patrons would be reminded on the way to mass of their mortality and that redemption must be had—sort of a scare tactic if you will. The same held true with the Church's art.

"A cardinal of the Church ordered a tapestry version of this triptych called *The Garden of Delights*. The artist, Hieronymus Bosch, was said to have been greatly inspired by the disturbing text of Revelations. All you have to do is look at it to see that it was meant to frighten . . . to impart that the indulgent life leads to the fiery gates of hell."

Kylie stared down at the Boschian depiction of the horrific realm. Twisted bodies fell upon one another in human torture.

"The statues also bespeak punishment," Eva said, gazing up at the glowing beasts. "But while their lesson is none the less brutal, it is intended for the redeemable. In the Apocryphal Text, or the Testament of Abraham, Michael—who was not only an angel of life, but an angel of death—was thought to be able to save one's soul from eternal damnation even after death. He could punish the wicked, thus bringing their redemption."

"Purgatory?" asked Amelia.

"Yes," said Eva. "The pain you see in their faces tells us that they are unwilling victims caught within a type of retribution . . . a purging, so to speak, where they serve a thousand years of service to work off the misery they caused others . . ."

"Like in Revelations?" asked Amelia. Her voice was soft, her dark eyes waiting yet withdrawn.

"You must be a girl who knows her Bible," said Eva with a smile.

For a moment, the dim light of the room seemed to close in on the sitting area. Kylie could see her friend's discomfort, not only at the rhetorical question but at the ever-mounting information that wove the lineage behind the creatures tighter and tighter. No longer was the monster confined within the memories of a friend, it roamed freely through the pages before her. With each passing word her shoulders closed inward as though her body were shrinking from the abhorrence of the creature's existence.

"The idea that one's soul could be saved even after death was attractive to both the Church and its patrons," continued Eva. "For the people it gave them hope and for the Church it brought significant revenues in indulgences and paid prayer."

"What do you mean paid prayer?" asked Arlin.

"Well, you could diminish the time your loved ones spent in purgatory by contributions to the Church," she explained. "The whole concept of purgatory and the fact that it was being used as a fund-raiser was one of the final points of contention that started the Reformation. Under the scrutiny of the newly formed Protestant sect, the Church strengthened its stance by canonizing much of the Apocrypha that supported their position on purgatory, while ridding itself of anything belonging to pagan beliefs because they had become so controversial. Though lost after the Reformation—shapeshifting ... messengers of death taking the form of animals ... angels serving penance as a means of retribution were all beliefs that had originated long before the Middle Ages. Russian folklore and also Ancient Greece had similar messengers of death."

"This one is entitled *Odysseus and the Sirens*," said Eva, placing yet another book before them. The picture that filled the page was labeled: DETAIL FROM A GREEK RED-FIGURED STAMNOS FROM VULCI, EARLY FIFTH CENTURY B.C..

Kylie was immediately seized by the image. A nude man stood tied to the mast of a ship while huge birds with human heads swooped down upon him. She looked to Amelia who stared with white lips down at the painting. In spite of the cool room, tiny wisps of perspiration had formed at the base of her blonde hair.

"As punishment for their rebellion, the goddess Aphrodite turns the souls of the dead to birds," explained Eva. "They then reside in the spirit world where they lure the living to their deaths. Odysseus," she said, pointing down to the bound man, "is forewarned that the angels of death are coming so he ties himself to the mast of the ship so that he won't follow them to his death."

Kylie instantly thought of Gavin Collins and of the fateful step he had taken to his own demise. Like the man in the painting that could not trust his own will, Collins had been lured by the mistrustful face of death. A dark river of dread ran over her, for even two thousand years earlier, the Greeks had known of the creatures and of their uncanny deceit.

"The Sirens were said to have beautiful voices that could lure their victims," said Eva. "Other times they made a screeching, terrifying noise, much like the Irish Banshee or the Ankou of Celtic Folklore."

"A shriek?" asked Kylie, her stomach sickening. She thought of the piercing cries Julius Vanderpoel had made that day in the school and that night at her father's.

"Yes, a mournful wail," said Eva. "A cry of death or perhaps misery.

Even the more traditional angels are known to make shrieking noises," she mused.

"Another role of the Siren," she said, turning back to the painting of Odysseus, "was to dispense pleasure in death . . . the idea that one is carried to heaven in painless bliss is also depicted by the Hindu Apsaras who share the same form as the Sirens. Sort of dispensers of euphoria you might say. Lilith, the original goddess of death, was the first true angel of mercy."

The book lay open to a bas-relief of a half-woman, half-bird creature that was dated 2,000 B.C.. "2,000 B.C." gasped Kylie. "My God," she whispered, for it was a time that was unfathomable yet, still, the creatures had been documented.

"If you notice," said Eva, leaning in closer to flip through some of the pages, "Phoenician mythology, Assyro-Babylonian mythology, Egyptian mythology . . . all of them depicted the presence of half-human creatures that were linked with the dead and thought to dwell in the underworld."

Turning from one page to the next, Kylie saw that the creatures were documented clear back to the time coined as the "cradle of civilization"—back to the time of Mesopotamia where the King Assurbanipal was said to have seen an entire underworld filled with winged figures.

"As you see," said Eva, relaxing back onto the sofa. "Nathaniel Roth's creations were not so outlandish as one might initially think. He was simply giving expression to the beliefs that had survived thousands and thousands of years."

Kylie closed the book and tried to put it back onto the table but her mind was so inflamed by the images that she couldn't bring herself to release them. They were all images she had seen before, that she had studied in college in pursuit of her degree. She should have pieced them together long before the night of the fire. She should have known that rainy day in Dr. Jordan's office that her mind was not creating but merely reassembling and confirming the myths and theologies of societies long past. If she had only thought sooner, maybe Jack would be alive. If she had only opened one of her textbooks and thumbed through the photos—

The resonate voice of the woman abruptly pulled her from her thoughts. "The Renaissance shifted society's focus away from spirituality to science and mathematics. Pieter Brueghel the Elder made a great deal of money with Boschian type depictions—*Fall of the Rebel Angels* among them—but other than that, very few portrayals of these angels have been received well since the Reformation."

"But there have been some?" asked Kylie.

"Yes, but none that have reached any notoriety," said Eva. "In fact, I have a few paintings from a contemporary artist who depicted the angels true to their medieval form and—even today—his work is considered confrontational. I was thinking last week that, well—if Dora decided not to take the other two statues—then a couple of his pieces combined with the one you purchased may create a striking ensemble."

The suggestion brought a groan from Arlin. "Please tell me you're not speaking of that lunatic Hector Haynes."

With mere mention of the name, the light in the room seemed to dim. Eva flashed an acerbic glance in the direction of the comely man, cleared her throat and rose from the couch.

"I think Dora may appreciate the artist's work," she said. As she crossed to the far wall and began thumbing through a group of paintings that leaned together, an uncomfortable silence settled over them. Amelia reached nervously for another cigarette, but then stopped. She took a deep breath and began chewing at her nails that were already so short they looked as if they could bleed. Kylie shifted in her seat, while Arlin poured himself a second cup of coffee.

"You'll have to excuse us, ladies," said Eva, her back remaining toward them. "Arlin and I have a . . . well," she hesitated, clearly choosing her words carefully. "Hector Haynes had certain ideas that Arlin found offensive."

Arlin sighed, his pretty mouth forming into a pout. "The man was a complete . . . oh how shall I say . . . psychopath," he said pointedly.

Eva turned back with a wry smile. "Aren't most creative types?" she quipped, the black smudges of eye-liner that defined her glassy eyes narrowing.

While the two bantered between them, Amelia's gaze wandered to the telephone against the wall. With a quickening of her heart, Kylie too noticed the black phone that was silent and waiting: Dale Benson had yet to call. Amelia turned purposely to Kylie; her message was frantic and pleading. Though no words were spoken, Kylie knew her intent. She wanted to leave, to escape the oppressive room. They didn't have time to shop through other artists' work on the pretense of a buy. Time was of the essence.

"This is one of my favorites," said Eva, breaking the silent discourse. She had withdrawn a painting and placed it against the wall for the group to view. Kylie politely got up and though Amelia remained behind, she knew the very moment that her friend saw the painting. Her soft gasp echoed through her ears, the sound more shrill than the screech of a scream.

"IT's entitled *The Deceptive Hands of Death*," announced Eva.

The painting was of a bright tunnel of light that cut through a thick blackness. At the far end of the spiraling tunnel stood a small angelic child in a pretty pink dress. She was a perfectly beautiful little girl with the exception of clawlike hands that reached outward to the viewer as though inviting them inward.

"Much like a contemporary rendition of the Odysseus and Siren myth," said Eva, "the artist attempts to show that there is a dark side to death, a deception that lures people toward it."

Amelia had moved forward but she immediately glanced away, her eyes catching Kylie's as she turned. "It was them," she whispered, nervously rubbing her hand against her hot brow.

Kylie instantly knew what she meant, for she too had thought of Amelia's grandmother and of her deathbed vision. Her heart faltered as she looked back to the painting, at the animalistic claws that sent chills screeching down her spine.

Arlin, who had noticed the interchange, nodded his head. "It's pretty unsettling, isn't it," he commented.

Kylie smiled a hollow acknowledgment as Eva pulled another canvas from the group and leaned it alongside the other. "This is a self-portrait of the artist. It's actually more of a sketch I guess I should say."

A balding man in his late fifties to early sixties stood within the shadowy light of a warehouse, his thick arms folded tightly across his chest as he stared forward. His smooth face was strained, his haunting eyes dark and nervous.

"One night, a few years ago, I was giving a lecture at Harvard when he showed up," said Eva. "He asked a lot of questions, in particular about the angels which I had yet to retrieve from Europe. I bought some of his paintings thinking they might sell, but, well, most of the well-to-do aren't as open-minded as your client."

With resignation, she turned her back to the paintings and took a seat on the couch. "You're more than welcome to look through them if you're interested," she said, lighting herself another cigarette. "There's five of them altogether."

Amelia's anxious glance urged Kylie toward the paintings.

Kylie hesitated a moment, the room around her suddenly closing in. Like a darkened forest threatening to engulf the sitting area, the gargoyles, paintings and tapestries edged up to the island of light, throwing shadows across the walls and ceiling. With the horrid feel of the stiff sandals she moved to the wall and began sorting through the canvases in search of Hector Hayne's work. After several generic landscapes—simple green fields to fill a dull office or hotel room—she came upon three that were clearly done by the disturbed artist. The first was another rendition of the tunnel of light; the same girl stood at the end only a sickening smile had been added to her face. The next was of a crouching beast hunched in a dark alleyway, with human feet and hands, his face and body contorted into a nightmare. And the last—the most hideous of all—sent adrenaline prickling to her fingertips. She carefully removed it from the group and placed it alongside the self-portrait.

"This one is interesting," she said as casually as possible.

"It's entitled *The Kingdom of Shadows*," said Eva from across the room, a puff of smoke hanging languidly about her shadowed face.

Silence once again took hold of the room, as all eyes, including Arlin's, focused on the painting.

A man stood crouched within a closet, his large body jammed within a tight space as spiders and rats oozed between the cracks in the floor and ceiling. Long bony fingers reached in from the door beneath sending shards of light cutting across the man's horrified face. Amelia's voice broke the silence.

"My God," she uttered, looking toward the self-portrait. "It's the same man."

At first thinking that the artist had merely cloned the man in the closet after himself, Kylie was startled to see that the features in the two paintings were identical.

"Again," said Eva. "One must look to the life of the artist in order to understand. Hector had suffered from a near-death experience. A bad one," she said quietly. "When he first brought the painting to the shop he wouldn't discuss what had inspired it. It wasn't until after I had met with him a couple of times that he invited me to an NDE group . . . he said that it would not only lend insight into his work, but perhaps to some of the other pieces I have . . ."

"Please," she said, motioning the two women toward the couch.

"At the group, most of the experiences people described were very positive," she continued. "They see their relatives, a bright light, they feel a warmth. The specifics of each experience varied from person to person, but there were similar characteristics, one in particular. Everyone in this group said they were given the option to come back if they wanted. All with the exception of Hector. He had been resuscitated from a fatal heart attack fifteen minutes after he had lost consciousness. He had a very bad experience. He claimed to have seen all kinds of things—horrific things that the doctors blamed on lack of oxygen to the brain. But Hector didn't buy it. He was certain he hadn't imagined it all and he said he had proof. He was a very nervous, odd man, and he had a theory. He was convinced he had been wrongly brought back—that the doctors had resuscitated him when they shouldn't have. He believed that modern science was screwing with the balance, as he called it. That people were being resuscitated when they were destined to die and that a type of underworld was seeping up to reclaim them," she said, her eyes resting on the harrowing depiction within the closet. "He had statistics about all kinds of things where accident victims and others are brought back from the brink of death. He invited me to his apartment one night and showed me a whole book of articles he had clipped. There were drown victims, cardiac-arrest victims, accident survivors—everything you could imagine—who had either miraculously escaped death or who had been resuscitated after a long period of time. Then he had follow-up obituaries where a good number of them had died within only months of their survivals from some freak reason."

With a deep breath, Amelia restlessly got up from the sofa, her palm pressed against her chest as if to relieve some pressure. Though she escaped to the shadowed part of the room, Kylie noticed the tremble in her friend's hands.

Unaware of the mounting tension that her words evoked, the woman beside them continued. "Hector was convinced that he would be one of those people. He said that only one-fifth to one-third of all patients who are brought back after cardiac arrest ever leave the hospital and a substantial number of those die within a year. He became very paranoid. He was terrified to be left alone. He made his wife stay with him practically every minute of the day. It was very unnerving to watch . . . to see him—" but her voice broke off as she paused in contemplation. She took a long drag from the cigarette and exhaled heavily, staring through the smoke as though the scene were still within reach. With a nod of her head, as if to dispel her thoughts she repositioned herself on the sofa. "Arlin cringed every time he came into the shop."

"I couldn't help it," Arlin contended. "All that talk of death got under my skin." He turned to Kylie to implore her understanding. "I just hated it when he talked about . . . well, you know, seeing things. In his room at night and . . . ugh," he shuddered with a wave of his hand.

"Well, maybe he really was seeing things," said Eva. "It wouldn't be the first time that someone had come back from death with a heightened sense of perception."

"Oh honey," sighed Arlin, not unkindly. "He had gone mad, plain and simple."

"Maybe so," said Eva, snubbing the cigarette into the ashtray. "But the whole thing aroused enough suspicion in my mind to follow up on some of the things he was saying."

"Like what?" asked Kylie.

Eva paused for a moment before answering. "He was convinced that Ancient Egyptians were leagues ahead of us in their knowledge and understanding of the afterlife. He said there was a small secretive society of nobility called the Cult of Osiris. Osiris Khenti Amenti was a death god who also appeared in the form of the bird Bennu. This secretive cult that adopted his name used near-fatal suffocation to create a near-death experience so that they could explore the afterlife . . . partly in hopes of defying death. Before one could become a god-king, he was required to take the journey in order to properly lead the people. The ritual took place in the underground chambers of the Great Pyramid and would be attended by a priest and several other members. The prospective king was placed into an airtight sarcophagus sealed with wax where he would remain for about eight minutes before the lid would be removed and the rushing air would revive him. I did a little research, and he was right. According to Egyptologists, detailed accounts of the religious ritual were documented in their hieroglyphics and some even believe that their findings are responsible for many of the chapters in the *Book of the Dead*." She looked toward the painting of the man in the closet. "They reportedly found an underworld, a place where the dead reside. In Greek mythology it's called 'The Kingdom of Shadows'. Hence, the title of the piece," she said reflectively. "Hector believed in cracks of entry... that this underworld was seeping up to reclaim him."

"What do you mean, 'cracks of entry'?" asked Kylie.

"It's when the physical world can be entered by the spiritual," said Eva. "New Year's Day, midnight, season's change, mirrors, thresholds are among a few of them. The symbolism of himself inside the closet is meant to signify the cracks of entry."

Amelia stood before the disturbing painting with her back to the group, when Kylie noticed that her friend's breath had grown short and sporadic. "Amelia," she said gently. "Are you—"

"I'm fine," she said, pivoting away.

In the glimpse as she turned, Kylie saw the fear and overwhelm choking the very breath from her friend. "Maybe you should sit down," she suggested.

Arlin stood from the couch. "Honey, you look positively peaked."

"It's just a little stuffy in here," said Amelia, her voice struggling.

"I'll turn up the air and see if that helps," offered Arlin.

"Thanks," said Amelia, her gaze meeting Kylie's in a silent plea to let it drop.

As Arlin got up from the couch and went to the thermostat, Amelia turned to Eva with a thin, hollow smile. "So what happened to him?" she asked, swiping the dew from her brow with a trembling hand. "This Hector Haynes?"

After an uncertain moment, Eva answered. "He became obsessed," she said softly.

"That's putting it mildly," said Arlin, taking a seat once again at the couch.

"Obsessed with what?" asked Kylie.

"With escaping death," answered Eva.

The answer cut sharply through both women.

"He took to reading ancient scriptures looking for clues. I think he knew every word of The Book of Enoch by heart."

"The Book of Enoch?"

"It was part of the Apocrypha that the Church rejected—an apocalyptic foray into the afterworld," explained Eva. "The last time I saw Hector he was ranting about it and about Germanic mythology. He was convinced that if he killed the spirit when in the guise of its earthly body that the spirit would also die. He was crazed, out of his mind," she said. "He killed every living spider, or bird, or rat that he came upon. Even his wife became terrified of him."

Within the sudden silence, the sound of Amelia's breath had grown increasingly strained. Kylie looked helplessly to her friend who had begun to pace about the room, her gaze fixed on the bleak portrait of the artist.

"I wouldn't mind talking to him," said Kylie, trying desperately to hide the silent frenzy rushing beneath her own skin, "If Dora likes his work, then maybe—"

"I'm afraid that's impossible," interrupted Eva softly.

Amelia suddenly stopped and turned to the couch.

"Why not?" asked Kylie, her heart crawling into her throat.

"Just like he predicted, he died within six months of his resuscitation."

"There's nothing strange about that," said Arlin uneasily. "He died of a weak heart."

The comment hung suspended before them like a bird that had suddenly lost its wings. "No Arlin, he didn't," said Eva, gently. "He drowned in his own bathtub."

THE ATTACK erupted suddenly and forcefully, piercing through the lingering silence. For a paralyzing moment, Amelia stood transfixed, clutching her chest and gasping inward. As she tried to wrench the oxygen from the thick air, the faces around her mirrored her fright.

"Amelia?" said Kylie, standing quickly.

"I can't . . . breathe," she gasped, digging her hand into her sternum. She began moving back and forth across the floor to outrun the tightness clamping down on her lungs, but with each fruitless gulp she became more and more frantic. "I can't . . . breathe!"

"Is she asthmatic?" asked Eva rushing forward. "There's a pharmacy—"

"No," said Kylie. "She's not. Amelia, what is it?"

"I don't . . . know," she gasped. "It's . . . like yours."

Kylie knew instantly what she meant. The panic attack bore the same characteristics as her own brought on by claustrophobia . . . the pressure on her sternum, the sweating, the fright, only Amelia's had clearly been incited by unmitigated fear. "Arlin, do you have a small paper bag?" she asked.

"There's one up front," he answered moving quickly from the room.

"This room's a little tight," said Kylie.

"I'll open the back door," said Eva.

Amelia's clammy hand pressed down on Kylie's in an entreaty to stay close. Tears suddenly flooded her cheeks and were falling downward when the glimmering light streamed into the room. Like a giant stark hand it reached inward, its long razor-sharp fingers cutting through the darkness, needling its way to the macabre faces of canvas and stone. With the horror of the room brought into full light, her gasping escalated. The terror closed in and increased its volume, as she glanced from corner to corner like a caged animal.

"Melia," said Kylie sharply. "Melia," she repeated calmly but firmly, forcing her friend to meet her gaze. "Sit down here on the sofa."

Through the continuing gasps, Amelia obediently crossed to the couch and sat back as Arlin brought the bag.

Kylie quickly opened it. "Breathe into this," she instructed.

Amelia quickly clasped it to her lips and began to breathe, the bag collapsing and refilling with her own breath.

Eva brought forth a glass of water.

"Thanks," said Kylie, setting it aside. "I think she just needs some space."

Eva stood within the curtained doorway, the lines of her face clarified by the harsh daylight. "Let's go up front and let them alone," she
said, taking Arlin's arm.

Kylie settled to her knees and took her friend's hot hand into her
own. She massaged it gently, just as Amelia had for her years earlier.
The calmness of others was the only thing that ever eased the gasps
into a steady breath. "Shh," she whispered. "It's just a little panic attack. It'll pass, you just have to trust it. Shhh . . ."

As Amelia's breathing slowly returned to normal, she lowered the
bag, her crimson eyes searching out Kylie's. In the aftermath, dark
lines of mascara streaked her cheeks accentuating the underlying terror that had brought on the attack. "Did you hear what she said?" she
asked painfully, the tears rushing to her eyes once again.

"It's okay," said Kylie. "Don't think about it—"

"He drowned to—" but her words were choked off by her emotion.
She looked to the painting of Hector Haynes and his closet of torture
when the black phone drew her attention once again. Like a harbinger
of doom it remained silent, glistening within the newly found light. At
once, the overwhelming fear in her face disintegrated into dark defeat. "I have to know," she said softly.

The resolve that abruptly glazed the blue eyes sent an icy tremor
through Kylie's thoughts. For a moment she felt as though she were
staring at a stranger—a small sickly girl. "Melia," she said, gently
clutching her hand.

The distant eyes looked toward her like a deep abyss of ruby wine.
"We'll take your father's truck to Hamilton," said the strange voice
before her.

A deep raw ache moved its way into Kylie's gut. "Give him time,"
she said, turning away. "He's famous enough that if anything happens
it will be on the news."

Amelia sat up in preparation for departure. "We can't wait," she
said with frightening calm. "I have to know . . . I have to see for myself."

Nineteen

As the blue wash of the approaching night turned the white pickup to gray, the '82 Ford rattled along the two-lane highway that cut through the New England hillside. With deep orange glimpses that broke through the blackened woods, the summer night was descending with the day's sweltering temperatures in tow.

Kylie rolled the driver's window within an inch of closure to escape the blasting hot air. After only thirty minutes on the road, her cheeks were already throbbing with wind burn. They had taken Highway 1A through Salem, past Beverly and the small town of Wynham and soon they would reach the sleepy little community of Hamilton, Massachusetts.

As the heat trapped the scent of tobacco and old vinyl within the cab, Kylie focused her parched eyes on the road, contemplating the truck that trembled around her. It had been years since she had been behind the wheel, when her father had lent it to her and Jack. They had gone to a party out at Cochichewick Lake, before making love in the old bed that clattered behind her. With the promise of a sweet harvest dancing around them, they had gazed at the stars and planned their future, their easy laughter drifting up toward the glowing moon. But the sound was but a whisper on the whistling wind. Kylie's heart constricted, for the present remained with the cruel finality of time.

Amelia was silent, staring through the passenger window watching the darkened woods tremble by. In the vast space between them lay the remains of a half-eaten sandwich and some chips they had grabbed from the house. "We're going for a ride, Daddy," Kylie had called, as her father made his way down the dock toward his boat. "Whatever you want, love. Whatever you want."

The flickering lights of Wynham disappeared in the rear view mirror, the searing pavement passing beneath them in a hum. Like a warm hypnotic dream imparted by the devil, the Ratchford Art Boutique moved a million miles away. The Pandora's box faded further and further into the distance like a fantastical voyage into hell they had abruptly escaped. Kylie gripped the wheel tightly, wandering what would happen if she just kept driving through the sunset and into the night. Perhaps they could outrun whatever fate had in store—but the lights of the small town of Hamilton were already blotting the horizon. With each yellow line the town drew nearer, bringing a new kind of horror shivering over the heat of the wind.

Would the attorney be alive, and if so, what would they say to him?

"We'll just watch and see," the voice said in answer to her mind's query.

When she turned, she was startled to see the dull eyes of Amelia staring back at her. Her friend had barely spoken a word since leaving the shop.

"We'll just watch and see," she repeated, before turning back to the darkening hillside.

JUST NORTH of town, Sagamore Farm Street intersected with Bay Road.

"Take a left at that last stop light . . . go three and a half miles past a wooden bridge, then you'll find it on the right." Those had been the directions from the overalled attendant at the station. Sure, he had heard of the attorney. "He represented those rich brothers that killed their parents . . . Cut both of their heads off and stuffed them in an icebox." Seemed to him that was what he had heard, anyways. And yes, he was certain the attorney lived alone. "The Missus moved out about six months ago."

A few miles inward, the paved road abruptly turned to gravel. With the truck vibrating beneath them, Kylie reached down and flicked on the head lamps, the harsh beams blasting against the mosquitos and white rocks. Far in the distance, a bloody line sliced across the horizon and swallowed the last glimmer of day. The road suddenly narrowed bringing the trees crowding inward into a darkened tunnel.

Just as the attendant had promised, they found the ranch-style house in a clearing to the right, within perfect view of the road. It was set back no more than fifty feet, but the manicured estate that stretched behind it seemed to go on endlessly.

Both women leaned forward, peering through the bug-spotted windshield of the idling truck.

"He's there," Kylie said, with equal parts relief and apprehension.

The door on the left of a two-car garage stood open with a warm light illuminating its contents. It boasted a white Cadillac sedan with gold trim resting quietly in the roomy space. The trunk was propped open as though someone were unloading it. A duffle bag, a kerosene lantern and a few other items lay on the cement behind the car, yet no one was in sight.

"Can you see anything?" asked Amelia, her voice already lighter.

Kylie looked from window to window searching for movement behind the glowing curtains. Though slightly more subdued than she would have imagined, the house bespoke wealth. Two stately pillars led up to an arching entrance, while French windows and doors spanned the sides of the long tan-brick dwelling. "He's obviously in there somewhere," she said, sliding her foot off the brake.

"Let's wait a second," said Amelia. "Maybe he'll come back out."

Kylie pulled toward the sloping ditch, hit the lights but left the engine to idle, sending an angry cricket into protest from a nearby bush. With a heavy breath she looked back to the windows, wondering what Dale Benson would do if he caught the two women parked at the end of his drive spying on him. Her last conversation with the man could hardly be deemed cordial. While she was still in the hospital he had called her directly to cess out the story she would relay to Drew Dodson of the NTSB in a subsequent phone interview. He had used the slippery tact of an attorney in twisting her words and her vacillating memory—anything to relieve himself of the responsibility of the lost lives. With a pang she noticed the skis hanging neatly along the wall inside the garage. "It didn't take him long," she muttered, feeling the attorney's life had scarcely been affected by the tragedy that had devastated so much of her own.

"What did you say?"

"Nothing," she said, shaking off the resentment. She impatiently put the truck into gear. "Let's get out of here."

With one last steady look, they idled past until the house was behind them, then she hit the gas and pulled the head lamps back on. In the beam of the sudden light, a dog was abruptly before them, lying still in the middle of the road.

"Watch out!" gasped Amelia, gripping the dashboard.

Kylie barely had time to brake before the animal was beneath the front of the truck.

"Oh Jesus!" she exclaimed, instantly putting the Ford into reverse to back away from it.

"You didn't hit it," said Amelia. "It's too low to the ground."

The body of the dog slowly appeared in front of them, in the same position as before. Kylie jammed the truck into park, her legs shaking so forcefully she could barely keep her foot on the brake.

For a stunned moment, both women were silent, staring at the still animal. Then the head of the dog lifted and looked lethargically back at them. What looked to be dried blood covered his white face. As the women quickly climbed from the truck and rushed toward it, it began to hobble to its feet, its hip clearly injured. Kylie immediately saw that the dog was dehydrated, for foam had formed at its lips.

"Be careful," she said, raising a warning hand. "He might bite."

But as they drew near, the dog began to whine and thump its tail. With sad, pathetic eyes he looked up at them. Kylie gently touched his head.

"Shh, it'll be okay," she said soothingly, all the while assessing the damage. From what she could tell, there were no injuries that could have produced the blood on its face. "I'm not finding anything," she said running her fingers slowly around his ears. "He's a Brittany spaniel—a hunting dog. My uncle used to have one that liked to roll around in the blood of her prey."

"I don't think so," said Amelia. "Look at that." She was pointing to the dog's side which was raw and exposed.

"It's a buckshot wound," said Kylie, recognizing it from the game her uncles brought back from the woods in Georgia. With a dull feeling of dread, she reached carefully through the matted hair to the dog's tag. It began to whimper as she worked the small piece of metal loose from a clump of bloodied hair. She pulled the tag into view of the headlights, her throat tightening with the words. "His name is Ben," she said softly and then read the address. Just as she had feared, the dog was Dale Benson's.

BEFORE approaching the daunting pillars the women settled on two scenarios that had given them the courage to move forward: either the dog had been hurt in the attorney's absence and Benson had yet to discover the mishap, or the dog had been shot while hunting and the attorney was unpacking before taking him to the vet. While the latter explanation was crude at best, it was not exactly out of the scope of the attorney's temperament.

Beneath the heat of the entry light, Kylie pressed the doorbell two times and then waited. With the dog at their feet, the women were silent, both equally hesitant. If and when the attorney answered they would simply tell him they just happened to be in the neighborhood when they stumbled upon the injured animal—their friend's name was Terri Greiner and she lived down the road. The attorney would hardly buy the story considering the message she had left for him earlier, yet it was the best they could come up with.

Kylie swallowed dryly and pressed the white button once again. The bell chimed with a regal chord, but the only sound that followed was the faint voice of a television that echoed from some distant room. As the moths fluttered about the lights crashing their heads against the glass of the lantern, the women continued to wait. With each passing second, Kylie's apprehension mounted. She stared at their distorted reflection in the black peephole, with visions of the attorney lying bloodied on the other side.

"Let's go around to the garage," she suggested, turning away from the immense door.

As the cool grass moved across her bare ankles, her heart began to thunder. On the drive lay the remains of several dead birds that had been ripped to shreds. Flies buzzed around them, the last scavengers on the totem pole to collect their meal. She glanced back at the dog that waited by the front door.

"He must have eaten them," she said, the fear building inside of her. The dog was thirsty and tired, its injury perhaps days old. But the garage was open and the car half-unloaded as though only a moment earlier the task had been started.

"Hello?" she called out, turning the corner into the garage. The side door to the house was open, with the keys still in the dead bolt. "Hello?"

Still no answer, only the sound of the television that had intensified. Jack and Chrissy of *Three's Company* bantered to one another about their rent, while the laughter of the audience clattered between punch lines.

"What do we do?" asked Amelia, her voice reaching up Kylie's back like an icy hand nudging her forward.

The terror in her friend's eyes made Kylie's limbs begin to tremble. She moved closer to the door and slowly peered inside, her first glimpse a long narrow hallway that led deep into the house. She leaned inward and rapped sharply on the door. "Hello?" she said, her voice sounding impatient. "Mr. Benson?"

The Brittany suddenly brushed past her bare leg and limped into the house. It went a few steps and then turned back as if waiting for the women to follow.

"Do we?" Kylie asked, though her feet had already made the decision for her. She started at the sound of her own sandals stepping onto the shiny wooden floor. As she moved into the hallway, she could see to the far end to what appeared to be a den. A deer's head was mounted on the masculine papered wall, the shadow of its antlers moving with the faraway television. "Mr. Benson, we found your dog," she called, but with the continuing silence, her words had lost their commitment.

The Brittany had stopped in a pool of light that spilled from a door on the right. With Amelia close behind, Kylie moved past an open kitchen with a marble floor and gleaming appliances. A bluish light shone from above the stove, yet the room remained empty. "Hello?" she said, her voice dropping to a near whisper as she turned back to the corridor.

The Brittany limped further away, toward the glowing light of the television. The women followed, past two closed doors and the open one on the right where the dog had first paused. It was a shadowy, dignified study with volumes of books forming the walls. A deep green lamp was lit, yet again the room was empty. When the women turned back to the hallway the dog had disappeared.

"Where'd he go?" Kylie asked.

Then they heard the whimpering from the den.

The women remained frozen as the dancing antlers and sound of the sitcom, beckoned from the end of the corridor.

"Mr. Benson?" Kylie demanded, forcing her voice from a whisper, but her heart thudded so loudly that it drowned it to a murmur.

Their eyes remained riveted on the light that pulled them forward.

As they approached the arching doorway, the sound of laughter bounced from the walls and echoed back at them, while the head of the deer was joined by a wall of mounted animals of exotic nature. A huge eagle appeared to be taking flight, but it was merely an illusion created by the shadow that moved behind its spread wings. A leopard was in full leap with its claws drawn, the blue of the television dancing in its lifeless eyes. With one more step forward, Kylie saw the double-barreled Winchester on the floor and the Brittany that had hit a pointing position toward something on the other side of the sofa. With every muscle she willed herself forward. As her sight cleared the edge of the couch the stench hit her so forcefully that she instinctively grasped her mouth. Even before she saw the faceless body sprawled across the floor buzzing with flies, her stomach began to heave. It convulsed and twisted as her eyes locked on the mangled head attached to the torso by a mere string of flesh. She forced herself away, but her eyes went from one gruesome sight to another. Blood was splattered from one end of the cream carpet to the next, while chunks of what appeared to be flesh and hair had clumped on the screen of the glowing television. For a moment she heard nothing but the sound of the sitcom with Janet and Chrissy icing a cake. As the retching pulled her stomach to her throat, she doubled with the vomit that rushed her nostrils and mouth. Her eyes gorged with blood and somewhere in the back of her mind she heard the cries "No! . . . No! . . . NO!" Her thoughts were spinning, muffling the sound, until the final heave when she realized the voice was Amelia's and it had turned to one long agonized scream.

Twenty

"ESSEX COUNTY SHERIFF'S DEPARTMENT. DEPUTY RHODES SPEAKING."
   Kylie spoke softly for fear the call would be recorded. "Yes, I'd like to report an injured dog. He's been shot and needs immediate attention."
   "Well, ma'am, for that you'd need to call the animal—"
   "There's also a dead man . . . he's inside the house."
   "Excuse me?"

"The address is 12944 Sagamore Farm Street. It's in Hamilton."

"Ma'am could you please give—"

"Did you get that address?"

There was silence over the line.

The deep voice of the deputy grew slow and steady. "Ma'am I want to help you. But I need your—"

"12944 Sagamore Farm Street."

Kylie pressed the receiver back onto the pay phone and stood silently gripping it. She leaned her head against her hands and took a long steady breath of the warm salt air. Sea gulls circled overhead, cawing at the night.

"God, help me," she whispered, glancing back to the silhouette that awaited inside the truck. If she had to face the painful silence once again, her heart would surely burst. The dainty hands of her friend had twisted and turned, yet she hadn't spoken a word since they had left the house. They had driven all the way to Pickering Wharf before stopping, putting as much distance between them and the ravaged body as possible before reporting it. Kylie let her grip fall and with an aching head and a sick taste in her mouth, she turned for the pickup. With leaden feet that smarted from the new sandals, she paused at the driver's door and leaned into the open window. The idea of getting inside was simply unbearable.

Amelia looked over at her, the blue cast of the nearby docks sinking into the crevices beneath her eyes. Her lips formed a thin smile and even before she spoke, Kylie knew what she would say.

"I'm going home tonight. I can take a red-eye to Atlanta and be home before dawn."

The tears welled in Kylie's eyes so sharply that she nearly choked on her own breath. A breeze wafted off Salem Harbor, only instead of relief from the oppressive heat, it brought a chill burning deep into her bones.

"I wish you wouldn't," she said softly.

Amelia looked away, her focus resting forward. "I don't have a choice," she said numbly. "I have to see Dix. I have to get my life in order."

"Not yet," said Kylie. "If we keep searching—"

"It won't matter," said Amelia certainly. "God wants us dead."

"Melia, don't give up. Not yet anyway. Remember how you told me after my mother died that God would never want us to give in . . . to just let go . . . to just—"

"It's the will of the Lord," said Amelia.

The voice was dull and resigned and it sounded so foreign that it brought a start to Kylie. Again she felt the strange presence of some-one else within the flesh of her friend—a small frightened child full of shame and remorse.

"Melia?" she said gently. "Melia, look at me."

Slowly the silhouetted face turned toward her, but like a cold, drafty house that's been condemned, the eyes were vacant and shuttered.

Kylie swallowed back her tears. "Okay then," she said.

With every muscle in her body fighting her, she reached a heavy hand and pulled the handle. The rickety door screeched with protest, as the cry of the restless gulls fluttered overhead.

Twenty-One

IT WAS ONLY 6:35 A.M., YET NAHANT BAY WAS ALREADY EMPTY. IN HER father's oversized robe, Kylie watched the stern of the *Miss Lila* disappear out to sea. It shrank to a mere spec of red before it was swallowed by the vast blue line where the sky and ocean kissed. Certain the boat was completely out of sight, Kylie turned to an old wooden bench that butted against the cottage, and removed the morning's newspaper from beneath the planks. Fearing that the paper would say more than she cared to tell, she had risen early to hide it from her father; for the last thing she wanted was to add more worry to his already troubled brow.

She placed the bulky paper onto the rail of the dock and unfolded it beneath the sun. Just as she had expected, the attorney's death had made the front page of the *Boston Globe*. The headline read: ATTORNEY DALE BENSON FOUND DEAD IN HAMILTON HOME and it occupied the bottom right hand portion of the page.

With the sound of the ocean lapping against the dock, she read the article.

Thursday, May 30th
Attorney Dale Benson, who represented and brought
forth an acquittal for the Shelford brothers in the double-
murder trial of Rex and Bonnie Shelford, was found shot
to death in his Hamilton, Massachusetts home late last
night. Due to the attorney's recent personal and business
difficulties, authorities believe the death was a result of
suicide.

On the evening of May 27th, Benson returned home
from a hunting trip at Quabbin Reservoir in Central
Massachusetts, and though it is believed that he died
soon after his arrival, his body was not discovered until
Wednesday evening when an anonymous call was made
to the Essex County Sheriff's Department to report an
injured animal.

While authorities maintain that the death was a result
of suicide, a spokesperson for the Benson family estate
claims it was accidental. A double-barreled shotgun was
found at the scene and the family believes the attorney
may have been cleaning the gun, unaware that a shell was
still lodged in the second chamber.

"In determining the cause of death, one must look at
all of the contributing factors," stated Coroner Shep
Gilmartin. Not only was the attorney recently separated
from his wife, but he was facing charges of witness coercion in the Thomas vs. Tradecore suit. Benson, who was
indicted last winter by the Massachusetts Bar Association, was scheduled for a deposition on the very afternoon of his death.

Aside from the impending threat of criminal charges,
Benson was suffering financial woes due to litigation
over the crash of the Benson, Graves & Sneed owned
Merlin IV that took six lives on February 20th earlier
this year. Several pending claims brought forth by the
victims' families have recently shaken the long standing
firm of which the attorney has remained co-chair even
after his recent retirement.

A Brittany spaniel was also found at the scene, suffering from dehydration and a wound to its side. Investigators report that the animal was in the line of fire, sustaining minor injuries from the blast.

Kylie closed her eyes against the glare of the paper, but the dark words remained in the back of her lids. *Two days*. The body had been there for two days. Her stomach clenched with the malodorous scent that lingered within her memory and the sight of the headless corpse and the bloodied dog standing stiffly over it. "Damn," she gasped, thrusting her eyes open into the bright sun. The ocean stretched endlessly before her, as blue and as clean as the sky, yet it couldn't erase the feeling of black that had settled into her soul.

Repeatedly, she saw the gun being thrust into the attorney's mouth as his grasping hands pleaded for mercy. She shook it off—the gruesome, ruthless image—replacing it with one that was easier to accept. Perhaps the attorney had known nothing of his demise: he had simply felt a tug and his life had ended.

She pushed her palm into her forehead and then brushed it back through her hair, her eyes resting on the article once again. It mentioned the anonymous call, but nothing of the clues that could have led the curious to her doorstep. Her name was on Benson's recorder, her vomit in his rug, and there was a gas station attendant who could surely identify her, yet in the course of the tragedy, the particulars had fallen to simply meaningless. And if they hadn't, what would they have proven? "That you're gutless," she said softly. "You stumbled upon a dead man and ran like a coward."

A feeling of dread pressed upon her as she turned for the cottage door. There was much to be done, but only one way in which it would be accomplished. She drove all thoughts from her mind and moved from one task to the next. First, she cleaned the kitchen, methodically and meticulously, then the living room, the bedroom and—at last— the bathroom. With her lower back aching and a renewed bout of nausea, she stripped from her clothes and stepped beneath the cool rushing shower, letting it take the scent of cleaners from her skin.

She dressed in the cotton sundress she had worn the day before, then packed a bag—a small duffle that she found in the bottom of her father's closet. She lay it by the door and then sat down at the table to write her father a note. For a silent moment, she gazed about the small cottage—at the precious life she had been invading. Her father had pulled himself up after the death of her mother and Tucker and had made a life for himself. He had friends, so many friends and a cozy place to call his own. Jack's death had drained him. She had seen it in his eyes; even his walk had become more labored. She knew that if she stayed in the house a day longer, it would be to her father's detriment. He needed his life back and she needed to find her own.

Put things in order. The words were Amelia's and they had been the last she had spoken before she turned down the long corridor to the 747.

With the salt of her friend's tears still moist on her cheeks, Kylie had refused to say good-bye. "We'll see each other again," she had vowed, for she would not give up so easily. She would continue to fight.

She wrote the note in her best hand, keeping it simple and to the point. She would stay at Dora's until she found a place of her own. The house was empty and would remain so until the renovations were complete.

Taking in the feel of her father one last time, she stood by the door for a lingering moment. Her fingers touched the knitted sweater that hung upon a hook waiting patiently for the winter months to return. Pressing the wool against her cheek, she breathed in the rich scent of it. "I'll see you soon, Daddy," she whispered, though the words bore a vacancy inside of her. What if it was a promise she would not keep? What would become of the man who had been broken so many times? Death had snatched so ruthlessly in her father's direction, that she was not certain he would withstand another blow. "God please," she said aloud, her words tight and acrid. She took one last look around the tiny cottage, her heart continuing to fall. *Let me win this*, her mind whispered.

With the entreaty left dangling in the still room, she picked up the bag, locked the door behind her and walked silently down the long, narrow dock.

PART FIVE

Twenty-Two

FATHER MATT ALDERMAN SHOVED THE CAR DOOR OPEN WITH HIS foot, pulled the hood of his sweat jacket over his head, then dashed toward the rectory. The pelting rain was coming down in sheets forming a streaming river that transcended the curb, gushing up to the pink oleanders that lay sodden against the east porch. He quickly knocked on the door and waited, even though there was a key in his left pocket that fit the lock. He would take residence of the rectory after the cathedral was restored, but in the meantime wanted to give Dix and Amelia Blackwell their privacy. After a long moment, the side door swung open, revealing the shadowed face of Dix.

"Oh, man, I'm sorry Father," he said, quickly pushing the screened-door open. "I hope you haven't been standing there long."

"No, not at all." The priest stepped inside, stomping his soggy tennis shoes onto the mat to loosen the mud. "You would think after ten years of Savannah summers I would get used to the daily dousings," he said, pulling his drenched sweatshirt hopelessly away from his skin.

Dix handed him a kitchen towel. "No rain in D.C.?"

"Not like here, no," said Father Matt, wiping his face. "I guess this is only the beginning of it. I heard on the radio that another storm is moving in tomorrow afternoon. I thought I better come by to—" but his voice broke off when he caught a glimpse of the young man's red eyes and grave expression, "—to check those rain gutters."

Dix moved away from him into the dark kitchen, rubbing the top of his arm across his face.

Father Matt brushed the towel through his wet hair, knowing that a smooth approach would have to be rendered. The father had always liked Dix and admired his sense of self, yet knew that if confronted head on, Dix would never confide in him. Even though the priest was only a few years older than Dix, their worlds were dimensions apart.

Dix carried himself with the walk and talk of a rebel. His exterior was tough, yet he possessed the sensitivity to create some of the most moving music Father Matt had ever heard; it was not through Dix's words, but through his art, the Father had glimpsed a true sense of the young man's character.

Dix Hamilton had been raised by a poor widow, living in and out of the streets of New Orleans before settling in Savannah. Through sheer determination, he had put himself through college after which he had met Amelia. Father Matt had been the officiating pastor at the couple's wedding—a day that he himself would never forget. With the family of the groom on one side and the bride's on the other, the temperature inside the church had reached an all-time high. Dix's meager gathering had the disheveled look of a family that possessed one suit, a polyester blend meant to last a lifetime. The father even recognized a few of them from the Inner City Night Shelter he visited on Fridays. On the opposite side of the aisle, the wealth of the Blackwells was daunting. Mamie Blackwell remained at the helm, her lips uncharacteristically tight through the entire ceremony. She held steadfast in her disapproval to the marriage, even after a bargain had been struck the evening before to ease the tension. Father Matt had made the unusual proposal that had kept the Blackwell family from splitting at the seams. In the South, where a name and heritage can mean everything, Dix Hamilton became Dix Blackwell and had managed to hold onto his pride in the process. Still, it wasn't enough for the Blackwell matron, who through the following years managed to make the young couple's life hell.

When Father Matt saw the duffle on the kitchen floor, packed to capacity, his first thought was of Mamie Blackwell.

"You headin' somewhere?" he asked casually.

Staring thoughtfully out the rain-smeared window, Dix took a cigarette from a pack of Camels that lay on the counter. "Yeah," he said, gesturing absently back at the duffle. "I've got a load of antiques I need to take to L.A. . . . Smoke?" he asked, holding the pack out.

"No, thanks," said the priest. "I've got that health thing going. Do you mind?" he asked, reaching toward a cup that rested in the dish drainer.

"Help yourself," said Dix.

As Father Matt filled the mug with tap water, he could feel the eyes of the young man upon him. The priest suddenly felt stodgy with his closely trimmed hair and clean shaven face. Secluded within his vocation, he lived a life apart from the rest of society and though counseling and guidance were part of his calling, he always felt a profound sense of ineptness when dealing with the private lives of his parishioners. How could the young man possibly be expected to confide in him—to speak about a world that the priest knew nothing about?

"Father Matt," said Dix slowly. "I hate to bother you with this, but I don't know who else to . . . I don't know who else to talk to. You've always been kind of like a friend."

Father Matt smiled. "Thank you, Dix. What is it?" he asked.

"It's Amelia," he said, looking fretfully away. "I don't know what to do." The concession brought a wave of uneasiness within the young man. He moved nervously back and forth from the kitchen to the side door, wrestling with his thoughts. "You know how her and Kylie have been friends for a long time?" he asked.

"Yes," said the priest with a gentle smile. He had only seen the friends together once, at Amelia's wedding, and he had admired the way they cared so deeply for one another.

"Amelia trusts in her," continued Dix, "and that's understandable. But sometimes I don't think Kylie realizes how impressionable Amelia can be. When Kylie called her the other day to talk about her husband's death—she told Amelia that she saw some things that she couldn't possibly have seen. She was obviously just hysterical but she put these ideas . . . these insane ideas into Amelia's head . . . and damn it, I just don't know how to deal with it," he said with frustration. "Excuse my mouth, Father, I—"

"That's alright," said the priest. "I want you to speak freely."

Dix took a drag from the cigarette and moved restlessly to the other side of the counter. "When Amelia got back yesterday morning I thought everything was okay. But then she wouldn't eat . . . she wouldn't sleep. All she wants to do is work on the church. She was up all night and she's out there now. I know this is gonna sound strange, but I think she's scared that she's gonna die. I think she thinks something is gonna happen to her and she wants to finish the church before it does."

Father Matt set the cup gently onto the tile counter. "Well, considering that the plane accident wasn't that long ago and that her best friend's husband just died, fear of death is a completely natural reaction—"

"No," said Dix, shaking his head. "There's more to it than that." He paused a moment, clearly hesitant to continue. He moved a few steps as the sound of a faraway siren cut through the drone of the rain. "You know Kylie and Jack were also in the plane with us . . ." he said softly.

"Yes. Amelia had mentioned that."

"They were all hurt much worse than I was. If it hadn't been for the guy who rescued us, they would have probably died. After Jack's death Kylie had Amelia convinced that . . . that their survival was a mistake—that God had intended for them to die." He turned away, seemingly troubled by the admission. "It sounds crazy, I know," he said, shaking his head fretfully.

Father Matt thought of the floods that had hit the South a few years back. He had been assigned to the relief efforts wherein he had witnessed the same type of symptoms—survivors who had fared well, only to collapse months later. "Feelings of guilt for having survived . . . mistrust and anger toward God for having taken your loved ones are all common responses when tragedy strikes," he said.

The young man stopped to face him, the fear in his eyes startling, his lips disintegrating to thin lines of frustration. "She's not just wrestling with her mortality, Father," he said. "She thinks that God's gonna send someone to kill her."

Father Matt was startled. "I'm sorry, but I'm afraid I don't understand."

"She thinks that some kind of evil spirit set the fire that killed Jack. And that he's gonna come back for her and Kylie too."

The priest was silent, trying desperately to digest the bizarre information.

"They both believed it, at first anyway," said Dix, wiping his forehead with the back of his arm. "Amelia was really shaken when she left the other night . . . out-of-her-mind shaken. Even though they caught the guy that did it, she wouldn't listen to reason. I almost called you but then I thought that once she had time to think it all over, she would realize how—how ridiculous it all sounded. She was supposed to have stayed a week in Boston . . . then all of a sudden, she shows up at the doorstep yesterday morning. She hasn't slept a wink. I don't know what's going on with her. I know she's still upset but I can't get her to talk about it. When I asked her if Kylie had reconsidered the whole matter—whether or not she was thinking more clearly, Amelia said 'yes'."

"Have you spoken to Kylie about it?"

"I tried to call her but her home was destroyed. She was staying with her father, but I have no idea where she is now. I thought that maybe if she knew how seriously Amelia had taken what she said she could talk to her but—"

"Maybe I can help," said the priest. "Would you like me to talk to Amelia?"

Dix turned toward him, his honey-brown eyes pleading and unsure. "Would you?" he asked softly. "I need to make this trip. If I don't, we won't be able to make ends meet. I pulled the engine out of my car and I need money to fix it. But I just can't leave her like this. I'm afraid of what she might do."

"It'll be alright," Father Matt said steadily, resting a hand on his shoulder.

"I'm afraid, Father," he said unabashedly. "Without Amelia, I have nothing. I've never seen her like this. She's not herself. She's not the same. It's almost as if someone else has moved into her body. I was just out there, trying to talk to her and she got so worked up that she couldn't breathe. She had some kind of panic attack or something," he said, his voice choking with the grip he tried to keep on his emotion.

He dropped the cigarette butt into the sink, then gripped the edge of the counter. The shadowed glow of rain trickled along his frightened face, as the sound of spatters fell on the foliage outside.

"There's something wrong, Father," he said quietly, his eyes glassing with tears. "I think she may be losing her mind."

WITH the gray stormy weather draining the light from the day, St. Vincent's appeared somber and empty. Father Matt perused the dark pews, and was just about to turn away when he heard the muted sound of prayer coming from the other side of the altar. He took a few steps forward along the chancel, when he saw Amelia crouched on her hands and knees scrubbing with a sliver of sandpaper against the bottom of the alter railing. She was in the midst of the Lord's Prayer, her voice hoarse and incessant. "'. . . and forgive us our trespasses as we forgive those who trespass against us . . .'"

Father Matt stood silently by, startled by the determination with which she worked. She grated the paper with such frenzy, that it appeared her intent to force the petition into the paling wood.

He took a few steps forward and cleared his throat, yet still she remained lost to his presence. "Amelia?" he said gently.

When she turned toward him, it took a moment for his face to register within her own.

"Father," she said, rising to her feet, clearly shaken to find someone else within the church. The father was amazed at the hollowness of her cheeks and eyes. It had been merely a week since he saw her last, yet she appeared to have dropped twenty pounds from her already slender frame.

"I'm sorry if I startled you," he said. "I came by to look at the drains and to get you that check for Stockton Electric."

"Thank you," she said, reaching a willowy hand to take it.

She glanced away, clearly feeling his scrutinizing stare. As she lay the check on a pew next to some tools, the Father saw that the tips of her fingers had been rubbed raw.

"It looks like you've been working hard," he said.

"Yes." She took a deep breath, but the exhale seemed to disappear within her tense body. Her shoulders were so tight that it gave her the drawn look of a troubled teenager.

"Why don't you sit down for a moment," said the Father. "I want to speak to you."

From the moment she touched the bench, the tension drained from her body like rapidly melting ice. Even before the priest spoke, her eyes filled with tears.

"Dix asked you to talk to me, didn't he?" she asked.

Father Matt took her small hand into his own. "He's very worried about you. He tells me that you haven't slept in two nights."

She seemed confused, as though adding up some figure in her head. "I had a flight that took all night," she said. "Last night I was just . . . I have too much to do." She looked worriedly about the church, from the light fixtures to the altar. "I'll get the electrical wiring—"

"Amelia," he interrupted with a gentle smile. "I know that finishing the church is very important to you, but I don't want it to take precedence over your health. You have to eat and sleep and take time to relax—"

"Yes," she said, slipping her hand from his fingers. "Yes, I'll do that."

He continued, slowly and carefully, for he could see that she didn't want to confide in him. "When someone we love passes away, it's very difficult to understand. We all need to find a way to cope."

"Yes," she said distantly.

"I understand that your friend, Kylie, had some concerns when her husband first died."

She hedged away from him, avoiding his eyes. "What do you mean?" she asked.

"Because of her devastating loss, she was very vulnerable," he said slowly. "I knew a woman once by the name of Carmen. She lost her entire family in a boating accident. Naturally, she was hysterical. For awhile she even lost trust in God. She began to see him as vengeful and untrustworthy."

"Like Job," she said.

"Yes," he said with relief, for he had struck common ground. "Like Job."

"'They shall lie down alike in the dust, and the worms shall cover them'," she quoted.

"Yes," he said uneasily. "Job 24:19."

"My mother used to quote from it," she said with a touch of bitterness. "I want to be cremated, but my mother is against it. She says that the Catholic Church forbids it. Is this true?" she asked fretfully.

He started to answer, but then smiled. "Amelia," he said lightly. "There's no need for you to worry about such things right now. You're a young and healthy woman. You've got a long and prosperous life ahead of you."

As he spoke, her attention wandered past him, to the scaffolding behind them. He squeezed her hand slightly to try to regain eye contact but she remained concentrated on the gray boards as though they were of importance.

"If and when you die," he conceded, for he could see that he was losing her. "You may be cremated if you wish. Canon law is no longer opposed to it. But soon you'll see that life goes on, and that you have nothing to fear."

"Also from Job," she whispered, "'Fear of the Lord, that is wisdom.'"

A shudder prickled over the priest's skin for the voice sounded hauntingly like her mother's. There was no mistaking the struggle within her eyes ... the worry and self-doubt placed there by a fire-and-brimstone touting mother.

"You're a good person, Amelia," he said steadily. "You have no reason to be afraid of God or death."

As he said the words, darkness spread across her face, glassing her eyes. The shift was so sudden that he instinctively turned around, expecting to see that someone had entered and was standing silently behind him; but he found that the doorway remained empty.

"What is it?" he asked, unnerved in spite of himself.

She stood and looked nervously away, twisting her mouth within her fingers. "Nothing," she said softly.

Father Matt looked back to the wall and even though he saw nothing to fear, a feeling of trepidation scurried through his chest. He walked to the scaffolding and looked behind it, but there was nothing there. When he turned back, he saw that Amelia had picked up the sandpaper once again, her chin trembling.

"I'm sorry, Father," she said. "But I need to get back to work."

"Amelia," he said, trying to break through the terror that had clearly gripped her. "Amelia, please look at me."

He spoke no longer as an authority figure, but as a friend. He cared deeply for her and didn't want to see her suffer, especially at the hand of her own thoughts.

When she met his gaze, he was startled by the calmness that had suddenly taken hold of her.

"I promise I'll rest," she said with a smile.

The wall had been erected with such swiftness that the Father felt as if he had been belted across the face. Within seconds, she had shut him out and was now dismissing him. The priest had to look away from the set eyes and stony expression for he barely recognized the person behind the face. A sick feeling turned his breakfast to acid, for he knew that he had failed.

He looked absently about for his satchel, or was it his coat? *It's summer*, he reminded himself. He started for the doorway that led toward the rectory, but then turned back to the young woman who was already busily sanding once again. "Amelia," he said softly.

She paused for a moment and looked up at him.

"You're a fine woman," he said quietly. "You have nothing to fear."

Twenty-Three

"'THERE IS NOT ANY PRESENT MOMENT THAT IS UNCONNECTED WITH some future one. The transition from cause to effect, from event to event, is often carried on by secret steps, which our foresight cannot divine and our sagacity is unable to trace.'"

"Joseph Addison, 1723," Kylie whispered, her finger pressed upon the volume before her.

All morning, the quote had been rolling through her mind, along with the words of the counterfeit Ducker. *It's all interconnected, Georgia. Jack had to die or he would have gone on affecting lives that he shouldn't.*

"Is it what you were looking for, dear?"

Kylie struggled to pull her attention to the little librarian, to the soft crinkled eyes magnified by bottle-thick glasses. "Yes, thank you Ms. Hopkins."

"Let me know if you need anything else," said the elderly woman, before shuffling behind her desk once again.

Kylie stared blankly ahead, at the students and professionals who spoke in hushed tones at computers and work tables. *It's all interconnected*, the voice inside of her whispered. *You, me, all of it.* Julius Vanderpoel had not only been speaking of the world she saw, but of the one she didn't. It was no coincidence that he had been brought back into her life or that he had been among the mountaintop creatures to deliver her—it was all interconnected, closely, seamlessly. And as surely as her survival had affected the balance of her own world, it had affected his. With her shoulders pinching inward she tried to grasp onto a furthering thought. Julius Vanderpoel had entered another existence—one with its own set of rules of physicality.

He had a weakness—she saw it in his eyes, his manner. His physical rendering was inconsistent—at times solid . . . as real as any person standing before her, yet at other times weakened by her thoughts, or by his own. If his world had limits, limits that could be broken, perhaps it could even be destroyed.

She shook her head and turned away. There was something there – some semblance of hope – but like a scent on the wind it remained intangible and elusive. Pinching the skin between her eyes, she closed the volume and turned to the vast room of the Widener Library. After a day of gathering essentials and settling in to Dora's mansion, she had lain awake most of the previous night, searching her mind for clues, anything that would bring hope or understanding to a world she could not see or touch. Repeatedly, she had gone over the words of Eva Ratchford, deciphering the information again and again, her mind stopping at the same point each time: Hector Haynes. She thought of his paintings, of the beast crouching in the alleyway. Like Julius Vanderpoel, there had been a weakness to the beast, the tilt of the head, the eyes. Hector Haynes had far surpassed her in understanding, his final days narrowing his search to one source. He had been obsessed with an ancient scripture and she had come to the library to find it. She couldn't remember the name of it, or even who had written it, but she knew Ginger Hopkins would be able to help.

Though lacking a Harvard education herself, the Widener librarian was an unwavering pool of knowledge. Kylie had made the priceless acquaintance when Dillon was at the university years earlier. Whenever doing research for one project or another, Ms. Hopkins was always the one to point her in the right direction.

"Yes, dear?" said the little clerk, the soft blurry eyes once again looking up at her.

"I'm searching for a book that someone recommended, but I can't remember the name of it," said Kylie. "It's an ancient scripture . . . some kind of apocalyptic text that was rejected by the Catholic Church. It was called *The Book* of something or other."

The final clue brought a bright smile to the seasoned face. "Ahh," said Ms. Hopkins, lifting a finger of understanding. "You must mean *The Book of Enoch*."

With mention of the name, Kylie's throat constricted. "Yes," she said quietly. "That's it."

"Follow me," said the clerk as she set out on her path across the huge library. Kylie followed her along the south wall until they reached a section on the far end.

"It was discovered in 1773 in what is now called Ethiopia," said the clerk as she scanned the shelves in front of her. "But it was actually written about the middle of the second century B.C.—before Christianity," she said, with a pointed glance to Kylie. Her slender hands rested on a black volume with gold lettering. "In fact, passages were even lifted from it and put into the writings of Saint John." She handed the slim book to Kylie as though passing a dirty magazine. "You're going to like it," she said, with a sly smirk. "It's got some really fun stuff about the Watchers."

The old woman saw the question in Kylie's face.

"Oh, you'll see," she promised. "Hmmm," she mused, her attention returning to the shelves. "If you want cross referencing, this is the spot." She thought for a moment and then grabbed a couple of other books. "*Origen of Alexandria* would be good. He makes repeated reference to *The Book of Enoch*."

As she dumped several more books into Kylie's arms, a young student gingerly approached. "Ms. Hopkins," she whispered. "I was looking for something on the gardens of Versailles . . ."

The librarian gave Kylie a wink and then whisked the student to some other part of the library.

Kylie turned to a small table at the end of the aisle and lay the heavy stack of books upon it. She pulled the black book from the bottom, her fingers tingling with the feel of it. THE BOOK OF ENOCH THE PROPHET, TRANSLATED BY RICHARD LAURENCE was scrawled across the worn cover. When she opened it she found the title page yellowed and dingy. It had been published in London in 1883 by Kegan Paul, Trench and Company, with the latest release by Wizards Bookshelf under the *Secret Doctrine Reference Series*. As she held the ancient text between her fingers, she again thought of Hector Haynes. He too had grasped the same information. He too had chosen to fight, yet had failed. *I'm scared*, came the desolate words of her friend. She had spoken to Amelia before leaving Dora's that morning, and the bleakness in her friend's tone had stayed with her all day. When she thought of the faraway voice so resigned to death, a chill wrapped itself around her like a cool snake. Perhaps she was foolish to delay bringing order to her life as Amelia had advised. She had postponed an important meeting with the insurance agent to come to the library, yet if something were to happen to her, the money could slip through the cracks. *Tomorrow*, she promised herself. She would call Dillon later and schedule the appointment for tomorrow. In the meantime, she would not let fear and panic get the best of her. Hector had been obsessed with the book for a reason. Perhaps within it, he had found hope and understanding, or better yet, a weapon with which to fight.

Twenty-Four

THE FADING SUN CAST LONG SHADOWS ACROSS THE FRONT OF THE Greyson five-story federal-style mansion. With her arms cramping from the heavy load of books, Kylie paused at the curb to catch her breath, her heart racing from the heat and the strenuous walk up Pickney Street. As she looked toward the tall, ivy-framed windows of the second-story drawing room, her stomach crawled with apprehension. She had no desire to enter the empty home. She had already spent one lonely night within the silence and the thought of yet another was simply unbearable.

For a moment she pondered the stately bowfront row houses that cascaded down the narrow street to the bottom of the hill. Even though the rippling effect of the red-brick facades was breathtaking, there was a vacuousness to the orange-splashed homes. The neighborhood around her was still, with only the faraway sound of traffic to break the quiet.

She had always felt a sense of isolation when entering Beacon Hill, but now more than ever it felt like a cocoon of solitude. With its narrow cobble-stoned streets the historic district was a piece from the past, a nineteenth-century village cut off from the rest of the city by its dense elms, hidden gardens and narrow passageways. And while the effect was usually charming, within the heat of the stifling day it felt claustrophobic. The air was so thick and muggy that Kylie couldn't quite catch her breath. The scent from the flower boxes was stronger than usual, the sweet texture sending a wave of nausea quivering through her.

After one last glimpse at the vacant windows, she willed herself forward. "Let's go," she said aloud, forcing her tired feet up the steps to the recessed entryway.

The door swung smoothly open, the sweltering dusk spilling into the darkness. She flipped on the entry light and entered slowly. She wasn't sure what she was expecting to find, only that she couldn't bear to face it.

Standing perfectly still within the expansive entrance hall, she listened for sounds and looked for anything out of the ordinary. Directly ahead of her through a set of open double doors stood the formal dining room. A stack of paperwork was piled upon the shiny surface of the mahogany table just as she had left it that morning. To her right was the reception room with its chair-lined walls and to her left, the dark-wooded handsome stairs ascended in a mural-lined spiral. She stepped forward and peered upward to the progressive landings. Murky light from the rounded skylight smudged each floor, dimming with its descent. She could see just the door to the library that spanned the entire back half of the second level, while the drawing room took the breadth of the front. The third floor contained three bedrooms—one master and two smaller ones, while the fourth floor held a music hall that had been converted into a gym along with a dressing room and an elaborate bath. And lastly the attic, which used to be the servants quarters, had been transformed by Kylie and Jack into a cozy den replete with a stone fireplace and an intimate inglenook.

Kylie stared through the spiral as her mind scanned the many rooms, but the house was so huge that even a loud sound would not penetrate the heavy walls. She drew a breath and forced herself to calm, for all seemed in place. It would be ridiculous to go room by room looking for something that she would not find. "Just relax," she said to herself, as she slipped off her sandals then shut and latched the front door.

Twenty-Five

MATCHING THE QUARTERED OAK OF THE COVE CEILING AND THE wainscoting of the study, the vast desk stretched six feet by four, yet it was barely large enough to contain the sprawled books. With tired, aching eyes, Kylie looked up from her reading and focused on the gold clock that ticked from the mantel. She was startled to see that it was only 11:15 P.M. for it felt like two in the morning.

The sun had gone down hours earlier, yet the heat remained trapped within the brick walls of the mansion like an oven. She had been reading for so long that the lamplight reflecting off the text seared the black type into her aching head. She pushed her hands slowly across her hair fastened in a wayward knot, and took a deep breath, her eyes staring blankly at the text.

It was a parable. A fantastical story, to say the least. *The Book of Enoch* had clearly been a precursor to the Bible wherein many of the concepts had found a home. But like the Bible, much of it seemed an allegory, not to be taken literally but metaphorically.

It was an apocalyptic piece, wherein the prophet Enoch journeys through the spiritual realms. Guided by angels he tours heaven and earth, and the dominion of eternal fire all the while transcribing his visions.

While the story was interesting, and at times reaffirmed much of the information Eva Ratchford had given, Kylie couldn't find what Hector Haynes had found so pertinent. For over an hour she had re-treated back through the text, time and again looking for clues, but had found mere remnants. Chapter XXII, which read surprisingly like Revelations, described the punishment of the corrupt, but again, it was mere confirmation of what they already knew.

With a sinking feeling of defeat, Kylie's gaze was drawn to the long windows, to the quiet alley that separated the rear of the Greyson home from the next. There was no breeze, only silence and a blue moon that glowed from the still treetops. In a smaller house across the way, a young couple stood within a dark kitchen digging in the refrigerator for a snack. Loneliness took hold and Kylie's chest began to ache. What she wouldn't give to just go back to the way things were.

She dragged her eyes away from the window, forcing her attention once again to the waiting book. Perhaps she was missing some-thing—some analogy that was yet to be drawn. The text was opened to the last chapter, wherein Noah and the Great Flood are described in haunting detail. She had been so startled to find the Biblical story within the ancient doctrine, that she had pulled Dora's Bible from the shelf and was cross-referencing the two accounts.

As she began reading Genesis, she was surprised to find that the Bible not only acknowledged Enoch as a prophet, but as the great-grandfather of Noah as well. The text read: "When Enoch had lived 65 years he became the father of Methuselah... When Methuselah had lived 187 years he became the father of Lamech... When Lamech had lived 182 years he had a son. He named him Noah."

Clearly Genesis was acknowledging Enoch's existence and involve-ment, but as she read further she found that the Biblical version of the Flood had some striking omissions from its predecessor.

While both accounts spoke of the debauchery which the flood was meant to eradicate, it was *The Book of Enoch* that pointed an unwaver-ing finger toward the culprit from which Eden fell—a group of angels called the Watchers, or Nephilim. This special task force of angels was sent to earth to instruct man, but could not resist the sensual temptations of human flesh. Though forbidden to mix human and an-gelic genes, "they took wives from the progeny of men" and as a re-sult, these women bore monstrous giants which became known as the Grigori.

"Those who were from heaven disregarded the word of the Lord. Behold they committed crimes; laid aside their class, and intermingled with women... And the women conceiving brought forth giants, whose stature was each three hundred cubits. These devoured all which the labour of men produced; until it became impossible to feed them; When they turned themselves against men, in order to devour them; And began to injure birds, beasts, reptiles, and fishes, to eat their flesh one after another, and to drink their blood. Then the earth reproved the unrighteous."

After these fallen angels had brought tyranny to the lower regions of Eden, the task of their destruction was commenced.

"To Gabriel also the Lord said... destroy the children of fornica-tion, and the offspring of the Watchers from among men. Exterminate them from the earth..."

Kylie looked across to the Bible, where mere mention of the angels was given in Genesis 6:4: "The Nephilim were on the earth in those days, and also afterward, when the sons of God went to the daughters of men and had children by them."

The Bible only hinted at the presence of the fallen angels, whereas in the secret doctrine, not only was the angelic involvement instrumental, but in Chapter CV it is questioned whether Noah himself was one of the descendants of the Watchers, or Grigori.

"His colour is whiter than snow . . . the hair of his head is whiter than white wool . . . his eyes are like the rays of the sun; and when he opened them he illuminated the whole house. His father Lamech feared, and fled to me, believing not that the child belonged to him, but that he resembled the angels of heaven . . ."

Later in the book, Lamech's mind is set at ease.

"Now therefore inform thy son Lamech, that he who is born is his child in truth; and he shall call his name Noah, for he shall be to you a survivor . . . Then explain to him the consummation which is about to take place; for all the earth shall perish—"

Kylie squeezed her eyes shut; the words had begun to blur. As she sat back in the leather chair and took a long, deep breath, giant, barbaric angels laughing and drinking blood flashed into her mind. The scene was heathenish and dark, with women and beasts locked in coitus in strange twisting positions. She opened her eyes once again and shook her head with dismay. "Damn," she whispered. She was grappling in a world of the absurd. A dark cloud of dread settled over her with the heat. She was certain that the story was an allegory, one from which wisdom was to be extracted, but it was so far removed that she couldn't see what it had to do with reality. *Reality*. She had to smile. In the drawing room across the hall stood an image of what her reality had become. It was hidden beneath the brown cloth in which it was delivered, the tip of its wings peeking through the rough fabric.

"Reality," she said with a sardonic smile. There was no such luxury; for nothing was sane anymore.

Twenty-Six

Amelia blinked slowly, the inside of her lids scraping against her eyes like paper. Once again, the night had wrapped itself around her like a dark molten sarcophagus. It seeped into the spaces between the dresser and the wall, the bed and the doorway, bringing with it the sounds of the uncertain. Her gaze had been focused on the shadowed ceiling for so long that her eyes had begun to burn. For over an hour she had been waiting for the moment to come, for the sound of Dix's breath to slow to deep slumber, but now that it had, she felt frozen, unable to move.

With her head remaining still, she glanced to the narrow doorway, certain she could feel the presence that silently awaited.

She slowly reached her fingers to the sheet and pulled it away from her naked body, then quickly grabbed the cotton robe from the floor. After having sex she had covered herself to the neck in spite of the heat, for all through their lovemaking she was certain she could feel the eyes of someone or something upon her. She had tried to relax, to tell herself that there was no one there, but in spite of herself, Dix had detected her apprehension. He had abruptly stopped moving, keeping her tight within his grasp. "Bluebird," he whispered. "What are you thinking?" She wanted to answer, to confide in him, but her lips dared not move. Just as Father Matt would never have understood why she needed so desperately to finish the cathedral, that it was her only hope at redemption, Dix would never understand that the darkness was coming for her. If she told him, she chanced his siding with her nemesis through virtue of his disbelief. "Bluebird?" he had said, his eyes brimming with tears. When she didn't answer, he had abruptly climbed from atop her and turned on his side away from her.

She looked over at him, the sound of his soft breath intensifying the loneliness in her heart. She had to get out, to escape the stifling bedroom. Sleep was a mistake; she needed the precious time to work.

Standing slowly, she fastened the robe and began making her way across the creaky floor. With each step the thunder in her chest escalated, the darkness oozing tighter around her. When she reached the hallway, she flipped on the light and stared for a moment toward the staircase at the end of the landing. Death could be crouched just over the crest of the first step, waiting to plunge her downward. She pictured herself crumpled at the bottom, her neck broken and her head twisted to the side. *A simple accident*, the coroner would say. *Just a misfortunate step.*

Cold sweat trickled down her back and her legs shook. "Keep going," she whispered, her voice piercing the silence.

Slowly and methodically she made it to the head of the stairwell and peered downward. The narrow corridor that led from the bottom step was empty. If she could just make it down and past the door on the left, she would be fine. She tried to remember if she had closed it, but her memory escaped her.

As she stood breathless, the prayer began on its own, droning through her mind like the comforting words of a friend. *Our Father, who art in heaven . . .* With newfound strength she stole down the stairs and into the long corridor that led to the church. *Forgive us our trespasses as we forgive those . . .* The cool floor kissed the bottom of her feet as she drew closer and closer to the kitchen door, to the room that had once been a place of comfort but had now become a haven for the enemy. Within seconds it would pass and she would be on her way, but as it drew nearer the voice inside died away. Her sight cleared the oven and the long tiled counter that led beneath the window. She heard nothing but the sound of her own breathing and the rustling of the wings in the tree outside. Just as she feared, the bird was waiting, staring through the glass with its beady eyes, the blue of the moon reflecting off its shiny black feathers.

Her heart bolted and she nearly lost control of the scream, but she quickly swallowed it, back into the depths of her beating heart. For a moment, long and still they watched one another, until the bird cawed a few times and then took flight.

Twenty-Seven

STEAM DRIFTED UP FROM THE CLAW-FOOTED TUB, FILLING THE BATHROOM with a misty cloud. Kylie sank into the water, the warmth caressing her stiff shoulders and back. She took a deep breath and tried not to think of the huge mansion beneath her, of the vacant rooms and shadowy hallways.

It had taken all the courage she could muster to shut down the house for the night. After folding back the sheets within the master bedroom, she had set about the task of latching windows and turning off lights. To her dismay, she had been forced to make the long descent to the basement where she had left on a lamp earlier within the kitchen. It was then, while in the depths of the five-story structure, that she felt the expansiveness that moaned and settled around her. It was then that she felt not only fear, but a profound loneliness and a longing for Jack.

The sound of the faucet's drip echoed around her, sending gooseflesh over her in spite of the heat. The washroom was her least favorite of all the rooms yet to be refinished, for the chamber was narrow and dungeon-like. The paint-chipped walls were an emerald green topped by a ceiling mirror that hovered above the antique tub, like an ever-watchful eye, reflecting her every move. Shaking off the heaviness that had once again taken hold, she concentrated on the task at hand. She reached for the razor, then glided the shiny surface over her calves until they were smooth.

The pipes moaned within the walls as she turned the hot water on once again. She pulled the clasp from her hair letting it fall loose and then rested back into the warm liquid, immersing her head until her ears filled with nothing but the drone beneath the water. The mirrored image of her naked body swayed above her, while her long hair danced within the gentle waves. She felt strangely removed from the voluptuous form that appeared pallid and lifeless, her still hands dangling next to the patch of auburn curls between her legs. A cadaver. Within the tunnel-like image of the dark encroaching walls, she appeared a cadaver floating in a pool of soft light. Even the sad eyes belonged to someone else, to a strange being that merely housed her conscious. Her lashes closed inward and brought darkness, as the hot edge of the water swayed up the sides of her cool breasts that remained exposed to the softly moving air. The heat from beneath dulled the pain that churned within her stomach, while the coolness from above titillated her senses. She thought of Jack standing beside the tub, his gaze full of lust as it roamed over her nude body. The swaying surface became his hot fingers gently stroking her bare skin. The warmth stirred between her thighs, caressing and gentle, bringing a wave of sensual desire. Her hand moved to the wet locks and massaged downward until her fingers found the warm folds between her legs and pressed inward. "Jack," she whispered, imagining the penetrating flesh to be his. Her breath caught as the tremors of pleasure overshadowed the feeling of loneliness. She made no sound as her arousal continued to mount, only her breath that echoed through the small room betrayed her indulgence. For a brief few seconds there was no death, no pain, no empty mansion looming around her. For a brief few seconds she felt nothing but the contractions as they took hold and released her. But on the other side of the rapture, its counterpart awaited; for as the pleasure died away it left a void more excruciating than before. At once she felt dizzy as the heat and the emptiness consumed her. She felt chilled and alone, lost within the hollow room.

She sat up to regain her bearings, covering her face to silence the despair that threatened to overtake her. Jack was gone and no amount of wishing would bring him back. She remained still for a long moment with only the sound of an occasional drip to break the silence. With the emotion finally quelled, she brushed the wisps of wet hair from her forehead, then reached for the handle to the hot water. The heat had become too much and had begun to make her feel woozy. Her balance swayed as she glanced to the rack for a towel to get out of the steaming water.

That's when she noticed a bright smudge seeping beneath the door from the hallway; a light had been turned on somewhere downstairs. Adrenaline shot through her body, for someone else was within the house as silent and waiting as she.

You must have missed one, her mind whispered, but in spite of the attempt to reassure herself, her hand trembled as she reached for the robe on the towel rack. Without drying, she pulled the fabric around her and stood frozen, debating whether or not to move forward.

She waited five minutes before she was able to force herself to the door. Stepping slowly into the hallway, she glanced to the darkened bedrooms, then turned for the banister. An updraft from the spiraling stairwell sent a chill scampering over her damp skin; the light was coming from the library on the floor beneath. Her first thought was of the research that she had left sprawled across the desk, for she knew who awaited: Julius Vanderpoel had come for a visit.

HE STOOD at the unlatched window on the far end of the library, facing out to the garden beneath. Like a scene from a Rembrandt painting, his maroon smoking jacket and distinguished stance were as natural within the library as the antique pieces, the volumes and the Axminster rug upon the parquet floor. The cove ceiling bowed inward, enveloping the room and its occupant in a delicate light that gave the ageless impression of time standing still.

Kylie waited motionless in the doorway, and though the shadowy figure did not turn, she was certain he could feel her presence. She at once felt the outsider, a voyeur glimpsing into a private moment between a mansion and its true master, for his very presence commanded the room like a prince. His smooth hands were clasped behind his back, as though he were pondering something. A fragrant breeze drifted in and for a long moment there was only silence.

"You were to have died this morning," he said gently, his back remaining toward her.

At the sound of his voice, Kylie's pulse halted. The statement had been made with such calm, that it felt as if a cold hand had reached between her ribs and gripped her heart.

"It was 9:52 at the Downtown crossing," he continued. "A homeless man approached and begged for a quarter."

The filthy face of the bum was instantly before her, his flesh swollen and his eyes drunken with delirium. She could hear the roar of the train as it approached and the tremor of her heart as she dug through her purse to appease his mumbled plea. Just as her fingers had grazed her pocket book, the man had staggered dangerously close. She had frozen, certain he would force her into the rocky crevice as the train thundered down the tracks, but at the last moment he had retreated. She had dismissed the incident, attributing it to the stumblings of a drunk, but now that she re-examined the haggard face, she felt a flutter of recognition within the eyes.

"I would have slipped into the crowd," said the creature as he finally turned toward her, the warm light creating a sheen along his silken hair and jacket. "Within the chaos, a homeless man would go easily unnoticed."

In spite of herself, fear—cold and dark—shuddered through her. Her time had come even quicker than she had anticipated. "Why didn't you?" she asked, challenging the pale gaze.

For a moment there was only silence, and though he didn't speak she knew the answer; she was his only link.

As the thought found a firm place within her conscience it brought guilt, for her very effort at the being's destruction lay exposed on the desk behind him. Terrified that he would hear her thoughts, she tried to calm her throbbing pulse.

Neither confirming nor negating her apprehension, he turned for the dark shelves that ran along the east wall. "My father had a study, much like this," he said, his fingertips brushing along the old books. "I remember it all quite well now. I had a mother and a father. A wife and a son. A son," he repeated softly, hesitating slightly to consider the thought.

As he continued through the shadowed room, Kylie sensed that something in him had changed. He was more composed than he had been over the past few visits, no longer fighting with the matter around him; his elegant movements effected the solidity of a cultured man. His expression warmed as he paused at a shelf filled with old photos.

"My mother was an enchanting woman by the name of Mary Wolcott," he said. "In your line of work, I would assume you're familiar with the surname."

"Yes," answered Kylie, her voice so thin she barely recognized it as her own. She knew the name from her studies on Boston's Back Bay. The family had been instrumental in the monumental project to fill the low-lying swampland that later became occupied by Boston's elite.

"She ran our household, a handsome mansion on Commonwealth Avenue. It was much like this one," he said, stopping in the center of the room as if to breathe in the structure. "The floor plan very similar." He turned toward her, pivoting only slightly as if to study her.

Kylie felt the absurdity of the moment, of the creature trying to engage her in idle conversation.

A smile, ever so faint, tugged at his pink lips and just as she was certain he would respond to her thoughts, he wandered to the wall of books once again.

"My father loved his reading," he mused. "Harland Vanderpoel. He was a wealthy man. A man of 'principles,'" he said, bitterness singeing the edge of his words. "Principles that is, until it came to my wife. Her name was Greta. Unbeknownst to me, she and my father were quite taken with one another." He stopped and looked upward to the chandelier that twinkled within the dim light. His face darkened, yet his eyes remained detached. "After my arrest, they found her hanging in his study."

The image of a woman, blonde and delicate, streaked through Kylie's vision. She hung limp, her neck blackened and stretched from a rope that squeezed around it. Gasping, Kylie turned away, uncertain from whence the effigy came.

When she looked back, the creature had drawn dangerously close to the desk and the text that would reveal her intent.

"Even in death, she betrayed me," he said, his eyes resting on the material before him. "She took my seven-year-old son with her . . ."

Startled by the charge, Kylie tried not to see the tiny boy of which he spoke, of the shadowed figure that lay silent within a coffin, yet the dim impressions of the past waved through her like a chill.

She shuddered at the vehemence that had filled the gray eyes of the father. For a long moment, dark and sinister, he remained in thought. His fingers toyed with the thin pages of the Bible, the paper moving so gently it could have been fluttering in the breeze. Kylie's body began to tremble as she tried to focus on the text. She saw no words, only lines of script when abruptly a crimson droplet spattered upon the page. She looked to the dimly lit face, startled to find that a bright trickle of blood ran from his nose, the ruby stain in sharp contrast to the ash of his skin.

He turned slightly away as he pulled a handkerchief out of his jacket and wiped the blood from his face. "An unfortunate side effect I'm afraid," he said, examining the cloth. Taking note of her again, he flashed her an amused smile. "You can relax my dear," he said with a touch of affection. "I forgive you for your . . . how shall we say? Instincts of survival. If you had only completed your homework, my little rose, you would understand my predicament." His head bowed slightly as he eloquently recited from the text before him. "'I urge you as aliens and strangers in the world, to abstain from fleshly lusts which war against your soul.'"

The intensity with which he looked up sent a rush through her limbs. He was alive and vibrant, his cheeks suddenly flushed with color. "But I remember the flesh," he said, his voice practically a whisper. "I crave the tastes, the colors, the memories. Therefore, like the Nephilim, I will fall."

His eyes dropped once again as his hand brushed across the volume of Origen. "As the imperfect spirit falls closer and closer to earth, it becomes solidified and walks again as man. It continues to fall downward into the depths of darkness, to the core of the earth until it dissipates into nothingness. As you can see," he said with indication to the handkerchief, "my destruction has already commenced." He replaced the cloth to his jacket, then took a step forward, openly facing her. "Like you, my love, my time is limited."

Fear jetted into her belly and pulled her downward, deeper into the depths of darkness; she had given him back his life and in turn would see his destruction to fruition, yet like a victim chained to a drowning man, her time would be limited to that of his own.

As the solidity of the hideous bond closed around her, she searched the gray eyes for malice but found only sadness. *I crave the flesh* whispered across her skin, as the directness of his gaze filled with unequivocal desire. Under the intensity of the knowing eyes, she felt suddenly naked and exposed, for only minutes earlier her own yearning had consumed her within the heat of the water. Her face turned crimson at the thought that he had heard her silenced moans.

The twinkle in his eyes instantly affirmed her reflection.

"I hear your every breath," he said softly.

She became intensely aware of her body, of the shivers that had risen all over her damp skin. In spite of herself, the desire was reawakening for she was certain he could feel her now. Disgust at her own weakness rose within her throat, yet she was unable to stop the warm flush that spread between her thighs.

"Like mine, your body betrays you," he said kindly. Then he no longer spoke, yet she felt his words, caressing and kneading as surely as if his hands were upon her. *We're connected, Kylie Rose. We've always been connected.*

No, her thoughts whispered, yet the dark seed of doubt had been planted. His witness to her hidden lust aroused her, and though she had known that he awaited, she had made the descent of the stairs with her yearning still alive beneath her gown.

She felt suddenly a child, caught peering through the janitor's closet—at the bare, muscular torso that had thrust upward into the folds of her teacher's dress. "This will be our little secret," her prince had whispered, as the strange new feeling had tickled between her legs.

Startled by the memory, by the child who had once longed for the dangerous man, she edged backward, away from the powerful figure that had fixed his appetite upon her. Their gaze remained locked, and though the want smoldered within her belly, her fear eclipsed it. She gripped the wall that was suddenly behind her; she was trapped—utterly and irrevocably trapped—for within the depths of the mansion they were alone.

The shadows played within his wanton eyes, yet he remained still, his stance calm and all-knowing. Like a hunter gently observing his eventual prey, a slight smile fixed upon his lips. He would not take her then, but she knew he would return. She wanted to break away, but her legs would not carry her. She felt only her breath and the scent of roses that wafted from the garden beneath them.

Abruptly, the clock upon the mantel came alive, ripping through the moment with the tolling of the hour. The golden chimes spun in a whirlwind sending prickles of light against the milky mirror behind it.

Kylie stepped to the side, for the creature's restraint over her had been broken; the pale of his eyes had become distant, as though pulled to some faraway voice. Though he still appeared solid, he seemed to lose some of his essence.

Then, like a whisper, he was gone. As surely as if a screen had passed across the air his image dissipated.

Kylie moved forward and then looked behind her to the shadowed hallway. There was no trace, no lingering feeling; he was simply gone. She looked back to the mantel, where the clock had silenced when she realized that her own breath had stopped. *Cracks of entry*, her thoughts exerted, as she stared at the two hands facing upward. Midnight had been among the points of entry Eva Ratchford had mentioned, where the doors to the spirit world were thrust open. He had not needed the wings of a bird or the legs of a spider to carry him.

Feeling vulnerable within the darkened room, she wrapped her arms tight against herself and looked to the spot in which he had stood. She felt ashamed and empty.

We're connected, Kylie Rose. We've always been connected.

A thought, dark and ominous, worked its way into her mind: she had summoned the creature through her own loneliness. While grieving for Jack, she had beckoned him and he had come. "Oh Jesus," she whispered. Perhaps from the very first moment, she had forged the connection. From the moment in the cottage in which she had been seized by the familiar gray eyes—she had wanted to find him, to put a face to the phantom.

"It's nothing to do with you," she said aloud, for the events would have unfolded nonetheless. If she had remained closed, she would now be dead. She would have died in the fire alongside Jack. With a turn of her stomach, she thought of Amelia, who could not see within the shadows, the dark presence that would be watching. It would take her and then vanish without so much as a trace.

"Without a trace," she whispered, as her gaze seized upon the Bible that lay exposed beneath the lamp. She went quickly to the desk and turned back the pages, where she found that the red stain remained. She ran her finger over the wet surface that had smeared between the pages. Unlike the feather which had left a mere imprint within her locket, the substance was tangible. Her stomach constricted with the sweet scent of it, with the texture of human blood.

Sinking within the leather chair, she watched the wetness solidify and dry. As she had suspected, the creature's very essence was changing; in his own words, his destruction had commenced. But while the creature's demise bought her time, it brought her no comfort; for unlike herself, Amelia had no reprieve. With a heavy heart she looked toward the darkened window and thought of her friend across the vast miles of night.

Twenty-Eight

THE DISTANT RINGING PRICKLED INTO HER DREAMLESS SLEEP, DRAGGING her to the light. Her neck was cramping, her back aching as if she had been beaten. When Kylie opened her eyes, she found that she was hunched over the desk in the study where the morning sun stretched in fragmented pieces across the dusty room. Two floors beneath, the phone was demanding an answer; her first thought was of Amelia.

She bolted down the stairs, through the dining room and to the bottom of the kitchen stairwell where she found the phone beside the microwave where it had been abandoned. Before she could reach it, she heard the answering machine retrieve the call from the entrance hall. "Hello. This is Dora Greyson. I'm not—"

"Yes," cried Kylie, cutting the recorder off in mid-sentence. "Hello."

"He's gone," said the soft voice on the other end.

"Amelia? Melia, what are you talking about?"

"Dix. He left a couple of hours ago on his trip."

Kylie glanced to the clock, her eyes still struggling to focus. It was 8:35 A.M.

"I woke you, I know. I was going to wait until nine, but I just couldn't take—" the words fell off as she struggled to complete the sentence. She was softly crying.

"It's alright, Melia," Kylie said. "Just take a slow breath."

There was a strained sigh as her friend followed orders.

"You don't sound good," said Kylie. "Did you get any sleep?"

After another labored moment, the voice responded. "A little," she said faintly.

Even through the line, Kylie could feel her friend's attention drifting away. There was only silence and the eerie sound of her tight breath. "Melia," she said. "Talk to me."

"It's watching me," she whispered. "It's outside the window right now, watching me."

"What's watching you?"

"I closed the curtains but I can still see its shadow, its head and its beak are pointing toward me."

With a sudden sting, apprehension rose in Kylie's throat. "Maybe it's just a bird," she said uneasily. "A mother protecting a nest."

"No," Amelia whispered darkly. "They're watching me. I can feel it. I was painting last night and I saw a rat . . . its eyes . . . Oh God."

"Just take it easy," Kylie said, rubbing her hand across her forehead trying to erase the lingering effects of a hard night's sleep. "Amelia, listen to me. Go into the other room." She waited a moment. "Where are you now?"

"I'm in the hallway."

Kylie took a deep breath and tried to think what to do. "How long is Dix going to be gone?" she asked.

"He's driving to L.A.. He says it'll take four days but there's no way. It's too far."

"You shouldn't be there alone. You should go stay with your mother."

"No. I don't think so. Mama would take one look at me and—" she laughed tightly, but in the next moment her voice was shaking like a child's. "Dix thinks there's something wrong with me. And Father Matt. They all think there's something wrong. There's not, Kylie. There's not . . . It's just so dark. So black. I don't think I can face it."

"What do you mean?"

"Mama Mamie was right. All that time I didn't believe. Sister Emerita and all the rest of them were right. I turned my back on God . . . And now it's too late." Amelia's throat choked with the tears, and as Kylie tried to find the words to comfort her, she heard the frightened, incessant whisper of prayer. "God forgive me, forgive me . . ."

"Melia," she said, emotion filling her own eyes at her friend's desperation. She imagined her crouched within the hallway like a crumpled doll that had been degutted. "Melia, please stop. Whether or not you believed what they wanted you to believe, you've done nothing wrong."

"'Whatsoever is not of faith is sin'," gasped the voice through the tears.

"But you're an angel. A saint. You've never hurt anyone except yourself."

"But I have," she sobbed. "You don't understand. You think I'm good, but you don't know. You don't know. God will never forgive me."

"For what?"

"I can't tell you," she cried. "Please don't make me tell you!"

Taken aback, Kylie faltered in her response. The two had been the best of friends all their lives; they had shared the most intimate of secrets. To hear that there was something she didn't know, some deep dark transgression that Amelia had held back, filled her with pain. She started to respond, to tell her friend that there was nothing she could have done that would be so dreadful, when her words were cut off.

"It's too late for me," cried the beaten voice. "It's too late."

"Melia, please," Kylie begged, trying desperately to break through. She thought of the ashen, hollow face that had disappeared down the airline tunnel, and knew her friend would never survive four days alone. "Melia, please listen to me. You've got to stop thinking like this. You've got to just rest. I'm gonna book a flight," she said. "I can be there by this evening."

There was a moment of silence, wherein Kylie could feel her friend's shock. Since the death of her mother and Tucker, the two friends had always met in the nearby Charleston or Atlanta.

"I know how you feel about this place," said Amelia.

"I can't stand to hear you like this," Kylie insisted. "I want to be with you."

Though she could tell her strength had begun to quell her friend's tears, Kylie couldn't bear to hear the struggle; she felt helpless, the miles between them insufferable. "You need to just put this from your mind for now and get some sleep."

The suggestion brought a resurgence of emotion. "I need to keep working. I have to finish the church."

"Well, sleep first."

"No, I can't. I can't." Her voice rose as she began crying once again. "There's no time."

"You don't know that," argued Kylie. "You don't know how long we've—"

"No, I can feel them. They're getting closer. I have to keep working."

"Okay, Melia. It's okay," said Kylie. "Go ahead and work. You can sleep when I get there. I'm gonna hang up now and book a flight. I'll call you right back, okay?"

After Kylie disconnected the line, she immediately dialed the airlines. To her dismay, the earliest departure she could get was 5:15 that evening. When the reservations clerk read the time of arrival, fear slithered into her throat like a cold slug; she would not make it to Savannah until 9:49 that night.

Amelia answered the phone, her voice sounding small and frightened.

"I've got a flight," said Kylie.

"Are you sure about this?"

"I want to come," she said. "I wanted to get there sooner, but the earliest flight I could get doesn't arrive until almost ten."

"Dix pulled the engine out of our car—"

"Don't worry about meeting me. I'll take a cab from the airport." As she glanced to the clock to organize her thoughts, her stomach fell, for she had completely forgotten about a meeting with the insurance at nine. "Damn," she said, looking at her disheveled reflection in the toaster oven. "I've got a meeting with the claim's adjuster. Dillon's gonna be here any minute to pick me up."

"I'll let you go then."

"Melia, you're gonna be fine," said Kylie steadily. "I'll be there before you know it."

Twenty-Nine

ACCOUNT AGENT HAROLD GREENE REMAINED IN SILHOUETTE, HIS GRAY suit melding with the steel girders that rose behind him through the tinted glass. The harsh light of the day was subdued by the thick windows, giving a muffled shine to the bald patch at the crown of his head. His shoulders were narrow and appeared even slighter by the daunting, black desk that stretched between him and his clients.

"Five percent interest compounding on a half a million dollars gives us reason to try to resolve this matter as quickly as possible," he said. "Now that we have the death certificate and this statement of acknowledgment verifying that you're Mrs. Jack O'Rourke and that you're the beneficiary . . . there's just one more matter to take care of before we conclude all of this."

Dillon, who had been listening intently, leaned forward. "One more matter?" he asked. He glanced to Kylie for her reaction, but her attention remained distant, focused on what lay beyond the window. They were on the thirty-second floor of the insurance building, surrounded by the reflective edifices of the financial district. The Old Customs House rose between the glass structures, its huge clock facing toward them. With its stone tower bound by winged gothic figures, the landmark seemed strangely out of place within the forest of glass and chrome.

"Why, yes," said the agent, with a strange smile. "Because the policy is only a year old, we plan to contest it."

Dillon felt his face warm with anger—the insurance companies could never make anything simple. As a doctor, he witnessed patients receiving inadequate care because of the penny-pinching corporations; to have them dispute a life insurance policy after the fact was simply too much. "What do you mean, contest it?" he asked.

"Well," said the agent. "We have to know what sort of physical health the client was in."

"My husband died in a fire," said Kylie, her focus pulling back to the agent. "What's that got to do with his health?"

"According to the two-year-contestability clause—everything," said Greene, clearly affronted that she had once again joined the conversation to challenge him. "The policy is less than two years old— therefore still contestable. We have the right to make sure that he gave us valid information in the first place . . . that the policy wasn't purchased under false pretenses. If, for example, he had a heart disease we were unaware of, we wouldn't have issued the policy in the first place."

"Well isn't that something you should have thought of before you handed out the coverage?" asked Dillon.

"I'm sorry, but it's standard procedure," said the agent. "Unless Mr. O'Rourke had something to hide, you should have nothing to worry about. It should only take a couple of months to investigate."

"She's lost everything," said Dillon, pinching the skin between his eyes. "What's she supposed to do while you guys 'investigate'?"

"Well, aside from the life insurance, there's the matter of the homeowner's policy," said the agent. "I'll make sure the claims adjuster settles it in a quick and timely manner. In the meantime, there will be a provision of $8,000 for living expenses. When you meet with Agent McMartin at the site, she'll explain the details of that policy and also provide the check. Did you bring the photos she requested?"

The question had been directed to Kylie, but her attention had wandered once again to the old tower outside. Peregrine falcons were noted nesters in the tall peak and when Dillon followed Kylie's line of sight, he saw there were several swooping down into the squared valleys between the buildings.

Dillon touched her hand. "Kylie?"

"Yes, of course," she said. But she looked blankly toward him.

"Do you have the package we picked up at your safety deposit box?"

"Yes, I'm sorry," she said, reaching into her bag for the manilla envelope. "I have an article," she said, opening up the package. "*Boston Style* ran a story that featured the inside of the warehouse. Jack and I thought it would be a better representation than trying to photograph the contents ourselves."

"Yes, yes," interjected Greene. "That should work nicely. So many times clients are unprepared. I mean, just because you say you have an eight-foot nineteenth-century armoire with gold inlays doesn't necessarily mean that you do."

"These are additional pieces that we acquired after the article ran," said Kylie, thumbing through a small stack of photos.

Dillon noticed her sudden hesitation. He glanced down at the picture between her fingers and his stomach rolled; it was of Jack wearing a baseball cap. He was leaning over a large dining table, looking toward the camera with a smile. Dillon had taken the photo himself, the day the couple had found the antique. The three of them had been at a Red Sox game in Fenway Park when they had stumbled upon an estate sale on their way home.

"Why don't you have my secretary xerox those before you leave," suggested Greene gently. "I think Agent McMartin will be okay with that. As long as the photos match up to your claim, then you should have the money for the cash value of the contents within a couple of days. The structure will take more time. In the meantime, we can provide you with a room in a comfortable hotel that—"

"That won't be necessary," said Kylie.

"Very well, then. I suppose I better let you catch your meeting with Agent McMartin."

After a few handshakes, Kylie and Dillon headed across the white carpeting toward the glass door.

"There's just one other thing," said Kylie turning thoughtfully back. "If something were to happen to me in the interim . . . I mean, before all of this is settled—"

"We're not talking a lifetime," interrupted Greene, standing with a smile. "If all goes well, everything will pay out within a couple of months."

"Mmm," said Kylie, clearly not satisfied by the agent's response.

Dillon saw the shadow pass through her eyes raising a moment of concern within his own. He instantly thought of the stalker and wondered if the situation truly had been resolved as she had led them to believe.

"We can add another beneficiary right now, if you'd like," said Greene. "If it would set your mind at ease."

"Yes, it would. Thank you."

Thirty

"I DON'T KNOW WHY IN THE HELL I DRIVE IN THIS CITY," MUTTERED Dillon. "Only idiots are dumb enough to attempt it."

The eleven o'clock sun was blasting through the windshield scorching the black interior of the BMW. The bumpers ahead of them stretched all the way down Congress Street, past Faneuil Hall to the old Union Oyster House.

"It's got to be at least a hundred degrees," said Dillon, loosening his tie.

He looked over at Kylie, but she remained lost in her own thoughts. She was distant and quiet, as she had been from the time he had picked her up that morning. Her neck was dewy beneath the pale peach pant suit and even though she appeared calm and composed, she looked tired, her eyes squinting from the sun.

"There's a set of glasses in the glove box, if you'd like."

"No, I'm fine, Dill," she said with a hollow smile. Then after a moment, "Thanks for helping me with all of this. I know this is hard on you."

A knot instantly formed at the base of his throat. "Don't thank me," he said, turning his attention back to the bumper ahead of them. With a sickening feeling, he tried not to think of his brother's words—of the bitter accusations that had led to the nasty brawl. "Please don't thank me," he repeated softly.

He turned onto Hanover Street where the BMW picked up speed, yet Dillon scarcely felt the car move beneath them. He felt only the silence of his brother's absence and a longing for the way things had been. Rarely had there been a moment when they had all been together, when they weren't joking and laughing or entrenched in a heated debate about one thing or another. But now there remained a thickness to the air, a sadness and an empty aching. The woman next to him was no longer his brother's wife, but his brother's widow. She was broken and frayed, and he of all people had been left behind to pick up the pieces. *Little brother to the rescue*, his mind goaded. It seemed a nasty twist that the bloody hand of providence had brought Jack's prediction to fruition.

As the buildings moved past, the darkness he had felt in the insurance office oozed into his thoughts once again.

"Kylie," he said gently.

Her emerald eyes turned toward him, absorbing him in their gaze. "Yeah?" she asked.

"If the man who had been bothering you showed up again, you would tell me wouldn't you?"

Though she smiled, Dillon noticed that a blush came into her cheeks.

"Of course I would."

"Then what was that business with Greene?" he asked. "Why would you be worried that something might happen to you?"

"You just never know," she said quietly. She was silent for a moment, as though pondering the possibilities. "I would hate for everything that Jack and I worked for to slip through the cracks. We put a lot of—" but her words were choked off the moment she gazed back through the windshield. The energy drained from her eyes so quickly that it was as if someone had opened a hatch at the bottom of her feet and sucked it out.

Dillon looked into the glare of the sun, to the giant monster that seemed capable of crushing them with one merciless step. The warehouse stood naked before them, rising up from the ashes like a blackened skeleton.

JACK'S JEEP remained at the curb, in the exact spot he had left it the night of the fire.

Dillon pressed on the brake and pulled to the side of the street. "Are you sure you're ready for this?" he asked.

In spite of her screaming heart, Kylie forced herself to look at the devastation that awaited them. From fifty feet away, she could see there was nothing left inside, only blackened stone that formed the walls and rose into the white hot sky. The yellow tape of a police line remained stretched across the perimeter, fallen in places like the streamers of a party whose guests had long since dissipated. It drifted slightly in the breeze that wafted off Boston Harbor, over the hardened tracks of firemen who had trampled through chaos and mud. For a brief moment, Kylie heard the roar of the sirens and saw the face of the paramedic she had fought so desperately to escape.

"We can do this another time if you want," said Dillon.

"No," said Kylie, her gaze hardening against her heart. "Let's get this over with."

SOOT trickled from above like black snow dancing through a patch of sunlight. They had entered through the front door, stepping across the spongy, charred floor into the living room where lumps of black had taken the place of furniture.

". . . As you can see, the interior is a total loss," the agent was saying. "The foundation is in good, solid shape which makes this a lot easier. We ask that you get separate bids from three contractors of your choice. We pay in installments. Of course there's the question of your mortgage. We'll need . . ."

Kylie heard the words of the agent, but they had long since dissipated into jumbled sounds in the back of her mind. She couldn't remember the name of the woman or why exactly it had been necessary for them to go inside. All she could think of was the blackened stairwell before her, and the voice of Detective Binaggio. *We found him at the bottom of the stairs—trying to get out* . . . With a tremulous hand she reached for the rail where pieces of it broke off and crumbled to the floor.

"Mrs. O'Rourke?"

The appeal pulled her from her thoughts, and even though she wanted to turn, to respond to the agent, her body simply wouldn't budge. Dillon gently touched her arm.

"Are you okay?" he whispered.

"Yes," she said, turning away, trying to escape the acrid smell that drifted up from the ash. The heat pressed upon her, sending a trickle of sweat between her breasts. "You were saying?" she asked.

For the first time, she noticed the agent was surprisingly young. She was thin with stylish glasses, her black hair resting flat against her head. "There's the question of rebuilding," said the woman. "Without even asking, I just assumed that you would want to."

"Rebuild?" said Kylie, stunned by the thought. She hadn't even considered such a thing. It had taken them years to turn the old warehouse into a home. "When we found it, there was nothing," she said meeting the woman's questioning eyes. It was absurd to think that the world she and Jack had created could be recaptured. "No," she said, her voice shaking with her response. "No, I think not."

"It's something that you may want to reconsider," insisted the woman. "If you don't rebuild we could only give you the cash value of the home—minus the cost of the land value, of course."

Kylie moved to the side, but there was nowhere to go. She caught a glimpse of the kitchen, of the cracked tiles Jack had laid the night they moved in. Her head felt light and the heat was relentless.

"The demolition alone will cost you twenty percent of what it costs to rebuild. Sometimes people don't realize that to tear out a foundation—"

"No!" said Kylie, anything to shut the woman up. "Goddamn it, I said no!" The exclamation had escaped so fast that she hadn't had time to stop it.

The woman's lip puckered, but the pout was quickly covered by indignation. "I'm only trying to help," she said.

"I'm sorry," said Kylie as the threat of tears stung her eyes. "I'm sorry."

Dillon stepped in, smoothing out the rough edges as he whisked the woman away. ". . . It's just a little early," she heard him saying as the woman disappeared back through the doorway.

When Kylie glanced back, she caught her shattered reflection in the mirror that lay against the bottom of the fireplace. The devastation loomed behind her, her waning figure swallowed into its belly. She moved closer to the mirror, her gaze running along its gold frame. She thought of Julius Vanderpoel, of his pained face that had reflected in the glass. With his silk jacket, he had fit into the surroundings more surely than Jack. Then a sickening thought came into her mind: she had built it for him. The canary lounge—the scarlet drapes that clung to the top of the room like dried blood. It had been for him. *Someday I'll marry you. And so I shall wait.* He had waited. He had waited.

"Hey there."

She turned to find Dillon gingerly approaching.

"Dillon," she said. "I'm so sorry."

"She understands," he said, holding out a card. "She left this for you. She said to call whenever you're ready."

He was studying her, assessing her mood. "You should come to the house and stay. Theresa's there. She moved in a few days ago and it would give you someone—"

"No," she said. "I can't."

"I hate the thought of you staying in that empty house all alone."

"I can't, Dillon," she said with a sigh. "Really, I can't. There's too much to be done."

Dillon shuffled nervously, his eyes avoiding the devastation around them. He nodded toward the street where the Jeep remained. "I can come back later with Theresa to pick up the Cherokee," he said. "I'll store it in my garage until you decide what you want to do with it."

"That would be nice," said Kylie. She forced a smile to ease the tension, but the stagnant air became thick with an awkward silence.

"Well, I'll meet you in the car," said Dillon.

As he turned and ambled sadly toward the door, Kylie lingered for a moment, unable to bring herself to follow. Though the wreckage brought an incredible aching inside, she couldn't let it go; her last look at the life she once had could not end like this.

Emotion stung into her eyes, but she gently closed them and listened to the sounds of the harbor. As a slight breeze cut through the acrid air, she took a deep breath and tried to hear the hum of the fan that had brought her so much comfort. Tears escaped past her lashes and trickled down her face, yet she remained silent and patient for she knew that if she concentrated hard enough it would come. Then for a brief moment, a flashing glorious moment, it was there. The blades whirled overhead while the vast dark harbor sparkled through the towering windows. There were no ghosts from the past, no scars or demons to be fought. She was within the safety of her bed. Jack was beside her and the house as it was.

Thirty-One

THE STUDY BLURRED BETWEEN HER HEAVY LIDS, AS AMELIA'S HEAD lulled backward toward the sofa. While her thoughts twisted through the tunnels of her drowsiness, faces and moments lurched out at her in fragmented pieces: Her hands were at once gripping the sandpaper that ground along the wood, her fingers aching so painfully they felt as if they would snap. Then the face of Eva Ratchford took a long drag from a cigarette and looked downward to the tangled body of Dale Benson. With the buzzing of flies, a wall of darkness moved toward her. Just as the huge black wave threatened to consume her, Amelia snapped herself upright, forcing her eyes wide against the craving to sleep. She needed another glass of tea, a stronger one this time, for after three nights with little rest, the exhaustion vied to overtake her. The pitcher in the refrigerator was empty, and it would be several more minutes before the boiling of the teapot would sound.

Just a few more hours, she told herself. Kylie would be there, and then she would sleep. But it was only eleven o'clock in the morning. *Eleven o'clock*. She was already so tired that she simply couldn't think. Only minutes earlier, she had been staining the rail in the choir when she had imagined one of the pews moving forward, as though it had sprouted legs and was crawling after her.

The breeze from the central air tickled across her bare arms and though the temperature outside was sweltering, she longed for the warmth of the couch. As she sank back onto the sofa, the cushions opened up like a warm mouth to devour her. Just a few minutes, that was all. Just a quick nap before the whistle of the kettle would awaken her and she would go back to work.

She lay to her side, lowering her head onto the armrest. The candy dish on the coffee table appeared a foot tall, while the study behind it swayed as if she were on a rocking ship. "Just a few minutes," she whispered as her stomach fell deeper and deeper into the divan. Even before her eyes closed, her mind drifted to the halls of St. Mary's Elementary with its shiny floors and smell of crayon. Her back was to a wall, her classmates lined shoulder to shoulder next to her, while Sister Fran rapped her ruler against the bricks above them. Fear welled inside her chest as the nun moved slowly down the line toward her, for she could not remember the last of the psalm which they had been assigned. "'The Lord is my shepherd; I shall not want,'" she whispered as Sister Fran stopped in front of her next victim. "'He maketh me to lie down in green pastures...'" Over her own frantic words, she could hear Tommy Jordan struggling with the recital, then the crack of the ruler as it came down on his upturned hands. But she dare not look, she dare not linger on his pain for the black-cloaked nun moved closer. "'He leadeth me in the paths of righteousness for His ... for His name's ...'" The thick bosom was before her with the smell of Mentholatum stinging her nostrils. "Amelia Blackwell?" Her heart thundered so loudly that she couldn't hear her own voice grappling for the words. "'Yea, though I walk through the valley of the shadow of death, I will fear no evil ... for Thou art ... Thou art—'" Her quivering hands lifted as the bite of the ruler came down.

WHAT FELT like seconds later, she bounded out of the darkness with a gasp. Something had awakened her, had dragged her up to a seated position, but she stared numbly forward trying to place what it was. Her back was damp and her pulse banged against her head like a sledgehammer. She stared blankly toward the shiny telephone, but it remained silent. It had been ringing, she was certain of it, but something else had shattered the darkness. Her lips, her cheeks, her entire body was numb and her head felt as if it had been stuffed with cotton. The room had changed, the light was different. She couldn't place the time, the week, or even the year; all she knew was that she needed to act. She was in the study, but couldn't remember why she had come into the rectory. Rising from the sofa, she looked blankly about the room, her heart fluttering with disorientation. The air. There was something about the air that was off, an odor, thick and pungent. Then like a blast of ice bursting behind her eyes, she remembered the kettle on the gas stove. Hours had clearly passed but there had been no sound, no whistle to awaken her.

She dove forward, but her limbs remained sluggish as though she were moving through a vast space of liquid. The hallway was before her and though it was only a few steps, time stretched endlessly before she was standing in the doorway staring into the dim kitchen.

From across the room, she saw that the red kettle was in place but there was no flame beneath it—only the near silent hiss of spewing gas. Her flesh crawled along her slackened face as the words of her mother throbbed through her skull.

Tell Father Matt to get rid of that old stove—it's gonna blow you to pieces one day. Just one little spark will do it . . . Just one little spark.

Her stiff legs carried her to the stove, but it felt like someone else's hands that stretched from her sides and fumbled with the white knob. The fingers were slender and ineffectual, groping until the hissing finally ceased. A vacuous silence spun round and though the sound of the poison had stopped, the chill of danger remained. Like the soft wave of an ocean, the gas clung to the air, billowing around her body, permeating every crevice within the room. She was suddenly aware of her own breath, of its labored rhythm taking in the gas and expelling it. *Just one little spark*, her mind taunted as her shoulders tensed against the impending blast. Her eyes darted along the counter, and to the open broom closet behind her, searching for a silent stalker, a movement or a shadow that would bring the final blow. Then a sound, hideous and dull, broke the beat of her heart: the thump of wings rustled within the tree outside. Like the bars to a medieval dungeon the terror slammed down around her, trapping her within her own adrenaline.

Without even looking she could feel the glint of its eyes and the cock of its knowing head, observing from the window like an arrogant little demon, puffed with delight.

Just a bird, her mind whispered. *Just a mother protecting its young.*

Moving only her head, she looked slowly toward the window where the wallpaper was speckled with the tree's flowing shadow. The distorted line of the bird's body waved against the closed curtains—its head elongated and beak sharpened into consummate evil and haughtiness.

Just a bird, her mind chanted. *Just a bird.*

She felt drugged, unable to move, unable to think. She needed to ventilate the house, to open the doors and the windows, but her reflexes were deadened.

With her eyes remaining fixed on the abhorrent form, she edged slowly backward, then along the wall to the hallway. With each shaky step, the shadow was recast, as though the bird's gaze was following her across the floor, its beady eyes penetrating through the slit in the curtains. It remained eerily silent, until the moment she reached the doorway, when its wings fluttered ominously within the branches.

With a gasp, she passed through the doorway, leaving the kitchen and its horrors behind, but when she turned, she found that the tunnel-like walls of the hallway stretched for miles to the dim glow at the end—to the murky light that spilled through the fanlight above the thick door. Defeat sliced through her like a dagger; for she would never make it to the entrance in time. A spark would surely flare and she would be blasted to bits without even feeling it.

The petulant caw of the bird shrieked behind her, chastising her desertion.

You turned your back, Amelia Blackwell. Now the day of reckoning has come.

She felt the presence, thick and hungry, pressing inward. The walls waved in and out, and the floor slanted from beneath her. As her unsteady legs carried her further, she concentrated on the light, willing herself through each faltering step.

At last her cold hand touched the latch and pulled it downward. The door swung effortlessly open and the warmth rushed in on her in a blustery wind.

Without feeling herself move over the porch, the cool lawn was beneath her where she sank to her knees. Crouching forward onto the grass, she rested her head into her hands. As her racing heart began to calm, her shoulders trembled with the wave of tears that slowly over-took her. She had been frightened and on edge for so long that she could simply take it no longer.

After a long struggle to bring her emotions under control she wiped her eyes and looked up again. She searched the square for suspicious figures, but the street remained eerily empty. The only sign of life was the wind that scampered around her, through the live oaks and the palmetto, the leaves clattering amongst each other like tiny voices in the gales. In the sudden calm, a voice of self-doubt exerted itself. *You did it*, it whispered, as she clutched her arms tight around herself. She had put the kettle on the stove and forgotten to light the burner. "A harmless blackbird," she said aloud. That's all the shadow behind the curtain had been.

Yet in spite of herself, her back prickled with the feel of the open door behind her. She had the sudden impulse to run, to go somewhere, anywhere, for she knew that if she reentered the house, she would never make it through the night. Whether or not the spewing gas had been a mistake of her own, she felt the darkness drawing inward near-ing its conclusion. Abruptly standing, she looked to Dix's degutted Mustang. She could walk down to Casey's Drugstore and call some-one. She could call her mother. But as the chill of an approaching storm wafted toward her, she knew she would have to stay. No matter what, she could not abandon the cathedral. Not only did she need to air the rectory before the forecasted rains hit, but the cathedral was prone to leaks and would have to be watched closely if her work was to be protected.

You'll be fine, she said silently. All she had to do was stay awake and remain alert until Kylie's arrival. But as she stood shakily to her feet, her insides came alive like a nest of worms. Her panic was over, yet the after-taste of terror remained.

Thirty-Two

WITH THE WARM CUP OF COFFEE GRIPPED TIGHTLY BETWEEN HER PALMS, Kylie stared at the small monitor that hung high above the bar. The voice of the CNN weatherman rose just above the hum of the airport, as he pointed to a radar screen behind him.

"As you can see, folks, the weather pattern has moved into the southeastern part of the country bringing heavy winds, rain and in some places flooding. After wreaking considerable havoc over Tennessee and Alabama, the storm has now crossed over into Georgia where . . ."

"Not a pretty sight," drawled a deep Southern voice from beside her.

Kylie turned to find the bloated face of a business man smiling over at her from two stools down.

"Not you of course," he said with a tilt of his glass. "The storm." He shook his head and took another pull from his beer. "I don't know about you, darlin', but I'm not exactly lookin' forward to flyin' through that mess."

Kylie's mouth was so dry her throat burned. "No," she agreed quietly, nausea rumbling in her stomach as she looked from the dim bar.

To her right stretched the bright, sunny terminal and just beyond that rested the DC-10 that awaited final boarding. With the heat pounding mercilessly down upon the runway, it was hard to imagine that a fierce storm raged over nearly a quarter of the nation. Not only would her flight take her directly into the bad weather, but Amelia was beneath it. Kylie had tried all afternoon to reach her, but to no avail. She looked toward the pay phones at the edge of the dark haven and decided to try one last time before her flight.

Just as she lifted her purse to dig for change, the steward's voice came over the loudspeaker.

"This is the final boarding call for Delta flight 211 bound for Atlanta. We now ask that all passengers board the plane."

"That's us," said the man at the bar, dragging his briefcase from the counter. "They're not gonna hold it any longer."

Kylie slid off the stool, resting onto hesitant legs. When she reached for her duffle she tried to ignore the tremble of her hand.

"You can do this," she said quietly, slinging the strap of the bag over her shoulder.

Diverting her attention from the window, she kept her eyes on the dark burgundy carpet, watching her sandaled feet take progressive steps. Amelia had done it, so could she. She had flown all the way from Savannah without a glitch and then had flown back. She had bravely stepped inside the plane, stowed her carry-on and then buckled the seat belt . . .

"Oh Jesus," Kylie gasped, stopping in the middle of the seat-lined terminal. She wiped her brow with the sleeve of her pantsuit jacket. "Get a hold of yourself, Wylie," she whispered impatiently.

The steward was staring at her from across the way.

"I just want to make a quick call to my friend," Kylie said, her voice so slight that she was certain it had not carried the distance, but the disgruntled look on the young man's face told her it had.

"I'm sorry ma'am, but—"

"It's really important that I reach her. I've been trying to contact her all—"

"Sorry," he insisted. "Final boarding."

Thirty-Three

CROUCHED AGAINST THE HEADBOARD OF THE BED, AMELIA HAD BEEN waiting in the darkness for the storm's reprieve. When it finally came, the battery-operated clock atop her jewelry box read 9:40 P.M.

She listened toward the window that was slightly ajar, expecting the soft drip of the dissipated rain to turn once again to a downpour; but the curtains swayed only with a cool moist air and the stillness of night.

Loosening the grip she had kept on her knees, she stretched her stiff legs to the side of the bed and looked toward the dark hallway. It was so dark that she could scarcely see the shapes around her. Without even checking, she knew that all of the lines were still down. Dix had promised to call at seven but the phone had yet to ring.

A weak flash of lightning abruptly lit up the room, and she caught her own blue reflection within the dresser mirror. She was startled by the sight of her shadowed, tense eyes and blonde hair. Her tank top and frayed jean-shorts hung limply on her thin body.

"One one-thousand, two one-thousand . . ." she whispered.

Not until the fourth count, did the thunder rumble from the distant horizon. The wall behind her resonated gently and the perfume bottles upon the dresser jingled together like delicate wind chimes. The head of the storm had passed over, yet a westerly grumble promised that it was merely taking a breather in its brutal attack. Only minutes earlier the thunder had split down upon the rectory so forcefully that it sounded as if a giant sledgehammer were crashing against the roof. Pulled tightly into a ball, Amelia had felt as though an enormous hand would break through the ceiling at any moment to crush her. She had begged and pleaded for the storm to cease, but now that it had, she found the eeriness of the silence even more unsettling. Without the shattering noise of the storm to block her sound, she became too frightened to move for fear of somehow drawing attention to her presence.

The old springs of the bed creaked, as she nervously reached for a cigarette from the bed stand. Unable to see clearly, she fumbled with the matches before the tiny flame hissed to life. Her face drew inward as she took a long drag, the nicotine burning deep into her lungs. Though never having smoked in the rectory before, she needed something to hold onto, anything to bring her reassurance.

With the exhale, she sat stiffly back against the headboard and stared toward the dresser mirror. It was only a matter of time before Kylie would be there, but the thought brought little relief. Like herself, Kylie was wrapped in the same hideous nightmare. Perhaps the storm would delay her flight; or even worse, maybe it would somehow consume her. Guilt spread across Amelia's thoughts; she should never have allowed her friend to travel so far. It had been selfish of her to even call. Dix would be gone for four days, yet Kylie had lost Jack forever.

Her eyes constricted with the image of herself. Her outline smudged into the blue shadows like a figure in an impressionistic painting. She found it strange that her mascara was smeared beneath her eyes, for she couldn't even remember applying it. Staring at her pale lips and gaunt cheeks, she felt as though the darkness around her had somehow seeped inside of her—as if her lungs, her heart, every fiber of her being had been filled with black ink. She wanted to just disappear as she had when she was a child, to vanish into the silence where no one would ever find her. Even before she could speak, she had faded into the walls of her parents' giant house. She would hover in the crawlspace behind her bedroom for hours, yet no one ever came. Within the brutal solitude of the Blackwell home, she was simply never missed. Though painful to admit, she was a mere shadow, an afterthought of inconvenience born to older parents that had years prior drifted apart.

With a pang, she thought of her father with his quiet resignation, of all the conversations they should have had but missed. While Leonard Blackwell was a kind and thoughtful man, he was weak. His wife had ruled with the disarming grace of a Southern woman, yet her mollifying tone never softened the sting of her tongue. Amelia had taken after her father, swaying with her mother's current so as not to cause disruption. Submitting into the silence, she had followed the rules and lived by her mother's hand; even her eventual rebellion had been a quiet sort of mutiny.

At the age of fifteen, she denounced her parents' circle of wealth, traded in the pretty dresses and long flowing hair of the South and began a decade long romp from one harmful relationship to the next. When she finally found peace with Dix, she also found a place within herself. She soon made amends with her mother, but there was one major contention between them that was never resolved—she had turned her back on the Church and had never refaced it. While at first the denial was born out of defiance, her failure to return was incited by doubt. The wrathful God in which her mother had taught seemed suddenly fictional, a cruel figure meant to control and suppress. But in the confusion of her recent fear, her mother's convictions had found a home and the merciless God had reappeared vowing unforgiveness. With the tyranny of her mother's voice commanding her thoughts, what had once been moral became suddenly diabolical. What at once had been a selfless decision made on a sad day long past, had become a transgression so fierce she feared it would condemn her to the fiery pits of hell.

As the black ink inside of her churned, Amelia took another drag from the cigarette and then another. Her pulse had suddenly quickened. The darkness was coming and she was certain it would not behold mercy. With a shiver she felt it within the moist air that fluttered through the curtains.

Amelia, you're a fine woman. You have nothing to fear. They were the words of the priest, yet she could not find comfort in them. He had not understood her blistered hands or desperation to finish the church. He had not known her need for retribution; that she was in a race with death for the salvation of her soul.

We want you to think about this Miss Blackwell, demanded the stern lips of her past. *Think about the repercussions.*

The shadows melted to that sunny day long ago when she had considered the consequences and agreed to the price. Her fingers twisted together like wires, for she was merely fifteen and yet to control her nervous energy. "My mother would have to raise it," she answered softly, knowing that in Mama Mamie's eyes the child would never be anything more than a product of sin. It would be taught shame and fear and loneliness.

"Miss Blackwell, you must be fully aware of what you're about to do. Are you certain you won't consider adoption?"

"No. I want rid of it." She wanted to dispose of the seed before it became human, before it became a helpless child that she could no longer save. "I want rid of it," she whispered through her tears.

With the memory, the black of night squeezed tighter and seeped deeper inside of her. She wanted to run from her own feverish thoughts, but she knew that the sensations would follow. As she gazed into the steely mirror, the iciness of the table came back to her and the sharp odor of antiseptic stole her breath away.

The nurse hovered over her as the words of her conscience sought to qualm her thudding heart. *It's nothing more than a fetus, a tiny piece of tissue . . . a tiny . . .* but as she stared up at the bright lights, her head swimming with sedation, she had heard the sound of the suction. She felt the tug of its tiny legs and arms, its delicate hands being ripped from her belly. In the horrifying seconds before the job was complete, a murmur of regret had passed through her lips. She wanted to cry out but her own weakness and youth had kept her silent.

"God forgive me, forgive me," she whispered into the cool night. She pulled the smoke deep into her lungs and tried not to think of the demons that would be coming. She needed to stay calm, to push the thoughts from her mind, but the secret had been locked deep inside for so long, that like the spoil of rotted meat, it had festered and mutated into something unspeakable. The child had not died that day in the clinic; its dismembered body had been resewn and placed into the arms of her recent nightmares. It was visiting her in the night and in the shadows of the day, speaking to her about what might have been and condemning her for what wasn't . . . condemning her to the darkness she would now have to face.

Now the wrathful God would punish her. And even more severely than the slaying of the unborn child, he would punish her for her desertion. Instead of begging for forgiveness, she had turned her back and now the day of reckoning had come.

Her mother's face twisted with the grief and the proclamation of her daughter's fate: '*No murderer hath eternal life abiding in him.*'

"It wasn't a baby. . . not a baby," Amelia argued into the silence. It had no heartbeat, no pulse; it was a mere seed that had yet to sprout into life. Shaking her head, she tried to find the clear thoughts, to return to the voice that had once been her own, but her mind remained febrile. She had lost certainty in all, except for the darkness.

As she took another drag from the cigarette, she noticed the tremor of the tiny glow. Her hand was shaking. She held it out before her and looked at it with suspicion. Perhaps the darkness had already arrived and was simply waiting for her to bring her own death. By turning on the gas and then leaving it, her body had already proven capable of defying her. Even her breath, which had broken into a labored rhythm once again, could not be trusted.

She extinguished the cigarette into a Coke can, and though she tried to breath easier, her throat fluttered with sudden anticipation. While the rain had raged, a constant banging had sounded from somewhere deep within the cathedral, but she had not been able to summon the courage to investigate. The cathedral was prone to leaks and had suffered considerable damage in the rains of '96; and though she had hired the most experienced carpenter she could find for the restorations, the work had yet to be tested by a storm of this magnitude. Now that the storm was in remission, the nervous flutter in her chest told her that it was time to take a look.

Moving rigidly to the side of the bed, she stared toward the black hallway; she had been in the bedroom for so long the thought of leaving it was paralyzing.

With a quick glance to the glowing red digits she saw that it was

10:25 P.M. Kylie would soon be there. If she waited, they could check out the noise together.

Just a few more minutes, she bargained with herself. If Kylie didn't arrive, she would descend into the darkness alone.

In spite of what might lay within the shadows beneath, the church remained her only hope. If she protected it to the end, perhaps then and only then, God would have mercy.

Thirty-Four

ON THE FIFTEENTH RING, KYLIE HUNG UP THE PHONE AND STARED blankly at the rotating carousel. It spun round and round with one lone bag that had yet to be claimed. Her head still pounded from the hellacious landing into Atlanta, the fluorescents stabbing into her eyes like needles.

The elderly man at the phone next to her was grumbling to himself. He had been stuck in the airport for as long as she, waiting on the same flight. "You tryin' to call Savannah too?" he asked gruffly.

"Yes," she answered, rubbing the knot between her eyes.

"My daughter lives just outside of there," he said, shaking his head. "If the winds are as bad as they are here, the lines are probably down."

"Probably so," she answered softly. She imagined Amelia alone within the darkened rectory and her heart sickened.

"It's damned irritating," the old man muttered, shuffling off in the opposite direction.

After gathering her belongings Kylie stood for a moment, uncertain where to turn. She was desperate to get across the remaining 252 miles to Savannah, but there were no more flights going in or out of Atlanta due to the storm. The only way to Savannah that night was by car and none of the rental agencies had one available. She had gone from counter to counter, where she was met with the same response. "We're fresh out of cars. Did you have a reservation?"

She didn't even have a valid driver's license, but that was one point she had dared not mention. That morning, she had found her license in her safety deposit box, and though it had been revoked two years earlier, there was nothing labeling it to that effect. She was hoping that with any luck at all, the Georgia and Massachusetts computers would not interface. Just as she decided to try Budget once again, a polite yet hesitant voice addressed her from behind.

"Excuse me, ma'am?"

When she turned, she was puzzled to find the first clerk she had approached standing before her. He was a slim young man who looked shyly over at his Hertz counter. "I just had a cancellation, if you don't mind a sedan."

Kylie grabbed her bags and smiled weakly. "I'd take a tank right now, if that's all you had."

Thirty-Five

PARTING THE CURTAINS, AMELIA LOOKED TO THE WET STREET BELOW; there were no cars in sight except for Dix's Mustang hidden beneath a tarp. The street lamps were off and there were no lights coming from any of the old houses across the square on Charlton Street. The entire area remained in blackout.

A flash of lightning abruptly cut across the bedroom, followed immediately by a deep groan more powerful than the last. She could hesitate no longer, for the storm's reprieve was nearing its end.

You have to go, Melia. You don't have a choice. If the roof of the cathedral leaked, the fresh varnish would buckle and the moisture would turn the old wood black. *Just a quick trip down and back.* She would assess the damage and then swiftly return to the safety of the bedroom.

When her bare feet touched the cool floor, it sent a chill traveling up her legs into her spine. She lifted the flashlight from the bed but made a conscious decision not to turn it on; she would descend the stairs in darkness. If the presence was waiting, she would not give it fair warning.

Moving like a shadow, she descended the stairwell without the aid of the light. She continued quickly down the long hall toward the back door, but as she drew near the entrance to the kitchen she slowed. Pausing at the edge of the doorway, she stared toward the curtained window. There was no sound, no movement, only an eerie stillness and the occasional drip from a sodden tree branch.

Go quickly, her mind urged.

She obediently turned for the rear entry where she unlocked the door and stepped into the stone passageway.

Entering the church from the back side of the altar, she rounded the communion rail into the heart of the cathedral. For a moment she froze, overwhelmed by the blackness. The stained-glass windows were mere smudges of dim light against a wall of ebony. She switched on the flashlight, the light streaking in a weak beam across the empty pews. Scanning the altar behind her and the statues to her right, she saw nothing out of place. It wasn't until she felt the icy liquid swirl between her toes that she saw the water to her left and the open clerestory window swinging on its hinges.

She quickly propped the flashlight on the front pew, dragged the tall ladder beneath the window, then started up the metal rungs. As she neared the top, the ladder teetered like an unstable ride of a traveling carnival. She gripped with both hands and looked down at the swaying shadows. A sense of vertigo wavered her balance forcing her to look up again. She quickly reached for the window and pulled it shut, then made her way back down to the solid floor. With her eyes lowered and her shoulders rigid, she went immediately to the corner where she retrieved a rag and a bucket. She returned to the puddle and got down on her hands and knees to mop up the water.

Just as the rag touched the floor, the dim lights of the old chandeliers flickered on and then off before settling on once again. She took a deep breath and looked about the murky church. Only four of the twenty chandeliers had been wired, lighting a small section along the north side of the nave. Though no one was there, the hair had risen on the back of her neck. She was certain she had heard a shuffling sound within the scaffolding when the light had flashed on. Her eyes scanned the boards, but she saw no movement within the shadows. After a long breathless moment, she crouched once again to the puddle where her own reflection rippled back at her with empty eye sockets and hollowed cheeks. She looked like a mad skeleton. The darkness behind her swayed menacingly within the current. With a swish of the rag, the haunting image dissipated.

"God please, please," she whispered, but instead of comfort the entreaty forged the fear inside of her forward. The tense face of Hector Haynes clouded her vision as her chest tightened with trepidation. Like herself, he had known about his fate but had been unable to run. She pictured his crumpled body within the closet of torture and the terrified screech of his face.

Her pulse drummed through her ears, as she moved faster, swishing the dirty cloth through the endless puddle. She wrung it within the bucket and bent once again, when she froze with the feel of the presence, of its dead cold stare fixing upon her.

She lifted slowly to an upright position, facing straight into the eyes that sparkled from between two scaffolding planks. The rat remained frozen as she locked within its gaze.

For a silent moment, there was no breath, no air, only the sweet gamey odor of the rodent's proximity. Then in the second in which she blinked, the creature was gone. Forcing her gaze deeper into the crevice, she waited for the sound of its movement but there was only silence.

As she lifted slowly to her feet, the rag fell to the water with a soft splash. The church creaked and moaned but there was no sound of the intruder, only the beat of her heart skipping frantically beneath her breastbone.

Go back to work, her mind urged. *It was only a rat.*

The church had been plagued by the rodents for years, but when she tried to force her stiff legs to bend they merely trembled. Her breath was working itself into a silent frenzy, and her lips and fingers had begun to tingle. She turned for the dark opening of the door, when the distinct sound of movement scuffled behind her.

She pivoted to the empty pews that stretched into blackness. "Who's there?" she demanded, her voice echoing between the stone columns. As her eyes leapt from one side of the statue-lined wall to the next, she was certain that the shadows had shifted inward. The stone eyes of the saints were upon her, mocking her from their perches.

'*Oh ye of little faith,*' they silently taunted.

She began to edge backward, the terror mounting so fiercely that she could no longer feel her legs or feet beneath her. *Nothing's there*, she tried to tell herself, but she could feel it breathing softly from the shadows, just beyond the statues and the edge of dim light.

"Who's there—" she repeated, but her fear choked off the last of it.

She turned to run, but as she bolted toward the door, the slick floor slid from beneath her. The weight of her body fell backward, pulled heavily toward the wet puddle. Her head popped forward as it hit the pew, her torso slamming against the unyielding marble. Pain, agonizing and sharp, burned through her skull forcing her entire body to constrict. Tears of fright drenched her cheeks, while the warm feeling of blood flooded into her mouth. Staring blindly into the darkness, the hellish pits of Hiernonymus Bosch filled her vision. A huge rat devoured a man's neck and shoulders while a bird pecked flesh from his legs. "No!!" she screamed, but the effort was a mere murmur that drowned within her choking throat. With all of her might, she rolled onto her side, when something stirred within the shadows to her left. Out of the corner of her eye, she saw a murky silhouette scamper beneath the pews.

At once, hysteria took hold, stealing ground against all reason. A high-pitched whine started within the base of her throat. Her body was squirming, grasping toward the pile of boards but her mind had grown numb, filled to the brim with delirium. They would not take her into the light, but pull her downward, further and further into the darkness—down into the abyss of maiming tortures.

As her hand touched the two-by-four, the sudden hiss of claws scampered behind her, moving across the marble toward her. When she turned, she did not see a rat, but the beady eyes of a demon and the hairy body of a devil. It closed inward as she scrambled on her hands and knees to her feet. Pivoting with one long steady scream, she lifted the board above her head and brought it forcefully down.

FATHER MATT pounded one last time on the rectory door. Peering through the curtains into the darkened hall, apprehension rose in his thoughts.

"You shouldn't have waited," he chided himself. In keeping his promise to Dix he should have skipped the game to check on Amelia sooner.

When he slid his key into the dead bolt, he was startled to find it unlocked. Just as he began to edge the door open, he heard the harrowing scream from the cathedral. His first thought was of Amelia under brutal attack from an intruder. He immediately abandoned his keys in the lock and began running to the rear entrance of the church. When he yanked back the heavy door, the sound of frantic breathing and a repeated dull thud echoed from within. As his shoes slid around the back of the altar, he braced himself for the worst, yet nothing could have prepared him for what he found. Within the dim light of the shadowy nave, he saw the demented figure of Amelia Blackwell standing over a pile of boards. With all of her might, she pounded a two-by-four down upon a smashed form, each blow bringing a dark liquid spurting upward. Recognizing it only from its tail, for the upper body had been pulverized, he saw that it was a rat.

"Amelia!" he called sharply, freezing her in mid-swing.

With eyes filled with dementia she turned toward him, her mouth gaping with adrenaline and horror. Blood ran from her bruised lip down her chin and her clothes were wet and smeared with dirt.

"It's okay," he said softly, raising a shaky hand to steady her. "It's okay, it's dead."

Her arms were trembling and her grip was so tight that even in the dark he could see there was no circulation in her hands. A dark stain of blood had sprayed up on her tank top and was trickling down her arms. "It's okay," he repeated softly. "Just put the board down."

With faltering steps, she edged away from the slaughtered form as though it still posed a threat. Not until she was several feet away did she release the board to clank upon the marble floor. Still she turned from side to side, peering toward the dark corners, her gaze settling on the statues behind them.

Following her line of sight, Father Matt looked to the empty darkness then back to her fear-ridden face. Surely the dementia that remained was not caused by the mere rodent; she had worked in the church for almost a year without fear of the rats.

"Amelia?" he said gently.

SHE TRIED to find a word, a sound of response, but she merely looked to the priest with spent horror. She knew that her eyes were wild and frantic but still couldn't calm herself.

Father Matt immediately moved forward, his shaking hand touching her arm. "Sit down here for a moment," he urged, guiding her toward the front pew.

She rested back onto the wooden bench squeezing her eyes shut against the darkness, willing her racing heart and breath to calm. *You're fine*, the hot voice inside of her whispered, as tears of relief flooded her eyes. It had been a mere rat. She had been so convinced that her moment had come, that it had turned to a demon. But Father Matt was there beside her. With him by her side, no monsters would appear and take her into the shadows. She was safe.

"Everything's okay," he said, resting his hand onto her hot back. "You're gonna be fine."

She had been wrong about the night, for Father Matt would see her through safely, yet when she reopened her eyes, she was certain she could still feel the cold presence waiting beyond the statues.

"Dix mentioned these attacks," said the father. "You just need to relax."

She suddenly realized that she was gasping for air, her dry lips sticking together like paste. What felt like minutes passed, yet her breath continued to elude her. *It'll calm in a moment*, she told herself. As it had a few days earlier and the day in the boutique, she just needed to concentrate on breathing slowly. But as she continued to wait, her lungs sunk deeper and deeper into the airless abyss. She began to gulp desperately, but still couldn't pull enough oxygen from the air. At once, the fear began to creep back inward. She grabbed for the flashlight and shined it into the shadows, but saw no one.

"It's . . . getting . . . worse," she cried, getting up from the bench.

Abruptly a flash of lightning cut through the stained-glass windows, illuminating the dead form that lay at her feet. She moved further from the slaughtered mess, for its sickening smell was choking her.

"It'll pass," said Father Matt. "If it stopped before, it—"

"No . . . it's different," she heaved. "It feels like there's . . . something stuck."

She kneaded her hand into her breastbone to dislodge the knot, when she felt the strange wetness on her palm. Pulling it out before her, she was startled to find the red stains on her hands and chest. It was the blood of the rat and for a brief hellish second, she was certain it was sinking into her skin. She gaped at the stains in horror, when a hideous voice inside of her whispered, *It's crawling inside of you.* Jolting backward, she looked to the mangled form—to the dead lump that lay upon the marble only a few feet away. Though the rat's head had been smashed, the rodent still possessed a form—a hideous, unspeakable shape that for a second seemed to be breathing in sync with the shadows behind it. "No," she moaned, rubbing the blood from her throat. *No*—it was insanity! Yet the lump inside grew sharper with each breath.

"What is it?" asked Father Matt.

The palm of her hand kneaded harder against her breastbone, but it brought no relief. "There's something . . . inside of me," she said, her voice rising with terror. "There's something . . . stabbing me."

Father Matt slowly edged toward her.

"They've done something to me!"

"Who's done something?"

She tried to answer but the pain was becoming unbearable.

"Just calm down," he said reaching his hand out to her. "You're just excited—like before."

"No!" she suddenly screamed, retreating away from him. "It's not . . . the same!" Gripping her chest, she pivoted back to the dead rat. It wasn't possible. It couldn't be possible, yet the hideous sensation jabbed inside of her. She had been prepared for a knife, for the deadly blow of a blast, never for the demons to attack from within, to crawl beneath her skin where the outside world could not see. "They're going to . . . kill me!"

"Who's going to?" pleaded the priest.

"They've put something . . . inside of me!" she gasped. She pushed her hand deeper between her breasts until the pale skin above her tank top had turned bright red. She had been right all along—it was the night. It was the night they would take her! "You've got to . . . help me," she begged, clutching the Father's wrist. "They've put something . . . under my ribs!"

Though the priest had not thought it possible, her eyes had grown even more feral. Tiny beads of sweat streamed down the side of her face and her lips were turning blue.

A coldness moved through his belly: he could not handle this on his own. "I'm going for help," he said steadily, but the words did not reach her. Her attention remained riveted on the shadows as if she expected at any moment to be sucked into them.

He edged toward the door, then with one last look, he abandoned her within the murky church.

WITH everything he had, the priest sprinted toward his car on the street. Yanking open the driver's door, he grasped the phone and hit 911. He gave the operator the information, the address, instructions for the rear entrance . . . "The front door is chained with renovations," he heaved, "so they have to go to the rear of the church behind the hedge."

"If the entrance is easily missed, you'll have to wait for them, sir," instructed the operator.

"I have to get back . . . I have to—"

"Just stay calm, sir, and wait. Our unit will be there shortly."

With adrenaline rushing against his eardrums, he listened for the ambulance. Shuffling anxiously beneath the street lamp, he looked to the cathedral behind him with its black windows; there had been no sound from within. Caught between the impulse to return to Amelia and the operator's instructions, he forced himself to remain steady. Just as he was about to hit redial, he heard the whine of the siren. Within seconds, the flashing lights swirled around the wet street and stopped at the curb.

Even before the feet of the medics hit the ground, Father Matt had already begun running back to the darkened entry. "Over here!" he called, waving his arms. "This way!"

He burst through the heavy door and slid around the front of the altar. Though Amelia was nowhere in sight, the sound of her strained breathing pulled him toward her. She lay crouched against a wall, her frantic gaze fixed forward.

"I'm here," he said, touching her burning skin. "It's okay."

In the short time he was gone, her condition had turned drastically worse. Beneath the smeared mascara, her eyes had swollen to mere slits of misery, while every inch of her body seemed to be grasping for breath. She remained frozen in the same spot, so lost within her struggle that she seemed oblivious to his presence.

"You're gonna be fine," he said. "The paramedics are here."

"This way!" he called, standing and waving to the medic team. "She's over here!"

OUT OF the darkness, the hushed tone of Father Matt's voice drifted toward her, prickling against her hot skin. ". . . She's been very distraught . . . very paranoid lately. Her husband's away and—"

"Ma'am?" said a female voice sharply. "Ma'am? Can you tell us your name, please."

The intense brown eyes were searching out her own, demanding an answer.

"A . . . melia," she struggled, trying to see past the pain to the paramedic's face.

"Okay, Amelia, we need you to calm down. You're very excited and we need to get your vitals. Will you let us do that?"

At once, the silhouettes descended upon her, poking and prodding at her. She was startled to find herself on the stretcher, for the last that she remembered was crouching within the darkness. Her head was pulled forward with an oxygen mask strapped to her mouth yet it brought no relief; it only added to the blind terror that gripped her.

As her eyes locked on the black chandelier, a flash of light burst into her left eye, and then into her right.

"Pupils are reactive . . ."

There was a tug at her tank top then a high-pitched beep melded with the frantic rhythm of her heart.

"Amelia," said the female voice snapping her attention back to the brown eyes. "Father Matt tells us that you've had these attacks before?"

She tried to shake her head, to tell them that it was different, but the darkness hovered over her pressing her into the cool stretcher. "The pain," she managed to say, her breath cracking across her dry tongue.

"It's nothing to worry about," said the paramedic. "It's common with these sort of attacks. We just need you to relax. Your anxiety will only intensify it."

"Please," she whispered. They didn't understand. She was going to suffocate if they didn't remove the wedge that had been embedded in her chest.

The detached gaze of a male EMT stared down at her, inspecting
her as though she were a specimen beneath a glass. "This is Med-Star
7. We have a 34 year old female with a prior history of panic attacks.
Patient presented with acute shortness of breath, diferetic with pre-
cordial . . ."

"Please," she implored. "It's—"

"Just breathe through the oxygen," said the paramedic.

She stared in horror as they continued calmly around her, dismissing her pleas as the mere rantings of a lunatic. She tried to sit up, to
pull away from the stretcher but the EMT tightened a strap around
her.

"Vital signs: b.p. 100 over 80. Pulse 130 . . . respiration at 32 . . ."

Through the flashing lights and moving bodies, Father Matt's hand
slipped into her own. "You're gonna be fine," he said, but she knew
that he was wrong. She was going to die. While those around her
moved in oblivion, the vise on her chest was tightening. It was only a
matter of minutes before the darkness would claim her, before she
would be dragged into the heinous pits. As the wave of black terror
moved through her she sought the comfort of the priest's eyes.
"Help . . . me," she begged, her feverish mind struggling to remain
focused. She needed to tell him, to confess, for there would be no time
for requital. "I have to . . . confess!"

In spite of the hollow smile that was fixed on the priest's face, his
expression grew darker. "There's no need for that now," he said.
"You're gonna be fine."

"No . . . I need to . . ." *tell you about the baby.* But she had not said
the last of it aloud. She tried again to speak, to find the thoughts, but
they had begun to jumble.

The sounds and the voices became whispers as everything around
her slowed and became more pronounced. The stretcher was suddenly moving, past the altar and through the rear entrance. The backside of the cathedral rose behind her with flashing red lights cutting
across its edifice. The wheels of the gurney squeaked round and
round, vibrating into the passageway and then silencing across the
grass. As a soft rain drifted down from the black sky and trickled
across her hot skin, she thought of her mother and father, of Dix so far
away. What she wouldn't give to have him beside her, to hold her hand
and tell her the darkness could not take her. She thought of Kylie and

the emotion burst through her frenzied breath. "Kylie," she whispered. Perhaps like the rest of them, she was already dead.

With a gray smear, the inside of the ambulance blurred across her vision, the EKG reverberating within the tight space. The female paramedic moved in beside her with a radio in hand.

"This is Med-Star 7. We're settling the patient in preparation for transit . . ."

The voice, along with Amelia's own thoughts and senses, melded with the beeping of the monitor. A dark wave moved toward her, bringing the last tremor of fear. She was nearing the end, she knew. When the final blow came, there was no breath, no light, no reprieve. Like a current of electricity the pain ripped through her chest, through her arms and into her back.

In the paralyzing moment, she saw the shadow move across the face hovering over her.

"What's going on?" came a confused voice from the front of the ambulance. "Are we ready to go?!"

"No!" cried the paramedic. "I need you back here!"

As the beeping noises grew abruptly sporadic, the driver's face joined the woman.

"Check the leads! Maybe they're loose!"

They were suddenly fumbling with the wires, their confusion and panic mounting. "What the hell is it?!"

They couldn't see the relentless hold bearing down on her heart and lungs, squeezing the very life from her body.

"Her blood pressure's dropping!"

"Amelia? Amelia can you hear me?!"

As the voices grew tighter and tighter, she suddenly felt their thoughts, their confusion and fear. The bodies were moving, their breath warm on her face. Their words jumbled into one collective conscious that beckoned and petitioned, yet she had abandoned the fight. Through the shifting shadows and the pain, she abruptly felt the release. At once she was apart, away from the agony and the frantic voices. The dark leaves of the trees fluttered around her as the white top of the parked ambulance glowed beneath her. Father Matt stood at the open doors, his shoes sinking into the mud beneath him. With the faint, distant sound of the cardiovert, he began edging from the door. She saw the pain on his face and she felt pity. He was watching her death, watching her body jolt with the electricity. She wanted to tell him that it was alright, that she felt nothing but warmth but she knew that he would not hear her.

When the familiar hand came, she did not question it—she did not remember the fear or the deceit. She knew only that it was her grandfather's and that he had come to take her away.

"WE'VE got a flatline!"

For a stunned moment Father Matt stared at the thin green line that stretched across the screen. It wasn't real, it couldn't possibly be happening. One minute she was breathing and the next her heart had stopped. His own heart was pounding crazily and his mouth was dry. He needed to do something, to help, but he was so stunned by the turn of events that he remained paralyzed. He reached to the pocket of his sport jacket . . . he was a priest . . . he had refused her the rite of penance and now she was dying. He looked helplessly to his car that was a mere shadow within the rain; there was no time to retrieve the kit with the holy oil and his prayer book. He would have to make do without it. He tried to find the prayer, but his mind had gone blank, filled to the brink with the violent screech.

"I'm going to intubate!" called the paramedic, reaching behind her to grab a Laryngoscope. She put the lighted blade into the slack mouth, then threaded a tube down the opening. As a trickle of blood oozed down the side of the pale face, Father Matt's legs weakened. A dull roar pressed down upon him, when he suddenly realized that the gentle rain had turned once again to a downpour.

"Father!"

Within the sharp light of the ambulance, the EMT was staring expectantly out at him.

"Get in, if you're coming with us!"

In the next moment he was inside the ambulance. The EMT had shut the doors behind him and the ambulance had finally begun to move. Suddenly trapped within the chaos, the smell of blood, of medicine and of sweat was overpowering. The eyes. He could not look at the eyes. It was Amelia—Amelia Blackwell. But with her breasts crudely exposed from the cardiovert and her neck turning blue, she resembled more a cadaver, a freakish mannequin incapable of embodying life. Like some twisted child of Frankenstein, wires ran from her chest and her arms giving the nebulous hope of life. Liquids dripped into her veins while the paramedic pumped rhythmically on her breastbone.

Looking away, the priest rubbed his hand across his dry lips. The prayer, he needed to return to the prayer. "May God . . . May God open . . ." he grasped for the verse, for the point in which he had ceased, but another voice inside of him was stronger—*She's dead.* The woman before him was dead. Though he could no longer see her face, her hand had fallen to the side, blue and lifeless. As the sound of the siren screeched behind his temples, the priest stared at the limp fingers that moved gently with the ride. "I absolve you in the name of the Father, and of the Son and of the Holy Ghost," he said quietly. "'Yea, though I walk through the valley of the shadow of death . . .'"

As the priest prayed, the ambulance swayed from one corner to the next, all the while the paramedic fighting a battle which had already been lost. Father Matt was not certain how much time had passed when he finally touched the arm of the medic.

"Please," he said gently.

Though she did not look up, the paramedic hesitated. Winded and sweating, she stared down at the still body. She pushed the handle of her radio, the exhausted sound of defeat replacing the frenzy in her voice. "This is Med-Star 7 in transit with 34-year-old female. Current ETA 5 minutes. Unsuccessful in resuscitation efforts. Request orders to cease and desist."

After a long tenuous moment the answer crackled over the radio. "I concur with assessment and request. Discontinue effort."

As the paramedic rested back, away from the body, Father Matt saw the empty eyes that stared upward. Tears filled his own as his stomach turned in upon itself. Remorse and self-loathing seeped into his veins; he had failed her. She had cried out to him but he had not heeded her pleas. He had turned his back on her confession, forcing her to cross over with a burdened heart.

"Father?"

He looked up, startled to find that the paramedic had been speaking to him. "Yes . . . I'm sorry. What did you say?"

"Was she one of your parishioners?"

"Yes," he said, the answer choking within his throat.

"I'm sorry," said the paramedic.

There was a moment of silence as the ambulance rocked and swayed.

"I thought it was just panic," the priest said helplessly. "I thought she was just imagining something."

He looked to the paramedic, who clearly shared his bewilderment.

"I wish I could tell you what just happened here," she said, wearily shaking her head. "But I can't."

As the priest's eyes returned to the still face, there was a tightening in his throat. They had been beside her all along, but had somehow missed the true battle. The echoing of the young woman's terror made the sting in his gut grow sharper; she had been forced to face it alone.

He touched his hand to her warm forehead, then closed her eyes, putting an end to the hideous stare. Within the seconds that followed, the face before them softened. The fear and anguish washed from the hollowed cheeks, leaving behind a beautiful still girl who appeared no more than sixteen.

"Go in peace, child," said the priest softly.

Thirty-Six

"THIS ONE'S FOR ALL YOU FOLKS OUT THERE IN THE LOW COUNTRY tonight looking forward to a little drying out. Put away those buckets and umbrellas cause the sun's on its way and it's gonna be a scorcher."

Kylie straightened her stiff back, as the song, *"I Can See Clearly Now,"* floated from the sedan's speakers. The upbeat voice of Johnny Nash made the black night that hung suspended within her headlights appear even emptier.

Highway 204 stretched before her like a long black snake slithering through the wooded pines and cypress swamps, past overgrown cotton fields and abandoned plantations. There were no cars ahead of her nor behind. The storm had passed, leaving a moonlit night.

Forced to drop down to the two-lane highway when an overturned rig spilled oil all over the Interstate, she would be entering Savannah from the southwest, the highway taking her within a couple of miles of her old home near the Skidaway River.

With each passing mile, she felt the sickening pull on her heart intensify, for there was no denying the road beneath her, nor the place for which it led. Like entering into an old dream, where memories had since faded to the mere shimmer of illusion, she would no longer be afforded the reprieve from the bittersweet pain which time and distance had given her.

It had been years since she had last visited Savannah, and even then it had been for a mere two days. She had flown in for Amelia's wedding, staying not a moment longer than was necessary. And while Savannah was most certainly the loveliest, most splendid place in her thoughts, the loss of her mother and Tucker had tainted the South forever.

As much as the lobster-rich, snow-covered sea of Boston belonged to her father, the balmy marsh and fragrant rivers of Savannah were her mother's. Southern Georgia did not exist without Lila Gascoyne McCallum; it was simply unbearable to imagine. Savannah belonged to her and to her alone, for it was the earth from which she was made. Born to impoverished parents of French descent, she was raised alongside two brothers in the swamps outside of Savannah. They worked in the cotton fields of others, while planting rice crops of their own on the twenty acres they had managed to purchase over the years. Kylie had been raised on that same land, surrounded by the love of the Gascoyne family. But soon after Lila's death, the family dissipated. Kylie's grandparents succumbed to old age, while her two uncles sold their share of the land and found homes elsewhere: one on Sapelo Island where he ran a shrimp trawler; the other in Macon, Georgia where he married a woman and took a job in a textiles factory. The remaining acreage, along with the house in which Kylie was raised, was abandoned and had remained so ever since. Neither she nor her father had ever considered otherwise. To live there was unthinkable, to sell it—inconceivable.

To Kylie, Savannah was a graveyard. A fragrant garden whose swamp honeysuckles, wild azalea and wisteria had become too sweet.

A garden whose warm breeze carried a shiver and whose rich soil stung her feet. Were it not for Amelia, she would never return.

Now, the very route that carried the most painful memory of all—that of her mother and Tucker's death—was her very egress into the past. She had been on her way home from New York the night she saw the flashing lights on the highway and the smashed old Ford beneath the grid of the semi-truck. In her subsequent visits, she avoided Highway 204 at great pains, but the detour sign stretched across the interstate had made that impossible.

As she passed over the Ogeechee River, only two miles from the fateful site, she was startled to see that she was going eighty-five. Not only was she anxious to reach her friend, but perhaps to slip as quickly and quietly as possible down the highway. In spite of the churning sense of urgency, she let off the gas, for the last thing she needed was to be pulled over with a suspended license. As the red line of the speedometer edged downward, she glanced to the glowing numbers of the dashboard clock. It was 1:40 A.M.

With the falling speed, her stomach sank. *You'll get there.* While the voice of hope told her that Amelia would be asleep, she knew in her heart that she wouldn't. She would be waiting. Waiting in terror.

After the red needle had fallen well below the speed limit, she returned her foot to the gas. It was then that she saw the two small figures skipping across the highway ahead of her. Barely visible within the shadowy night, one sank down onto the side of the road, while the other froze within her approaching headlights. In the split second before Kylie could react, the small face was lit with the bright beams, her round face filled not with terror, but curiosity. Kylie's foot smashed onto the brake while her entire body cranked the wheel to the side. The heat, the dark swamp and the glistening highway spun into one solid smear. The car swirled wildly, for under the slick pavement the wheels could not find a grip. With the turning force slamming her up against the driver's door, Kylie braced herself for the certain crushing of the roof, for the grinding of metal around her, but the vehicle did not flip. At last it caught onto the graveled shoulder and spun out into the ditch where it came to rest within the tangled underbrush facing into the dense cypress.

For a long breathless moment she remained still, her hands gripping the wheel. She could not move—she dare not, for fear of what lay on the highway behind her. Over the abrupt stillness, the silky words of the deejay came over the airwave... "That was Johnny Nash, folks, bringing the promise of brighter days. Put away those blues, cause the old man sun—"

Open the door, her mind whispered. She had to get out of the car. The child could lay mangled, in need of help. With a shudder she thought of a small deer she had once hit. It had spread into pieces, part of it caught beneath the hood of the still purring engine.

"... comin' at ya' now with B.B King's *Days of Old* and that..."

With a turn of the keys the radio silenced, replaced with the sound of the bayou. "Move," she whispered. She had to see. When she touched the cool latch, the door swung effortlessly open with the slant of the car, the grass moist on her exposed ankles. She held her breath and turned back to the darkened highway. The pavement glistened in the distance, but there was no sign of the child, no lifeless figure laying on the silvery road. The emptiness made her heart pound even heavier. She looked to the hood of the car, to the wet tires, then bent slowly to the ground to look under. *Nothing*. The engine felt hot but the axle was clean.

The child had been still, had not moved with the approaching headlights—surely the sedan had hit her. But there had been no impact, no sound of a thump. If she had struck the child, surely she would have heard something. When she had hit the deer the noise had pounded against the car so loudly that it was deafening.

At the front of the car she found no dent, only scratches from the underbrush. A palmetto leaf hung limply from the grill.

Again she turned to the empty highway and began moving in the direction of the children, her sandals crunching over the grit of the wet pavement. "Hello?" she called. "Is anybody there?" There was no response. She stopped at the spot in which she was certain the child had been and looked into the bushes on both sides of the highway. "Hello?" Nothing. Only the cadenced shriek of the bayou—a familiar sound, so much a part of a time long forgotten. As she stood in the center of the highway, trembling with relief, her breath caught with the familiar feel of the moment. Much like that night, there was a stillness to the air, the trees were covered in the satiny sheen of the newly fallen rain. For a second, the maroon sedan that lay silent in the ditch, became the smashed remains of her mother's old Ford, while the smell of burnt rubber became the scent of her loved one's death.

The words, *Welcome home*, whispered through the thick air. She quickly began to move, to bring her thoughts back to the present.

With little maneuvering, she was able to get the car out of the ditch. Gripping the wheel with both hands she breathed a sigh of thanks. As the moon peeked from beneath the dwindling clouds, glossing the pavement ahead of her into a shimmer, she slowly began to gain speed once again.

Thirty-Seven

WITHIN THE SILENT CHURCH, FATHER MATT COULD NOT TAKE HIS EYES off the bloodied lump that lay beneath the old rag. He could not bring himself to simply scoop the rodent up and throw it away. For more than an hour, all he could do was sit on the pew and stare down at it.

The hospital had been a nightmare. Mamie Blackwell had been distraught, so pained that for a moment the nurses feared she would slip into shock. And while Mamie lamented her grief, Amelia's father, Leonard Blackwell, stood silently by, his face so empty that it tugged more fiercely at one's emotion than if he had burst into tears. "Tell me why, just tell me WHY?!" Mamie had insisted. But the doctors did not have the answers. Father Matt did not have the answers. He couldn't even find the proper words to comfort the distraught parents. Amelia Blackwell was dead, and as of yet, there was no explanation. No explanation, that is, except for the one that she herself had given moments before her heart stopped. A shiver moved up the priest's spine, yet he refused to look away from the blood-stained rag. The notion that some unseen force had shoved something beneath her ribs questioned the very boundaries of reason, yet it was the only account that had been put forth. Something had caused the death. Young women did not die simply because they feared that they would. Young women did not predict their own deaths with the accuracy of predicting the rise and fall of the sun. But Amelia had and there was no denying it.

Abruptly he remembered the look of terror in her eyes. *She's not just wrestling with her mortality, Father. She thinks that God's going to send someone to kill her.* They were the words of her husband, spoken just the day before.

Father Matt shook his head, weakened beneath the burdening thoughts. To even consider such ideas was surely sacrilege, perhaps even madness; yet there was no denying that whatever had taken the young woman, had done so swiftly and ruthlessly, and she alone had seen it coming.

For a long while, the priest remained on the pew, silently waiting until he had the energy, the strength to get up. When he heard the door beyond the altar open and close, his shoulders tightened. With a start, the priest realized that—for the first time ever—he was frightened to be in his own church. His throat constricted as the soft footsteps came toward the nave, then one of the most beautiful women he had ever seen emerged from the darkness. At first he was too numbed to recognize the auburn hair that curled wildly, or the vibrant green eyes that stared toward him. But when she spoke, the smoothness of her voice awoke him and he knew. It was Kylie O'Rourke and she had come for her friend.

THE MOMENT Kylie saw the priest's blood-shot eyes, she wanted to turn the other way and leave. Clearly he was there for a reason, one that she dare not surmise. He looked tired and worn, his jacket crumpled as if he had been wearing it for days.

"I'm sorry, I didn't mean to interrupt," she said, gesturing toward the altar.

"That's alright," said the priest, standing slowly to his feet.

"Father Matthew—isn't it?" She recognized the friendly face and unassuming manner from Amelia's wedding. He was a tall athletic man, whose good looks defied his profession.

The priest ran his fingers through his hair and moved toward her. "Yes, yes. And you're Kylie."

She took his extended hand. "I knocked on the rectory but there was no answer," she said. "I guess Amelia must be asleep, I know she was tired and . . ." Her voice trailed off as she studied his face.

There had been trouble, she could tell. He was looking away from her, avoiding her eyes. Perhaps Amelia had confided in him, recruiting him to stand watch, to guard against her terror. "What is it?" she asked.

The priest drew in a breath as if to muster his courage. "There was a problem," he started slowly. "When I found Amelia here in the church, she was having trouble breathing. She complained that . . . she said that something was crushing inside of her . . ."

"Where is she?" asked Kylie. "Is she asleep?" She began moving toward the door.

"No."

When she turned back, the priest was gripping the pew. "I'm sorry to tell you this, but—" and though he wavered in mid-sentence, she knew it was grave. The conciliatory tone of his voice said it all.

She took a step back, for she could not bear to hear the rest. She became suddenly aware of the church around her, of the scaffolding and the tools, of the sandpaper and the paint. It was Amelia's place. *Amelia's.* She could feel her in the room perhaps only a moment earlier, sanding and painting. "Where is she?" she repeated, the fear inside of her building.

"I'm sorry but . . . the paramedics couldn't save her," he managed to finish.

A slow drip fell from above, plopping hideously into a bucket. She played the sentence back in her mind, for surely she had misheard. "You mean she's dead?" she asked faintly.

"I'm sorry," he said gently.

A pounding, a screaming started from deep inside of her, yet her lips remained still. She turned to the shadows as the fleeting lines of the highway flashed through her mind. The deafening sound of the bayou screeched behind her temples when the voice of the priest cut into her thoughts.

"She's at the coroner's office now. They're doing an autopsy to determine the cause of death."

Cause of death. The words sounded so strange, so ridiculously out of place, just misplaced syllables that had somehow slipped between them.

But the priest was still gripping the pew as if to steady himself. "I thought it was a panic attack," he continued, sounding strangely confused. "When I found her, she was beside herself . . ."

At once an image—dark and heinous—eclipsed her thoughts: *they found their way to her.*

Kylie turned to escape, when the wall of anger began low, from somewhere deep within. Like the rumbling of a train, it trembled up her legs and into her stomach. As she bit back the vehemence that stung into her throat, the screaming within turned to a long wailing moan. They had found their way to her. Just as Amelia had predicted, they had taken her that night. At once her friend was crouched before her trembling in terror. Her friend's final hours had been spent in terror. She turned to the side but there was nowhere to go. *I was on my way. I was on my way.* With a shudder she felt the power of the walls around her. The walls that would not allow it, had not allowed it. They could have waited, they could have given her time to make the journey. It was a joke. A hideous joke. "A sick joke," she said aloud. She was speaking, turning. "I was on my way. I was on my WAY!!" she suddenly screamed. The priest was moving toward her, but she backed away. "She was alone! Alone, damn it!!" The fury, the tears were streaking down her face, choking her. Smothering her. She was backing to the door. Running, running, when the arms were suddenly around her. The grip was firm, pulling her back, holding her within.

When her tears finally subsided, there was nothing left inside. No more grief, no more anguish, only an icy dullness remained. She was sitting on the pew, the priest standing against a nearby pillar. He was watching her, his face pinched in deep thought.

"Will you be staying for the funeral?" he asked, breaking the long silence.

"I'm not sure," she said, staring numbly at the altar railing. She noticed a small piece of sandpaper that had fallen beneath the wood. The job had meant everything to Amelia and now someone else would finish it.

"I'm sorry for your pain," said the priest. "I know that you've also just lost your husband."

"Thank you."

"If I may speak candidly—I know that your grief is still fresh, but I fear I won't have another chance to talk to you."

Kylie pulled her eyes from the sandpaper to the shadowy face of the priest. He was clearly reluctant, wishing to say something that he feared would upset her. "What is it?" she asked.

"Dix mentioned that you had some ... some spiritual concerns when your husband first died."

Kylie's face instantly reddened. "What do you mean?" she asked.

"That you thought maybe the plane accident had something to do with your husband's death. That maybe God wanted you and some of the other survivors dead."

"I'm sorry, Father, but I have no way of knowing what God wants." The bitterness in her voice was startling.

"I understand. I also understand that these concerns were expressed during profound grief. I just hate for Amelia's passing to cause these same sort of fears to resurface. While, granted, it's unusual that two survivors from the same crash have perished in such a short time—"

Three her mind whispered, but she did not voice the number.

"I hate for you to ... to be frightened by a pattern that doesn't exist." He took a few steps and ran his hand fretfully through his hair. "If I've learned anything as a priest, I've learned one thing for certain. Death has no set limits or patterns. It comes when we least expect, and when we're least prepared. I don't know the reason behind Amelia's passing. In one moment she was breathing and in the next ..." He shook his head. He remained silent a moment, clearly having thoughts he would not share. "I'm sure that the coroner will have a logical explanation," he said wearily.

Kylie was struck by the reservation in his words. "I'm sure that he will," she said. "I have no doubt that he will. Now if you'll excuse me," she said, standing to her feet. "I could use some fresh air."

Thirty-Eight

DILLON HAD BREWED THE COFFEE AS STRONG AS HE COULD MAKE IT, YET it still left him groggy. The caffeine could not combat the sleepless nights, nor the thick cloud that had muddled his thoughts since Jack's death. He was staring numbly down at the dark liquid, when Theresa walked into the kitchen with the cordless phone in hand. A tightness had taken hold of her features. "It's Kylie," she said quietly. When Dillon took the phone, Theresa turned away to the counter. For a confused moment he looked to the clock. It was 5:06 A.M.

"I didn't wake you did I?" The voice was soft, empty.

"No, of course not," he answered. "You know we doctors never sleep."

"I didn't even think about Theresa being there. I'm sorry. Please tell her that I'm sorry."

"That's okay," he answered, avoiding the questioning eyes that had turned toward him. "We have a surgery at seven." Theresa moved across to the refrigerator, and though she was facing away again, he saw that her movements were terse. She grabbed the orange juice but then returned it to the shelf. Then picked it up once again.

"You don't normally call this early. Is everything okay?" he asked, the coffee beginning to sour in his stomach.

"I just wanted to hear your voice."

"Where are you? It sounds like you're outside."

After a long moment there was a heavy sigh. "Dillon, I'm sorry. I don't know why I called."

He quickly sat forward. "Don't hang up." He could hear the moment of uncertainty on the other end. "Where are you?" he repeated.

"I'm in Savannah," she said.

A cold silence drifted through the line. "Kylie?" He could hear that she was crying.

"I didn't know who else to call. You and Daddy are all I have left."

"What's happened?" he asked.

As she proceeded to tell him of Amelia's death, his mind suddenly felt more tired and heavy. Though it was a new day, it seemed as if it might be midnight, the sky through the kitchen window still as black as coal. Amelia Blackwell was dead. He had not known her well, but through Kylie, he too had come to regard her as a friend.

"I'm coming down there," he said. "I'll get a colleague of mine to do the surgery."

His eyes caught Theresa's as she looked up from the stove.

"No," said the voice on the other end. "I'm fine, Dillon. Please don't come. I just needed to hear your voice. I just needed someone to talk to. I've been walking, trying to get out of my head, but just the

idea of Amelia at the coroner's office—" She tried to finish but the
tears choked her words back.

"Don't think about that. Don't—"

"They didn't need to cut her open," she gently sobbed. "She
wouldn't have wanted that."

Dillon felt at a loss for words. He knew that the autopsy was necessary—if nothing else to clear the paramedics of wrongdoing. "It's
mandatory in cases of unexplained death," he said weakly. "They need
to know what happened."

"You mean what they think happened," she said bitterly. "Dissect-
ing her won't give them the truth."

"What do you mean?"

"Nothing, Dill," she said, the emptiness returning to her voice.
"Nothing. I'm just tired. So damned tired."

"Wylie," he said tenderly. "Are you sure you don't want me to come
down?"

"Positive. I'll be back in a couple of days."

When Dillon hung up the phone, he felt the weariness of the call
settling over him. His insides ached. With resentment, he thought of
fate, of the heinous hand that Kylie had been dealt. Not only had she
lost Jack, but now her best friend as well. After a long while, he looked
up, startled to find that Theresa was still in the kitchen. She was leaning against the counter staring at him, her eyes cold and ungiving.

Anger suddenly shot through him.

"What, for Chrissake?" he snapped. He took a long drink from his
coffee, forcing his voice to calm. "What do you want me to say?" he
asked quietly. "We've been friends for ten years. She was my brother's
wife. Am I supposed to just forget that I ever knew her?" He had
turned the question back to her, but her face remained blank. As he
stared into the jealous, resentful eyes, he suddenly felt depleted, more
exhausted than he could ever remember being. His gaze went to the
window, where a purplish light began to break over the backyard.

"I can't even begin to compete with this," she finally responded. "I
thought that I could, but there's just no way."

"That's just it," he said gently. "You don't have to."

"Please," she said, tears suddenly trickling across her olive skin.
"Ever since the accident I've known. From the moment they first

wheeled her in . . . from the moment those doors swung open and you came through with her, I knew. I'm not trying to hurt you. I know that you're still grieving over Jack, but it's not just his death that you're dealing with. You're in love, Dillon. And it's not me you're in love with."

"You're wrong," he said, bitterness stinging his throat. He turned away as the emotion flooded into his eyes. "We were friends. We . . . the three of us ... we were best friends. You know that I ... You know how I feel about—" he was moving toward her but she quickly retreated.

"Please," she said, holding her hand up to silence him. "Don't even say it. Stick to the deal, okay? You made it clear from the beginning. You're not in love with me and you never will be. I'm thirty-eight years old. I don't have the luxury of waiting around anymore, hoping that'll change."

He stared into the violet eyes, wanting with all of his might for the right words to pass over his lips, yet something inside, some gnawing unidentified pit, kept him silent. He suddenly felt like a fake, a deceitful bastard incapable of conducting a conversation let alone a relationship.

Theresa turned for the door. "I'll move my stuff out tonight. After my shift."

Dillon took a step forward, but she was already gone.

Thirty-Nine

At the far end of the shady lawn, Kylie paused to collect herself. She pulled her hair back within a barrette and smoothed her wrinkled pants to try and make herself more presentable. Her clothes were damp and her feet blistered. She had been walking all night, through the darkened wet streets of the historic district, past the old homes and warehouses, and along the commercial riverfront. She had waited until the sun had fully risen before driving to the Blackwell home.

It had been years since she had last seen Mamie and Leonard Blackwell; to meet again under such conditions filled her with apprehension. She wasn't quite ready to face the grief that surely awaited beyond the black door, so for a few minutes she lingered beneath the ancient oaks, taking in the place where so much of her childhood had been spent.

The Blackwell estate had graced the west bank of the Skidaway River for over one hundred and fifty years. It was a beautiful, old home—a white two-story mansion with black trim and a bi-level porch that stretched the entire perimeter of the house. Old money had built it, and old money had kept it alive. Though Leonard Blackwell had descended from a long line of attorneys it was his father's great-grandmother that had mounted the Blackwell fortune through the planting and exportation of cotton. In order to protect the plantation when the Civil War erupted, she had taken in Yankee officers with the condition that the house not be burned. And in the Reconstruction that followed, while those around her lost their fortunes, her empire remained intact. Unlike her neighbors, who awoke one day to discover their Confederate currency worthless, she had the foresight to invest in U.S. Federal Bonds. Over the ensuing generations, the land was subdivided but the house remained the same; even the black and white colonial-style paint survived.

The vast lawns with plush green grass and giant trees were a child's dream, a fantasy playground much different from the home that Kylie herself was raised in only a couple of miles west in the bayou. The first time she ever laid eyes on Amelia hadn't been at St. Mary's where they had attended elementary, but from the woods that stretched beyond the estate. Kylie had stood at the edge of the property and spied on the shy little girl who lived in the beautiful house. Little had she known that same child would become the dearest friend she would ever know, and that she would return one day to mourn her loss.

BY THE TIME Kylie summoned the courage to ring the bell, her hands were trembling. With herself so unsteady, she feared she would not be much comfort to the parents.

When Mamie Blackwell pulled back the huge door, Kylie was stunned by how much the mother had aged. While Amelia's parents had always been older than her own, it was the first time that Kylie had ever considered one of them elderly. Mamie's upswept hair had turned silver and her once thin figure had expanded, yet age had not softened her tight lips or scrutinizing gaze.

"Hello, dear," she said, taking Kylie's hands into her own. "We've been expecting you. Father Matt said that you left the church some time last night. Where in heavens have you been?"

"I was walking," she answered softly, kissing the mother's cold cheek.

"Oh for heaven's sake," said Mamie, shaking her head with disapproval.

From the entry hall, Kylie was embarrassed to see that Father Matt was sitting within the parlor. Clearly he would see that she hadn't slept or showered since she had last left him. Self-consciously brushing a stray hair from her face she followed the mother. As they moved toward the expansive room, the muffled sound of an ensuing conversation drifted toward them.

Kylie recognized the man speaking as Doctor Maurice Sauvage, a renowned cardiologist who was a longtime friend of the Blackwell family. Sitting across from him on the divan was Amelia's father. She was saddened to see that he had grown thin and stooped, and that a vacancy had settled in his eyes.

When the women entered, the three men rose formally.

"Hello Kylie," said Mr. Blackwell. "Father Matt told us you were in town."

As she kissed him on the cheek, she could smell Scotch on his breath.

"You remember Dr. Sauvage—"

Kylie took the hands that were offered and then quietly found a place on the sofa. As if the years had never passed, she felt like a child before her elders. Only Father Matt, whose gaze had settled on her, seemed an equal, his sunken eyes mirroring her own fatigue. "We were just discussing the coroner's report," he explained hollowly.

A knot leapt into Kylie's throat. Throughout the night's long walk she had been anticipating this moment, anxious for the explanation that would be proffered. The particulars surrounding her friend's death were vague. All that Father Matt had told her, was that Amelia was having trouble breathing. But the report would have to say more. Perhaps there would even be evidence of foul play, with another

"Clyde Tremblay" to shoulder the blame. "What did it say?" she asked faintly.

Dr. Sauvage turned his attention toward her. "They found a massive blood clot blocking the main artery to her lungs. Your friend died of a pulmonary embolism."

"A blood clot?" she repeated, for it could not be that simple.

"I'm afraid so," said the doctor.

Kylie stared into the crinkled face, trying to digest what he was saying. There had been no fires or bullets or strange twisted accidents to eliminate her friend; she had died of natural causes. "Where did the clot come from?" she asked, trying to keep her voice from trembling.

"During her bed rest following the plane accident, a deep vein thrombosis—or blood clot," the doctor clarified, "formed in her thigh. Last night, her heart carried the clot to her lungs, where it cut off the blood supply and oxygen."

Kylie felt numbed, her mind rendered blank by the directness of the information. She had expected evidence of choking or smothering, traces of arsenic or asphyxiation, never had she anticipated the enemy to come from within.

"Doctor Warner assured me she was in good hands," muttered Amelia's father. "I insisted that he give her a thorough examination before releasing her. I specifically asked about this danger."

"Leonard, surely you remember the testimony in the McCormick case," said Dr. Sauvage. "Half of the deep clots can't be detected in a physical examination."

"But one of this magnitude," said Mr. Blackwell, ruefully shaking his head.

"It was that accident," interjected Mamie, her eyes dark.

"It's usually those that we least expect," mused Dr. Sauvage. "Those that make a miraculous recovery that die later from complications."

With a shiver, Kylie felt the truth in his words.

"Of course, there were warning signs," admitted the doctor.

All eyes turned toward him.

"The breathless attack that her husband witnessed a few days ago was actually an embolic episode where a shower of smaller emboli—or clots as you will—broke loose and traveled through her bloodstream.

As they passed through the filigree of her lungs they temporarily cut off her oxygen but were not life threatening. Had we known about these attacks sooner, the clot could easily have been identified and treated with an anti-coagulant drug."

"God, if we had only known," groaned Mr. Blackwell. "I wish to hell Dix would have said something to us."

"What about when she visited you?"

The question had been directed toward Kylie, but her thoughts were on the day in the boutique, on Amelia's frenzied eyes as she struggled for breath. "Pardon?"

They were all watching her expectantly.

"When Amelia was in Boston, did you notice anything out of the ordinary?" asked Dr. Sauvage. "Any breathlessness?"

"Yes," she replied softly. She had been certain the attack she witnessed was prompted by fear, but perhaps she had been mistaken. "She had trouble breathing one afternoon and—" She stared down at her hands, for she had been the one who had told Amelia that it was merely panic. Through her own misconceptions, she had advised her friend to ignore the very symptoms that had killed her. The warm sting of tears abruptly trickled down her cheeks. "I'm sorry, I—"

A sun-spotted hand clasped down upon her own. It was Amelia's father. "You couldn't possibly have known," he said.

"The symptoms of a pulmonary embolism are identical to those of an anxiety attack, or even to an asthmatic attack," interjected Dr. Sauvage. "It's commonly overlooked or misdiagnosed. Especially when concerning patients of a more delicate nature."

"If there's anyone to blame, it would be myself," said the priest, his voice low and thin. "I'm the one who told the paramedics it was panic."

"Yes, but they may very well have reached the same conclusion on their own," hedged the old doctor.

"Had they known, could they have saved her?" asked the priest point blank.

"Quite possibly," admitted the doctor. "They could have done an emergency bypass while awaiting a pulmonary embolectomy."

Kylie got up from the couch feeling ill and confused. Her head was pounding and her stomach in knots. Never had she expected this turn of events. They were all to have died from accidents or bizarre twists of foul play. Jack had died of a fire, Dale Benson a gun, yet Amelia's body had simply given way. The outside forces had not tampered with her fate—had not needed to.

"There is one matter that I found puzzling," said Dr. Sauvage, interrupting her thoughts. "There was another type of blood found on the body."

The statement settled over the room like a sheet of ice.

"What kind of blood?" asked Mamie, her face the color of gray wax.

The old doctor looked to the parents as if reluctant to say.

Father Matt took a nervous step forward. "I didn't want to distress you with the details."

"Please," said Mamie, her voice tight. "We've lost our only child. We want to know everything."

The priest began to fidget, adjusting his jacket and then readjusting it. "You must understand. When I arrived at the church Amelia wasn't herself . . . she seemed to be, well, hallucinating things," he said carefully. "The church is prone to rats. Normally that didn't bother her but . . . when I found her she had a board in hand—"

"A board?" said Mamie, her voice rising with indignation. "What did she do? Smash one?" The mother's eyes were full of horror, her lips quivering and wet.

The priest nodded his head. "The blood splattered onto her in the process of . . . of killing it."

Kylie's stomach abruptly churned and flipped as if she were on a topsy turvy ride. She was suddenly facing downward, beneath the bright colored surface of what appeared reality—to the dark grinding engines that moved the illusion. With mention of the rat a completely different picture began to assemble itself before her. Perhaps Amelia's doctor had found no clots for there had been none to find. Perhaps the deadly clump had not been formed by mere bed rest, but by the dark force that had somehow found its way inside of her.

Doctor Sauvage was speaking once again, his words comforting the distraught mother. "Mamie, your daughter wasn't herself, you just have to remember that. Low oxygen to the brain—hypoxemia as it's called—would cause panic or bizarre behavior. It can cause feelings of impending death or even hallucinations."

As Kylie listened to her friend's fears so easily dismissed, she felt twisted within, her own thoughts manipulated and bent. Only a moment earlier even she had been convinced that her friend's panic was medically induced. Without a doubt, the attack she had witnessed had been prompted by fear—she was certain, for she knew from whence the terror came. Perhaps through that very fear, the answer had been found. Amelia had been so convinced that she would die soon, that a pulmonary embolism was the perfect way out. Not only would it eliminate her, but the hypoxemia would explain her seemingly irrational fear of dying. Amelia was weak and emotional—no one would question why she hadn't been taken for treatment. The paramedic and the attending physicians would not suffer malpractice claims, for the condition was commonly misdiagnosed. And her frantic words would not linger in the minds of her loved ones, for they would be logically dismissed.

When she looked back to the room it was through different eyes. A calmness had settled over everyone; the questions had been answered, the emotions placated. Father Matt caught her gaze and held onto it a moment as if to say, "You're going to be fine." Clearly his mind had been set at ease and expected that Kylie's had been as well.

"I'm going to rest," said Mrs. Blackwell, exhaustion dragging her voice to a low. Father Matt had taken her hand and was leading her to the hallway, while Doctor Sauvage spoke to Mr. Blackwell about the funeral.

For a long while, Kylie stood staring at the emptied parlor. It was over. Like a tide, the physical had washed over the spiritual, erasing all discerning prints. They had quietly come and gone and taken her beloved friend with them.

Whether the clot had been there all along or not—the pieces fit. They fit so smoothly and snugly that even she would never know for certain what had happened. And whether she had a hand in her friend's death by advising her to ignore the attacks, or whether she had merely corroborated the history of the attacks, she herself had become part of the web.

She felt the exhaustion of having been sucked in and spun around. Lingering guilt remained alongside whispering fear. Only she had prevailed and it was only a matter of time before the wave would wash over her as well. She wondered what death she would succumb to, if there would be pain and how it would affect those left behind.

"You must stay with us, Kylie."

The voice of Amelia's father brought her from her thoughts. He was standing in the doorway with Clarie Jackson beside him. The plump woman's hair had grayed, but Kylie was warmed to see that the Blackwells still employed the old housemaid.

"Miss Clarie," she said, rushing forward and succumbing to the woman's soft arms.

"There, there, child," said Clarie. "Good heavens, your blouse is damp." She pulled Kylie out to an arm's length and surveyed her clothes. "You need a nice warm bath and some sleep."

Kylie started to protest, but Clarie quickly cut her off.

"The Missus wouldn't have it any other way," she said. "I've already prepared your old room for you. Now, come along. Father Matt can bring up your luggage."

As Kylie obediently followed the brisk-moving woman up the long staircase—she felt once again the sense of fleeting time. Though it had been over two decades since she and Amelia had last scrambled at the heels of the housekeeper, it seemed only yesterday.

When they reached the landing, a nervous flutter tickled through her throat: Amelia's old room lay silent on the left. As Clarie disappeared down the darkened corridor on the right, Kylie paused by the closed door. It creaked softly open with a voice from the past.

Don't fall asleep, okay? Amelia's eight-year-old face was vibrant and clear, her long hair combed perfectly back. *I'll be there in five minutes. I promise.*

As the memory patted away in purple slippers, Kylie felt the same tug of separation she had felt so many years before. Mamie had always insisted that the girls sleep in their respective rooms, but once the lights were out and the parents had adjourned to their section of the house, there was nothing that could keep them apart.

Standing outside the white door, a sudden rush of fear and loneliness came over her; for the first time since she had stood at the edge of the woods, she was without her cherished friend. Once again she would have to face the corridor on the right, only this time, there would be no gentle knock in the middle of the night. The separation would be final.

Forty

FILLED WITH THE SCENT OF LAVENDER SOAP, THE GUEST ROOM WAS JUST as she remembered it. The same old canopy bed rested along the west wall—even the lace curtains and ivory bedclothes were the same. In spite of the cool central-air flowing from the vents, the windows, along with the door that led to the veranda, were open, allowing the warm muggy air to drift in from the bayou.

As Clarie laid out a towel in the adjoining bathroom, Kylie's attention was drawn to the dressing mirror which had been draped with a white cloth.

"Pay no mind to that, honey," said the maid, emerging from the bathroom to turn down the sheets. "Josephine Parker was over here bright and early to instill her will over the rest of us. I couldn't keep up with her, raising all the windows, covering all the mirrors. I tell you, someone should have put that woman in a sanitarium long ago. But you know us folks in the South, got to look out for our feeble minded."

Kylie knew the woman of whom Clarie spoke. The eighty-year-old eccentric was known throughout Savannah as the "Deadkeeper" and there were only two reasons that the babbling woman with the crazed eyes and rotten teeth entered one's home: either a loved one was on the doorstep of death, or they had already passed over. Bearing a cross and reeking of herbs, Josephine Parker performed a set of rituals to insure that the soul of the newly departed would have easy egress from the dwelling and would not come back to haunt it. While she opened windows and doors, sprinkled salt and hung horseshoes over thresholds, the homeowners stood patiently by. Not only was the service tolerated but to refuse her entrance was considered bad luck.

"Superstitious old fool," muttered Clarie, as she pulled down the cloth and then slammed the windows and door shut. "The Missus gave her free reign, but Mr. Blackwell pays good money to cool this rickety old place."

Like Clarie, most considered the old woman to be merely insane, a derelict who had been driven mad at the tender age of seven by the death of her twin sister. Yet even before Kylie was born, the woman's name—which had become synonymous with death—had reached legendary proportions. Nurtured around campfires between the frightened whispers of children, the story of Josephine Parker and her sister Jessie had become the story of the "Deadkeeper." After slipping into a well, Jessie's comatose body had been retrieved but her lost soul remained trapped in the underground springs. For six months her body lay in a coma before succumbing to death, leaving her soul behind to haunt the bayou. It was said that Josephine's babblings were to her sister's ghost, and her life's work was to insure that no more souls became trapped or lost.

While Kylie had often seen the old woman rambling through the swamps and the streets of Savannah, the only time she had ever spoken to her was after her older brother Aidan had died. In the early morning after his death, the ghastly knock had come to the door. Though Lila had graciously invited the old woman into their home, she had stayed at the door. "There's nothing to be done," the old woman had muttered, then turned away. There was no need to prepare the house, for Aidan's body would not be coming back: he had overdosed on heroin in a warehouse downtown and the viewing was to take place at the mortuary.

"What was she doing here?" asked Kylie. "She only comes when the body is in the hou—" Her breath suddenly stopped, for the full bearing of the woman's presence finally hit her: Amelia's body was to be viewed in the parlor beneath her.

"That's right, honey," said Clarie, noticing the stricken look on her face. "They're bringing the poor baby in later today."

Kylie suddenly felt the need to sit. "But she wanted to be cremated," she said weakly.

"Now surely you wouldn't think the Missus would go for that. Father Matthew tried to convince her but she wouldn't hear of it. That body's on its way and there's not a thing any of us can do about it."

As Kylie lowered onto the bed, her reflection appeared in the dressing mirror that had warped with age. Like Josephine Parker, her own grave image did not belong in the place of her childhood. The room around her seemed suddenly dingy and old—the carpeting worn and the wallpaper faded with the hideous passage of time.

"Is there anything else you need, honey?"

Even the once bright eyes of Clarie had dulled.

"No, I'm fine," she answered softly. "Thank you."

As the maid closed the door behind her, Kylie looked to the swamp that had been silenced by the glass. Contrary to the walls around her, it had not dimmed or grown sparse, its vibrancy remained. If anything it had grown even more powerful with age. Though the morning cut through the twisted cypress it remained murky and dark—a foreboding emanating from its shadows. Resting back into the sheets, Kylie squeezed her eyes shut. She would not look at the woods, would not think of the memories that lay tangled within its vines or its highways beyond. The past had become a graveyard and if she lingered on the lives it had devoured, she would not be able to bear it. As she closed her mind against itself, acrimony stung into her heart. Once again she had returned to the South to be greeted by death.

Forty-One

WITHIN THE LABYRINTH OF HER DREAMS CAME THE DISTANT HUM OF THE bayou. Abruptly, she stood within its shadows—within its heat and its sweat. Long tendrils of Spanish moss hung all around her, encasing her within a stagnant cocoon. A tiny chigger dropped down upon her chest and began to move upward. Then another fell and another. She tried to swat them away, but the moss had formed around her hands like larvae. As she watched in horror, the parasites buried their heads in her veins and began to consume her.

With a gasp, Kylie wrenched herself from the nightmare. Her eyes were suddenly open, staring at the rose wallpaper. The glow of morning remained, yet the room had dimmed. Confused by the deepening of shadows, she turned to the windows. The trees outside were filled with a burning red, only the light was not coming from the east but the west. She suddenly bolted upright. The deep sleep had not only carried her through the day, but into the dusk.

She noticed the sound of voices coming from somewhere beneath her, perhaps the parlor. Undoubtedly, others had arrived to offer their condolences. Struggling against the lingering fatigue, she untwisted her wrinkled pants and dropped her feet to the side of the bed. In spite of her grogginess, she needed to put herself into motion. First she would bathe and dress before joining her hosts, but when she looked about the room she saw that Father Matt had not delivered her duffle as Clarie had promised. She would have to venture out to the car to retrieve it herself.

Within the mirror she saw that her hair lay tangled around her shoulders and her face was creased with the hard sleep. She found a brush in the dresser drawer and then patted her cheeks to bring the blood back into them.

As she turned for the door, her entire body stiffened—the voices beneath had joined in unison. For a moment she remained silent, certain she wasn't hearing correctly, but when she pulled back the knob, the warm draft from the hallway confirmed her trepidation. Not only did it bear the scent of candles, but it carried the sound of prayer. While she had lain sleeping in the room overhead, Amelia's corpse had arrived and her Rosary commenced.

THE HOUSE beneath her had been transformed by the flickering candles and fading dusk into a dreamlike vision less tangible than the nightmare from which she just awoke. Paralyzed at the top of the stairs, Kylie stared down to the gray entryway, and to the archway that led into the glowing parlor.

"'Glory be to the Father and to the Son and to the Holy Spirit . . .'"

The chant was soft and low, its voices filled with a strange emptiness, an almost sinister rote.

As the heat rose with the reverberating sound, the stairs before her seemed suddenly steeper. Clutching the railing, she steadied herself.

Go back to your room, the voice inside of her urged.

She had no place near the gathering. She did not want to see the body, or to join in the ritualistic prayers. Amelia's wish was to be cremated, not to be filled with embalming fluid and put on display.

Wanting nothing more than to hide from the abhorrent night, Kylie started back for her room, when she heard another sound coming from the corridor behind her. It was that of a child softly singing. Even before she turned, she knew from whence the song came. Amelia's door stood open, the sweet melody emanating from its shadows.

• • •

THE GLOW from the coming twilight lit the room from within. As she approached the doorway, Kylie saw that the striped wallpaper had not changed, nor the piles of books and stuffed animals along the north wall. They were just as Amelia had left them years before. A sudden movement within the shadows caught her eye, yet it was merely a curtain fluttering within the bayou's breath. With a twist of her heart, she saw that the windows had been opened and the long dressing mirror cloaked with a white sheet. Though the room was now in full view, it wasn't until a glint of light caught a head of shiny curls that a figure was revealed within the shadows.

Crouched on the far side of the canopy bed, the child was facing away from her, the sound of the swamp melding gently with the haunting tune. As she drew deeper into the room, she saw that it was a little girl, her fingers brushing tenderly over the hair of a rag-doll that rested against the bedpost. Kylie silently watched her, until the creak of the floor disclosed her presence. The child quickly turned, then stood to face her. Kylie instantly recognized the wide brown eyes and dark corkscrew hair, it was the little girl from the highway she had nearly struck the night before.

"Hello," said Kylie. "I'm sorry if I frightened you. You have a very lovely voice."

The child remained silent, gazing with the same curious stare that had been trapped within the headlights.

"You were on the highway last night," continued Kylie gently. "It's very dangerous to play there, especially after dark. I was afraid that I had hit you."

With sadness, she noticed that the little girl's dress was tattered and old. Clearly, the child was from a poor family that couldn't afford the kind of toys the room boasted. "Do you live in the woods?" she asked.

But the child did not respond, she merely looked past her as if Kylie were suddenly invisible. Then she took a few steps, turned and spun into a pirouette, her thin arms extending gracefully outward. Kylie watched her a moment, then turned for the door.

"I know who you are," announced the child from behind her.

Looking back, Kylie saw that she had landed in a perfect plié.

"My friend told me," she said, her chin tilted proudly upward. "We saw you from the bushes."

"I see," said Kylie, amused that the children had spied on her from the woods. She had been so shaken that she was certain she had looked ridiculous. "And who's your friend?"

"Somebody you know," declared the child assuredly. "Well, you used to know him," she reconsidered, extending her arms once again. As her graceful body did another pirouette, Kylie noticed that she had no shoes. "But probably you forgot about him too. His mama and daddy forgot about him. Now he doesn't have anybody but me."

"What happened to his parents?"

"They left him by the accident and never came back."

"What accident?"

"The one on the highway. You know," she insisted.

As the little girl stilled and looked expectantly toward her, a strange feeling overcame Kylie. Within the darkening room, she struggled to see the child's eyes but the light had grown too dim.

"You know," the child repeated. "Him and his mama were driving one night. She was mad at him 'cause he forgot his books. Then the big truck came."

For a breathless moment, Kylie merely stared at the child's silhouette. She had been speaking of a friend, but clearly she meant another. Clearly she had been told of the collision that had claimed Tucker's life, yet she had somehow misunderstood his death. Perhaps the only way she could comprehend it was to envision him alone and lost without parents or friends.

"Yes," said Kylie, the word passing from her lips in a painful admission. "I knew a little boy who got hit by a truck. A very dear little boy. Only his parents didn't forget about him—he died. But that wouldn't be your friend in the woods." A rush of sorrow came upon her so quickly that she had to look away. To hear that her young brother's death had become the chatter of children filled her with anguish. "He had a very sweet name," she said weakly. "Did you know he was called Tucker?" she asked.

The child looked at her strangely and then began to giggle. "Well of course, silly-billy. He told me himself."

. . .

As THE response nettled between her temples, Kylie blinked once and then blinked again. For a horrifying second, the outline of the child seemed a mere whispering in her mind. The figure was smiling, she knew, yet there was no form to her features.

"Miss Kylie?"

She pivoted around—the voice having come from behind her. The overhead lights were suddenly on, Clarie's fingers lingering on the switch.

"Who in heaven's name are you talkin' to?" the maid asked.

When Kylie turned back she saw the little girl had vanished. Only the doll remained at the side of the bed, its black eyes staring forward.

"Miss Kylie?" Clarie repeated.

Kylie looked to the closet and to the dark space behind the flowing curtains, then quickly went to the bathroom door and looked through. A sewing room adjoined to the other side. When she had turned, the child must have slipped between the rooms.

"Yes, I'm sorry," she finally responded.

Clarie had moved toward her, her fleshy face pinched with concern. "Honey, you don't look well," she said. "Are you alright?"

"Yeah, I'm okay," she said, though she felt drained by the strange conversation with the child.

"You need to eat," said Clarie. "You haven't had a bite all day."

With the maid's observation, Kylie suddenly realized her hunger. The pang in her stomach was so intense it had turned to nausea. "Really, I . . . I'm fine," she said, for she couldn't bear the thought of passing the gathering downstairs.

"Now, now," said Clarie detecting her reservation. "You just pay no mind to what's goin' on down there. We'll go straight to the kitchen by the rear stairs. No one will ever see us. Now come along." With her last order, she promptly left the room.

Left within the shadows, Kylie took one last glance around before following the maid. By the time she reached the hallway, Claric was already halfway down the corridor toward the slender stairwell that led to the kitchen. As the full figure disappeared into the darkness, Kylie felt the chill of someone behind her, but when she turned back she found that the hallway was empty. What appeared to be ten gaunt men all dancing in a row was merely the candlelight throwing the shadows of the banister upon the wall.

You're imagining things, her mind whispered, suddenly aware of her grogginess. She wasn't thinking clearly, she knew. In her clouded state, the child had managed to unsettle her. She needed to speak with her again, to clarify her last remark. It would have been impossible for the girl to have known Tucker, for she wouldn't even have been born by the time of his death.

"Well?" Clarie called from behind her.

The maid remained at the end of the hall, her hands expectantly upon her hips.

"Coming," said Kylie, beginning in the maid's direction.

Within the kitchen, Clarie went immediately to the refrigerator. "Have a seat," she said quietly, nodding to the breakfast nook. "I'll have a chowder whipped up in no time."

From where Kylie stood, she could see the edge of the gathering through the dark archway that led to the parlor. She turned to the kitchen table and to the screened porch behind it, anything to avoid the muttering voices and guests dressed in black.

The kitchen's heat and humidity were unbearable. As in the rest of the house, the windows had been lifted and the back door opened. Her attention was drawn by the flutter of bugs that bound out of the blackness and smashed against the screen. With their determination to get inward, Kylie suddenly remembered her dream—the tiny little insects embedding into her skin. Caught between the din of the swamp and the relentless prayer, a cold sweat shivered over her. She pulled a chair from the table and sank downward.

"'. . . As it was in the beginning, is now and ever shall be. World without end . . .'"

Amelia's body was in the next room. But she could not think of it, could not bear to imagine it.

"Is there anything I can do?" she asked softly, but Clarie did not hear her. She continued at the sink, scrubbing and chopping vegetables. Kylie noticed for the first time that she too was wearing black. It seemed utterly aberrant, for the kitchen around her was rich with memories, the table beneath her, the butcher's block to her left, even Clarie busied at the sink was a familiar sight. But their warmth was now twisted into the grotesque by the gathering in the next room.

"'Holy Mary, Mother of God, pray for us sinners . . .'"

In the undercurrent of worship, Kylie suddenly heard the child's melody once again, but from where it was coming she could not tell. She looked reluctantly toward the archway, where the melody grew in intensity, yet it was slowly distorting, the voice turning gruff and hoarse. As she stared into the contorting shadows, an image moved in unison with the abrasive voice. Something or someone was shuffling along the wall toward the kitchen. It hunkered unnaturally forward, its long cloak dragging along the floor. The figure was muttering nonsensically . . . pieces of the melody mixed with uneven words and sounds.

As if sensing her gaze, the creature turned toward her, the startling image of the face emerging from the darkness. It was the visage of the child gnarled and twisted into that of an old crone. The corkscrew-curls had grayed and thinned into limp ringlets, while the wide-set eyes that had once been enchanting, had deepened and hazed with cataracts. As if seventy years had suddenly passed, the hideously-aged counterpart of the child had stepped into the light and it was Josephine Parker. The mere sight of the macabre woman sent Kylie's entire body quivering.

"'. . . Hail Mary, full of grace . . .'" chanted the voices behind her.

"Grace . . . grace," the old woman muttered. Then the tune again, the melody of the child.

As the notes melded with the freakish sight, Kylie stood slowly to her feet. She was not seeing correctly, could not possibly be. The ghost of Jessie Parker was a myth, a mere tale invented by children; yet there was no denying the horrid juxtaposition of youth and age and the similarities between the two. With a deep chill, she thought of the style of the little girl's dress. It was pleated at the bottom, like those of an era long past.

She abruptly stepped back, the heat pressing into her clamoring skull—all around her the living and the dead seemed to press into one. If the child truly was Jessie Parker, then the words of Tucker may have been uttered in truth. *They left him by the accident and never came back.* As the scent of burnt rubber stung into her memory, Kylie thought of the limp figure that had been pulled from the wreckage. "He's unconscious but alive," the paramedic had cried. But perhaps like herself, who had perused her own likeness within the cold stillness of the plane, Tucker had remained apart. The thought of him lost and alone, caught in some heinous limbo, filled her with horror.

She needed to get out, to find the little girl once again, but when she stepped toward the archway, she found that the eyes of Josephine Parker had fixed upon her.

As if awakened by Kylie's thoughts, the old woman's gaze had grown abruptly focused. She was shuffling into the kitchen, her lips moving and chewing. "I can hear you," she said between the twisted words and grunting sounds.

Kylie tried to look away, but the muttering wretch was nearly upon her. As the space closed between them, the pungent odor reached into Kylie's throat and grasped her breath.

"What are you doing here?" the madwoman demanded, her clouded eyes growing suddenly enraged. Her breath reeked of a foul stench, a hair standing off of her chin. "You have no place here," she goaded. As she pulled her crinkled lips inward and chewed between her thoughts, Kylie tried to back away but the woman continued to pursue her, her voice rising. "You don't belong here, I said!"

From somewhere beside her, Kylie felt Clarie turning toward her, her hands dripping from the sink. Her mouth was moving but Kylie did not hear her words. She heard only the embodiment of death that had set its icy focus on her.

"You don't belong here!"

Clarie and another woman were suddenly there, grasping the lunatic's shoulders. The women were guiding her away, one of them scolding her and trying to get her to leave the house.

"Dead . . . dead," the old woman was muttering. "She belongs with the dead."

Kylie put her hand to her temple, for the tiles beneath her had begun to jumble. The prayer had stopped, silencing all around her. Through the doors, the glow of the votives highlighted the grave faces that had turned toward her. And through the aisle of parted guests, Amelia's pale profile pointed upward, her smooth features stroked by the candlelight. As the lights began to smear into one, Kylie felt certain she would faint.

As she started to weave, the unified stare of the guests was joined by the hiss of whisper. With heavy limbs, she started for the sanctity of her room—but a chair was suddenly before her. Stumbling over it, it screeched across the floor. She grasped for her balance when a firm hand suddenly caught her.

A face of concern filled her sight.

"I'm fine," she tried to say, but at once she was moving . . . running toward the stairs.

Forty-Two

A BOWL OF CORN CHOWDER SAT ON THE BEDSIDE TRAY, YET KYLIE couldn't bring herself to touch it—the mere smell of it turned her stomach. Though she had already showered and wrapped herself in her robe, the tears simply refused to stop flowing. The old woman's stench seemed to have settled in her pores, while the words of the little girl would not leave her.

They left him by the accident and never came back.

She could think of nothing but Tucker's hand within her own as his ravaged body lingered within a coma. The doctors had been certain he would live, yet the light had never returned to his eyes. If they hadn't given up on him—possibly, just possibly—he would have found his way back. But the excruciating thought, one that had plagued her for years, was simply too much.

"You could be wrong," she whispered, trying to push back the pain. She could be mistaken about the little girl's identity. While there was no denying the relation between the child and the old woman, the bond could be less binding than she had surmised. Perhaps they were merely grandmother and granddaughter. Or great-aunt and niece. Her head swam with the contention, as she started to pace.

When the knock came to the door, she quickly rubbed her face with her sleeve and looked about the room for something to busy herself with. "Yes?" she said. "Who is it?"

"Dr. Sauvage."

Kylie knew instantly what the doctor wanted. More than likely, her ridiculous display had raised concerns for her health. Only out of respect, did she unlatch the door.

"Yes Doctor, come in," she said, retreating back within the room to dry her eyes.

The elderly doctor gently closed the door behind him and turned to her with a sigh. As she had expected, he held a medical bag within his grasp.

"There's a small committee downstairs insisting that I speak with you. Perhaps even have a look at you," he said.

"I'm okay," she said, turning away from the watchful eyes. "Really."

Though her gaze went to the veranda door, her own reflection was all she could see in the black glass. With her face puffed from tears and her arms wrapped tight around herself she looked like an obstinate child. "I was just hungry," she said, relaxing her hands to her sides.

"I see," said the doctor, looking to the cold dish of chowder. "Then I take it, that's your second bowl of soup."

Kylie smiled weakly. "I just haven't gotten to it yet."

The doctor laid his bag on the dresser and flipped it open with a snap. "I must tell you that I'm a little concerned about you myself. When I saw you this morning I was surprised by your pallor. You've always been so vibrant and healthy," he said warmly. "We've already lost one of our Georgia beauties, we can't afford to lose another."

Without further discussion he took a stethoscope from his bag and looked expectantly toward her. "Why don't you have a seat here," he said, gesturing to the chair at the dressing table.

Though reluctant, Kylie followed orders.

"Breathe," he said, placing the scope to her chest. "I would like to take some blood, if you don't mind. I fear you may have some sort of vitamin deficiency. You're much paler than you should be and your eyes—"

"It's nothing," she said patiently. "I haven't been eating as much—"

"Clearly, no," he interrupted. In spite of her hesitancy he was already preparing the needle. "I understand the trauma that you've had to face," he said, his eyes resting on the scar on her chin. "Mr. and Mrs. Blackwell told me of your husband's death."

With a sharp prick, the tube filled with crimson blood.

"It all may be a bit much for a young woman to take. I have some Valium that I'm going to leave with you. Perhaps it will help you get a good night's sleep."

As she pulled the sleeve of her robe back down, he laid the container with the pills upon the dresser before her.

"As far as Josephine Parker goes," he said, "her nephew asked that I deliver an apology on his behalf. He was here to keep an eye on Josephine, but he got distracted with his own two children."

Startled, Kylie looked up. "His children?" she asked.

"Yes. Apparently, they're quite unruly."

"Was one of them a little girl?" she asked weakly.

"I really couldn't say. Why do you ask?"

"Oh I . . . just saw a child that . . . that resembled Ms. Parker," she said.

"The poor dear," groaned the doctor with a mischievous grin. He snapped the medical bag shut and shifted its weight into his hand. "Will you be staying in Savannah long?" he asked.

"I haven't really decided," she answered, trying to pull her thoughts back to the moment. She noticed the doctor studying her again, his kind face crinkled with concern.

"I'll have the results of the test back in a few days," he said. He reached into his pocket and pulled out a card. "If you have any questions, you can reach me at this number. If you're not here, is there somewhere I can reach you—"

"Yes," she said and proceeded to give him Dora Greyson's number.

As the old doctor lingered at the door, Kylie's heart warmed. With his abounding white hair and thin goatee, he had always reminded her of Colonel Sanders. Though she had rarely spoken with him, he had been a comforting presence at nearly every Blackwell gathering over the years.

"It's been nice seeing you again," he said kindly. "Perhaps you can pay the Blackwells the occasional visit. I know they think dearly of you."

"Yes," she said sadly. "And I of them. Thank you."

As the doctor quietly slipped from the room, melancholy filled her heart. She felt certain it would be the last time she would see the old gentleman. She looked at the white card, the elegant black letters so simple yet dignified.

For a long while she remained at the dressing table, listening as the guests beneath took their leave. Her eyes rested on the pills. Though the bottle had been full when the doctor had pulled it from his bag, he had emptied most of them into another container, leaving only two behind. Clearly he had not trusted her with more. Perhaps with reason. The thought of sleep, of a long endless space of black where there was no pain or loss, was enticing. The old woman was right—she belonged with the dead ... with Jack, Amelia, her mother and Tucker. *Tucker*. Her stomach dropped.

They left him by the accident and never came back.

"It wasn't her," she said aloud. The child was clearly a great-niece, not a voice from the grave. The girl was simply confused about Tucker's death, nothing more. "Nothing more," she whispered to drive the thought home.

Feeling depleted, she flipped off the light. Within the darkness, her fingers grasped for the pills, for there would be no chance of sleep otherwise. She felt too raw and exposed, her thoughts careening against her will.

The pills were tart against her tongue, but she quickly washed them down with the water Clarie had left. Amazed by her own thirst she nearly drank the whole glass without a moment of breath.

The room around her slowly came into focus as her eyes adjusted to the dark. Within the blue light her hair coiled into black wire, her eyes mere smudges of coal. As she stared into her own emerging image, she got the sudden feeling of being watched. She looked behind her to the bed and the empty space around it. No one. But on second glance to the mirror, she saw something behind her through the window— two small figures standing at the edge of the swamp staring toward her.

At once she bolted to her feet, the empty glass tumbling to the floor. She stood silent, unmoving and scarcely breathing. Slowly rotating to the windows, she peered out to the moonlit swamp, but the figures had vanished.

Going quickly to the veranda, her sight followed the left curvature of the lawn to where she was certain they had been standing. There, upon two trees that stood side by side, a glowing light lifted up toward the moon, but it was merely foxfire giving the luminescent impression of two bodies.

Again, it was her imagination getting away with her. Just her mind that had created the rim of light around their taut little shoulders, around the set stance of the girl and the curly head of the boy.

It wasn't him, her reason argued, yet her heart refused to listen. The thought of him near, in any form or capacity burned through her like lightning.

Tucker. It had been her dear sweet Tucker.

He had emerged from the darkness to find her.

WITH a few short steps she was there, at the edge of the black swamp where the figures had been. A bittern that had perched above the foxfire froze with her approach, undoubtedly its tiny heart beating as frantically as her own. Her eyes searched between the cypress and the moonlit vines, yet saw no one.

"Hello?" she said, her timid voice barely breaking the silence. She stepped forward, through the thick growth, when she realized that it was the head of the path that led to her old house. Her heart constricted, for it was a passage that Tucker would have known.

Though stepping cautiously at first, she began moving faster and faster down the once beaten trail that had grown tangled and dense. The moon followed her into the swamp, but its light was soon choked by the branches closing inward. It became progressively darker yet her mounting conviction drove her forward. She tried to control her excitement, yet with each passing step she became more and more convinced it had been Tucker. He had stood at the head of the familiar path, for he had known she would follow.

"Tucker!" she gasped as she fell deeper and deeper into the bayou. He would be there, she was certain, for it was home. He had needed her desperately and now she would come. He would be waiting at the house . . . sitting on the porch as he had so many years before. Waiting sweetly. Ever so sweetly. Through the clearing, not more than a mile, he would be there.

Branches and twigs brushed past her legs, snarling within her gown and scraping against her skin, yet she scarcely felt them. She scarcely noticed the chatter around her or the warm moist earth at her bare feet. Her only thought was of the tiny hands, of the brown eyes filled with wonderment, and of the impish little grin. Tears of joy, of a deep burning love wet her cheeks. She would see him again! She would touch him and hold him close. Never again would he fear or be alone. Never again would she release him.

With her pulse beating so fast that she could scarcely breathe she rounded the last bend into the clearing. She tried to call out, but the anticipation choked her voice. When she saw the edge of the gate, her legs became so weak she feared she would not make the last few steps. Then it was before her, the walkway—the porch ... the rushing silence ...

At once she stopped, her heart thundering forward without her. Within the dark night the house appeared an abandoned shack. The windows that had once sparkled with sunlight were all broken, the glass shattered upon the bayou floor. The swamp had moved inward, vines twisting along the porch railing so thickly that she could scarcely see the dilapidated floor beneath.

"Tucker?" she whispered. He was nowhere in sight.

Out of the shadows, a long black snake slithered over the porch step and disappeared into the underbrush. It had vanished to the left where all that remained of her mother's garden was a broken gate hanging crookedly on its hinges.

At once she felt emptied, gutted by the dreadful sight that lay before her. She became aware of her own breath, of the sweat trickling over her shaking body. Like a desperate fool she had cut her way through the bayou without shoes, crying like a madwoman. Her feet were bleeding and her gown was ripped. Tucker was not there, just as he had not been at the head of the path. She had been so consumed by thoughts of him, had wanted him so desperately, that she had turned foxfire to flesh.

She looked for a shape, the familiar face ... she listened to the sounds, but the diminishing voice in her soul was all that was clear. *He's gone, Kylie. He's gone for good.* His swing hung rotted through, the rope that held it in place frayed to a mere string.

Again she felt the loss—the bitter yearning for the sweet child. For a brief moment he had lived. She had almost felt his hand within her own, had comforted and loved him only to have him ripped away and sent back to the dead. The shadows around her shifted, yet she did not turn, for their emptiness held nothing but sorrow.

Standing before the place that had once brimmed with life, agony crawled from the depths of the soil and nestled within her. The slashes in her feet stung. She had been out of her mind, near hysteria—hoping to find that which no longer existed. It was the South, with its intoxicating scent that had pushed her over the edge. Or perhaps it had been her own reluctance to let go that sent her screaming into the woods. Perhaps somewhere deep inside she had come to Savannah expecting to find Tucker... even her mother and Aidan, for as long as they roamed the bayou of the past, they were not lost to her. Somewhere deep inside she had believed that if she were to cut back through the woods far enough, if she searched deep enough, they would all be there still living the life they once had. But the windows on that existence lay dark and shattered.

Abruptly, she cast her eyes away from the dreadful sight, but her feet would not carry her farther. She was frozen, unable to move forward or back, for there was nowhere to go and no one to go to. She was home.

Kylie! Kylie! Bet you can't catch me!

With a shriek, the voice whisked past, but it was merely a memory. The air around her changed as another took its place.

Hold it steady now, don't move. She could feel her father on the porch behind her, and Aidan, not more than fifteen, beside him. The hammer clanked as the shutter was nailed into place, but when she pivoted back, there was nothing but the dark. The reproachful form remained silent. The shutter lay crumpled upon the ground, the paint chipped to the ashen rot of wood.

The life had vanished. All that remained were the bones, its flesh consumed by the night. In the starkness of its decrepitude, there was no denying its reality. Never again would her loved ones gather beneath the roof. Never again would Amelia appear at the gate, or her mother sit quietly on the porch. Aidan's whistle would not sing through the trees, just as Tucker would not follow her to the river. It was all gone, her father now living in a beaten-down cottage, broken and alone.

In a black void, the pain inside expanded consuming all in its wake. At once she was moving back through the snapping woods. She was not thinking or breathing, her only thought was of flight. As the emotion choked within her throat, the hideous setting vanished into the depths from which it emerged. Not until she was halfway to the clearing, did it occur to her that no refuge lay ahead, only more of the same darkness. Amelia's body would be waiting within the parlor beneath the flicker of candles. As the tears flooded into her eyes, her step blurred, her feet tangling beneath her. The soil was at her knees, in her hands for she had stumbled to the ground. She struggled to get up, but like a lion in pursuit of its prey, the grief had caught up to her and was devouring her. It ripped through her limbs, through her gut, through her very being. All around her, the screaming of the gloomy thickets closed inward. It promised that no matter what the light would bring, it would all come to the darkness, to the snakes and the rats, to the night and the soil. A hopelessness such as she had never felt trembled over her sobbing body. Like the ice of a frozen lake that had cracked, her defenses had finally given, allowing the frigid waters of doom to flood in. Despair took hold and for a long while she was lost within it, unable to break free.

It was the steady thumping, that abruptly pulled her from the lamenting. It caught her breath and forced her gaze upward, to the moss that hung overhead. A great horned owl was perched in the cypress, its yellow eyes locked upon her. Beneath its claws a small squirrel thrashed about, its quiet screaming joining that of the other sounds. At sight of the convulsing form flopping helplessly, Kylie's sorrow turned to fury. At once, she grasped for a rock at her feet and with all of her might, she flung it toward the owl.

"Get away!" she screamed.

As the stone ricocheted off the tree, the bird took flight and glided lithely away, its victim in tow. Only the blood remained, oozing smugly down the side of the tree. Beneath the soft *coos* of the bittern and the single *kwawk* of the heron, death was laughing, mocking her.

"What do you want from me?!" she screamed, swirling on the empty bayou. "What do you want?!"

But even before the words left her lips, she knew. Death would never show mercy. It would taunt and torture, saving the strongest game for the last. It would take what it wanted, settling on nothing less than her soul.

You belong with the dead, came the voice from within.

She took a step back, her moonlit shadow stretching before her. She had become a mere ghost treading through a life that no longer existed—its other players long since moved on: her mother, her brothers, her best friend. Even Jack was now gone. It was only a matter of acceptance that she join them.

It's what God wants, whispered the voice of Amelia.

As the words settled over her like a cool blue river, a resolution and understanding took hold. Whether it was the calming effect of the Valium, of the doctor's pills he had so carefully guarded, or simply surrender—she knew. The fight was over. Her life, her past, her hope were all dead.

Within the truce, she sank down upon a tree stump and for a long while remained silent. After nearly an hour with her thoughts, she gathered the bottom of her gown into her fingertips and continued slowly down the path. When she reached the end she would pack her bag and say good-bye to her friend. She would not wait until after the funeral to leave, for she didn't have the luxury of time. There was too much to be done, to prepare for, and valuable time had already been lost. In spite of Amelia's warning she had continued to fight. But she could no longer refute the truth: her extinction was imminent. It was time to think of her father, for he would be the survivor, the one left behind. She needed to do everything in her power to prepare him, to ease the blow. Without the distraction of her own survival, she would concentrate solely on his.

Forty-Three

AS THE FIRST GLIMPSE OF MORNING SPREAD ACROSS THE HORIZON, KYLIE shoved her duffle into the trunk and closed it quietly. With one last look, she turned back to the mansion, to the dwindling light within the parlor. Amelia's pallid face was still with her, the beautiful visage that had been even more lovely in death. After gathering wild flowers from the path, she had laid them at the breast of her friend. Though it had taken all of her courage to approach the casket, she had not looked away. Instead, she memorized the stillness of the features. She touched the coolness of the hand. "I'll be there soon, Melia," she had promised.

Standing before the silent mansion, Kylie could already feel the absence of her own footsteps, of her own voice, her own laughter. While she was still at the curb, life had shifted forward without her. As the hollow feeling took hold, she held her gaze forward. In a sudden moment of clemency, the pain was eclipsed by the past. The sun was suddenly high, the emerald lawn bursting with the laughter of two friends. Amelia Blackwell and Kylie McCallum danced beneath the sprinklers, their tiny hands intertwined in alliance.

Forever friends, they vowed, as they spun round and round, their laughter rising up to the sky.

"Forever friends," Kylie whispered, as the sun faded back to an amethyst glow. All was still again, the porch light dim with the approaching dawn.

Without a moment's hesitation for fear she would falter, she took a seat in the car and pulled away from the curb. As the mansion faded into the twilight, she didn't look back. With a deep breath, she continued forward, leaving the past, with its ghosts, with its pains and its joys behind.

PART SIX

Forty-Four

HARDEN TRUTHERS, OF TRUTHERS & BASTIEN MORTUARY, CONFORMED to every negative stereotype ever conceived about his profession. The black suit hung impeccably from his lanky frame, his manner pristine and rehearsed. The lines of his face were harsh, his cheeks sallow, his eyes mere slits of red. And like a vampire going in for the kill, he knew his figures. His elongated fingers danced over the keys, the calculator ribbon singing forth in a cacophony of dollars and cents.

". . . transfer of remains $200.00, funeral vehicle $175, transfer of flowers $55.00—all within a 30-mile radius, of course. Additional distances will be billed at $2.00 per mile. Death certificates $8.00 each, permit disposition $7.00, clergy to perform graveside service $75.00, musicians and singers—"

"No, those aren't necessary."

"Pardon?"

"No musicians and no singers."

The mortician turned toward her, yet Kylie's expression remained resolute.

"Very well," he acquiesced with a sigh. "A simple service. Let's see, we still have dressing and casketing . . . bathing and handling, hair-dressing, cosmetology—"

"I'd like to just skip all of that."

"Pardon?"

"Skip it. I would rather not be 'handled' so to speak."

"Surely, Mrs. O'Rourke, you would like to be bathed and dressed," he said, the slight upturn of his lips betraying the discreet tone of his voice.

Kylie shuddered at the very gleam in the mortician's eyes. Feeling suddenly naked, she pulled her sweater tighter around her.

"However I arrive here," she said, steadily, "that's how I want to leave. No washing. No make-up. Whether I'm in one piece or twenty, just put me in the casket and lock it."

A stiff smile melted over the wet lips. "Very well, then," he said, turning back to the calculator. "Refrigeration at the very least is a must," he asserted. "That'll be $290."

As the calculator hummed once again, Kylie's attention was drawn to the clock. To her dismay, it was almost five—little time was left to complete the day's tasks.

"You have your choice of the vinyl, leather, or solid hardwood memorial booklet. Those run from $25.00 to—"

"That's not necessary."

"Okay. What about service folders and prayer cards? Those are—"

"Really Mr. Truthers, none of that is necessary."

"Crucifix. Surely you'll desire the crucifix. It's solid brass and only $15.00."

"Fine."

With one last firing of keys, the tally snaked out onto the desktop. "I think you'll find this more than reasonable," he said, folding the receipt into a small envelope and handing it to her. "All that's left now is the choice of casket. If you'll just follow me into the showroom," he suggested.

Up until that moment, the arrangements had been a matter of a simple business transaction transpiring within an office. The idea of going any deeper into the mortuary sent Kylie's nerves into a frenzy.

"This way," the mortician urged.

As Kylie trailed behind the willowy man, she kept her eyes on the floor and tried not to breathe the strange odor that permeated the hall. Four doors had shivered past when the mortician stopped in front of one and extended his hand graciously inward.

"If you please," he said.

When Kylie stepped into the room, she found that it was filled with coffins.

"This silvery beauty is our sleekest, most top-of-the-line design," said the mortician, smoothing his hand over a lid and then raising it.

At sight of the pillowy innards, a cold sweat shot up Kylie's back.

"If you run your hand through it, you can feel the level of comfort," he said.

The mortician had seemed a mere absurdity—an amusing eccentric with a lascivious grin—but standing before the open casket, the glint in his eyes suddenly took on new gravity. In the words of the brochure, they were "planning her eternal rest."

"If you'll just step over here," he coaxed, "you'll find that it's not quite so daunting as it may seem."

But the terror of claustrophobia had already settled in. In Kylie's mind she lay submerged within the satin, the closed lid mere inches from her face.

"Excuse me," she gasped, turning for the door.

"Mrs. O'Rourke," called the mortician.

Once into the hallway, she stopped. "Yes, I'm sorry. Please just pick one that's . . . simple. Inexpensive."

She tried to wipe her brow but found that her hands had somehow slipped between those of the mortician's.

"Rest assured, I'll find the perfect one for you. It's been a pleasure serving your pre-needs. Hopefully it will be some time before we see you again."

"Yes," said Kylie, regaining her hands.

"I'll get back to you on the choice, so that—"

But Kylie did not hear the last of it. She was already out the heavy door, back into the warmth of the sunlight.

Forty-Five

BY 9:00 P.M. MOST OF THE SHOPS HAD CLOSED. KYLIE WALKED ALONG Charles Street at the edge of Beacon Hill, weighted by packages filled with boots and sweaters, hats and belts; everything her father would need to make it through another harsh winter. In the eight hours since her arrival back to Boston, she had arranged her own funeral, met with an attorney to devise a will, scheduled the demolition of the warehouse, and secured a year's worth of provisions for her father's boat. Her every muscle ached with fatigue yet she kept walking. Though the night had settled over the city, the streets still buzzed with activity. As long as she kept shopping, remaining lost within the stream of bodies, she would not have to face Dora's mansion that waited atop the hill.

Though the resolve she had found in Savannah had stayed with her, fear had begun to seep back in. Fear of the dwindling hour and of the final moment when her life would cease. But the biggest dread of all lay coiled within her stomach like a snake. She feared the long nights ahead within the darkened mansion. There she would be alone and most vulnerable, with no doors or bolts to bar Julius Vanderpoel's return.

As she paused at a streetlight, her eyes were drawn to a shelf of bright bottles within a liquor store window. Even from half a block away, she recognized the shape of the Courvoisier, of the Jack Daniel's and Grand Marnier. A craving came over her so intensely that her mouth began to water. To taste them, to be lost within their warmth would be all that she needed. Drinking in the past had caused her grief. It had taken her drive and sent her life spiraling downward. But now, there was nothing left to destroy. Perhaps even, if she drank enough, Julius Vanderpoel could not reach her. It would numb her so effectively, that she would make it through the long night.

"Excuse me, miss, are you going?"

An old woman was behind her, waiting impatiently for her to cross the street.

"No," she said, stepping back out of the way. She looked to the liquor store again. *No*, her mind sighed. She had to remain sharp until all of her tasks were complete. Repositioning the packages, she saw that her skin was wearing raw from the corded handles. With resignation, she looked to the slope of Beacon Hill. Mustering all of her remaining strength, she began the climb up Pickney Street. The serpent within her belly stirred, yet she continued toward the mansion.

Forty-Six

THE FRANTIC SUCKING OF HER OWN BREATH AWAKENED HER. SHE WAS sitting upright, her eyes fixed toward the open window. Her groggy mind struggled to adjust, to find the figure that had been standing there, watching. A gentle breeze drifted in, yet she saw no one. "Just a dream," she whispered, to reassure her fumbling thoughts.

Kylie pulled the sheet up around herself and slid from the bed. Her heart hammered with a vague sense of urgency, yet she remained lost. There were errands and meetings, yet she had been sleeping. She looked to the clock. It was 3:45 A.M. *Nothing to be done at this hour,* she told herself.

Within the bathroom she rummaged through the boxes. There were pills, she was certain. Dora had left them. Bottles toppled out onto the floor . . . razors and hair gel . . . then the secobarbital. Just to help her sleep—to put an end to the churning inside of her. She looked at the date. They were old but not expired.

She popped two in her mouth and bent to the sink. The water was cool on her lips, on her cheeks, her eyes.

Grabbing a towel from the rack, she turned for the hall. The silence of the mansion was unbearable. She stood at the head of the stairs where there was nothing but darkness beneath. At once, she remembered a task, an insignificant errand that had weighted her mind. Descending to the study, she pulled on the light. The library books from Harvard lay strewn across the desk, in the exact spot she had left them before leaving for Savannah. Quickly gathering them together, she carried them to the bottom of the stairs and placed them by the front door. She would return them tomorrow. As she turned back for the stairs, her eyes caught the message light on the recorder. She had been so tired upon her arrival home that she hadn't noticed the light.

She hit the red button and turned for the kitchen. A cup of chamomile tea would help her sleep.

"Playing message number one," announced the electronic voice.

"Kylie, it's me."

At once she froze, the thin voice of Amelia bolting through her.

"I was just . . . oh God, I know you're probably on your way to the airport but I just had to talk to you. I just woke up and the gas . . . the gas was on in the kitchen. I don't know if I did it or . . . Oh God, Kylie. I can't think anymore . . . They're coming for me. I can feel it. I keep trying to close my mind to it. But it's here, I can feel it . . . Jesus, listen to me. I sound like a madwoman, don't I? . . . I just need to relax, I know. Panicking. That's what I'm doing. I even reconsidered going to

Mama's until you get here, but we both know how that would end. I'm gonna stay here and stick it out. That's the only thing I can do. Stick it out. God, I can't wait to see you."

With a shrill beep the message was silenced.

"End of messages," concluded the electronic voice.

Kylie found herself gripping the handrail, her legs trembling so fiercely that she sank to her knees. "Melia," she whispered. The snake in her stomach was twisting, despair closing inward. The voice had been so frightened, struggling for breath.

Again the craving for the colorful bottles took hold—for the warmth and numbing of pain. There was one in the kitchen, far beneath the cabinets in the back—a forgotten bottle of vodka she had noticed one night when shutting off the water valves. She was already moving toward the kitchen, when she stopped. Her father. She had to remember her father. She had to stay focused on the tasks at hand. *Keep it together, Wylie*, came the voice from within. She was too close to the end to lose strength now.

Forty-Seven

O'BRIAN'S PUB AND GRILL WAS SITUATED AT THE END OF THE DOCKS, overseeing all of the incoming boats. Through the cloudy windows, Kylie could see most of Nahant Bay, stretching from the northeast shoreline of stately houses, to the cove of cottages where her father resided. The tavern was conveniently located—a cozy haven where the fishermen gathered after a long day's work. It was her father's favorite hang-out, his home away from home.

Many an afternoon, Kylie had waited inside the pub for her father's boat to dock, listening to the chatter of Rick and Tim Hoover, Declan O'Connor, Billy Johnson, and Sal Wardoff. Not only were they her father's closest friends, they were his family. They had been his support and his life, when all else had failed. After the death of his wife and both of his sons, Sean had relocated to Swampscott a broken man. It wasn't until he started frequenting the tavern that he found his strength again. There he gained the support of friends, but most importantly, he found Ruby O'Brian.

Though a plank inscribed MICK O'BRIAN PROPRIETOR still hung above the door, the pub was now operated by his widow. Ruby O'Brian was forthright and friendly, jostling the fishermen as if she were one of their own. But from the moment Sean had walked into the bar, Ruby had addressed him differently, never razzing him the way she did the others. One who didn't know better would think the two disliked each other, but Ruby and Sean had a connection. They had a bond, Kylie knew, an understanding that only widowers could share. And while Sean had never mentioned it, Kylie was certain that they were lovers. Ruby O'Brian cared deeply for her father—more so than anyone else that Kylie could think of—and it was for this reason that Kylie had come earlier than usual to the pub.

She was staring out at the sun-speckled water, at her father's empty dock, when Ruby approached the booth.

"Here you go hon'," said the stout woman, setting a soda on the table before her. "Your da' should be comin' in any time now."

"Thanks," said Kylie. "I actually needed to talk to you, first."

"To me, lass?" she asked with surprise.

Kylie noticed a nervous twitch in the big blue eyes and rosy cheeks. Though Ruby was friendly to her, there had always been a silent wedge, a strange energy between them.

"What would you be needin' with me?" Ruby asked.

"It's about my father," said Kylie.

A look of alarm spread over the freckled face. "Your da?" she asked. "What's the matter—"

"Nothing, nothing," Kylie quickly interrupted. "Daddy's fine. It's just that . . . I was . . . well. Could you sit down for a minute?"

Ruby looked about the bar, then anxiously rubbed her hands on her apron. "Sure hon'," she said, sliding onto the bench across from her. "What is it?"

"Ruby, I . . . I don't really know how to put this. I just wanted to know if . . . if anything were to ever happen to me . . . say if . . . well, if anything were to ever happen, you would look out for my father, wouldn't you? He doesn't really have anyone else, you know."

"Is something the matter, lass? Are you sick or—"

"No, nothing like that," Kylie said, forcing a smile. "I'm fine. I just got to thinking, worrying about what would become of him."

After a long thoughtful pause, Ruby answered. "I'll shoot straight with you, hon'," she said. "I didn't really think that you cared for me much. Sean has told me how close you were to your ma. Daughters don't usually take kindly to their da's . . . you know . . . lady friends."

When she said the last of it, her eyes glanced away.

Kylie's face reddened; for the first time ever, the friction between them had been given voice. It was true that she could never picture her father with anyone other than her mother, but she had never imagined anyone knew how she felt. With growing shame, she thought of the many times she had avoided inviting Ruby on their outings.

"I'm sorry," she said softly. "I never even realized how—how it must have seemed . . ."

"That's alright, lass," said the woman, patting her hand. "No crime in loving your ma. If I had a daughter, I'd expect the same. But there's really no need to be worryin' about an old gal like me. Your da' still loves your ma with all his heart. She was the love of his life. Mick was the love of mine. But me and your da', we got a nice thing," she said with a pensive smile. "We're buds, me and your da'. I wouldn't let him hurt, child. I wouldn't let it happen."

Through the windows, the *Miss Lila* had eased into its boat slip, and Sean was out on the wooden planking, hoisting the ropes onto the dock. At sight of his stooped shoulders and weathered neck, tears suddenly welled in Kylie's eyes. Her father appeared an old man, forced into the labor of a twenty-year-old. He worked long hard days to return to a shabby little closet of a house.

"Hey," said Ruby. "Are you sure you're alright?"

Kylie wiped her face. "I'm fine," she said, her gaze roaming past the docks, to the fine houses on the far shore. "I was just thinking that Daddy needs one of those nicer homes. Something with proper plumbing and central air."

In spite of herself, Ruby let out a snort of laughter. "And where would the sweet lug get that kind of money?"

Though Kylie said nothing, her heart lifted. Her estate would assure that her father would never have to work another day in his life. "Well, if he ever does," she said. "Encourage him to get one of those nice houses."

"You got it," said Ruby, with a grin. "But I have to warn you, lass. If your da' ever moved to that side of the shore, he'd have every bloke in here fightin' to be his roomy."

Kylie smiled. "Worse things could happen," she said. She looked to the packages beside her. "Well, I better be gettin' out there." She started to scoot from the booth, but then hesitated. "Ruby, can we keep this between us? I don't want Daddy—"

"Not to worry child. My lips are sealed."

KYLIE paused at the end of the dock, watching her father move across the planking. With the sun cast across his features, he looked alive and young again. His hair was tousled and glowing like fire, his strong arms flexing with the weight of a trap. It was a familiar sight—one of the first that had been emblazoned into Kylie's memory as a child— her father happily at work, with the afternoon sun on his shoulders. When he finally turned and saw her, a big smile broke across his face.

"There's my girl," he said proudly.

"Hi Daddy," she said, dropping the packages on the dock as she moved toward him. In spite of his soiled shirt she wrapped her arms around his neck.

"You're gonna ruin that pretty blouse of yours," he said.

"It doesn't matter," she said, holding tight. "I love smelling like sea dredge."

"What's this?" her father asked, when he saw the tears in her eyes.

"Nothing Daddy," she said. "I'm just happy to see you. I brought you some stuff, some sweaters and things."

"Good heavens, love. What have you been up to?"

"Just a little shopping," she said. "Another package will be delivered tomorrow."

He pulled out a red cap and slid it down over his head. "I don't know what to say, love. You shouldn't be buyin' me—"

"Now Daddy," she interrupted. "There's no sense protesting. You know it makes me happy."

Though the bill of the hat threw a shadow across his face, Kylie saw the distress in her father's eyes.

"Well, I'm glad to see you're alright," he said. "I was wondering where you'd been off to these last few days."

Kylie quickly looked away from the trusting eyes. She hadn't told her father of Amelia's death. There was no sense worrying him, for he would learn soon enough. "I've been dealing with the insurance and all that kind of stuff," she said.

Her father was studying her, looking for signs of depression, she knew. "You'll tell me if you need anything, won't you, love?" he finally asked.

"I will, Daddy," she said. "Dillon's been helping," she added weakly.

Satisfied with the answer, the awkward moment passed.

"Well, let's get this belle going," her father said, stepping back onto the boat. "I got some bread and potatoes and a couple of fat lobsters to butter up."

As the *Miss Lila* headed back out to sea, the water remained calm, the afternoon clear and blissful. Standing upon the deck, Kylie looked to the open sheet of the waveless Atlantic. With the beauty of the endless sky, with the rich smell of lobster and the sound of an Irish melody floating up from the cabin, she felt hope, promise that she was not leaving her father to ruin. He had friends and he had Ruby. He had the *Miss Lila* to lull and soothe him, to welcome him into her belly and carry him out to sea.

Like herself, her father was a survivor. He loved life and would fight to the end to keep it. The loss of his only remaining child would be a blow, but one he would surely survive.

As she looked out at the rippling sea, a quiet relief settled over her; her tasks were now complete.

With the sun on her face, she took in the moment, the comfort of her father's proximity, the serenity that the sea imparted and felt peace. For a long while she remained still, her gaze purposely avoiding the horizon. She didn't want to see the moon, the silvery wedge that had risen into the blue sky, the promise of the night to come.

Forty-Eight

WITH HER HAND HESITANT UPON THE LATCH, KYLIE PAUSED AT THE heavy door to the Greyson mansion. The smell of the ocean was still fresh in her hair, yet it didn't stop the foreboding from spreading inside of her. She had felt safe and alive on her father's boat, but the night had brought the return of the uncertainty. She looked to the west, to the lights of the city. Dusk had fallen thick and heavy, the heat seeming to intensify rather than abate with the disappearing sun. In the distance she could hear the gala sounds of the Cambridge River Festival, of laughter and of dance, of boats ringing through the Charles River, yet the lively sounds made her feel all the more isolated and ghostlike.

Upon leaving Swampscott, she had once again felt the strange absence of her own presence—as if time had already erased over her. No sooner had she left the docks, when the sensation had caught her breath. The *Miss Lila* was bobbing in the water, her father lost in a conversation with Declan O'Connor. In seconds the morrow had come, and she was no longer in it. Lingering outside of the mansion, she felt the empty crevice before her, the dark hole into which she was slowly succumbing.

With a twist of the key, she was inside and the door was bolted behind her. She left the lights off, for the moon illuminated the stairwell and the floors overhead. The message light was blinking, yet she hesitated before touching the play button for fear of hearing Amelia's frightened voice again. She had not erased the call, had not been able to bring herself to it. She hit the button twice and waited for the voice. "Playing message number two."

"Kylie, this is Dr. Sauvage. I've got the results of your blood test and everything looks fine. I would still like to talk to you. If you could, please give me a call at—"

Kylie hit the reset button and stood staring pensively at the machine. Her blood was fine. There were no lurking diseases to abruptly snuff her life. If only it had been that simple. She looked upward, through the dark tunneling stairs, a shudder running through her. "Don't," she whispered. If she allowed herself to wonder, to dwell on what her demise might be, she would never make it through the night.

Slipping off her shoes, she ascended slowly, step by step.

BY THE THIRD glass of brandy, the edges of the room had begun to soften. Kylie stood by the bed, unsure where to turn next. Again she went over the checklist in her mind. It was all complete. There would be no complicated messes for her father to deal with; the estate was in order. She had even purchased a suit for him to wear to her funeral.

She took another sip of the brandy, the sting of the liquor melting inside of her. While her body had begun to numb, she was hoping that her mind would soon follow. With no more chores to occupy herself with, she didn't want to be left at the mercy of her fear. The house was strangely quiet, just as it had been the night before. There were no creaking boards, or moans of settling, just an unnerving silence.

Quickly pulling her blouse over her head, she turned her attention to the simple task of bathing. Instead of a lengthy soak in the master-bathroom, she would shower across the hall. She wanted to be in bed as quick as possible, to drown her trepidation in slumber.

Within minutes she was stepping from the shower, when her eyes caught a pair of gloves wedged just below the rungs of the gas heater. As she bent slowly, she saw they were Jack's—ones they had searched endlessly to find.

Taking them into her hands, her throat pulled tight with sadness. "Jack," she whispered, feeling the worn leather, wrapping her fingers within their grasp. They were merely old work-gloves, but they had been his favorite. Thinking back, she now realized how they had vanished. The couple had been finishing the room's renovations when Jack had become distracted. She had been painting along the floor-board when he had reached his hand up her shorts and felt beneath her panties.

"Go back to work," she had laughed, pulling away from him, but he had been relentless. He had taken her on the floor, on the cool tiles at her feet. In the midst of their passion he had slid the gloves from his hands and tossed them away.

In remembering the night, she could still hear their lovemaking echoing within the small chamber. She could see the spent lust in his eyes as he had sweetly bathed her and wrapped her within a towel. He had nestled behind her and turned her toward the mirror.

"Round one," he had whispered.

Ensnared by the memory she turned to the glass, only it was not her husband's wanton face that stared back at her, but the red eyes of the mortician.

Surely Mrs. O'Rourke you would like to be bathed and dressed. At once the gaunt figure leaned over her, his sweaty fingers crawling across her skin, slithering inside of her.

"Oh Jesus!" she gasped, pinching her eyes shut. The image had come from within, yet it startled her as surely as if Harden Truthers had materialized behind her.

When she reopened her eyes, the scene had vanished, yet it left her shivering. In truth, the next hands upon her would not be Jack's, but the mortician's. The lecherous man would be the one to pull her clothes from her body, to do with her as he willed.

She imagined herself laying naked and waxen upon a steel table, vulnerable to his probing eyes and hands. She would have no control, no way of even knowing what was done to her, for she would no longer have dominion over her own flesh.

Staring into her own frightened eyes, she reached out and touched the glass. "It doesn't matter," she whispered. "It would no longer be you." But instead of relief, the thought brought a deeper kind of terror. The image before her was the only proof—the only physical evidence of her being. It was how people related to her, how she saw herself. With that gone, Kylie O'Rourke as she now knew herself would cease to exist.

As the terror within her deepened, she turned away. She thought of the brandy, of the pills on the bedside table. Her insides were trembling and she needed something more to quell her, but as she looked to the door, her thoughts went to the last time she had bathed within the dark mansion. She was alone within the room, yet she couldn't say the same for the rest of the house. Julius Vanderpoel could be roaming beneath.

Standing silent, fear began to overtake her. She had made it to the room undaunted, but the sudden thought of leaving it rendered her immobile. She reached for her robe, but then suddenly had to grip the counter behind her to catch her balance. The brandy had seeped into her veins more effectively than she had thought. Her ears were ringing and her heart was tripping ahead of itself.

Just relax, her mind instructed. She had heard no sounds, and there were no tell-tale lights coming from the corridor as before.

Stepping into the hallway, she peered to the floor beneath. Though the study remained dark, she kept her eyes focused on the stairs as she passed back to the master bedroom.

Once inside, she quietly shut the door and latched it, yet even as she pulled the bolt over she knew—no lock could stop the one she feared most.

ATOP the bed she felt exposed, the vast room stretching in each direction. In spite of the heat, she left her robe on and pulled the curtains of the canopy shut. Closing herself inside of the four-poster bed, it felt suddenly safer, a tiny fortress against the outside perils. As she lay back within the sheets, the bed suddenly shifted and took a dip. She tried to relax, to slow her thudding heart, but when she closed her eyes, she was suddenly sinking downward.

Whether I'm in one piece or twenty, just put me in the casket and lock it.

Her eyes were instantly open, staring up at the canopy above her. It was a directive she had given, yet she was now startled by its consequence. She would be trapped within the heavy vault and then lowered beneath the earth. There would be no light, no air. At once the sheets beneath her became the satin of the coffin, while the sinking feeling became the disintegration of her skin.

With a deep breath she sat upright, yet the horrid thought remained: her cheeks, her shoulders, her breasts, would all soon be rotting within an airless tomb. The bed seemed suddenly constrictive, the burgundy material moving inward to suffocate her. Pulling back one of the curtains, she dropped her feet to the side of the bed. The legs that stretched before her were not rotted and gray, but long and supple. Her arms were smooth and toned.

With a tremulous touch, she ran her hand over her hips, up her stomach and across her breasts. She was alive.

"Alive," she whispered. She was alive, yet she had been abandoned—left for death. Bitterness stung in her throat. Though her body was still young and vibrant, she would never again make love. She would not be allowed to give birth or live to see herself grow old. Like an animal caught within a trap, she had been left for the darkness to feast upon.

As she rubbed her hand against her hot forehead, she was startled to find tears running down her cheeks.

Reaching to the bedside table, she grabbed the Secobarbital. As with the night before, they would stop the harrowing thoughts, bringing a haze into which she could sleep. She filled the glass again with brandy, and swallowed two of them down. She took another long drink and then another. It was an old habit she knew, but one she had learned well. If enough of the liquid burned inside of her, it would silence all.

Connecting the gap in the curtains, she lay back again. She would not close her eyes, she would merely rest, and wait for the pills to take her.

IT WAS the sound of breathing—a deep heavy rhythm—that pulled her from the black sleep. Her eyes fluttered open, to the bed that rose over her, the curtains distorting upward into a red tunnel. Her body was chilled from her own sweat, yet she didn't move, didn't reach for the robe that had fallen from her bare skin. She lay paralyzed, intensely aware of the folds of the canopy, for the breath that had awakened her had not been her own, but one from the other side of the thick fabric. Through the corner of her eyes, she could see the silhouette moving slowly along the edge of the bed.

Her pulse shrieked as the figure stopped at the footboard and turned toward her, yet she lay perfectly still and unblinking. Julius Vanderpoel had come at last. Like a hungry animal, he waited behind the thick curtains, his shoulders silhouetted against the night.

At once, her mind was fumbling over itself. She had known this moment would come—she had known that night in the study when he had locked her within his bestial gaze—yet she lay vulnerable, her reflexes deadened at her own hand. Whether he had come for her flesh, or the clock to her final hour had been started, there would be no escape. To the far left lay the door, yet she would never make it past the figure in time—her head was too heavy from the booze and barbiturates. Once again the canopy around her became her tomb, while the figure before her, her taker.

With a gasp she was suddenly moving, fumbling through the blackness. She was bolting outward, through the break in the curtains on her right. She found the floor at her feet and could feel the wall at her hand, yet when she turned for the opening, the figure appeared within the passage in front of her. Recoiling back, she was trapped within the corner, the sheet pulled tight around her.

At once, her head was swimming, the looming figure tilting off balance. Her breath had nearly stopped, yet her heart thundered mercilessly, hammering through her body.

"You have no reason to fear, Kylie Rose," came the smooth voice. "I didn't come for your death."

The promise whispered against her ear. It burned through her head, through her limbs, yet it didn't stop the tremor inside of her. She thought of the night in the study, of the hunger within his eyes. Even without seeing his face she could feel it now—the determination behind his breath. He had not come to end the nightmare, but to pull her deeper inside of it.

With her focus trained on the black silhouette, she could see the door to the left—a mere smudge of black in her peripheral vision. Gripping the sheet tighter, she prepared to run, but in the next moment the figure stepped aside, the moonlight ebbing across the pale face.

"I won't stop you," he said, opening the path before her. "I would never take you against your will."

With a start, she saw the desire in the gray eyes. They were focused upon her, yet they were controlled and waiting. His hair was disheveled, and like a heroin addict in need of a fix, he seemed to struggle with the very instincts that drove him, yet he remained still.

"You're free to go," he whispered.

The words were so gentle they slid through her hazy thoughts like silk. His eyes were locked upon her, but as promised, he was simply waiting and watching. He was giving her escape, and in her mind she was moving past him, through the door and into the night, yet she had not taken a step. Something further, deeper beneath her will kept her riveted.

Within the rhythm of her own breath, everything around her seemed suddenly a dream—a distorted, crystallized dream. She became aware of the open window, of the breeze that carried the sounds of the city. An entire world hummed beyond, yet she stood alone, no longer part of its existence; all ties and roots had been slowly severed. She tried to think of Jack, of the warehouse, of the life she had once had, but it seemed a mere blur. It had all vanished, disintegrated into the twisting darkness.

All that remained was the shadow before her—the familiar counte-

nance and grace that had lain hidden within her thoughts for so long.
Through her childhood, through Savannah and her marriage, a silent
ghost just beneath the surface, guiding her, drawing her back. All the
rest had been a mere sidetrack, avenues and bridges returning her to
him, to a treaty formed long ago within a dim hallway—to an inter-
marriage of trust and brutality, of a child's innocence and desire.

"You're mine, my little rose. You've always been mine."

He had resurrected from the past to claim her at last.

And like a prisoner to the pact, she had prepared herself for him.
She had lain naked beneath the robe, she had taken the pills and the
booze. She had given him the door in.

"You've been waiting," he said softly.

The heat of the night became suddenly unbearable, pressing upon
her, confusing her senses. She tried to look away, but the lustful gaze
would not release her. Like a mirage promising refuge, the sensual
lips ebbed in and out of the light, drawing her inward. She became
suddenly aware of her bare shoulders, of the chills rising all over her
skin. She was not rotting within a tomb; she was alive and naked beneath the sheet. He was craving her, and though his hands were not
upon her, she was awakening with desire.

"Please," she murmured, her head at once light and swirling.
"Please—"

But the supplication had come too late; he was moving toward her
through the shadows, the warmth of his hand sliding behind her neck,
pulling her inward.

"I can't," she gasped, but his lips were upon hers, tasting her, warm
and moist.

"Shh, my little rose," he whispered, his breath hot against her skin.

Within the heat of his touch, the air was suddenly moving, the ceiling above her blurring within the shadows. It wasn't real, it couldn't
possibly be happening. He was a mere whisper, a mere ghost, yet his
body was pressing against her, hungry and strong, his heart beating
faster . . . more thunderously than humanly possible—a quick, ravenous beat that drove from beneath. The lips were suckling her, consuming her like a much-needed opiate. The sheet was parting, his
touch smoothing across her thigh, between her legs. She clutched the
hand, but it had already found her. With a start she felt her own
warmth, her flesh giving as she accepted his touch.

At once the fever was devouring her, rushing against her senses. Her lips were quivering, searching out his own, the taste of him, the feel of him, her will defeated—taken prisoner within her own flesh. It all blurred into one desperate need, a voice, a small desperate voice, a crying whimper wanting more, taking more.

They were moving back upon the bed, when beneath the frenzy of her own breath sprang an icy vein of lucidity. There was a moment of terror, a deep resonating terror in which she knew: she wanted it— she had always wanted it. The gray cold eyes, the brutality behind the gentle touch . . . Julius Vanderpoel. The prince of her childhood, the prince of her dreams.

Tell us about the man, Kylie McCallum. Tell us about the rose.

There were no more discerning lines, dividing the darkness. She was no longer trapped within the vents, hiding, cowering in fear. She was no longer running from the darkness, she was embracing it.

"Kylie Rose."

Forty-Nine

JUST AFTER SUNRISE, THE TRUCK FROM TANDY'S BOAT & SUPPLY PULLED up to the dock and began unloading in front of the *Miss Lila*.

Sean was on his way back from coffee at the pub when he saw the three men piling boxes at the edge of his dock.

"What's all this?" he asked, stepping out of the way of a crate that had sprouted legs.

A beefy man turned back, the cigar in his mouth leaking ashes onto his sweaty tee-shirt. "Are you McCallum?" he asked, squinting into the sun.

"Yeah."

"I was just about to come down and get ya'," he said, dropping the load onto the dock. "We're from Tandy's. Your neighbor said you were down there eatin' breakfast, so I thought we'd go ahead and start unloading."

Sean looked with dismay at the bustling workers. "I hate to tell you this, but I didn't order anything," he said. "I haven't been in Tandy's in over a month."

The man wiped his brow and unraveled a pink slip of paper. "It's from a . . . Kylie O'Rourke. Ring any bells?"

"Yeah, that's my daughter," said Sean. "But she couldn't have ordered all of this."

"Well," said the man. "It's right here on the invoice. Gill nets, mesh bags, rubber boots, rain gear—"

"Then there's been some kind of mistake," interrupted Sean. "My daughter said I would be getting a package today. She didn't say anything about a whole truckload of stuff."

"Well, actually we were just supposed to deliver one of the crates— the rest she wanted put on account for you."

"On account?"

"Yeah—prepaid. Said she was goin' away and wanted to make sure you were outfitted through the winter. But we're not a storage house. We need the space." He turned again to the crate and continued onward. "Don't worry," he said, glancing back over his shoulder. "You won't get stuck for the delivery. When someone shells out this kind of dough, the delivery's on us."

"Just hold on a second," Sean said, stepping in front of him. "I'll pay your delivery charges, but you're gonna have to take all of this back—"

"Sorry buddy, but you don't have much of a choice. Even if I wanted to take it back, we don't have room for it."

Sean pointed to the ever-mounting stack of traps. "The last time I checked, those were running at $55.00 apiece."

"Sixty," corrected the man.

"How many of those are you unloading?" he asked.

"A hundred."

"That's over six thousand bucks," said Sean. "My daughter doesn't have that kind of money."

"She paid cash," said the man, as though it were the definitive answer. "Sign here," he said, thrusting a pen and a clip board into McCallum's hand. "She also put a trap hauler on the account. Said your hydraulics had gone out on it. We won't have that in stock for a few days but as soon as we get it in we'll give you a call."

He took back the pen and pocketed it. "If you ask me, you're a lucky man," he said, shaking his head. "My boy's too cheap to even buy me a cigar, let alone stock up my boat months in advance. Everyone always wants a boy, but girls—they know how to look after their old pops. I shoulda had a girl. That's all there is to it," he groaned, hopping up into the cab of the truck. "Must be some trip she's takin'," he said leaning out the passenger window. "Those supplies'll last you a year."

With a wave of his hand, the truck pulled away, a dust cloud rising in its wake.

For a long moment Sean stood silent, the morning sun warming the back of his neck. As though a leaden wrench had slid down his throat, his stomach had grown heavy. He turned back to the dock, to the neat pile glistening in the sun. Not only had his daughter not mentioned a trip, but she had meant for the overwhelming purchase to remain a secret. Had the supplies not been delivered, it could have been months before he would have gone in to Tandy's. While the faulty hauler was in dire need of replacement, the new traps would not have been needed for some time to come.

Must be some trip she's takin', lingered the man's words. *Those supplies'll last you a year.*

"What are you up to, love?" uttered Sean, his brow fretted with consternation. "What the devil are you up to?"

Fifty

THE MORNING OOZED BETWEEN HER PUFFY LIDS, THE RED SEA OF LIGHT fingering into her deadened senses. With a groan, Kylie turned her head, the pain shooting through the base of her skull.

"Jack?" she murmured, her mouth pasty, her hand reaching to the sheets that lay crumpled beside her. He had been there a moment earlier, the weight of his body pulling the side of the bed down, the roll of the mattress intensifying the nausea within her. Digging her fingers into her brow, she struggled to place the night before—images spun past, but vanished without cohesion. Beneath a layering of dreams, there were faces, Jack's friend Freddy and the rest of the old gang. Alice Newfield had been there laughing, her ruby lips spewing obscenities. "You were fucking him, you know," she howled. "Fucking him!"

At once a memory bore out of the fog, one of flesh upon flesh, of Julius Vanderpoel's silhouette rising above her.

With a sudden feeling of doom, Kylie thrust her eyes wide. Her face was pressed against the pillow, the morning screeching to a halt in front of her. She was not in her own bed as she had surmised, but in Dora's, the covers strewn across her midsection. She was naked, the feel of sex dried between her legs.

"Oh Jesus," she murmured, sitting upright, the moment settling over her in a black mist. Like a drugged dream, the night continued to elude her. She remembered only fragments of the figure coming to her, of her passionate moans and his darkened eyes as he had moved into her. Atop the night stand lay the uncapped bottle of pills, and the brandy glass she vaguely remembered emptying.

With tremulous fingers she reached for the robe and pulled it around her. From across the room, an oval mirror imitated her movements, but the image that corresponded was too beaten to be her own. Her face was frightfully drawn, her hair matted.

With a sudden churn of her stomach, she noticed a shape behind her, a pale figure sitting silent in a chair. She turned back, the reflection seizing the form of Julius Vanderpoel.

He was staring toward her, the morning light resting hesitantly upon his calm face. Like a reflection of her own disintegrating spirit he had changed, somehow faded. He was no longer the lustful beast that had taken her within the night, but an aging man. As though time were accelerating, tiny lines had formed along his eyes and mouth. His hair had dulled and tapered at the temples, as if several years had passed within the dawn.

"You're very observant, my dear," he said softly, his voice dry and raspy. "Time has begun again—my fall precipitated."

Kylie was reminded of his recount of Origen's theory—of the willful spirit falling closer to earth—pausing only briefly to walk again as a man—

"—before reaching extinction," he finished with a slight smile. With a kerchief he dabbed at his nose, where blood had begun to seep. After a thoughtful moment, he pulled the white cloth out before him and surveyed it. "'Headlong themselves they threw down from the verge of heaven, eternal wrath . . . Burnt after them to the bottomless pit.'" Then a sardonic smile, a moment of self-irony. "I never cared for John Milton, but his words bear a certain veracity, I'm afraid."

Kylie was silent, unable to assimilate words or a response. The pale lips and flaxen hair did not belong within the light of day, but in the illusory effect of the night. The dim room seemed suddenly too bright, the light crude in its unveiling of the shadows.

"It won't be long now," he continued. "For either of us." His gaze drifted, as if to other words and phrases etched upon the walls of the dim room. "Another has already been sent. She watched you as you slept."

Kylie was startled. She felt suddenly exposed, her adrenaline surging. "Another?" she asked, barely able to choke off the word. She looked behind her, half-expecting to see the specter of which he spoke.

"My time with you is finished," he said simply, rising to his feet.

When she saw that he was preparing to leave, an unexpected panic came over her. He was leaving, saying good-bye. The end was near, perhaps mere hours away, yet he would not be the one to take her. For the first time, she saw clearly the link that bound them. Although he had brought misery and fear, without his shield, she would be forced to face the darkness alone.

His eyes warmed, as if her thoughts amused him. Moving toward her, he paused within inches of her. She felt his breath, and though she still fought it, her body flushed with his proximity.

"I'll miss you too, my rose," he said, stroking her cheek.

He lingered for a moment, a finale to the life-long bond—the life-long torment. His face had softened, his eyes startling in their tenderness. Then he moved apart from her, and walked to the door.

As if in afterthought, he turned back, his face filled with genuine regret. It took him a moment to speak, but when he did, his voice was low, fatherly. "I'm sorry for what you're about to know. It wasn't meant to be. There was never a soul for the child."

The words were strange, stirring the nausea within her. She grasped the bedpost to steady herself. She felt off, disoriented, the lingering effects of the night battering against her raw senses. "What child?" she meant to ask, but his lips had already parted in response.

"Your husband's. It's been growing inside of you."

With the jolt, she drew back, her hand instinctively touching her abdomen. She was silent, for nothing could have stunned her more.

"It wasn't meant to be," he said steadily. "You were to have already been dead when it was conceived."

As she stared blankly, the words, their implication lingering around her like a faint scent, the figure passed from the doorway. The sound of his footsteps descending the stairs was labored, slow.

Alone within the room, she remained still. Her pulse was racing, yet she didn't move. She was struggling to grasp, to comprehend or simply to believe. It couldn't be. It simply couldn't be. She was trying to think back, to remember her last period—through the weeks that had passed, yet she could not decipher the time. It was all a haze of trauma and emotion. She became suddenly aware of her tender breasts, her swollen belly. She had felt the changes but had been so consumed by all around her, that they had not registered. She thought of Dr. Sauvage's message, which abruptly took on new relevance. Though all was well, he had wanted her to call, perhaps to tell her, to—

She immediately went to the dressing table, to find the card, the number. For a moment she merely stared at the receiver, before lifting it to dial. When the receptionist answered, her voice brightened with Kylie's name. "Yes, Mrs. O'Rourke, he's been expecting you," she said, and then promptly put her through to the doctor.

"Good morning, my dear," he said. "You got my message about your tests?"

"Yes," she answered, her throat tight.

He was hesitant, clearly preparing to relay something difficult. "I hope you don't mind, but I ran a couple of extra tests . . . a pregnancy test—"

With the word, she faltered. Her head was reeling, yet the doctor's voice continued. He was congratulating her, yet his tone remained serious. He wanted her to see a physician, to make sure that everything was okay. "I'm sure you're fine," he was saying. "But it's still wise to see an obstetrician as soon as possible . . ."

"Yes," she answered distractedly.

With the perfunctory good-byes, the phone rested neatly back into its cradle.

Again she was motionless, grappling to comprehend that a being had somehow formed inside of her, Jack's child. As if in response to her thoughts, a pull shot through her abdomen. "Oh God!" she gasped, her fingers pressing to her lips, her stomach.

Jack's child was inside of her. Even after his death he had been there all along, growing inside of her. Suddenly the faintness and the ever-present nausea she had taken for grief had clarity: she was pregnant.

"Pregnant," she whispered aloud. As the overwhelming thought found a home it brought a twinge of elation. Jack was with her; she need only touch her belly to be near him. It brought a moment of comfort, yet when she noticed her reflection within the gray morning light, her heart tripped.

The child will not live, came the totality of her thoughts. It was only a matter of hours before they would both be dead.

Clutching her robe, her eyes dark and desperate, she appeared a mere step away from it. With her veins still pulsing with the liquor and pills, she resembled less a mother, than a whore after a long and brutal night. Again she felt the soreness between her legs, an aching from the vigorous sex; not only had she forsaken Jack, but she had forsaken their child. She quickly turned away but there was no escaping it: their very nemesis was still inside of her. While the stained sheets were strewn across the bed, the stench of her infidelity, of the unnatural and twisted union was within her.

Her stomach was suddenly churning, heaving, for there was no turning back. With the nausea smothering her, pulling her breath, she turned. She was running, fumbling toward the bathroom. As her hands grasped the cool porcelain, she sank to her knees, the dry heaves overtaking her. When the retching finally subsided, she was sobbing. She went to the bathtub and drew water, cold and hot blasting at full volume. Filling her hands, she splashed it across her face. She stepped inside of the basin, and sank downward. She grabbed the soap and rubbed it across her lips, her breasts, then slid it between her thighs.

It wasn't until she sat back, until her tears fell away to a quiet weeping, that she sensed the child inside of her again. She could not feel its movement, but she imagined it growing, changing with every beat of her heart. She wondered how big it was and if its tiny little hands and feet had formed. Though she could not see or touch it, she felt an instant bond. She tried to remain firm, to tell herself that there was no chance for the child, but the tide of longing was too strong. Against all logic and reason, hope ebbed inward—hope that she could somehow survive and that the baby would be carried to term. She imagined herself at six months and then nine, then holding the child within her arms, a rosy-cheeked little baby smiling up at her. But just as she allowed herself to think it, to indulge in the precarious fires of fantasy, she felt a cramp and saw the portent of the agony to come. Like a thin red ribbon, blood seeped from between her legs—a tiny trickle staining the clear water red.

Fifty-One

"IT'S PROBABLY JUST A LITTLE BREAKTHROUGH BLEEDING MA'AM. There's nothing to be alarmed about." The receptionist's voice was monotone, indifferent.

With feverish hands, Kylie gripped the counter of the emergency-room window. "Please," she said. "I want to see a doctor. I need to see a doctor."

"I'm sorry ma'am," said the young girl. "If you'll just take your seat in the waiting room—"

"But it's taking so long. Why is it taking so long?" Kylie looked past the window, but there was no one in sight. Again she felt the seeping of blood from inside of her, the last remnant of Jack fading away. "Please, can I just talk to someone? Maybe the nurse or a resident doctor?"

"We're going as fast as we can," said the receptionist, with a perturbed sigh. "You just have to be patient."

"But you don't understand," Kylie begged, her voice breaking with emotion. "There's something wrong. I know that there's something wrong."

"Ma'am, just take a seat and I'll call you—"

"Please—"

"Take your seat and—"

"No!" Kylie shrieked, pounding her fist onto the counter. "I'm gonna miscarry, goddamn it! Can't you hear what I'm saying?!"

Abrupt silence fell over the clinic; even the distant typing stopped.

A security guard appeared from within, eyeing her warily. "Please step back from the window, ma'am," he said.

Kylie saw the fright in the receptionist's eyes and released her hands from the counter. "I'm sorry," she murmured, smoothing her hair from her face. Through their appraising stares, she suddenly realized how she must appear. With her red eyes, rumpled dress and pores reeking of booze, she could have been a lunatic or a drug addict or one of the many homeless that wandered through the door into the small clinic.

The stuffy room became even tighter, the patients lining the walls all staring at her. An Asian couple avoided her gaze while a sickly child, nestled within the crook of his mother's arm, was frowning with fear.

"I'm sorry," she repeated.

The receptionist was still staring, when a nurse approached her from behind.

"It's alright, Brittany," said the nurse. "I can take it from here. Come on back, Mrs. O'Rourke," she instructed with a smile.

Still shaking, Kylie retrieved her bag from the bench, and entered the door on her left.

"This way," said the nurse brightly, turning down the long corridor before them.

The clinic was dirty and much dimmer than Massachusetts General, which Kylie had avoided for fear of seeing Dillon. Though she would have felt better at the familiar hospital, she wouldn't have been able to face him, to explain the guilt in her eyes or the seemingly irrational conviction that the pregnancy was doomed.

"If you'll undress from the waist down," the nurse said stopping before an open door, "the doctor will be in shortly to examine you."

Left alone within the room, Kylie tried desperately to collect herself. She went to a small sink in the corner and splashed cool water on her face, looking only briefly at her weary reflection. Without even realizing it, she had lost weight. Her cheekbones were more prominent, her eyes somehow brighter. "Pregnant," she said aloud. The word still seemed foreign, yet a maternal instinct had already taken hold, quicker and more powerfully than she had ever imagined possible. More than life, she wanted the child, but with the flow of her own blood her body was betraying her. As her lips began to quiver, she bit down on the emotion and turned to the task of changing. Just as she pulled off the dress and wrapped the paper robe around her, a knock sounded at the door.

"Come in," she said.

"And how are you today, young lady? I'm Dr. William George." The portly doctor smiled cheerfully. "I understand that you're having some problems?"

"Yes," she answered softly.

"Well, you're in good hands," he said kindly, patting the top of her hand. With his round little glasses and gray hair, Kylie instantly thought of a grandfather—of a Santa Claus whose optimism and cheer assured that no one in his care could ever face misfortune.

"I suppose congratulations are in order," he continued. "That is, assuming this is a wanted pregnancy?"

"Yes," she said.

"According to your last normal period," said the doctor, looking at the clipboard in his hands, "you should be seven weeks along." He closed it, turning a scrutinizing eye toward her.

Kylie was once again aware of her appearance, of the faint odor of liquor. "I didn't know I was pregnant," she said. "I had some brandy and . . . pills," she added, unable to meet the doctor's eyes.

"What kind?"

"Sleeping pills. Secobarbital, I believe."

"Barbiturates and alcohol. That's an unwise combination, my dear."

"Yes."

"Well, that should be the end of that. We want a healthy pregnancy, now don't we?"

"Yes, of course," Kylie said with a wan smile. Under the doctor's attentive gaze, she dared to feel hope once again. She could almost imagine that there was no danger, no unseen force moving against her, that she was merely a mother at her first prenatal visit.

"Well, let's have a look," said the doctor, putting the clipboard aside.

Kylie lay back on the examination bed and put her feet in the stirrups.

As the doctor placed the cold speculum inside of her, she winced with the soreness. Closing her eyes in mortification, she was certain that the night's rough intercourse was evident.

"Let me start off by telling you," said the doctor slowly, "that nearly half of all pregnancies experience a little bleeding in the first few months. Usually, it's nothing to be alarmed about. Your cervix is not dilated, which is a good sign." He removed the speculum and stood between her legs. Placing two fingers into her vagina, he pushed down with his other hand on the outside of her pelvis. "The uterus feels the right size," he said, releasing her, then moving to the sink. "You can sit up now."

As she slid back up on the table, Kylie pulled the paper-wrap around her.

"Everything looks fine," he said cheerfully. "Just as a precaution, though, I would like to do an ultrasound scan. It's a very safe procedure wherein ultrasound waves are reflected from the fetus to give us an image on a monitor. That way we can actually see what's going on. You may have heard of a sonogram?"

Kylie nodded.

"It'll allow me to rule out one last concern. Because of the pain, I want to make sure that it's not an ectopic pregnancy."

"Ectopic?"

"Stuck outside of the uterus, in the fallopian tubes or cervix. While it's highly unlikely, it deserves a look. Ectopic pregnancies can be life-threatening to both the fetus and the mother, so they're not to be taken lightly. Again," he said quickly, "it's just a precaution. I think with bed rest, the bleeding will subside. And the soreness, well, I think we both know where that might have come from." He looked at her over the rim of his spectacles like a disapproving grandfather. "Perhaps lovemaking could be a little gentler next time," he said.

"Yes," said Kylie sheepishly.

"Well, let's get you set up for the sonogram. This'll give us a good excuse to see how handsome the little devil is," he said. "In fact, we'll see if we can't print out a photo of it for you to take home to your husband."

Kylie's breath caught, for she had not marked "widow" on the patient questionnaire.

"That would be nice," she responded.

• • •

WHEN she saw the head, the back, the tiny legs within the gray moving image, her heart leapt. It was there, as sure as her own hand, it was there.

"Very good," mumbled the doctor, moving the transducer over Kylie's bare abdomen. "Very good. The fetus is in the uterus where it should be. If you look closely you can see the head, the spine, the belly."

Within the cathode-ray monitor, the black and white details were faint yet detectible. Tears trickled down the side of Kylie's face as she watched the beautiful image. She longed intensely for Jack, just a few more seconds of his life to see what she was watching.

"It's the right size and length for seven weeks, and it appears to be developing nicely," said the doctor. "The head is still comparatively large in relation to the rest of the body. You can't see them clearly, but the eyes are formed, the hands and feet and all of the major internal organs have formed."

With every movement of the wand, a different aspect of the image was revealed.

"Is it too early to know the sex?" Kylie asked.

"Yes," he answered distractedly, his eyes enthralled with the image. "I'm looking for movement, which you wouldn't be able to feel yet, but should be detectible . . ." His voice trailed off, a look of puzzlement on his face. With a sudden lump in her throat, Kylie noticed his expression had changed, become more concentrated.

"Let's look for the heartbeat . . . shall we?" he said, moving the transducer over a different part of her abdomen. "Breathe," he said softly.

Without even realizing it, Kylie had been holding her breath. "Can you see it?" she asked, her eyes riveted on the little head, the rounded belly. "Can you see it?" she asked again, turning to the doctor whose face was lit with the glow of the monitor.

The doctor was not answering, the cheer having melted from his features. "The heart beats strongly by the sixth week and should be visible at this stage," he finally answered, "but that doesn't necessarily mean that it hasn't started."

He finally faced her and smiled, but there was something missing, some discomfort that he would not disclose.

"Our equipment is not exactly state of the art," he continued, looking away from her. "It's possible that we just can't detect it yet. An obstetrician would actually be able to tell you more—"

"But the movement, you said there should be movement."

The doctor had flipped off the monitor and was turning away. A nurse had entered the room and was standing behind him. "The pregnancy is intrauterine," he said to the nurse. "So there's no life-threat to Mrs. O'Rourke. You'll be fine," he said, turning back to Kylie.

As abruptly as flipping a switch, everything had changed. The doctor no longer resembled optimism, but a weak man incapable of delivering bad news. As if unwilling to sever the hope he avoided her eyes, and spoke in generalities with no further mention of the sonogram photo.

"Bed rest," he said, flashing a weak smile in her direction. "Plenty of bed rest, and schedule an appointment with your regular doctor as soon as possible. Don't wait any longer than a few days. Hopefully he'll be able to recommend an obstetrician," he said without conviction. "You'll be fine Mrs. O'Rourke. Terri will take care of you from here."

Without another word, the doctor left the examination room.

Left on her back to stare at the blank monitor, Kylie remained motionless. All thoughts, all hope and pain melded into one solid void, as cold and lifeless as the black picture before her. *There's no soul for the child*, came the pitying voice of Julius Vanderpoel. He had tried to warn her, to prepare her.

"It's dead, isn't it?" she asked, even though she knew by the doctor's cowardly exit, by the way the nurse was avoiding her gaze. She sat up, trying to regain her breath. "It's dead," she repeated, this time to herself, to the last flicker of hope dying inside of her.

"That's not what the doctor said," the nurse said gently. "Yes, Mrs. O'Rourke, he's uncertain. At this stage, the heart may have started and he was simply unable to detect it. It happens. All you can do is wait and see and let nature take its course."

"It already has," said Kylie, her tongue numb within her mouth.

"You can take Tylenol for the pain," said the nurse. "Other than that there's really nothing we can do if a spontaneous abortion does occur. You can remain within the comfort of your own home, or you

can come in. Either way, you'll need to see a doctor afterwards to assure that all of the fetus has been expelled."

Fetus expelled. The words were crude, perfunctory. It was no longer
a child to be nurtured but a foreign object to be ejected.

"Good luck to you Mrs. O'Rourke."

With that said, Kylie was left to face the agony alone. Her arms
were tight around her, her head down. Again no one could help her, no
one could see. No child existed, for its parents were to have already
been dead when it was conceived. There was no soul for the child for
it was never meant to be.

Fifty-Two

SEAN STARED INTO THE DIM FOYER OF THE MANSION, DEBATING WHETHER
or not to enter. Upon his knock, the front door had creaked open; the
handle had been locked, but someone in their haste had left it slightly
ajar. He stepped back off the porch and checked the house lettering
once again: 822 PICKNEY STREET. It was the address Kylie had given the
morning she had moved out—some society woman's house she had
been renovating—a Ms. Greystone or Greyson.

"Kylie?" he called once more into the stillness.

Noticing a pair of his daughter's sandals at the foot of the grand
staircase, he stepped reticently inward and looked up through the
landings. The house was so vast that if she were on an upper floor she
would not have heard him.

"Love?" he called even louder. Still no response. He hesitated a bit
longer. He thought of leaving, of going to a nearby pay phone and dialing the house, but when he clutched the doorknob and went to close
it, he felt uneasy about leaving after finding it ajar. Someone could
have snuck in while his daughter lay sleeping—

"Kylie? Can you hear me?" he shouted a little sterner. He glanced
toward the dining area, to the halls that branched off to each side, and
then began mounting the stairs. Once to the second floor, his eyes
were drawn to the bedroom.

"Hello?" he called, approaching the open doorway. Still nothing.

The bed was disheveled, the sheets strewn halfway across the floor. From where he stood he could see a bottle of liquor on the bedside table along with some pills. He noticed the faint odor of sickness—of vomit.

"You alright, love?" he asked quietly, the question to himself for the room was clearly empty.

Without will, his gaze was drawn to the sheets, to the center of the bed, where a murky stain, seemingly tainted with blood had formed in the shape of a pear. As a sharp image went through his mind, he looked quickly away. He felt suddenly embarrassed—an intruder, peering into his daughter's private life. He regretted entering the mansion and felt an urgency to get out.

Just then, a sound startled him so, that a deep groan escaped from his chest. It was a telephone, ringing from the entry downstairs. As he stood listening, a recorder picked it up. The voice was muffled, a woman's, greeting the caller.

Closing the door behind him, Sean moved away from the bedroom. He tried to put it from his thoughts, but the sight of the room had put a pit in his stomach. The disheveled bed, the stained sheets could mean only one thing: less than two weeks after her husband's death, his daughter had been with a man—a stranger perhaps—someone she had met at a bar or on the street, undoubtedly brought to her bed to assuage her grief. While on the *Miss Lila* she had maintained a smile, yet when alone, she was aching.

"Damn," Sean cursed aloud, wishing nothing more than to erase the last few minutes. He felt suddenly empty and ineffectual as a father. His baby girl had grown up; she was a woman in pain, searching for consolation in ways that he could not help her. As he began his descent of the stairs, a long beep sounded and then another voice echoed from beneath. It was a man's, thin and persnickety.

"Kylie, this is Harden Truthers, of Truthers & Bastien Mortuary. First off, I want to thank you again for coming to us for your pre-needs. I also wanted to let you know that everything has been taken care of concerning your casket . . ."

Seized at once, Sean stopped on the stairs.

"I think you'll be happy with my choice. It's from our most elegant line, with a rich damask lining—a sort of pale peach that I think will go quite nicely with your lovely complexion. So, you can rest assured that all has been taken care of, but if you feel the need to call, please don't hesitate. All the best to you, Mrs. O'Rourke," concluded the message.

Sean stood where he was, unable to move, unable to breathe. He suddenly dashed for the phone, but the line had already gone dead. He remained frozen a moment longer, his heart fluttering. He looked beneath the table for a phone book—then he remembered the number, one you could dial to get the last caller. He dialed "star," then hesitantly hit 69.

The same fastidious voice answered, tempered by a somber tone.

"Truthers & Bastien Mortuary... your place of heaven on earth. What may I do for you this morning?"

"Yes," said Sean, trying to remain steady. "You just left a message for my daughter, Kylie—"

"Kylie O'Rourke, yes. How may I help you, sir?"

"It sounded as though you've arranged a burial for her. You mentioned a casket?"

"Well, sir," came the cautious response. "Is Ms. O'Rourke present so that I might speak—"

"No, she's not. But I'm her father."

"Well, sir, a person's funeral arrangements are a private matter that—"

"What funeral arrangements?" demanded Sean, the fear building inside of him. "My daughter's not dead."

"No," said the voice patronizingly. "Of course not, but many choose to settle these matters before they pass away to make it easier on their loved ones—"

"My daughter's thirty-four years old," quipped Sean. "Not eighty."

"I understand that."

"She's got another forty or fifty years before she's gonna need your bloody services."

"You very well could be right, sir," said the mortician calmly. "We're simply trying to make it easier. In case something were to happen. You never know in this day and age—"

"What the hell's gonna happen to her?" demanded Sean. He stepped back, trying to control his anger.

"Sir," said the voice tartly. "Your daughter came to us. I merely provided her with what she requested."

"I bet you did. And at a fair price, I'm sure, you blood-suckin' shagger!"

"Sir, there's no need—"

"My daughter's fine! You got that? She's fine. She doesn't need your pre-need services and she sure as hell doesn't need your goddamned peachy casket!"

Sean slammed the phone into its cradle, then looked helplessly around him. "Bloody shagger," he cursed, wiping his lips. "Bloody shagger."

He paced to the right, and then to the left. He turned to the open door, to the sunshine and the world that moved beyond. As he stood silent, his anger was quickly eclipsed by fear. A small girl rode past on a bicycle but he did not see her. He saw only the booze, the pills, the huge stack of supplies resting on his dock. He saw his daughter's hollow smile, the pain in her eyes as she had hugged him "good-night."

"What would you be needin' with a casket, love?" he whispered.

Must be some trip she's taking, nagged the answer from within.

Fifty-Three

By THE TIME HE MADE IT TO CAMBRIDGE, SEAN HAD WORKED HIMSELF into such a fret that after he pulled the old truck up to the curb and cut the engine, he had to sit for a moment to calm himself. With a deep breath, he reached for the bottle of rye he kept stashed beneath his seat.

As he took a long pull from the liquor he studied the elegant brick house before him; all of the curtains and shutters were drawn. Over his right shoulder, he looked to the BMW parked in the drive. He was certain that the little black car was Dillon's. As the secretary had confided when he had called Dillon's office from the A & P, the doctor was home but was not accepting calls or visitors. "He's taken a leave of absence," she had said with more than a little distress in her voice. Though she had not elaborated, it was clear that the leave was not a vacation. When Sean had asked for Theresa Ollridge's number, for he knew of the close relationship between Dillon and the anesthesiologist, the secretary had been reluctant. "Mr. McCallum, I doubt she'll know anything more," she had said. By her crisp intonation he knew there must have been trouble between the couple.

In spite of the young man's wish for privacy, Sean had continued on to Cambridge without phoning. He couldn't take the chance that his call would be ignored, for there was no one else that could help him.

THE SOUND of the chime was shrill, intrusive within the still house. In the three days since Theresa had left, there had been nothing but silence. No television, no radio, no solicitors or gardeners. Just silence. For three days, Dillon had not wanted to see the light, to feel the outside presence of anyone.

As promised on the morning that Kylie had called from Savannah, Theresa had returned that evening for her belongings. With her sudden absence, the loneliness had hovered around him, choking him, sending him inward. Under the relentless introspection, there had been no more denying it. He had lied to himself and he had betrayed his brother. Though he had not intended it, had not wanted it, he was in love with Kylie O'Rourke. It was a disclosure that had hit him hard. He had taken a leave from the hospital with the intention of getting away, yet three days later he remained alone within the house.

The sight of Sean's truck was a brusque interruption into the blurred space of time. At first startled to see it parked at the curb, for Dillon was unaware that the fisherman even knew where he lived, he remembered that he had been to the house once before after Jack's funeral.

Without further hesitation, he unlatched the door. The older man did not smile or extend a greeting, the look on his face said it all: the visit was not a social call.

"Your secretary told me that you didn't want to be disturbed, but it's important."

"You're always welcome, Sean. Come on in," Dillon said, leading the way down the hall.

"I'm sorry. I hope I didn't wake you."

"Wake me? No," he said, though he knew why the question had been posed. It was mid-afternoon yet the house was dark. As he pulled back the shutters in the den, the light stung against the book-lined walls. "Make yourself comfortable," he said, pointing to a leather chair. "Would you like something to drink? I've got coffee or soda." He moved to the wet bar, but as he reached for a cup, he hesitated, then grabbed the whiskey glasses instead.

"I know you've got a lot on your mind," fretted Sean.

"Looks like I'm not the only one," said Dillon, handing him one of the glasses of whiskey. The father, who sat wringing his hands, had to unclench them to grasp it.

"What brings you out here?" Dillon asked, taking a seat before him.

"I need you to tell me the truth about something."

"I've always been straight with you, Sean, you know that."

The father stared toward him, took a sigh, then forced the question from his lips. "Is there something medically wrong with my daughter . . . terminally wrong?"

The question was so unexpected, that it took Dillon a moment to answer. "No," he said. "Not that I'm aware of. She made a complete recovery after the accident. Why do you ask?" he said, for his response had not seemed to ease the father.

Sean got up from the chair. "If there's nothing wrong with her, then I think she may be, well I think she may be thinking of . . . thinking of suicide," he finally managed to say.

Dillon was so stunned that he merely gaped at him.

"I may be jumping to conclusions," Sean continued. "But I don't think so." He proceeded to tell him of the shipment and of the conversation he had with the undertaker. Dillon stared into his glass of whiskey, silently adding his own assumptions to the father's.

"What is it?" asked Sean, noticing his reticence.

Dillon spoke slowly, cautiously. "When we were at the insurance office the other day, Kylie insisted on putting the claim into your name. She wanted to make sure you could collect the money . . . in case she died before it was disbursed."

"Bloody hell," sighed the fisherman.

In the silence that followed no doubt was left lingering: Kylie was anticipating her own death.

Sean shook his head. "My daughter's a fighter. She's a damn good fighter, but she's been through too much. I need you to help me, son," he said, turning to face him. "I need you to talk to her, see what she's thinking."

Though he had seen it coming, the request shot through Dillon's gut like fire. The idea of seeing Kylie, of speaking to her was more than he could bear. With the drink in hand, he rose from the couch and drifted toward the window.

"What's the matter?" asked Sean, puzzled by the stricken reaction.

Dillon stared through the open shutters, grappling for a response. "I don't think I'm the best one to handle this right now," he finally replied. "My interference might make matters worse."

"What are you talking about, son? You and Kylie are friends, you're family."

"I know that sir. It's just that . . . it's just that I'm not thinking clearly when it comes to your daughter right now. My head isn't where it should be."

The father leveled his eyes upon him, yet the young man could no longer meet his gaze. Sean looked to the darkened hallway, to the newly opened shutters. He sighed heavily, the weight of it filled with understanding. "Have you talked to her about it?" he asked. "About this?"

"No," answered Dillon quietly.

The father sighed again. "I guess that explains the leave of absence . . . the rift between you and Ms. Ollridge. Quite frankly, son, I'm surprised she stuck in there as long as she did when it was obvious you were in love with my daughter."

Dillon looked up, startled by his shrewdness.

"It's not that hard to figure out," said Sean. "Like most of us sorry blokes, you wear your heart on your sleeve."

Dillon moved away, unable to face even himself. The secret was out, freed from his aching chest, from the scraping inside of his head, yet it left him shaking with the bitter taste of shame in his mouth. "You can understand, then, why it's better if I back off. She was my brother's wife," he said, the admission twisting through him like a knife. "My brother's wife," he repeated. "The least I can do is let her grieve in peace."

Sean took a step back, looking away from the unbearable anguish. He rubbed his hands across his eyes, across his brow. A long while passed before he began to speak again. "She may have been your brother's wife, but there were times when I wished to God she wasn't."

Dillon looked up, smarted by the remark. "Excuse me?" he said.

"I cursed myself for it," admitted Sean, shaking his head, "but I wished it none the same. More than anything a parent wants his child to be loved, to be looked after. I saw how you cared for her in the hospital . . . how you took her hand into your own, how you studied her face. Never once did I see that kind of love from Jack."

Dillon started to respond, but the father held up his hand to silence him.

"Don't get me wrong. Jack meant the world to me," he said, his voice low. "I loved him like a son, but his death can't change the truth about him. He was a troubled young man. He let my daughter down time and again. I saw the pain, the grief. I imagine you saw it too, son. Whether you care to admit it or not, you saw it too. When Kylie was in the hospital, when she was lying there in agony, Jack was nowhere to be found. It was you I saw beside her bed . . . who held her hand through the long nights. It was you, each and every time."

"Jack was hurt—"

"Even after he was released," interrupted the father, "you were the one. If your brother had been looking after his own wife, you wouldn't have had to do it for him. If you fell in love with her in the process, it was no one's fault but Jack's."

"With all due respect sir, my brother never mistreated—"

"Didn't he?" asked the father, his anger rising. "What about the night in Chinatown, when you had to stop him from manhandling her? You think I didn't see the police report? A man's daughter doesn't get a black eye without questions being asked," he said sharply. "Don't immortalize your brother because he's dead. You did the right thing by her, and no amount of guilt can change that."

Though it was hard to hear, Dillon knew that the father spoke the truth. He had been justified in protecting Kylie, yet he still could not forgive himself for falling in love with her. His own heart had betrayed him, had betrayed them all. "I went too far."

Again the father took in his words. "Only you and your conscience can answer that," he said gruffly. "All I know is that my daughter needed you then and she needs you now. A thirty-four-year-old woman doesn't buy a casket for the future. She buys a casket because she plans on using it. If you want guilt son, you just think about that," he said, the anger breaking from his voice. He paused for a moment, his head going down, his focus on the floor. "Whatever you have to do to find peace with your brother, do it, but don't punish Kylie. She's already lost enough. Don't abandon her now . . . not when she needs you the most."

Dillon could hardly bear the slump of the big shoulders, the tilt of the fisherman's head. He instantly thought of that night long ago, that cold bitter night when he had called upon the cottage in Swampscott with news of the plane crash. The big man looked crushed, just as he did now.

"I would never abandon her, sir," he said. "Never. I just thought it best if . . . if I kept my distance for awhile."

"That's not what she needs. She needs someone to talk to. I can't help her. She won't open up to me. But you, she'll listen to you."

Dillon knew that first and foremost he and Kylie were friends. She depended on him, needed him. Putting distance between them would not lessen the love he felt for her. "I'll talk to her," he said. "I don't know if she'll confide in me. She tends to keep things to herself sometimes, but I'll try."

The father rubbed his head in dismay. "You're all I've got," he said. "Kylie never did have a lot of close friends and Amelia's too far away to help. I thought of calling her but . . . I don't see the good in worryin' her."

Dillon looked to the father. Either he had not heard of Amelia's death or he had simply pushed it from his mind. "Sir?" he said.

When the fisherman turned toward him, it was evident that he had not heard the dreadful news. The father had known Amelia from the time she was a small girl, he had a right to be told of her death, yet Dillon knew that it was not his place to tell him, it was Kylie's. The fact that she had not, only substantiated the father's grievance that she would not confide in him. Just as she had tried to hide the prepaid account of supplies, there was no reason for her to hide the death. Once again there appeared a plan, a premeditated manipulation of facts and consequences. While her father would undoubtedly learn of the loss, perhaps Kylie had chosen to wait, thinking that in the wake of her own death, the tidings would be less onerous.

"What is it, son?"

"Nothing," said Dillon. He turned away unable to endure the deceit. He felt suddenly on edge, for the situation was perhaps more dire than either of them had supposed. Whatever Kylie was planning, she expected it to culminate soon; for she would not, could not maintain such deception for long. "I'll talk to her," he said with newfound urgency. "I'll do everything I can to get through to her."

Fifty-Four

THE HEAT WAS UNBEARABLE, YET KYLIE COULDN'T BRING HERSELF TO go to Dora's. Instead of the bed rest the doctor had ordered, she sat on the park bench watching the deepening of shadows, watching the long tendrils creep across the Boston Common toward the tips of her sandals. With her arms wrapped tightly around herself, around her tender belly, her mind remained fixed on the gray monitor, on the lifeless image. Repeatedly, she imagined Jack's response, the grief in his eyes. He had wanted a child so desperately and now it had come. Like a twisted, heinous joke, it lay silent and dead inside of her.

I want a family, Kylie. I want children. Can't you understand that? The words that had been embedded in her memory were never so sharp, so cutting. Never was her regret, her guilt so raw.

Tucker's dead, and he's not coming back! We deserve our own child, can't you see that?

But she had been unable to see anything other than the inevitable pain and grief. Instead of the happy family Jack envisioned, she saw Tucker lying muddied and limp on the blood-splattered highway. She saw the tiny coffin as it was lowered within the black earth. Because of her fear and grief, she had denied Jack what he wanted most. And now, in spite of her resistance, the pain had come. In some horrid twist of irony, she was now pregnant. Now, when there was no chance for its survival—with Jack already dead and her last hour approaching.

As she stared out over the green grass, anger stung her throat. The child could have been given to her earlier. In spite of her fear, she would have abandoned all reservation and loved it intensely. Or she could simply have died without knowing and been spared the grief.

"Why now?" she asked bitterly. Now that she was about to die. It could be nothing other than God's recrimination against her. Punishment for her bitterness, for her refusal to forgive Him for Tucker's death. She had forgiven her mother's and Aidan's, and now even Jack's and Amelia's, but never Tucker's. *Never.* He had been but a child, a sweet innocent child. To compound the loss with news of the pregnancy, mere days—possibly hours—before her death, merely drove her resentment deeper. Her only consolation, was that the end would soon follow.

With the sound of a distant bell tower, she looked to the sky, to the orange orb hanging just above the golden dome of Beacon Hill. The sun was beginning to set. Within an hour, another day would come to an end. A young man lay idly on the grass reading, while a boy chided a puppy whose leash had tangled around a bush. It was the picture-perfect setting to a summer's eve. There appeared no immediate threat: no shrieking figure coming at her with a knife, no ground opening up to swallow her, yet it was coming, she could feel it. Somewhere around her, it was coming. Somewhere deep in her soul she knew: the end was upon her. Like a cowardly beast it hunkered close by, refusing to show itself. It hid beneath the flowers and the sunshine, yet there was no disguising its scent.

"What are you waiting for?" she asked through tight lips. "What more do you want?"

Feeling suddenly exhausted, she picked up her bag and began to walk. Without a conscious decision, her feet led her up Pickney, to the mansion's doorstep.

It wasn't until she slid the key into the lock, that she heard the telephone's ring, and then Dillon's voice. He sounded tired, distressed. With a wave of tenderness, she suddenly realized how much she missed his smile, his comforting embrace. Dillon. The one who always made it right, made it all better.

"I know I'm driving you crazy with these messages, but I need to talk to you," the voice beseeched, "to see you . . ."

She lay her keys beside the phone, but didn't touch the small box. He had clearly been trying to reach her, but she couldn't see or talk to anyone, not now, especially not Dillon. He would hear it in her voice . . . the guilt, the shame. He would see another lover in her eyes.

"If you're there," he continued, "please answer. It's important."

There was a pause, a moment of uncertainty. Then a heavy sigh. "It's about your father. He came to see me this afternoon. He was very upset, Kylie."

Without further delay, she lifted the receiver. "It's me," she said softly.

Fifty-Five

THE JAVA HOUSE WAS UNUSUALLY PACKED FOR A WEDNESDAY EVENING. Like the rest of Harvard Square, it was booming with overflow from the annual Cambridge River Festival. Though it was well past seven o'clock, the temperature was still so intense, the humidity so high, that the tiny café was jammed with undergraduates and tourists trying to escape the heat.

In search of a breeze, Dillon had taken a table outside on the wooden deck where he could keep an eye on the surrounding streets as well as the door. From where he sat, he had a clear view of the subway exit located in the center of the square. He anxiously watched the small island, for it was where Kylie would be deboarding the train.

When she emerged from the tunnel, Dillon immediately saw that Sean had reason for concern. He was so taken back by the sight of her that for a moment he merely watched her. It was not so much her rumpled dress or disheveled hair that troubled him, but her movements were strained, tight. Her head was down, as if she had to will herself through each and every step.

When he called to her from the ivy-covered deck, her gaze caught his own and she smiled. But the gesture was empty, almost painful. As she worked her way up the stairs toward him, the sunlight caught her hair, yet her eyes remained dull, her face ashen.

"Thanks for coming," he said, his lips gently touching her cheek. "What can I get you to drink? An iced coffee . . . tea?"

"Tea would be nice."

Dillon went inside to the counter and ordered the drink. When he returned, he found her watching him. Her gaze had softened and she smiled genuinely, albeit sadly.

"What is it?" he asked, as he set the glass before her.

"We've been friends for so long, that... sometimes I forget how handsome you are," she said, "how much you look like Jack. You were so different from each other... your coloring, but really, your features are the same."

Dillon glanced downward, his embarrassment mixed with a sudden sadness. To be reminded of his and Jack's similarities, made their differences all the more painful.

"I'm sorry," said Kylie, the warmth of her eyes fading. "I didn't mean to—"

"Don't be sorry," he said. "Don't ever be sorry for talking about Jack."

For a moment, silence settled between them.

"I didn't know you were back in town," he said.

"I should have called."

"Your father is really worried about you."

"I'm fine." Swiping a strand of hair from her face, she looked immediately away. "It's madness down by the river," she said, clearly uncomfortable with the subject of herself. "They're having those crazy boat races again." She picked up a sugar packet, but her hands were so unsteady that she was having a difficult time keeping grasp of it. "They had one shaped like a hotdog with drunk kids squirting mustard all over the place..." Her voice dwindled. As she dumped the sugar into her glass, she stared at the crystals, her lips clenched tight as if a torrent of emotion might escape if they parted.

"He got the supplies, Kylie," he said. "All of them," he added gently.

She looked up at him, her cheeks coloring.

"He also knows about the casket you ordered. He went by the Greyson house this morning to talk to you and... he overheard a message left by a mortician."

She looked out over the square, then to the pillared entrance to Harvard Yard, clearly anything to avoid his gaze.

"What did he say?" she finally asked.

"He's terrified... naturally. I'm worried about you too, Kylie. You don't look well. I know you've been through a lot, but you can't let yourself become consumed by it."

She stared downward, pondering the thought. "I'm immersed in an ocean and you're telling me not to feel the water," she said softly.

"Feel it, just don't let it drown you."

A fly buzzed around the sugar packet, its hairy proboscis suckling the grains. "It already has," she whispered, her eyes riveted on the insect as if she saw something more, something heinous. "I've died and gone to hell."

Dillon reached out and touched her hand. "It'll pass," he insisted.

She shrank away from him, her arms wrapping tight around herself. "It'll pass," she repeated softly. "For years Jack said that to me. 'It'll pass, if you let it. If we have a baby of our own, you'll forget.' But death is something you never forget."

Dillon knew the death of which she spoke. He knew of Tucker and of the overwhelming affect he had on her life, on his brother's marriage. He remembered the tears, the embittered arguments, Jack's persistence in trying to force her past the loss of the child in order to have a family of their own.

"How do you forget the death of a seven-year-old child?" she mused quietly.

"You don't," he said. "You trust that he's gone on to a better place."

Tears instantly sprang into her eyes. "I couldn't," she whispered. "I just couldn't, Dill. A baby was the only thing that Jack ever asked of me, and I wouldn't give it to him."

Dillon's heart constricted, not only for her, but for his brother and his lost dream. Jack had always believed that she would come around, that one day he would have children. "I'm sorry, Kylie," he said. "It just wasn't meant to be."

She looked abruptly up at him, anger taking hold of her features. "That's a catch-all phrase, isn't it? To keep us quiet and content. We're shuffled around like pawns, God snatching what he wants and that's the best we get. He gives us loved ones, then crushes and mangles them. It's a game, really. Some kind of twisted punishment."

"Death isn't a punishment," he said. "It's a natural part of life."

"What's natural about a semi-truck? Or being burned to death in your own home?"

Dillon stared at her, at a loss. "You shouldn't be thinking about all of this," he finally managed to say. "We don't have the answers. All we can do is live our lives—"

"And wait." The coldness in her voice chilled him. Though she stared forward, he knew that it was not the iron railing that she saw.

"No," he said steadily. "We don't wait. We let the dead go and we continue onward. Death is not the enemy, Kylie. Giving up and not living is the enemy."

Again, there was silence. He searched her eyes for anything, some sign that he had broken through to her, but her gaze remained vacant. With a shudder he recognized the resignation, the look of departure he had seen time and again on the faces of his terminally ill patients.

"I want you to go in for counseling," he said gently. "I want you to talk to someone. If not Dr. Jordan, I can recommend someone else that can help you."

Her eyes were unfocused, lost within a dark cavern of thought.

"Surely, you must know how this appears," he said.

But she made no response, merely stared past him.

"You buy a casket, you put the insurance in your father's name. You fill his boat with enough supplies to last a year, you tell the owner of the business that you're taking a trip . . . Kylie," he said, to draw her gaze inward. "Ending it all, is not the answer."

Her brow furrowed, as if he were suddenly appearing before her.

"Is that what you think?" she asked. "That I'm going to kill myself?"

He said nothing, his silence serving as confirmation.

She seemed truly astounded. "Because of the casket?"

"Because of everything."

"And my father . . .?"

"That's why he came to me. That's why he wanted me to talk to you."

She took a sharp breath and then another. "I wouldn't do that to him," she said, her emotion quickly rising. "Surely he knows I would never hurt him like that. Dillon, you can't let him think that. He relies on you. He trusts you."

"Then what is it? Why did you keep Amelia's death from him?"

"I didn't want him to worry—"

"You knew he would find out sooner or later. Why later? Why didn't you tell him about the supplies? Why all the deception?"

She stared at him. "If I told you, you wouldn't believe me," she said, looking away.

He touched her hand. "Try me."

Beneath the weight of her stare he felt her testing him, searching his eyes, his face for the strength to confide in him. The truth was perched on the edge of her lips, it was filled with terror and anguish, but just as he was sure she would come forth with it, she swallowed it back. "I just wanted to be prepared," she finally responded, the words catching in her throat.

"Prepared for what?"

"In case something happened to me."

"Like what?"

"I don't know," she faltered. "An accident, or—"

"An accident?" he repeated, his heart plummeting. "If there was an accident," he said pointedly, "he would know."

She looked up, clearly startled by his inference. "But that's . . . that's not what—" she stopped. She looked suddenly ill, her face waxen. "Dillon, you've got this all wrong. If something happens to me, you can't—"

"If what happens, Kylie? What? Before you do something selfish, I want you to think about something. Think about the pain you're feeling right now, then think of your father. He has no one else but you. Not only is he a heavy drinker but he's not a young man anymore. If something happened to you . . . an 'accident' as you say, I doubt he would survive it."

Her breath caught as if he had struck her. "Don't you think I know that?" she gasped, her voice wrenching with anguish. "That's why I was trying to protect him . . . to give him . . . everything that he—" but she cut herself off again, sheltering her face with her hands.

"You think a few supplies are going to do the trick? A few traps and some rain gear are going to take the place of his only remaining child?" he demanded.

"No," she whispered, tears escaping past her hands, trickling through her fingers.

"You think all the money in the world is going—"

"Stop it!" she cried. "You think I want things this way! You think I want this?! That I want him alone, out there on that boat every day, every night alone. That I want him to ache and feel the pain I feel right now!"

"He doesn't have to, Kylie. It's in your control."

"No," she cried, shaking her head. "No, it isn't. You've got to believe me."

"Then let me help you."

"You can't!"

The greens of her eyes were swimming in pain, her face pinched with grief, yet he kept pounding, desperate to get through.

"I'm a doctor, Kylie, I've seen a lot of death. It can do ugly things to you. No matter how you die, your skin turns color, your eyes dry and sink inward. Morticians hide this stuff. But your father, he's your only next of kin. He would be the one called first. He would be forced to identify your body—or what's left of it. He would be forced to see his baby girl, distorted, twisted into something unspeakable."

With the assault, she pulled back, frozen, the horror of his words suspended between them. The anguish in her eyes was so violent, so gut-wrenching that he instantly regretted the approach. It was a cheap shot, but he had taken it. He had finally reached her, yet he had severed the bridge.

"Kylie, I just want you to understand—"

"I've . . . I've got to go—" she said, looking blindly, clamoring for escape.

"Kylie—"

"I'm sorry, but—" In the next second she was cutting her way across the deck. Before Dillon could stop her, she was gone, moving briskly through the street from the café.

WITH the familiar rocking of the train, Kylie's weeping began to subside. The dark casing was carrying her away, its rumble soothing her, helping her gain control of her breath. She tried to think of nothing, to push all images from her mind so that the emotion would abate. She found that she was instinctively clutching her abdomen. The bleeding had finally stopped, but a dull ache remained as a constant reminder that her body was no longer her own; it was inhabited by death. The voice was silent, yet constant, it brought her nausea and unsteadiness. She should have stayed at the house, instead of venturing back out into the heat. She felt sudden anger at Dillon. He had known just what to say to lure her to him; that concern for her father was her assailable point. He had known just the right tact to scale the wall she had erected. But he had not realized the true thrust of his words, had not understood that not only was her death imminent, but that a secret lay hidden beneath her flesh; that her father would not only lose a daughter, but a grandchild as well. At thought of her father's shaking hands and liquored eyes, the emotion swelled upon her again. In spite of all her preparations, she would not be there for him, to comfort him when he shouldered the loss. Perhaps Dillon had been right; perhaps he would not survive it. Again the sorrow threatened to overtake her, but she pushed it back. *Ruby will be there*, she reminded herself. She had to trust in that, to believe it.

Brushing her fingertips beneath her lashes, she took a deep breath. She stared forward where the blackened windows reflected her image against the rushing tunnel. With the stark overhead light she looked like a ghost, a hideously drawn specter with sunken eyes and colorless lips. An elderly man sitting diagonally from her was staring, but when she looked to him he glanced away. Dillon had also been staring earlier, her shocking appearance clearly adding to his misconception.

She had been so stunned by the notion of suicide, and then consumed with thoughts of her father, that only now did she appreciate how the mistake had been made. Everything she had done as of late could point to suicide. Even her conversation with Dillon had seemed to incriminate her. Though she had tried, she had said nothing to dissuade him; if anything, she had made it worse. It was as if for a moment she were captive within his perception, making an appearance just long enough to further it along; as if her words had been merely skimming the surface, while colder deeper shadows drove them from beneath.

A strange feeling tickled inside of her. She would not take her own life, had not even considered it, yet he had been so convinced. In spite of the heat, she felt suddenly chilled. It was the effects of the hangover, she told herself. Or perhaps it was the pregnancy, pulling at her insides, making her shiver.

She sat back, her head resting against the vibrating glass. To think of nothing was the key. Easing her mind into the dull rhythm would unclench her shoulders and soothe her raw stomach. The man seated next to her was pressed against her, his briefcase lodged securely between his legs. His cologne was sweet, strangely feminine. The smell of it twisted her stomach. She rolled her head to the side, looking blankly through the crowded train. That's when she noticed the woman. A gaunt woman, with long, dirty-blonde hair staring at her from the far end of the car. Her heart quickened, for she had noticed her earlier. Somewhere in her mind she had seen her before. Then it struck her: the woman had been standing by the Harvard Yard entrance, staring toward the café. She had seemed to be waiting. For a brief second the out-of-place face had caught in Kylie's mind, then it had faded back into the crowd of young students. Now she had appeared again, staring unabashedly, her face emotionless, her arms at her sides as if somehow removed from those around her. *She watched you as you slept*, slid the words from her thoughts.

With a deep tremor, Kylie rose to her feet. She had taken the subway, completely disregarding what Vanderpoel had told her that night in the study; that she was to have died a sudden, grisly death beneath the tracks of a train. "I would have slipped into the crowd," he had promised. "A homeless man would go easily unnoticed."

The dark and the light flashed across the angular face . . . in and out of the pulsing lights, but still the woman did not look away.

Kylie took a step back, just as the sway of the speed caused her to lose balance. Grasping hold of a dangling hoop she steadied herself, and looked up again, but the woman had vanished. The flickering light continued, but a businessman now stood in her place, reading a newspaper. Kylie's eyes darted through the crowded car but the passengers were shifting with the slowing train. As the gears grinded and screeched, they forged toward the exit. She found herself trapped within the current. She tried to turn, to see behind her, but the bodies were ever-moving. She was suddenly pressed against the glass doors, a hand at her back.

In a burst of adrenaline, an abhorrent thought hit her: she could be pushed from the train, yet it would appear as if she had jumped. They would not see the hand jet out from the crowd—her nemesis would slip quietly away. As though awakening outside of herself, all became clear. Perhaps Dillon had been right all along; she would not take her own life—yet her death would be deemed suicide. Consumed by her own grief, she had been in a haze, completely oblivious, unthinking, while her every word, her every gesture had been sealing her fate. Like an unwitting accomplice to her own murder, she had moved through the set-up: the insurance, the supplies, the funeral arrangements. Even in her denials, the groundwork for her extinction had been laid, her "cause of death" already written.

Just as Amelia's paranoia was attributed to a blood clot, just as the authorities had believed Clyde Tremblay's confession, just as Dale Benson's bloodied den was credited to a pending lawsuit and divorce, her death would not be questioned.

With the black-sooted ground whirling before her, her terror deepened into paralysis. She was entranced by the surging motion, the brakes screeching, the pull bringing the crowd with it. As the train howled toward the light of awaiting passengers, she started to turn, to cry out, when the rushing had suddenly stopped. The doors swished open and before she had time to think, to assess, she was stepping from the car, her every urge for escape. Though it was not her exit, she was moving quickly through the tunnel toward the light of the stairs. In a frenzy, she ascended the steps, bypassing the slow walkers, trying to make her way above ground as swiftly as possible.

When she reached the top, she pivoted back. In a sea of heads, the passengers moved toward her, parting only to pass. Out of the balding heads and baseball caps, brunettes and blondes, she did not see the woman. As the last of the passengers scattered, the dark tunnel wavered beneath her. Within seconds the entrance was abandoned.

For a long moment, she stood clutching the railing. The woman had not emerged from the tunnel, yet Kylie's thundering pulse did not abate. With the sun on her face again, the chill of sweat crawled over her skin. Her head was rushing, the sudden silence strumming against her eardrums. She noticed a man looking at her, then someone else loitering nearby.

"Miss?"

She turned to the fleshy jowls, the woman's skin shining with sweat. "Are you alright, miss?"

"Yes," she said. "Yes, I'm fine." Yet she continued to grip the railing.

She looked to the empty stairwell ... she needed to reboard the train to cross over the Charles River, but the fear inside would not let her. In the remains of the chaos she felt one thing for certain: her death would be deemed "suicide." While she wanted to believe that the woman was merely a passenger and that there was no plot, no plan, the facts would not relent. Everything she had done bespoke someone preparing to take their own life. Her mind raced back ... scraping through her actions and words, searching for something, anything that would disprove her theory, but instead found more incriminating evidence; clues to be unearthed later by family and friends to add credence to her despair.

"I should have known all along," Ruby O'Brian would say, as the fishermen gathered round. "She came to see me just before she did it, you know? Worried what would become of her da'."

The autopsy would reveal the dead fetus inside of her. "She had wanted a child, Jack's child," Dillon would confide. "It must be what sent her over the edge."

Even before her death, those around her were already convinced. The conclusion was drawn, now it was only a matter of its execution.

Abruptly, her eyes were focused and wide, aware of all around her. Wiping her brow, she looked up at the exit then to the long avenue before her. As if suddenly awakening in a mine-field, she was terrified of which way to step, for her annihilation could lay anywhere. If not pushed from the train, she could be nudged from the stairs or into a busy intersection. The hand could come quickly and unseen, her assassin vanishing without a trace.

She turned abruptly and was walking. She was at Kendall Square, only one stop away from her own. She would traverse the Longfellow Bridge by foot and then cross over into Beacon Hill. Within minutes she would be home.

Again the pull inside of her took her breath. As she made her way down Main Street, the din of the River Festival murmured toward her, the heat seeping into her skin, into her pulsing heart. She concentrated on her steps, forcing herself faster and faster. If she could just make it to Dora's, to the darkness of the mansion walls, she would have time to think. She found herself looking back, searching the faces, the smiles and the laughter, the bodies milling listlessly in the heat. Approaching the intersection of First and Main, she looked to the hands, to the shuffling feet, the smell of beer clinging to the humidity, choking her.

As the crimson light flashed green, the crowd poured into the street. Within minutes she made it past Memorial Drive and to the Longfellow Bridge. As she drew near the river, the muffled sounds turned to chaos. The boats were floating underneath. Whistles were blowing, instruments clattering. The festivities spilled over the bridge, blocking the street, swarming the walkway. As she was forced against the metal railing, the distance rippled beneath like a molten grave—the water deep and murky. Her wavering reflection was suddenly sinking downward, her face green, her eyes bulging.

I've seen a lot of death. It can do ugly things to you.

She saw herself pulled from the water, tiny worms filling her eye sockets.

Your father would be the one called first. He would be forced to identify your body.

She thought of Dale Benson—of the heinous smell, of his brains splattered on the TV glass. She imagined his family, his wife staring down at his missing head. Her own demise could be the same, her father facing the same carnage.

I doubt he would survive it.

Her stomach was suddenly turning, threatening to heave.

"Hey, watch it lady!" a fat man said, clinging tight to a dripping hotdog. The sweet smell of tobacco and pork wavered beneath her breath, but she pushed faster, past the street vendors and the drunken youth slopping their beers.

At last she broke from the crowd and was across the bridge. As she cut onto Charles Street she stole a glance back, just in time to see the woman emerge from the den of bodies moving toward her, her face still strangely fixed. At sight of the willowy figure, Kylie's legs nearly crumpled beneath her. The woman had not exited the train at Kendall Square, yet she had somehow caught up to her. With her adrenaline surging, Kylie cut into a grocer's on her left, the chimes on the door announcing her presence in a flurry of bells. The Asian man behind the counter smiled, but she took no time for pretext. She was making her way down the small cramped aisle toward the rear exit to Cedar Lane. Just as she reached the door, she stopped abruptly. Before stepping from the store's safety, she needed to consider the situation. She peered out to West Cedar—with the exception of a dozing cat, the street was empty. She could exit onto the side street and cut back the opposite way from the mansion. "And what?" she asked, wiping the sweat from the side of her face. There was nowhere to go, nowhere to hide. If the woman was truly who she thought, it was futile to run. If her time had truly come, there would be no escape. She felt dizzy, nauseated and needed to lie down. Without further debate, she exited the store in the direction of the mansion. She was only one block away,

just around the corner to safety. The mansion did not guarantee pro-
tection, but at least it was familiar.

As she made her way along the empty street, she felt all the more
exposed and vulnerable. Turning onto Pickney, she took a glance
back, just as a blasting horn screeched toward her. In the brief second
it passed, it pulled her inward with its force. She imagined herself
thumping beneath its axle and then being dragged along the street.
With a *whoosh*, the hooting teenagers were carried away.

The street was once again empty and the mansion was in sight, yet
the terror inside of her swelled. She was rushing up the hill, the grade
seeming to grow steeper with each step. Her breath was heaving,
burning through her throat. She was at the foot of Dora's walk, then
the steps were beneath her. She grasped the handle and with a jingle of
her keys, pulled the door back, then slammed it into place and latched
it. The sounds were instantly gone.

On the other side of the thick wood she slumped to the floor, trembling.

THE SHADOWS fell over the entry, over the dining room table and the
stairs on her left, until night was upon her. She had not moved, had
simply waited and watched as the darkness took hold.

With the disappearance of light, a calmness had settled over her,
her grip had slowly loosened, her panic ebbing away to a cool stillness.
Rising to her feet she peered through the side windows to the street
beneath her. For a long while she stared down at the wavering
branches, at the glowing sidewalk, finding and forming her resolve.
Though unable to speak it, even within her own mind, she knew what
she needed to do.

Looking toward the stairs, she remained unready, unwilling to approach it just yet. Instead, her thoughts turned sharply to her hunger,
to the twist in her stomach that she had been unaware of until this moment. Having not eaten a bite all day, she was suddenly ravenous.

When she flipped on the light in the kitchen, her heart lifted unex-
pectedly. As if seeing the room anew, she found the result of her and
Jack's labor sublime. The Merk and Daniels appliances gleamed silver
and sleek, Jack's cabinetry and intricate tile work providing color and

warmth. Though rarely visited even when she worked alone at the mansion—for Jack had been the cook not she—it was one of her favorite rooms within the house.

To her further delight, the kitchen was efficient and easy to use, even for a novice such as herself. Within minutes she had a steaming penne before her—olive oil, sun-dried tomatoes, basil and garlic. A simple recipe that Jack had showed her one night in the kitchen, when she had gone without dinner in his absence. She had been so consumed by her work in the attic room, that she had emerged at midnight to discover that all of the restaurants on Beacon Hill had closed.

"I can't believe you Wylie, this is pathetic," he had teased, throwing the ingredients in the pan as smoothly and as deftly as a chef. "I go to the races for a few hours and you starve?"

"I guess I'm hopeless," she had smiled, leaning into the median, savoring a glass of Cabernet along with the lesson. There had been such beauty in his movements when he cooked, his muscular lean hands chopping and sprinkling with abandon until the last twist of the pepper grinder added the finishing touch. The results were always magnificent, melting in her mouth with a sensuality, yet her truest pleasure had always been in watching him, admiring the brawny hands that yielded such delicate delights.

"What's my incentive to learn when you feed me so well?" she had razzed, swiping her finger through the last drop of sauce.

"Starvation, Wylie. Who else is gonna take care of you when I'm gone?"

When I'm gone.

With the words, the memory vanished, the room suddenly cool and empty. She continued eating slowly and deliberately, but an inescapable awareness of the night, of the insistent present, drifted through the open window.

Unwillingly her thoughts turned to the task before her, her appetite suddenly gone. She could delay no longer. She needed to act with precision and expediency, for time was of the essence. The woman could return at any moment.

Gazing out into the darkened alley, she went over it again in her mind, weighing the options, but finding no other. No matter what, she would not be able to spare her father the pain of her "suicide." If she stepped back out the door, she would be exposed once again. If she

kept running they would catch up to her. If she remained hidden behind the mansion walls they would still reach her. Perhaps the woman
would even take her that night. She would not know when or how,
only that they would find her and that a forced suicide would surely be
violent. Yet she could not simply sit back and wait for them to come to
her, to decide how to take her. She could not wait to be electrocuted in
the bathtub, or awakened to slit wrists with a knife in her hand. She
could not allow her father to find her bloodied or dismembered, to
allow death the element of gore with which to torture him. Dillon's
portrayal of the aftermath had been brutal; she could not chance its
accuracy.

Since her return from Savannah, she had accomplished all tasks . . .
there were no further arrangements to be made. Her time was long
finished. Piece by piece she had already abandoned herself, with one
last step, she would slip quietly away. Her choice of death would be
quick and painless. There would be no blood, no disfiguring aftermath for her father to face, no brutal images to haunt him in his grief,
for she alone could spare him this agony.

Even as she was formulating, accepting the plan as her own, she
saw the undercurrent. It was exactly what they wanted. Even before
she had conceived of it, the very tool they had provided lay silent and
waiting. No doctor in his right mind would have prescribed her barbiturates, yet Dora—the consummate pill-popper—had plenty to spare.
There was even the abandoned bottle of vodka beneath the sink with
which to wash them down.

With a bittersweet sigh she thought of the irony; her fate truly
would be to take her own life, to put an end to the ceaseless battle.
Never had she thought it would end this way, never had she imagined
she would die at her own hand.

As she dumped the balance of the pasta down the drain she mused
that the lost appetite was for the best. It was important that her stomach remain empty. After washing the dishes and returning them to
their place, she meticulously dried off the cabinet and sink. She
wanted it to look nice when Dora found it. With regret she would not
finish the mansion, but it was close enough, that nearly anyone could
step in and easily complete it.

With a flip of the switch the recessed lighting dimmed until a blue
glow settled over the shining room. Leaning against the archway she

took one last moment to absorb it—the carefully bordered cabinets, the pale-pink mosaic of roses in the backsplash.

"It's beautiful Jack," she said softly.

The life they had shared had been beautiful. It had been full of rough times and good times—the work, the love, the play—but she had little regret.

She felt strangely at peace, for at last she knew; at last the final chapter to her life had been written. There would be no more pain, no more black days or nights to struggle through. It was finished. Her last cause to fight for had been her father, now he would be the extenuation to surrender. Sean McCallum would not be called to bear witness to his daughter's mangled body, he would find her simply asleep.

With the forgotten bottle of vodka in tow, she turned and walked slowly toward the darkened stairwell.

Fifty-Six

IN THE QUIET, SHE FELT THE COLD LITTLE BEING INSIDE OF HER. SHE imagined its still body, the curve of its tucked head. She would not face the darkness alone. Even in its silence, they were united.

"Just you and me," she whispered.

There had been fifty-three pills in all chased down three at a time with the vodka. Along with the secobarbital, she had taken phenobarbital, codeine and even antihistamines—anything that she could find that Dora had abandoned. Beforehand, she had showered, dressed in her nightgown, then replaced the stained sheets. With her balance already beginning to sway, she had switched off the lamp and disappeared within the four-poster bed.

It wasn't until she began to feel her surroundings slipping away, that the fear began to snake back inward. The room around her was dark, too dark, yet she couldn't stand the thought of the light, somehow exposing her.

She would be revealed soon enough, her face drawn, her body stiff and cold. Dillon would call the next day, she was certain. Then he would come searching. At the thought of the abhorrent discovery, of the anguish it would inflict, shame overcame her. Her father would soon know what she had done, would suffer the seeming betrayal. She had written him a note and then shredded it. How could she ever explain, have convinced him it was the only way out? That death would have come nonetheless, she was merely meeting it halfway.

With a chill slithering from the heat, she rolled onto her side, wrapping the sheet in closer. Trying to stave off the shadows as long as possible, she concentrated on the table, on an empty bottle of pills she had absently recapped.

Staring into the black night, she was reminded of a time long forgotten, of another moonless, shadowless night, her first one alone after the murder of her teacher, after her crude introduction to death. Still aching and bruised from scampering through the vents, still reeling from the police and the cameras, she had lain awake the whole night through, staring into the darkness, haunted by the violent turn of her prince, by the still legs on the shiny classroom floor. Filled with guilt and shame, she had relived the paralysis that had gripped her— that had kept her from entering the classroom, from answering her teacher's cry. She remembered and felt it clearly now, the remorse, the terror, the breaking inside of her, the moment when the ghosts of Ellen Young and Julius Vanderpoel had slid into the shadows of her child's mind. At an age before comprehension, she had met death. Death. The one demon she had never been able to surmount. The demon that had haunted her most, had infected and navigated her life. Even now it held its grip, its reign of terror. In mere minutes she would face it—she would slip into the same unknown into which her teacher had vanished. At last she would know.

"It won't be long," she murmured, imagining the tiny body beneath her grasp silent yet listening.

With a start, a gentle gasp of breath, she realized her lids had fallen shut, the blackness moving in without notice. Forcing her eyes to focus, to lock on the pill bottles, her lips began to move, a song drifting into the silence.

> "Pumpkin shells and tinker bells,
> daffodils in June.
> They bow their heads in garden beds,
> waiting on the moon.

When night appears, they have no fears,
the stars will guide them through.
Past darkened sleep that threatens keep,
to morning skies of blue."

It was a lullaby she had sung for Tucker. "To help him sleep," she whispered, stroking her warm abdomen with her palm. "Just a beautiful sleep."

With the hum of her voice, the melody rolled through her mind to the past . . . to the feel of Tucker's hand within her own, to the soft words melding with the *whir* of the life-support as it was silenced. Beneath the beat of her own heart, she could still hear the softening of the clamor, the numerical lights switching to black, her father's stony expression as he turned away. Then the silence.

The unbearable silence.

In a black river, the regret moved over her. She had betrayed Tucker with the song, just as she was now betraying the child inside of her. She had held his hand within her own, held it tight, then led him into the darkness.

Stay with him Kylie. Don't leave his side. Promise me you won't leave his side.

I promise Mama. I promise.

She had not left his side, yet she had forsaken him. For years she had dreamt of the moment, had tried to see him, to connect, to pull him back, but each time failed. She was left with nothing but his voice, calling to her from some distant place, begging for her to come.

He's dead, Kylie, came the impatient voice of Jack. *You've got to let go.*

But she could never let go. Even now, the loss was insufferable. He had brought life to her parents, had brought salvation to them all. He had been life's promise of a new day, of the soft baby blades of grass . . .

A child is forever. You can never let go.

Stay by him Kylie.

It's not your fault.

Stay by him.

The incriminating eyes of the girl were before her. *They forgot about him . . .*

"No," she whispered. "No, I never forgot."

Through her incessant longing for Tucker, she had failed Jack, she had failed her marriage and even the unborn child inside of her. She had wanted Tucker and no other. She had no room for another.

"Forgive me," she whispered, her words slurring past her lips. But it was too late—time had irrevocably moved on.

With a sudden fluttering of her heart, she knew that the end was near. Her pulse was fading, her breath, her consciousness. Her weakening gaze moved past the table, to the room behind it. They would come for her soon. With all of her might, she stared toward the light of the windows, expecting the shadows to change, to shift at any moment, to see the blonde woman from the train . . . someone . . . anyone . . . perhaps disguised in her mother's flesh, or Jack's, beckoning her forward, toward some distant light. The fingers that lay touching her belly began to tingle, her skin melding into the bedclothes.

"Not long," she murmured, the resonance gurgling inside her head like water.

As she lay waiting for the hand, the touch to release her, her mind drifted back to the song.

> *Pumpkin shells and tinker bells,*
> *daffodils in June.*
> *They bow their head in garden beds,*
> *waiting on the moon. . . .*

Out of the long space of darkness she became aware of the heaviness, of the dark mass that held her submerged. As if in thick black waters, lucidity wavered above, intangible and uncertain. With all of her might, she forced her eyes open toward the light of the surface.

The canopy smeared across her vision, her body trembling. For a moment she could not think where she was, nor place the delirium in which she found herself. She felt the sheets beneath her grasp, her fingers knotted tight. Then she remembered the pills, giving form to the dreadful circumstance. She was in Dora's bed, soaked in an icy sweat. In a cornucopia of dark hues, the room was blurring and uncertain, the delirium casting a darker, less-defined corporeality than a nightmare. Time had passed—hours or mere seconds—she had no bearings, all she knew was that she remained.

With her slowing pulse, her veins had turned to ice, the cold reaching deep inside of her, edging through her limbs, curling into her stomach and chest. In search of the windows, she found only a dim smear of light. Her fingers and toes were chilled to the bone, her breath was but a faint afterthought. She had taken more than enough pills, yet there was no figure, no silhouette looming over her. Only silence. Something was wrong, deadly wrong. In a dark wall of dread, the doubt rose inside of her. What if she had been mistaken about the woman; that she had been merely an office worker returning home, or a mother on the way to meet her child? What if she had been wrong about the forced suicide; that some other death had awaited her—an "ailment" such as Amelia's, or an "accident" that would be deemed an accident. Even a violent death under those circumstances would cause her father less grief than suicide. Without knowing for certain, she had taken her life into her own hands, defying every rule she had ever been taught, her fear and panic driving her to the unspeakable.

Out of the deep chasm of shifting shapes and colors, came the stab of terror. It had been a mistake, a bad heinous mistake! She would die alone within the darkness, her forgotten soul slipping into an abyss, no one coming to collect her, to set her free.

Her adrenaline was suddenly surging. She looked to the blurring table, to the bedside where the outline of the phone vacillated in the dull light. She struggled to raise herself but her limbs had become leaden. Reaching outward, her fumbling fingers brushed against the table. She was grasping for something, anything in her vision, but all rules of the physical had been lost. The unbearable weight of her hand pulled it downward, the empty bottle of vodka toppling with it, thumping against the floor. Held captive within the stillness of her own body, she lay shivering, her indiscernible skin burning like ice. Her eyes and throat stung with remorse—in spite of her uncertainty, there would be no turning back. She would lay within the hell, listening to her labored body, to its destruction that she alone had effected, feeling the poison ripping through her cells, her flesh.

With a tightening of her throat, she remembered the child, the vague image of the fetus. *What have I done? What have I done?* Rolling onto her back, her heavy arm wrapped tight around herself, her fingers clutched against the trembling that was becoming unbearable.

"It's okay," she gasped, her voice thin and frightened. "Okay"—trying desperately to stave off the blinding terror. *It'll be over soon*, the promise flowing from her mind, but never reaching her lips.

The image of her brother Aidan was suddenly over her, his eyes glassy, a heroin needle protruding from his arm. "No turning back," he whispered, his eyes rolling white. As his features vanished, her own lips were numbing, disappearing. In a river of thoughts, the delirium was overtaking her. She was floating, moving over the waves of an ocean, then sinking downward, plummeting into the trenches of a sea, to the murkiest of waters, her thoughts careening and bashing wildly—the darkest moments of her life jetting out at her, reassembling—her mother on the highway reaching out to her, then the brutal force of a plane encasing her, her hand gripped within Jack's, the sound of prayer . . . of screaming.

Out of the stream of images, taunting and confusing, she was talking with her Aunt Clara, but when she turned to respond it was her mother, her warm fingers running through her hair, soothing her . . . "Kylie McCallum, you're a sight," she said with a click of her tongue.

"A sight," she muttered to the emptiness, her throat burning and dry, her lips cracking. Her body was drawing inward, holding tight, fighting against another wave of motion.

Beneath the chatter of her own teeth, she heard the sound. It came from beside her, strangely clear—clearer than her own heartbeat, her own thoughts. In some barren indefinable space a room had reappeared, the wavering ceiling dropping lower and then retracting. Her gaze streaked about the gaunt walls, trying to decipher the shapes, the movements. Again she heard it, the soft whimper, a painful weeping, cutting into her soul, for she had heard it before, time and again, in her thoughts, her dreams.

"Tucker?" she whispered.

The thick *strum* of silence enveloped her, her eyes wide, fighting, ever fighting. Then she heard it again, a small nearly indistinguishable whimper.

She looked above her to the wavering ceiling.

The cry grew abruptly clearer and louder, coming from somewhere above her or below. Coming from somewhere distant . . . somewhere outside of the room. He was lost and alone. She could hear it in his voice, the forlorn pitch. He was crying out, trying to reach her, to pull her to him, yet she remained paralyzed. The sobbing grew louder, penetrating the walls, the floorboards, the heaving black walls that had risen around her, thick and ungiving. It grew louder and louder until it merged into one long gut-wrenching wail.

Tucker! Tucker! With all of her being she was struggling to cry out, but her lips would not move.

It's not real, came the voice from within. *It's not real!* It was in her mind, her thoughts. It was the nightmare, resurrecting from the past—the blackened room, the beckoning cry. *It's in your head, Kylie. In your head!* Her own fear and guilt providing the munitions with which to torture her. The doctor's face and his words, prickling at her, jabbing . . .

We're disconnecting all support.

It's not your fault, Kylie! He would have died anyway.

But she had given up too soon. She had not held tight enough, begged hard enough.

You understand what this means.

You understand Ms. McCallum?

Yesssss.

Beneath the child's shuttered eyes and pale still mouth, he had been reaching out to her, but she had let him slip into the darkness, into the heinous torturous place where he remained, beneath her thoughts, in her dreams, crying out to her, pleading for her to come.

He's there Jack, I feel him! Just on the other side of the darkness. Crying out. The plea growing to a deafening intensity.

Tucker! Tucker!!

At once the shrieking descended upon her, a high-pitch careening of rubber and glass . . . metal twisting upon metal, flesh upon flesh . . . the tiny body bursting through the windshield . . . the screams . . . the brilliant colors of green, blue and blood.

Rising above the chaos came the dull thud of her arms, her legs against the sheets, her body fighting against itself. With a vague awareness that she was convulsing, she was sinking inward, into a black void. Until there was nothing but silence and darkness.

At last, there was no sense of the physical, no images, only her mind, her soul.

She was no longer cold or shivering, simply still. Again she felt the fear, the overwhelming sense of a mistake. They would not come for her! She would remain within the darkness forever, lost and alone.

"Mama?" she cried. "Mama!"

The voice was inside of her.

I can't help you, baby. You shouldn't have come.

She tried to reach out, to touch her, but there was nothing but black.

"God please," she begged, "please!" But God had forsaken her.

Out of the darkness, she felt a breath and heard the sound of the bayou, the twist of the hemp against the tree branch, back and forth, back and forth.

Tucker?

With haunting calm the melody came, like an anchor reaching out to her, tender and soft.

Pumpkin shells and tinker bells . . .

He was there! She was feeling his thoughts, his pain. He was waiting, ever waiting, just a mere breath away.

They bow their heads in garden beds . . .

Her gaze was pulled through the black to the hollow of a door.

Waiting on the moon . . .

He was just through the door on the other side.

When night appears they have no fears . . .

She need only believe, only a breath away . . .

Again she was sinking through the ebony, the voice becoming clearer, purer, pulling her, twisting her downward through the depths. She was slipping inward, into the darkest crevice of her existence . . . where dreams were made, where it was the beginning and the end. Where he had visited, had touched her, ever waiting . . . always waiting, just a mere breath away.

At once, she felt the release, the giving over. She was moving upward and outward, away from all that she had ever known, the voice reaching out, pulling her forward into one long sense of movement and focus. Streaks of light began moving past her, then images and faces . . . time moving, screeching past . . . moments, mere glimpses, pieces of the past flashing by her in broken fragments faster and faster . . . until the only sound that remained was the song. The beautiful melody pulling her toward it . . . the images merging into one long sense of movement and focus, a dark long tunnel, closing inward. She was fleeting through the tunnel, faster and faster toward the light at the end, the one singular voice focusing inward, tighter and tighter ... a clear distinct light pulling inward growing brighter and brighter until at last, she passed through. For a suspended moment— there was nothing but silence.

With a sigh, the highway appeared before her, the asphalt slick and wet beneath her. For a moment she remained still, the cool mist of fog on her face, touching, caressing. The solid world had reappeared, the familiar terrain, senses and sounds. The deep blacks, the emerald greens and pools of azure. The stars twinkled above her, bright and lovely, the night sharper, yet gentler than she ever remembered. The smells of the earth, of the bayou fragrant and intoxicating, the rotting soil as sweet and pungent as molasses, its gentle cadence but a mere whisper ...

Standing in the center of the highway, she remained transfixed, the yellow lines fleeting away from her in both directions. When all at once she felt the energy, the lights, the blast of warm air, the car roaring down the highway, ripping past her.

She had slipped into a world beneath, another dimension that somehow ran below and above the living. She had entered a place, so like the familiar but a counterpart. It was misty and soft ... shifting and changing, as malleable as the wind, as a thought. Again she felt the thread, the pull that had brought her ... "Tucker," she whispered.

She had been here before but she had not searched further or deep enough. She had not wanted to see, to face the shadows, the darkness. Yet he was there, waiting.

With a mere thought, the dilapidated house was before her. She was outside of it, then within ... she was beneath it and all around ... Her hands were touching the swing, the frayed rope, the shattered glass.

Home, Kylie. Home. But it wasn't real. Could not be real, for she was dead. Home no longer existed. It was gone ... melted away into the past. But no time existed here, just the countless ebbing and waxing of the moon—traces of moments caught within the tree branches, within the fluttering leaves. There was no time here ... only feelings and emotions ... no time ... only memories ... mere shadows of memories ...

A little yellow truck lay rusted on its side, a wheel missing. There was a bed, then no bed—time stacked without order, mere shadows no longer seen by the living yet remaining. She looked to Tucker's room, his toys . . . his thoughts. Once again, he had brought her to him. He was there among the memories and she had come to join him . . .

Even before she saw him, she sensed his sweet smell, that of the wind and the earth, his rosy cheeks and tousled hair . . .

"Tucker?"

The small figure moved from behind the house, his head lowered, his eyes looking shyly up at her.

Tucker. It was her beloved little Tucker. The moon highlighted the tiny freckles on the slope of his nose, the redness of his lips, his eyes staring out at her like two golden chestnuts.

"Daddy misses me," he said quietly, the phantom voice sweet, lost.

"Yes Tucker."

His hands moved to the wood, to the side of the house.

"And Mama . . . Mama is gone, isn't she?" he asked, picking at the paint, the chips falling to the earth like snowflakes.

"Yes."

He looked up at her, his face fretted, his lower lip puffing outward. "I waited." There was sorrow in his eyes. They were suddenly inside, the room filling with ice. "You forgot, but I waited here like you said."

The words repeated in her thoughts, building in gravity. He was there for her! She had asked him to wait, had begged him to return. Through the pain, the sorrow, through the long nights of beckoning him to stay, he had heard her voice. It had not been some monstrous force that had bound him! It's you Kylie, came the answer from within. You've imprisoned him in your grief.

"I couldn't leave you sad," the child said, his lips rounding, his eyes widening with compassion. "It was nobody's fault. Not the man in the truck, or Mama's or Daddy's. They just wanted me to leave. But I couldn't leave you sad."

He had lingered for her, waiting for her to accept, to understand, to move forth. But for her own pain and guilt she had been unable, unwilling to release him. Just as with the nightmare of Ellen Young, she had buried it deep inside, had been fighting what she envisioned as the faceless phantom of death, when all along she had been battling her own sorrow and contrition. He had remained within the gallows of her unacceptance, waiting. As closely as the wind to the earth they had remained connected. As surely as the night to the stars, he had spoken to her in her dreams, in her thoughts, a mere breath away to guide her through—if only she had been listening.

"Thank you, baby," she said softly. "Thank you."

A proud gentle smile touched his lips. "You didn't have to worry," he said bravely. "I was scared for just a minute, but then it didn't hurt at all."

With a pang she thought of the ravaged little body bursting through the car window.

"Aidan wanted me to come," he continued, "but I stayed here instead."

"Aidan?" she echoed, but Tucker was glancing about the room, his face filled with sadness. She became aware of the house around her, still cold and barren. It was as Tucker saw it—a place where they didn't belong. Once again she got the overwhelming sense of a mistake—a broken barrier where she should not have traversed.

Tucker was looking to the door, his face suddenly concentrated, taken with distraction. "They want me to go now," he said simply, as if answering some faint whisper. He looked back at her. "You'll come with me, won't you?"

She did not blink, for fear if she did, he would vanish like the makeshift walls around her.

"Yes, darling."

She was reaching out, her fingertips touching his own. "Take my hand."

The touch was soft, tender, his fingers slipping into her own.

"You'll be with me, won't you?" he asked, the entreaty singed with apprehension.

"Yes, Tucker."

"Always?"

"Forever."

The fireplace was suddenly warm, the room lighting from within. She pulled him into her arms, the feel of his little body beneath his soft clothing. She felt his cheek against her own, his arms wrapping tightly around her neck. She kissed his face, his lips. It could be nothing other than heaven . . . His breath was inside of her, filling her with his warmth. The cold feelings were instantly gone . . . there was nothing but warmth, a deep rapture enveloping, caressing her very being . . . rushing through her like a river, a warm golden river of bliss, touching her, easing her. She was lost within its beautiful tide, when it suddenly began to shift. Like the swift current of a river, it doubled back and began to tug against her . . . one dark thread that

*grew tighter and thicker. She felt herself pulling back, away from the eu-
phoria . . . the pulling turning to fire . . . a heaving, scorching flame. Then
all at once she flipped and was on her side, her head down, lower than her
feet. Then a light flashed bright and her eyes were staring wide, into the
brightness . . . all the while the pulling, the voices, the hands—her mouth
was stopped by something. They were pulling her back, away from him. She
could not scream, could do nothing. She was strapped!*

With the rushing and heaving of her stomach a checkered floor appeared beneath her, a red bucket filling with liquid, the smell of vomit,
the screaming inside of her head. They were pulling her back!

She tried to cry out, to scream—to stop them.

She became aware of her skin, cold and exposed, the light racking
through her system, blinding and painful.

"She's conscious."

Then another voice. "Kylie, lie still. We're trying to help you."

"Introduce the charcoal slurry . . . 200 grams . . ."

With a whirling motion she was on her back, a duller light probing
into her retinas. A figure loomed over her, his voice low, distorted.

"Welcome back, Mrs. O'Rourke," he said. She saw nothing but his
eyes, black and listless, the surgical fatigues. The intent staff milled
around her, adjusting, shifting, as her thoughts vanished back into the
delirium.

Fifty-Seven

A CONVERSATION FROM THE HALLWAY LINGERED AT THE EDGE OF HER
consciousness, a nurse discussing something about a chicken casse-
role with another. A murky light escaped from beneath the drawn
blinds, yet Kylie couldn't tell the day or the time. She was not certain
how long she had been awake, nor exactly when the haze had begun to
melt. Through her clearing vision, Dillon emerged at the foot of the
bed. First his figure, then the rest of him, the details of his face, of his
smooth white skin rendered nearly blue within the cool light, his brow
knit, as he stared at a book resting in his lap.

An oxygen mask had been clipped to her face, IVs attached to her arm. Her throat burned like fire, her stomach cramping. With the feel of a pad between her legs, she wondered if she were still pregnant, or if the fetus had been expelled in the trauma.

Like a prisoner taken hostage, she had been slammed back into the living. She felt the brutality of her arrival in the ache of her temples, in the horrid taste in her mouth. She wanted to yank out the tubes, pull the needles from her arms. Once again medicine had taken its own liberties, bringing life where it was not wanted—did not belong. Once again, man's intervention would prolong the hell. *What gives you the right?* she wanted to say, but pressed her lips tighter instead. The bitterness in her heart twisted her mouth downward, but her eyes remained cold and steady.

As if sensing her gaze, Dillon looked up, his face instantly a palette of emotion. Though he said nothing, she saw the agony, the anger, the pity all dueling it out behind the searching eyes. Resting the book to his side, he came around to the head of the bed and gently slid the mask from her mouth and took her hand.

"How do you feel?" he asked.

She slipped her hand and her eyes away, the emotion trickling down the side of her temple.

Clearing his throat, Dillon turned to a chart. "If you're having stomach cramps," he said, his voice low and clinical, "that's to be expected. They did a gastric lavage ... emptied and washed out your stomach, so to speak. The strange taste in your mouth is from charcoal that was used to absorb the remaining poisons. The IV drip is for rehydration and for the cerebral edema. You had a swelling in your brain ... you were having hallucinations ... bad ones."

"I was dead, wasn't I?" she asked, her eyes fixed on a cheap litho on the wall—a watercolor of yellow nodding daffodils.

"Your heart stopped in the emergency room." he answered softly.

"For how long?"

"Three minutes."

Three minutes yet it felt a lifetime. She had seen Tucker, had been there with him. He had trusted her, had placed his sweet trust in her. Now she had abandoned him once again, had left him to face the shadows alone. "You shouldn't have brought me back," she said bitterly.

She felt the grave eyes upon her, but it meant nothing. She was empty, void. She had finally been free, yet they had forced her back. Whether it was God's will, or man's intervention, she would not be allowed to leave on her own accord. She would be forced to wait in fear and anticipation of the next torturous ending. "You only delayed the inevitable. Next time it'll be worse."

She felt his shoulders pinching inward. He was clearly stricken by her words, yet she had no pity. She wanted him to leave, to simply go away, but he remained at her side as if willing to take whatever she had to give. With a sudden softening of her grip, she remembered the pain in his eyes, his supplications at Harvard Square. *It's not his fault, Kylie. He's only trying to help.* Still she could not face him.

He stood patiently by, watching her. "I don't know if you're ready for this or not," he said finally, "but there's something I need to tell you. They did some blood tests to check your liver . . ."

Within the cautious hesitation, she knew what would follow.

"You're pregnant, Kylie."

He waited for her response, but she had none to give.

"Did you know?" he asked, as if in her silence the thought had suddenly occurred to him.

"Yes."

The answer seemed more than he could bear. He turned away, the back of his hand covering his mouth, his head bowed low. "I don't understand this," he said, the words catching in his throat. "You said you wanted a child—Jack's child."

"I did."

"Then why this?"

She could not answer.

After a moment he turned back, but wouldn't look at her. "There was some bleeding," he continued, his voice again cold and professional. "They did an ultra-sound—"

She noticed his eyes glance to the side, to a glowing monitor beside her.

"I asked that they make a videotape of it, so that—"

"I don't want to see it."

He placed the clipboard aside and faced her. "I thought you might at least want to know—to see—that the baby is—"

"Dead," she finished, the flatness of her voice startling even herself.

His face was unchanged, staring. "No," he responded. "Whether you want it or not, it's alive."

The comment was so unexpected that she met his eyes.

"There's a heartbeat. You can't dispute a heartbeat."

He had hit a button, an image appearing on the screen.

"Your body's been through a hell of a trauma, but the pregnancy survived."

She merely stared at the gray image, unable to think, to believe. There had been no life, no soul for the child. *It can't survive*, came the decree of Julius Vanderpoel, yet there was no refuting the image. The angle on the tiny body was turning, the focus moving inward on the strange rapid rhythm. She was reaching out, her fingertips tracing along the shoulder, along the tiny bent arm. Along with her emotion, desire rose within her breast. The child was alive! She was gasping, tears streaming her face, but as soon as she felt the joy, the fear beat it back. She turned abruptly away, the wall rising once again. Death was imminent. To hope otherwise, either for herself or the child inside, was nothing short of torturing herself.

"Please turn it off," she said quietly.

As the monitor faded with a click of the switch, a sudden emptiness mixed with her dread. There was now a child to die with her, a living being destined to suffer. She felt the sudden need to get up, to move away from all around her, to run somewhere, anywhere, but as she remained with her hands clutching the gown at her side, her attention was pulled once again to Dillon. He stood with his back to her, his hand grasping the doorjamb, as if struggling with his own warring thoughts.

After a moment he spoke, his voice rimmed with sorrow.

"I can't keep you alive," he said softly. "I can't guard you night and day. If you really want to die, eventually you'll succeed. You almost did this time."

He turned slowly back to her, his face open and direct.

"You came close, Kylie. So close."

With his mouth clenched, he broke away, his hands in his pockets, wandering toward the windows. For a moment, the slatted light seemed to absorb him, his face in profile, his blue eyes dark yet concentrated. "I wasn't the one who found you."

She looked toward him, the silhouetted light making the creases of his mouth deepened and grave.

"After you left the square, I thought you needed time alone. I would have called you today. But today would have been too late. You would have already been dead."

A strange feeling of nausea came over her. She wanted to look away, but her eyes remained riveted.

"You may think some grave injustice has been done by your resuscitation," he said softly, "but you're wrong. You belong here, with the living. It wasn't the paramedics or the ventilator or the IV drips that saved you . . . it was something else, something more powerful that wanted you alive. As a doctor, I want to believe I can control life . . . that nothing as oblique as fate has the upper hand, but sometimes when I'm treating a patient, I get the sense that something more, something else is dealing the hand. That sometimes no matter what I do, the patient's future has already been written. I go through the motions never knowing the outcome, how the pieces will fit, but always with a sense that I'm part of it. I knew of a patient once that was in dire need of a heart transplant, but he had a rare blood type. His was a particularly heart-wrenching case. He was a father with two small children, his wife having passed away years earlier. At the last hour, a heart came in from a man that had been crossing the street when a stray bullet from a New Year's Eve party struck him. The blood type was a perfect match—the heart saved the patient. It wasn't until days later, they discovered the donor had been his estranged brother. Most of my colleagues argued that it was pure luck, sheer coincidence that two brothers who hadn't spoken or seen each other in twenty years were brought back together in such a way. But I don't believe that. I believe that it's all connected somehow. That there's a reason for everything."

He was facing her again, his shadow throwing his figure over the bed.

"At around eleven o'clock last night," he continued, "the neighbors reported a loud screeching coming from the mansion. When the police arrived, the sound led them to the attic where they found an old horn alarm, shoved into a corner of the room."

Kylie instantly knew the old security system of which he spoke. Nearly a year earlier, Jack had removed the door and window trigger switches, and tore out all of the wiring in anticipation of an updated system. "But the alarm had been—"

"—disconnected," finished Dillon. "Yes. But there it was boxed and disassembled, blasting at full volume. They found you in a downstairs bedroom . . . just in time."

Kylie was so stunned that she merely stared at him.

"When they pulled the alarm apart, they found that an old back-up battery was fueling the horn. They couldn't say for certain what triggered it—either some shift of movement, or a dwindling battery-warning activated the system; either way, they said that it was one in a million chance that it went off. That it was pure luck they found you. But it wasn't luck," he said with a shake of his head. "I've seen this kind of thing too many times. Call it fate, divine intervention, or whatever the hell you want, but you were spared, Kylie. And whether you were spared for yourself, or for your father, or for the child inside of you, there's a reason."

LONG after Dillon left the room, Kylie remained still, not daring to move, to let her thoughts speak too loudly. The lights in the hallway eventually dimmed, the glow of the sun through the blinds fading to darkness. Nurses had come and gone, but she had scarcely noticed them, had not replied to their comments or questions. It wasn't until all had calmed to silence that her fingers went slowly back to the monitor, to the image that lay just beneath the black glass. With a flick of the switch, the glow warmed before her. She hit the play button, and the fetus appeared.

"Hey," she whispered, swiping a tear from her cheek.

All afternoon her thoughts had been colliding, battling for position. She had tried not to speculate, to take comfort in Dillon's conviction that she had been spared. She tried not to ponder too fully that she had ventured into death alone, yet had emerged with another.

Take my hand, her memory whispered.

The cool glass was beneath her touch, yet it was Tucker's warm skin that her mind felt, his entreaty circling inward.

You'll come with me, won't you?

They want me to leave now. You'll come with me, won't you?

They had been embracing, their fears, their dreams, their souls merging into one. Tears obliterated the monitor before her, yet her fingers remained, the promise of her heart repeating again and again.

You'll be with me, won't you?

Yes, Tucker.

Always?

Forever.

With the focus closing in on the heart, she allowed herself to believe . . . "Is that you, baby?" she whispered. *Is that you?*

The movement continued rapid and silent. Her breath caught as the tape ended and the screen jumped to black. For a moment she remained staring into her own dark reflection.

"Hello love."

At the sound of her father's voice, her throat clenched tight. Dillon had called him against her will, for she couldn't bear to face him. She slowly looked to the doorway, where he remained hesitant and sad. "Daddy," she said softly, her chest caving at sight of his pain.

"I couldn't stand to lose you," he said, his voice breaking.

"I'm sorry, Daddy," she cried, her arms reaching out to him.

"What were you thinkin', lass?" he scolded, pulling her tight. "What the devil were you thinkin'?"

Fifty-Eight

FOR A LONG WHILE KYLIE STOOD WATCHING THE BLACKENED BRANCH beat against the side of the brick building, the summer storm drenching the walkway beneath. Once again she stood before the rain-streaked window within the psychiatrist's office, her arms crossed, her heart filled with confusion, her eyes worn from emotion, only this time, months had passed since that cold March day, as well as a lifetime worth of pain. This time, she was not alone. The child was inside of her, living, growing.

It had been three days since the suicide attempt, the first twenty-four hours filled with headaches and an overall achiness, but by the second morning, all symptoms had vanished. Though the pregnancy was effecting increasingly pronounced changes in her body, she felt physically better than she had in months. The nausea had left her, her appetite soaring. She had been sleeping soundly every night, a deep restful slumber. The dark circles under her eyes had vanished, her cheeks now tinted with a soft rose. Her breasts and stomach continued to swell, while evidence of increasing blood supplies had appeared beneath her skin. With her transforming body, her spirit was also changing. With each passing second, the dark cloud was lifting. With each passing hour, she moved further and further from the fear. She was no longer looking over her shoulder, expecting the shadows to shift. The intense urgency that had plagued her for months, seemed to have dissipated overnight.

Still, the numbness inside had not left her, the questions continuing to dog her, in her waking hours, her dreams: If she were truly to die, why hadn't they taken her? Why the alarm? Why had she been allowed to come back and had Tucker returned with her? During a prenatal workup that morning, she kept expecting the news, the vacancy to settle in the obstetrician's eyes, any sign that the pregnancy was doomed, but no such moment arose. When the due-date of December 30th had been given, it brought only one thought—would she and the baby be alive to see it?

Though life appeared as if it would continue, it was still too much to hope, to believe, that her destiny had taken a sudden turn, to trust in Dillon's certainty that fate wanted her alive and for a reason.

With her back to the doctor, she felt his scrutinizing eyes upon her. His brooding face was reflected against the droplets of rain that clung to the window, the warm glow of the desk lamp outlining his concentrated features. Within her silence, she wondered what theories he was extrapolating.

"Counseling is a must," Dillon had insisted, but she had confided nothing more than the bare minimum to the psychiatrist. Though she had revealed her experiences on the mountain so trustingly before, she had nothing to gain by divulging her innermost secrets now. She remembered too well the intrusive and threatening analysis before Detective Binaggio and had no desire to be doubted or classified once again as unsound of mind. She had allowed herself only one small reference to her past visit. By the time of her appointment, Dr. Jordan already knew of Jack and Amelia's deaths; she merely added to the tally with Dale Benson's and let him draw his own conclusions. Judging by the flinch in the doctor's eyes, he clearly remembered her fear of the accident's aftermath and her "unwarranted" paranoia concerning their survival. Just as she had foretold, Jack, Amelia and Dale Benson were now dead. Her own survival was the only negation to her prediction, yet it was enough for the doctor to cling onto and gain conviction of his own. With a wave of his hand and a clearing of his throat, he had dismissed it. After all, arson, suicide and a medical condition were hardly proof of a dark world seeping upward, snatching at will. With little more than a thought, the deaths were filed away in his clinical mind as a freak and unfortunate coincidence. From his perspective, she remained—not a woman who had been fighting death—but a widow who had been so desolate she had embraced it; who had abandoned all hope with the loss of her husband and friend.

"What's important," the doctor had replied kindly, "is that you're alive and that you must go on living."

But to go on living was a much harder feat than he could ever have imagined. For the first time since Jack's death, it felt as though life might continue; to envision it without him or Amelia was an impossibility. It was this point that she had been pondering for so long, staring out at the falling rain.

"It'll take time," the doctor said, breaking her reverie. "Let yourself grieve, but accept that your loved ones have moved on."

He was speaking of the recent deaths, yet it was Tucker who came to mind—the undying grief that had consumed her for so long. Even before the plane crash, she had been living in mourning . . . burying the pain through alcohol and a tumultuous marriage. Like Josephine Parker who refused to let go of her sister, Jessie, she had been living between worlds, straddling the line between life and death, inviting the spirit world in. Perhaps it had not been her mother's locket that had brought Julius Vanderpoel to her, that had opened her eyes to the dead, but her own unwillingness to let go, her own unwilling spirit to abide within the living.

"They hear us, you know?" she muttered to the falling rain. "The dead. They're connected to us. The lights, the sounds."

She was thinking of Josephine Parker, of her many incantations to release the dead—opening the windows, putting sheets over the mirrors—when it was not the physical world that bound her sister, but her own sorrow and unwillingness to set her free. There really was a limbo, but it wasn't a place, a physical location, but a place in the hearts of the living, a prison where both the living and the dead remained shackled together.

"It's time to let it all go," said the doctor gently. "There's not just yourself to think about now. You've got a child inside of you to consider. Your life's taken a different path now."

A different path. Had her life truly charted a different path and if so, was the child the reason? She thought of her father's visit, of the light in his eyes when he learned of the pregnancy . . .

Daddy misses me, came the haunting pronouncement of Tucker.

Was it her destiny that had been altered, or her father's or Tucker's? She placed her hand on her stomach and imagined the life within.

Turning to the doctor, she posed a gentle challenge of her own. "Do you believe that we have a chance to come back, if our time isn't finished?"

"Your time isn't finished, Kylie," he replied, mistaking the question to mean herself. "You're going to be a mother now. Your life is intertwined with another. What you do, affects it."

With a gentle breath, she contemplated his response. As surely as she had been worked out, had she been worked back in? And if so, for how long? Would she be allowed to love, to stay with the child? How would she live, not knowing when, or how death would come; if she would see the child through the pregnancy, through its adolescence? How would she live with the uncertainty?

With the encroaching tears, she turned away. "I don't think I can take it," she said, biting her lip. "To lose a child again. I don't think I can live with the uncertainty."

"You have no choice. None of us know, Kylie. None of us know how long we've got, or how long our loved ones will be with us. All we can do is cherish each moment and let death come when it comes."

"When it's meant to," she said softly.

"If you believe in fate—yes. Buddhists, Jainists and Hindus all believe that we're here to learn, to solve, to perfect, to become a purer energy. We stay only as long as we need to, for as long as it takes, until we're done with what we came for."

Kylie stared out at the dying rain, her breath clouding the window before her. She wanted the answers, but would have to settle for uncertainty. She wanted the agenda, but would have to be content with time.

Fifty-Nine

FALL DESCENDED UPON THE CITY WITH FREEZING RAINS AND FRIGID temperatures, but then in late October gave way to a brilliant Indian Summer.

The gold and crimson leaves danced along Newbury Street, the brisk New England sky blue and flawless. Sweater-clad pedestrians ambled along the sidewalk, a small cluster stopping in front of the Ratchford Art Boutique. Completely disregarding the sign posted BY APPOINTMENT ONLY tacked to the heavy wooden entry, they vied for a glimpse inside the clandestine shop whose doors usually remained bolted.

In a flurry of energy, Arlin appeared from within. "Excuse me," he chimed, shooing a man with a baseball cap and camera aside, before tugging the massive door shut.

"Tourists," he grumbled within the sudden darkness. "I can't even enjoy the seasons without all of the Nellies nosing around." With a swipe of his hand, he pulled the curtains back down over the open casement windows, a woman outside gasping with the rebuff. "By the stares we get, you would think we were torturing poor maidens in here, feeding their virgin souls to angry demons."

"What do you expect?" Kylie asked from the winged chair Arlin had dragged into the front room for her to rest in. "The outside of this place looks like some kind of medieval dungeon."

"You think?" Arlin asked, his brow crinkling in thought. "Well, let's keep them guessing, shall we?" he said with a mischievous grin.

"Who's guessing," Kylie groaned. "I've often felt tortured in this place."

"Nonsense, you love me."

"I adore you."

"Then why don't you bring me more clients like Dora? Art lovers with unlimited funds."

"Two months, Arlin. Just give me two months."

"You know, lots of women work right through their pregnancies. It's good for you."

"No," she said pointedly. "It's good for you. Now be happy with the business I'm giving you or I'll leave you to your tourists."

"Don't get testy. A fella's got a right to earn a living. Which reminds me, I've got a gorgeous—"

"Stop right there. I don't want to hear it. I told you I'm on a budget."

"Okay, okay," he said with a swift pivot toward the back room. "I'll leave you to your painting while I find something to wrap it in."

As he disappeared behind the heavy curtains, Kylie rose from the chair for another look at her new purchase—a nineteenth-century portrait by a Swede named Lovendahl. After acquiring a home in Swampscott, she had promised herself that the remainder of the insurance settlement would be used solely for furnishings and to set up a trust fund. With Dora's mansion long since completed and no other jobs in the waiting, the painting was the only expenditure on art she had allowed herself—a gift for her child. In her search for the perfect piece, the gentle hues and peaceful image had instantly caught her. It forged the limits of what she had allotted to spend, but once she had laid eyes upon it, there could be no other choice.

The painting was entitled *Elysium*, the reference of heavenly bliss not to a band of angels or golden gates opening outward, but to the peace found between a mother and child. A woman rested against a tree on a river bank, a small boy at her side. Neither the woman nor the youngster were smiling, yet the stoic tranquility within their eyes was breathtaking.

Tilting the painting out from the dark pieces that surrounded it, Kylie felt a surge of excitement. With a squint of her eyes, it was easy to imagine it above her living room mantel. It would be the needed soft touch within the masculine home which she had tailored exclusively for her father—a man of size. Though she herself preferred a more graceful interior, she had filled the house with sturdy hardwoods, rugged leathers and open spaces, even a recliner to ease her father's tired body—all of the amenities she had wanted so desperately for him and could now afford. It had been no small feat coaxing him from the cramped cottage to the North Shore, yet once he had settled into the larger home he found it much more to his liking—"a house a man could get used to" was how he had summed it up. The home was manly to say the least. The painting, with its gentle lines, would bring a nice balance, a softening of the edges.

With one last appraisal of the portrait and its gilded frame, Kylie started to rest it back, when her eye caught the edge of a familiar painting behind it. Leaning her own further forward, she saw that it was the depiction of Hector Haynes crumpled within the hellish closet, rats and spiders seeping inward.

The image was so brutal and startling she nearly lost her balance. At once that dark day with Eva Ratchford came rushing back to her, the sound of Amelia's desperate gasps for breath, the shroud of fear that had hovered over them. Shuffling through the next four paintings stacked behind it, she saw they were all Hector's. They had been placed in the "sold" section of the store, awaiting delivery.

"Can you believe we actually found a buyer for those?" Arlin said, peaking his head in from the back room. "Hector was such a freak, I thought they would never sell."

Kylie struggled to find her voice, but her thoughts were too leaden to speak. She wondered what poor soul had related to Hector's story, had seen their own experiences reflected within his depictions. She wondered if they too remained silent, fearful of ridicule and disbelievers.

Letting go of the paintings, she turned away from them. She was glad the shop would be rid of them—for she would never again have to look upon the artist's pain.

Lowering herself slowly, she let the soft chair ease her shaking legs. Until that startling moment she had not realized how the horrific memories had begun to fade, the events taking on the shade of distant dreams ... the shadows, the moments seeming mere glimpses of nightmares. Somewhere along the way, life had moved forward. Without notice, it had even gained normalcy. Only occasionally did she think of it now, did the few nightmarish months come into her thoughts, did the name Julius Vanderpoel roll into her silent dialogue where the secret would forever be cast.

"Julius Vanderpoel," she whispered aloud. As if conjuring a ghost, she saw vividly his features, his absorbing eyes. She remembered that blistering day in August, when the name and image had last crossed her path.

It had been late in the day on the west side of the Common. A small electronics store was having a sale on televisions—something she had been wanting to purchase for her father. As she cut across the street to the shop, she had smelled the smoke in the air but had thought little of it. It wasn't until she was standing before a wall of TV monitors that it took on significance, the news story blasting forth in varying volumes set in unison . . . "Father of Vanderpoel Strangler found burned to death in home," was the lead-in.

With locked knees and bated breath, Kylie watched the recap of the "late-breaking" news. A reporter stood before a blazing brownstone, her hair whipped about by the heat and wind. A suspicious fire had consumed the old Vanderpoel mansion, killing the eighty-eight-year-old Harland Vanderpoel. Arson was suspected, but details were uncertain at the time.

When the camera shifted to incorporate a crumbling pillar, it was then that Kylie noticed the face among the onlookers—an elderly man with stooped shoulders and pale eyes staring toward the burning building. It was Julius Vanderpoel, his features withered to that of an old man.

Anyone looking closely could have seen the resemblances between Harland Vanderpoel's photo and the man in the crowd, but he went unnoticed. As he turned and disappeared within the onlookers, Kylie ran from the store, her eyes tracing the trail of smoke into the sky. For a long while she remained outside of the shop, watching the thin strip of black evaporating into the sunset.

That night's news and the days to follow had been filled with the developing story. An autopsy revealed that Harland Vanderpoel had been dead long before the fire had been set, his neck sliced from ear to ear. Other than evidence that he had willingly opened the door to his assassin, there were no clues to his murder, yet Kylie had no doubt in her mind who had killed him. Julius's embittered words of his father's betrayal had stayed with her, along with the detailed image of his wife's suicidal hanging, alongside their seven-year-old son's. The father had finally been called to answer for the illicit affair, justice coming back in the form of a specter. She wondered how Harland Vanderpoel must have felt when he had opened his door to the aged visage of his long-deceased son. The shock alone would have been enough to kill him.

Mary Wolcott-Vanderpoel, wife of Harland and the matriarch of the troublesome brood, had also received mention. It was believed that the corpse of a small baby found buried within the walls of the mansion had been her own—the child having expired nearly sixty years earlier, several years before Julius's birth.

The layers of the story were more staggering and impenetrable than even Kylie had imagined, the newscaster echoing her sentiment on the final night of coverage . . .

"Though investigators continue to scour the premises for clues to this slaying and to the troubled past . . . the dark secrets of this infamous family may never be unraveled."

Kylie knew that at the very least, Harland Vanderpoel's homicide would go "unsolved," the authorities having little hope of tracking a murderer who had died decades earlier. At times, when she passed the darkened streets and subways, her eyes scanning past the homeless, the aged, she looked for him—but she never caught sight of him again. Julius Vanderpoel had vanished back into the shadows from which he had arisen, leaving an indelible mark in his wake.

"This ought to do it," said Arlin, reappearing with brown wrapping paper and a roll of twine. "I keep telling Eva I need more packing materials but she never listens."

As he began to wrap the painting, Kylie silently rested her hand on her stomach and took comfort in the child inside. With the feel of the tiny fingers rolling along the inside of her skin, the darkness melted. The child was what mattered. Above anything and everything—the past, present or future—her son eased all else. With his settling, she imagined him as she had last seen him, contentedly suckling his thumb within the sonogram monitor, the tiny bulge hanging from between his legs confirming his gender.

"What do you think?" asked Arlin.

Kylie was startled to find him staring toward her. "What? I'm sorry, I didn't hear what you said."

"I said that you should let me deliver this for you. There's no sense in you lugging it with you all the way back on the train."

Kylie smiled. "I'm pregnant Arlin, not an invalid."

"Honey, you can't even see your feet."

"I don't need to see my feet. Besides, I don't want to drag you to the 'ends of the earth,' as you so kindly put it on your last visit. The way you carry on, you would think Swampscott was in the Himalayas."

"Well it might as well be, darling. If I can't get there by foot I would just as soon fly. Besides, fish, families and fresh air? Not the sort of place for a night-prowler like me." He turned to her with a shrewd gaze. "Or you, come to think of it. Who are you and what have you done with my Kylie?"

"She's buried beneath twenty pounds of fat and swollen ankles."

"Fat, schmatt. Even pregnant, you're gorgeous—all chesty and raging with estrogen. I wish it would give me that kind of glow."

Kylie shot him an acerbic glance.

"Trust me," he said, "you're no worse for the wear. I saw the looks you were getting the other night at the theater. Speaking of which, what about that handsome brother you were with? Why don't you leave this here for now and get that stud-muffin to come down—"

"Dillon," she interrupted. "His name is Dillon. And I refuse to do without my painting just because you've got a crush."

"Don't look at me, honey. I'm not the one smitten."

Kylie turned to him, startled not only by his implication, but by the color rushing into her cheeks. "What do you mean?" she asked.

"The two of you. Eyes glued on one another all night."

"Arlin," she said. "He was Jack's—"

"Brother. Yes I know. I also know when someone's been bitten. The two of you are in love, honey, and you can't even see it."

Unable to find words, she looked away. Dillon was dear to her, so dear. It was true they had grown closer, but that was only natural in the wake of Jack's death.

Within her sudden silence, Arlin moved toward her. "I'm sorry darling," he said, stroking her hair gently. "You know I loved Jack and would never—"

"I know," she said, recovering herself.

"Sometimes I open my big mouth a little too wide. I just want you to move forward, to be happy. You clearly adore each other, honey. That's all I'm saying."

. . .

WITH the painting in tow, Kylie stepped back out into the blustery day. The temperature was dropping with the setting sun, the trees blazing with the colorful foliage. Wrapping her wool scarf around tight, she headed up Newbury, thoughts of Dillon still weighting her mind.

She thought of his gentle touch in Lamaze and the way his face lighted when they listened to the baby's heartbeat. She thought of the awkward silence that had settled between them when a nurse had mistaken them for a couple, and her own jealousy, as she had become more and more aware of the way women were drawn to him.

In truth, Arlin had merely given voice to the bewildering feelings that had been growing inside of her—emotions that confused and terrified her.

After her attempted overdose she had leaned on Dillon desperately . . . seeing Jack in his movements, his voice, taking comfort in his companionship, but slowly Jack had receded from between them and her feelings for Dillon had begun to clarify. In her dreams, he had become more than a friend, he had become her lover. After ten years of platonic friendship, the shift was discomforting.

Until Arlin had said it, she had not even allowed herself to consider that Dillon might feel the same. Out of survival of her marriage, she had denied within herself the attraction they had once felt for one another. When she had first met the brothers, it was Dillon who had caught her eye, but when Jack had won her heart, she had buried those feelings deep inside.

Dillon had always been respectful of her decision. Even when Jack had thought otherwise, he had never given him cause for concern. Even after Jack's death, he had kept his distance. At one point he had even seemed to be pulling back from her. It was she who had insisted on seeing him, on making him a part of the pregnancy.

Still, Arlin's words continued to pique at her thoughts. *Dillon*. Was there a possibility between them? If she were to open the door to something further, how would they make the transition? From friend to lover. There would be no turning back. The thought of losing him terrified her. Dillon was everything to her.

Yet it was more than the uncharted waters that frightened her, it was the small part of her that was still holding back. A part of her that remained on borrowed time. Though she cherished each moment, filling it with as much as she could, she remained constantly aware that it could be her last. Her fear of death had vanished, yet her fear of hurting the ones whom she loved remained. Perhaps all who had experienced death, felt the same. Perhaps they all treasured each moment, knowing that it could be their last.

As the train boomed through a dark tunnel, her uterus suddenly gripped tight. No matter how often the Braxton Hicks contractions came upon her, they always caught her breath. "It's perfectly natural," her obstetrician had told her. "It's just your body preparing itself—getting in shape."

"Hey little fella," she said, rubbing her hand against her belly. After a moment, the tightening subsided. As the train glided to a smooth halt, she looked to the opening doors and then down at her swollen ankles. "One step at a time," she said. "Isn't that right? Just one fat foot in front of the next."

Sixty

THOUGH CHRISTMAS WAS FIVE DAYS PAST, THE ANGELIC SONG OF carolers eased through the twilight. As the snowflakes danced from the grayish sky, the gas lamps along Union Street grew brighter. The lights of the season hung draped along the red-brick street, early evening commuters bustling to get home to their families, to the warm stews and fireplaces that awaited them.

Kylie took a seat on a bench in front of the Old Union Oyster House where she was to meet Dillon for dinner. In spite of the cold, she opted to wait outside, the evening air feeling fresh on her face. Snow had fallen thick and heavy throughout December without the brittle temperatures that usually accompanied it. The thermometer remained just below freezing with little wind chill, a perfect balance to the relentless warmth of pregnancy.

With the holidays nearly over, her due-date of December 30th had come upon her faster than she could ever have imagined. The day had been filled with anything and everything to distract her from the pregnancy. Lunch had been spent with her father, then a movie and a salon appointment to follow. At the advice of one of his nurses, Dillon had given her the gift of a pedicure—but the last thing she wanted was someone messing with her feet. The ploy was to distract her from the pivotal day, but her feet were so swollen it would have been torturous. Still, she went through the motions of the appointment, tipping the manicurist and swearing her to secrecy. Dillon worried needlessly about her blood pressure, her diet, her exercise, and needed no encouragement. In spite of his concerns, she felt fit and surprisingly energetic. The baby was healthy, no longer kicking, but squirming restlessly within the confining quarters. It was time to come out. She felt equal parts excitement and fear at the thought. She didn't want a pedicure, she wanted Dillon by her side. She wanted his hands on her back, her neck, his gentle stroke on her stomach, the soft voice in which he calmed her and urged her through the Lamaze exercises. She thought of the way the light had caught his eyes that morning, and the grip of his firm jaw as he had helped her from the train. She wanted him beside her, touching her, reassuring her. She wanted him near ... always, forever.

A nervous flutter came alive inside of her. He was surely on his way to her now, wondering what it was she wanted to discuss with him. He would have already left the hospital, having promised to come straight away after his patients.

"Shhh," she whispered aloud, the baby squirming, taking cue from her apprehension. With a deep controlled breath, she need only think of her father's encouraging words ... *He loves you, Kylie. He's always loved you.*

Tears had come into her eyes when she had heard them, for though it seemed that Dillon felt the same as she, he had made no move accordingly.

"Don't you understand, love? He can't," her father had confided. "The laws of brotherhood forbid it."

Out of love for his brother he had remained bound, unwilling to overstep the silent perimeter; and even though Jack now seemed the one pulling them together, remaining with them through the child, drawing them closer, the first move would have to come from her.

"Talk to him, love," her father had said. "Tell him how you feel."

Ever since lunch, she had felt an urgency to speak with him. She wanted him to know how she felt before the baby's delivery. From the moment of his birth, she wanted her son to have a father, to have Dillon.

When finally she caught sight of him across the street, the gray coat, his dark curly hair, his lips and nose red with the cold, her heart leapt. She quickly stood before he could see her, for she didn't want him to witness her awkward struggle from the bench.

"Is he the father?"

The craggy voice startled her. She turned to find a fragile old woman beside her, stooped with a cane. As Kylie looked into the warm hazy eyes, she felt something familiar, something soothing within the gaze that had fixed so attentively on her.

Do I know you? she wanted to say, but instead, followed the woman's line-of-sight back to Dillon, who now stood at the crosswalk.

As though sensing their attention upon him, he looked up and smiled. With the cars passing between them, he raised his hand in acknowledgment.

"He's beautiful," said the old woman. "Simply gorgeous."

"Yes," murmured Kylie, her pulse racing at the sight of him. The moment their eyes locked, Dillon's hopeful and sad, she saw the love, the fear. He clearly knew why she had called him there, and found peace within the silent dialogue that passed between them.

As she smiled gently back at him, something tumbled to the ground by her feet.

"Oh goodness," said the old woman, looking helplessly down at a bag she had dropped. "Aren't we a pair?" she said, feebly, eyeing her cane and Kylie's heavy belly.

Kylie looked to Dillon, still trapped on the other side of the street, and back to the bag on the ground. Wormer Books & Company was etched across the front of the sack, the fine paper quickly soaking up the dampness of the brick walkway. Though she dreaded the awkward bend, there was no other choice.

"I'll get it," she said.

With considerable effort she managed to grasp the bag between the tips of her bare fingers, the blood rushing so fully into her temples that the ground swayed. In a moment of light-headedness she tried to raise back up, when a pain jabbed from within her chest—a deep excruciating stab. As she groped blindly to upright herself, the cold sweat of fear gripped her; the pain was not a contraction, but the familiar knifing she had felt after the accident—a sharp dagger so excruciating that she could scarcely breathe. Something had gone wrong inside of her, something deathly wrong. The bag slid back down to the ground, her eyes staring wide. She found the crinkled face before her, distorting, the knowing eyes without surprise.

"I'm sorry, my dear," the old woman said softly. "It won't hurt long."

In that moment Kylie knew—what had been familiar about the old woman, was that she did not belong.

Somewhere behind her own gasps, she heard the blasting of horns, she felt her knees hitting the sidewalk, her shoulder slamming into the cement. She had managed to fall without hitting her belly, her arm wrapped tight around it. The baby was squirming, fighting, as if to escape the icy sidewalk beneath her. Still she could not breathe, could not speak, the pain was unbearable. Through her tears, she watched the woman's feet shuffle away from her, the fallen bag—used solely to precipitate her collapse—left abandoned on the walkway. It was then that she knew: the pain's source was to bring her death. From the thwarted angle, the cars roared past seemingly ten feet above her, the snowflakes fluttering downward, resting gently on her outstretched hand.

Trapped at the crosswalk, Dillon watched in horror as her body crumpled to the ground. From the moment he saw her clutch her chest, saw the ghastly way her eyes went blank, he knew what had happened. Without waiting for the traffic, he shot through the cars, narrowly dodging the blasting horns and screaming drivers.

"Kylie! KYLIE!"

Shoving the onlookers aside, he was before her. Her hair lay muddied around her ashen face, her lips tight as she struggled with the pain.

"Tell me where it is!" he beseeched. "Is it stabbing to your back?"

"Yessss," she managed to breathe.

The confirming answer brought a swell of tears to his eyes. It could be nothing other than the graft in her heart, given way beneath the stress of the pregnancy. Ten years of medical practice would not let him escape the odds. Without surgery, she had seven minutes, eight minutes tops. He was gathering her up, her warm breast against his thundering chest.

"Get back!" he was screaming, as he burst through the door, the tinkle of a bell distant, the warmth enveloping them. "Get me a phone! Get me a phone!" he was screaming.

Time seemed staggered, the receiver in his hand, his voice trying to articulate when his mind wanted nothing more than to scream. *Not enough time! Not enough time!* was all he could think, his lips forming the stats ". . . nine months pregnant . . . a ruptured aorta . . . Where are we?" he asked helplessly, his eyes darting around before remembering. "The Union Oyster House!"

As he relinquished the phone, Kylie gripped his hand tight. Without a word, he saw the fear in her eyes, not for herself but for the child. His touch followed hers to her belly, to the feel of the tiny limbs twisting beneath her flesh.

"He's going to be fine," he promised. "There's nothing wrong with him. It's your heart."

She gripped his hand even tighter. "He's what's important," she whispered, her hair dampened by the pain, tiny curls of auburn clinging to her ashen forehead. "Take the baby—"

"Shhh," he whispered, smoothing back her hair with his fingers. "It's not gonna come to that," he insisted, his voice faltering. "You can both still make it. We just need to get you into surgery . . . we just need to patch things up."

But she saw the truth in his eyes, in the terror he fought so desperately to hide. Her body had been stretched to its limit, the birth of the child its last giving. In spite of the pain, a calmness settled over her, for the answer to her question had finally come . . . it was Tucker. God had given her Tucker—a precious gift on borrowed time. Now that his life was beginning, hers was to end. With the deepening peace, she envisioned the journey before him. She looked into the eyes of the man to raise him, and saw the love he would give. Though her fate had been altered only briefly, Dillon's had changed for a lifetime.

"I want you to make him yours," she breathed softly.

The decree brought the tears choking into his throat. "We'll raise him together," he whispered desperately. He grasped her fingers within his hand and kissed them. He should have seen it! He should have seen it coming! The swelling was there, the signs, the symptoms. Everything to warn him.

"Beautiful Dillon," she said sadly, touching his lips to silence his thoughts. "You couldn't have stopped it."

Gathering her shoulders and head into his arms, he cradled her inward. He held her tightly through the fog of sight and sound, the long nightmarish dream without end. When the ambulance came he rode beside her, the female paramedic making her comfortable and then lingering back. "There's nothing more I can do," she whispered apologetically. "Nothing until she reaches surgery."

Within the silence, the lights of the city smeared past them, the red and blue siren swirling in a surreal glow.

In the years to come, he would look back on the moments, the minutes when there was so much to say, so much to tell her, words and feelings that would go unspoken.

"I know," she whispered, taking his face into her hands.

Gently she kissed his lips, his tears. "I know."

As he held her close, his cheek against her own, he felt her body easing . . . "You O'Rourke men," she breathed softly. "I've got such a weakness for you . . ."

She remained aware, long after the warm touch released her, long after the heart monitor began to screech, the paramedics rushing her inward, the fluorescent lights smearing overhead, Dillon's hand clutched within her own. She did not feel the knife, the opening of her flesh, she heard only the screaming monitor, and the frantic heartbeat of the baby. Like a feather, she was floating upward, abandoning the chaos. The body upon the table was foreign, the chest split open, the abdomen splayed wide, the eyes staring, empty. It was nothing more than the refuse of her life, an empty receptacle. It was the child she was drawn to, the small life bursting with energy. She felt the cries, his fear, his overwhelming shock at the new surroundings. She was whispering, touching . . . *It's okay sweet baby, I'm here.* The eyes turned, searching, hearing. *I'm here.*

For a blissful moment, everything else dissipated . . . There was nothing but the tiny being before her, squirming, his wrinkled fists clenching and reclenching.

Then at once he was moving away, his attention to a nurse, to the lights overhead, his lungs filling and refilling in a wail of emotion. She felt herself pulling away, lifting upward further and further from the scene beneath her, from the life that was no longer her own.

"Kylie?"

The presence was with her, beside her, guiding her toward the warmth.

EPILOGUE

Sixty-One

THE BLACK BMW GLIDED UP 1A FROM BOSTON TOWARD THE NORTH-east, the long stretch of highway hugging the coastline. Thirty-five minutes out of Cambridge, Dillon guided the car through the bend of Swampscott before reaching the North Shore.

Cutting the engine outside of the garage, he made his way up the long white staircase to the rear entrance of the ocean-side home. As he rose with the weathered steps, the blue shimmer of Nahant Bay on his right seemed to lift with him, the summer sun glinting off the rippling water. He noticed that most of the lobstermen had anchored for the day, yet several smaller boats still dotted the cove.

"Sean?" he called, peering through the open screened door, before grasping the handle. "Ruby?"

As he entered the cool house, the narrow hallway stretched before him, the hardwood floor gleaming like glass.

"Hello?"

Within the silence he mounted the side stairs that led to the bedrooms.

"J.T.?" he called, but found the room that was kept for his son empty. Toys lay neatly piled along the bay window, with no sign of the three-year-old.

"Anybody here?" he called, making his way back down into the expansive living room.

He thought maybe Sean had taken his grandson out on the boat, but he could see through the towering windows that the *Miss Lila* remained anchored at the dock in front of the old cottage.

"Hey . . . anybody around?" But the house remained quiet.

Crayons and coloring books lay strewn at his feet, a child's drawing atop the coffee table. Recognizing the same depiction that littered his own den in Cambridge—that of a father and son, stick figures with black eyes and straight lines for mouths standing alone in front of a house—he took a deep breath.

It's time, came the mandate from his memory. Several months back, Ruby had pulled him aside to speak with him. "The boy needs a ma."

Within the still house he felt a sadness settling over him, a melancholy that he had been battling all day. His gaze was drawn to the painting, the beautiful portrait of the mother and child that hung above the mantel. In the peaceful eyes of the woman, he often saw Kylie, felt her presiding over the home, watching her child on his visits to his grandfather, loving him. Though Kylie had not lived to see her son's birth, Dillon had witnessed the same serenity in her eyes when her hand had rested upon her moving belly.

"It's what she would want, hon," Ruby had insisted. "Sarah's a nice girl. J.T. loves her and she loves him."

Still, he felt the guilt inside of him, a small part of him unready to let go.

With a sigh, he turned to the matter of the messy floor beneath him, anything to busy himself, to distract him from the painting, from the delicate splashes of color, from the photo of Kylie that Sean kept by his chair. The house was meant for Sean, yet he still felt her presence, felt her laughter, her touch. He still felt the pain and wondered if he had made the right decision.

Gathering up the crayons and coloring books, he replaced them to their proper drawer.

Through the windows, he caught sight of Sean down at the cottage, the thick door opening and closing as he went to the boat. His pants were rolled up in an uncharacteristic show of white calves, his feet crimson from the cold water lapping onto the sand. For a moment Dillon stood watching him, until the small adjacent cottage now used primarily for storage and Sean's fishing gear, pulled his gaze. For a pensive moment his thoughts remained on the bungalow, on the thick door standing wide . . . remembering that cold harsh day long past. Another fateful day when he had come bearing news: *Jack and Kylie's plane has gone down, sir.*

Four years had passed, yet it seemed only yesterday, mere hours since he stood on the windblown dock, shivering, his chest filled with dread and fear. He had tried so desperately to hang on, but in the end he had still lost them. Ironically, it had not been the White Mountains to claim them, but the months to follow. In spite of his vigilance and all of his medical expertise, he had not been able to save either of them.

Four years had passed, yet the scars remained intact, the regret, the lonely days and nights when J.T. stayed with his grandfather. At times his heart ached when he looked at the child, when he would catch a smirk on his son's face that reminded him of Jack, or the light would catch his emerald eyes and bring Kylie to mind. He thanked God for the busy days when he was consumed with the job of parenting, when the minutes whirled by so fast, that there was no time to reflect.

With a slam of the back door, he turned toward the hallway. J.T. had clearly spotted his car, for he heard the patter of bare feet racing about in search of him.

"Daddy! Daddy!"

For a silent moment he took in the lovely sound.

"In here, son!" he called.

As the boy came bounding into the room, his face lit with the purest of love, Dillon scooped him into his arms. The child showered his cheeks with wet kisses, the tiny arms gripping his neck tight.

"Hey you little stinker," Dillon said, pulling the child out to get a good look at him. "What have you been into?" he teased, poking his finger into the plump belly that peeked out from the soiled tee-shirt.

"Grandma Ruru let me make a garden."

"She did?" Dillon smiled.

"It's right next to hers!"

"You don't say? Well let's go have a look at it."

With the child perched on the crook of his arm, he went down to the white gate that separated the yard from the sandy beach. "What's Poppy doing down at the boat?" he asked, pausing briefly to watch him rummaging through the *Miss Lila* and then back to the cottage. Even from a distance, Dillon could see that he was cursing.

"He's trying to find Alfred."

"What happened to Alfred?" he asked, pulling an ant from the child's light hair.

"Poppy fell asleep with him in his shirt pocket, and he ran away." Dillon smiled at the thought of the little lizard slipping out of the sleeping man's grasp. The boat and cottage were so cluttered that it could take days to find the pet.

Continuing through the gate, they found Ruby bent in the garden, her gloved hands gripping a small hand-shovel that she beat against the ground.

"Ants! They're nibbling my tomatoes off the vines," she said over her shoulder as they approached. "I don't know what to do with them," she groaned as she struggled to her feet.

"Somebody missed you last night," she said with a wink at Dillon and a tickle to J.T. "But Poppy made some ice-cream. The old-fashioned kind. The yummy kind. The kind that makes big people get stuck on their knees," she said, swatting the dirt from her ample thighs.

"See Daddy," the child said, wriggling free from his grasp. With finger pointing, he excitedly ran to a row of daffodils. "Those ones are mine."

"You don't say. What a fine job you did."

The proud child flopped down on his stomach in the freshly watered dirt, resting his chin in his hands.

"What are you doin', lad?" asked Ruby. "Basting yourself in mud?"

"Watching 'em sleep," whispered the child, his fingers tracing down the delicate flowers, his soft voice slipping over the breeze.

"Very well then. Watch 'em close," said Ruby, meandering toward the fence with her shovel in hand. "What about these roses?" she said, motioning Dillon to follow. "Do you know what would make them sallow like that?"

"No ma'am."

"I hate cutting 'em all back, but I guess there's no other choice."

As Ruby snipped at the vines, Dillon turned to the sea, his heart in his throat. It took him a moment to work up his voice. "I asked Sarah to marry me last night," he said softly.

Clearly startled, Ruby turned to him, her sun-burnt face squinting into the sun.

"She said 'yes'," he added quietly.

"Oh hon," she said, tears springing into her enormous eyes. Her red face grew even redder, as she swiped at her cheeks. "Oh hon, congrats," she said, yet her eyes remained sad.

"Don't worry," he said, resting his hand on her arm. "I'm not just doing it for J.T. She's a wonderful woman."

"That she is, hon."

Dillon's gaze returned to the beach, to Sean who was now lumbering toward them. His head was bent, the tiny lizard's tail sticking out from his brawny hand. For a silent moment they both watched him, his red hair threaded with silver, Dillon wondering how he would break the news to the fisherman. For nearly a year after his daughter's death, they had thought they would lose him, the grief shaking him to his core. Ruby had moved in to look after him, but it was through J.T. that the fisherman had come to life again. Through the child, he found his daughter again. Dillon feared that with the news, he would somehow feel he was losing her again.

"Don't be frettin' now," Ruby said, grasping his hand tightly. "He'll be happy for you, you'll see. And for his grandson."

"He's been through so much."

"Yes, but it's an accumulation of who he is, hon. When you get older, like Sean, you've accumulated a lifetime of loss, so much sadness that never dies. But you're left with the memories, the dreams, the gentle moments that they bring us. In our dreams love, they come to us. They make it better. They make us whole. They make us who we are."

"I don't want him to think that I've forgotten her. Or that J.T. won't know who she is. I'll always remind him."

"Of course you will, hon. She'll always be with him. You just have to trust in that."

Later that night in Cambridge, when he had tucked the child into his bed, Dillon broke the news to his son. "It's important to me to know how you feel about it. When I marry Sarah, she'll be your new mommy."

The moonlight rested soft on his son's face, his intense eyes narrowing as he mulled the new development. He lifted up on his elbow and turned to the photo of Kylie by his bed. It was one he had picked from an album of Sean's, Kylie surprisingly young in the picture.

"Will she sing me the night song?" he asked, his lips curled with fret.

"What song is that?"

"The one about the pumpkin shells and tinker bells? About the stars and the night?"

Dillon felt the emotion rush into his eyes. It was a small part of Kylie he had managed to give to him, the song that she had sang to him when he was still in the womb.

"No," he said, taking the boy's hand. "That's a special song just for you. Just like the painting, it's a gift from your mommy to you and only to you."

With a gentle kiss to the boy's cheek, Dillon laid him back and snuggled him into the sheets. Never had the child so completely resembled both Kylie and Jack simultaneously. His golden hair lay curled around his honey skin, his emerald eyes filled with understanding.

"Don't be sad, Daddy," he said softly. "It's okay to let Sarah come."

Acknowledgments

I owe a great deal to the following professionals, who provided important background information: my friend, Americo Simonini, M.D., who spent countless hours helping me to find medical conditions to support my story; Jennifer Collins, M.D. for her insightful suggestions; paramedics Billy Fields & Mike Carrell; pilot Gene Hudson, without whose help I never would have got the Merlin into the sky, much less out of it; Lieutenant Colonel Edward Cummins and Corey Kruse who also provided aeronautical expertise; Officers Brian Cunningham and Tom Kelly of the Boston Police Department; Captain Kevin O'Toole and Lieutenant Richard Splaine of the Boston Fire Department, Fire Investigation Unit/Arson Squad; Sooz Spruce of the New Hampshire Forestry Service; Tammy Wooster at the Divisions of Fisheries & Wildlife; Jane Weston of the Hamilton Town Hall; Stellgis Nichols for the colorful glimpse inside of Savannah; Ted Oldemans who provided insurance policy information; Eddie Hook of James Hook & Company for giving me run of the place; fisherman Derek Bennett who took me out on his boat and to his assistant Adam Foster; and to Greg Lovendahl for his expertise on gun-handling. My thanks to them all for their patience and generosity. Any errors or omissions are my own.

I would like to express my gratitude to my reading committee for their valuable insight: Cathy Armstrong, Janet Cummins, Tom Horton, Sue Riemer and Valerie Rupp. I'm thankful to Roger Eckholm & Laura Stephens for the mountain-cabin in which to sequester myself; and to those dear family and friends who gave moral support: Scott Welch, Andy Sands, Anthony Gallo, Mannie Rodriquez, Bill George, Larry Barsky, Kami Asgar, Barbara Horton, Curtis Foster, Jr., Don Schilling and Joseph Schilling; and to Jon McCallum for 24-hour tech support, for providing me with inspirational music by which to work, and for accompanying me to the coffee shop when the solitude became unbearable.

With final thanks to Eric Parkinson and Shari Lovendahl who read and reread the manuscript, offering criticism and advice. Without their love and tireless encouragement, the book would have ended after chapter one.

* * * * *

Massachusetts proved to be an open and friendly place to set this novel. While I tried to remain as faithful as possible to my research, I found it necessary to alter the floor layout of the Massachusetts General Hospital. The hospital staff, events and impressions depicted in this novel were solely from my imagination and in no way intended to reflect upon this fine institution. I also found it necessary to take creative license with the use of the Charles Street Jail in Boston. As this was a jail rather than a prison, there were never any executions at this facility. The Charlestown Prison was located across the river in Charlestown and has since been demolished. The last execution to take place at that facility was in 1947. Massachusetts has remained firm in its long-standing opposition to capital punishment, with no executions since that date.

References

The American Medical Association Encyclopedia of Medicine. Edited by Charles B. Clayman, MD. Preface by James H. Sammons, MD. New York: Random House, 1989.

BALL, ANN. *A Handbook of Catholic Sacramentals.* Indiana: Our Sunday Visitor, 1991.

BEERS, M.D., MARK H. and BERKOW, M.D., ROBERT. *The Merck Manual of Diagnosis and Therapy, Seventeenth Edition.* New Jersey: Merck Research Laboratories, 1999.

BLACK, JEREMY and GREEN, ANTHONY. *Gods, Demons and Symbols of Ancient Mesopotamia.* Texas: University of Texas Press in co-operation with British Museum Press, 1991.

The Book of Enoch the Prophet. Translated by Richard Laurence, LL.D. Archbishop of Cashel. California: Wizards Bookshelf, 1983. Original publication: London: Kegan Paul, Trench & Company, 1883.

The Egyptian Book of the Dead (The Papyrus of Ani). The Egyptian Text with Interlinear Transliteration and Translation, A Running Translation, Introduction, Etc. by E.A. Wallis Budge. New York: Dover Publications, 1967. Original publication by order of the Trustees of the British Museum, 1895.

BUNTING, BAINBRIDGE. *Houses of Boston's Back Bay.* Massachusetts: The Bellcnap of Harvard University, 1967.

DAVIDSON, GUSTAV. *A Dictionary of Angels.* New York: The Free Press, 1967.

GODWIN, MALCOLM. *Angels, An Endangered Species.* New York: Simon and Schuster 1990.

GROF, STANISLAV & CHRISTINA. *Beyond Death: The gates of consciousness.* London: Thames and Hudson, 1980.

GULILEY, ROSEMARY ELLEN. *The Encyclopedia of Ghosts and Spirits.* New York: Facts On File, 1992.

ILLMAN, PAUL E. *The Pilot's Handbook of Aeronautical Knowledge.* New York: McGraw Hill, 1995.

KASTENBAUM, ROBERT & BEATRICE, *Encyclopedia of Death.* New York: Avon Books, 1989.

The Larousse Encylopedia of Mythology. Translated by Richard Aldrington & Dalano Ames and revised by a panel of editorial advisors from the Larousse Mythologie Generale. Edited by Felix Guirand. First published in France by Auge, Gillon, Hollier Larousse, Moreau et Cie, the Librarie Larousse, Paris. Barnes & Noble, Inc. by arrangement with Reed Consumer Books, 1994.

LINDEN-WARD, BLANCE, *Silent City on a Hill: Landscapes of Memory and Boston's Mount Auburn Cemetery.* Ohio State University Press, 1989.

Pastoral Care of the Sick. Prepared by International Commission on English in the Liturgy, A Joint Commission of Catholic Bishops' Conferences. New York: Catholic Book Publishing Company, 1983.

STOCKSTAD, MARILYN. *Art History.* New York: Harry N. Abrams, Inc., 1995.

WALKER, BARBARA G. *The Woman's Dictionary of Symbols & Sacred Objects.* New York: Harper Collins, 1988.

WETHERELL, W.D. *The Smithsonian Guides to Natural America. Northern England—Vermont, New Hampshire and Maine.* New York: Random House/Smithsonian Books, 1995.

FOR THE BEST IN PAPERBACKS, LOOK FOR THE

In every corner of the world, on every subject under the sun, Penguin represents quality and variety—the very best in publishing today.

For complete information about books available from Penguin—including Penguin Classics, Penguin Compass, and Puffins—and how to order them, write to us at the appropriate address below. Please note that for copyright reasons the selection of books varies from country to country.

In the United States: Please write to *Penguin Group (USA), P.O. Box 12289 Dept. B, Newark, New Jersey 07101-5289* or call 1-800-788-6262.

In the United Kingdom: Please write to *Dept. EP, Penguin Books Ltd, Bath Road, Harmondsworth, West Drayton, Middlesex UB7 0DA.*

In Canada: Please write to *Penguin Books Canada Ltd, 10 Alcorn Avenue, Suite 300, Toronto, Ontario M4V 3B2.*

In Australia: Please write to *Penguin Books Australia Ltd, P.O. Box 257, Ringwood, Victoria 3134.*

In New Zealand: Please write to *Penguin Books (NZ) Ltd, Private Bag 102902, North Shore Mail Centre, Auckland 10.*

In India: Please write to *Penguin Books India Pvt Ltd, 11 Panchsheel Shopping Centre, Panchsheel Park, New Delhi 110 017.*

In the Netherlands: Please write to *Penguin Books Netherlands bv, Postbus 3507, NL-1001 AH Amsterdam.*

In Germany: Please write to *Penguin Books Deutschland GmbH, Metzlerstrasse 26, 60594 Frankfurt am Main.*

In Spain: Please write to *Penguin Books S. A., Bravo Murillo 19, 1° B, 28015 Madrid.*

In Italy: Please write to *Penguin Italia s.r.l., Via Benedetto Croce 2, 20094 Corsico, Milano.*

In France: Please write to *Penguin France, Le Carré Wilson, 62 rue Benjamin Baillaud, 31500 Toulouse.*

In Japan: Please write to *Penguin Books Japan Ltd, Kaneko Building, 2-3-25 Koraku, Bunkyo-Ku, Tokyo 112.*

In South Africa: Please write to *Penguin Books South Africa (Pty) Ltd, Private Bag X14, Parkview, 2122 Johannesburg.*